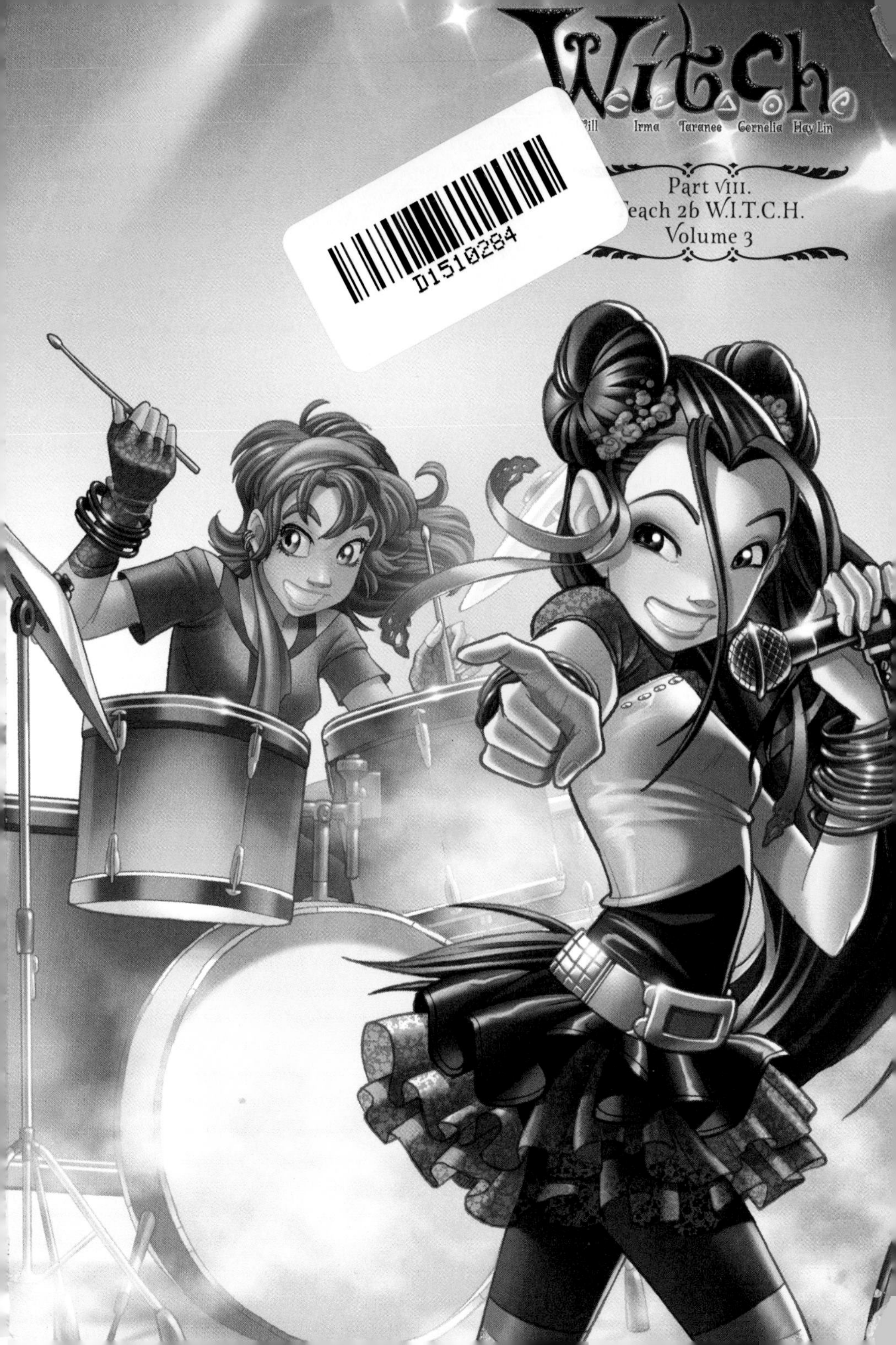
W.i.t.c.h.
Irma Taranee Cornelia Hay Lin
Part VIII.
Teach 2b W.I.T.C.H.
Volume 3

W.i.t.c.h.

Will   Irma   Taranee   Cornelia   Hay Lin

Part VIII.
Teach 2b W.I.T.C.H.
Volume 3

CONTENTS

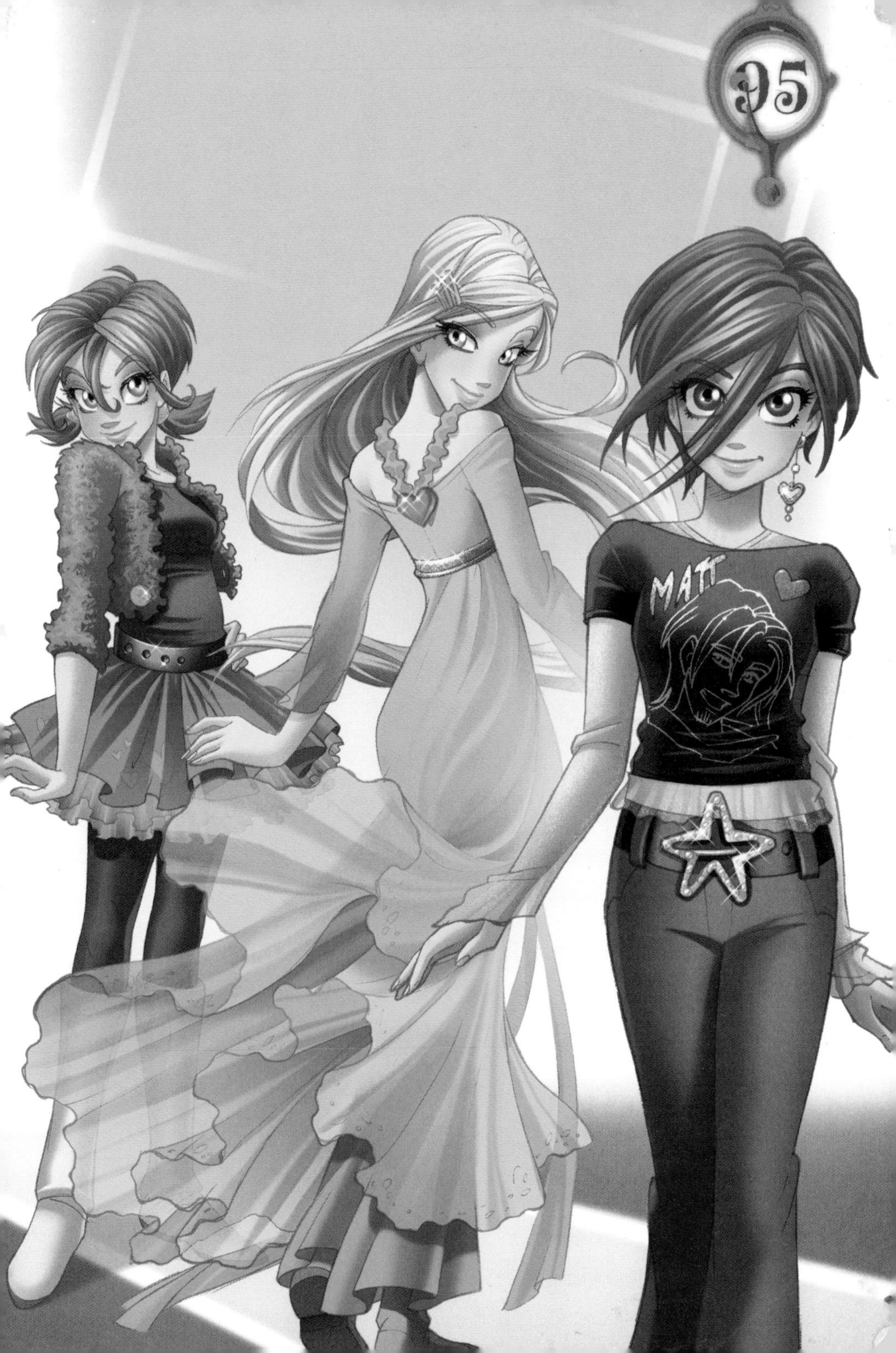
95
MATT

Countless Tears

"When you love, you can do unbelievable things."

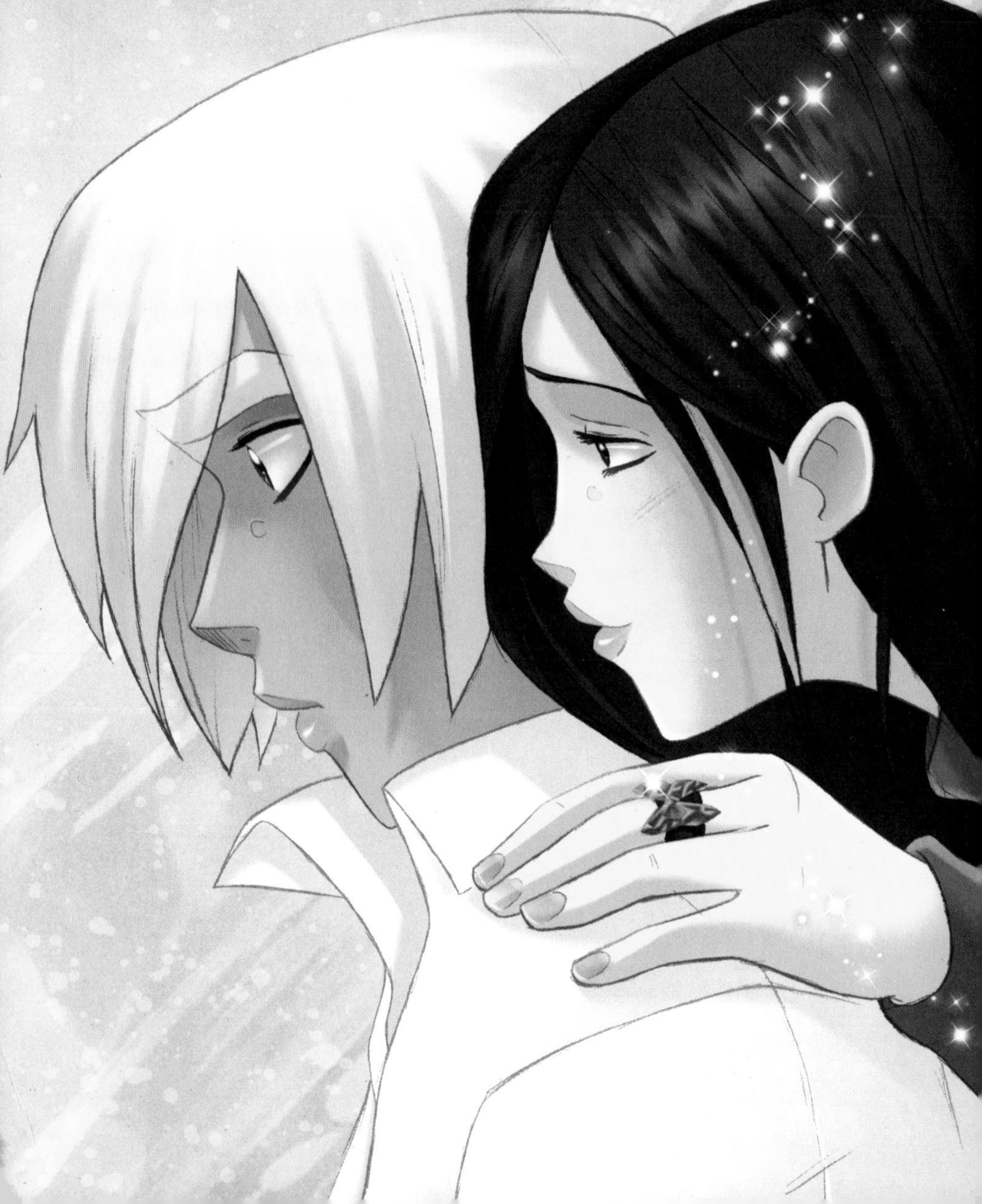

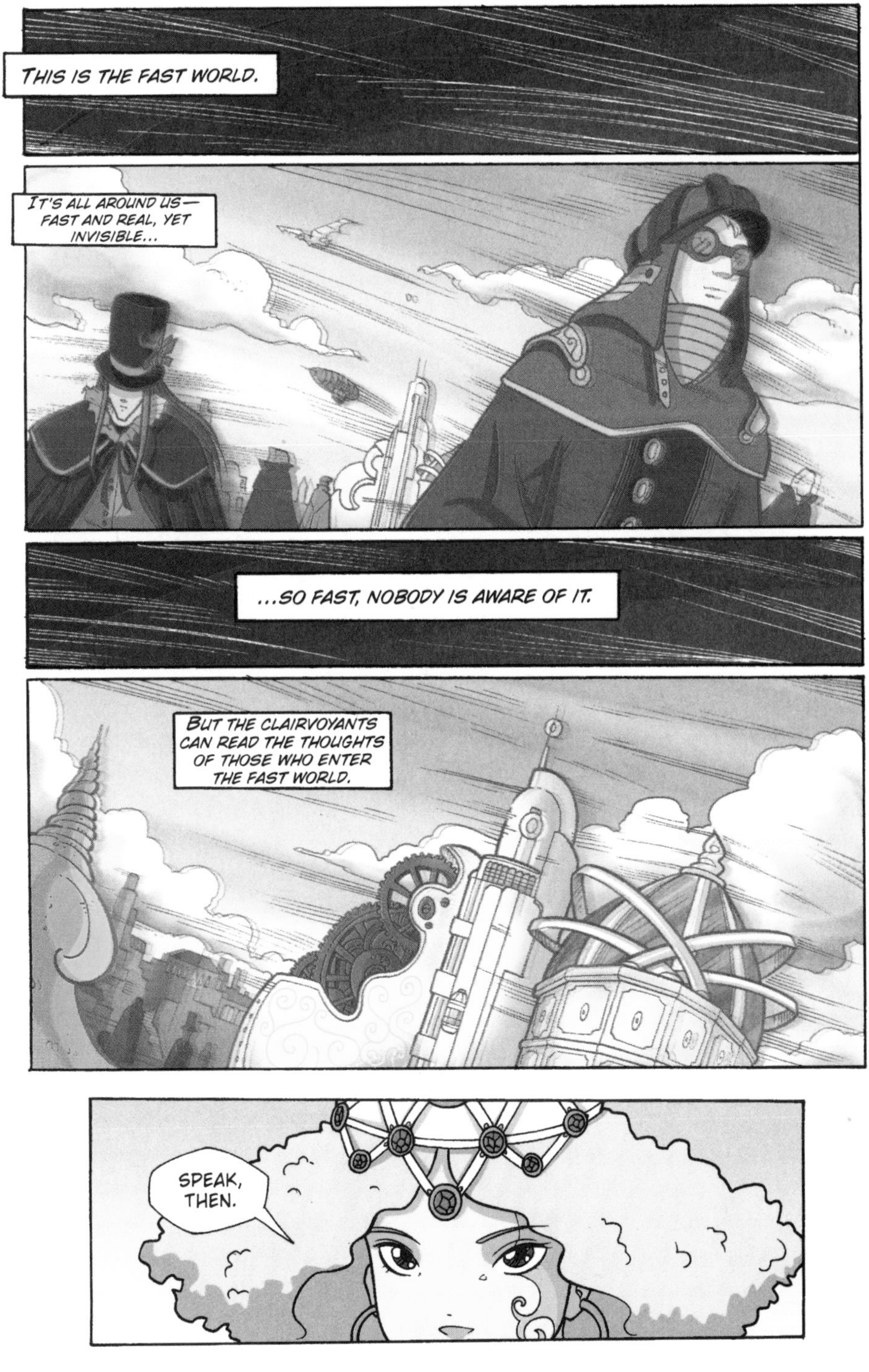
THIS IS THE FAST WORLD.
IT'S ALL AROUND US— FAST AND REAL, YET INVISIBLE...
...SO FAST, NOBODY IS AWARE OF IT.
BUT THE CLAIRVOYANTS CAN READ THE THOUGHTS OF THOSE WHO ENTER THE FAST WORLD.
SPEAK, THEN.

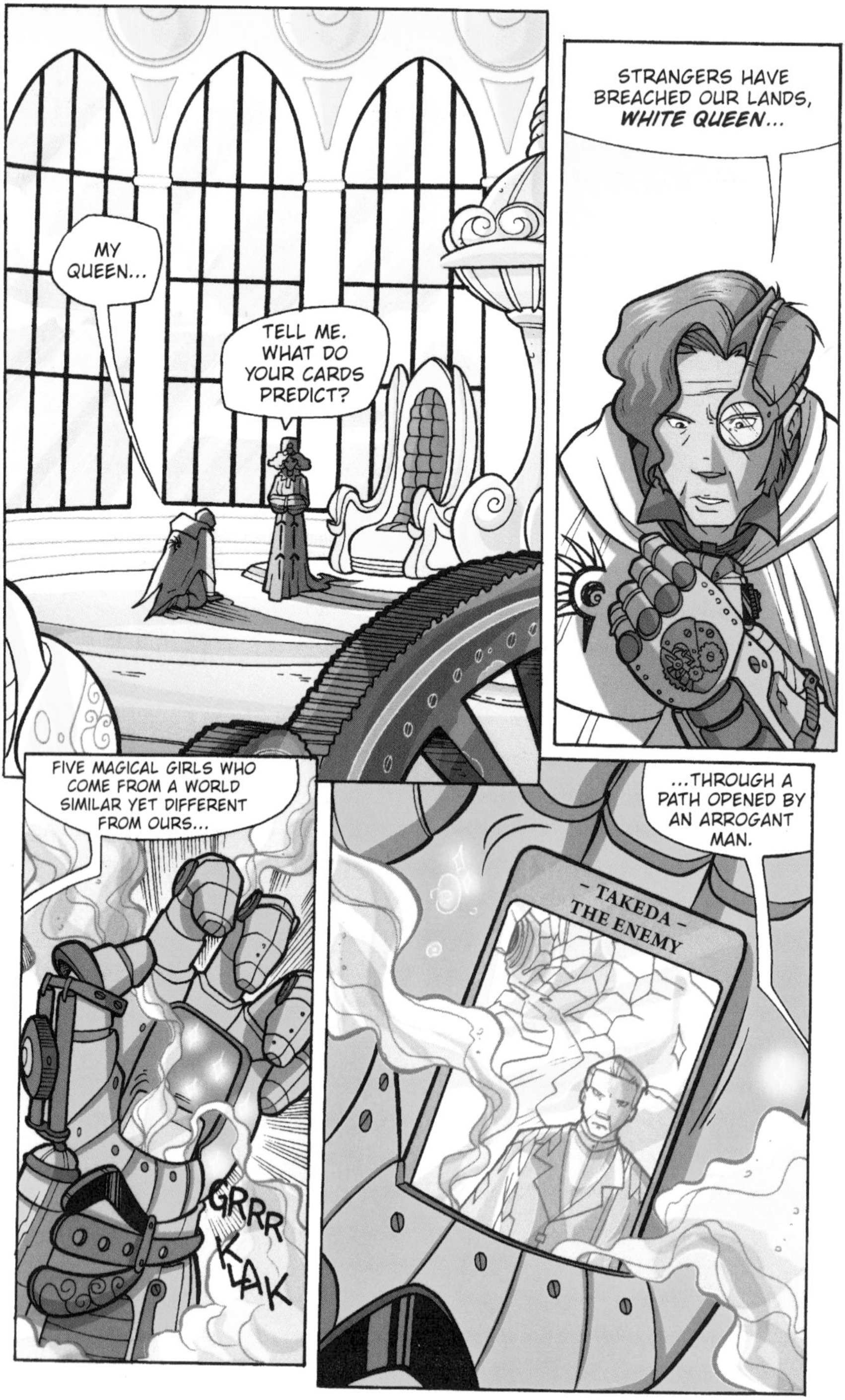
MY QUEEN...
TELL ME. WHAT DO YOUR CARDS PREDICT?
STRANGERS HAVE BREACHED OUR LANDS, ***WHITE QUEEN***...
FIVE MAGICAL GIRLS WHO COME FROM A WORLD SIMILAR YET DIFFERENT FROM OURS...
GRRR
KLAK
...THROUGH A PATH OPENED BY AN ARROGANT MAN.
- TAKEDA -
THE ENEMY

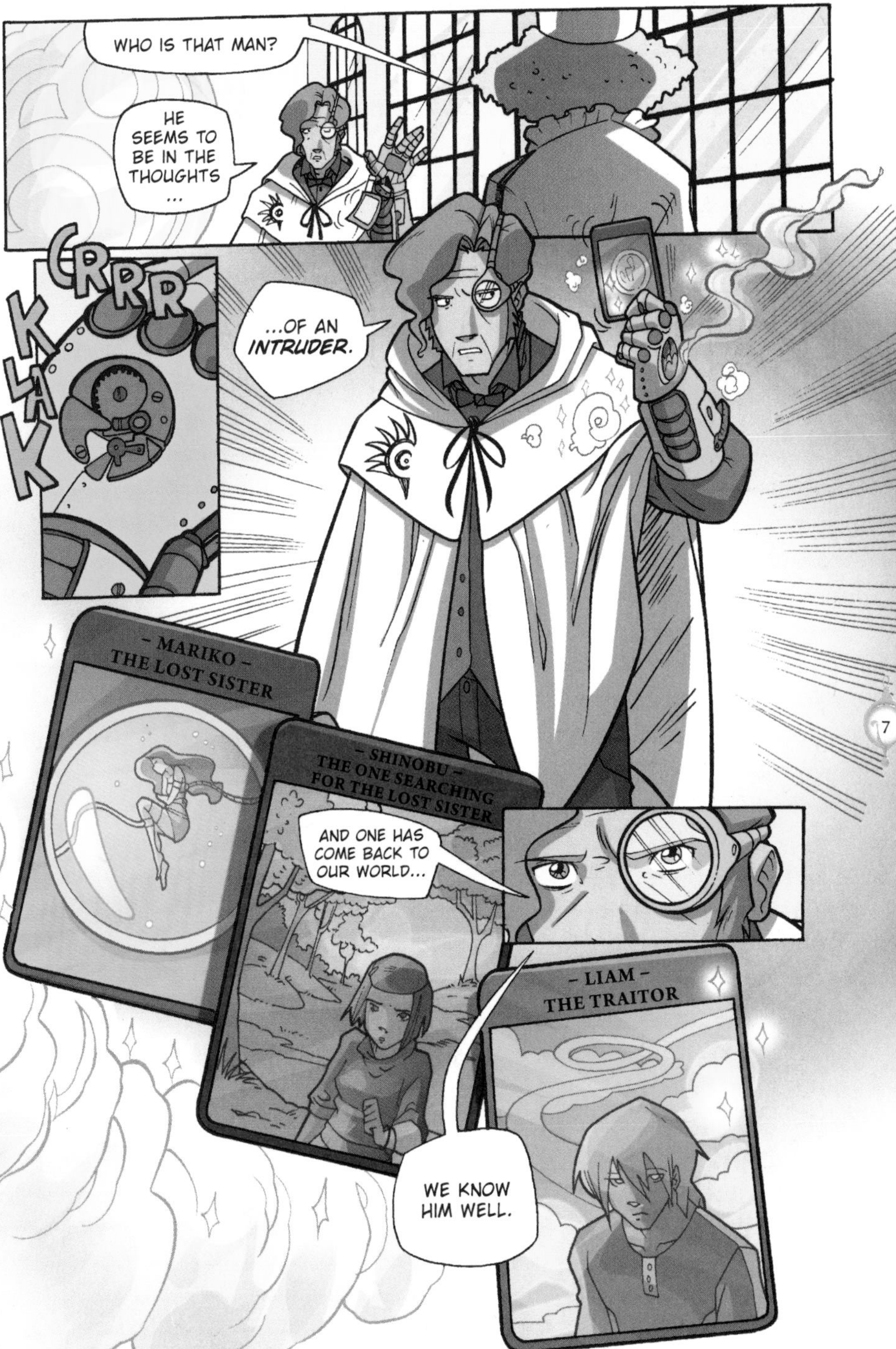
WHO IS THAT MAN?
HE SEEMS TO BE IN THE THOUGHTS ...
CRRR
KLAK
...OF AN INTRUDER.
– MARIKO –
THE LOST SISTER
– SHINOBU –
THE ONE SEARCHING FOR THE LOST SISTER
AND ONE HAS COME BACK TO OUR WORLD...
– LIAM –
THE TRAITOR
WE KNOW HIM WELL.

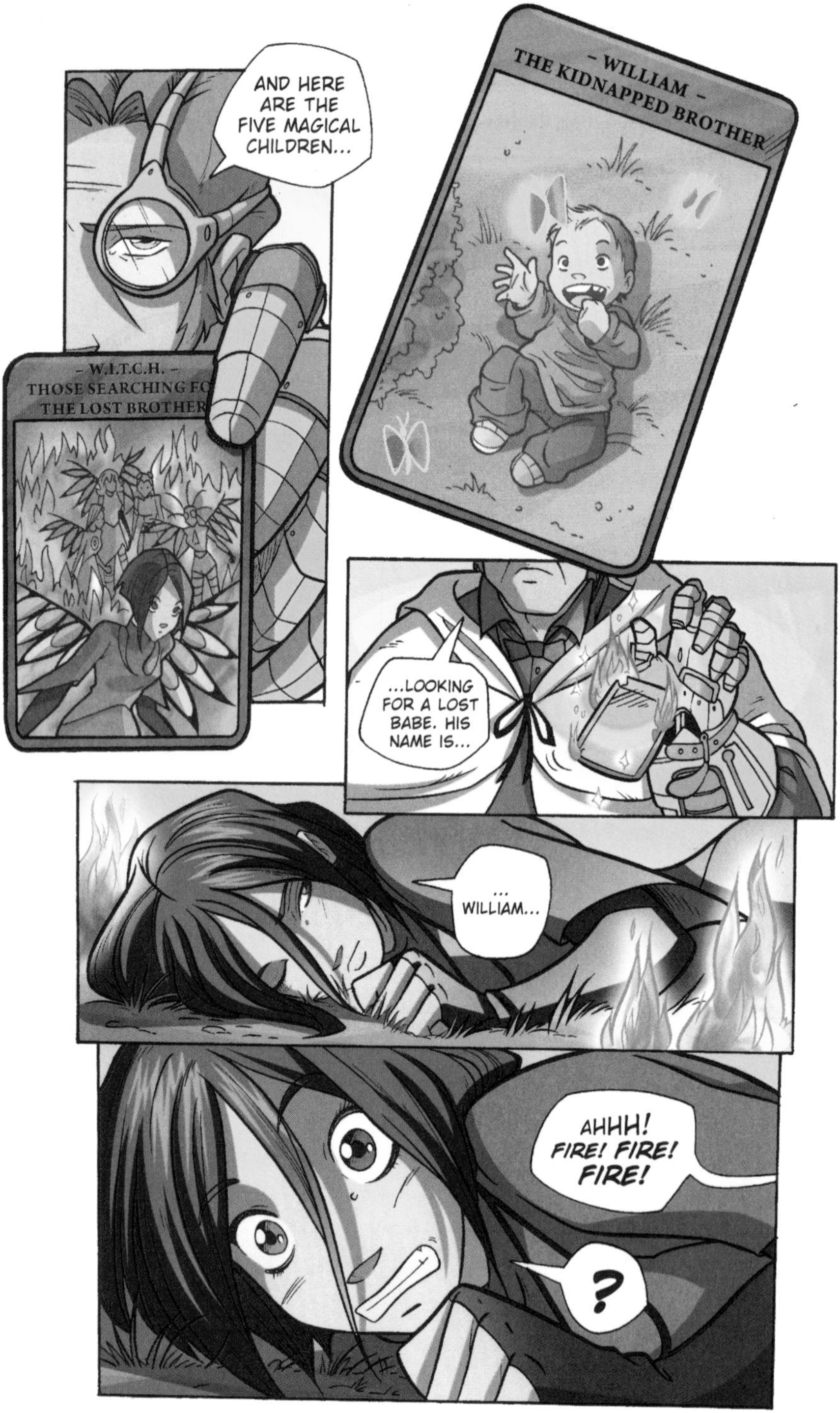
AND HERE ARE THE FIVE MAGICAL CHILDREN...
– WILLIAM –
THE KIDNAPPED BROTHER
– W.I.T.C.H. –
THOSE SEARCHING FO
THE LOST BROTHER
...LOOKING FOR A LOST BABE. HIS NAME IS...
... WILLIAM...
AHHH! FIRE! FIRE! FIRE!
?

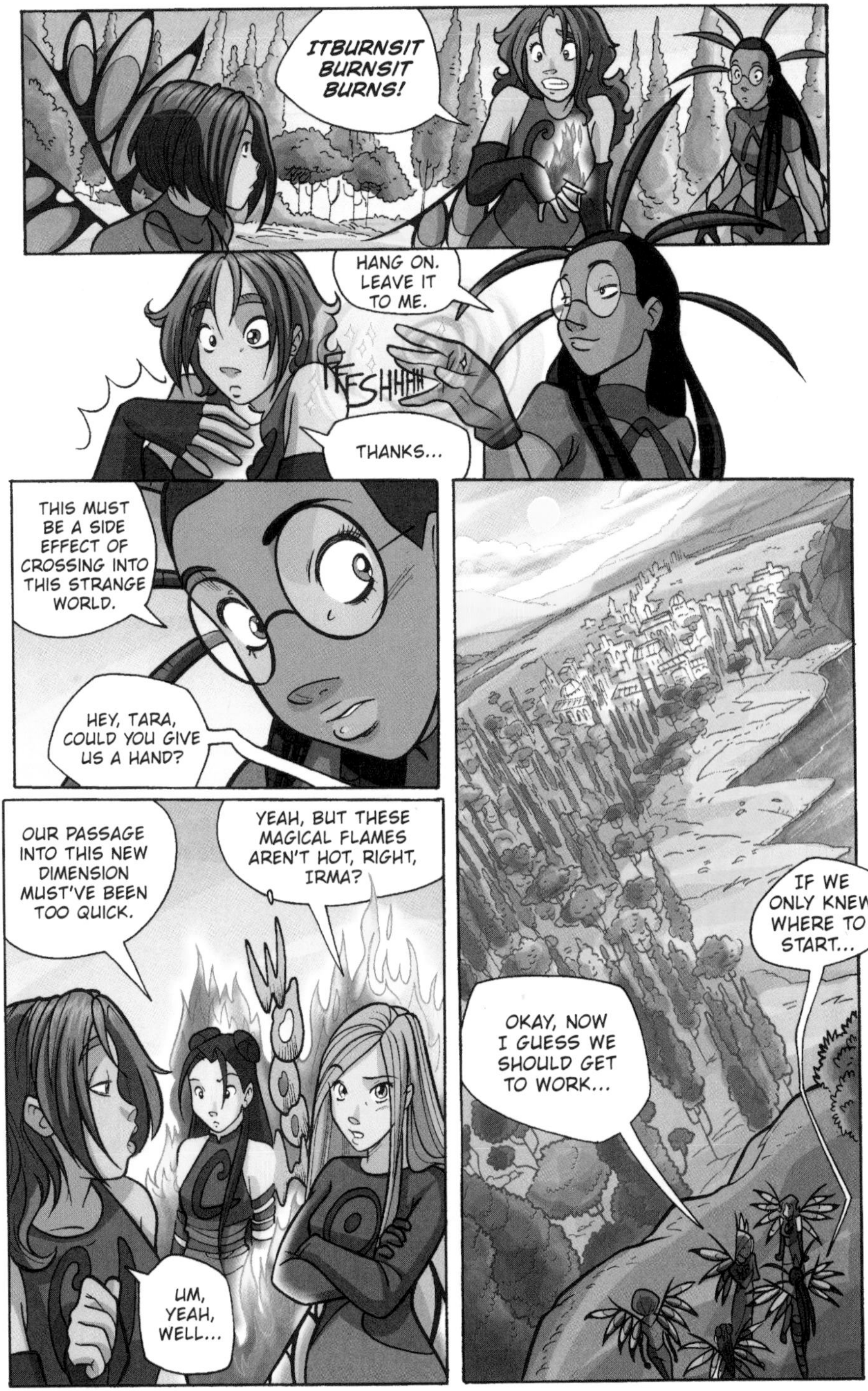
ITBURNSIT BURNSIT BURNS!
HANG ON. LEAVE IT TO ME.
FFFSHHHH
THANKS...
THIS MUST BE A SIDE EFFECT OF CROSSING INTO THIS STRANGE WORLD.
HEY, TARA, COULD YOU GIVE US A HAND?
OUR PASSAGE INTO THIS NEW DIMENSION MUST'VE BEEN TOO QUICK.
YEAH, BUT THESE MAGICAL FLAMES AREN'T HOT, RIGHT, IRMA?
UM, YEAH, WELL...
IF WE ONLY KNEW WHERE TO START...
OKAY, NOW I GUESS WE SHOULD GET TO WORK...

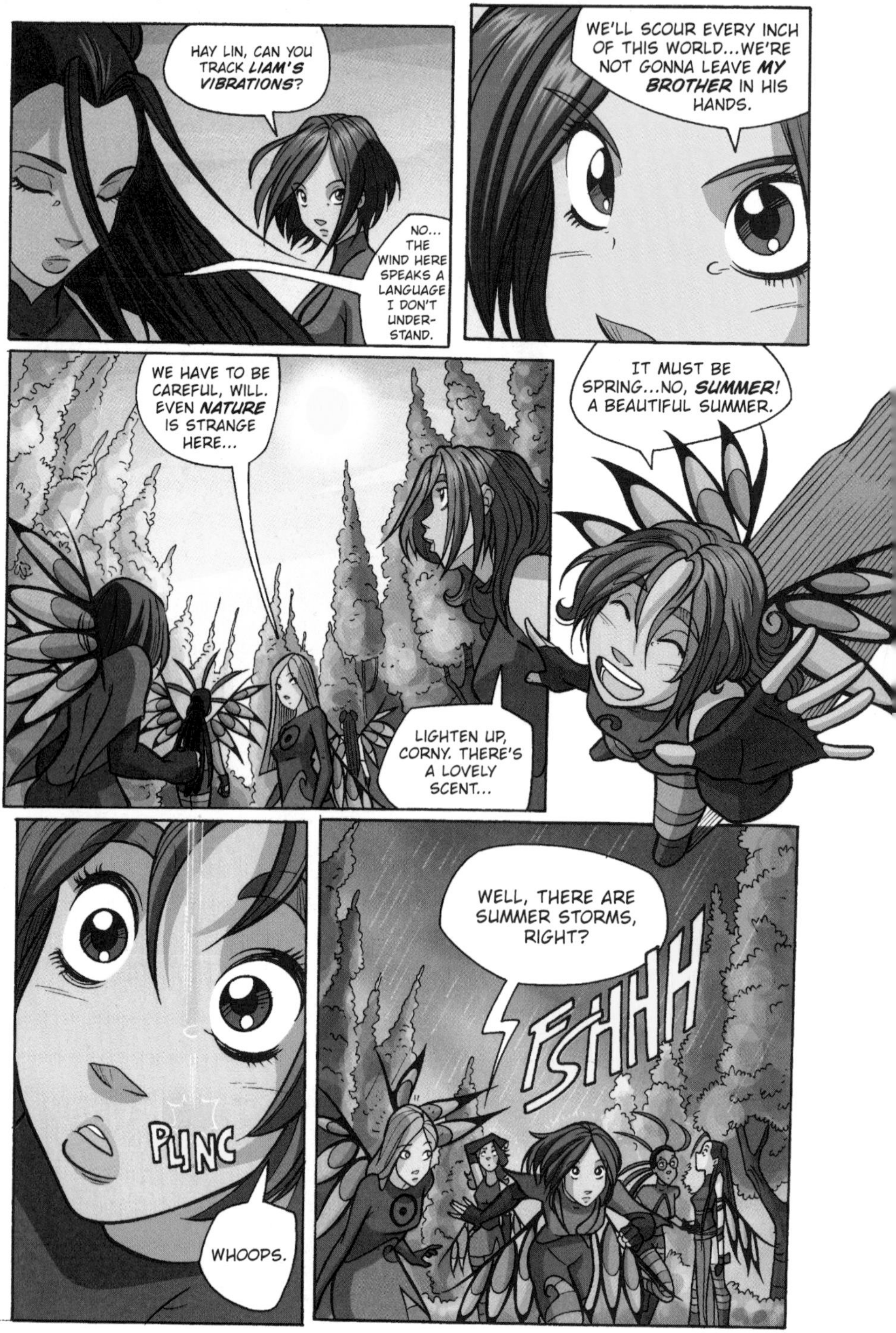
HAY LIN, CAN YOU TRACK LIAM'S VIBRATIONS?
NO... THE WIND HERE SPEAKS A LANGUAGE I DON'T UNDER-STAND.
WE'LL SCOUR EVERY INCH OF THIS WORLD...WE'RE NOT GONNA LEAVE MY BROTHER IN HIS HANDS.
WE HAVE TO BE CAREFUL, WILL. EVEN NATURE IS STRANGE HERE...
LIGHTEN UP, CORNY. THERE'S A LOVELY SCENT...
IT MUST BE SPRING...NO, SUMMER! A BEAUTIFUL SUMMER.
PLINC
WHOOPS.
WELL, THERE ARE SUMMER STORMS, RIGHT?
FSHHH

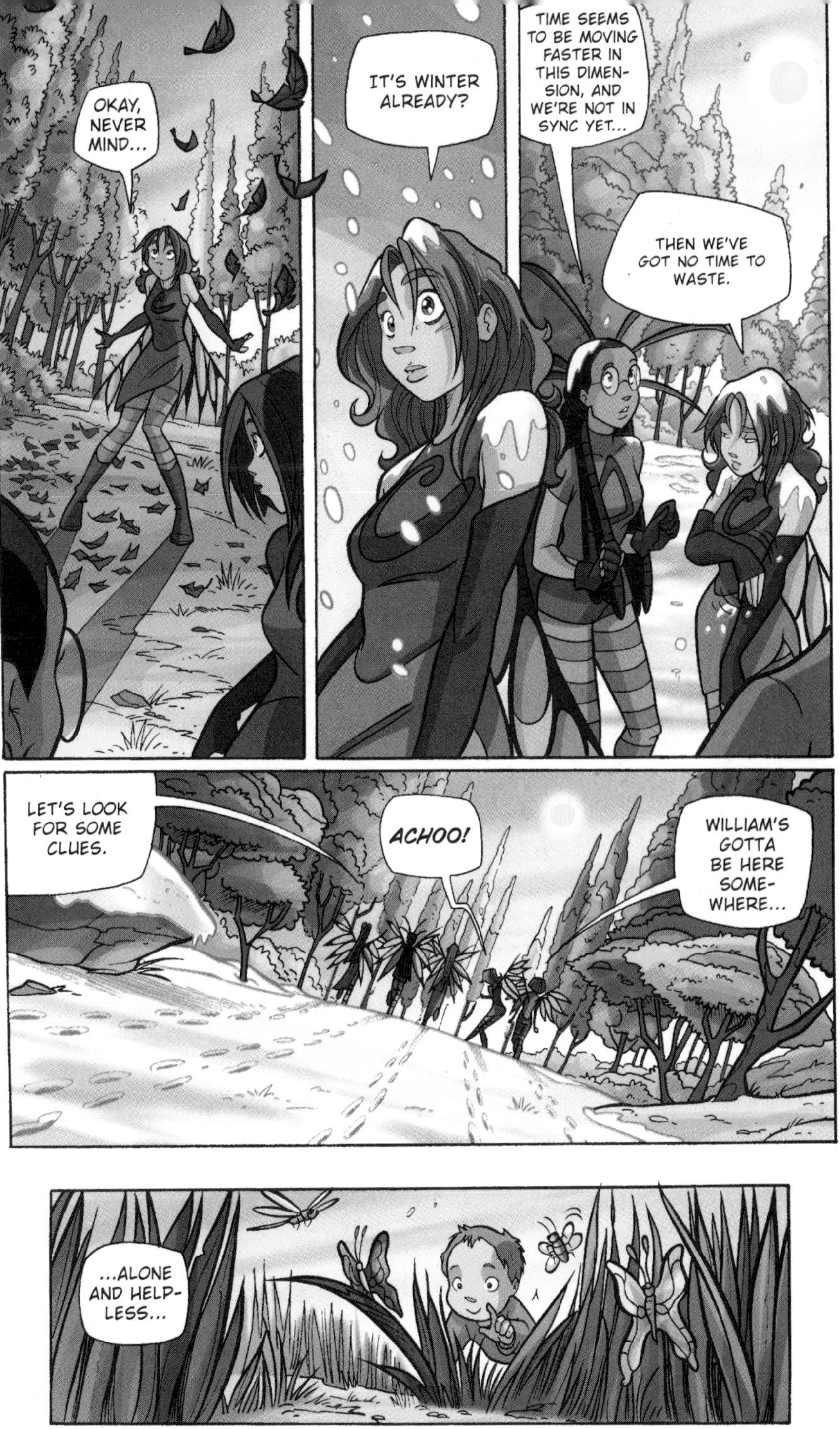

OKAY, NEVER MIND...
IT'S WINTER ALREADY?
TIME SEEMS TO BE MOVING FASTER IN THIS DIMENSION, AND WE'RE NOT IN SYNC YET...
THEN WE'VE GOT NO TIME TO WASTE.
LET'S LOOK FOR SOME CLUES.
ACHOO!
WILLIAM'S GOTTA BE HERE SOMEWHERE...
...ALONE AND HELPLESS...

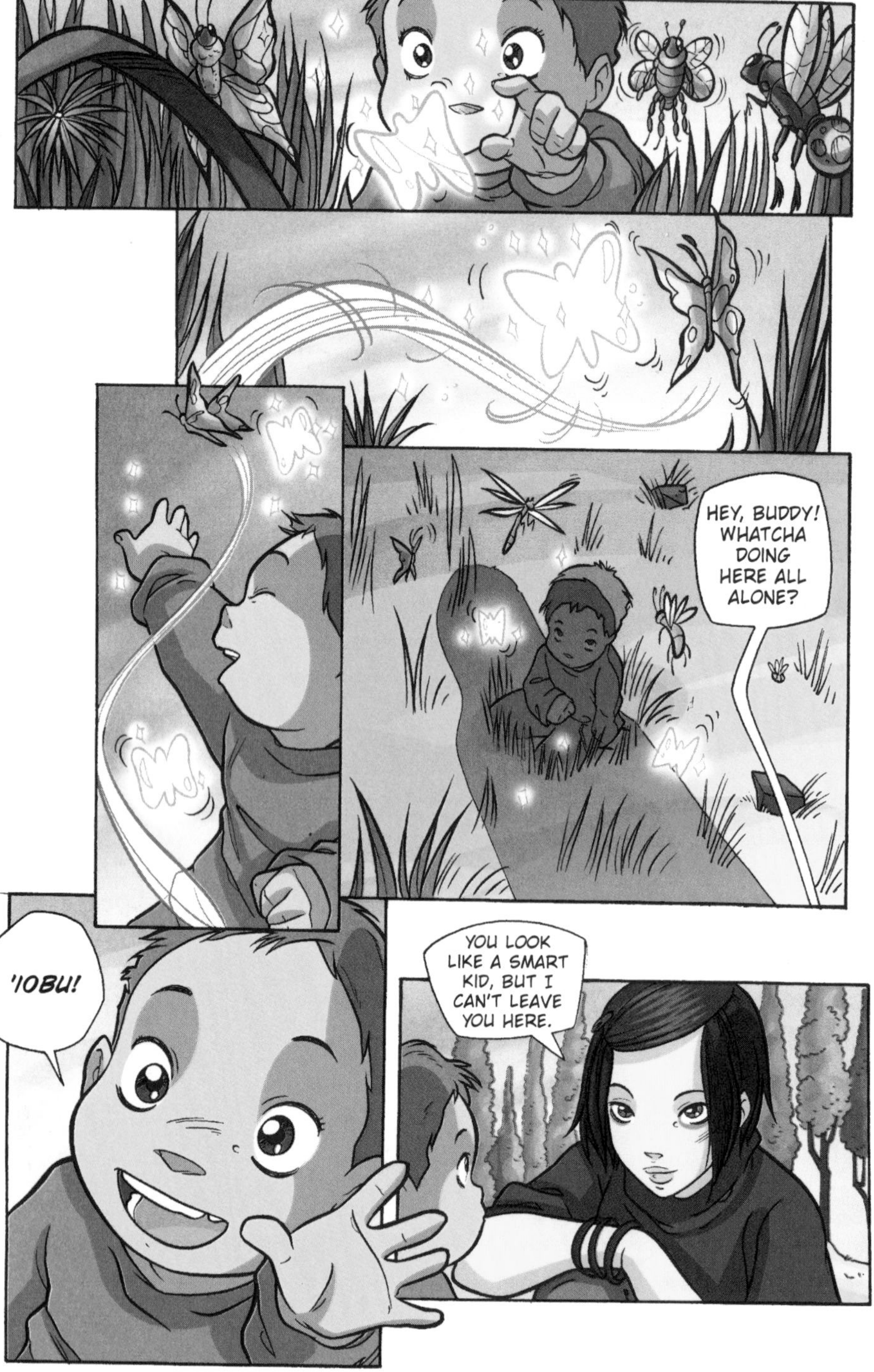
HEY, BUDDY! WHATCHA DOING HERE ALL ALONE?
'IOBU!
YOU LOOK LIKE A SMART KID, BUT I CAN'T LEAVE YOU HERE.

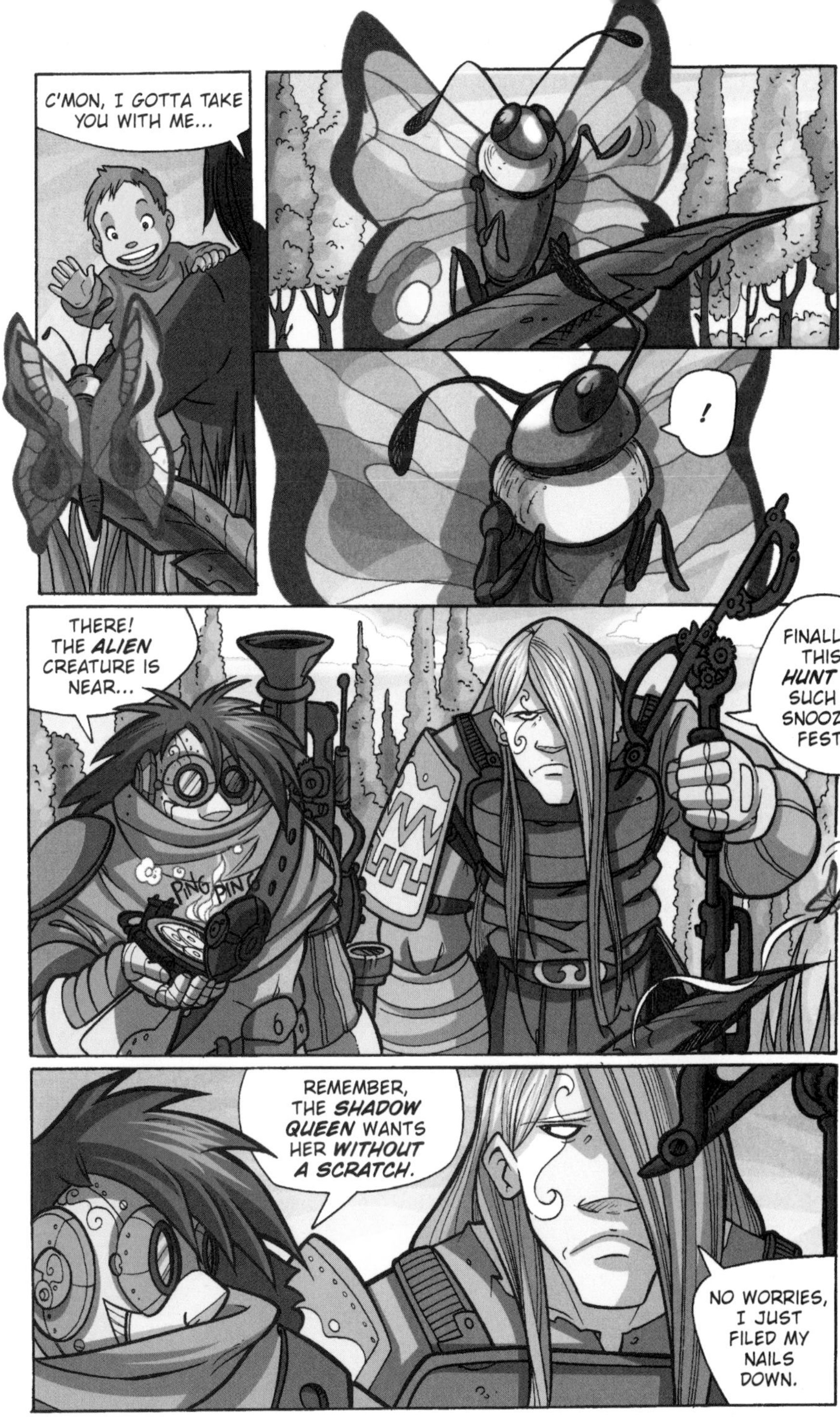
C'MON, I GOTTA TAKE YOU WITH ME...
!
THERE! THE ALIEN CREATURE IS NEAR...
PING PING
FINALLY! THIS HUNT IS SUCH A SNOOZE-FEST.
REMEMBER, THE SHADOW QUEEN WANTS HER WITHOUT A SCRATCH.
NO WORRIES, I JUST FILED MY NAILS DOWN.

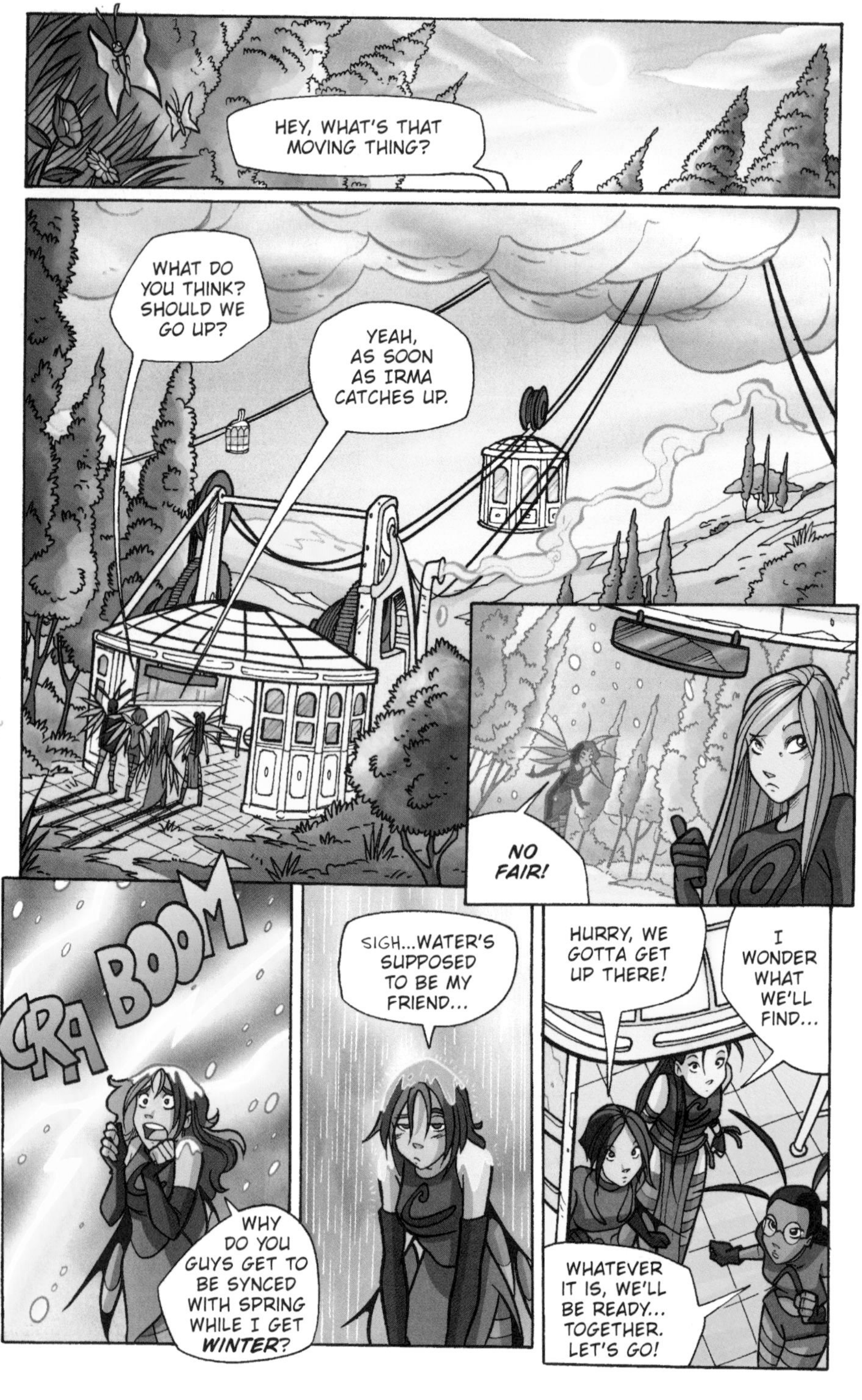
HEY, WHAT'S THAT MOVING THING?
WHAT DO YOU THINK? SHOULD WE GO UP?
YEAH, AS SOON AS IRMA CATCHES UP.
NO FAIR!
CRA BOOM
WHY DO YOU GUYS GET TO BE SYNCED WITH SPRING WHILE I GET *WINTER*?
SIGH...WATER'S SUPPOSED TO BE MY FRIEND...
HURRY, WE GOTTA GET UP THERE!
I WONDER WHAT WE'LL FIND...
WHATEVER IT IS, WE'LL BE READY... TOGETHER. LET'S GO!

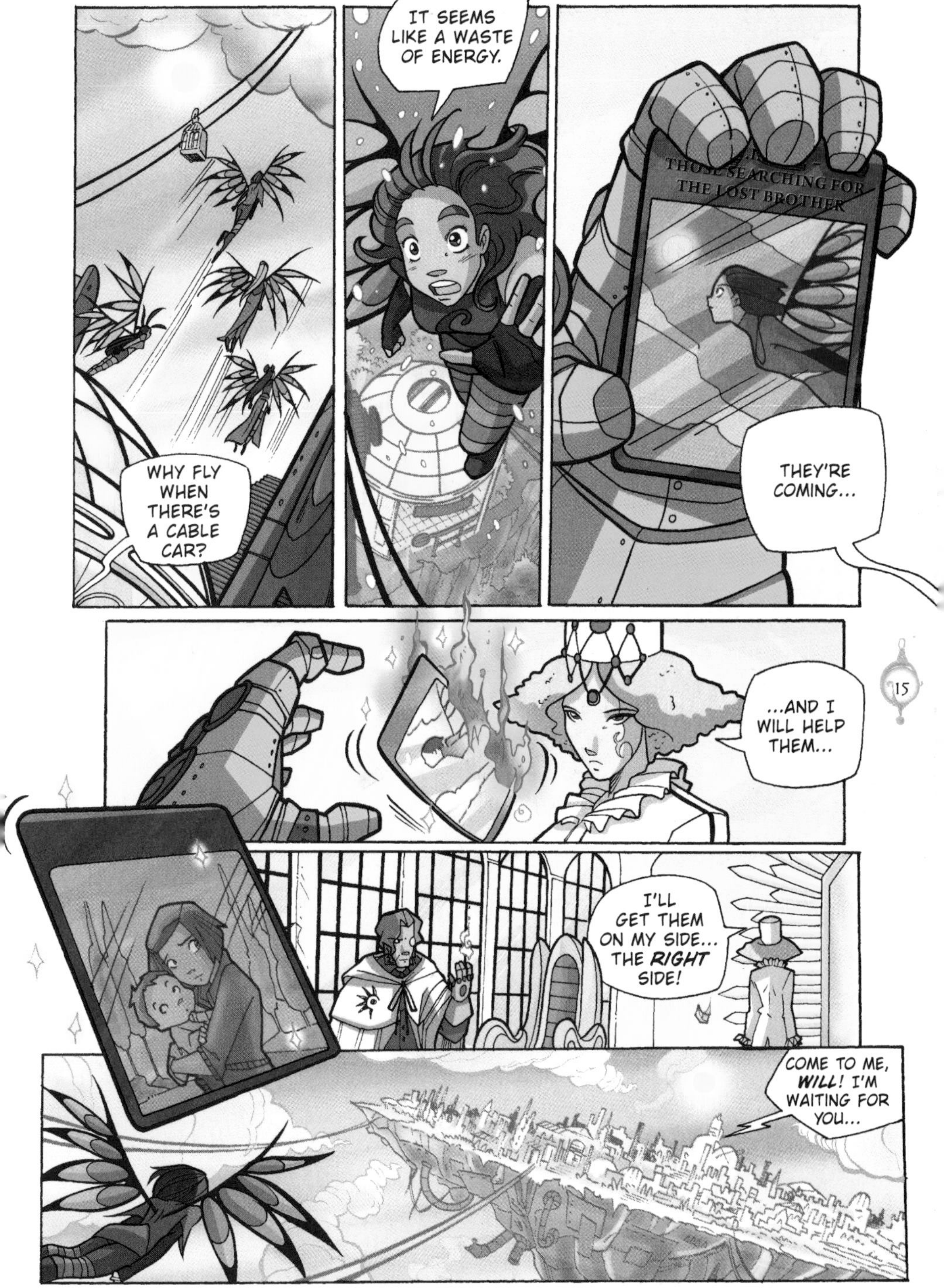
WHY FLY WHEN THERE'S A CABLE CAR?
IT SEEMS LIKE A WASTE OF ENERGY.
THOSE SEARCHING FOR THE LOST BROTHER
THEY'RE COMING...
...AND I WILL HELP THEM...
I'LL GET THEM ON MY SIDE... THE ***RIGHT*** SIDE!
COME TO ME, ***WILL***! I'M WAITING FOR YOU...

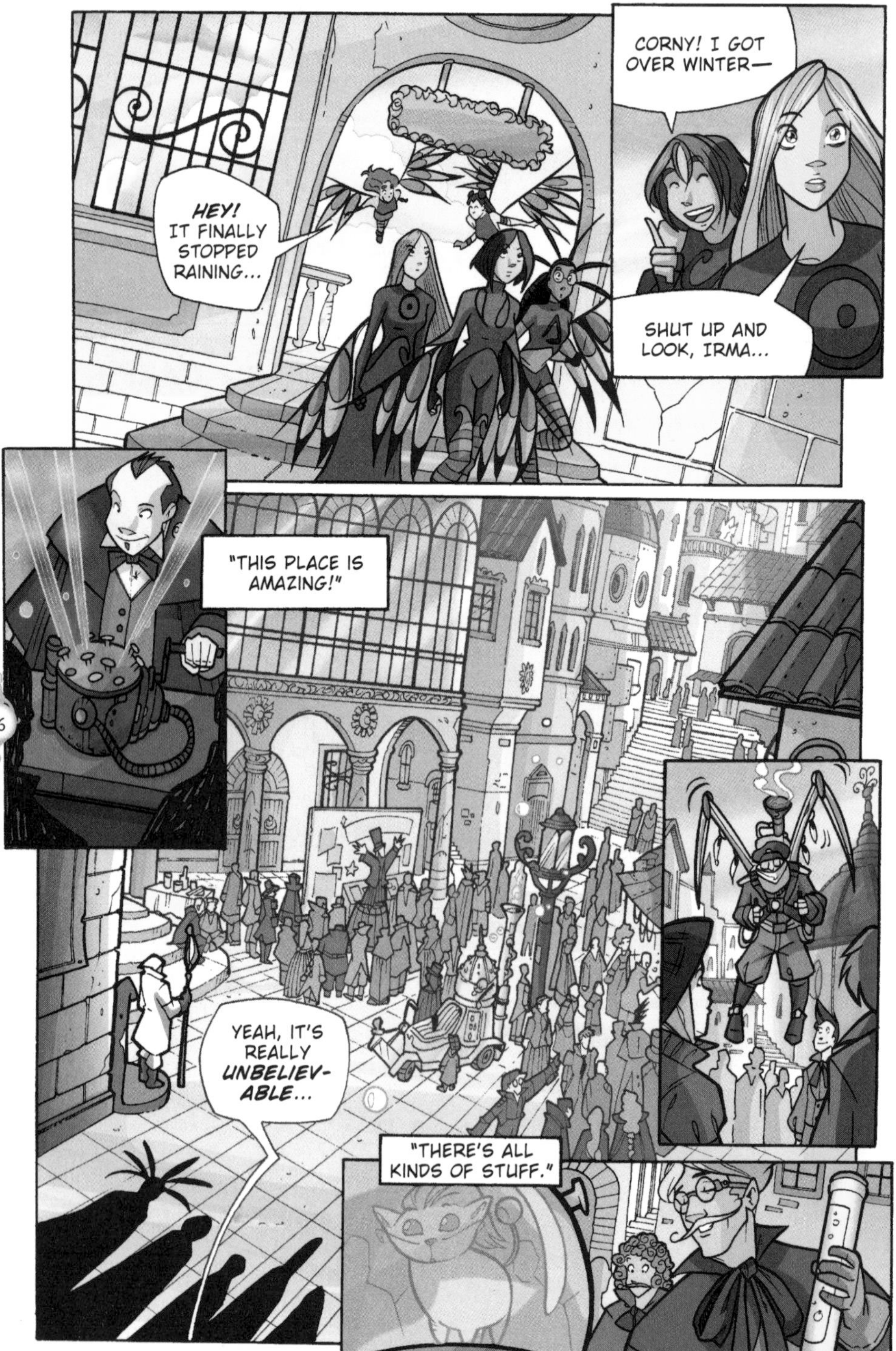
HEY! IT FINALLY STOPPED RAINING...
CORNY! I GOT OVER WINTER—
SHUT UP AND LOOK, IRMA...
"THIS PLACE IS AMAZING!"
YEAH, IT'S REALLY UNBELIEV-ABLE...
"THERE'S ALL KINDS OF STUFF."

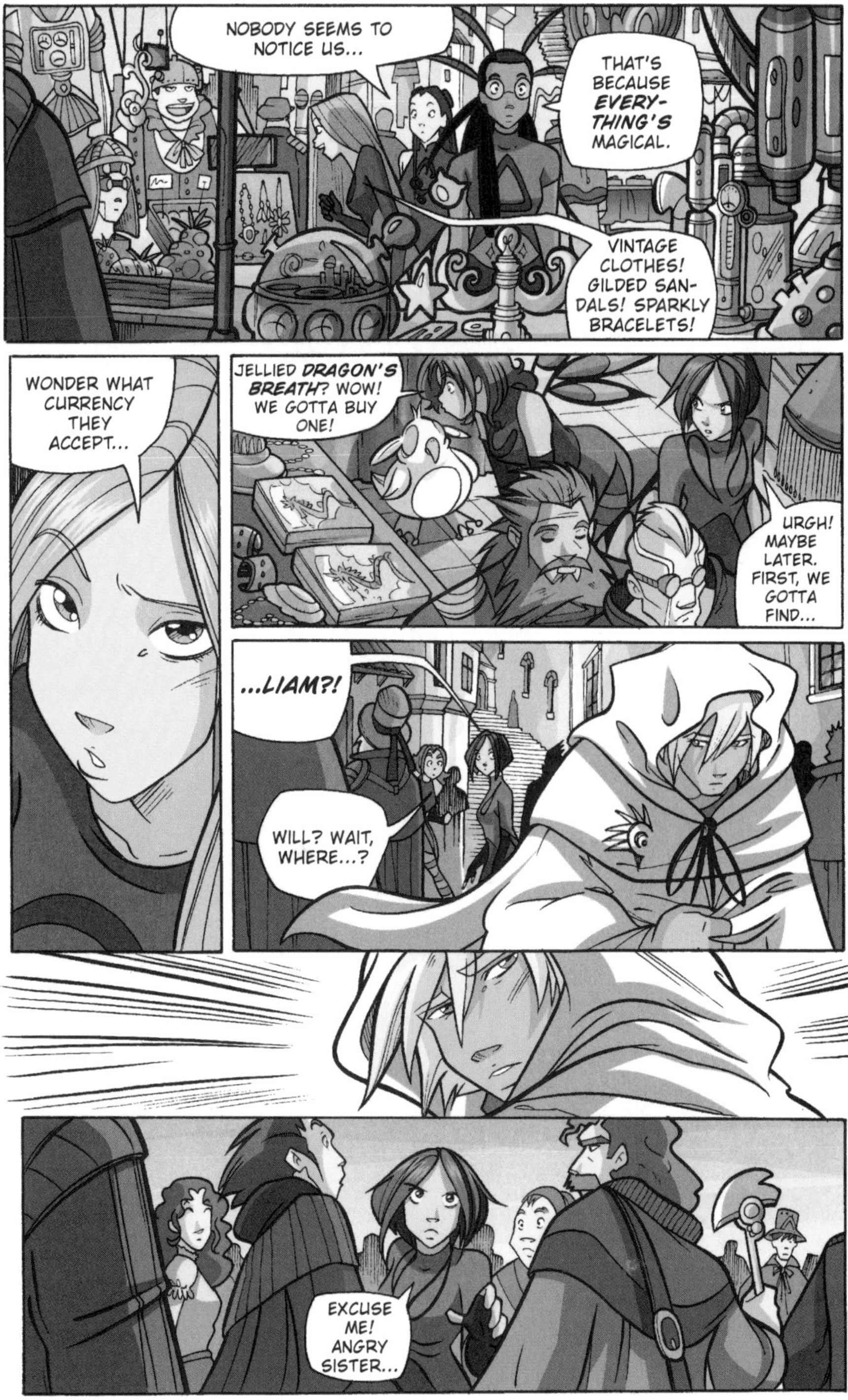
NOBODY SEEMS TO NOTICE US...
THAT'S BECAUSE EVERY-THING'S MAGICAL.
VINTAGE CLOTHES! GILDED SAN-DALS! SPARKLY BRACELETS!
WONDER WHAT CURRENCY THEY ACCEPT...
JELLIED DRAGON'S BREATH? WOW! WE GOTTA BUY ONE!
URGH! MAYBE LATER. FIRST, WE GOTTA FIND...
...LIAM?!
WILL? WAIT, WHERE...?
EXCUSE ME! ANGRY SISTER...

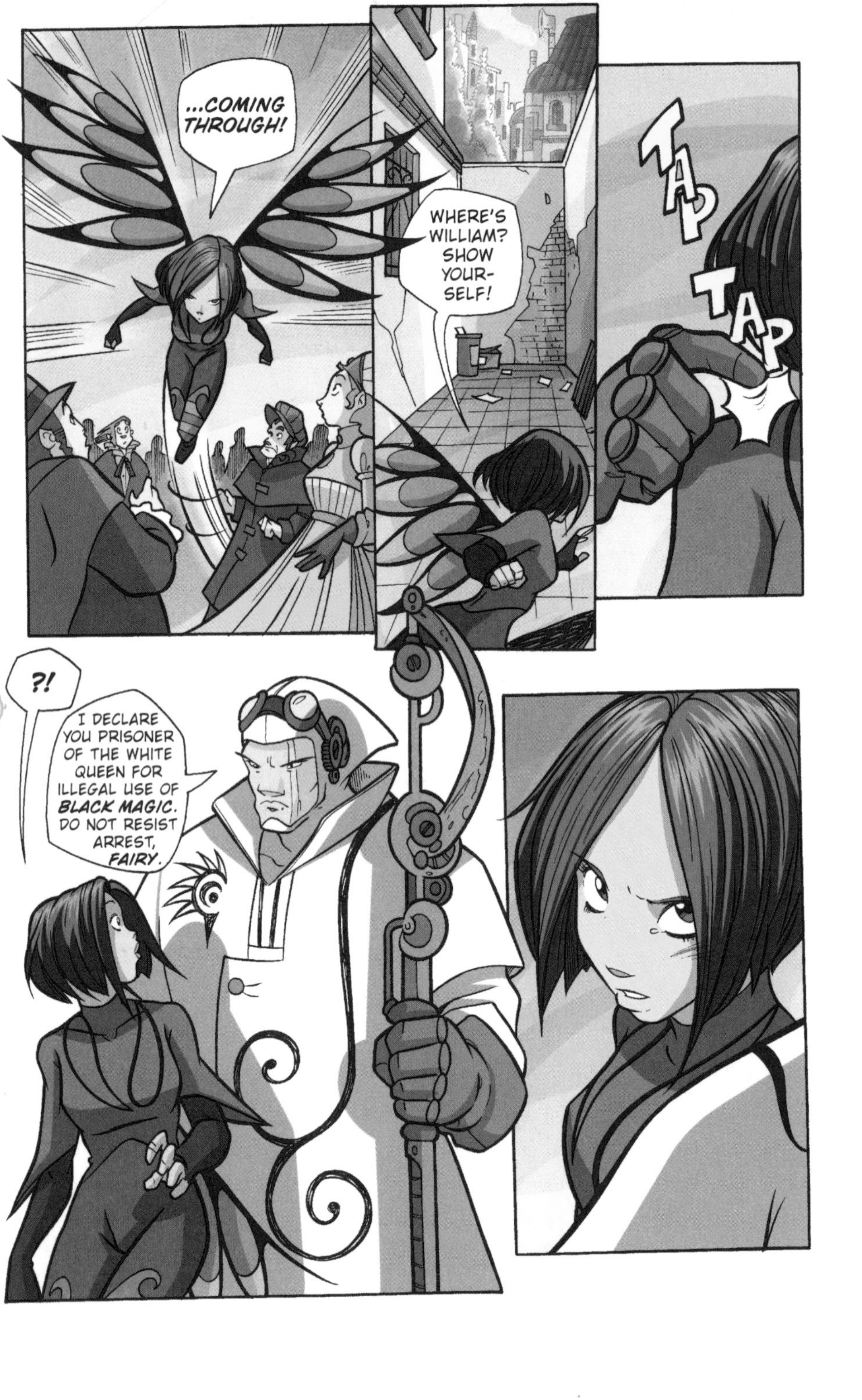

...COMING THROUGH!
WHERE'S WILLIAM? SHOW YOUR-SELF!
TAP
TAP TAP
?!
I DECLARE YOU PRISONER OF THE WHITE QUEEN FOR ILLEGAL USE OF BLACK MAGIC. DO NOT RESIST ARREST, FAIRY.

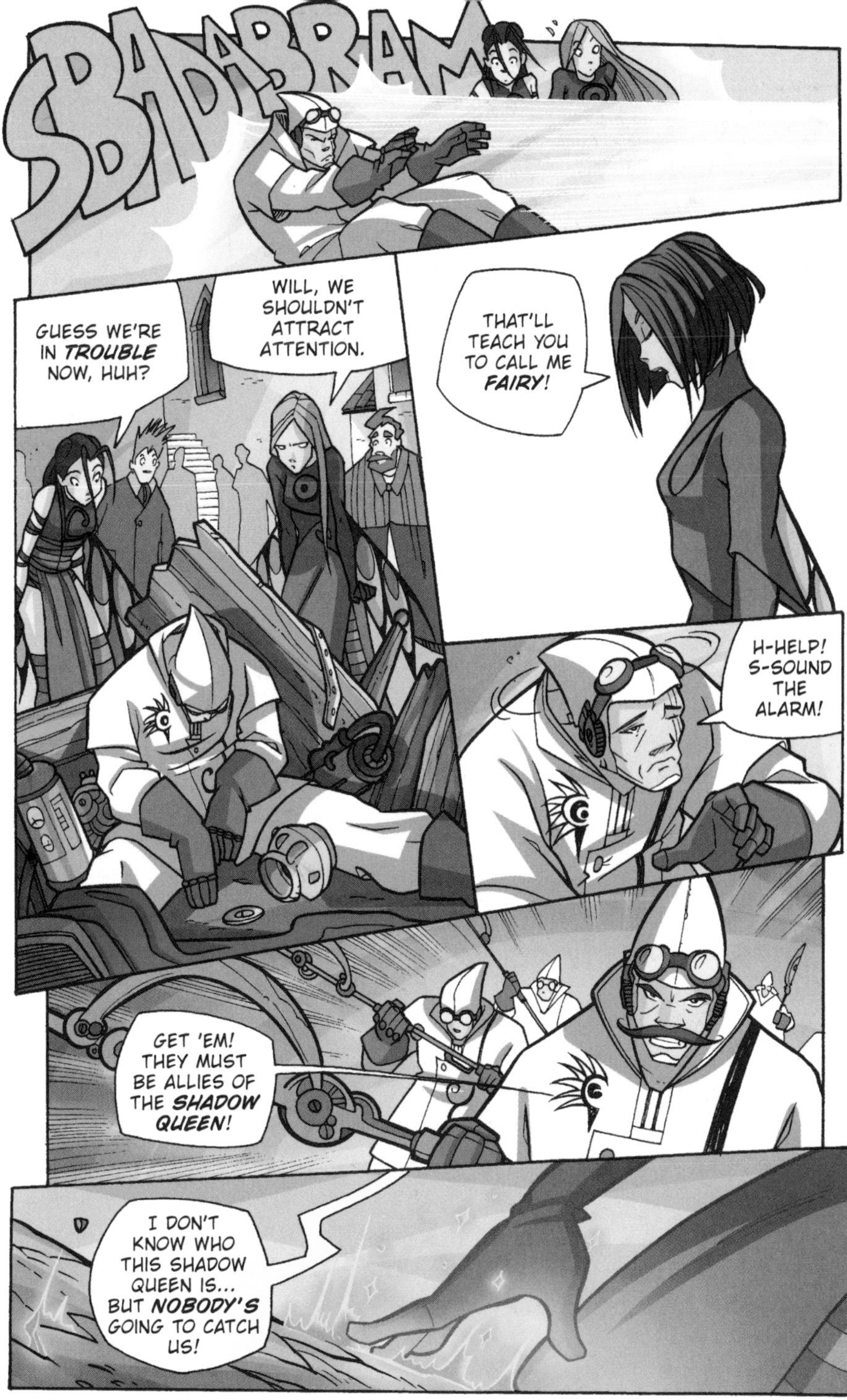
SBADABRAM
GUESS WE'RE IN TROUBLE NOW, HUH?
WILL, WE SHOULDN'T ATTRACT ATTENTION.
THAT'LL TEACH YOU TO CALL ME FAIRY!
H-HELP! S-SOUND THE ALARM!
GET 'EM! THEY MUST BE ALLIES OF THE SHADOW QUEEN!
I DON'T KNOW WHO THIS SHADOW QUEEN IS... BUT NOBODY'S GOING TO CATCH US!

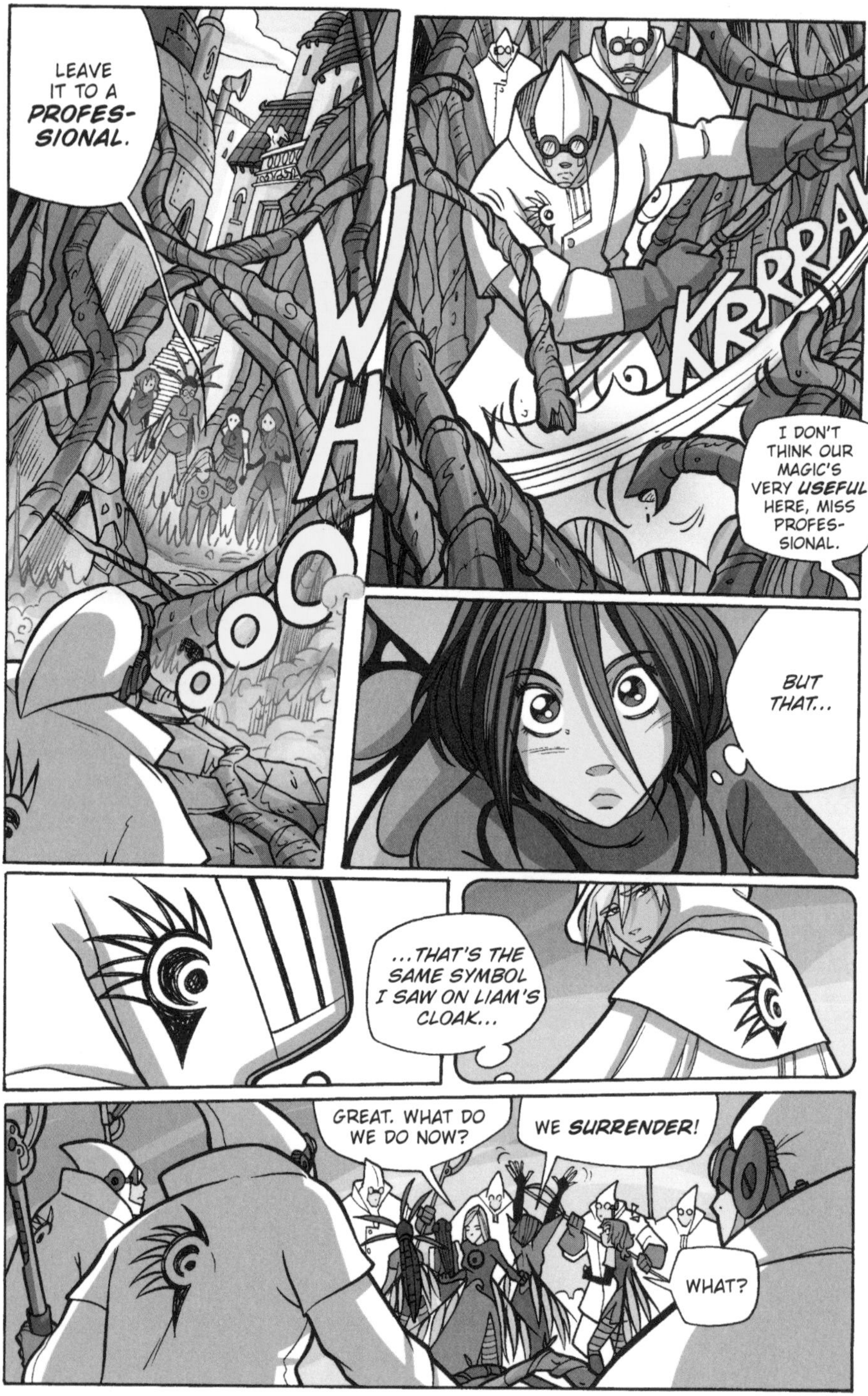
LEAVE IT TO A PROFES-SIONAL.
WHOOOO
KRRRAK
I DON'T THINK OUR MAGIC'S VERY USEFUL HERE, MISS PROFES-SIONAL.
BUT THAT...
...THAT'S THE SAME SYMBOL I SAW ON LIAM'S CLOAK...
GREAT. WHAT DO WE DO NOW?
WE SURRENDER!
WHAT?

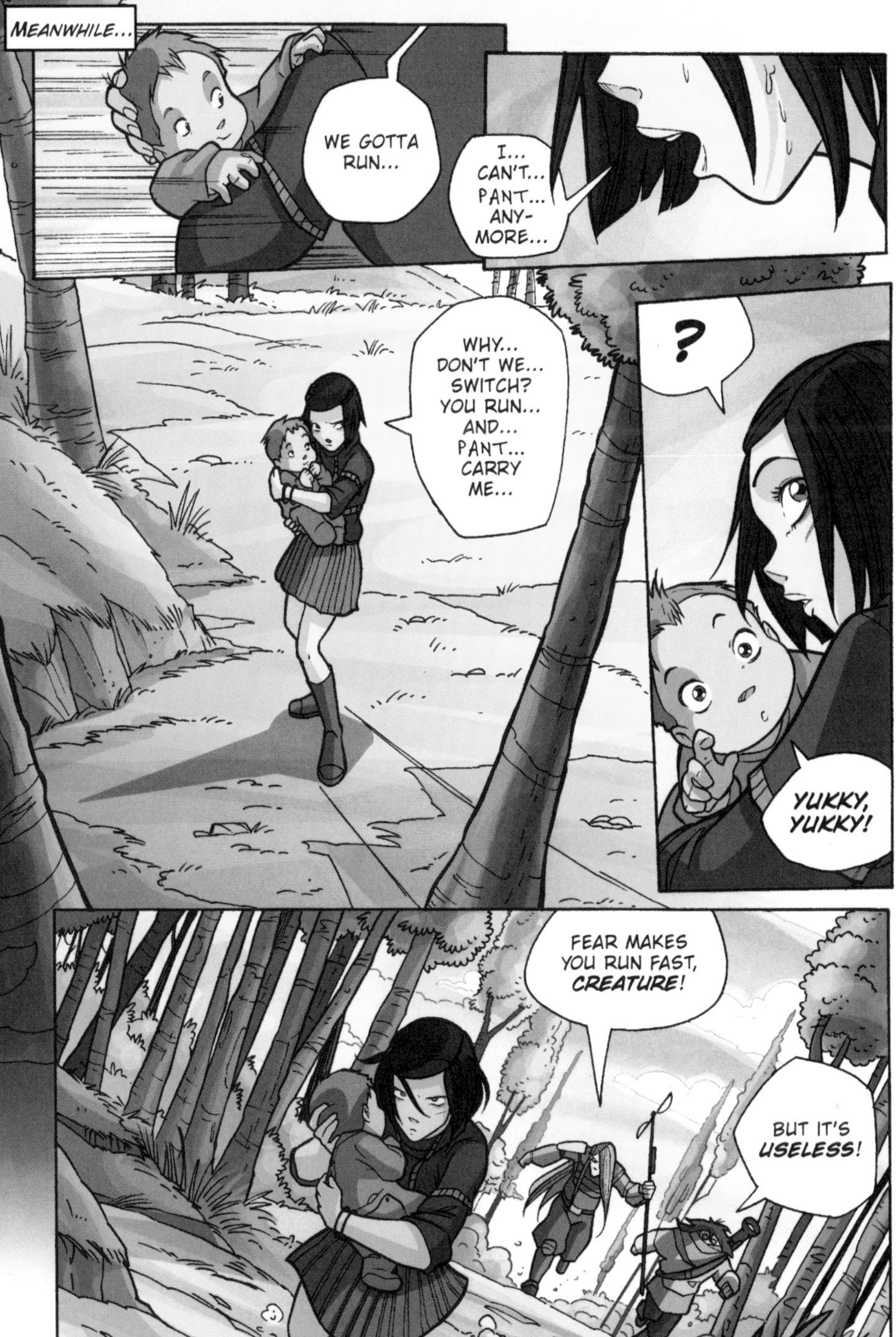
MEANWHILE...
WE GOTTA RUN...
I... CAN'T... PANT... ANY-MORE...
WHY... DON'T WE... SWITCH? YOU RUN... AND... PANT... CARRY ME...
?
YUKKY, YUKKY!
FEAR MAKES YOU RUN FAST, CREATURE!
BUT IT'S USELESS!

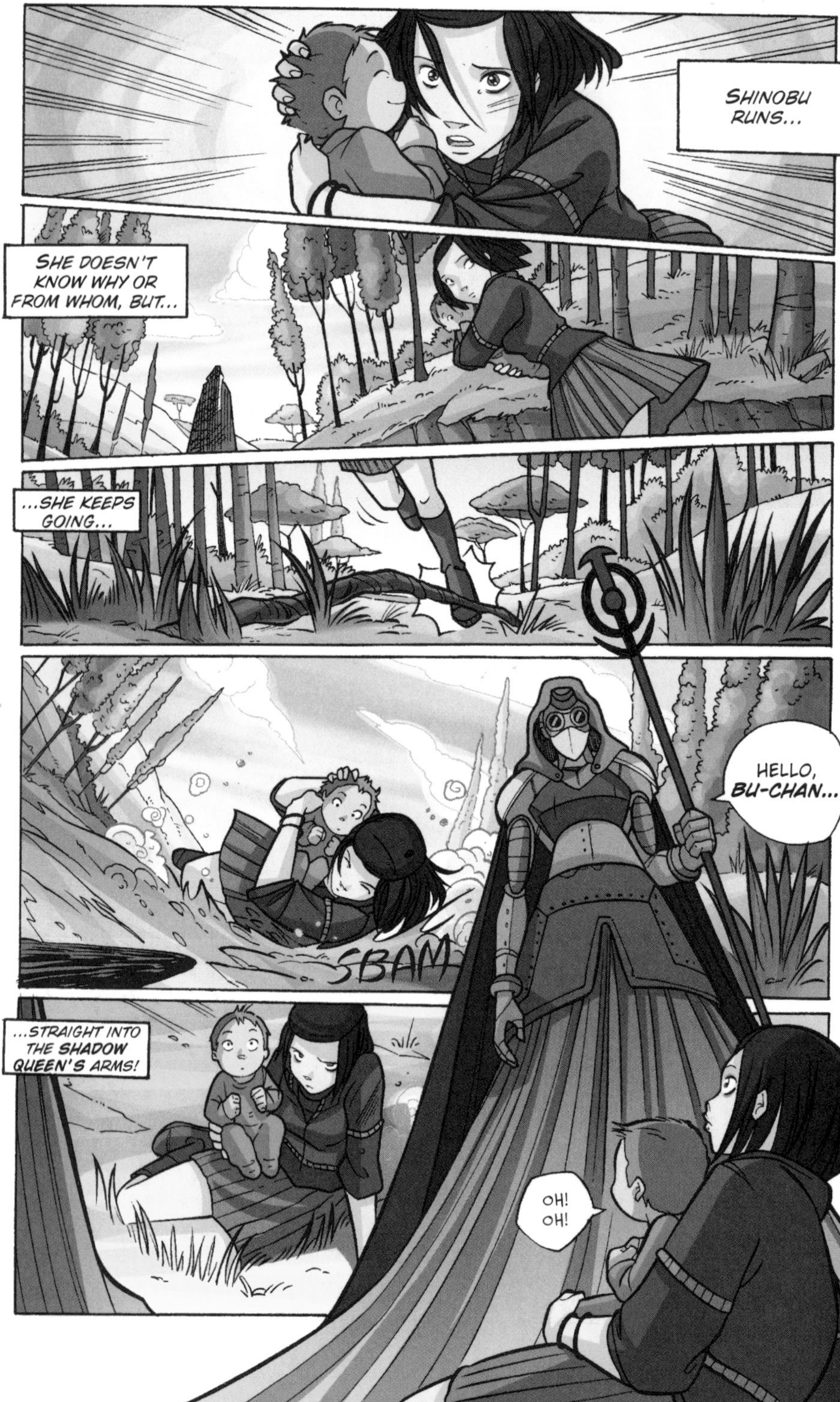

SHINOBU RUNS...
SHE DOESN'T KNOW WHY OR FROM WHOM, BUT...
...SHE KEEPS GOING...
HELLO, BU-CHAN...
SBAM
...STRAIGHT INTO THE SHADOW QUEEN'S ARMS!
OH! OH!

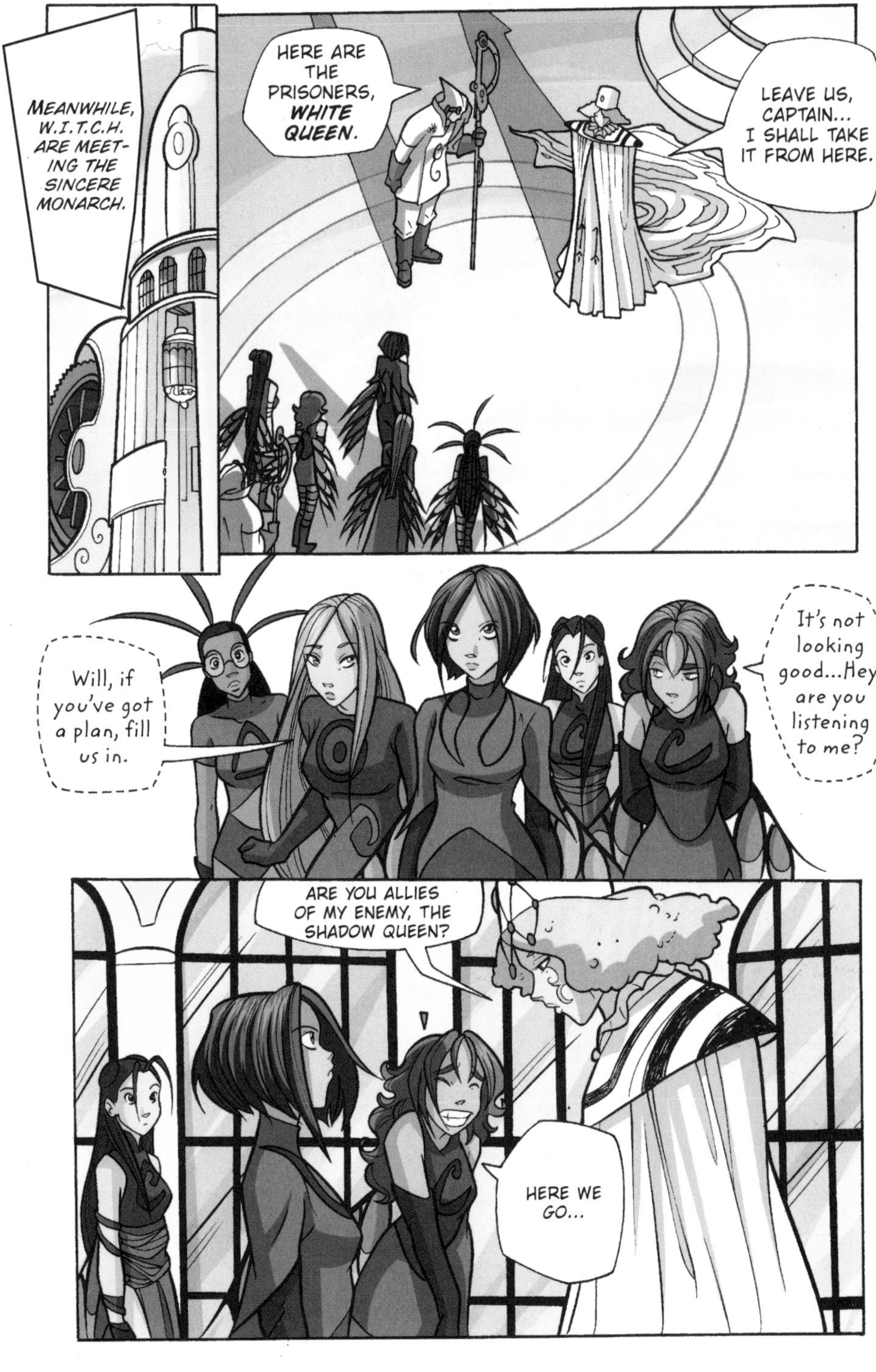
MEANWHILE, W.I.T.C.H. ARE MEETING THE SINCERE MONARCH.
HERE ARE THE PRISONERS, WHITE QUEEN.
LEAVE US, CAPTAIN... I SHALL TAKE IT FROM HERE.
Will, if you've got a plan, fill us in.
It's not looking good...Hey, are you listening to me?
ARE YOU ALLIES OF MY ENEMY, THE SHADOW QUEEN?
HERE WE GO...

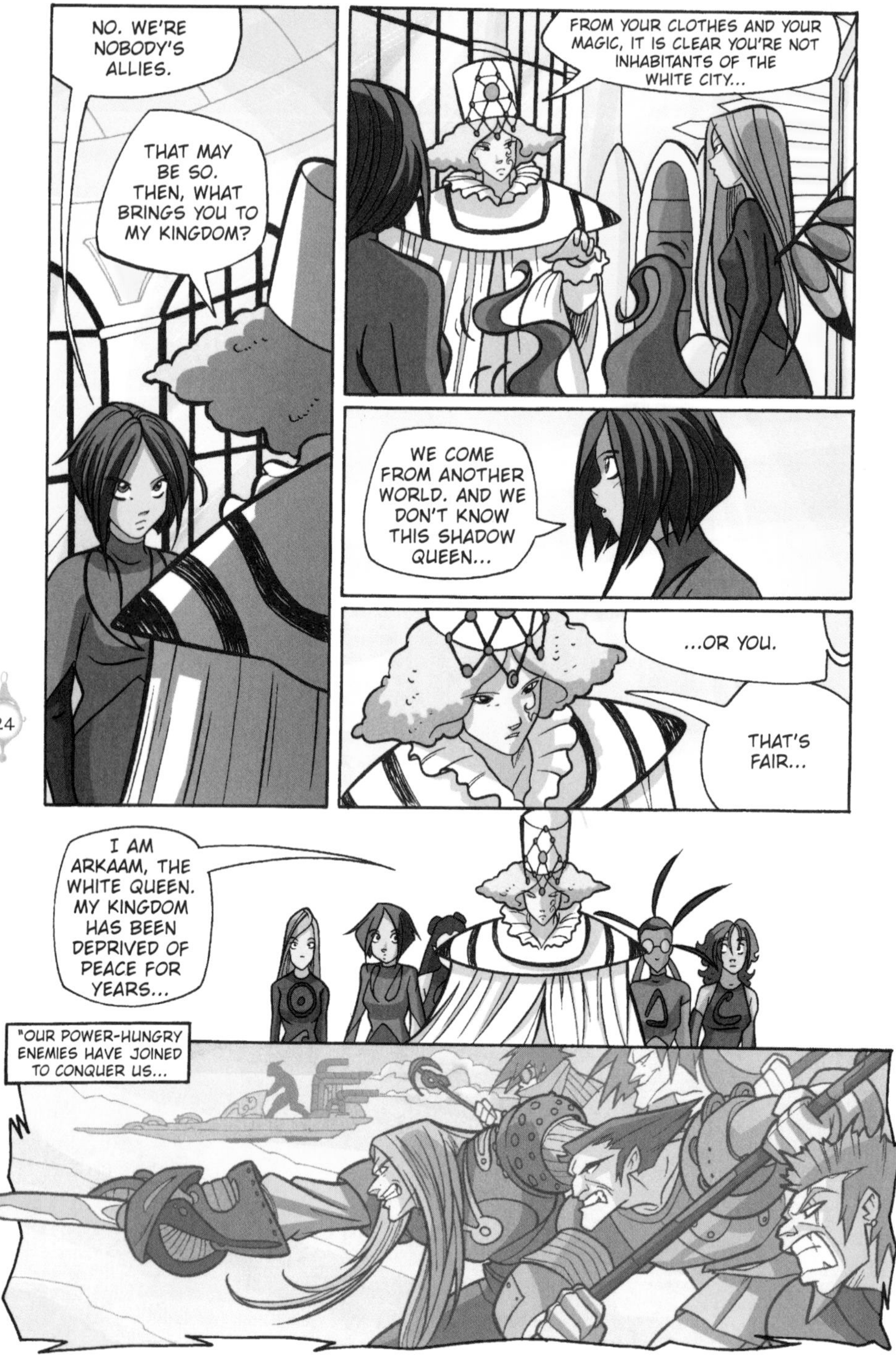
NO. WE'RE NOBODY'S ALLIES.
THAT MAY BE SO. THEN, WHAT BRINGS YOU TO MY KINGDOM?
FROM YOUR CLOTHES AND YOUR MAGIC, IT IS CLEAR YOU'RE NOT INHABITANTS OF THE WHITE CITY...
WE COME FROM ANOTHER WORLD. AND WE DON'T KNOW THIS SHADOW QUEEN...
...OR YOU.
THAT'S FAIR...
I AM ARKAAM, THE WHITE QUEEN. MY KINGDOM HAS BEEN DEPRIVED OF PEACE FOR YEARS...
"OUR POWER-HUNGRY ENEMIES HAVE JOINED TO CONQUER US...

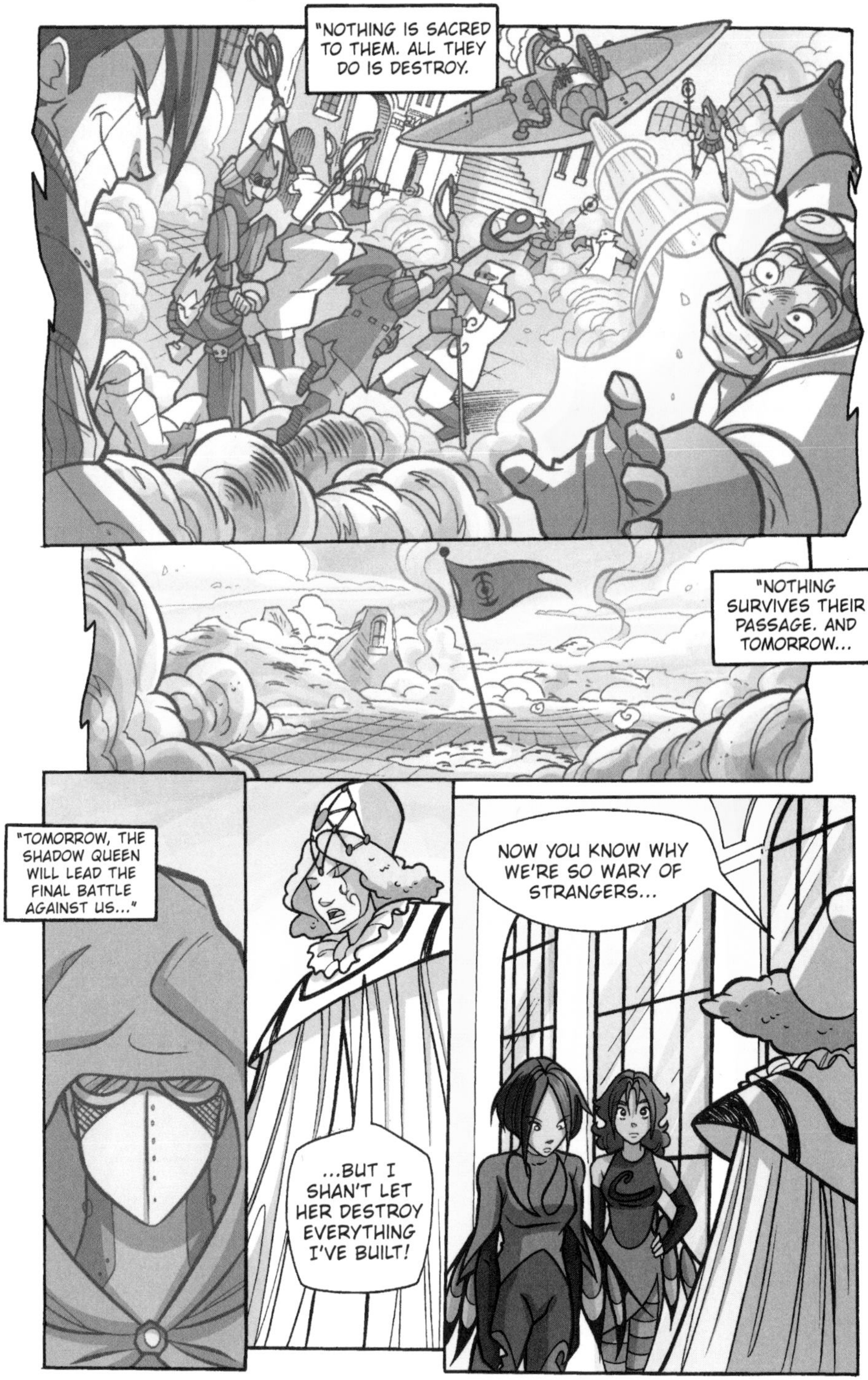
"NOTHING IS SACRED TO THEM. ALL THEY DO IS DESTROY.
"NOTHING SURVIVES THEIR PASSAGE. AND TOMORROW...
"TOMORROW, THE SHADOW QUEEN WILL LEAD THE FINAL BATTLE AGAINST US..."
...BUT I SHAN'T LET HER DESTROY EVERYTHING I'VE BUILT!
NOW YOU KNOW WHY WE'RE SO WARY OF STRANGERS...

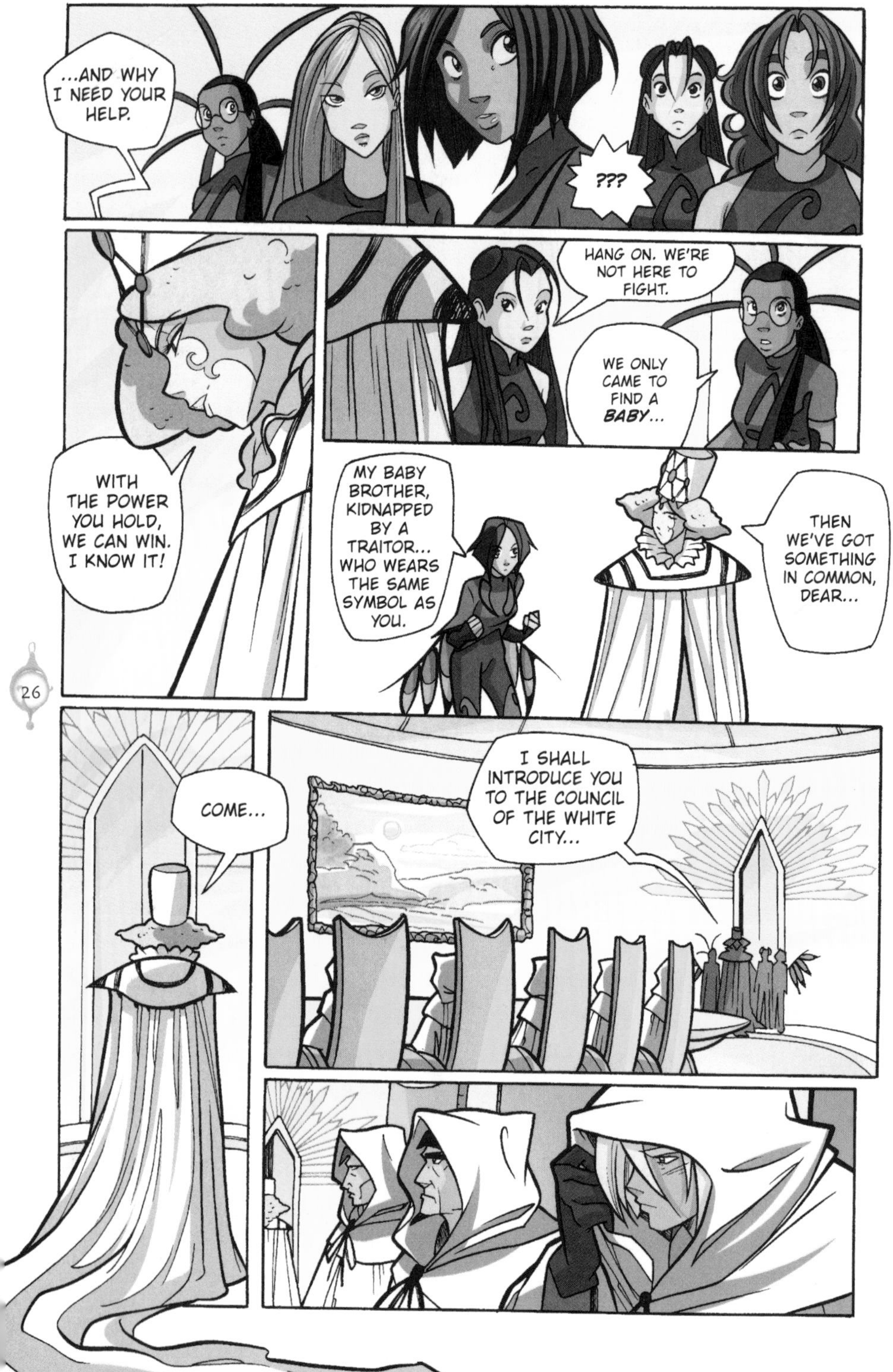
...AND WHY I NEED YOUR HELP.
???
HANG ON. WE'RE NOT HERE TO FIGHT.
WE ONLY CAME TO FIND A *BABY*...
WITH THE POWER YOU HOLD, WE CAN WIN. I KNOW IT!
MY BABY BROTHER, KIDNAPPED BY A TRAITOR... WHO WEARS THE SAME SYMBOL AS YOU.
THEN WE'VE GOT SOMETHING IN COMMON, DEAR...
COME...
I SHALL INTRODUCE YOU TO THE COUNCIL OF THE WHITE CITY...

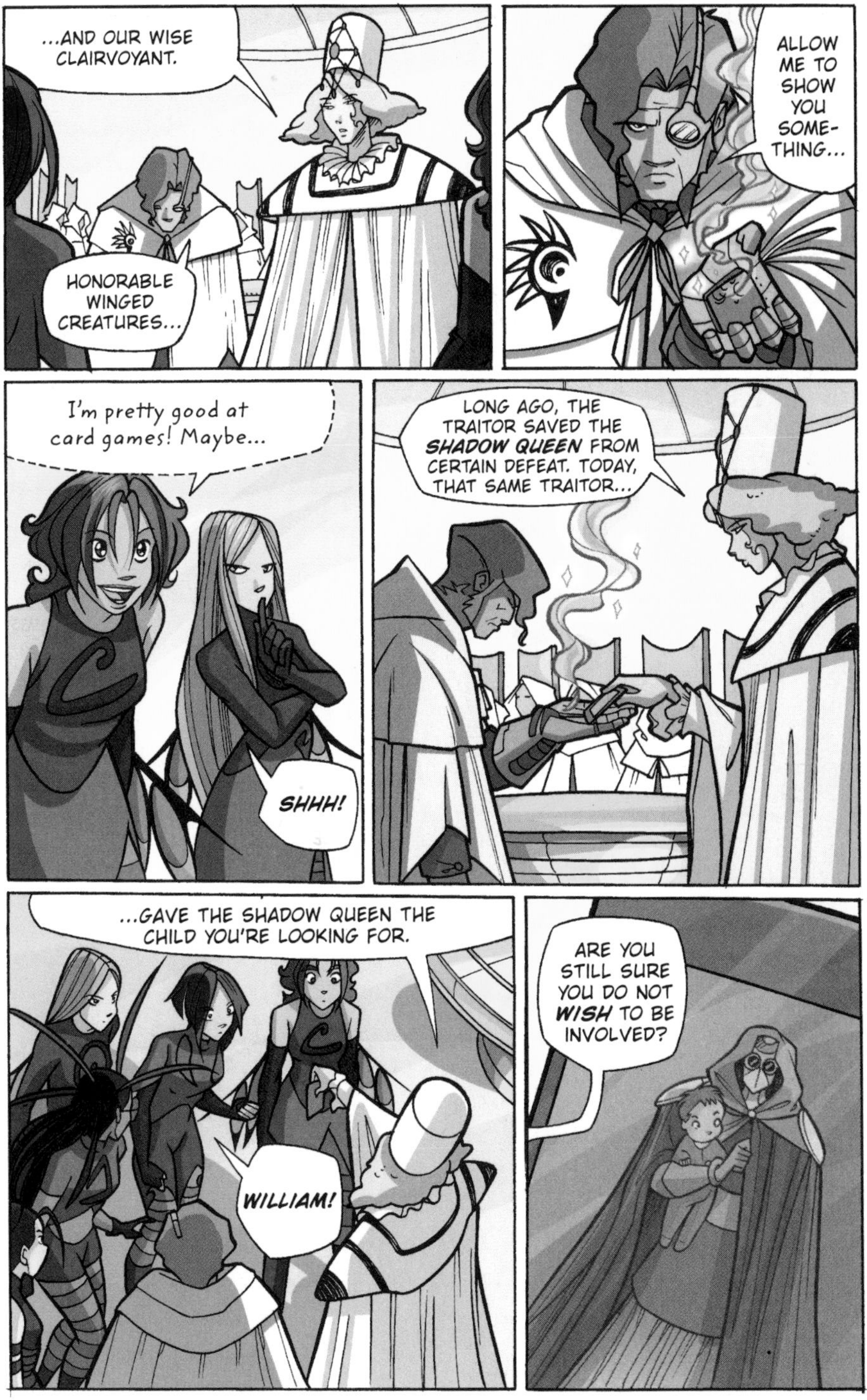
...AND OUR WISE CLAIRVOYANT.
HONORABLE WINGED CREATURES...
ALLOW ME TO SHOW YOU SOME-THING...
I'm pretty good at card games! Maybe...
SHHH!
LONG AGO, THE TRAITOR SAVED THE SHADOW QUEEN FROM CERTAIN DEFEAT. TODAY, THAT SAME TRAITOR...
...GAVE THE SHADOW QUEEN THE CHILD YOU'RE LOOKING FOR.
WILLIAM!
ARE YOU STILL SURE YOU DO NOT WISH TO BE INVOLVED?

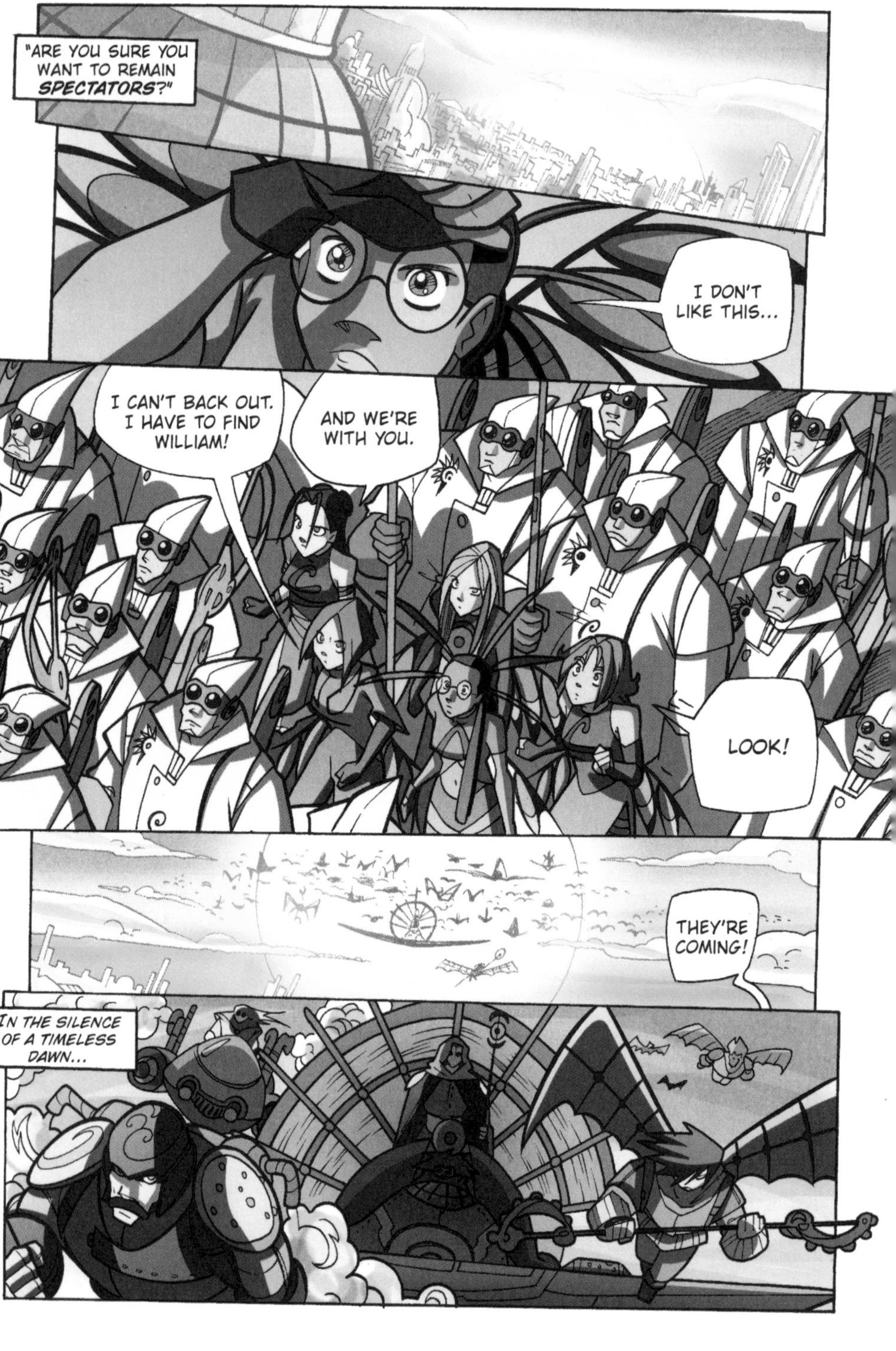
"ARE YOU SURE YOU WANT TO REMAIN SPECTATORS?"
I DON'T LIKE THIS...
I CAN'T BACK OUT. I HAVE TO FIND WILLIAM!
AND WE'RE WITH YOU.
LOOK!
THEY'RE COMING!
IN THE SILENCE OF A TIMELESS DAWN...

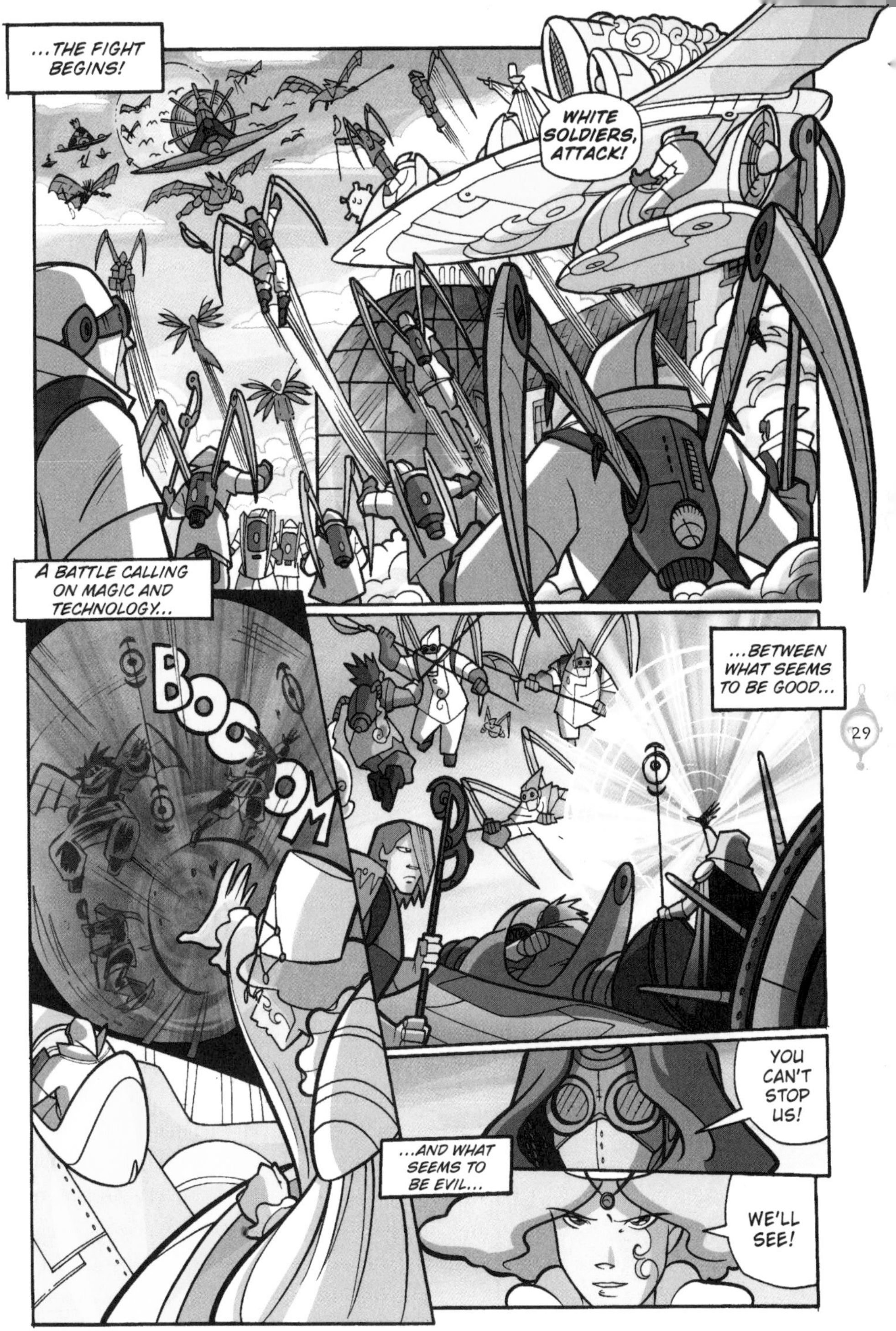
...THE FIGHT BEGINS!
WHITE SOLDIERS, ATTACK!
A BATTLE CALLING ON MAGIC AND TECHNOLOGY...
BOOOM
...BETWEEN WHAT SEEMS TO BE GOOD...
YOU CAN'T STOP US!
...AND WHAT SEEMS TO BE EVIL...
WE'LL SEE!

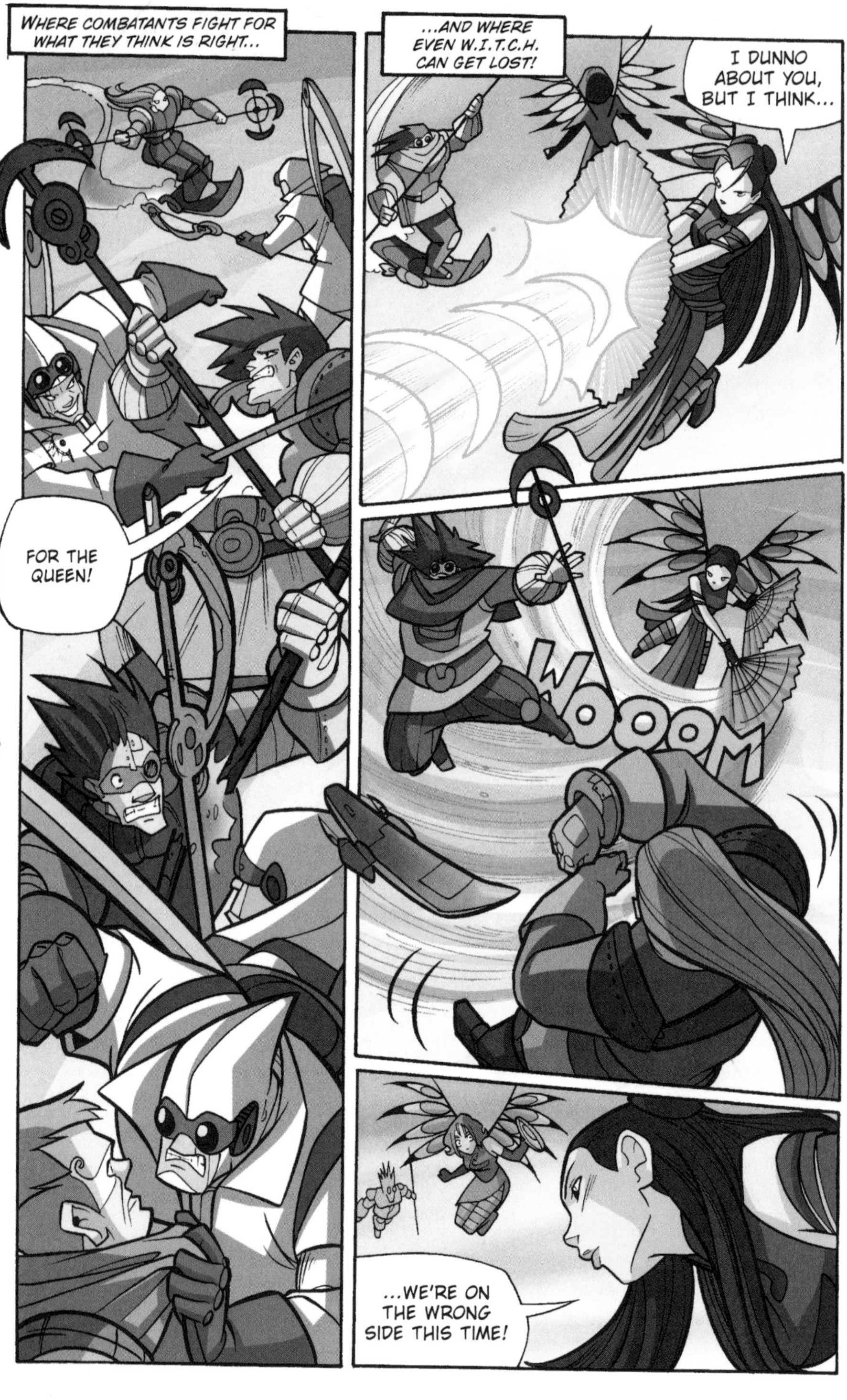

WHERE COMBATANTS FIGHT FOR WHAT THEY THINK IS RIGHT...
FOR THE QUEEN!
...AND WHERE EVEN W.I.T.C.H. CAN GET LOST!
I DUNNO ABOUT YOU, BUT I THINK...
WOOOM
...WE'RE ON THE WRONG SIDE THIS TIME!

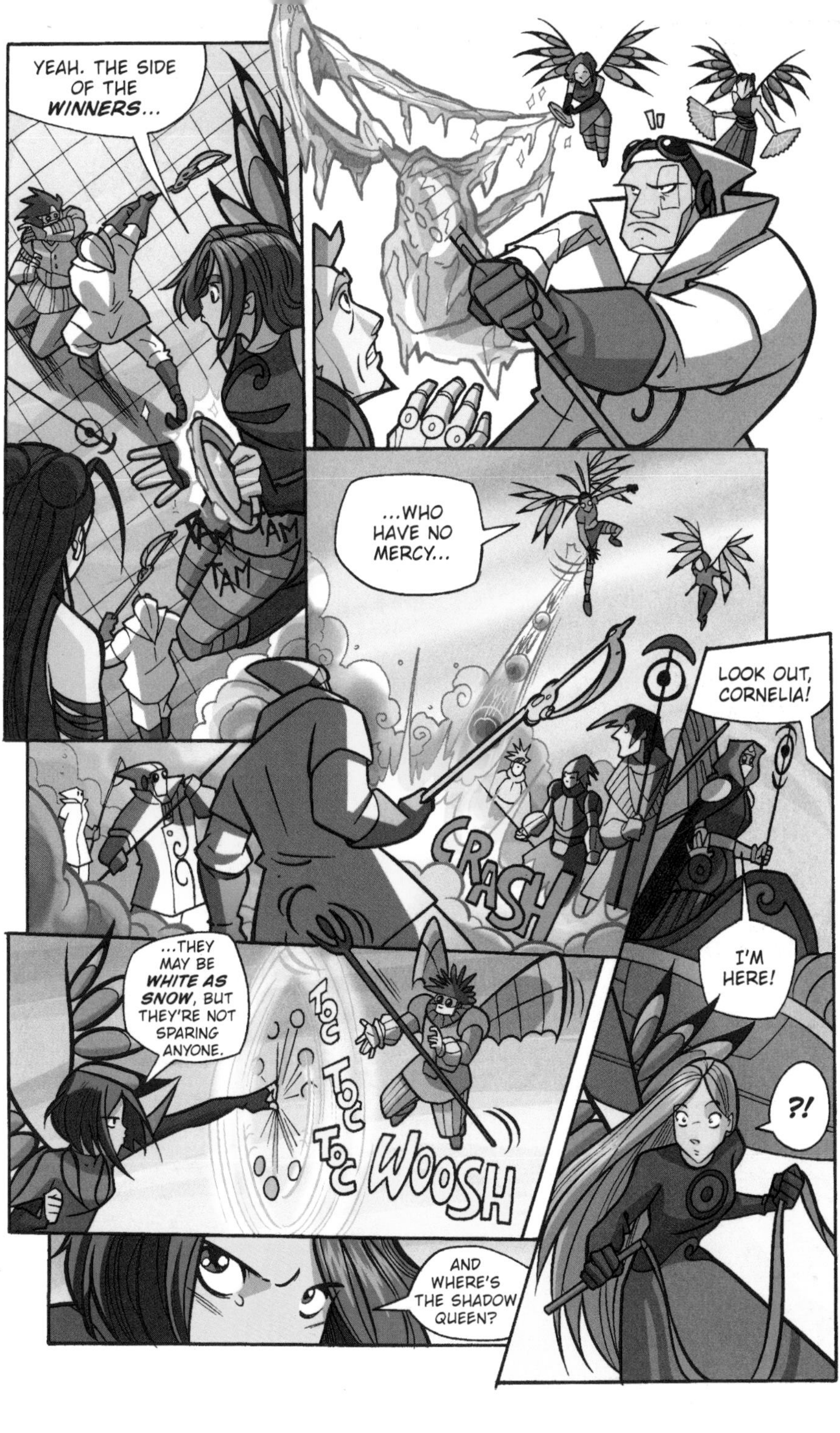

YEAH. THE SIDE OF THE *WINNERS*...
TAM TAM TAM
...WHO HAVE NO MERCY...
LOOK OUT, CORNELIA!
CRASH
I'M HERE!
...THEY MAY BE *WHITE AS SNOW*, BUT THEY'RE NOT SPARING ANYONE.
TOC TOC TOC TOC
WOOSH
?!
AND WHERE'S THE SHADOW QUEEN?

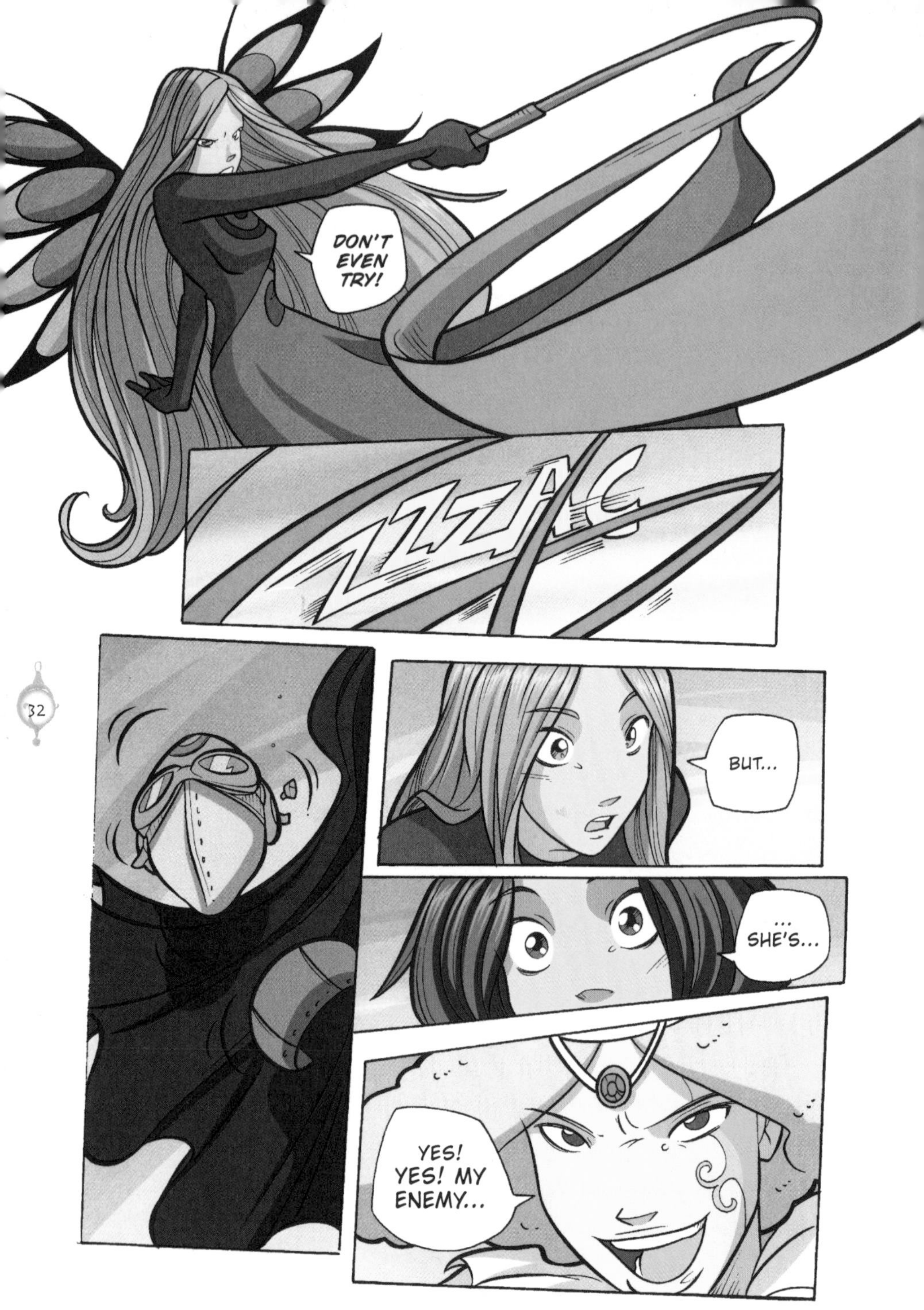
DON'T EVEN TRY!
ZZZAC
BUT...
... SHE'S...
YES! YES! MY ENEMY...

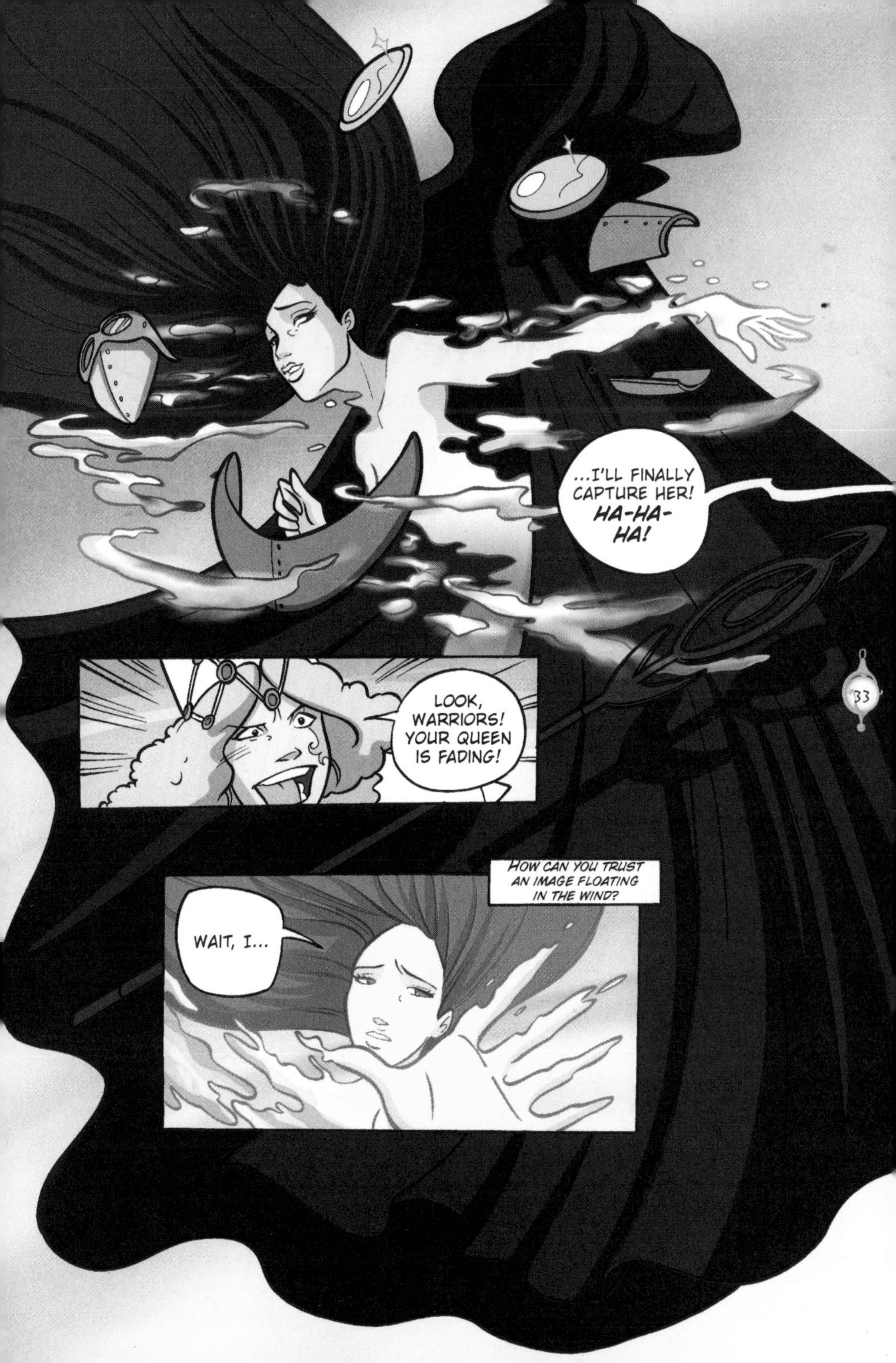

...I'LL FINALLY CAPTURE HER! HA-HA-HA!
LOOK, WARRIORS! YOUR QUEEN IS FADING!
HOW CAN YOU TRUST AN IMAGE FLOATING IN THE WIND?
WAIT, I...

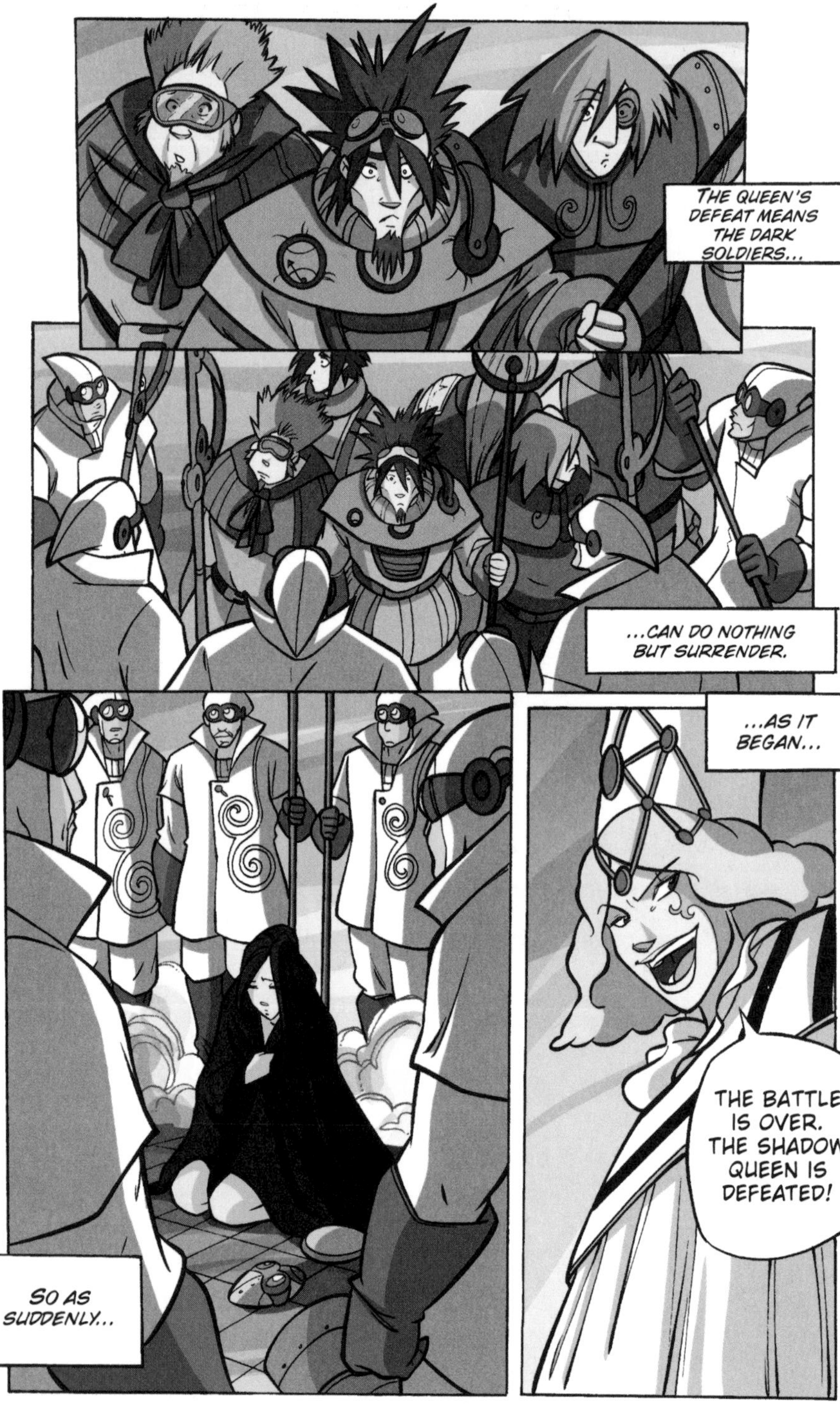

THE QUEEN'S DEFEAT MEANS THE DARK SOLDIERS...
...CAN DO NOTHING BUT SURRENDER.
SO AS SUDDENLY...
...AS IT BEGAN...
THE BATTLE IS OVER. THE SHADOW QUEEN IS DEFEATED!

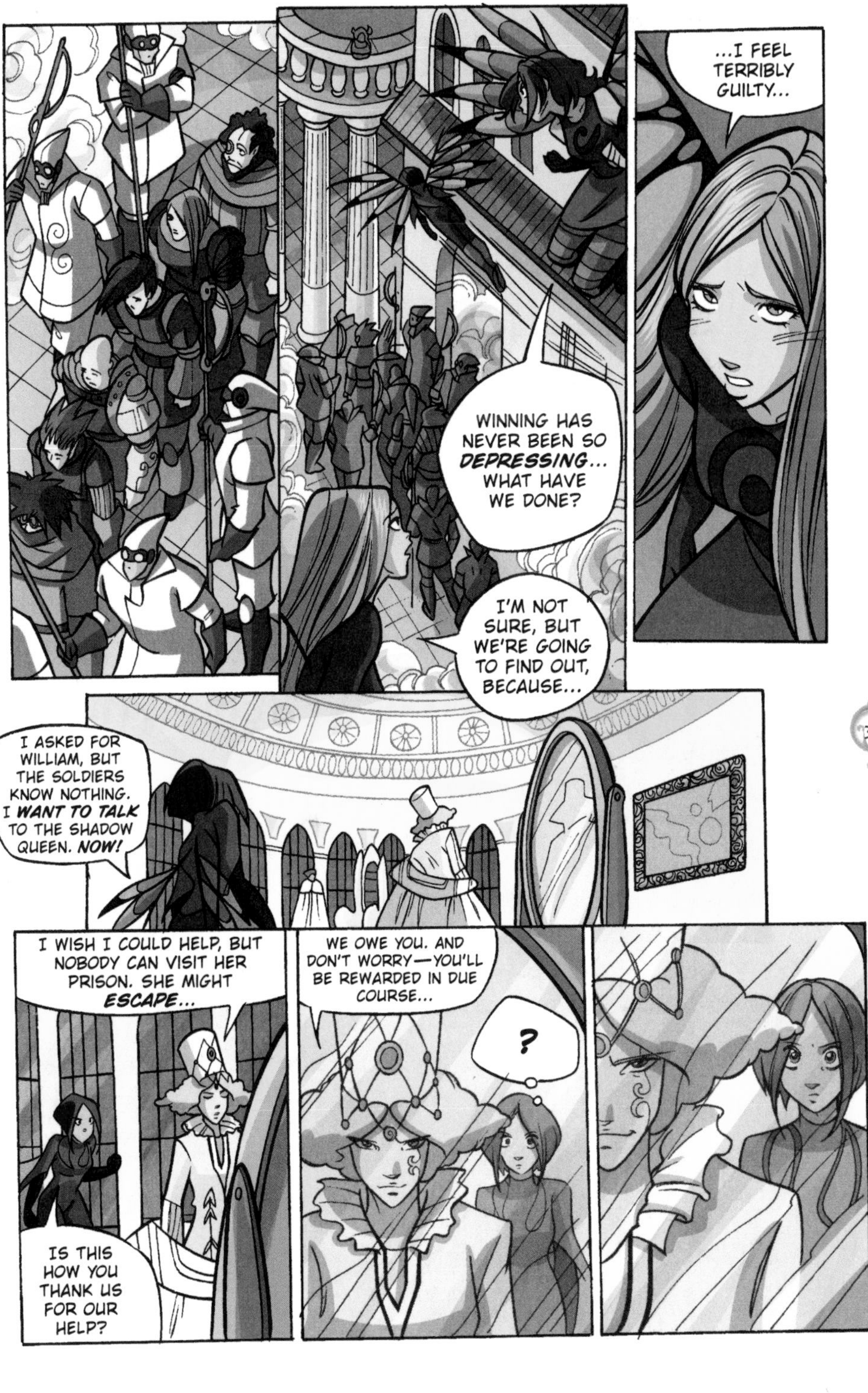
WINNING HAS NEVER BEEN SO DEPRESSING... WHAT HAVE WE DONE?
I'M NOT SURE, BUT WE'RE GOING TO FIND OUT, BECAUSE...
...I FEEL TERRIBLY GUILTY...
I ASKED FOR WILLIAM, BUT THE SOLDIERS KNOW NOTHING. I WANT TO TALK TO THE SHADOW QUEEN. NOW!
I WISH I COULD HELP, BUT NOBODY CAN VISIT HER PRISON. SHE MIGHT ESCAPE...
IS THIS HOW YOU THANK US FOR OUR HELP?
WE OWE YOU. AND DON'T WORRY—YOU'LL BE REWARDED IN DUE COURSE...
?

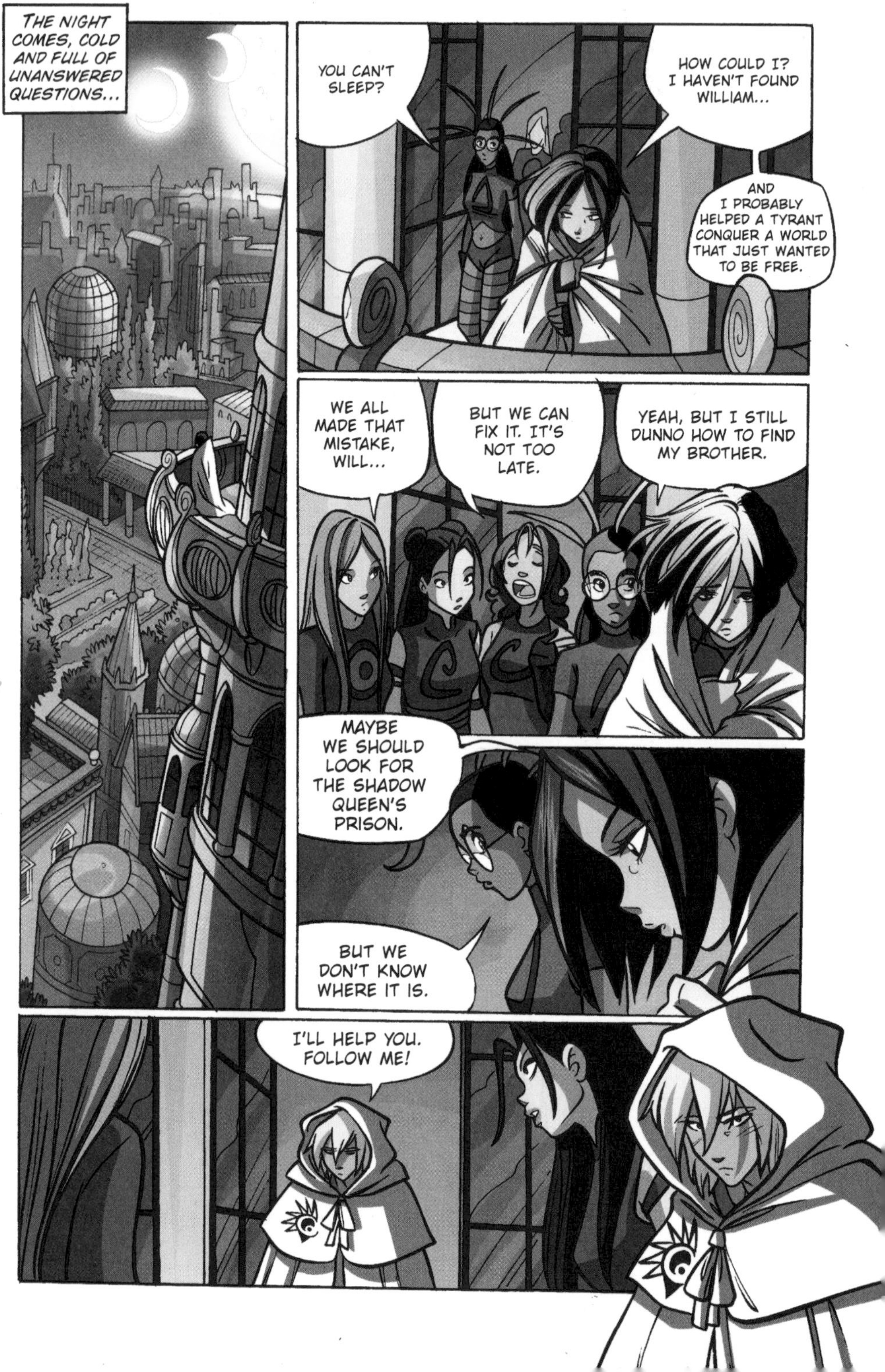

THE NIGHT COMES, COLD AND FULL OF UNANSWERED QUESTIONS...
YOU CAN'T SLEEP?
HOW COULD I? I HAVEN'T FOUND WILLIAM...
AND I PROBABLY HELPED A TYRANT CONQUER A WORLD THAT JUST WANTED TO BE FREE.
WE ALL MADE THAT MISTAKE, WILL...
BUT WE CAN FIX IT. IT'S NOT TOO LATE.
YEAH, BUT I STILL DUNNO HOW TO FIND MY BROTHER.
MAYBE WE SHOULD LOOK FOR THE SHADOW QUEEN'S PRISON.
BUT WE DON'T KNOW WHERE IT IS.
I'LL HELP YOU. FOLLOW ME!

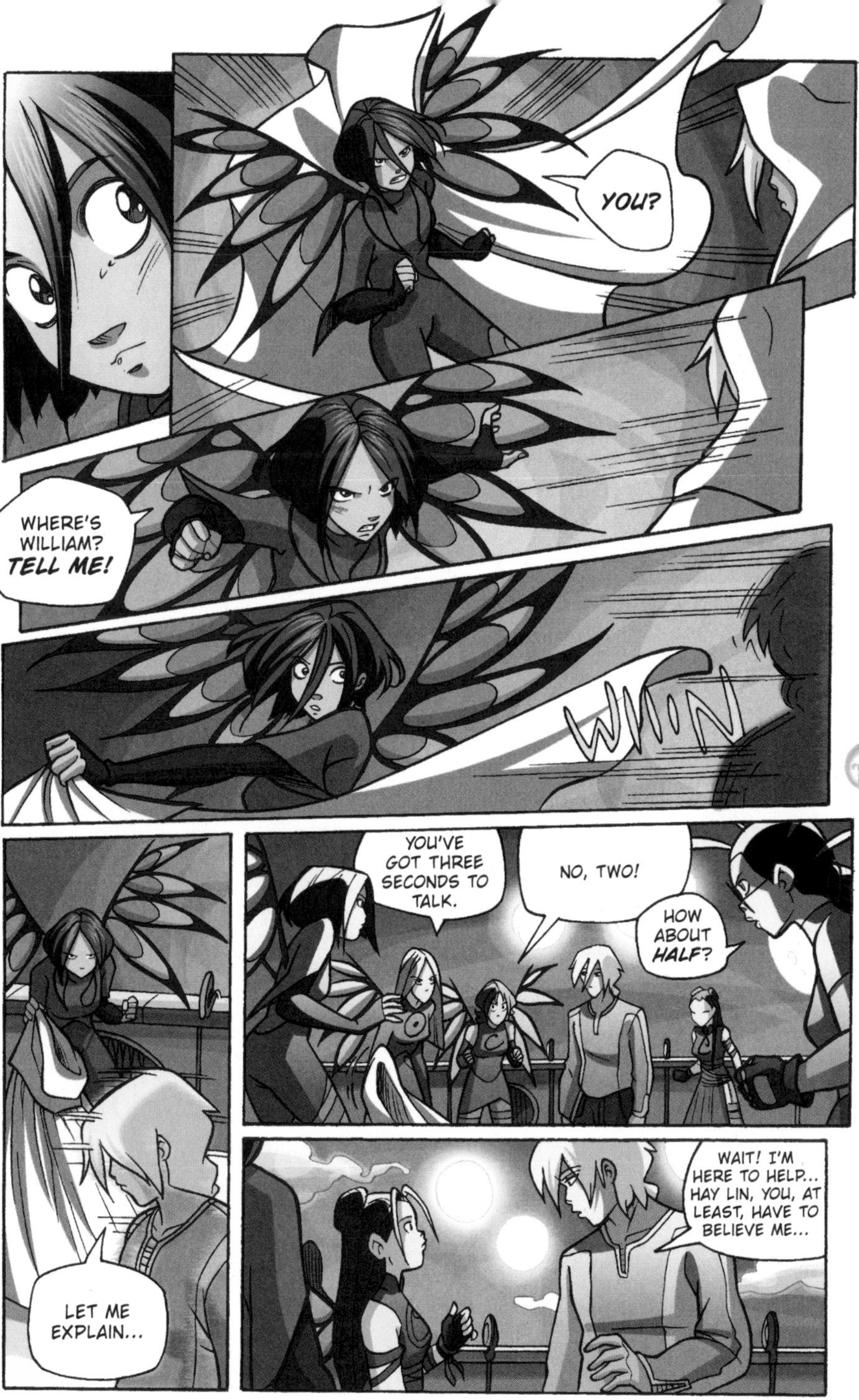
YOU?
WHERE'S WILLIAM? TELL ME!
WHIN
YOU'VE GOT THREE SECONDS TO TALK.
NO, TWO!
HOW ABOUT HALF?
LET ME EXPLAIN...
WAIT! I'M HERE TO HELP... HAY LIN, YOU, AT LEAST, HAVE TO BELIEVE ME...

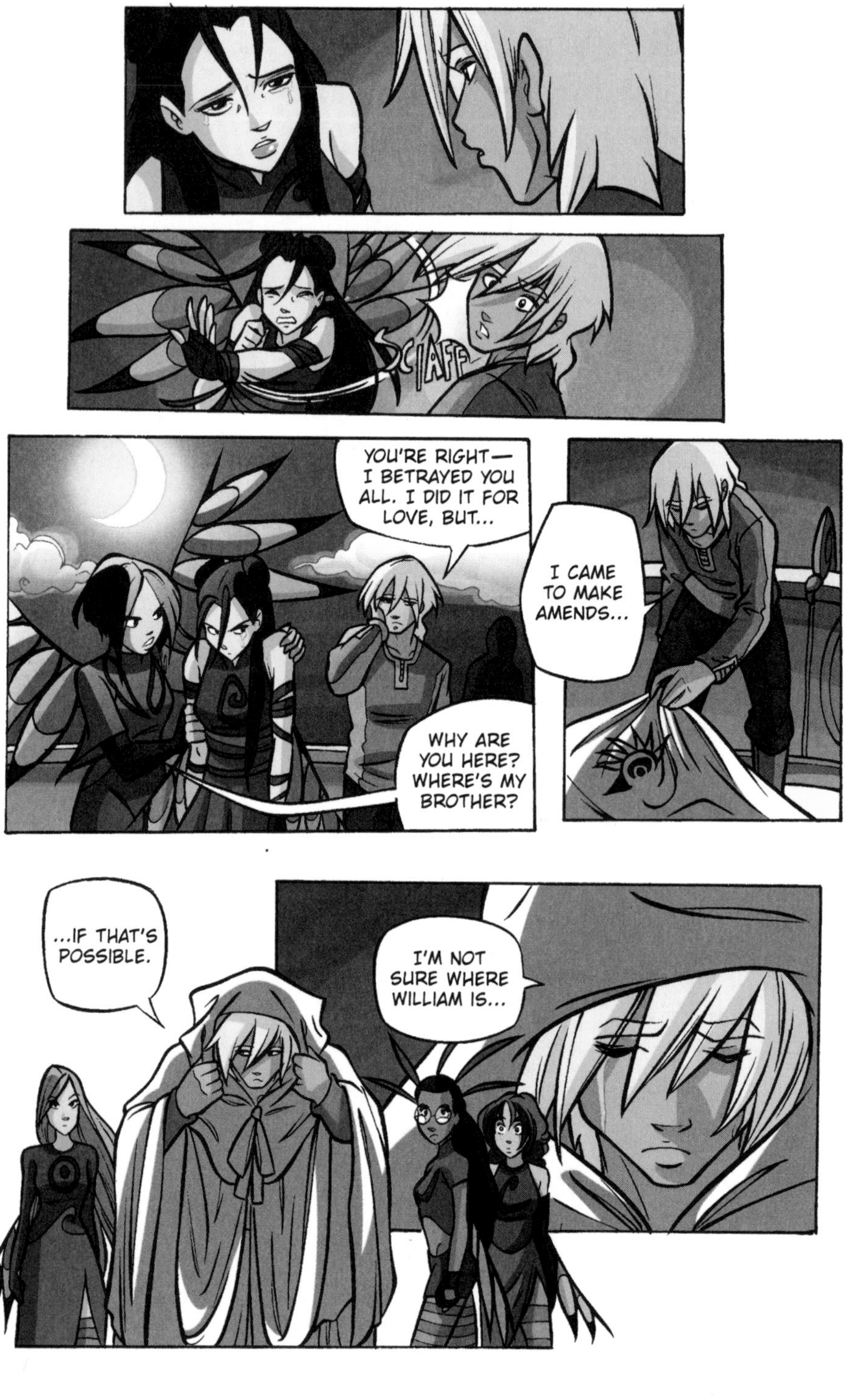
CIAFF
YOU'RE RIGHT— I BETRAYED YOU ALL. I DID IT FOR LOVE, BUT...
WHY ARE YOU HERE? WHERE'S MY BROTHER?
I CAME TO MAKE AMENDS...
...IF THAT'S POSSIBLE.
I'M NOT SURE WHERE WILLIAM IS...

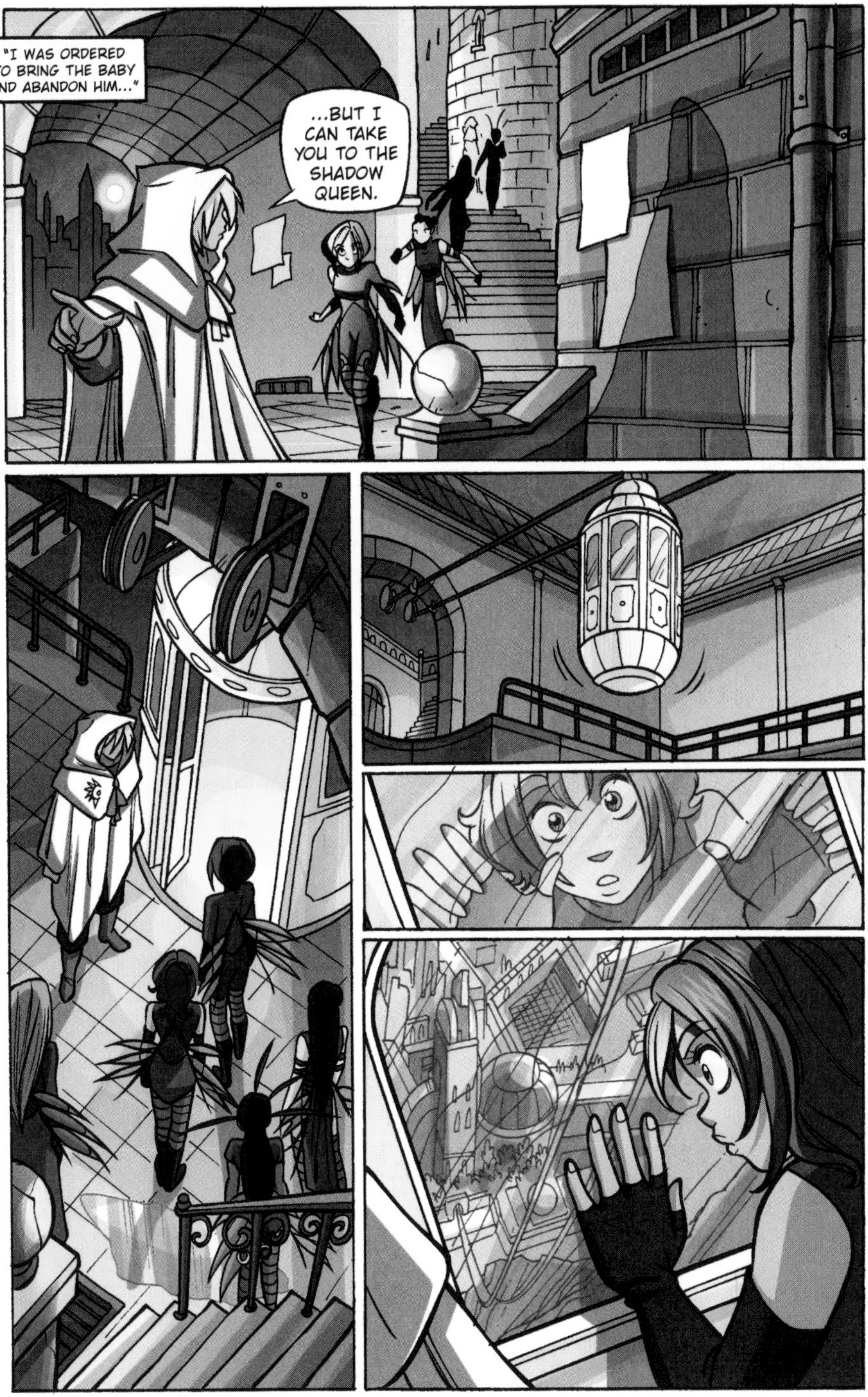
"I WAS ORDERED TO BRING THE BABY AND ABANDON HIM..."
...BUT I CAN TAKE YOU TO THE SHADOW QUEEN.

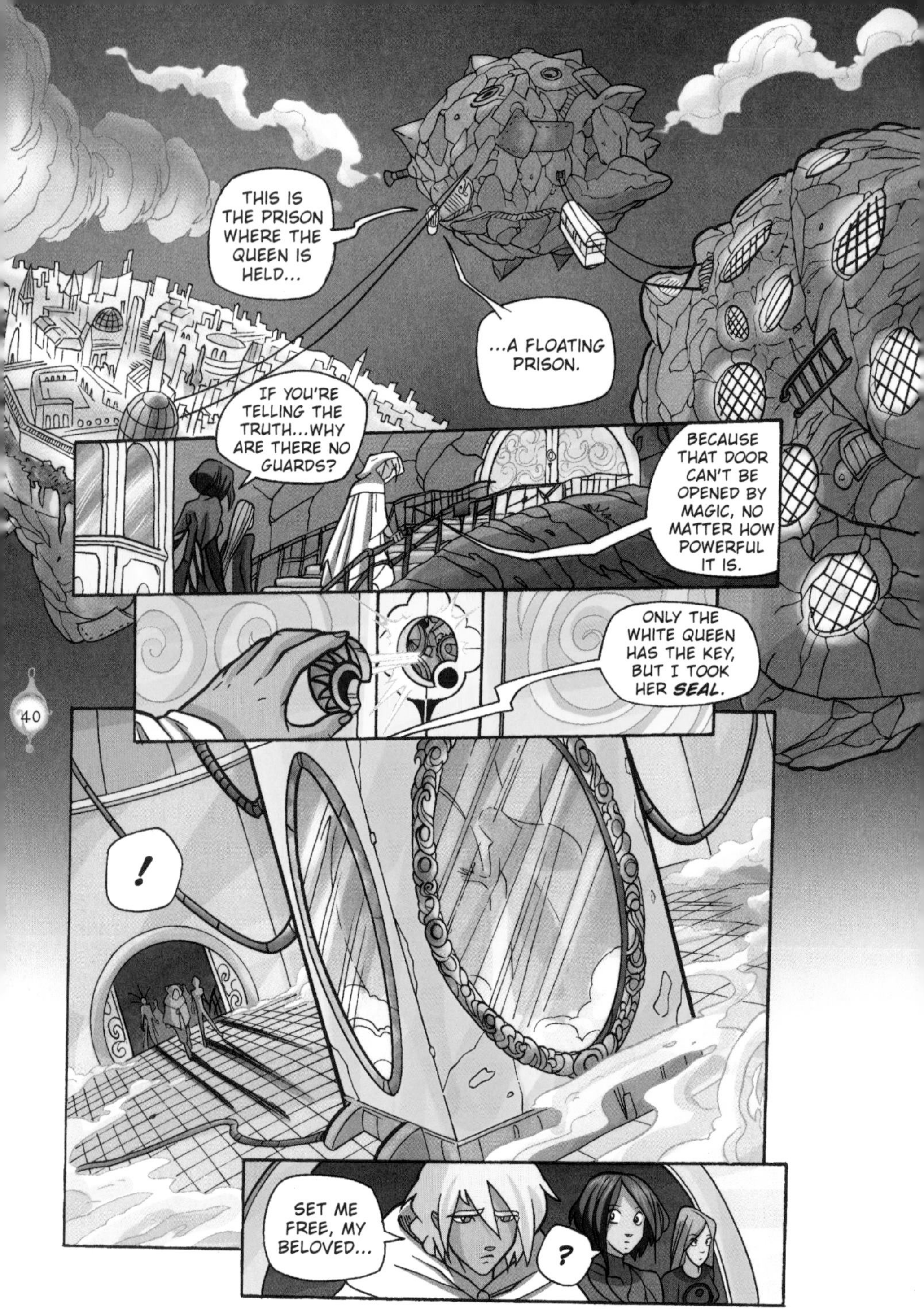
THIS IS THE PRISON WHERE THE QUEEN IS HELD...
...A FLOATING PRISON.
IF YOU'RE TELLING THE TRUTH...WHY ARE THERE NO GUARDS?
BECAUSE THAT DOOR CAN'T BE OPENED BY MAGIC, NO MATTER HOW POWERFUL IT IS.
ONLY THE WHITE QUEEN HAS THE KEY, BUT I TOOK HER **SEAL**.
!
SET ME FREE, MY BELOVED...
?

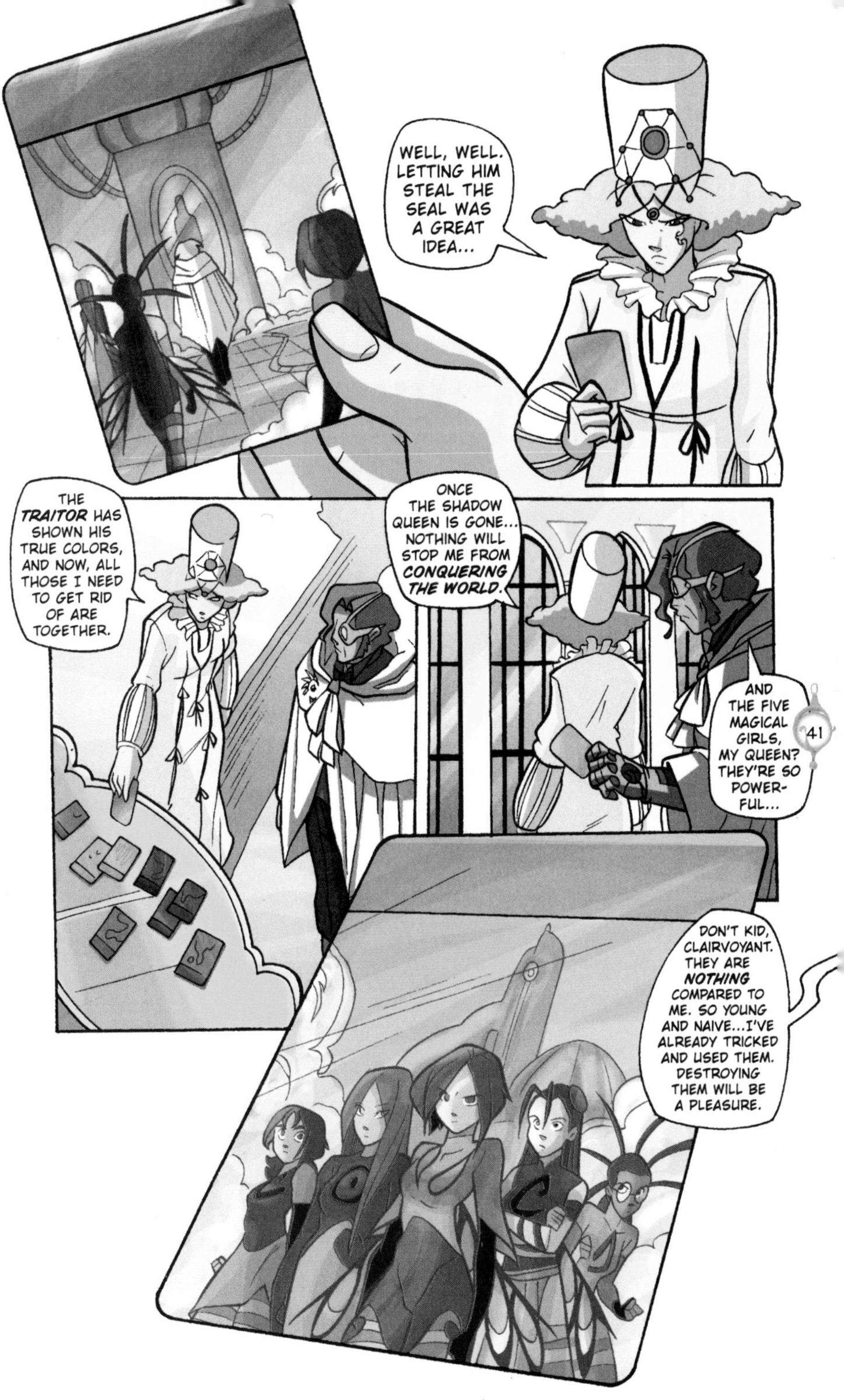

WELL, WELL. LETTING HIM STEAL THE SEAL WAS A GREAT IDEA...
THE TRAITOR HAS SHOWN HIS TRUE COLORS, AND NOW, ALL THOSE I NEED TO GET RID OF ARE TOGETHER.
ONCE THE SHADOW QUEEN IS GONE... NOTHING WILL STOP ME FROM CONQUERING THE WORLD.
AND THE FIVE MAGICAL GIRLS, MY QUEEN? THEY'RE SO POWER-FUL...
DON'T KID, CLAIRVOYANT. THEY ARE NOTHING COMPARED TO ME. SO YOUNG AND NAIVE...I'VE ALREADY TRICKED AND USED THEM. DESTROYING THEM WILL BE A PLEASURE.

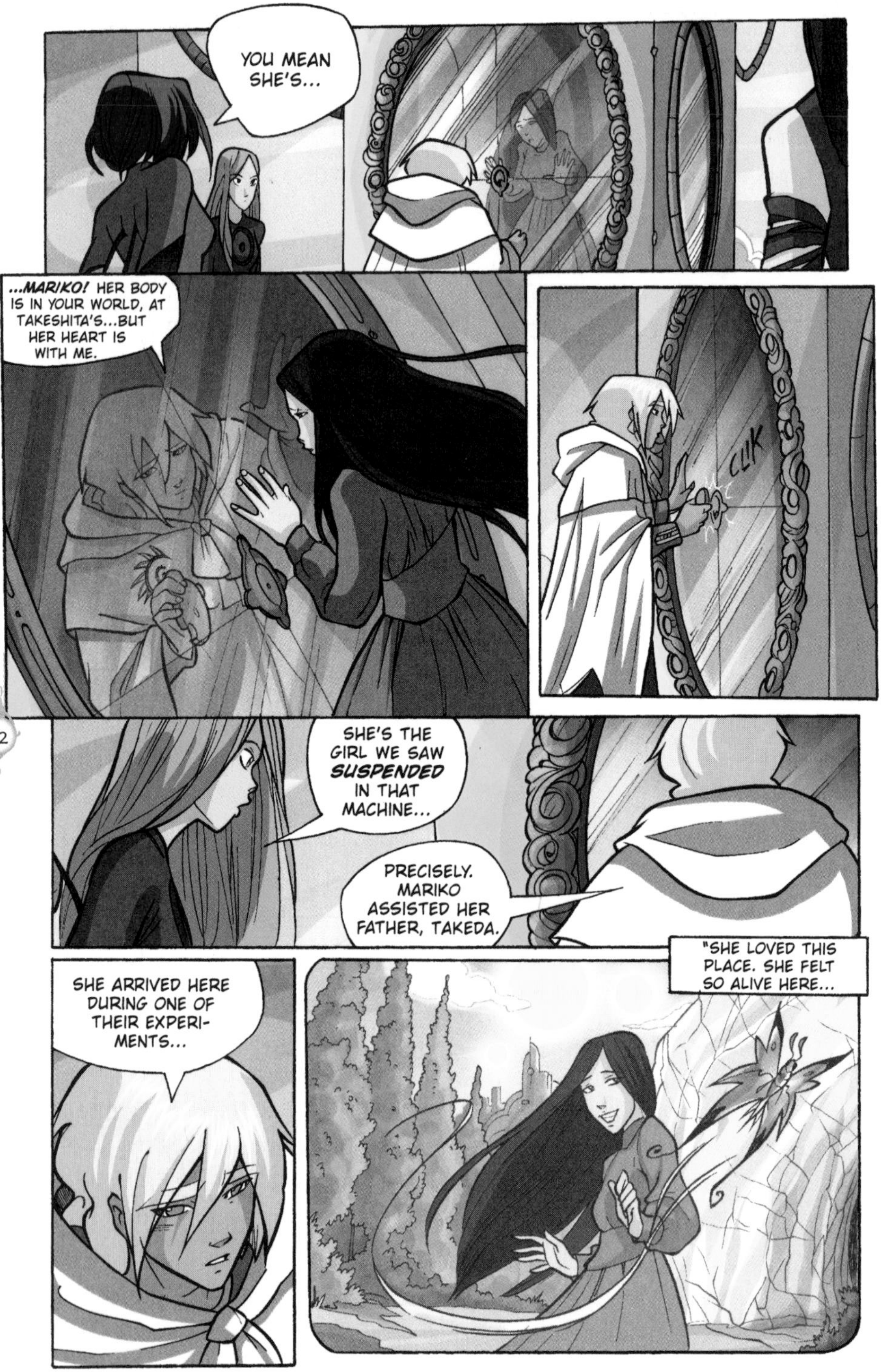
YOU MEAN SHE'S...
...MARIKO! HER BODY IS IN YOUR WORLD, AT TAKESHITA'S...BUT HER HEART IS WITH ME.
CLIK
SHE'S THE GIRL WE SAW SUSPENDED IN THAT MACHINE...
PRECISELY. MARIKO ASSISTED HER FATHER, TAKEDA.
SHE ARRIVED HERE DURING ONE OF THEIR EXPERI-MENTS...
"SHE LOVED THIS PLACE. SHE FELT SO ALIVE HERE...

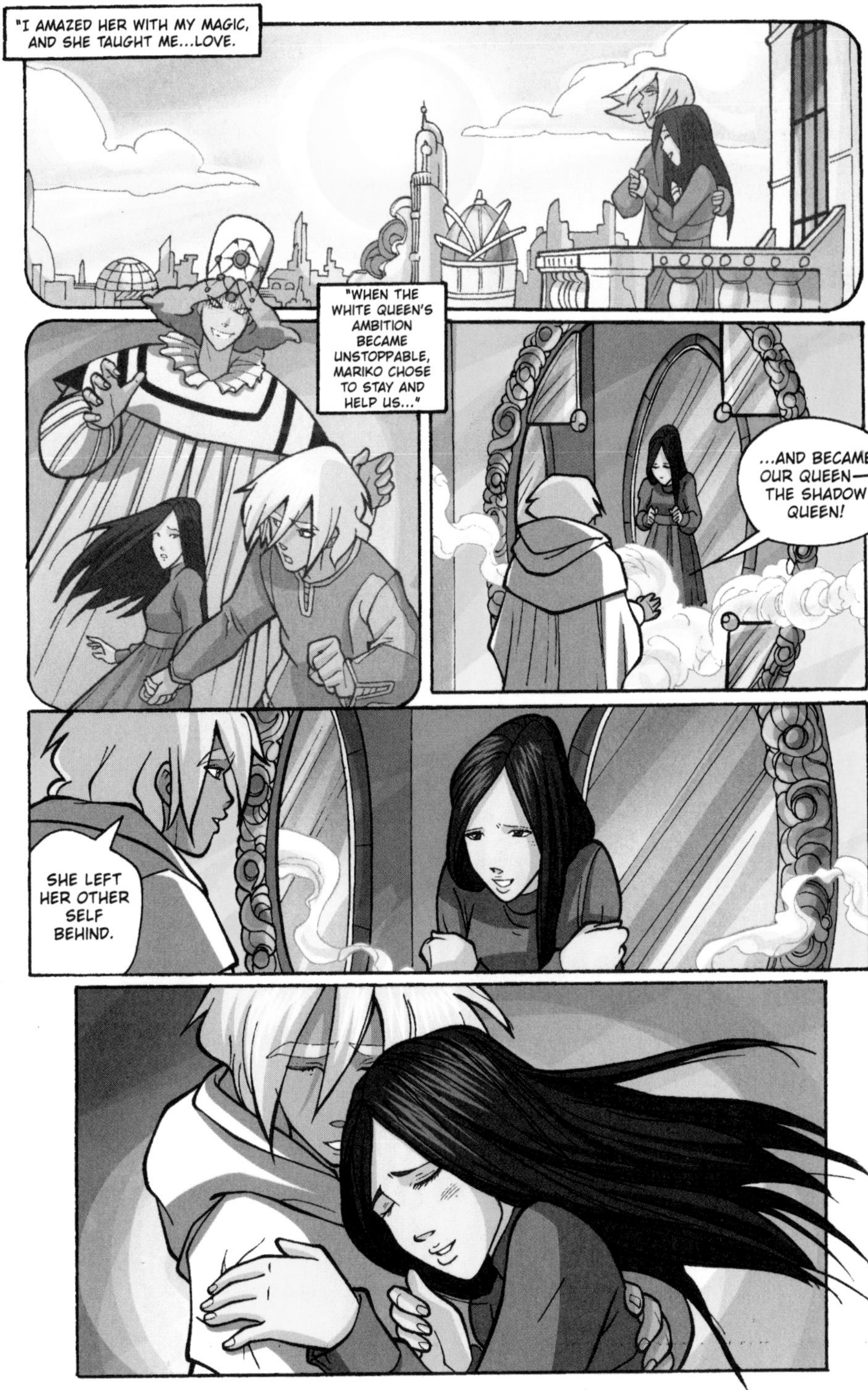
"I AMAZED HER WITH MY MAGIC, AND SHE TAUGHT ME...LOVE.
"WHEN THE WHITE QUEEN'S AMBITION BECAME UNSTOPPABLE, MARIKO CHOSE TO STAY AND HELP US..."
...AND BECAME OUR QUEEN— THE SHADOW QUEEN!
SHE LEFT HER OTHER SELF BEHIND.

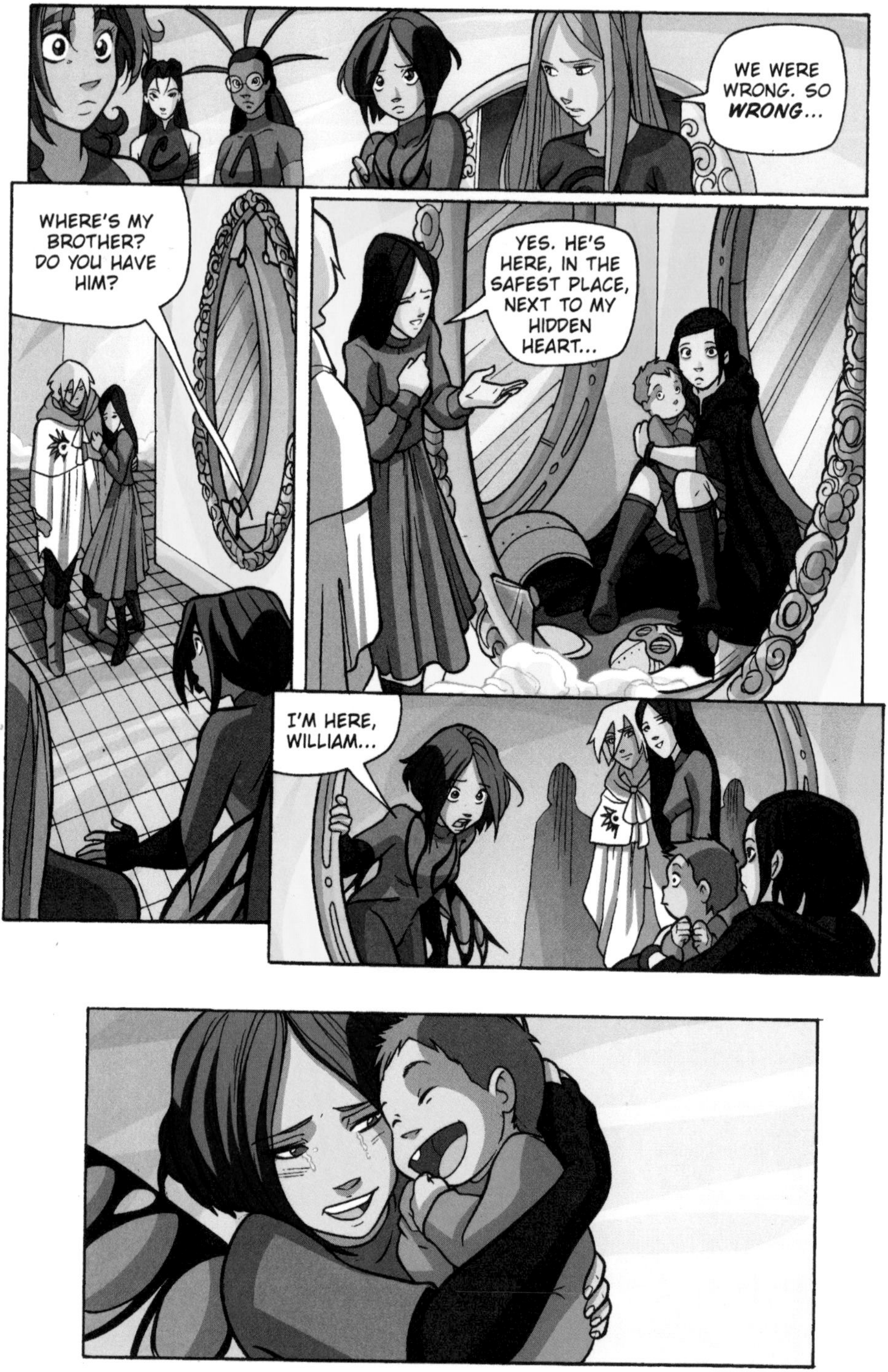
WE WERE WRONG. SO **WRONG**...
WHERE'S MY BROTHER? DO YOU HAVE HIM?
YES. HE'S HERE, IN THE SAFEST PLACE, NEXT TO MY HIDDEN HEART...
I'M HERE, WILLIAM...

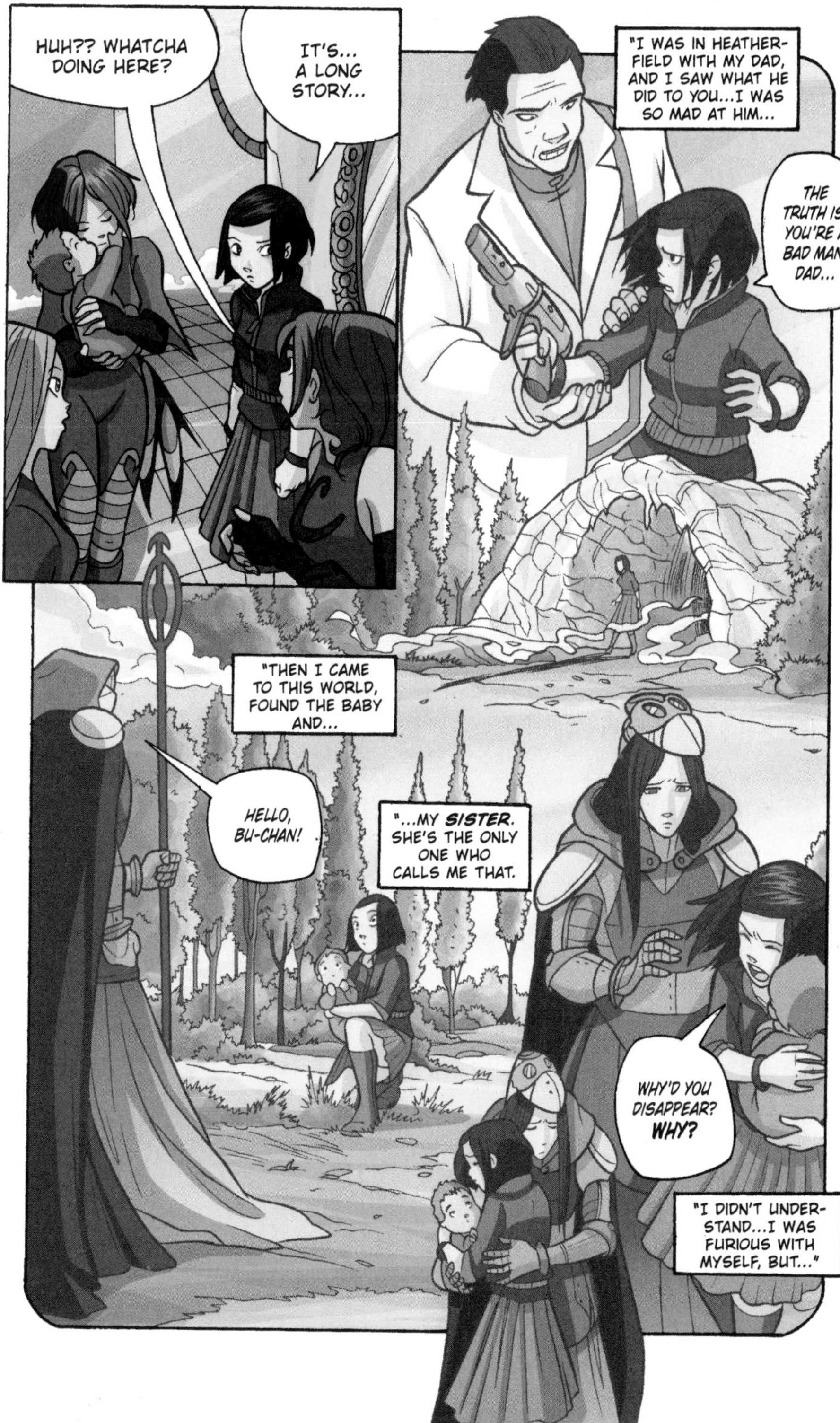
HUH?? WHATCHA DOING HERE?
IT'S... A LONG STORY...
"I WAS IN HEATHER-FIELD WITH MY DAD, AND I SAW WHAT HE DID TO YOU...I WAS SO MAD AT HIM...
THE TRUTH IS, YOU'RE A BAD MAN, DAD...
"THEN I CAME TO THIS WORLD, FOUND THE BABY AND...
HELLO, BU-CHAN!
"...MY SISTER. SHE'S THE ONLY ONE WHO CALLS ME THAT.
WHY'D YOU DISAPPEAR? WHY?
"I DIDN'T UNDER-STAND...I WAS FURIOUS WITH MYSELF, BUT..."

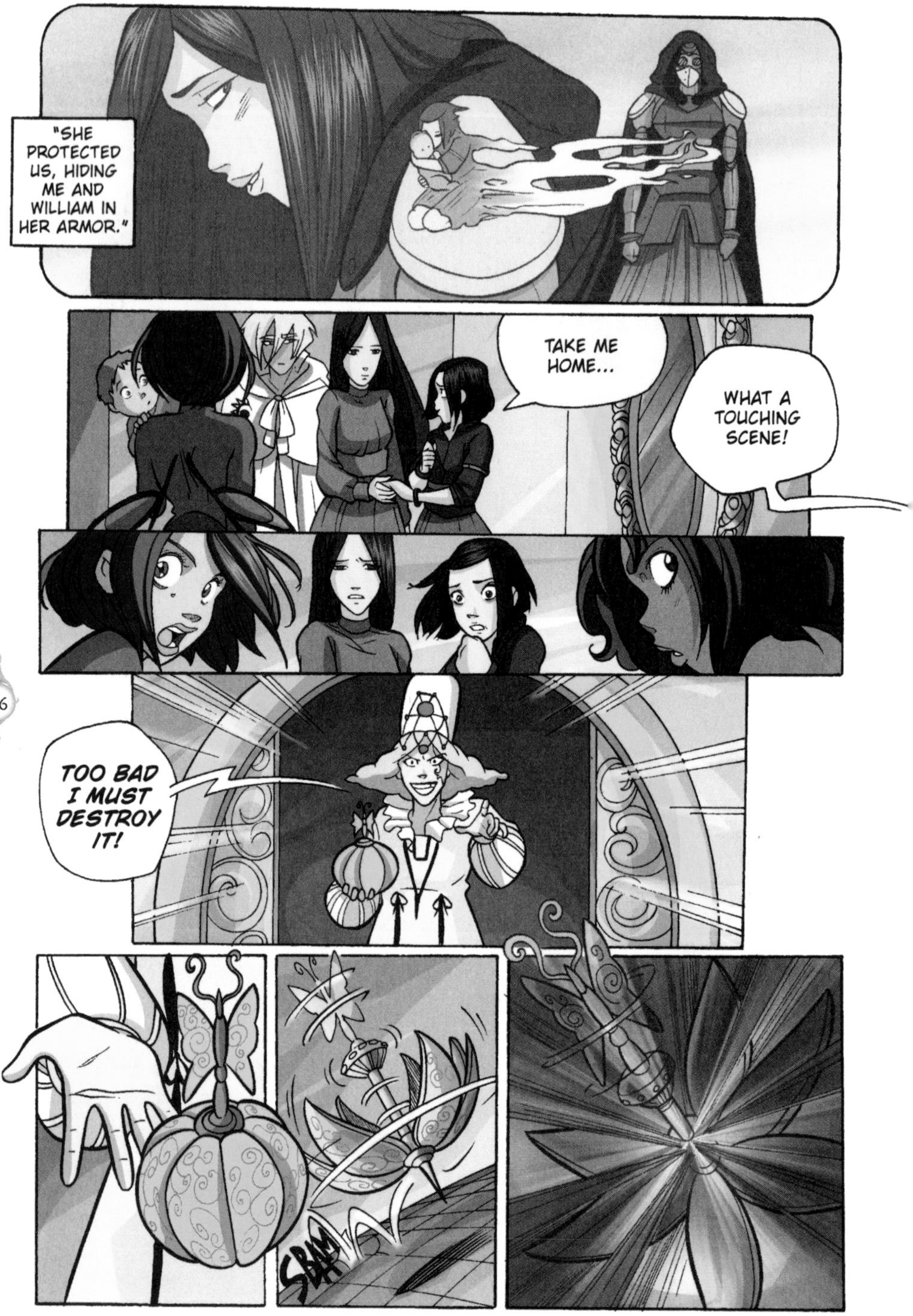

"SHE PROTECTED US, HIDING ME AND WILLIAM IN HER ARMOR."
TAKE ME HOME...
WHAT A TOUCHING SCENE!
TOO BAD I MUST DESTROY IT!
SBAM

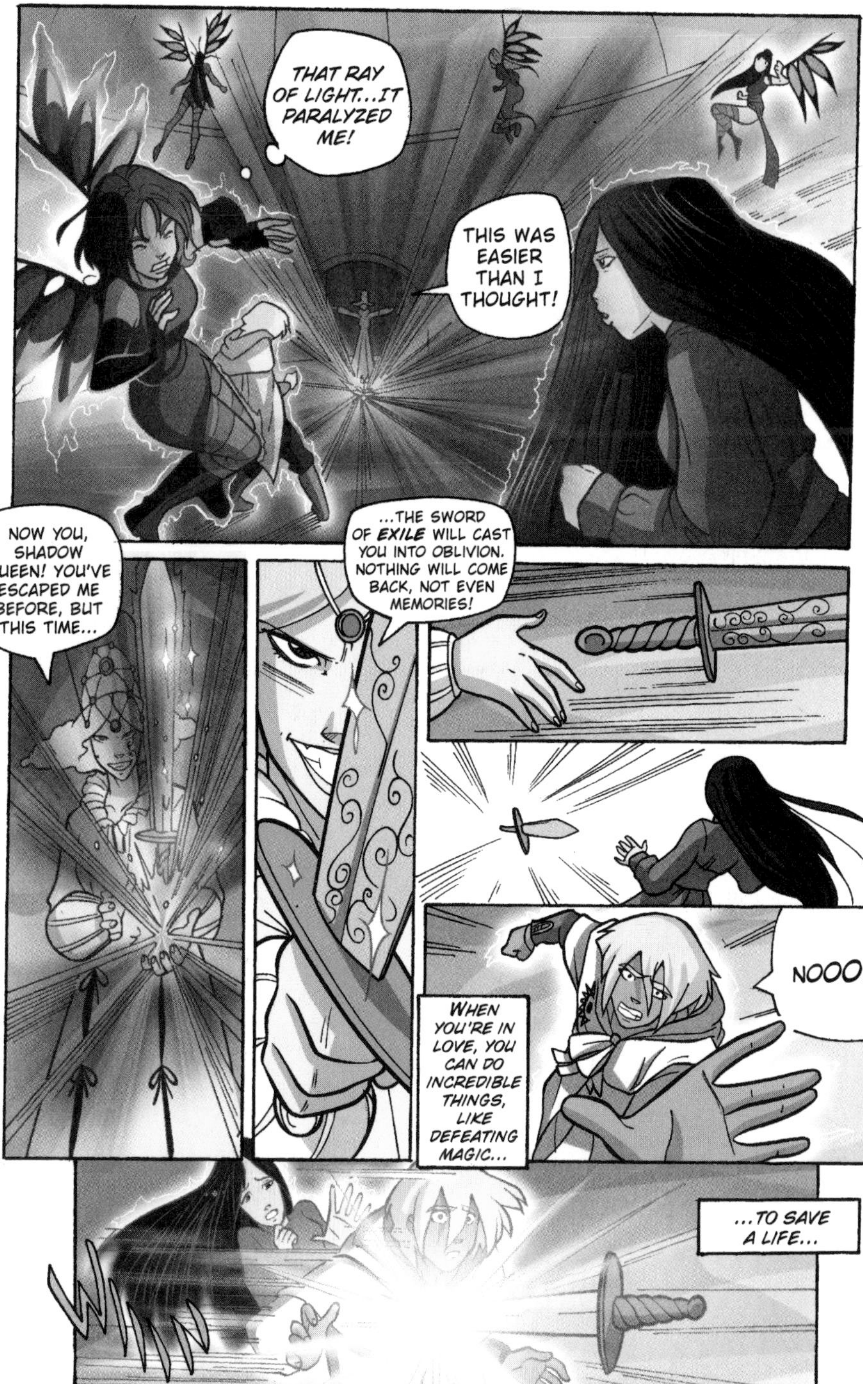
THAT RAY OF LIGHT...IT PARALYZED ME!
THIS WAS EASIER THAN I THOUGHT!
NOW YOU, SHADOW QUEEN! YOU'VE ESCAPED ME BEFORE, BUT THIS TIME...
...THE SWORD OF EXILE WILL CAST YOU INTO OBLIVION. NOTHING WILL COME BACK, NOT EVEN MEMORIES!
NOOO!
WHEN YOU'RE IN LOVE, YOU CAN DO INCREDIBLE THINGS, LIKE DEFEATING MAGIC...
...TO SAVE A LIFE...

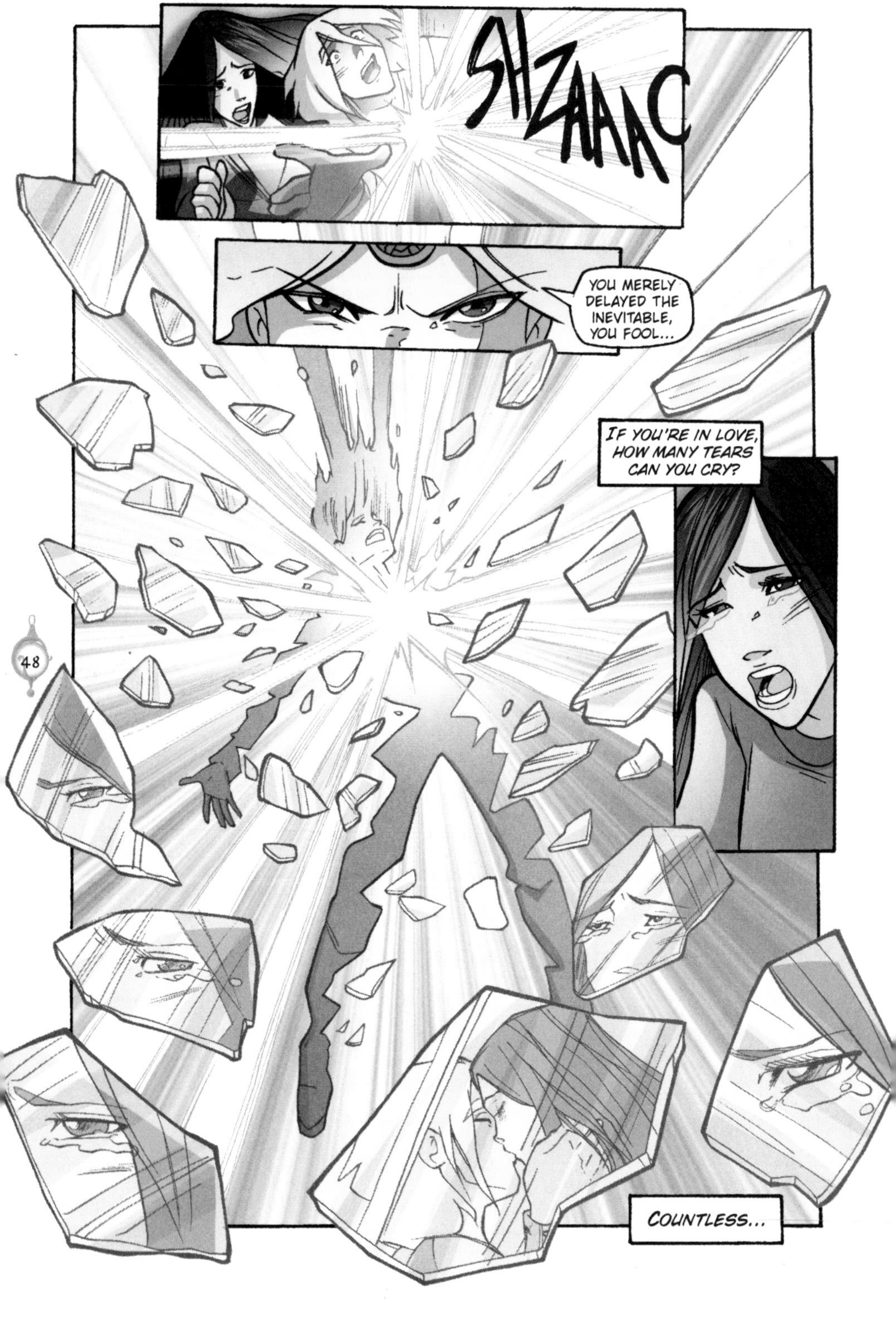
SHZAAAC
YOU MERELY DELAYED THE INEVITABLE, YOU FOOL...
IF YOU'RE IN LOVE, HOW MANY TEARS CAN YOU CRY?
COUNTLESS...

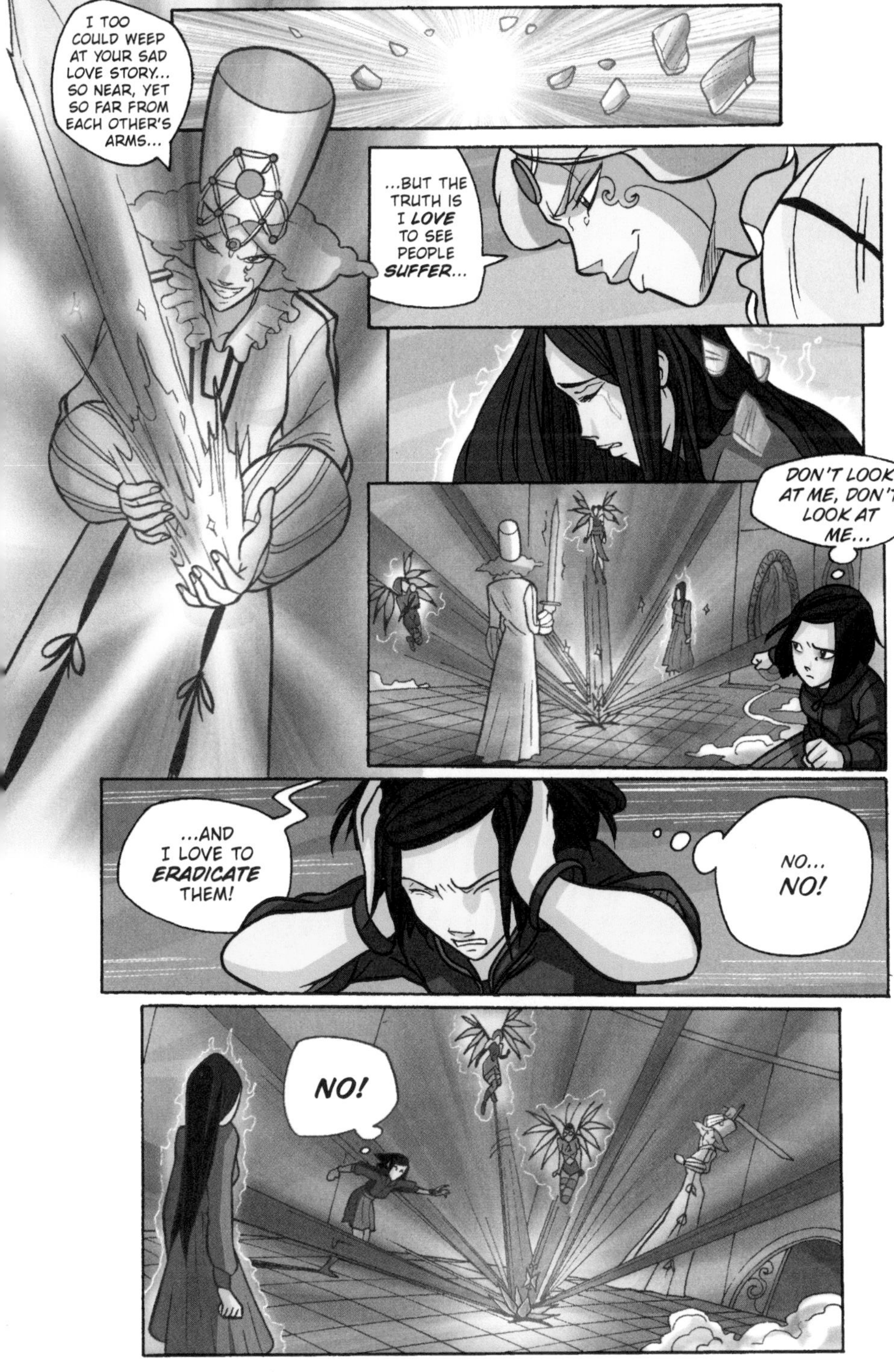
I TOO COULD WEEP AT YOUR SAD LOVE STORY... SO NEAR, YET SO FAR FROM EACH OTHER'S ARMS...
...BUT THE TRUTH IS I LOVE TO SEE PEOPLE SUFFER...
DON'T LOOK AT ME, DON'T LOOK AT ME...
...AND I LOVE TO ERADICATE THEM!
NO... NO!
NO!

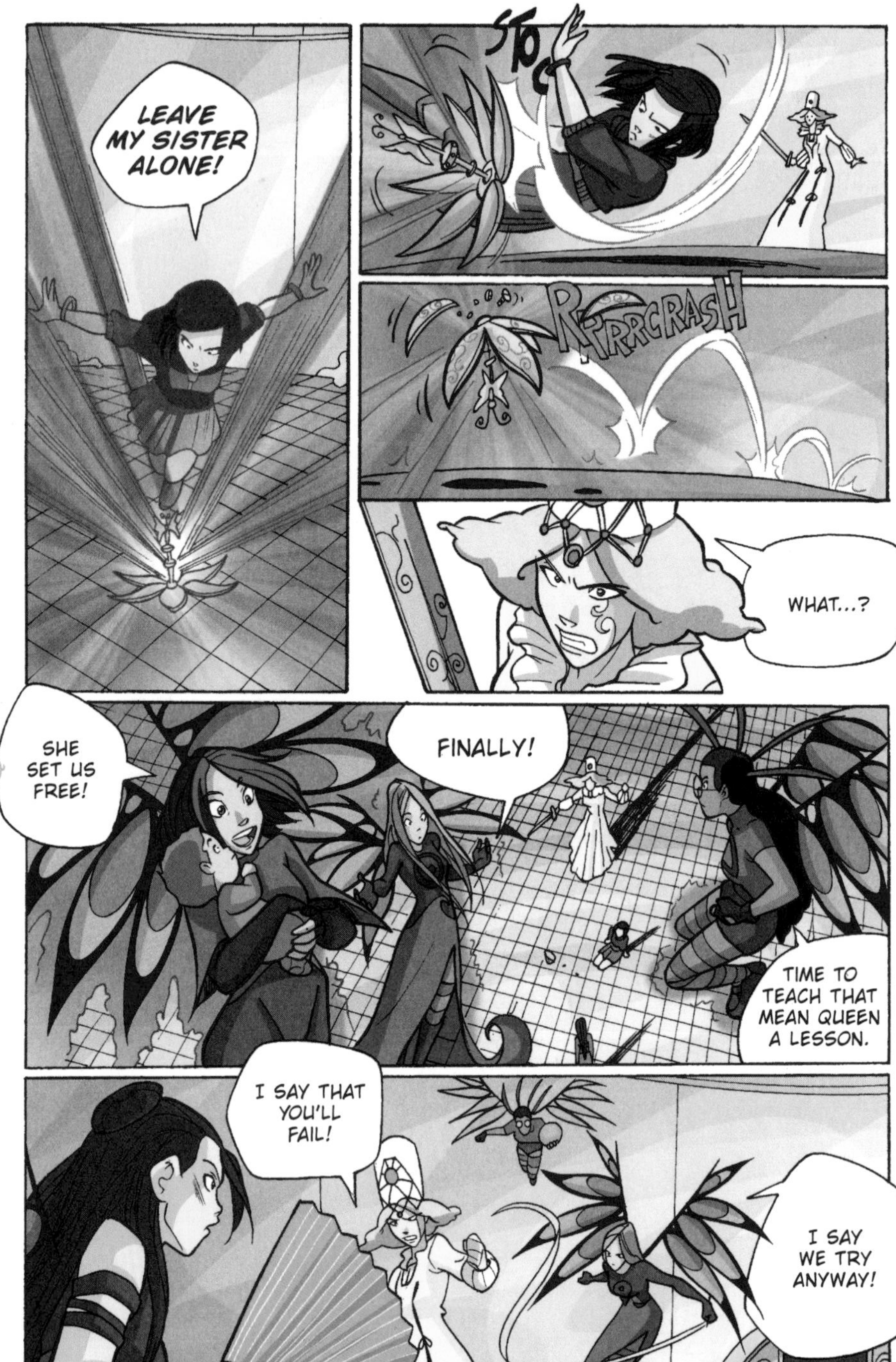
LEAVE MY SISTER ALONE!
STOC
R-RRRCRASH
WHAT...?
SHE SET US FREE!
FINALLY!
TIME TO TEACH THAT MEAN QUEEN A LESSON.
I SAY THAT YOU'LL FAIL!
I SAY WE TRY ANYWAY!

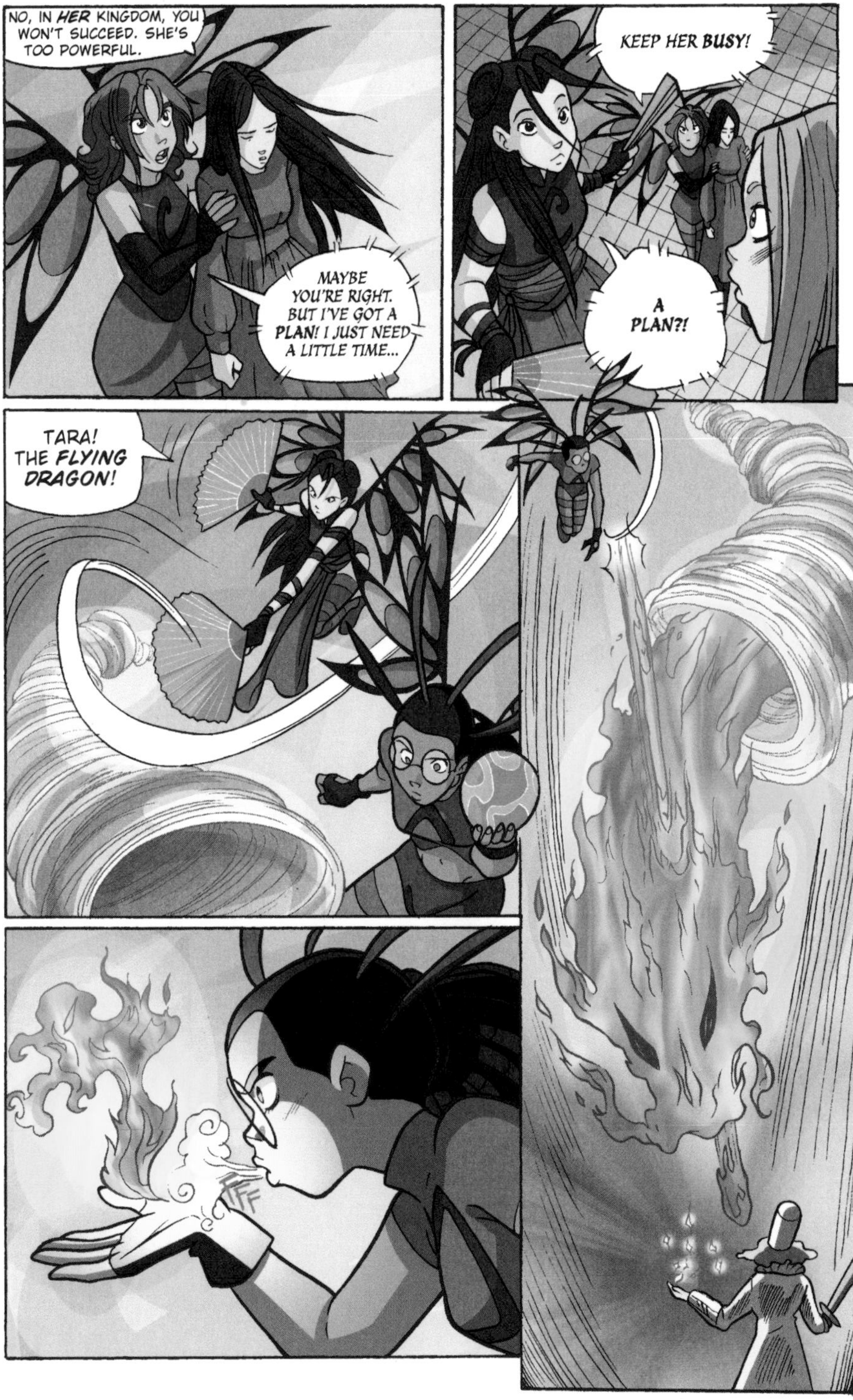
NO, IN HER KINGDOM, YOU WON'T SUCCEED. SHE'S TOO POWERFUL.
MAYBE YOU'RE RIGHT. BUT I'VE GOT A PLAN! I JUST NEED A LITTLE TIME...
KEEP HER BUSY!
A PLAN?!
TARA! THE FLYING DRAGON!
FFF

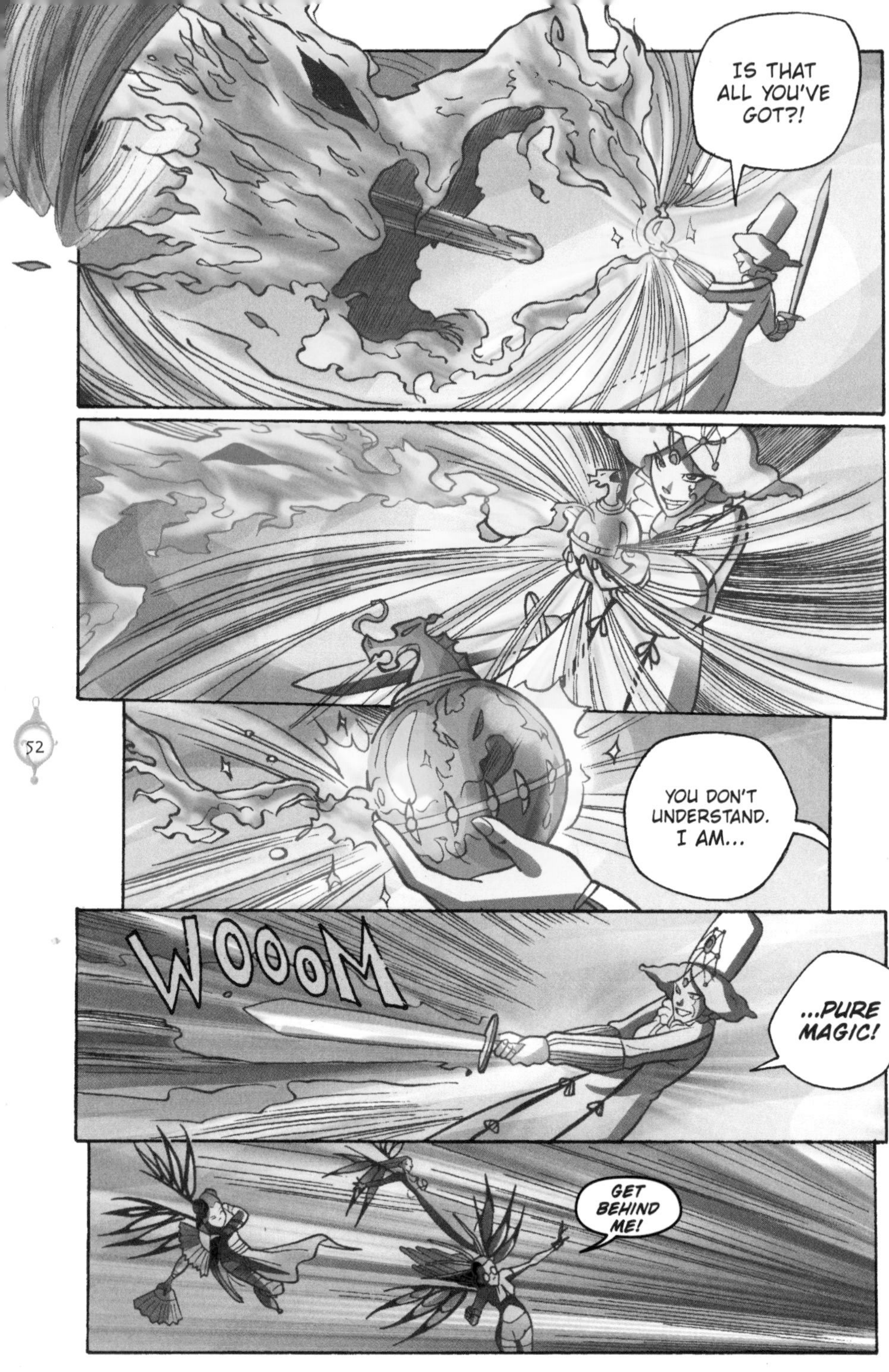
IS THAT ALL YOU'VE GOT?!
YOU DON'T UNDERSTAND. I AM...
WOOOM
...PURE MAGIC!
GET BEHIND ME!

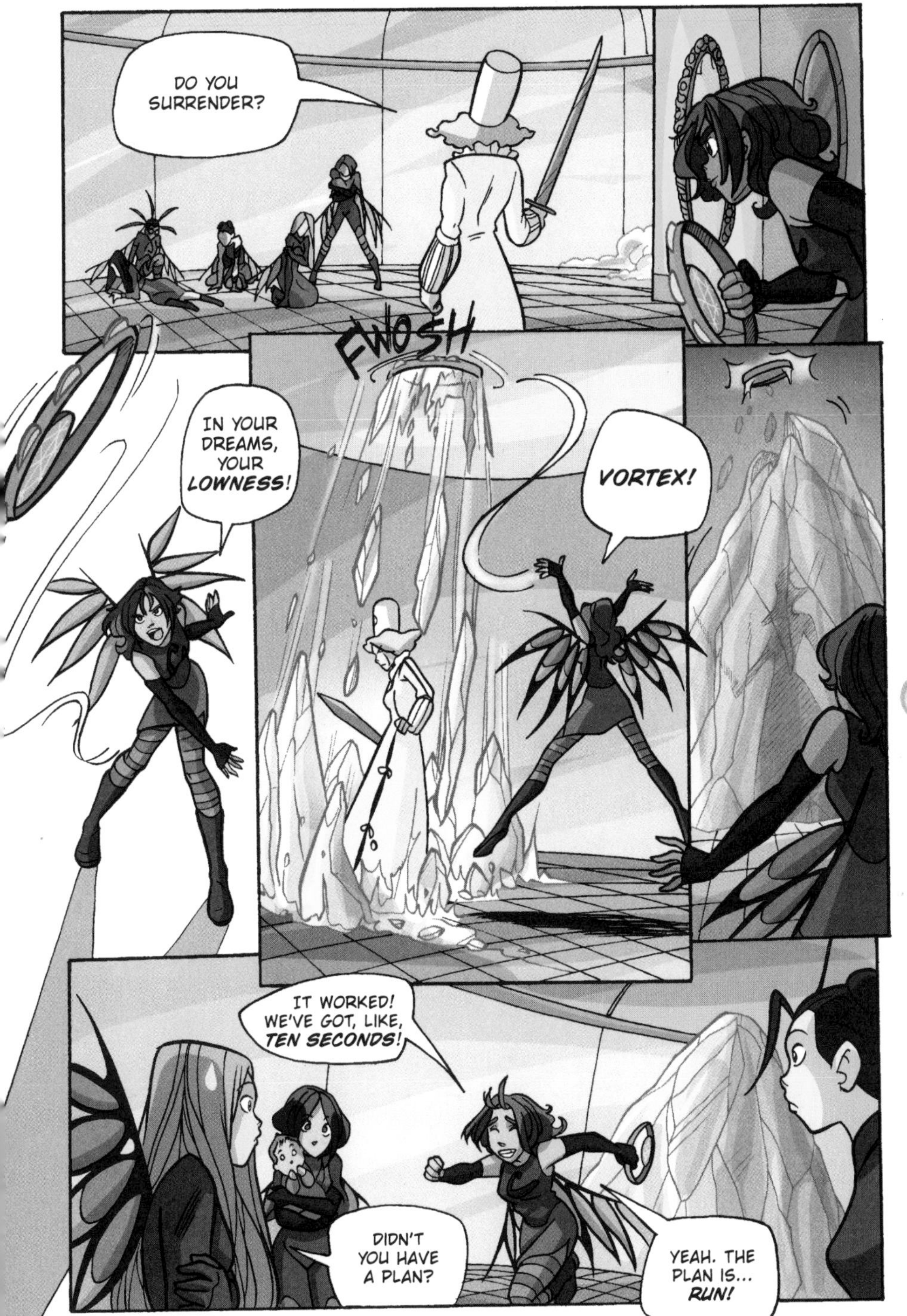
DO YOU SURRENDER?
FWOSH
IN YOUR DREAMS, YOUR LOWNESS!
VORTEX!
IT WORKED! WE'VE GOT, LIKE, TEN SECONDS!
DIDN'T YOU HAVE A PLAN?
YEAH. THE PLAN IS... RUN!

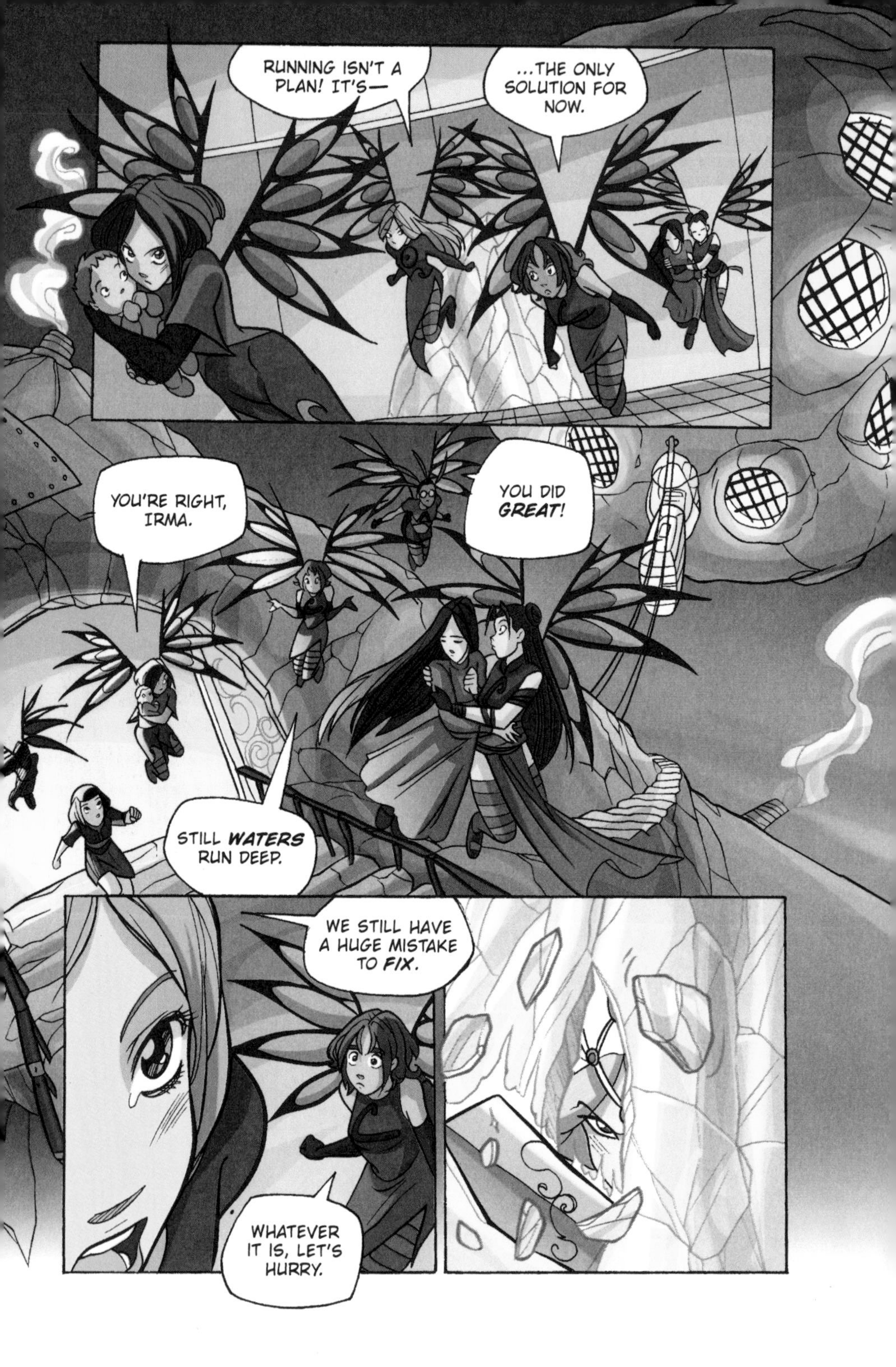
RUNNING ISN'T A PLAN! IT'S—
...THE ONLY SOLUTION FOR NOW.
YOU'RE RIGHT, IRMA.
YOU DID GREAT!
STILL WATERS RUN DEEP.
WE STILL HAVE A HUGE MISTAKE TO FIX.
WHATEVER IT IS, LET'S HURRY.

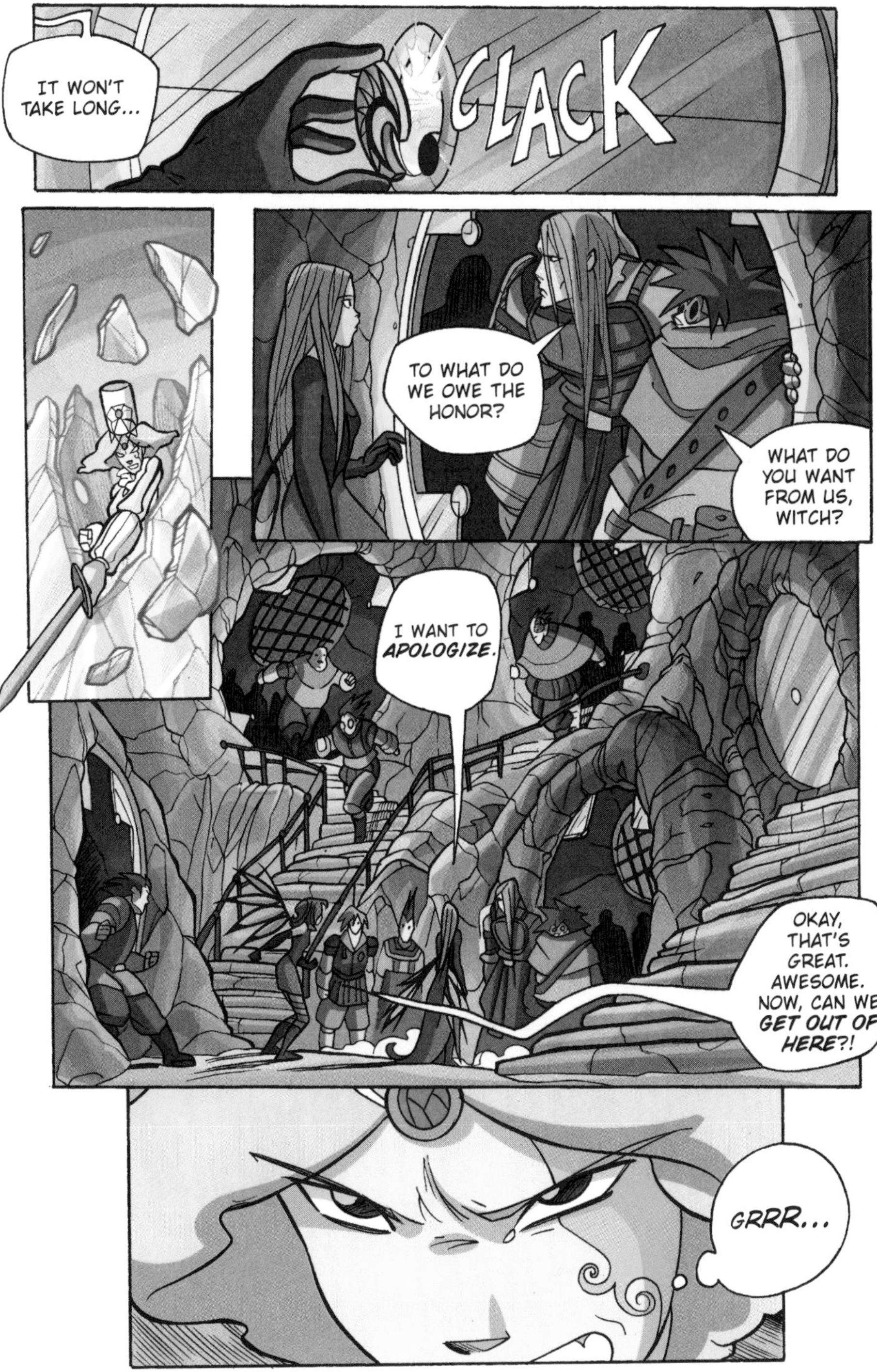
IT WON'T TAKE LONG...
CLACK
TO WHAT DO WE OWE THE HONOR?
WHAT DO YOU WANT FROM US, WITCH?
I WANT TO ***APOLOGIZE***.
OKAY, THAT'S GREAT. AWESOME. NOW, CAN WE ***GET OUT OF HERE***?!
GRRR...

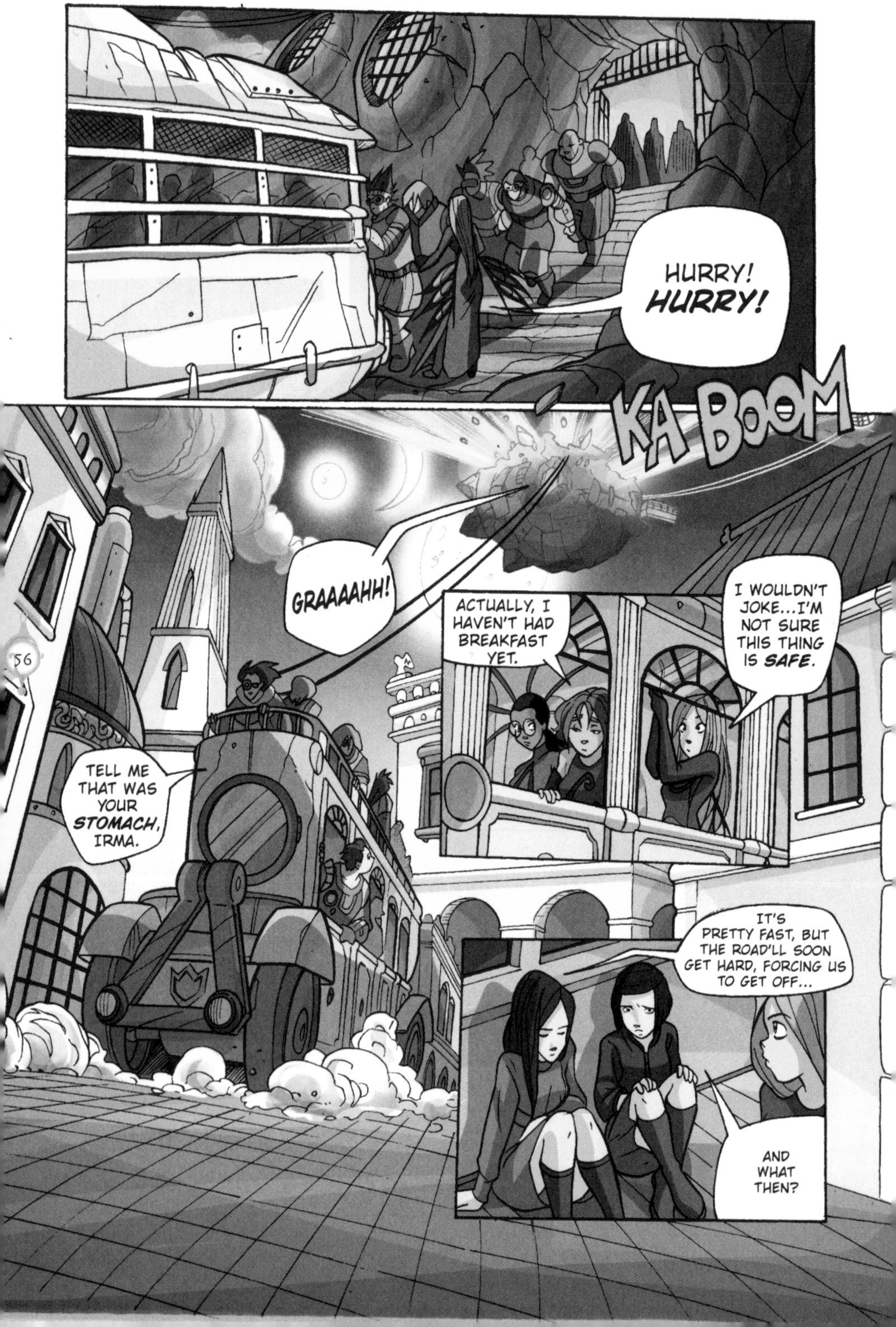

HURRY! HURRY!
KA BOOM
GRAAAAHH!
ACTUALLY, I HAVEN'T HAD BREAKFAST YET.
I WOULDN'T JOKE...I'M NOT SURE THIS THING IS SAFE.
TELL ME THAT WAS YOUR STOMACH, IRMA.
IT'S PRETTY FAST, BUT THE ROAD'LL SOON GET HARD, FORCING US TO GET OFF...
AND WHAT THEN?

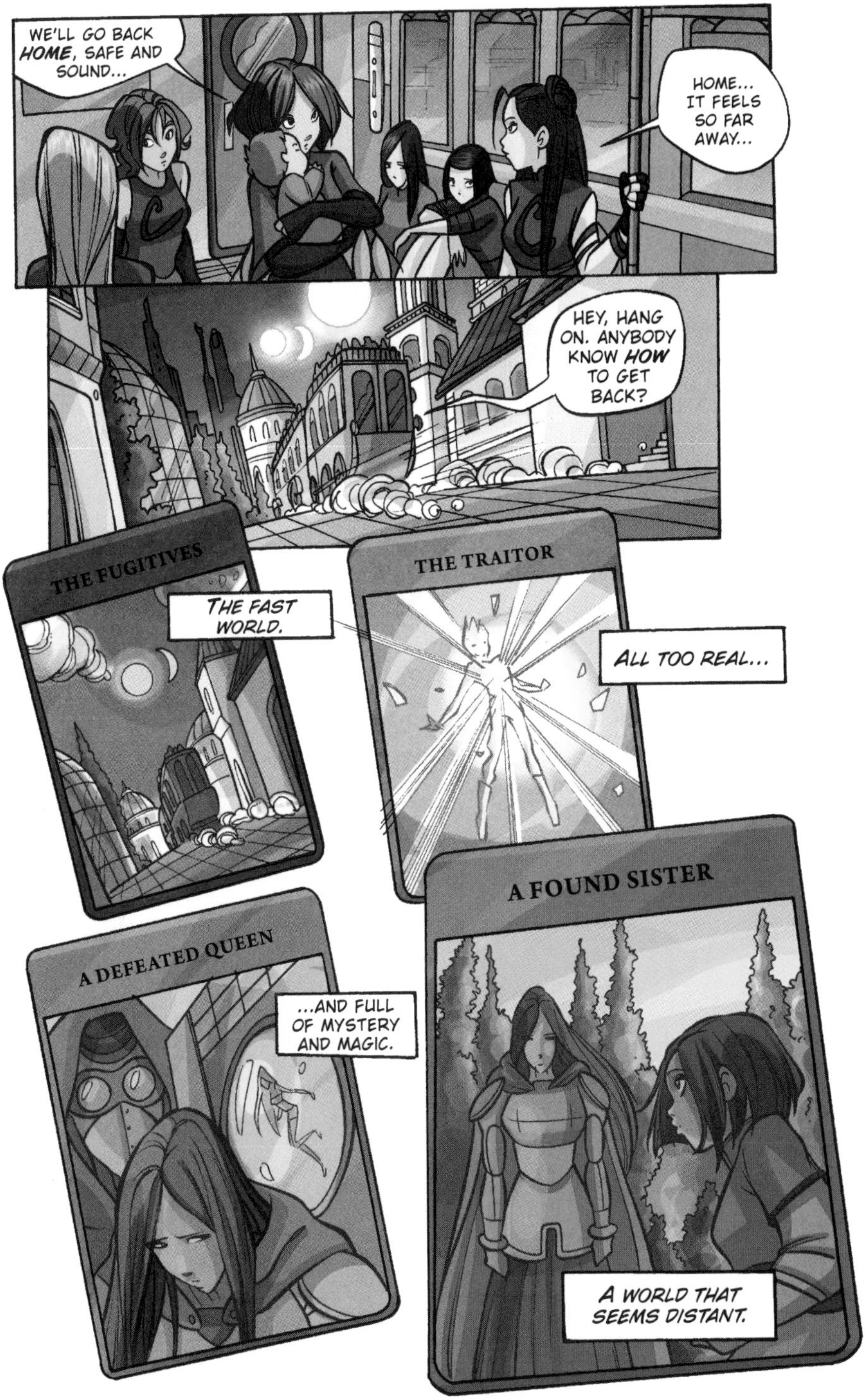

WE'LL GO BACK HOME, SAFE AND SOUND...
HOME... IT FEELS SO FAR AWAY...
HEY, HANG ON. ANYBODY KNOW HOW TO GET BACK?
THE FUGITIVES
THE FAST WORLD.
THE TRAITOR
ALL TOO REAL...
A DEFEATED QUEEN
...AND FULL OF MYSTERY AND MAGIC.
A FOUND SISTER
A WORLD THAT SEEMS DISTANT.

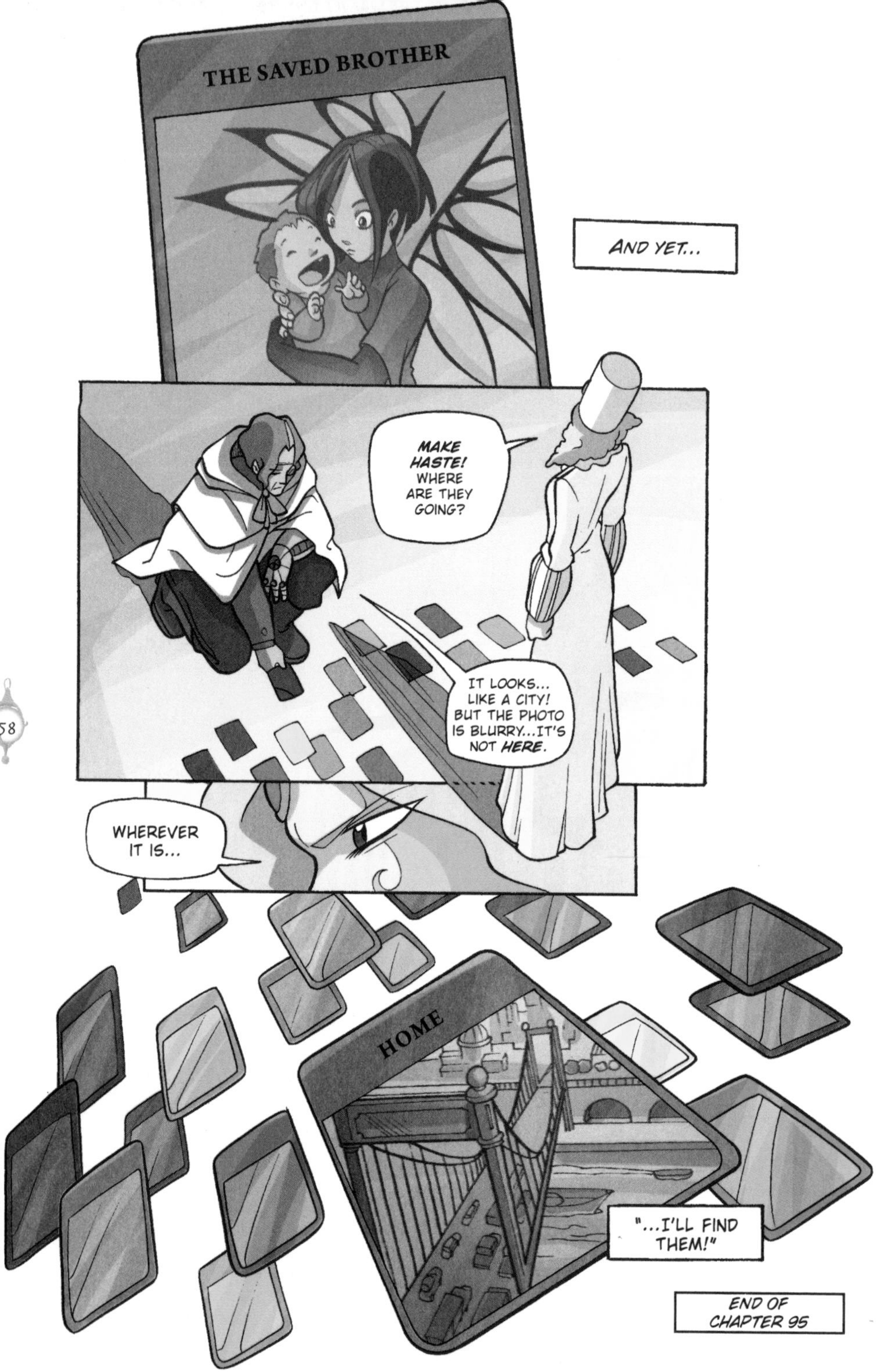
THE SAVED BROTHER
AND YET...
MAKE HASTE! WHERE ARE THEY GOING?
IT LOOKS... LIKE A CITY! BUT THE PHOTO IS BLURRY...IT'S NOT HERE.
WHEREVER IT IS...
HOME
"...I'LL FIND THEM!"
END OF CHAPTER 95

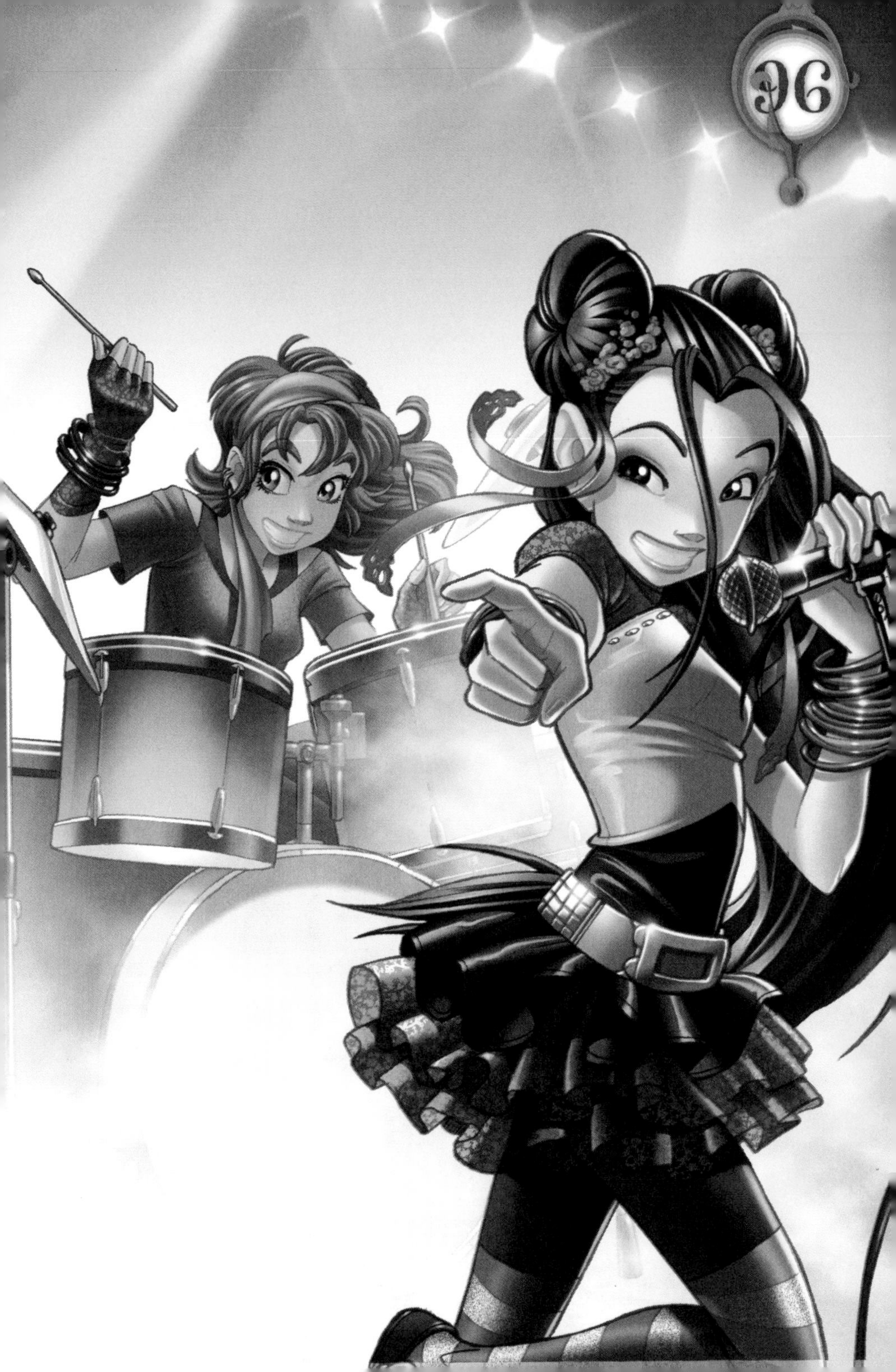

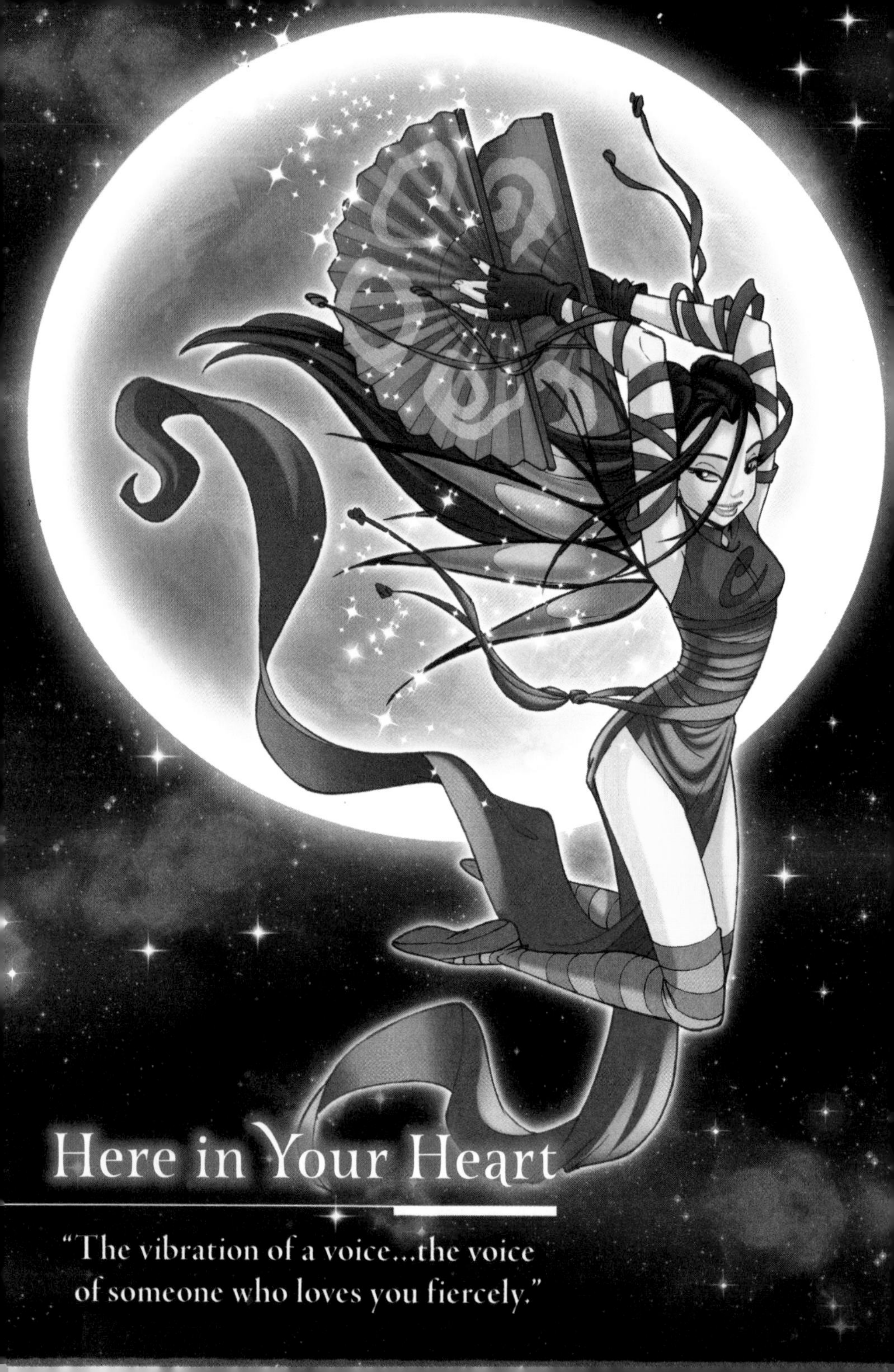

Here in Your Heart

"The vibration of a voice...the voice of someone who loves you fiercely."

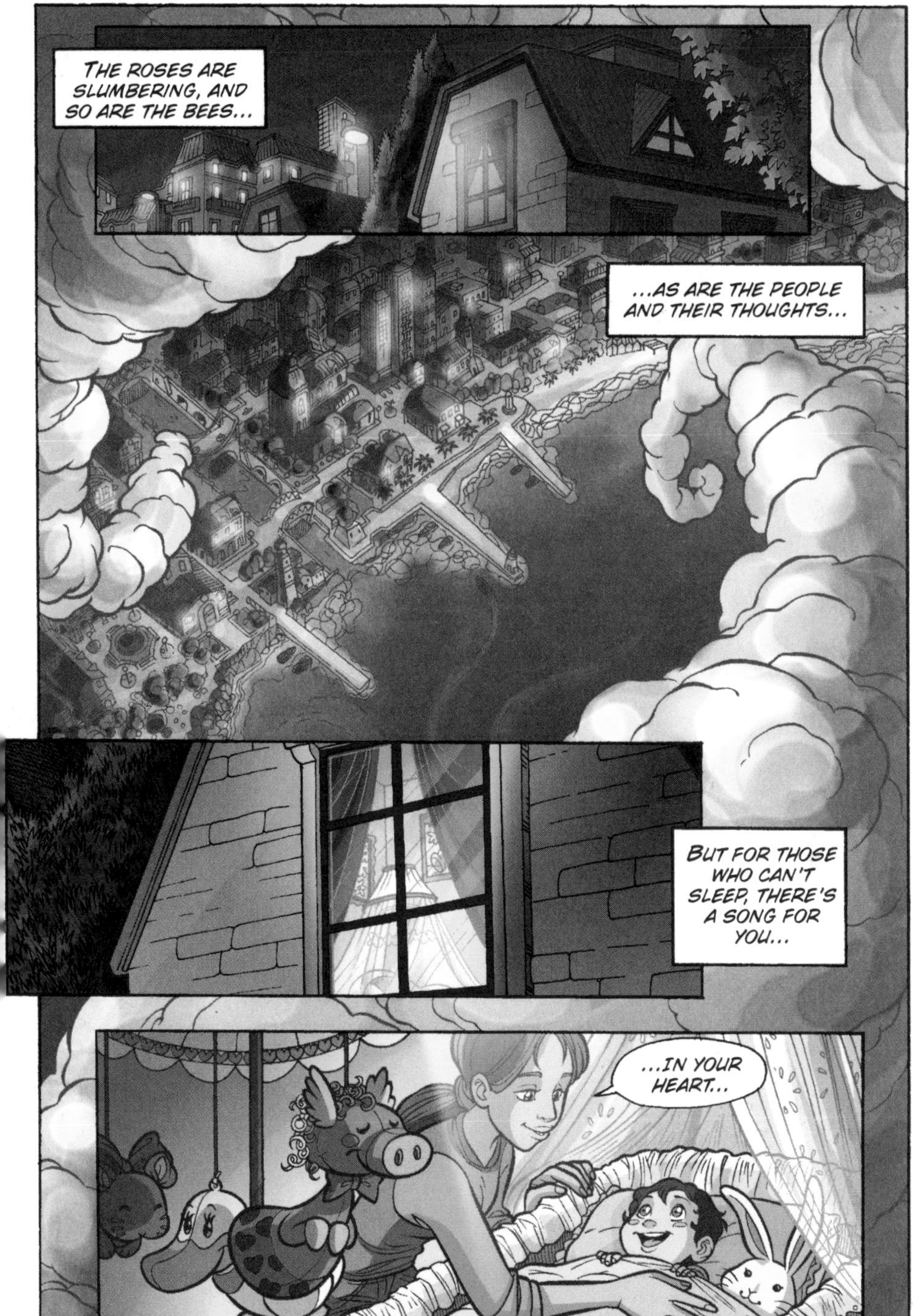
THE ROSES ARE SLUMBERING, AND SO ARE THE BEES...
...AS ARE THE PEOPLE AND THEIR THOUGHTS...
BUT FOR THOSE WHO CAN'T SLEEP, THERE'S A SONG FOR YOU...
...IN YOUR HEART...

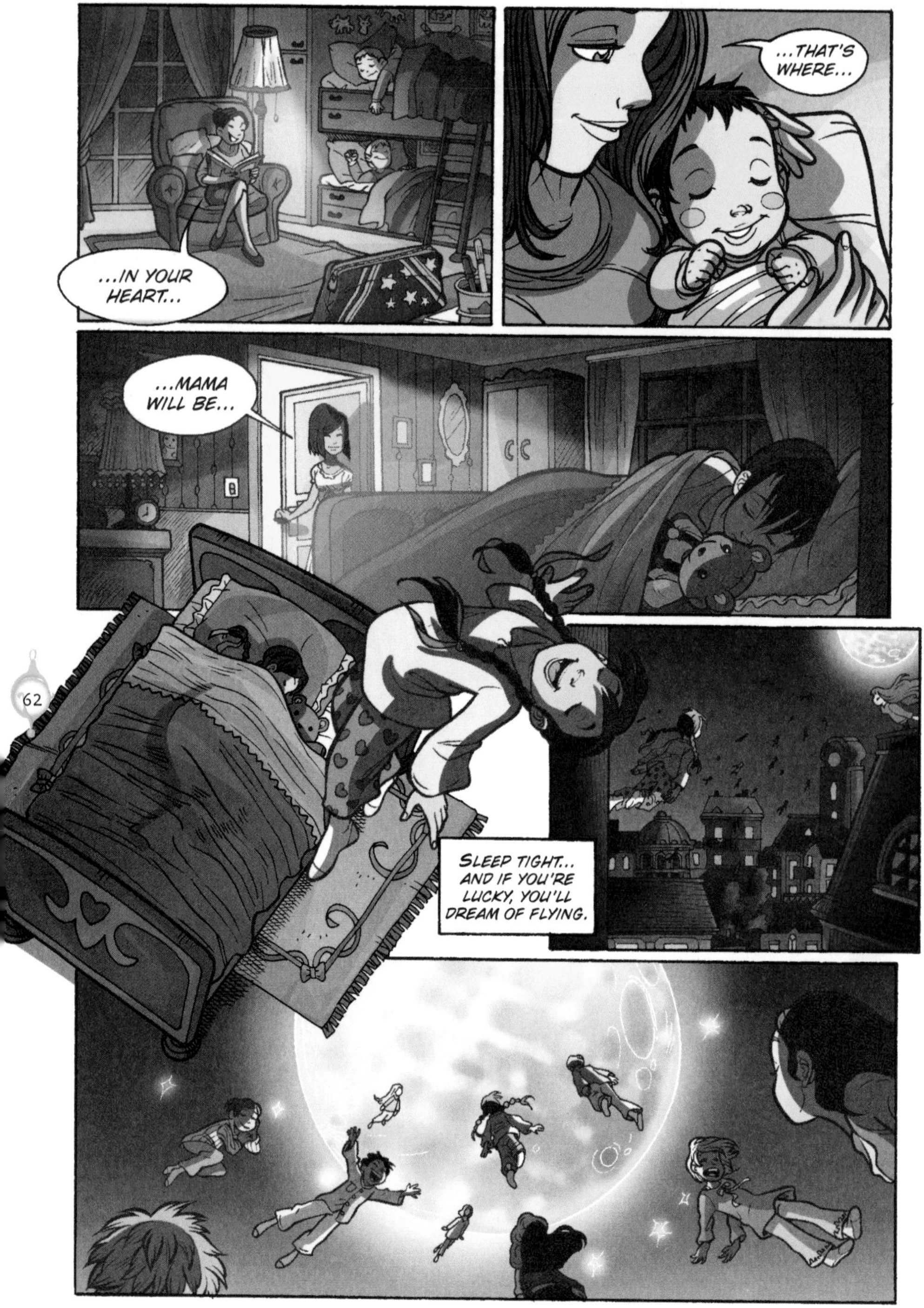
...IN YOUR HEART...
...THAT'S WHERE...
...MAMA WILL BE...
SLEEP TIGHT... AND IF YOU'RE LUCKY, YOU'LL DREAM OF FLYING.

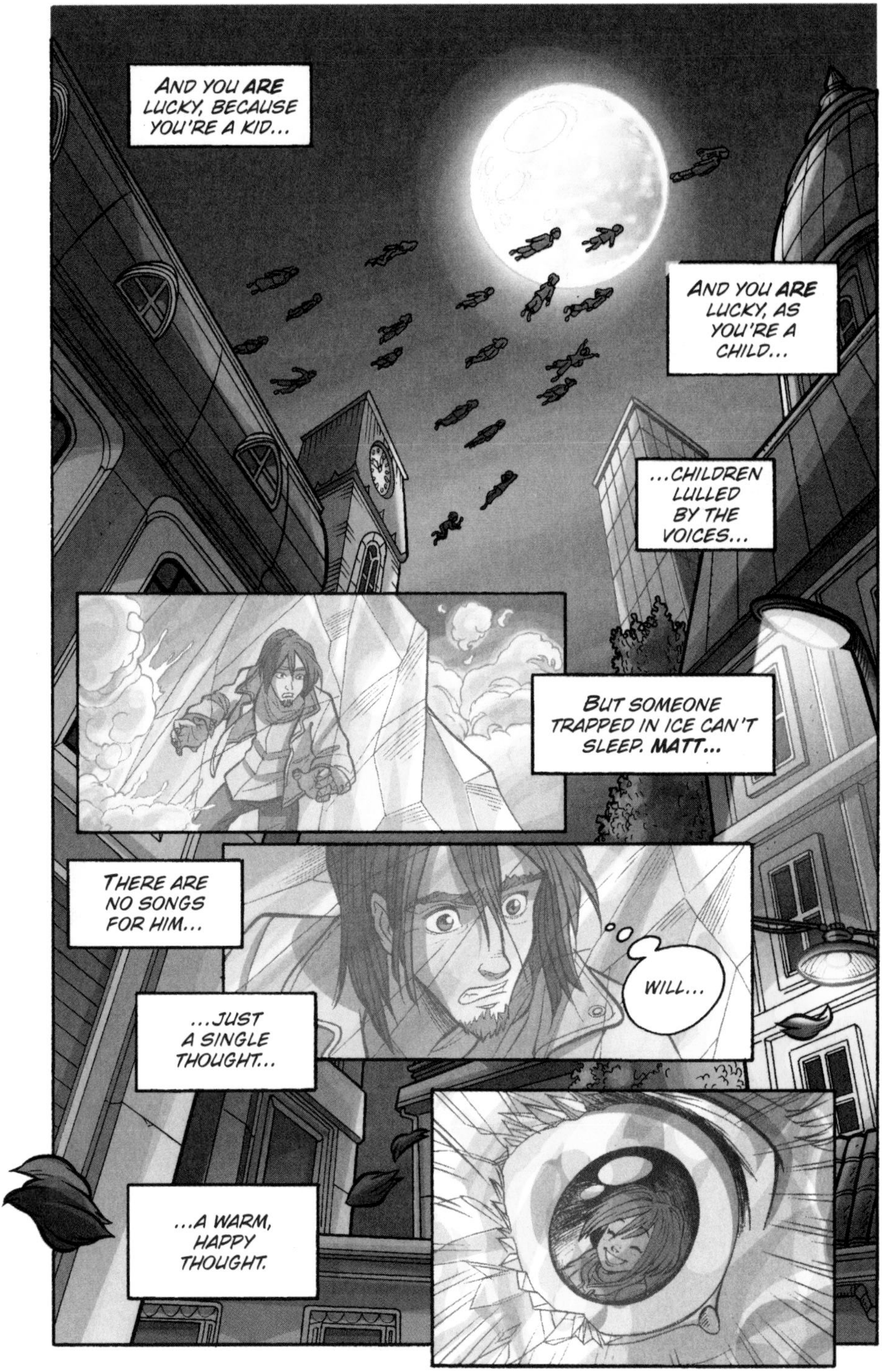
AND YOU ARE LUCKY, BECAUSE YOU'RE A KID...
AND YOU ARE LUCKY, AS YOU'RE A CHILD...
...CHILDREN LULLED BY THE VOICES...
BUT SOMEONE TRAPPED IN ICE CAN'T SLEEP. MATT...
THERE ARE NO SONGS FOR HIM...
WILL...
...JUST A SINGLE THOUGHT...
...A WARM, HAPPY THOUGHT.

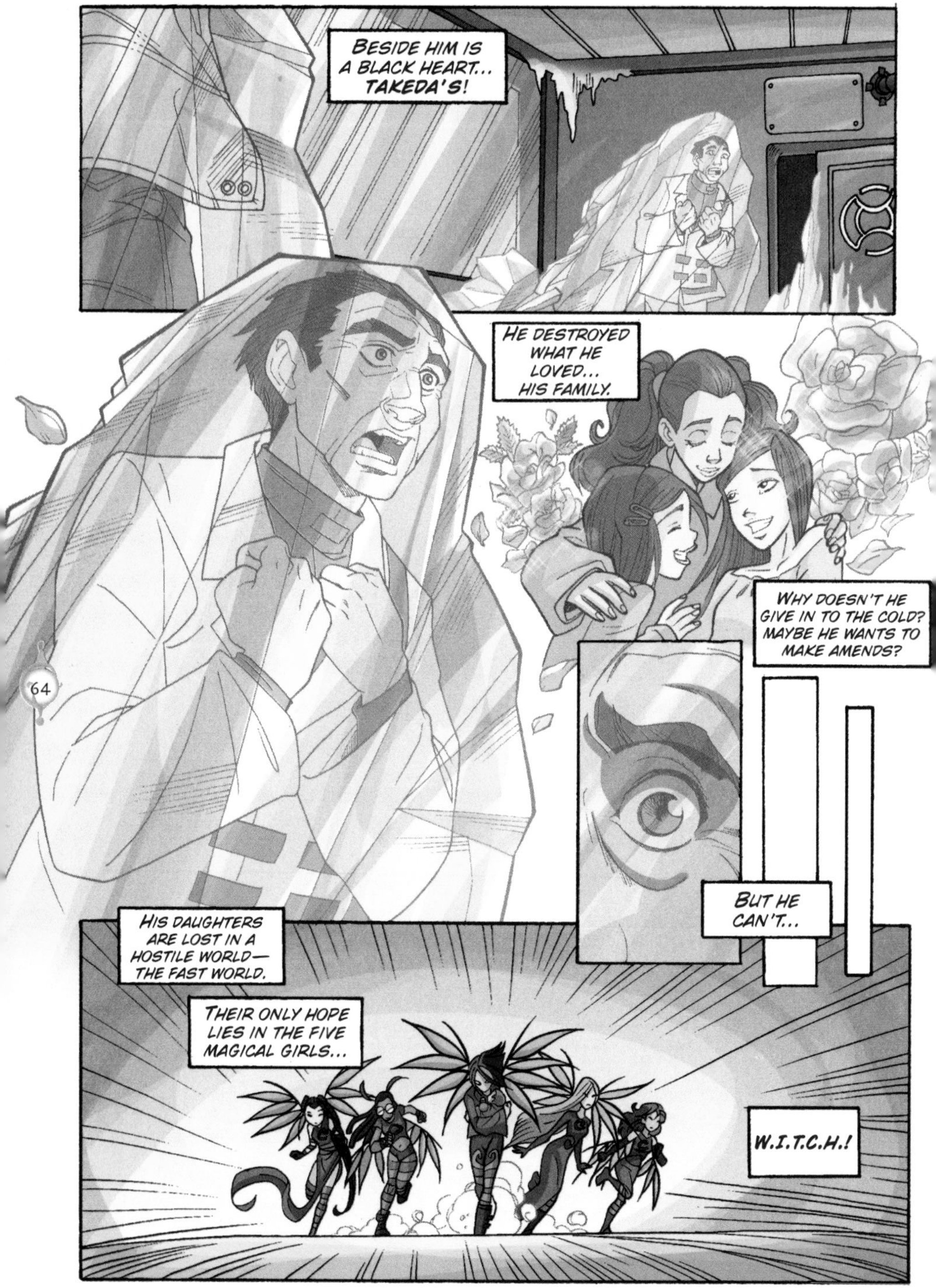
BESIDE HIM IS A BLACK HEART... TAKEDA'S!
HE DESTROYED WHAT HE LOVED... HIS FAMILY.
WHY DOESN'T HE GIVE IN TO THE COLD? MAYBE HE WANTS TO MAKE AMENDS?
BUT HE CAN'T...
HIS DAUGHTERS ARE LOST IN A HOSTILE WORLD— THE FAST WORLD.
THEIR ONLY HOPE LIES IN THE FIVE MAGICAL GIRLS...
W.I.T.C.H.!

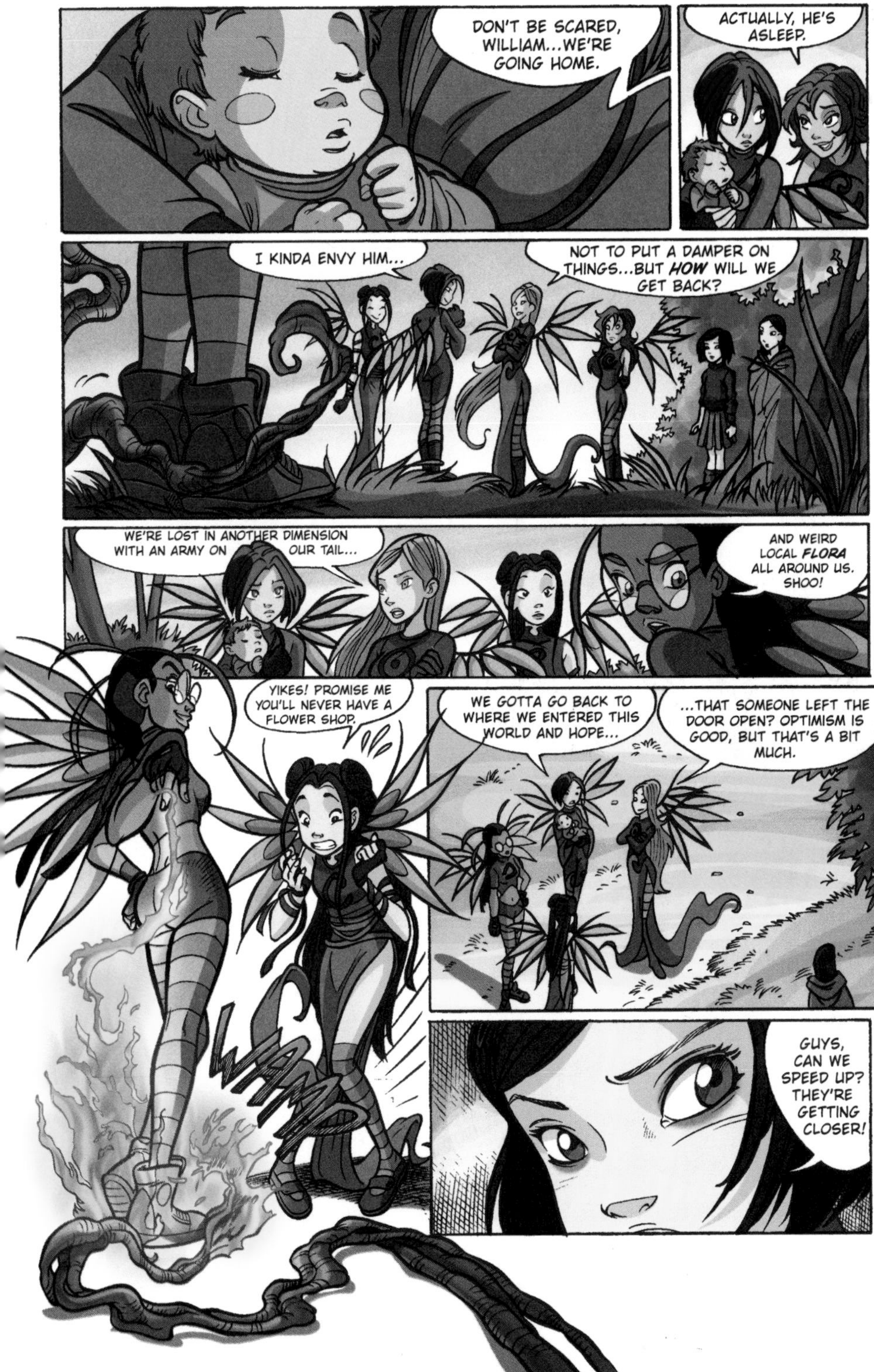
DON'T BE SCARED, WILLIAM...WE'RE GOING HOME.
ACTUALLY, HE'S ASLEEP.
I KINDA ENVY HIM...
NOT TO PUT A DAMPER ON THINGS...BUT **HOW** WILL WE GET BACK?
WE'RE LOST IN ANOTHER DIMENSION WITH AN ARMY ON OUR TAIL...
AND WEIRD LOCAL **FLORA** ALL AROUND US. SHOO!
YIKES! PROMISE ME YOU'LL NEVER HAVE A FLOWER SHOP.
WE GOTTA GO BACK TO WHERE WE ENTERED THIS WORLD AND HOPE...
...THAT SOMEONE LEFT THE DOOR OPEN? OPTIMISM IS GOOD, BUT THAT'S A BIT MUCH.
GUYS, CAN WE SPEED UP? THEY'RE GETTING CLOSER!

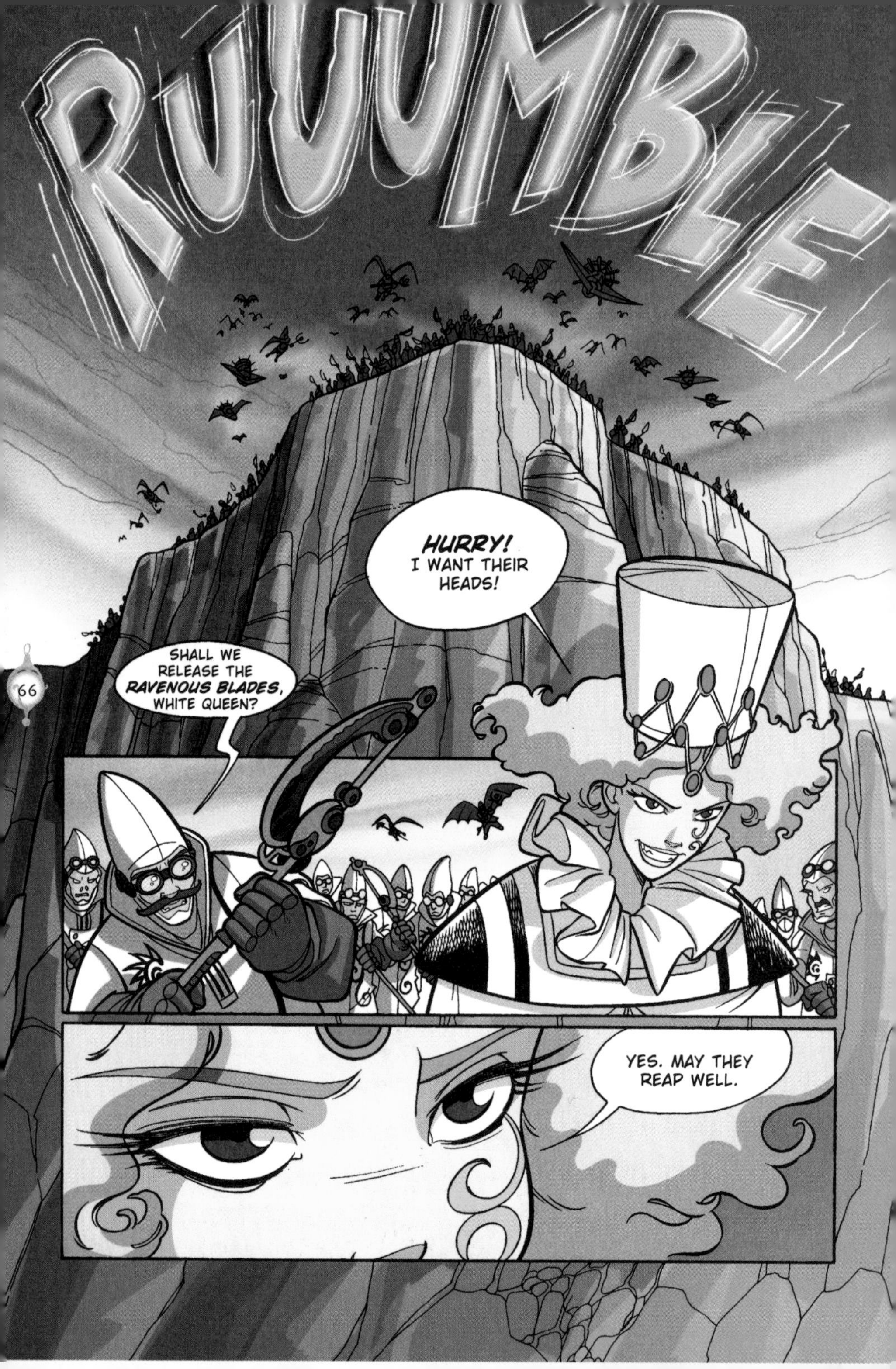
RUUUMBLE
HURRY! I WANT THEIR HEADS!
SHALL WE RELEASE THE RAVENOUS BLADES, WHITE QUEEN?
YES. MAY THEY REAP WELL.

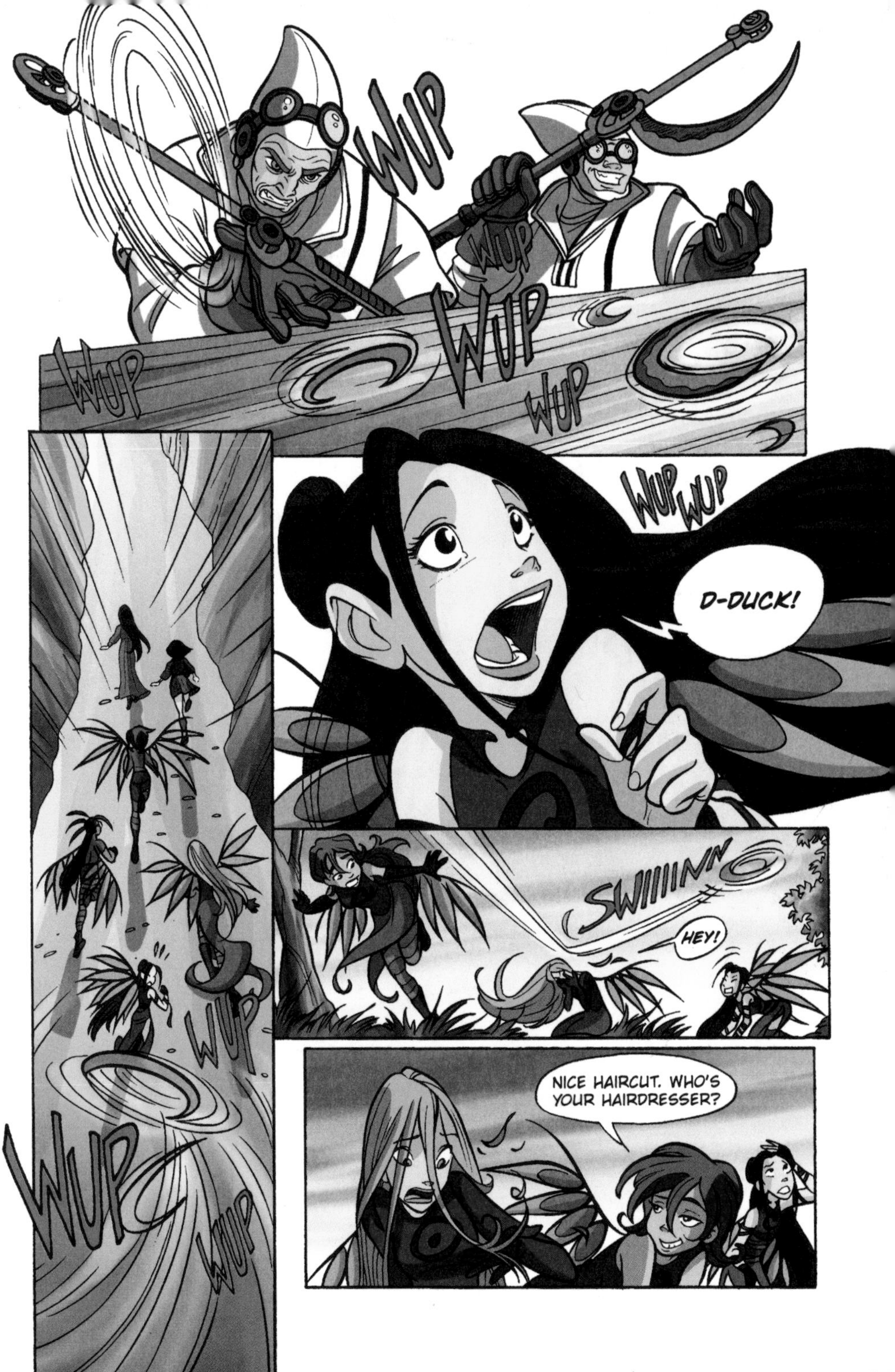

WUP
WUP
WUP
WUP
WUP
WUP
WUP WUP
D-DUCK!
WUP
WUP
WUP
SWIIIINN
HEY!
NICE HAIRCUT. WHO'S YOUR HAIRDRESSER?

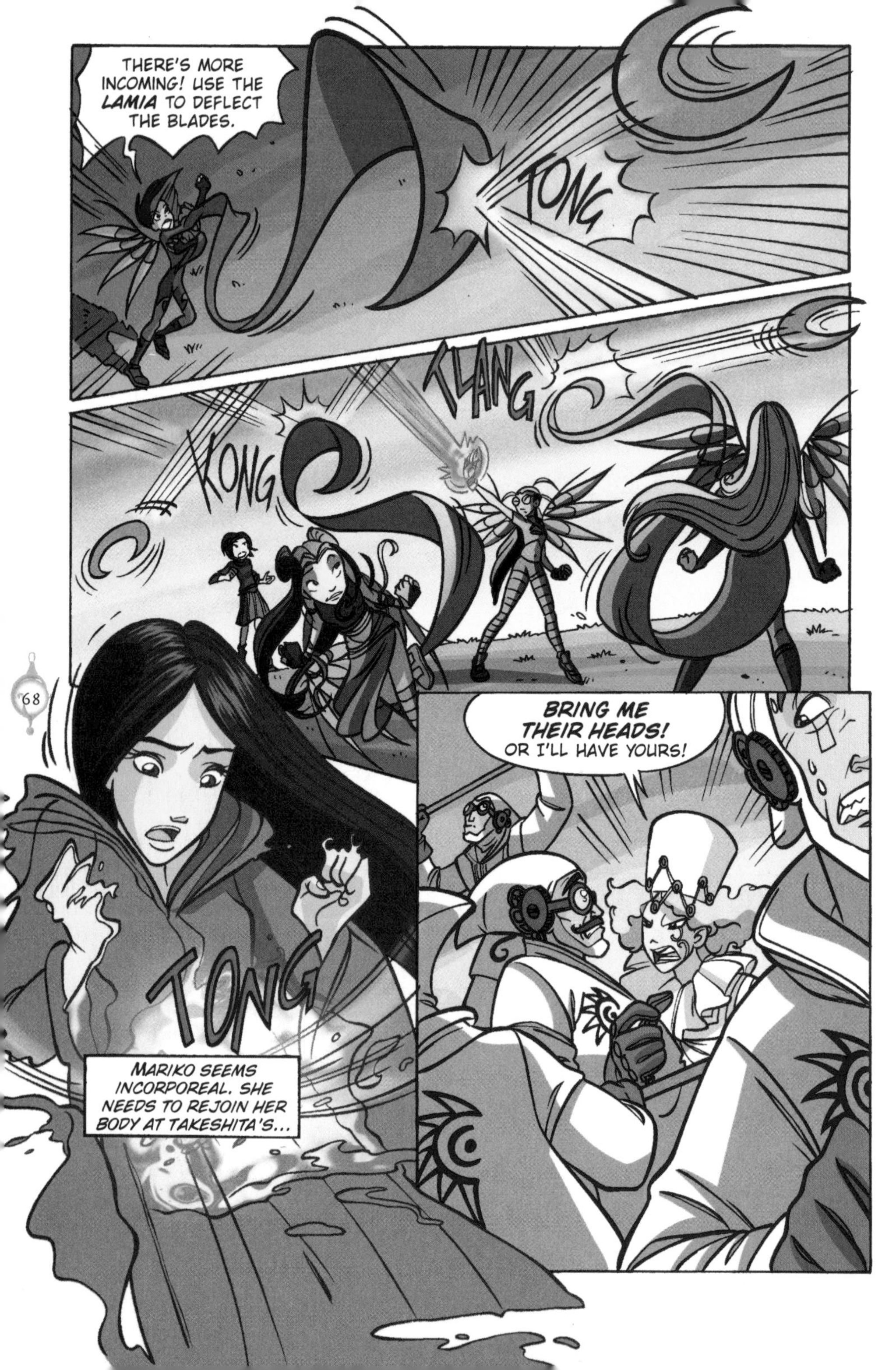
THERE'S MORE INCOMING! USE THE *LAMIA* TO DEFLECT THE BLADES.
TONG
KLANG
KONG
BRING ME THEIR HEADS! OR I'LL HAVE YOURS!
TONG
MARIKO SEEMS INCORPOREAL. SHE NEEDS TO REJOIN HER BODY AT TAKESHITA'S...

HURRY! THE PASSAGE HAS TO BE HERE.

REALLY? IT ALL LOOKS THE SAME TO ME...

I HAVE TO AGREE...

I'M TELLING YOU, *IT WAS* HERE.

A WARM THOUGHT... LIKE TEARS.

WILL...

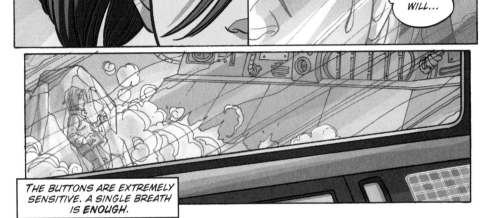

THE BUTTONS ARE EXTREMELY SENSITIVE. A SINGLE BREATH IS *ENOUGH*.

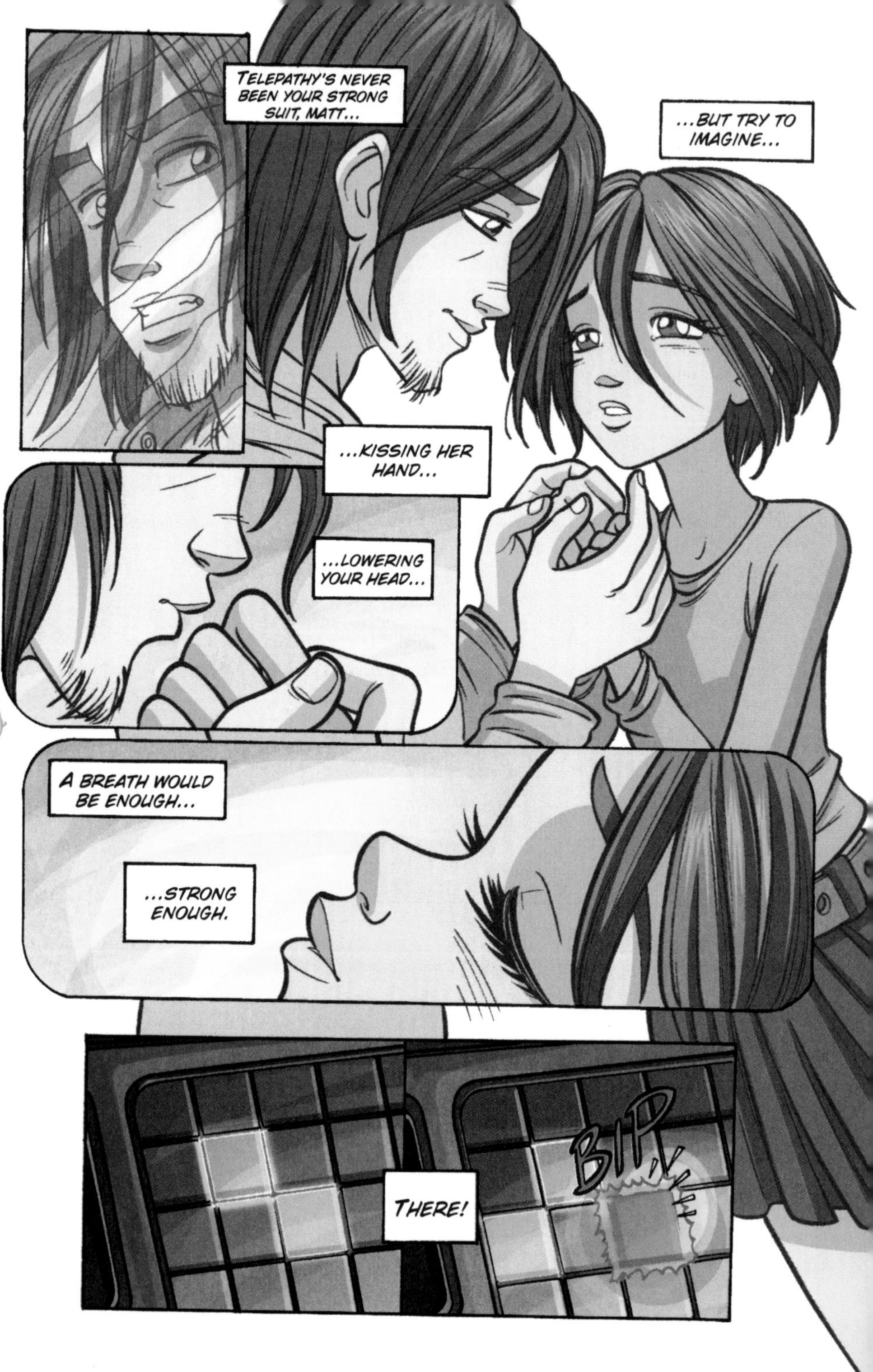

TELEPATHY'S NEVER BEEN YOUR STRONG SUIT, MATT...
...BUT TRY TO IMAGINE...
...KISSING HER HAND...
...LOWERING YOUR HEAD...
A BREATH WOULD BE ENOUGH...
...STRONG ENOUGH.
THERE!
BIP

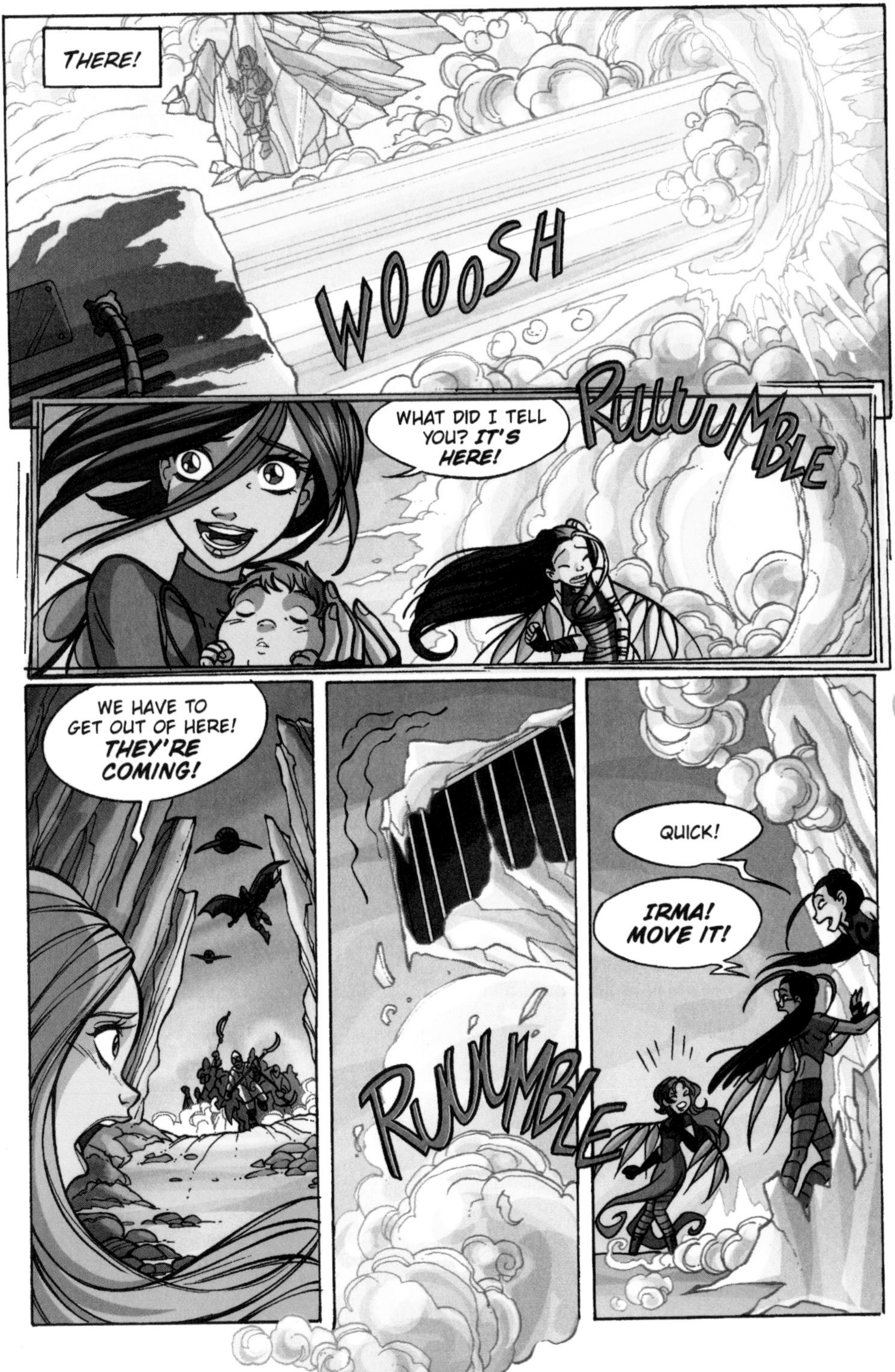
THERE!
WOOOSH
WHAT DID I TELL YOU? IT'S HERE!
RUUUUMBLE
WE HAVE TO GET OUT OF HERE! THEY'RE COMING!
RUUUMBLE
QUICK!
IRMA! MOVE IT!

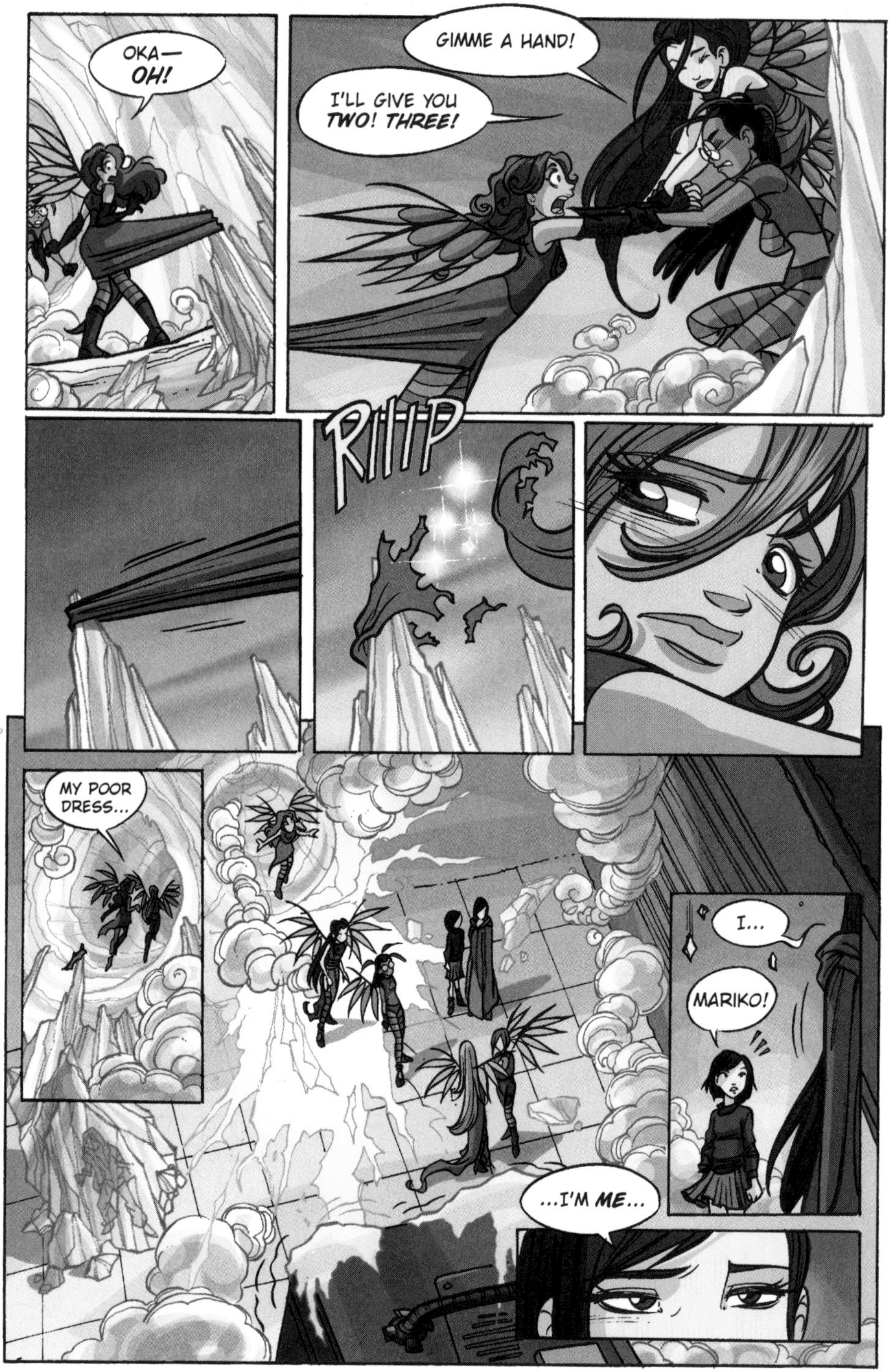
OKA—
OH!
GIMME A HAND!
I'LL GIVE YOU TWO! THREE!
RIIP
MY POOR DRESS...
I...
MARIKO!
...I'M ME...

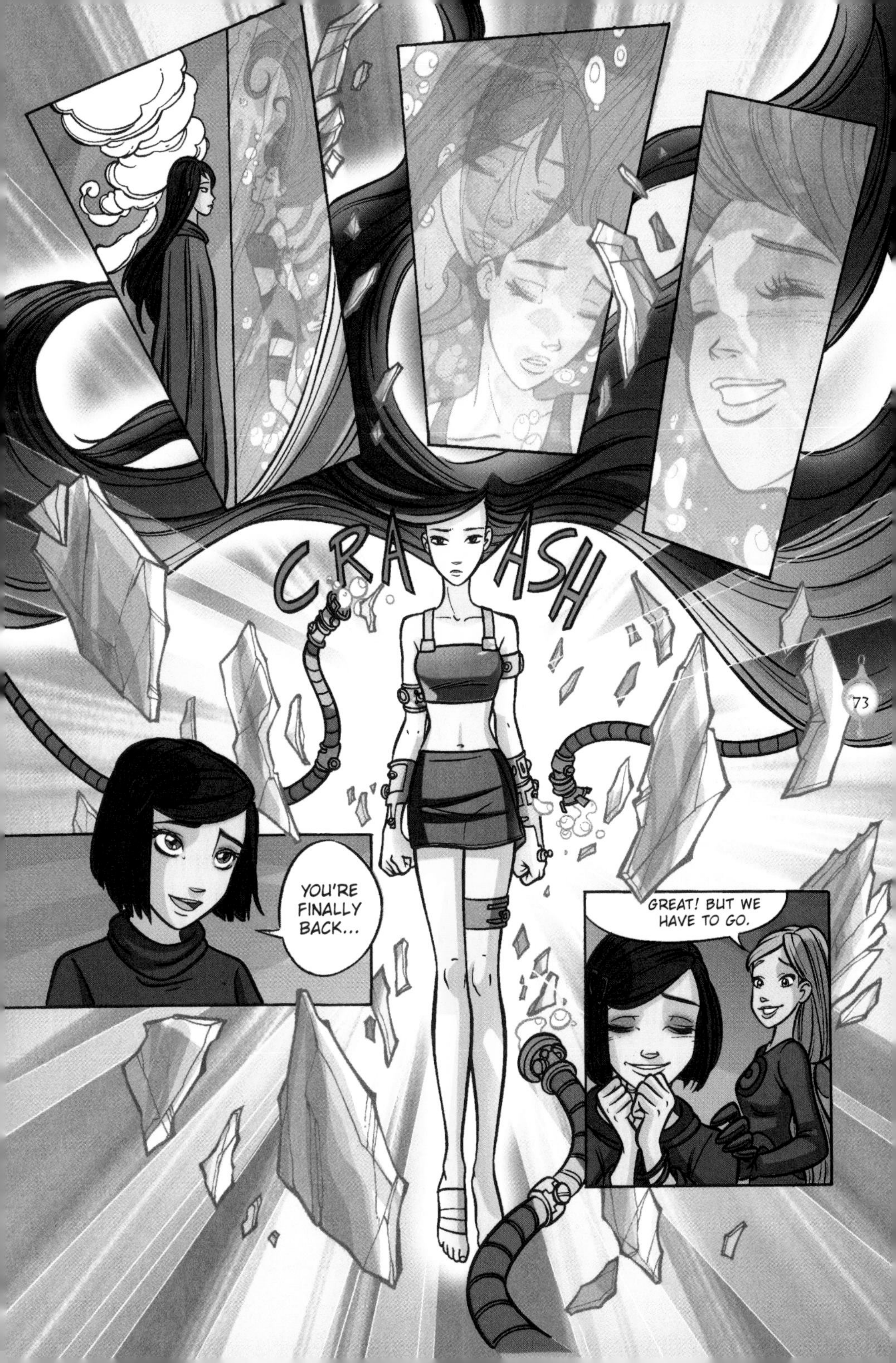
CRASH
YOU'RE FINALLY BACK...
GREAT! BUT WE HAVE TO GO.

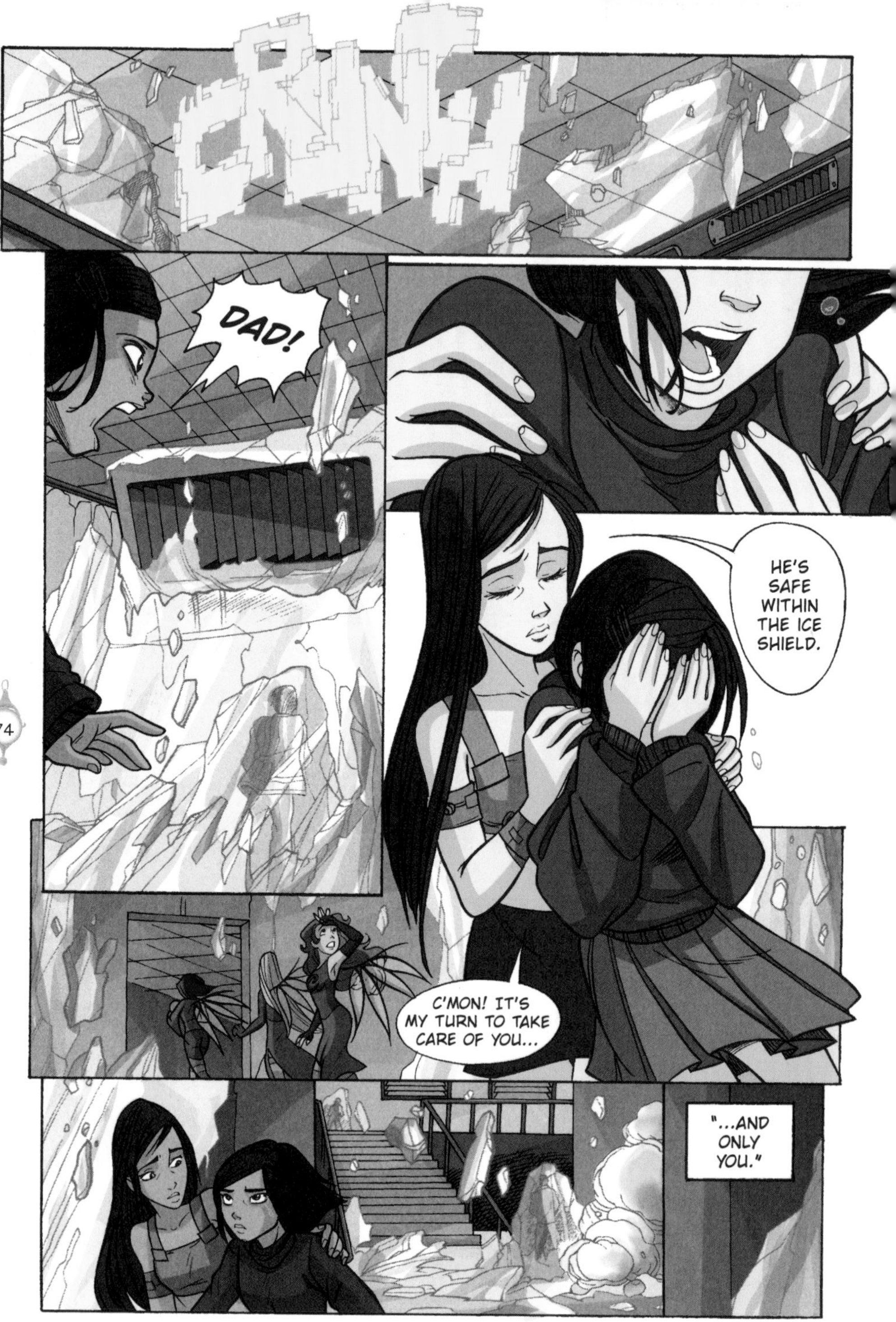
DAD!
HE'S SAFE WITHIN THE ICE SHIELD.
C'MON! IT'S MY TURN TO TAKE CARE OF YOU...
"...AND ONLY YOU."

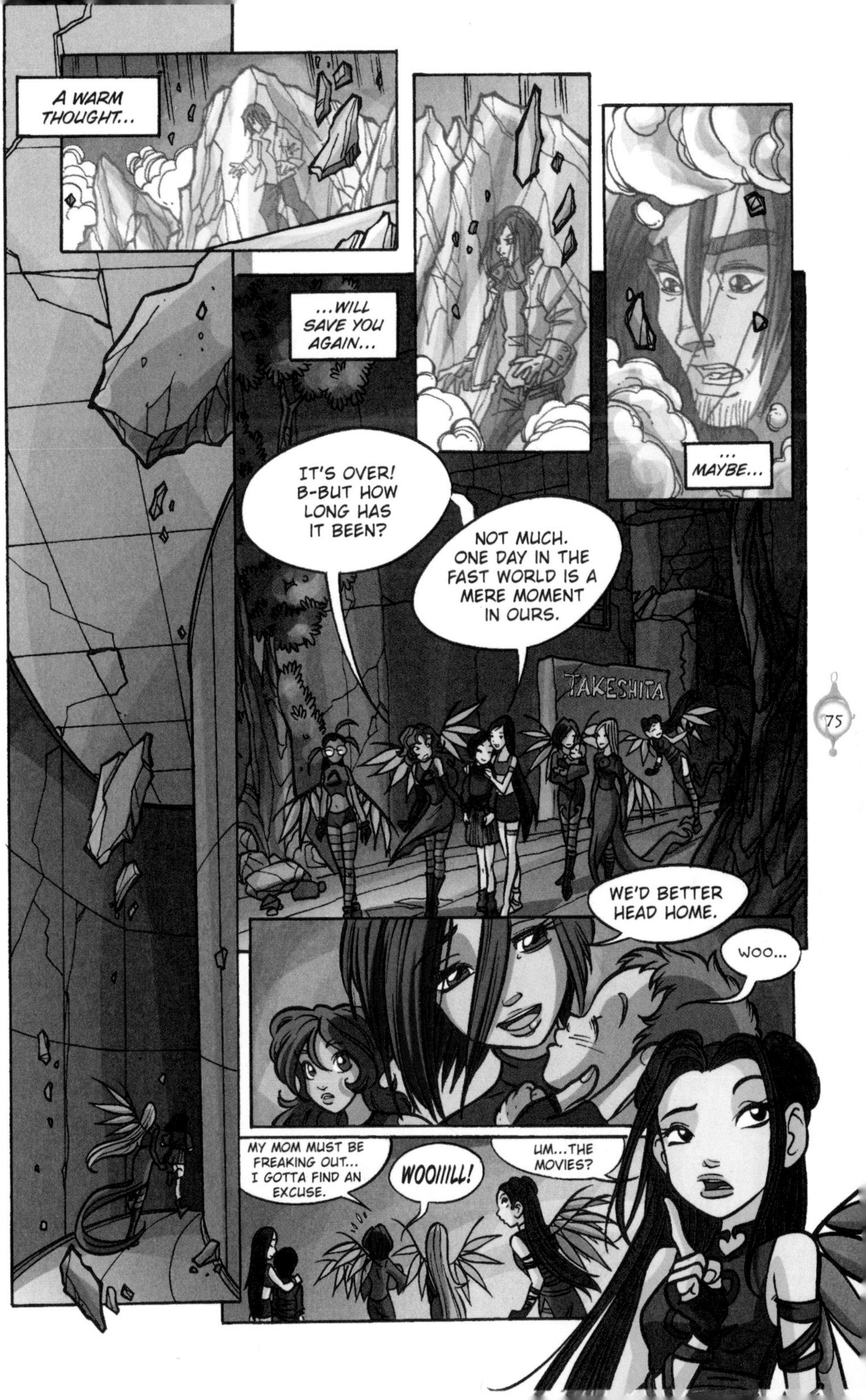
A WARM THOUGHT...
...WILL SAVE YOU AGAIN...
... MAYBE...
IT'S OVER! B-BUT HOW LONG HAS IT BEEN?
NOT MUCH. ONE DAY IN THE FAST WORLD IS A MERE MOMENT IN OURS.
TAKESHITA
WE'D BETTER HEAD HOME.
WOO...
MY MOM MUST BE FREAKING OUT... I GOTTA FIND AN EXCUSE.
WOOIIILL!
UM...THE MOVIES?

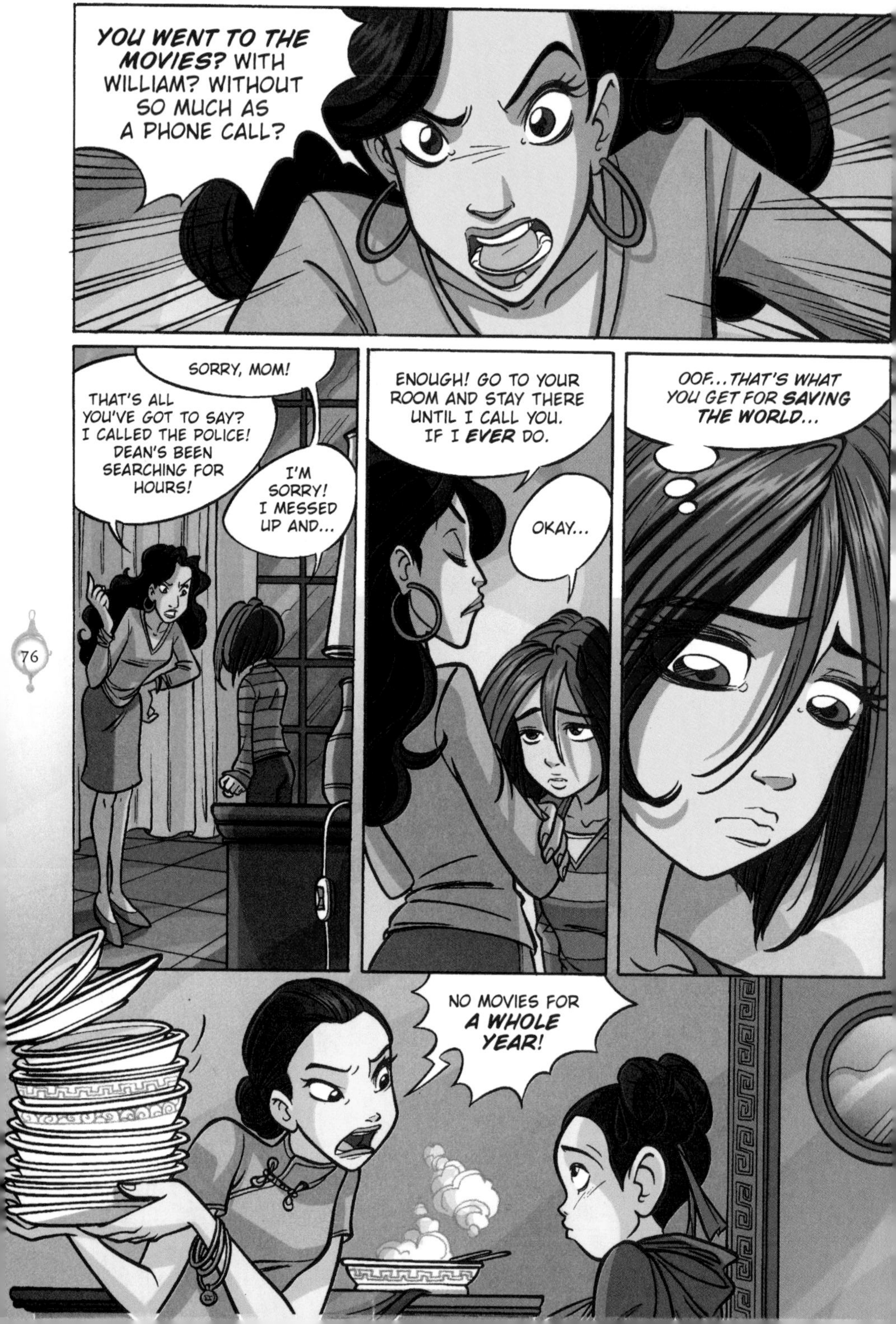
YOU WENT TO THE MOVIES? WITH WILLIAM? WITHOUT SO MUCH AS A PHONE CALL?
SORRY, MOM!
THAT'S ALL YOU'VE GOT TO SAY? I CALLED THE POLICE! DEAN'S BEEN SEARCHING FOR HOURS!
I'M SORRY! I MESSED UP AND...
ENOUGH! GO TO YOUR ROOM AND STAY THERE UNTIL I CALL YOU. IF I EVER DO.
OKAY...
OOF...THAT'S WHAT YOU GET FOR SAVING THE WORLD...
NO MOVIES FOR A WHOLE YEAR!

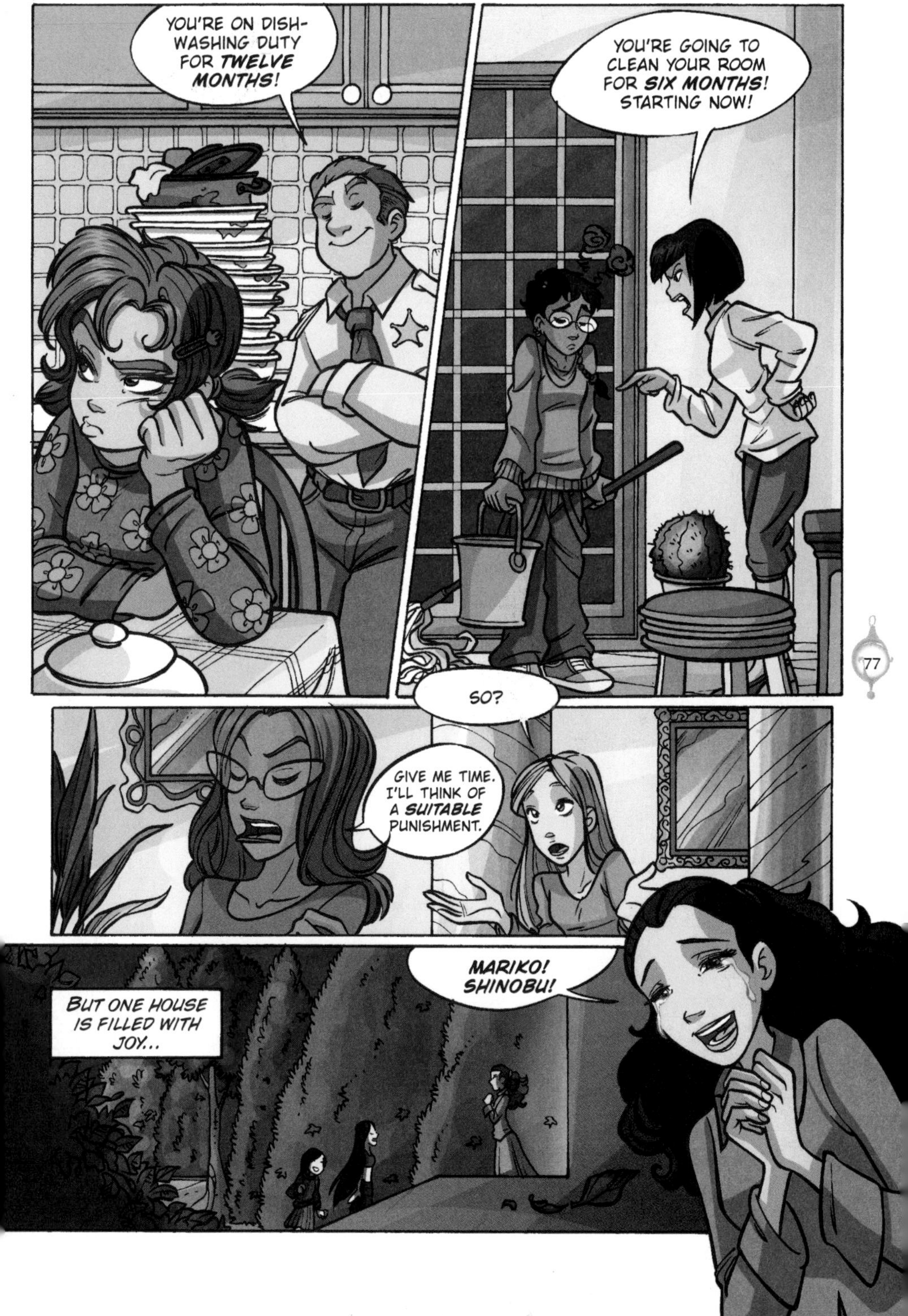
YOU'RE ON DISH-WASHING DUTY FOR *TWELVE MONTHS*!
YOU'RE GOING TO CLEAN YOUR ROOM FOR *SIX MONTHS*! STARTING NOW!
SO?
GIVE ME TIME. I'LL THINK OF A *SUITABLE* PUNISHMENT.
BUT ONE HOUSE IS FILLED WITH JOY...
MARIKO! SHINOBU!

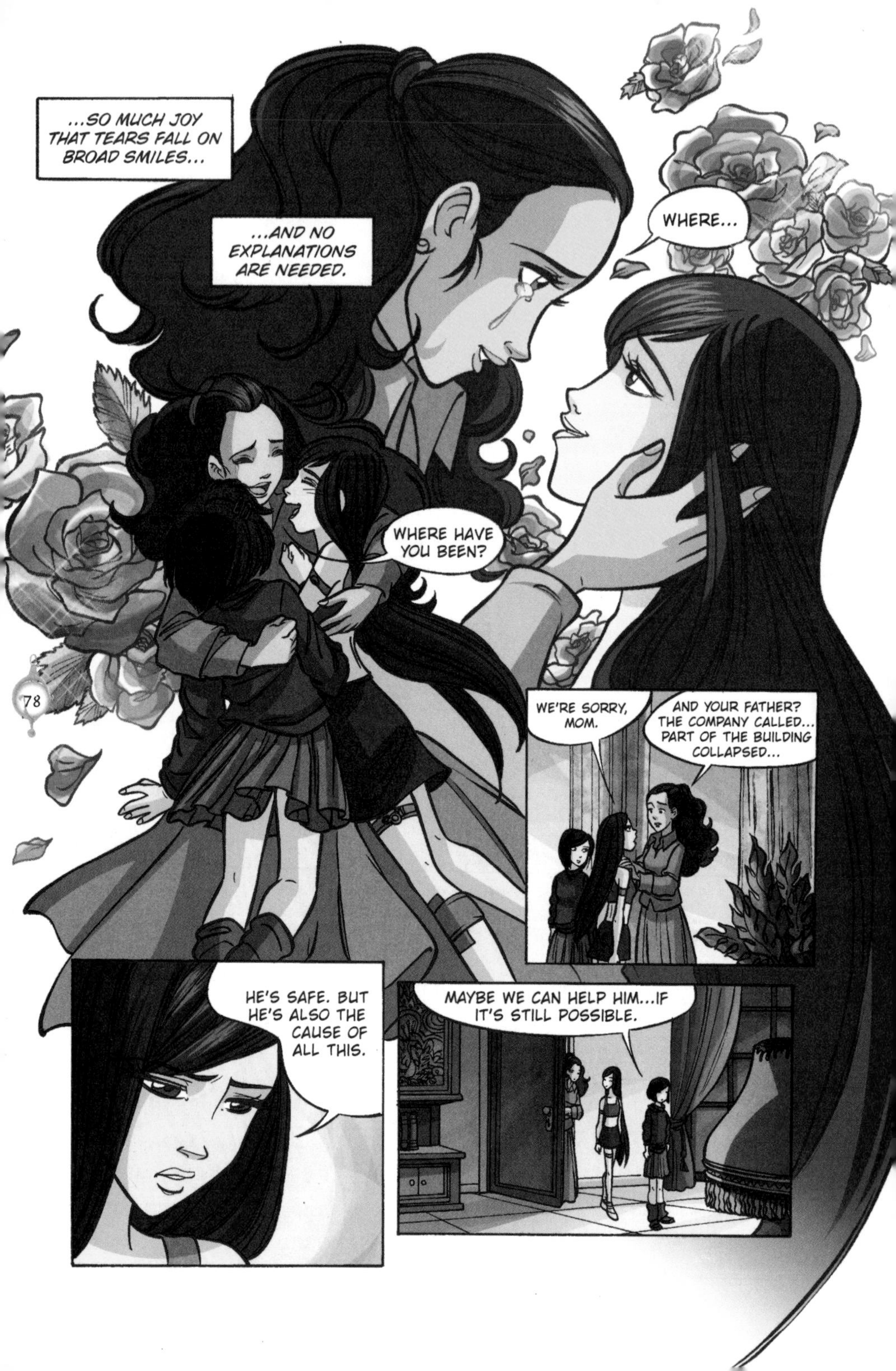

...SO MUCH JOY THAT TEARS FALL ON BROAD SMILES...
...AND NO EXPLANATIONS ARE NEEDED.
WHERE...
WHERE HAVE YOU BEEN?
WE'RE SORRY, MOM.
AND YOUR FATHER? THE COMPANY CALLED... PART OF THE BUILDING COLLAPSED...
HE'S SAFE. BUT HE'S ALSO THE CAUSE OF ALL THIS.
MAYBE WE CAN HELP HIM...IF IT'S STILL POSSIBLE.

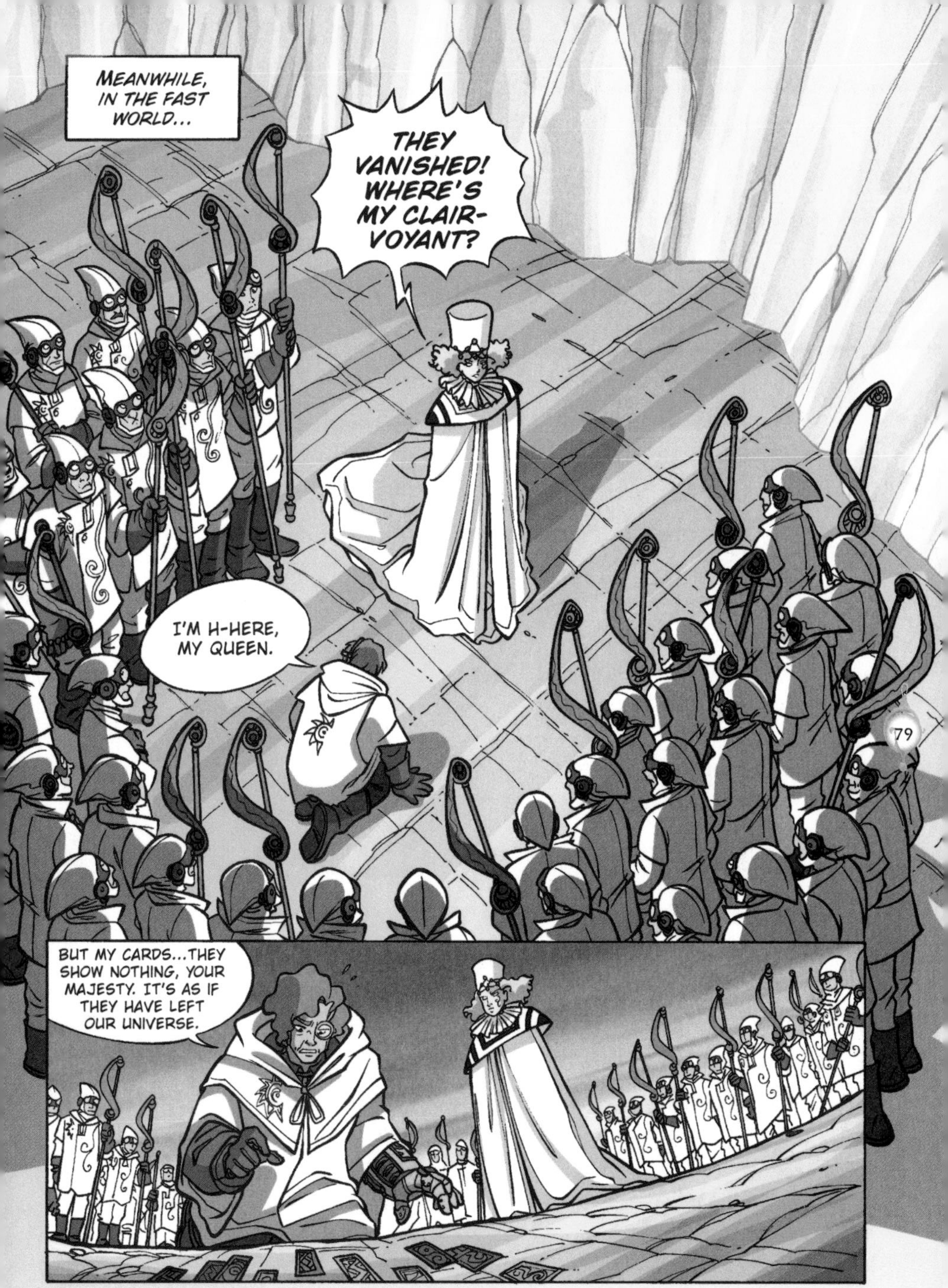
MEANWHILE, IN THE FAST WORLD...
THEY VANISHED! WHERE'S MY CLAIR-VOYANT?
I'M H-HERE, MY QUEEN.
BUT MY CARDS...THEY SHOW NOTHING, YOUR MAJESTY. IT'S AS IF THEY HAVE LEFT OUR UNIVERSE.

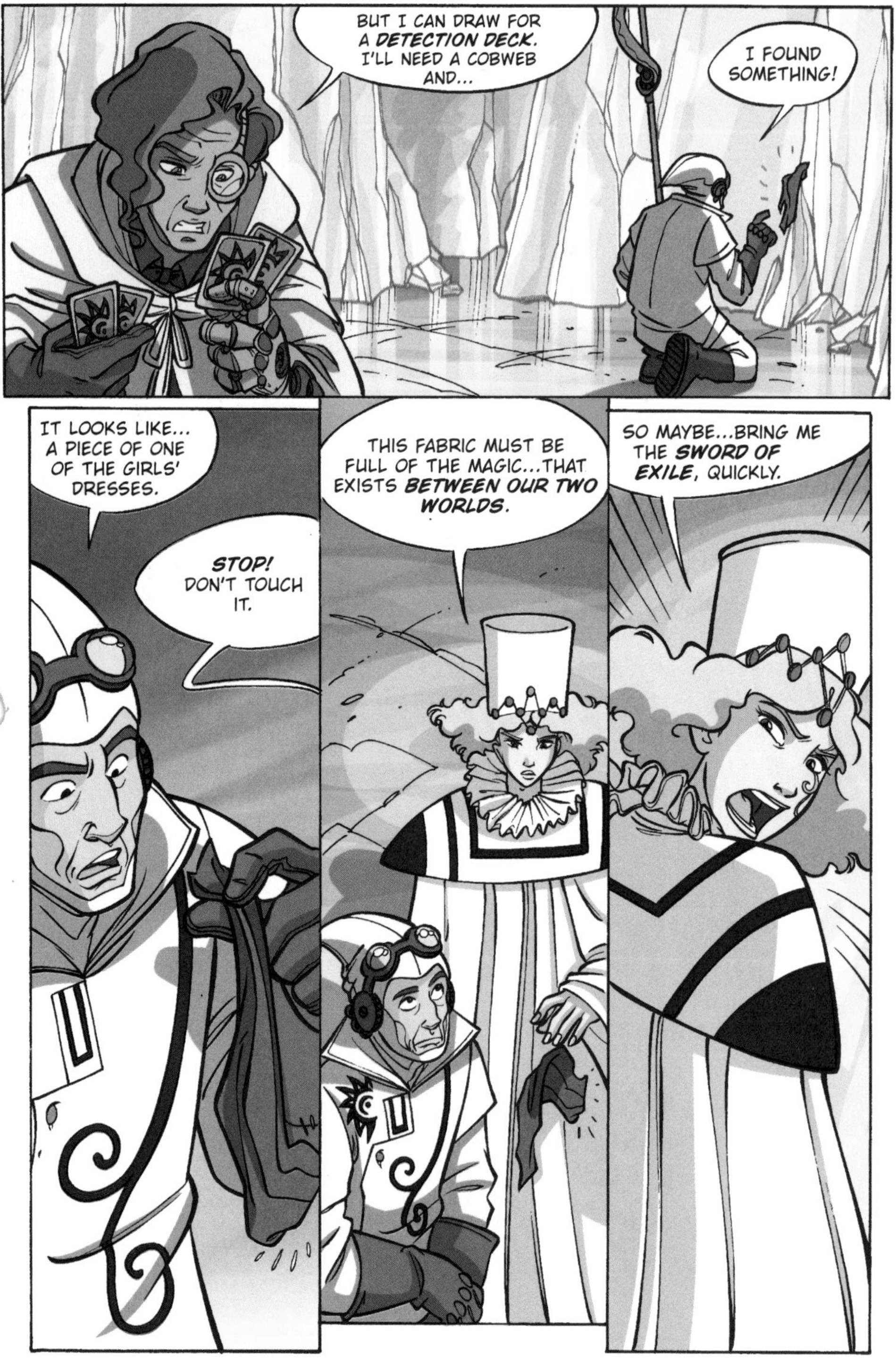
BUT I CAN DRAW FOR A **DETECTION DECK.** I'LL NEED A COBWEB AND...
I FOUND SOMETHING!
IT LOOKS LIKE... A PIECE OF ONE OF THE GIRLS' DRESSES.
STOP! DON'T TOUCH IT.
THIS FABRIC MUST BE FULL OF THE MAGIC...THAT EXISTS **BETWEEN OUR TWO WORLDS.**
SO MAYBE...BRING ME THE **SWORD OF EXILE**, QUICKLY.

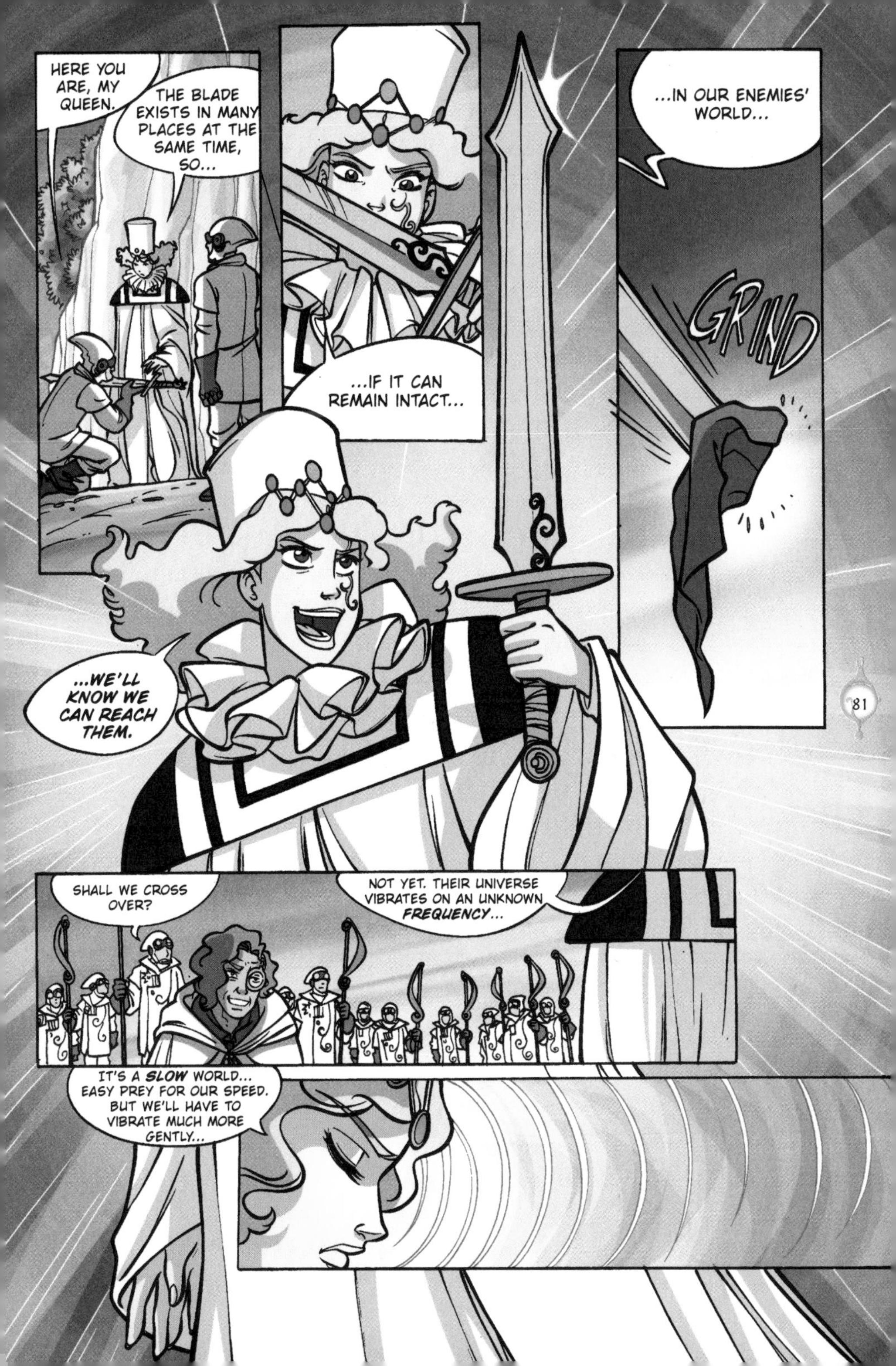
HERE YOU ARE, MY QUEEN.
THE BLADE EXISTS IN MANY PLACES AT THE SAME TIME, SO...
...IF IT CAN REMAIN INTACT...
...IN OUR ENEMIES' WORLD...
GRIND
...WE'LL KNOW WE CAN REACH THEM.
SHALL WE CROSS OVER?
NOT YET. THEIR UNIVERSE VIBRATES ON AN UNKNOWN FREQUENCY...
IT'S A SLOW WORLD... EASY PREY FOR OUR SPEED. BUT WE'LL HAVE TO VIBRATE MUCH MORE GENTLY...

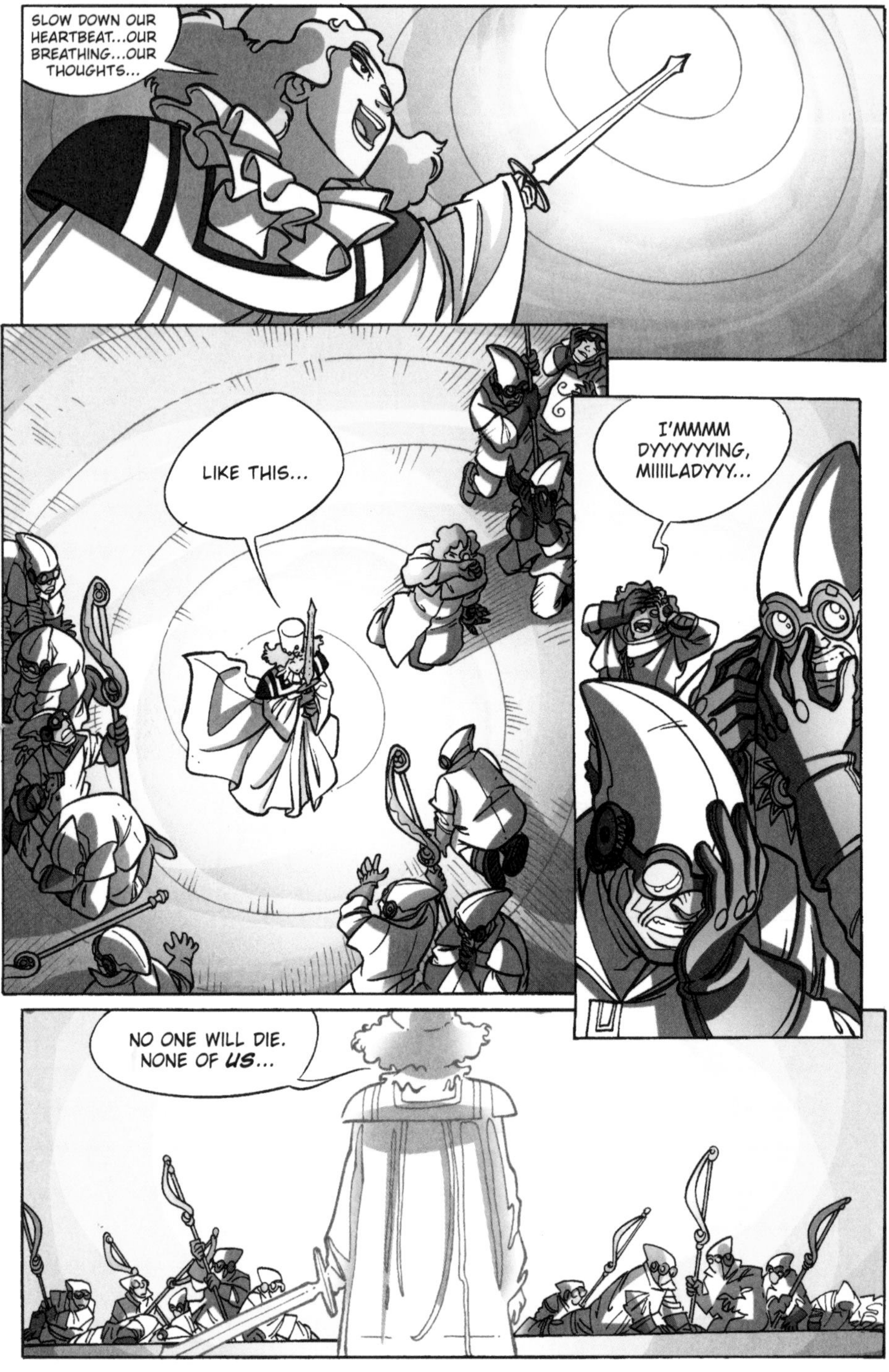
SLOW DOWN OUR HEARTBEAT...OUR BREATHING...OUR THOUGHTS...
LIKE THIS...
I'MMMM DYYYYYYING, MIIIILADYYY...
NO ONE WILL DIE. NONE OF *US*...

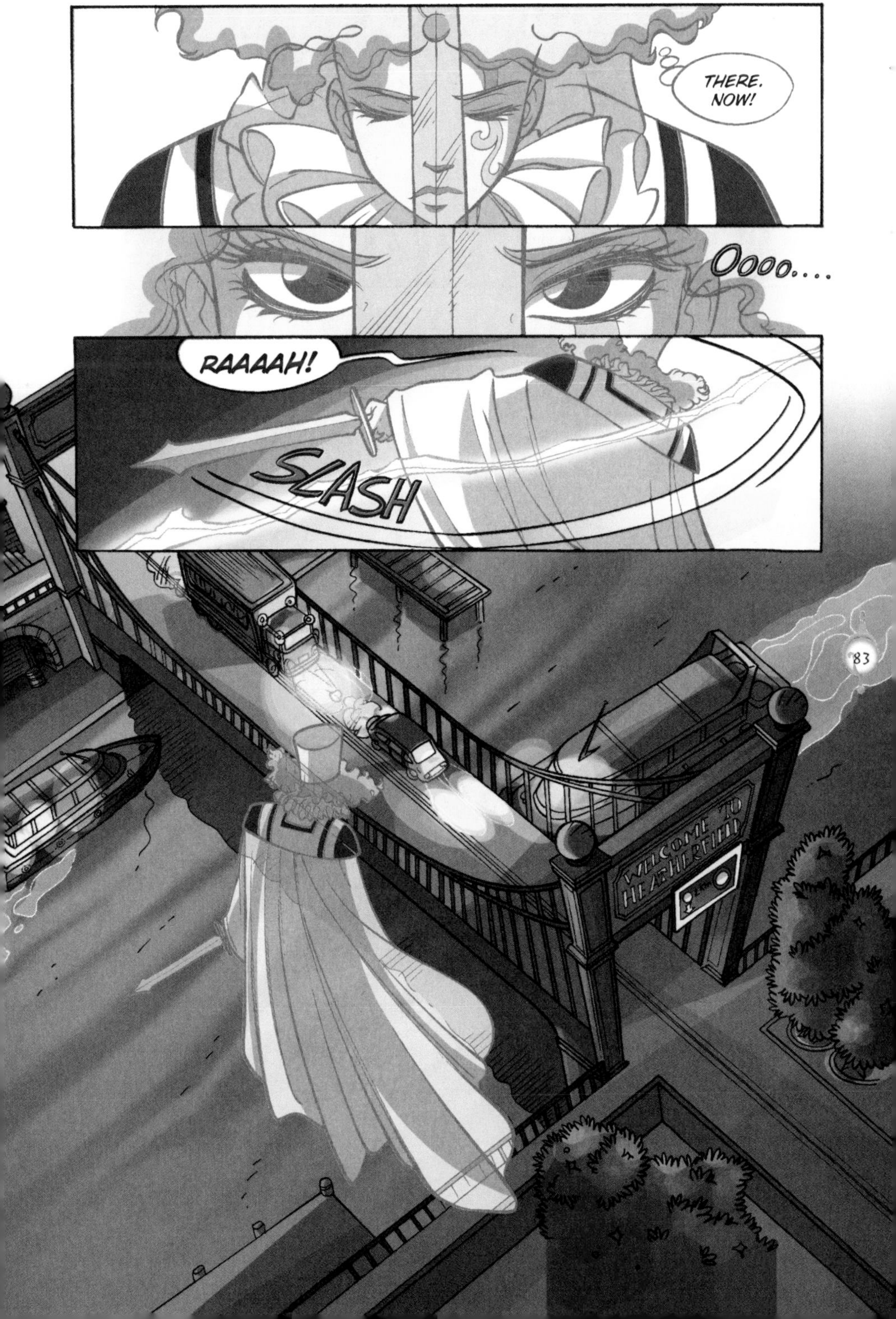
THERE. NOW!
Oooo....
RAAAAH!
SLASH
WELCOME TO HEATHERFIELD

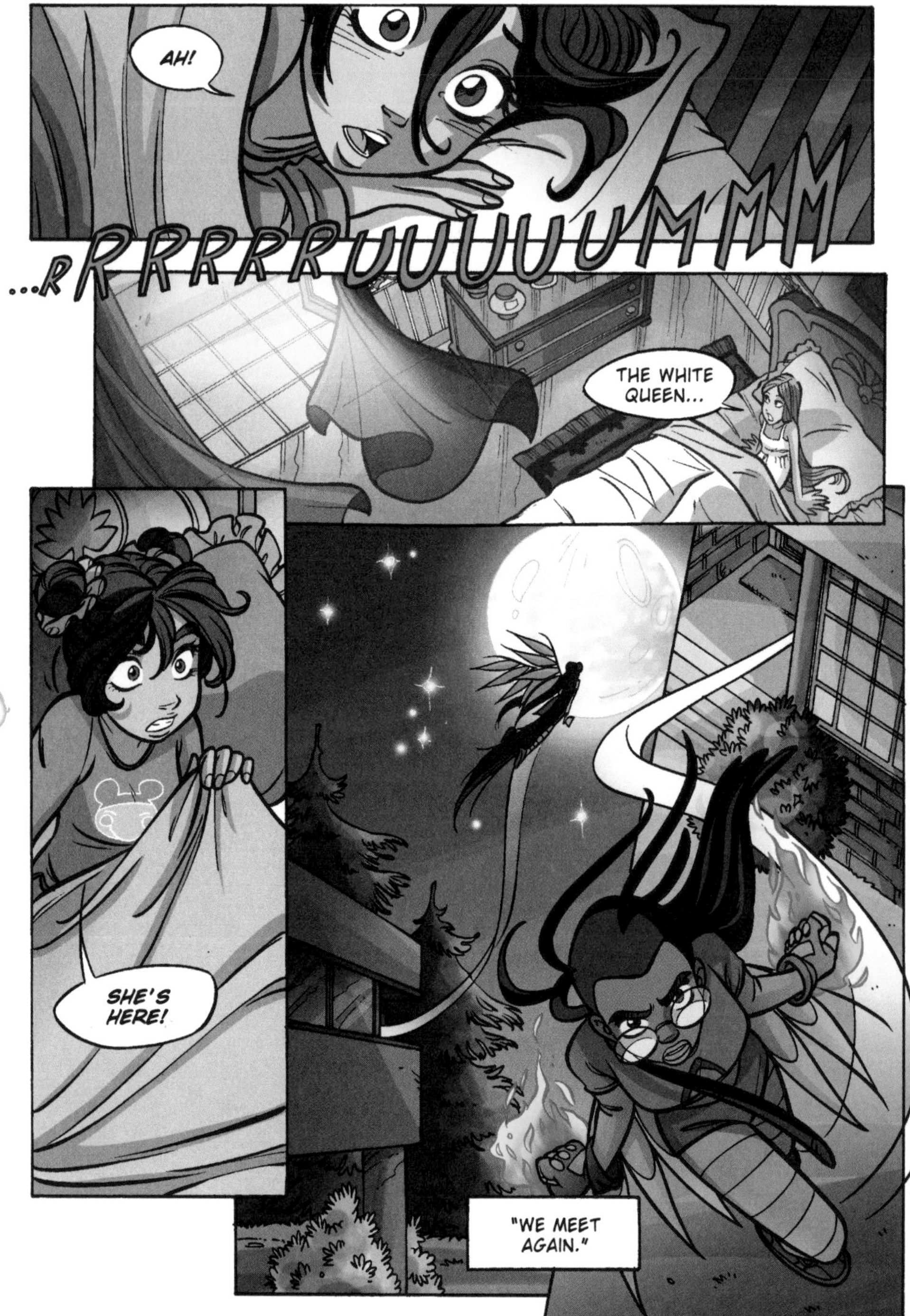
AH!
...RRRRRRUUUUUMMMM
THE WHITE QUEEN...
SHE'S HERE!
"WE MEET AGAIN."

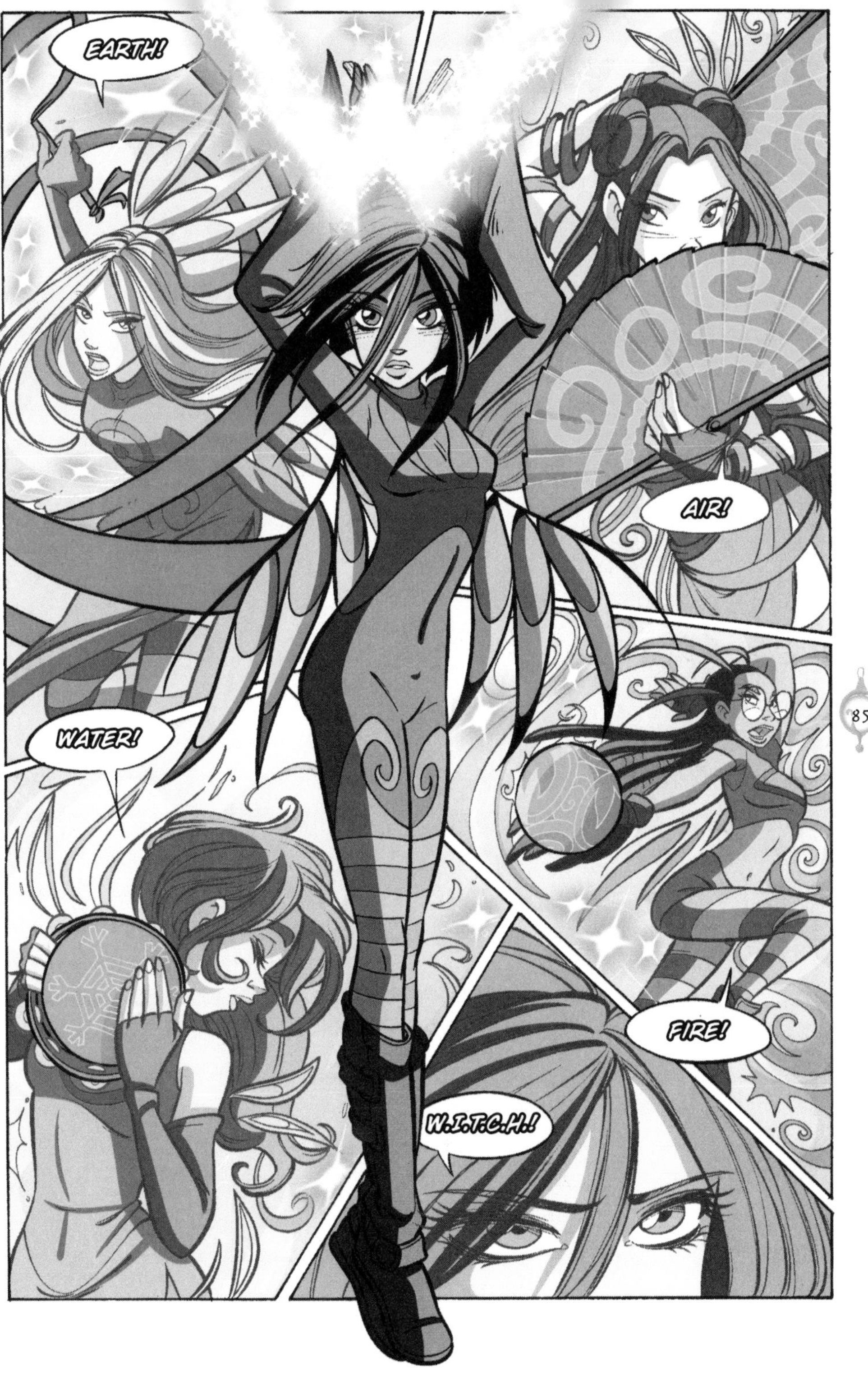
EARTH!
AIR!
WATER!
FIRE!
W.I.T.C.H.!

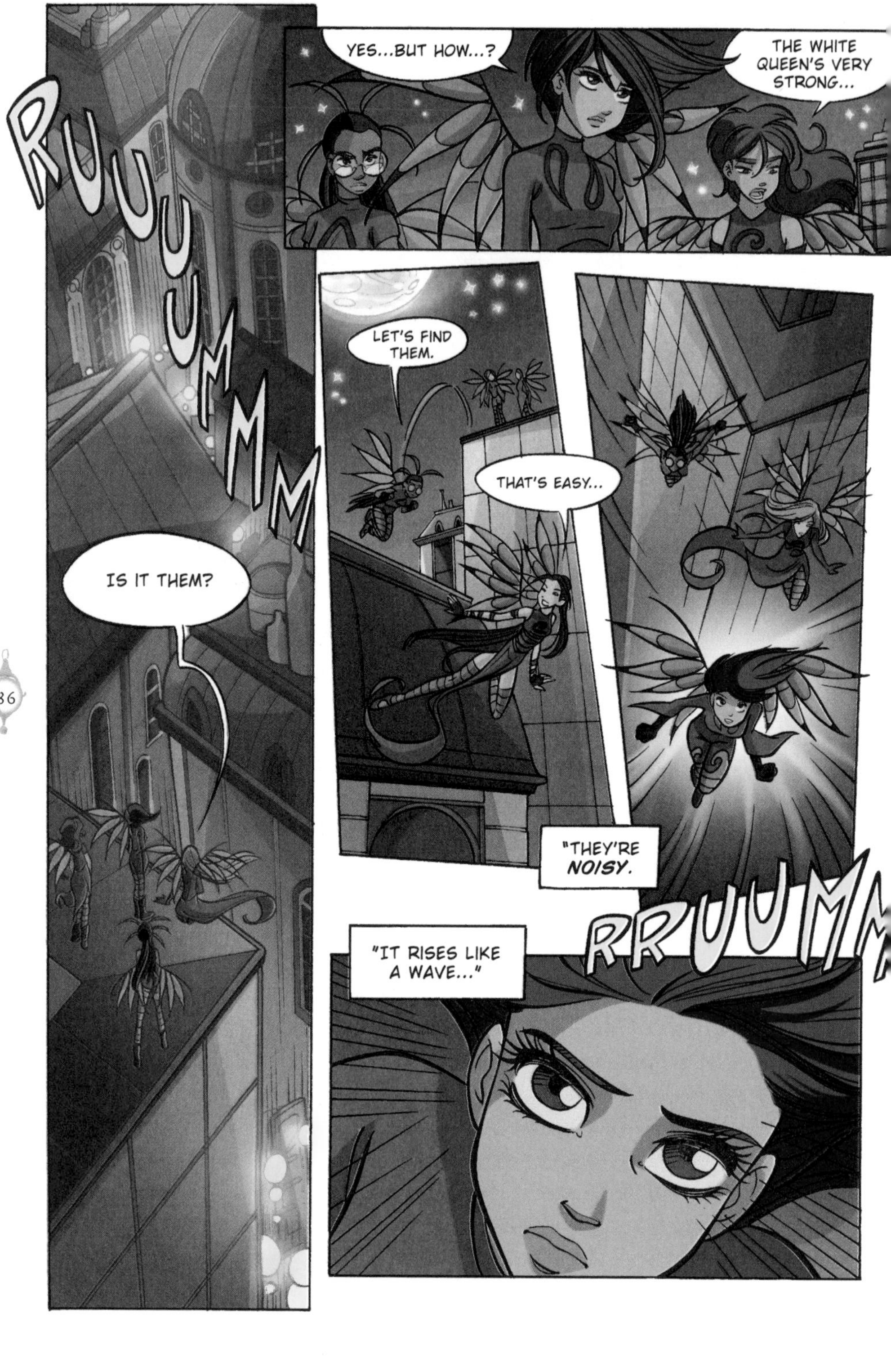
RUUUMMM
IS IT THEM?
YES...BUT HOW...?
THE WHITE QUEEN'S VERY STRONG...
LET'S FIND THEM.
THAT'S EASY...
"THEY'RE *NOISY*.
RRUUMM
"IT RISES LIKE A WAVE..."

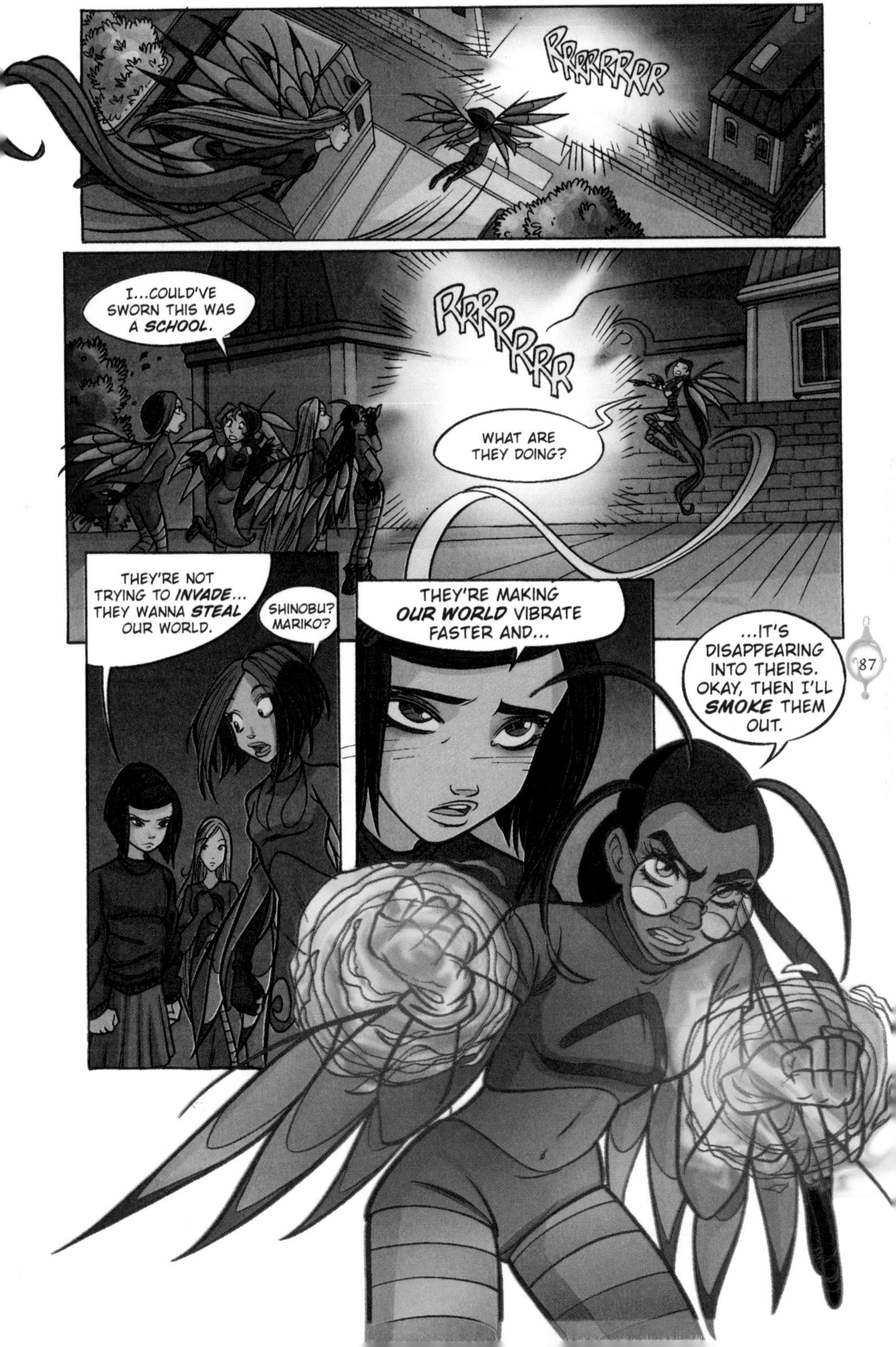
RRRRRRRR
I...COULD'VE SWORN THIS WAS A SCHOOL.
RRRRRRRR
WHAT ARE THEY DOING?
THEY'RE NOT TRYING TO INVADE... THEY WANNA STEAL OUR WORLD.
SHINOBU? MARIKO?
THEY'RE MAKING OUR WORLD VIBRATE FASTER AND...
...IT'S DISAPPEARING INTO THEIRS. OKAY, THEN I'LL SMOKE THEM OUT.

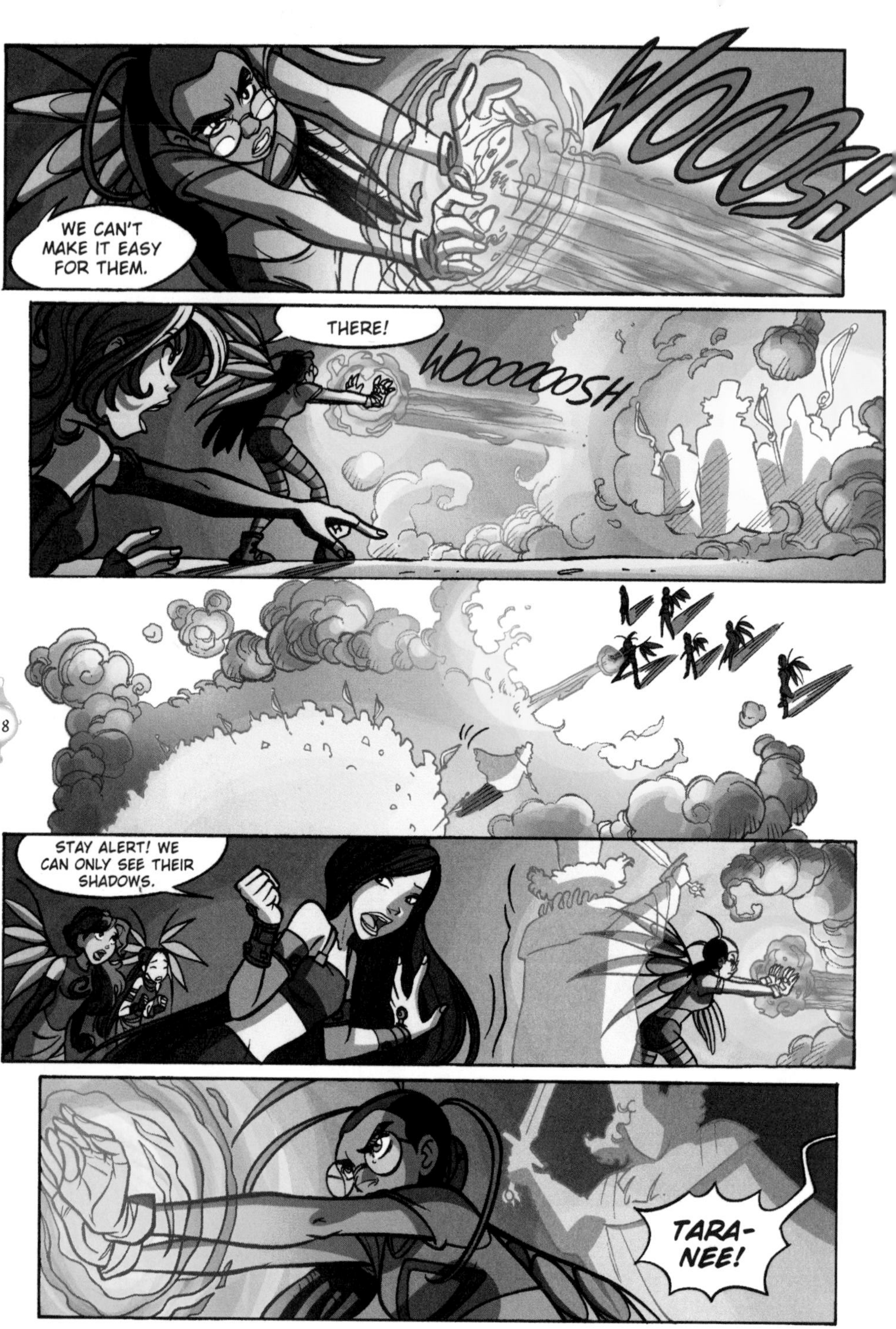
WOOOSH
WE CAN'T MAKE IT EASY FOR THEM.
THERE!
WOOOOOOOSH
STAY ALERT! WE CAN ONLY SEE THEIR SHADOWS.
TARA-NEE!

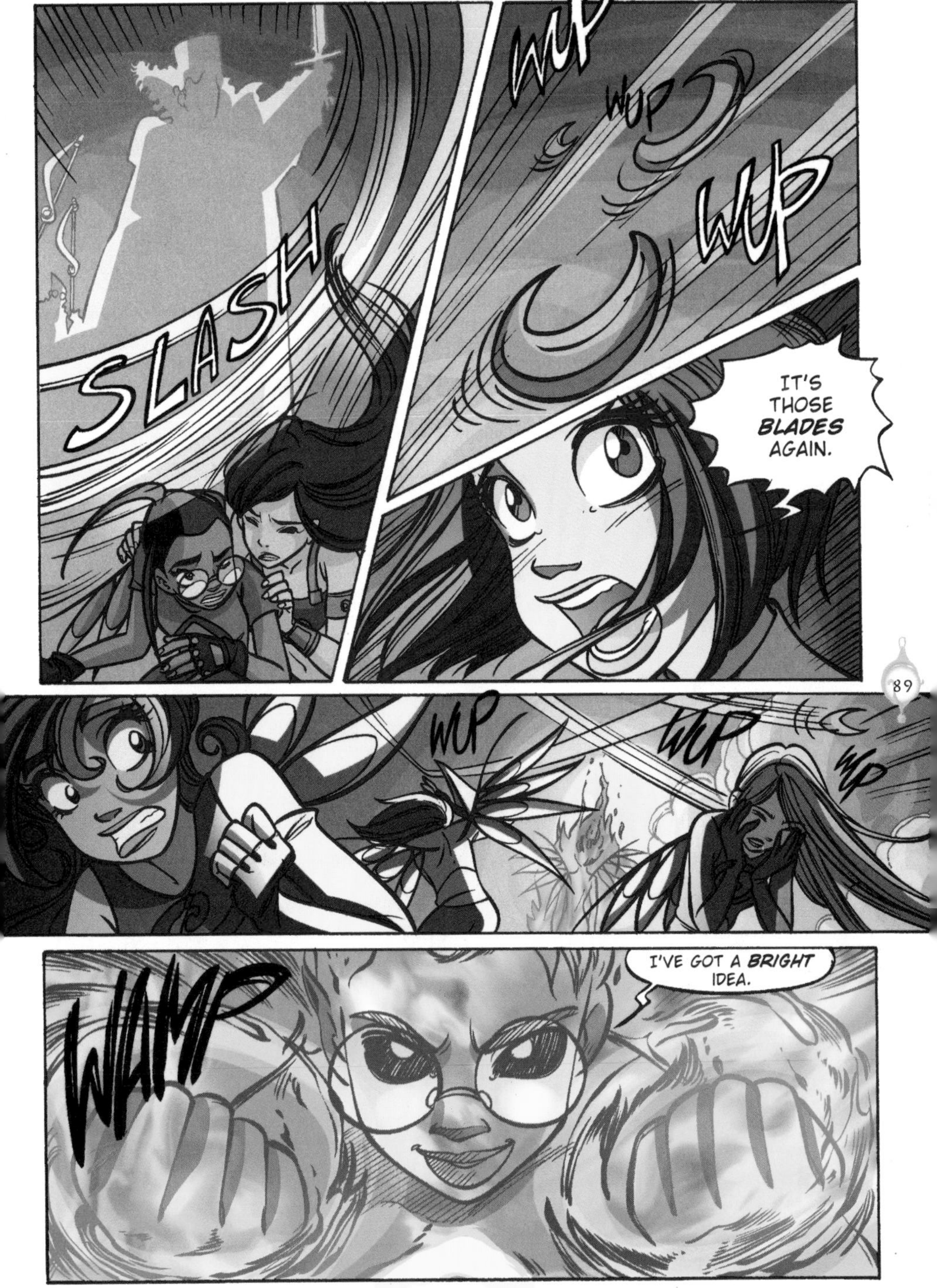
SLASH
WUP
WUP
WUP
IT'S THOSE **BLADES** AGAIN.
WUP
WUP
WUP
WAMP
I'VE GOT A **BRIGHT** IDEA.

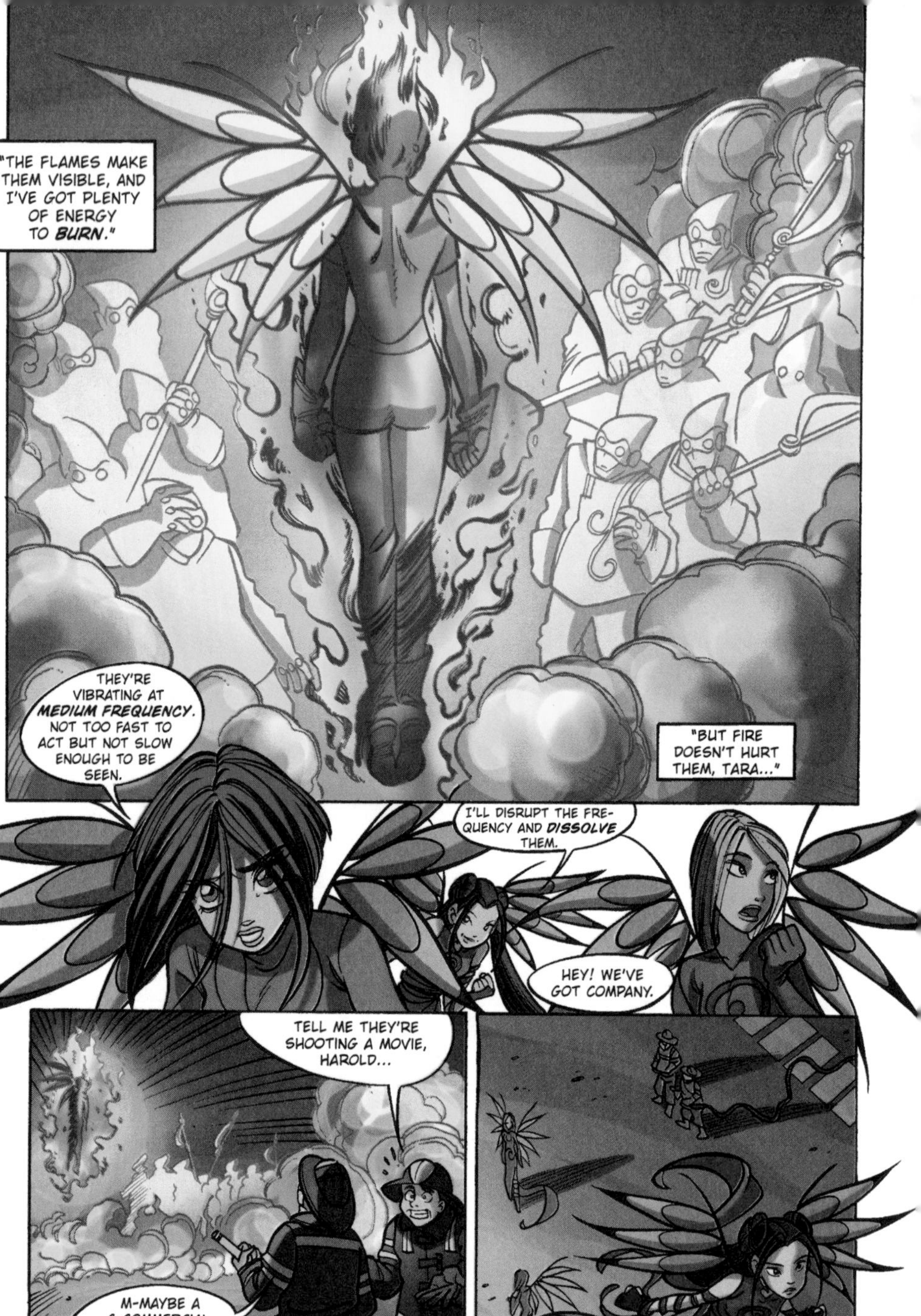
"THE FLAMES MAKE THEM VISIBLE, AND I'VE GOT PLENTY OF ENERGY TO **BURN**."
THEY'RE VIBRATING AT ***MEDIUM FREQUENCY***. NOT TOO FAST TO ACT BUT NOT SLOW ENOUGH TO BE SEEN.
"BUT FIRE DOESN'T HURT THEM, TARA..."
I'LL DISRUPT THE FREQUENCY AND ***DISSOLVE*** THEM.
HEY! WE'VE GOT COMPANY.
TELL ME THEY'RE SHOOTING A MOVIE, HAROLD...
M-MAYBE A C-COMMERCIAL, STAN, FOR SOME ***ENERGY DRINK***.

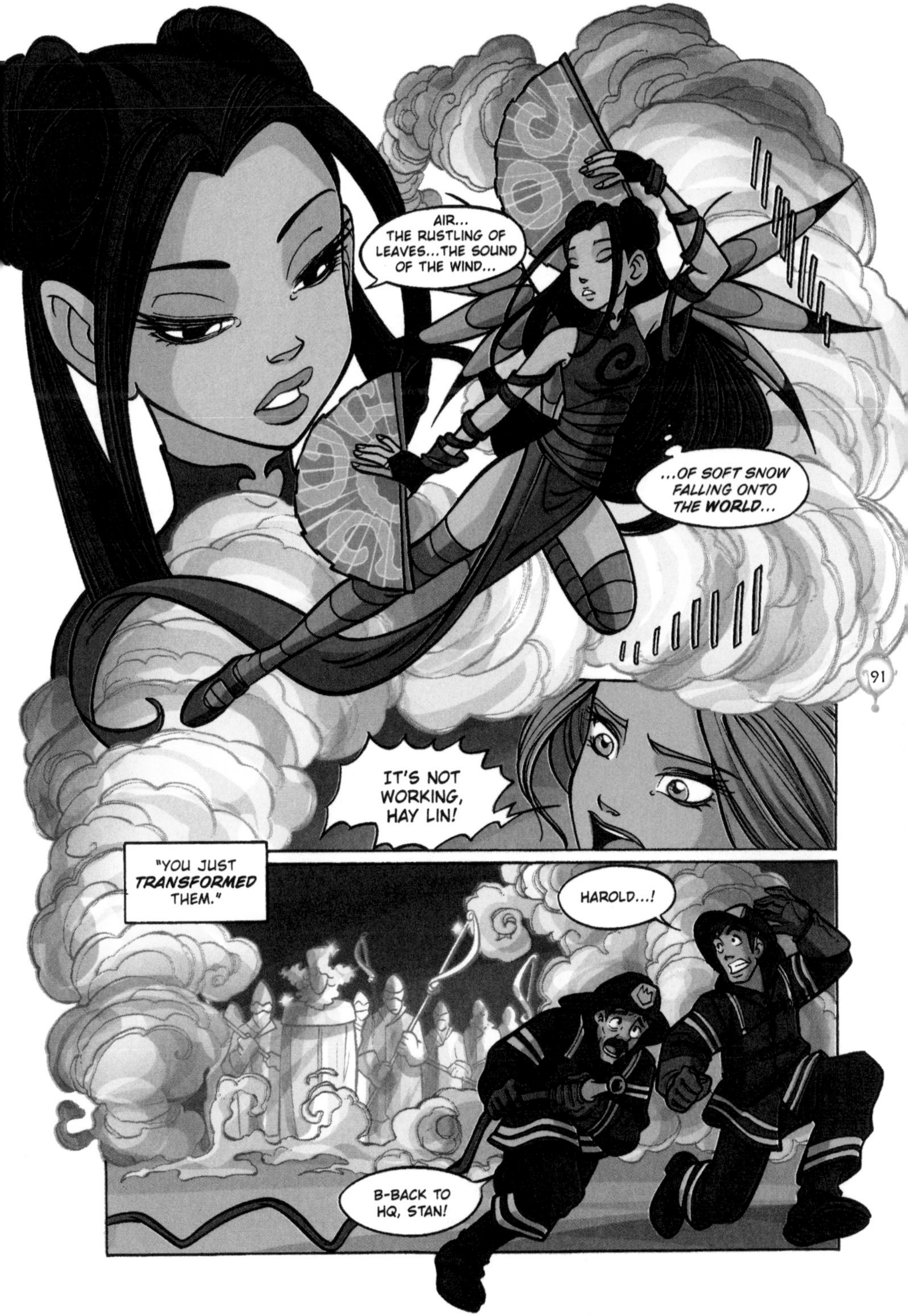
AIR...
THE RUSTLING OF LEAVES...THE SOUND OF THE WIND...
...OF SOFT SNOW FALLING ONTO THE WORLD...
IT'S NOT WORKING, HAY LIN!
"YOU JUST TRANSFORMED THEM."
HAROLD...!
B-BACK TO HQ, STAN!

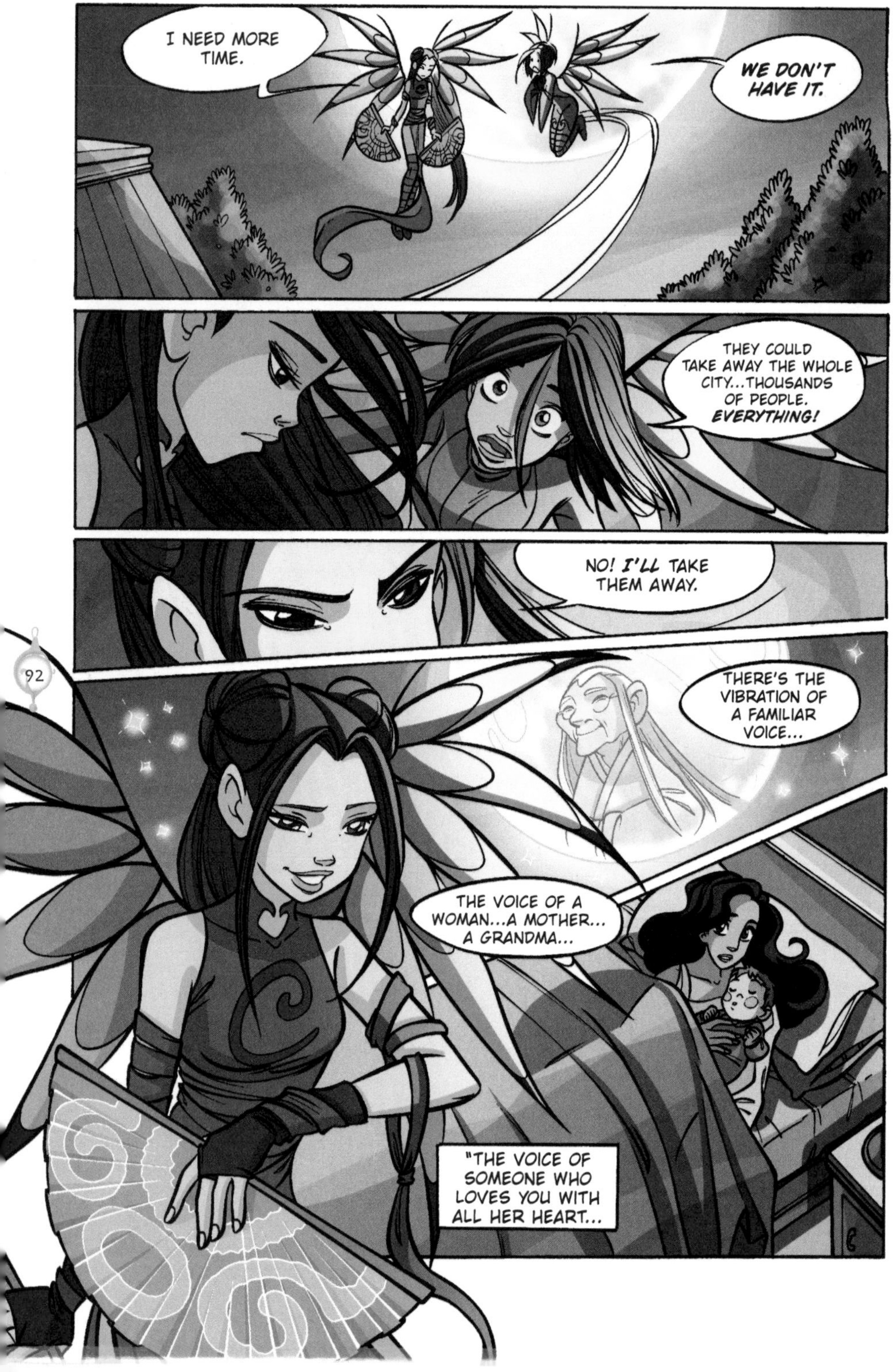
I NEED MORE TIME.
WE DON'T HAVE IT.
THEY COULD TAKE AWAY THE WHOLE CITY...THOUSANDS OF PEOPLE. EVERYTHING!
NO! I'LL TAKE THEM AWAY.
THERE'S THE VIBRATION OF A FAMILIAR VOICE...
THE VOICE OF A WOMAN...A MOTHER... A GRANDMA...
"THE VOICE OF SOMEONE WHO LOVES YOU WITH ALL HER HEART...

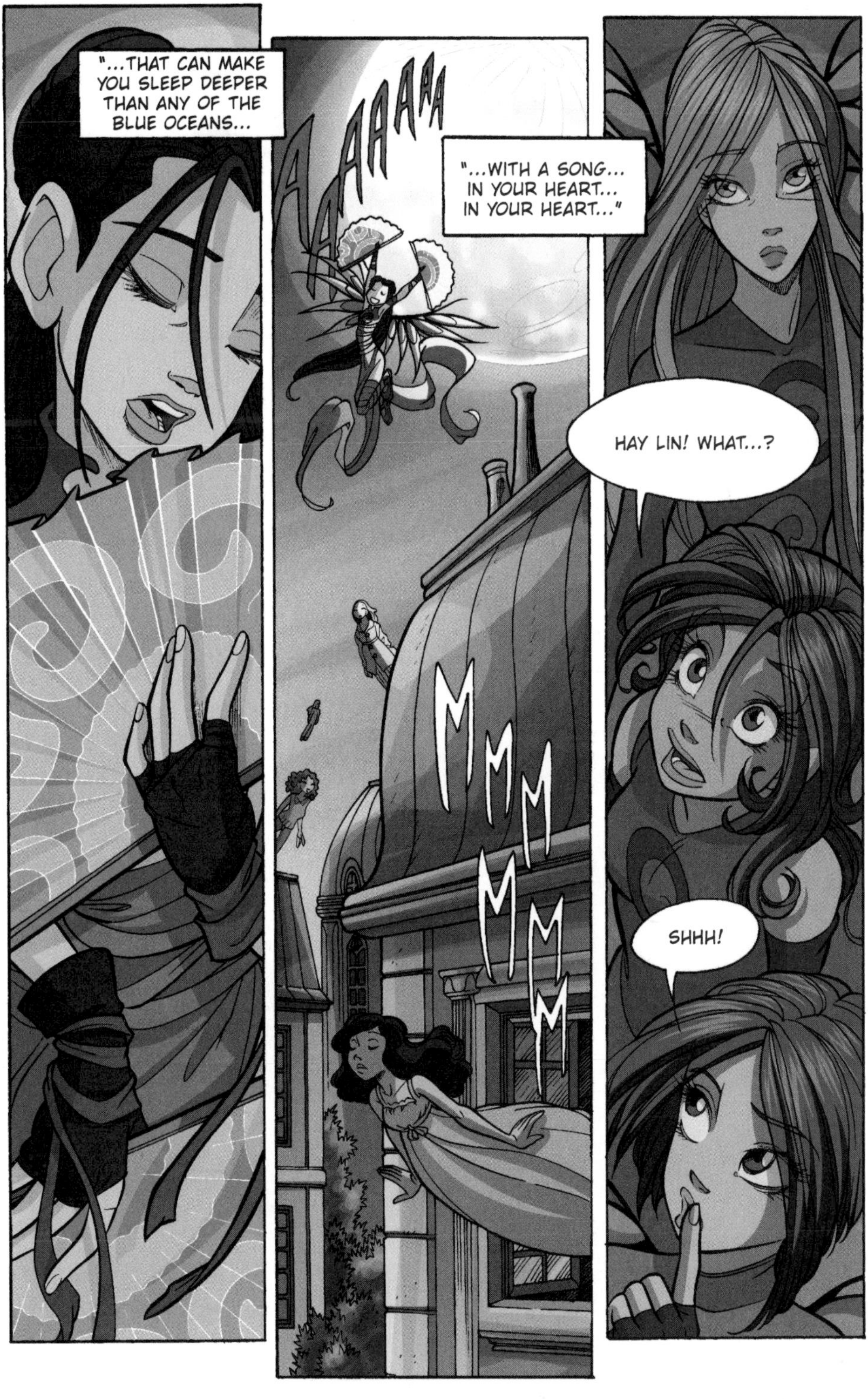
"...THAT CAN MAKE YOU SLEEP DEEPER THAN ANY OF THE BLUE OCEANS...
AAAAAAA
"...WITH A SONG... IN YOUR HEART... IN YOUR HEART..."
MMMMMMMM
HAY LIN! WHAT...?
SHHH!

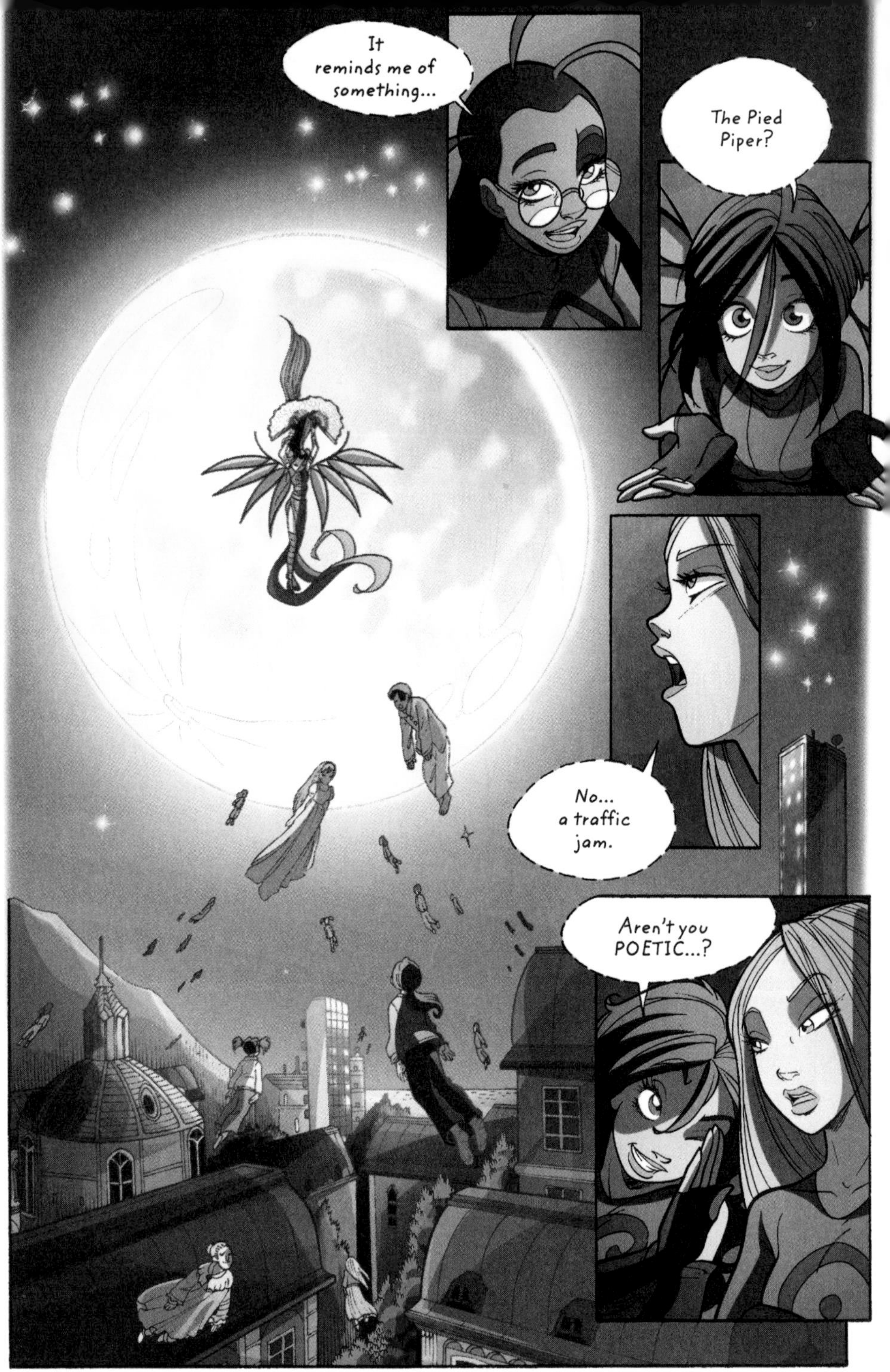
It reminds me of something...
The Pied Piper?
No... a traffic jam.
Aren't you POETIC...?

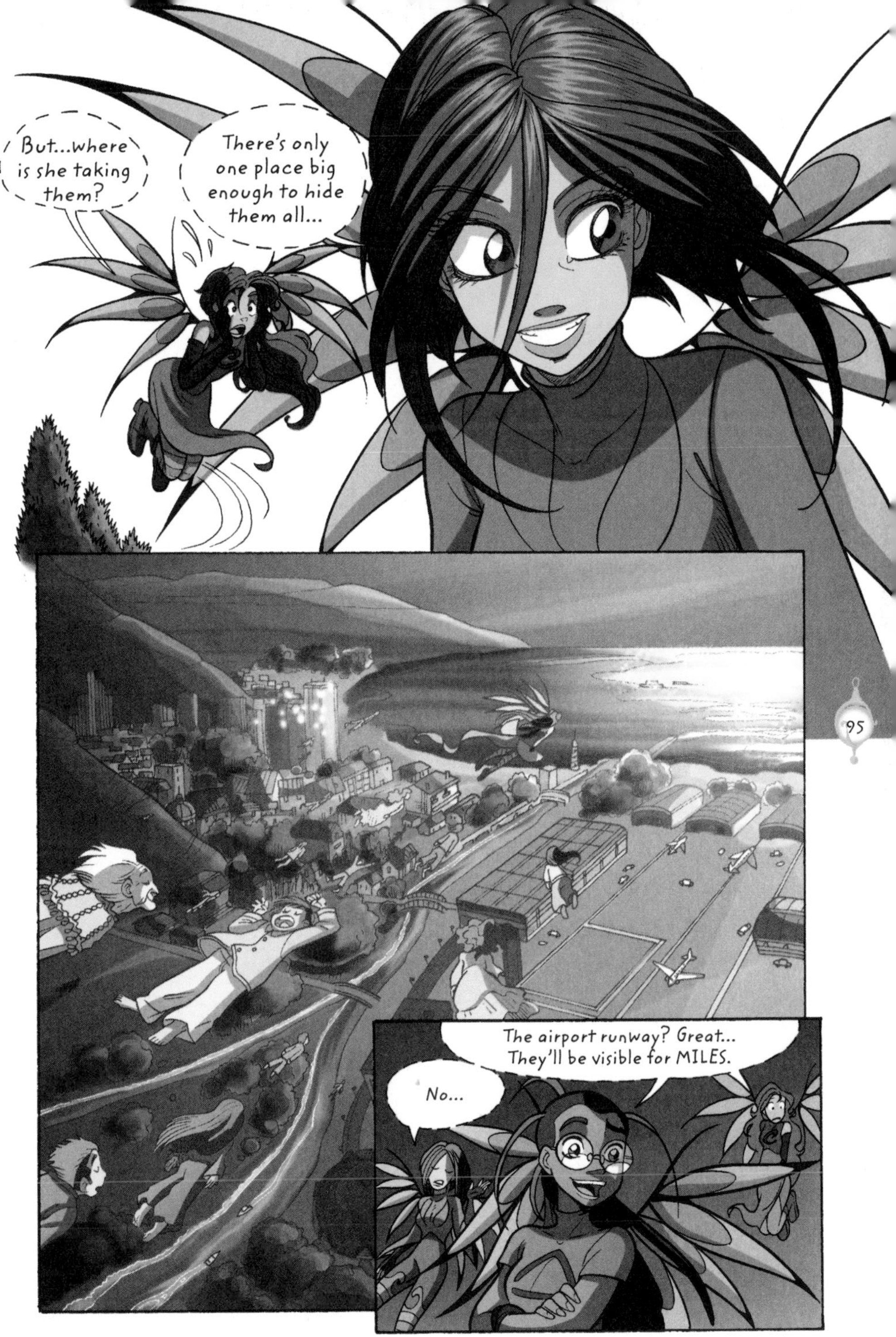

But...where is she taking them?
There's only one place big enough to hide them all...
The airport runway? Great... They'll be visible for MILES.
No...

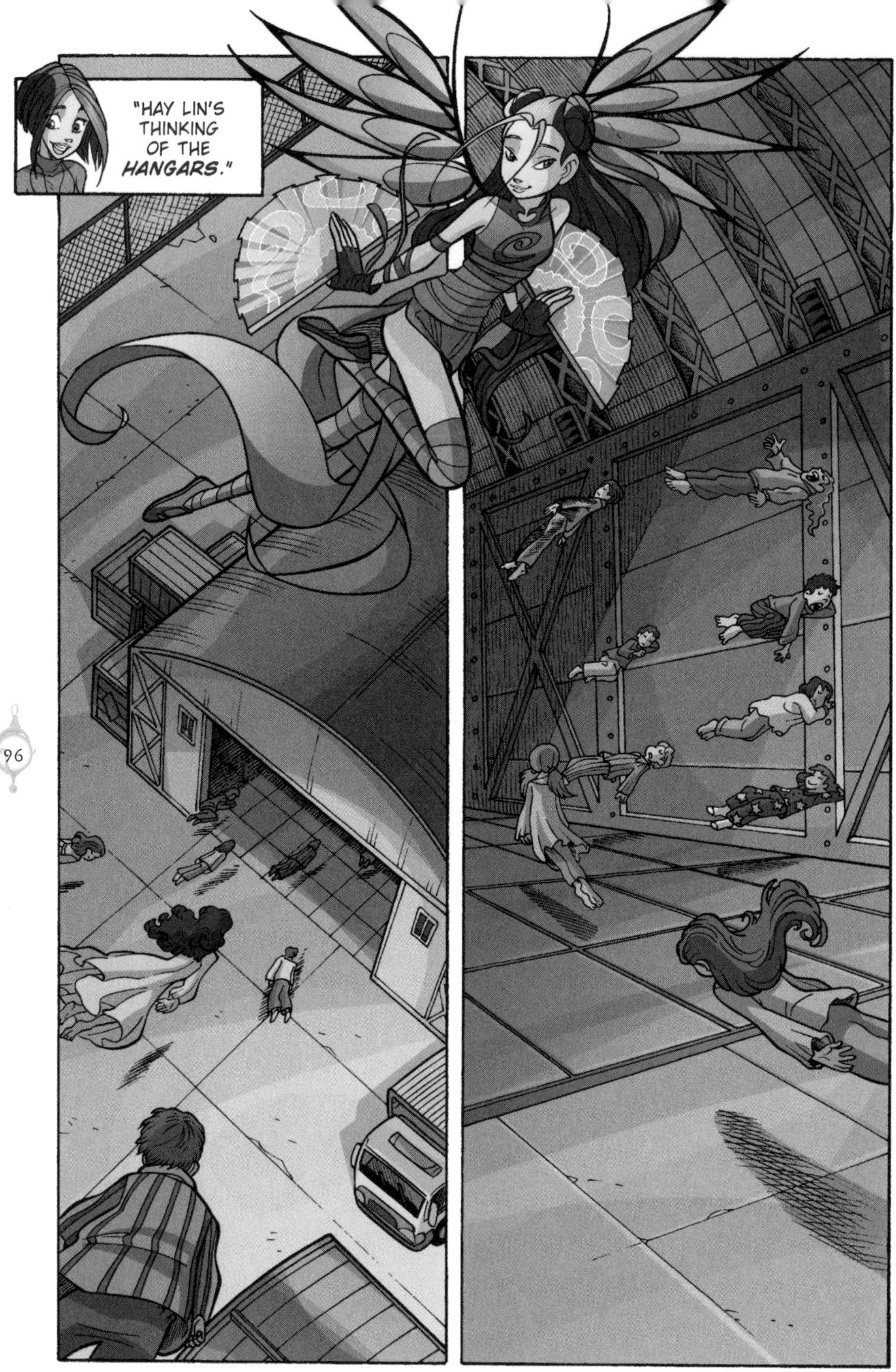
"HAY LIN'S THINKING OF THE HANGARS."

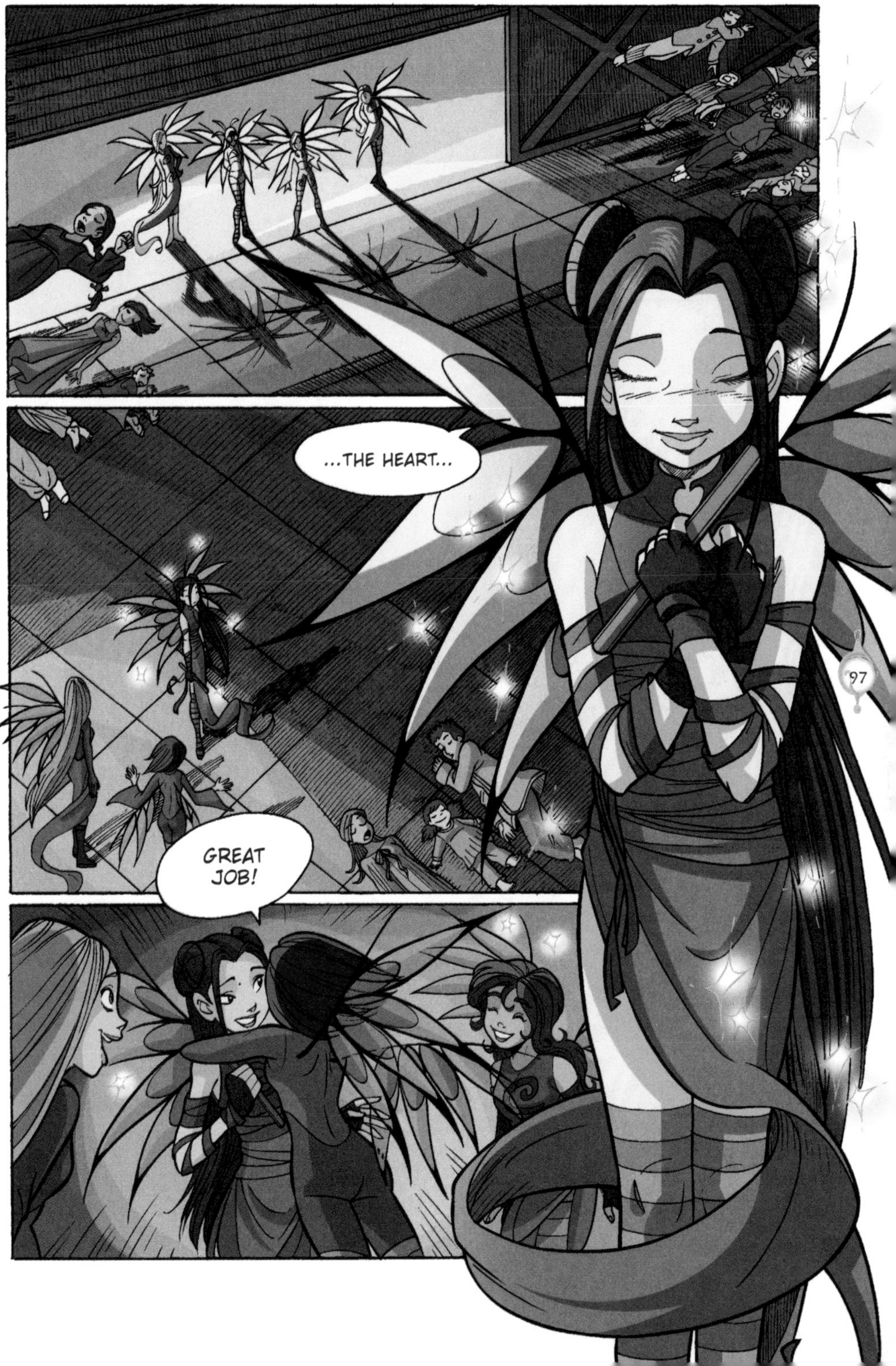
...THE HEART...
GREAT JOB!

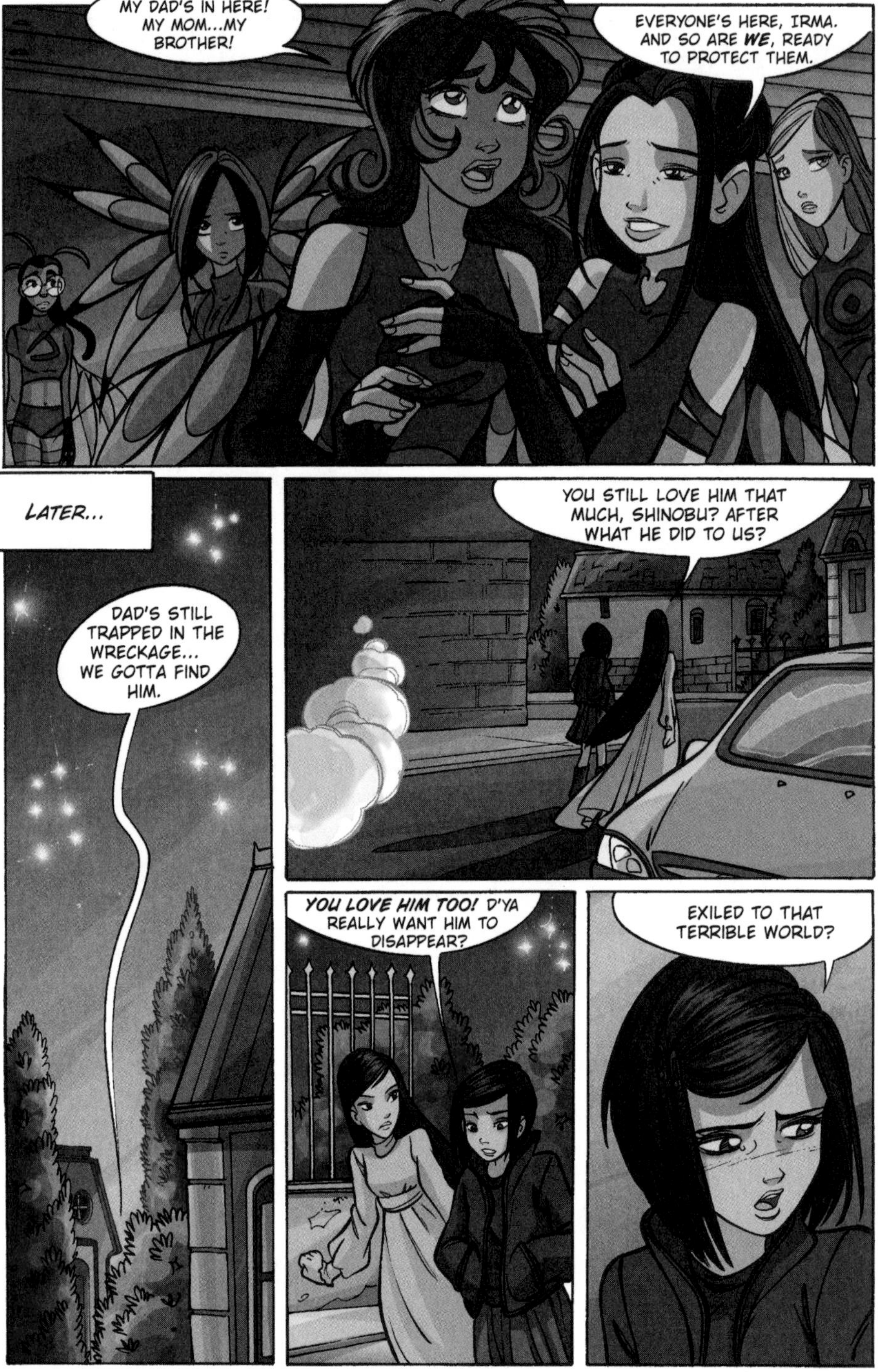
MY DAD'S IN HERE! MY MOM...MY BROTHER!
EVERYONE'S HERE, IRMA. AND SO ARE ***WE***, READY TO PROTECT THEM.
LATER...
DAD'S STILL TRAPPED IN THE WRECKAGE... WE GOTTA FIND HIM.
YOU STILL LOVE HIM THAT MUCH, SHINOBU? AFTER WHAT HE DID TO US?
YOU LOVE HIM TOO! D'YA REALLY WANT HIM TO DISAPPEAR?
EXILED TO THAT TERRIBLE WORLD?

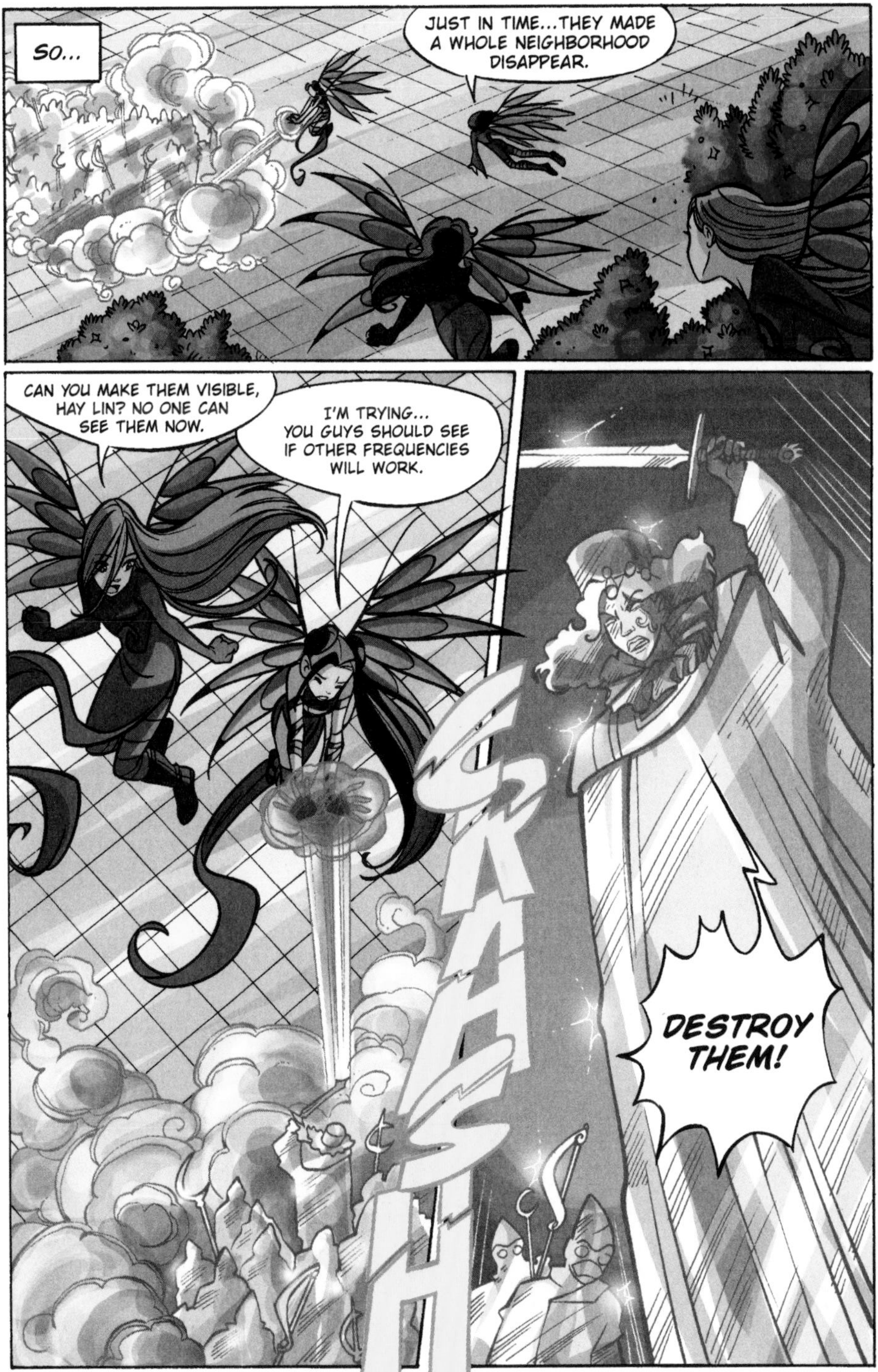

SO...
JUST IN TIME...THEY MADE A WHOLE NEIGHBORHOOD DISAPPEAR.
CAN YOU MAKE THEM VISIBLE, HAY LIN? NO ONE CAN SEE THEM NOW.
I'M TRYING... YOU GUYS SHOULD SEE IF OTHER FREQUENCIES WILL WORK.
CRAASH
DESTROY THEM!

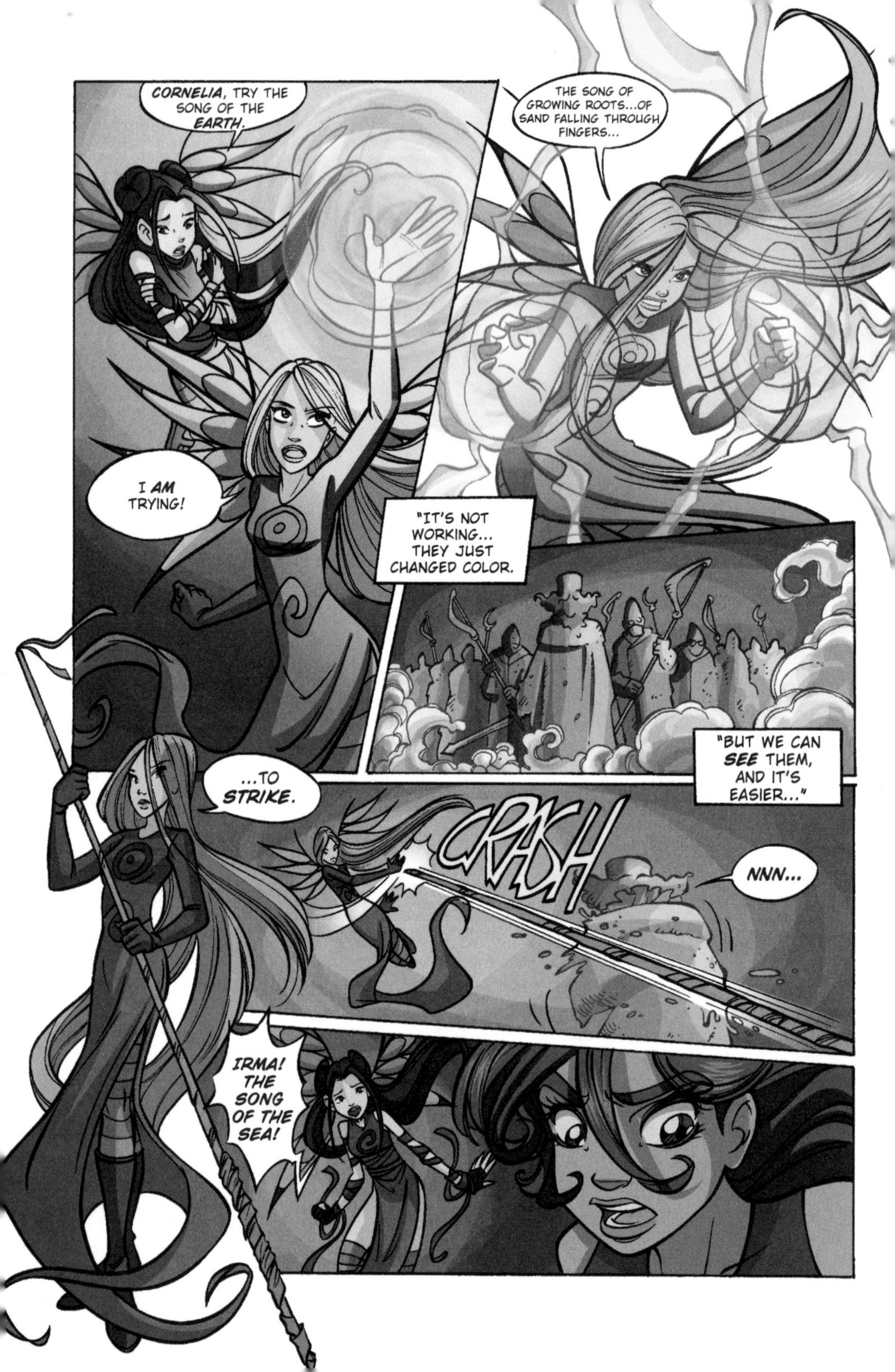
CORNELIA, TRY THE SONG OF THE EARTH.
THE SONG OF GROWING ROOTS...OF SAND FALLING THROUGH FINGERS...
I AM TRYING!
"IT'S NOT WORKING... THEY JUST CHANGED COLOR.
"BUT WE CAN SEE THEM, AND IT'S EASIER..."
...TO STRIKE.
CRASH
NNN...
IRMA! THE SONG OF THE SEA!

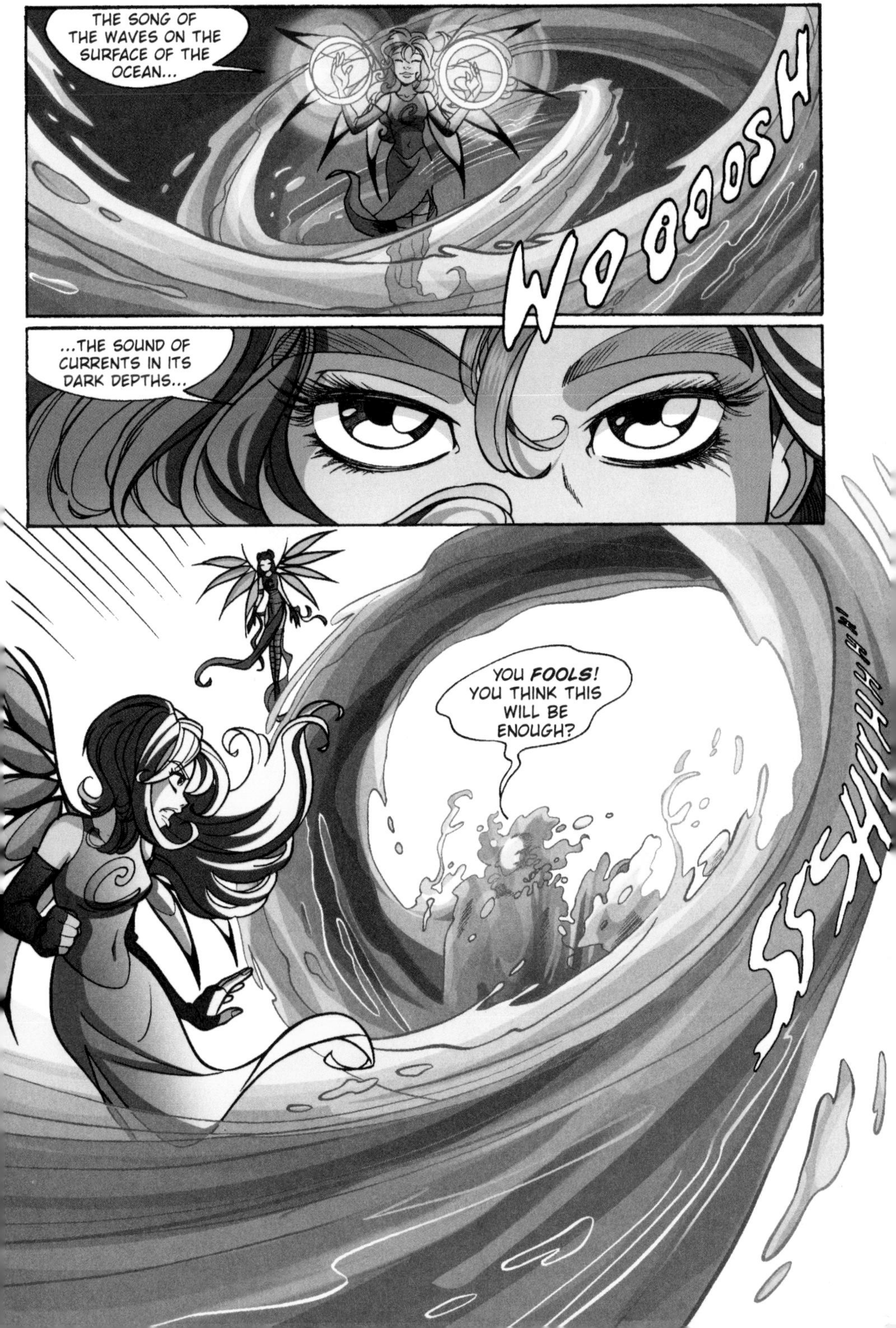
THE SONG OF THE WAVES ON THE SURFACE OF THE OCEAN...
WOOOOSH
...THE SOUND OF CURRENTS IN ITS DARK DEPTHS...
YOU FOOLS! YOU THINK THIS WILL BE ENOUGH?
SSHHHHHHH

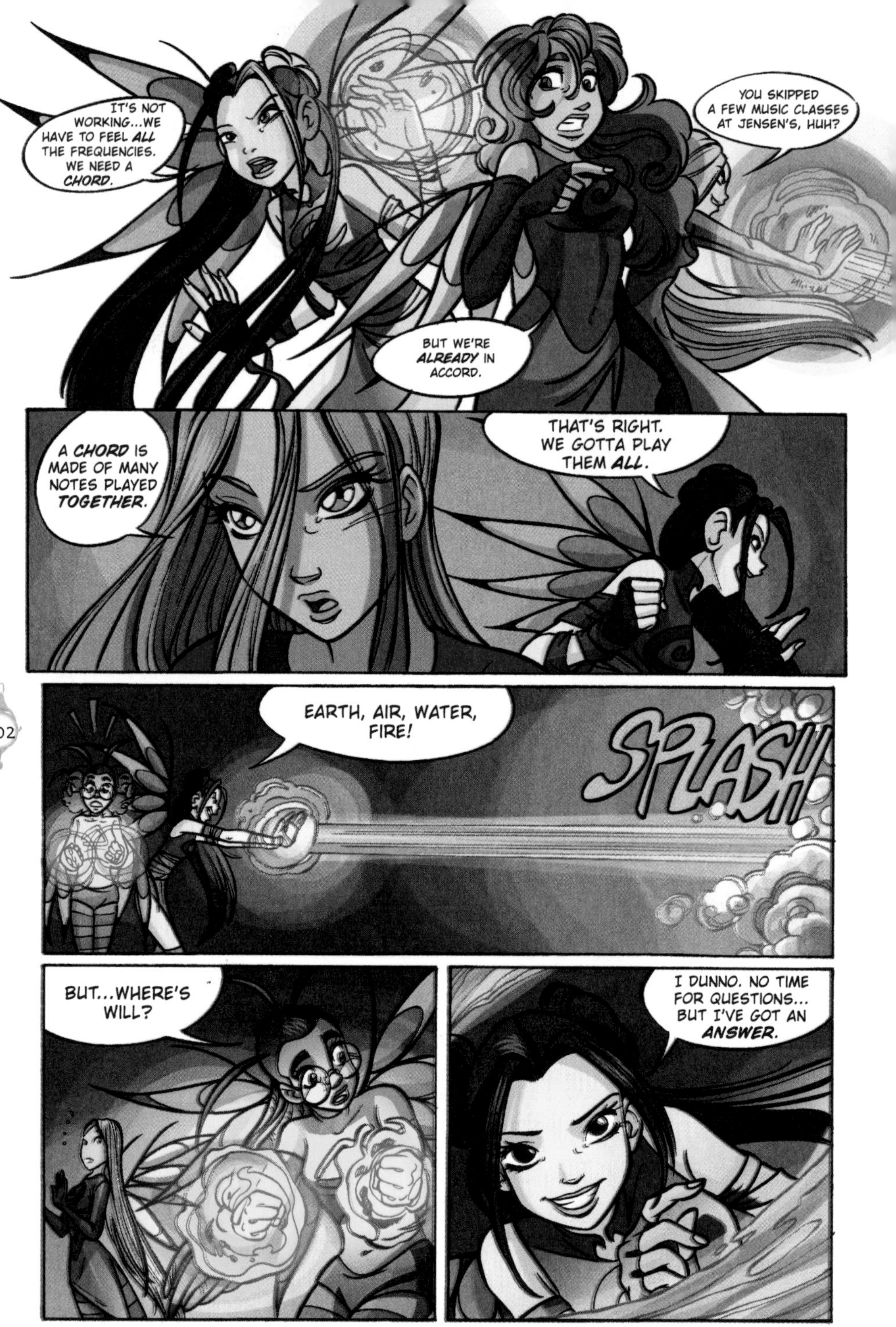
IT'S NOT WORKING...WE HAVE TO FEEL ALL THE FREQUENCIES. WE NEED A CHORD.
YOU SKIPPED A FEW MUSIC CLASSES AT JENSEN'S, HUH?
BUT WE'RE ALREADY IN ACCORD.
A CHORD IS MADE OF MANY NOTES PLAYED TOGETHER.
THAT'S RIGHT. WE GOTTA PLAY THEM ALL.
EARTH, AIR, WATER, FIRE!
SPLASH
BUT...WHERE'S WILL?
I DUNNO. NO TIME FOR QUESTIONS... BUT I'VE GOT AN ANSWER.

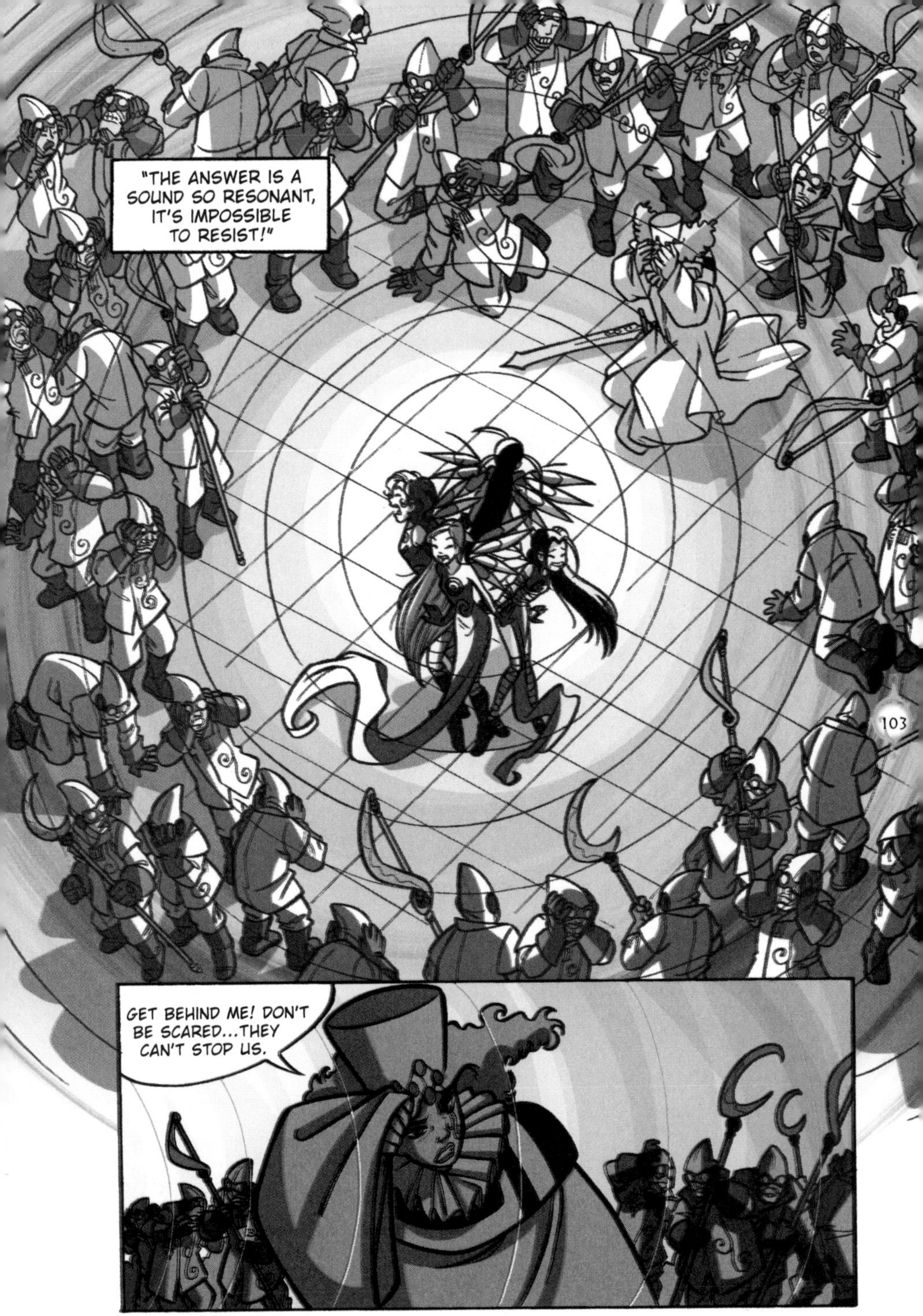
"THE ANSWER IS A SOUND SO RESONANT, IT'S IMPOSSIBLE TO RESIST!"
GET BEHIND ME! DON'T BE SCARED...THEY CAN'T STOP US.

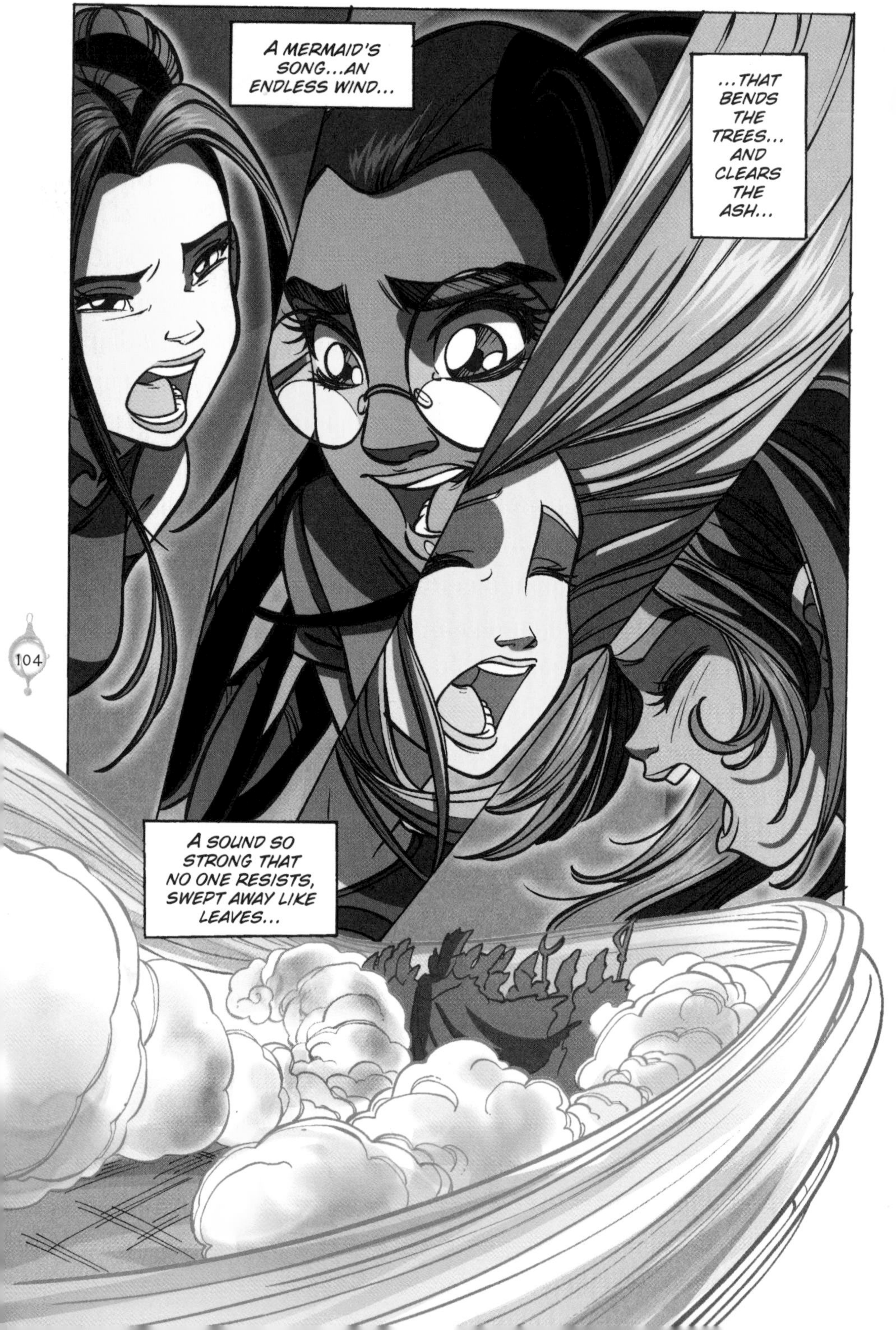
A MERMAID'S SONG...AN ENDLESS WIND...
...THAT BENDS THE TREES... AND CLEARS THE ASH...
A SOUND SO STRONG THAT NO ONE RESISTS, SWEPT AWAY LIKE LEAVES...

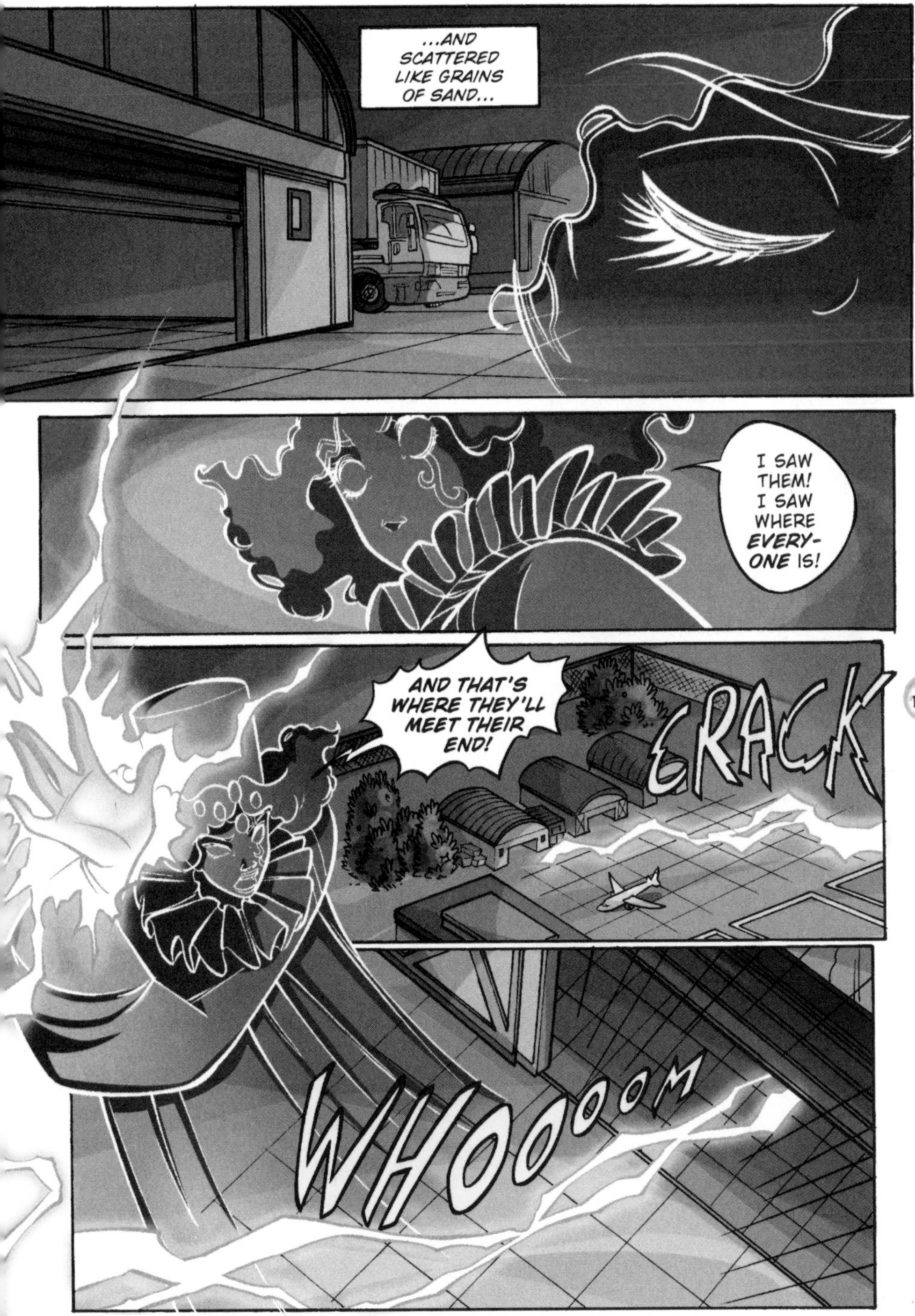
...AND SCATTERED LIKE GRAINS OF SAND...
I SAW THEM! I SAW WHERE EVERY-ONE IS!
AND THAT'S WHERE THEY'LL MEET THEIR END!
CRACK
WHOOOOM

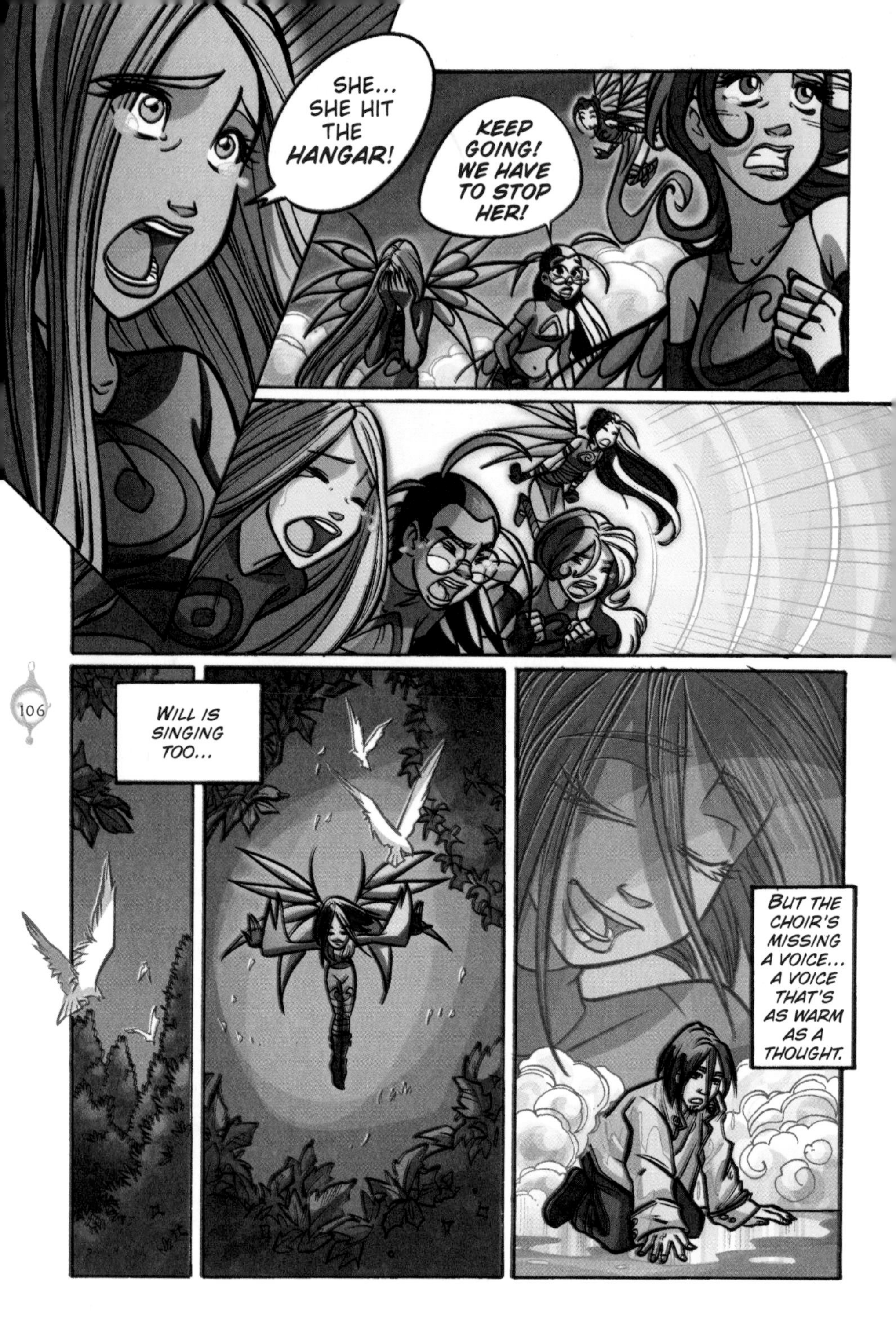
SHE... SHE HIT THE HANGAR!
KEEP GOING! WE HAVE TO STOP HER!
WILL IS SINGING TOO...
BUT THE CHOIR'S MISSING A VOICE... A VOICE THAT'S AS WARM AS A THOUGHT.

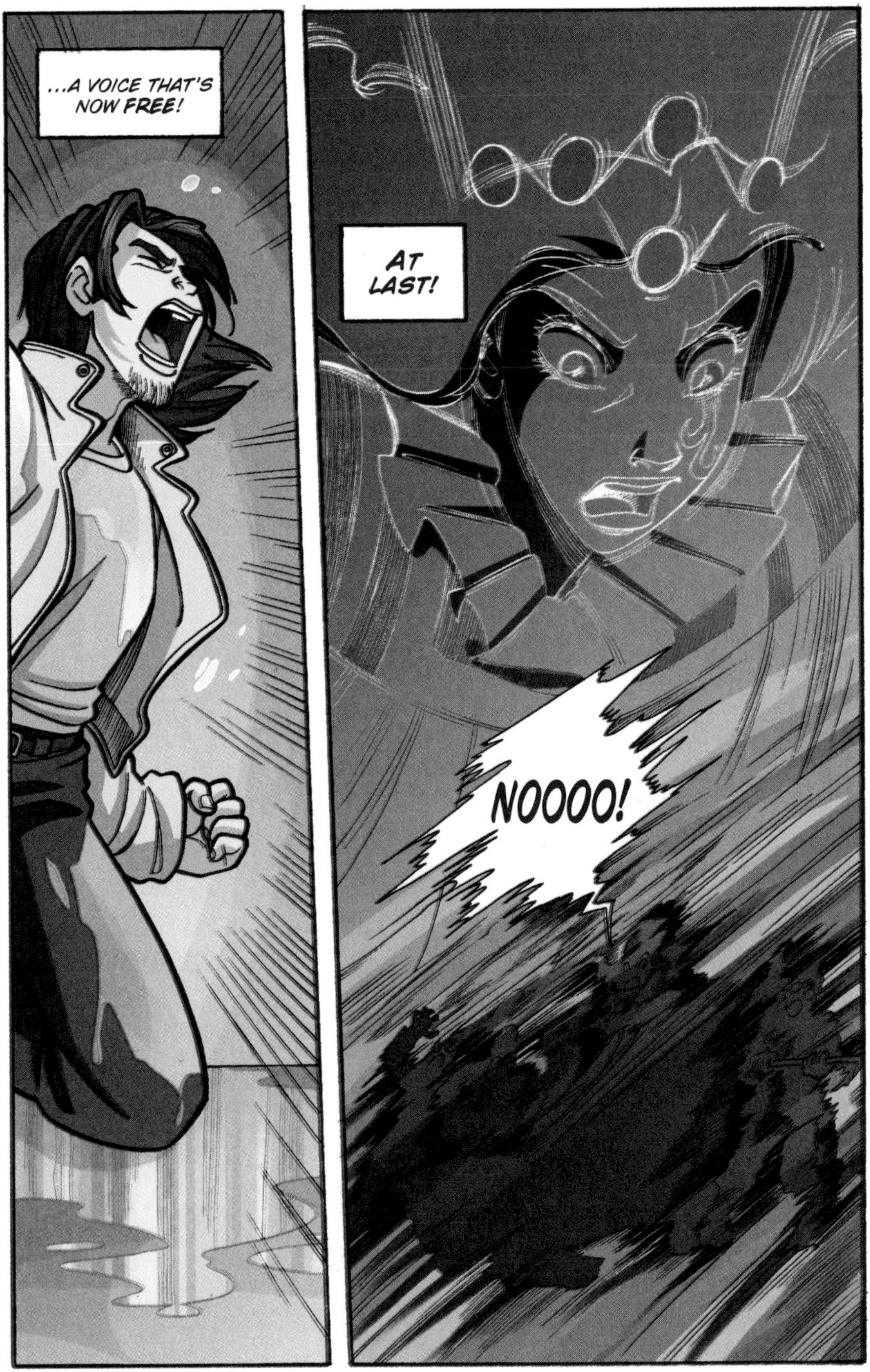
...A VOICE THAT'S NOW FREE!
AT LAST!
NOOOO!

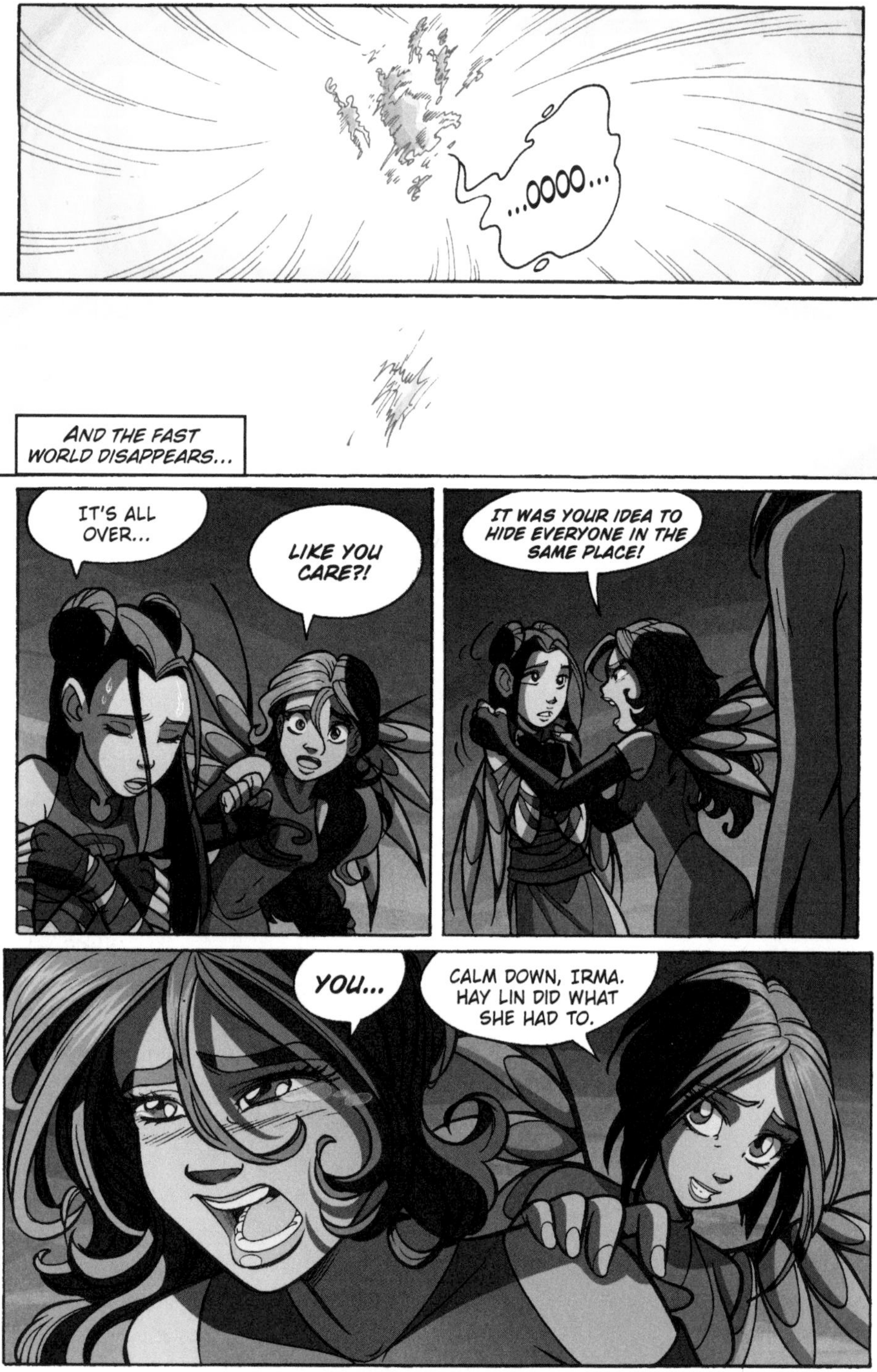
...OOOO...
AND THE FAST WORLD DISAPPEARS...
IT'S ALL OVER...
LIKE YOU CARE?!
IT WAS YOUR IDEA TO HIDE EVERYONE IN THE SAME PLACE!
YOU...
CALM DOWN, IRMA. HAY LIN DID WHAT SHE HAD TO.

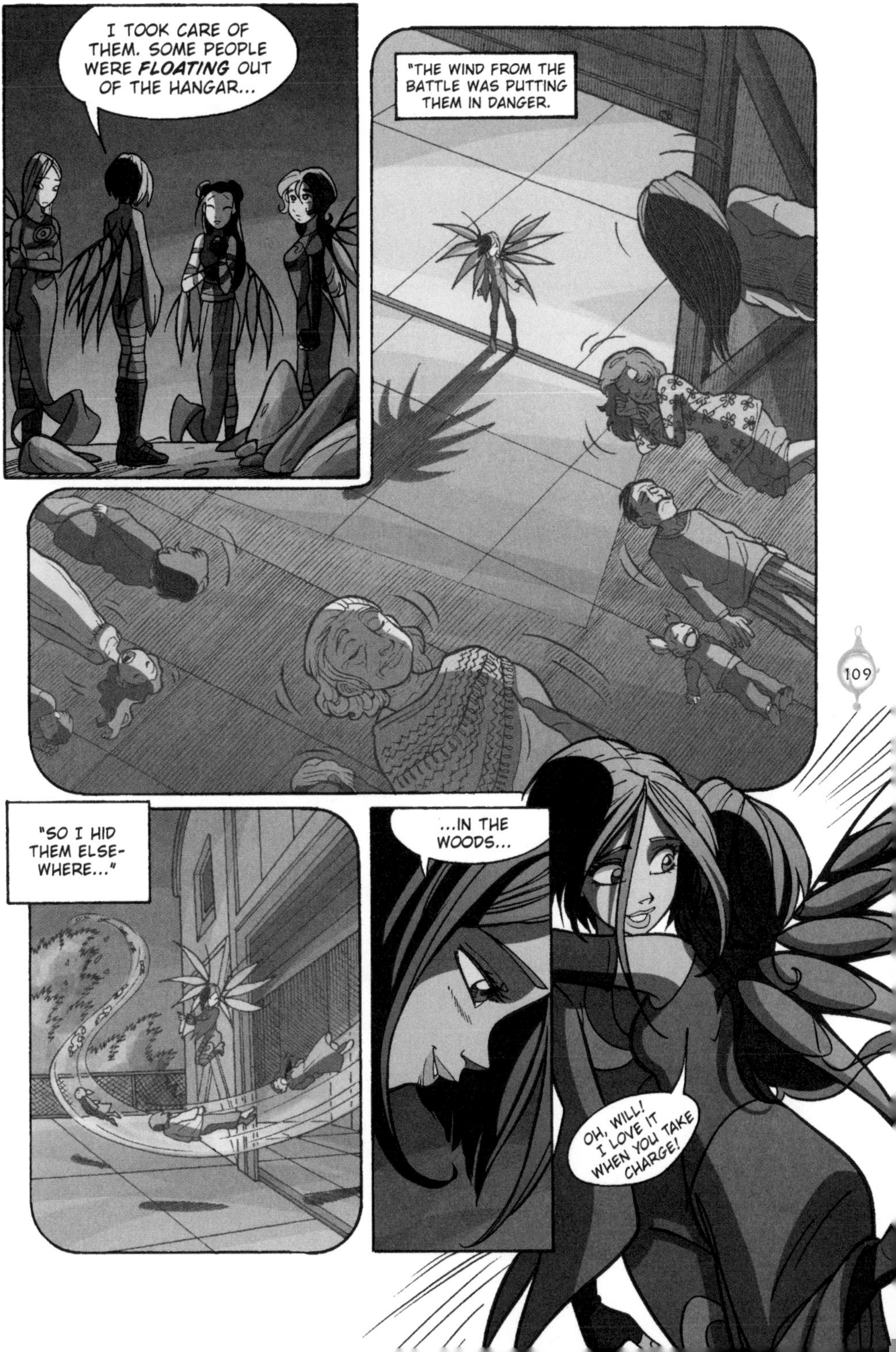

I TOOK CARE OF THEM. SOME PEOPLE WERE FLOATING OUT OF THE HANGAR...
"THE WIND FROM THE BATTLE WAS PUTTING THEM IN DANGER.
"SO I HID THEM ELSE-WHERE..."
...IN THE WOODS...
OH, WILL! I LOVE IT WHEN YOU TAKE CHARGE!

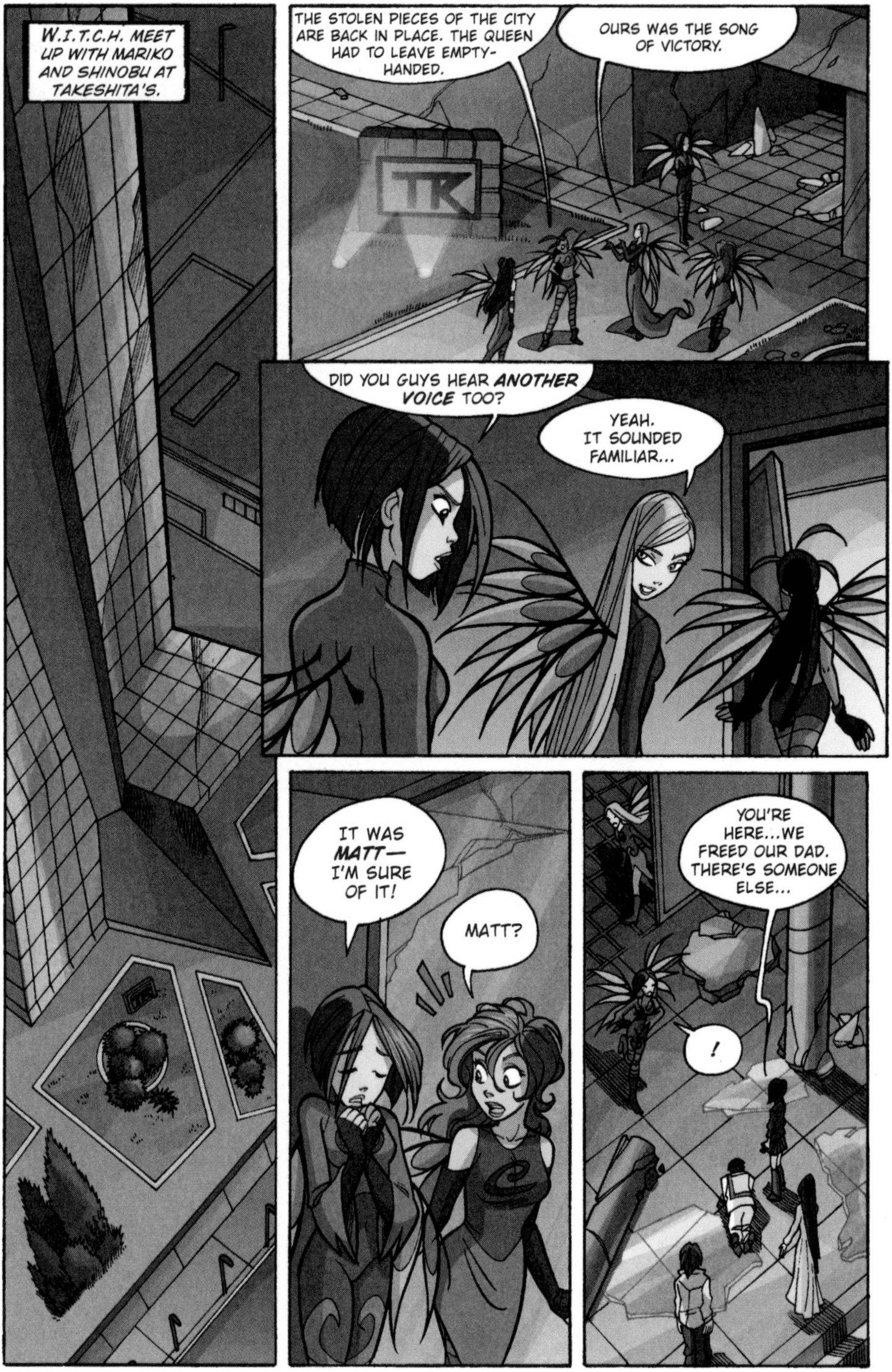
W.I.T.C.H. MEET UP WITH MARIKO AND SHINOBU AT TAKESHITA'S.
THE STOLEN PIECES OF THE CITY ARE BACK IN PLACE. THE QUEEN HAD TO LEAVE EMPTY-HANDED.
OURS WAS THE SONG OF VICTORY.
TK
DID YOU GUYS HEAR ANOTHER VOICE TOO?
YEAH. IT SOUNDED FAMILIAR...
IT WAS MATT— I'M SURE OF IT!
MATT?
YOU'RE HERE...WE FREED OUR DAD. THERE'S SOMEONE ELSE...
!

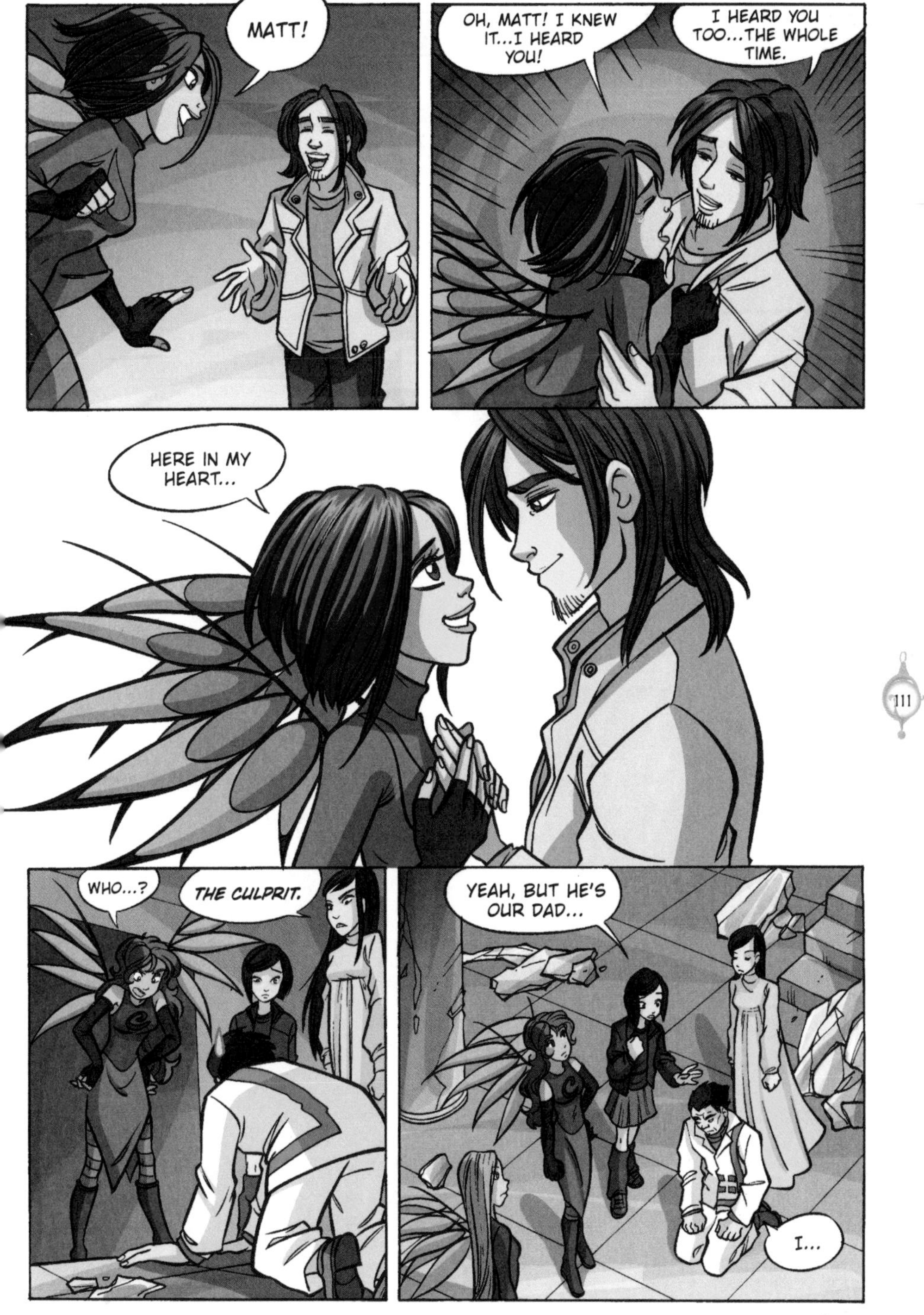
MATT!
OH, MATT! I KNEW IT...I HEARD YOU!
I HEARD YOU TOO...THE WHOLE TIME.
HERE IN MY HEART...
WHO...?
THE CULPRIT.
YEAH, BUT HE'S OUR DAD...
I...

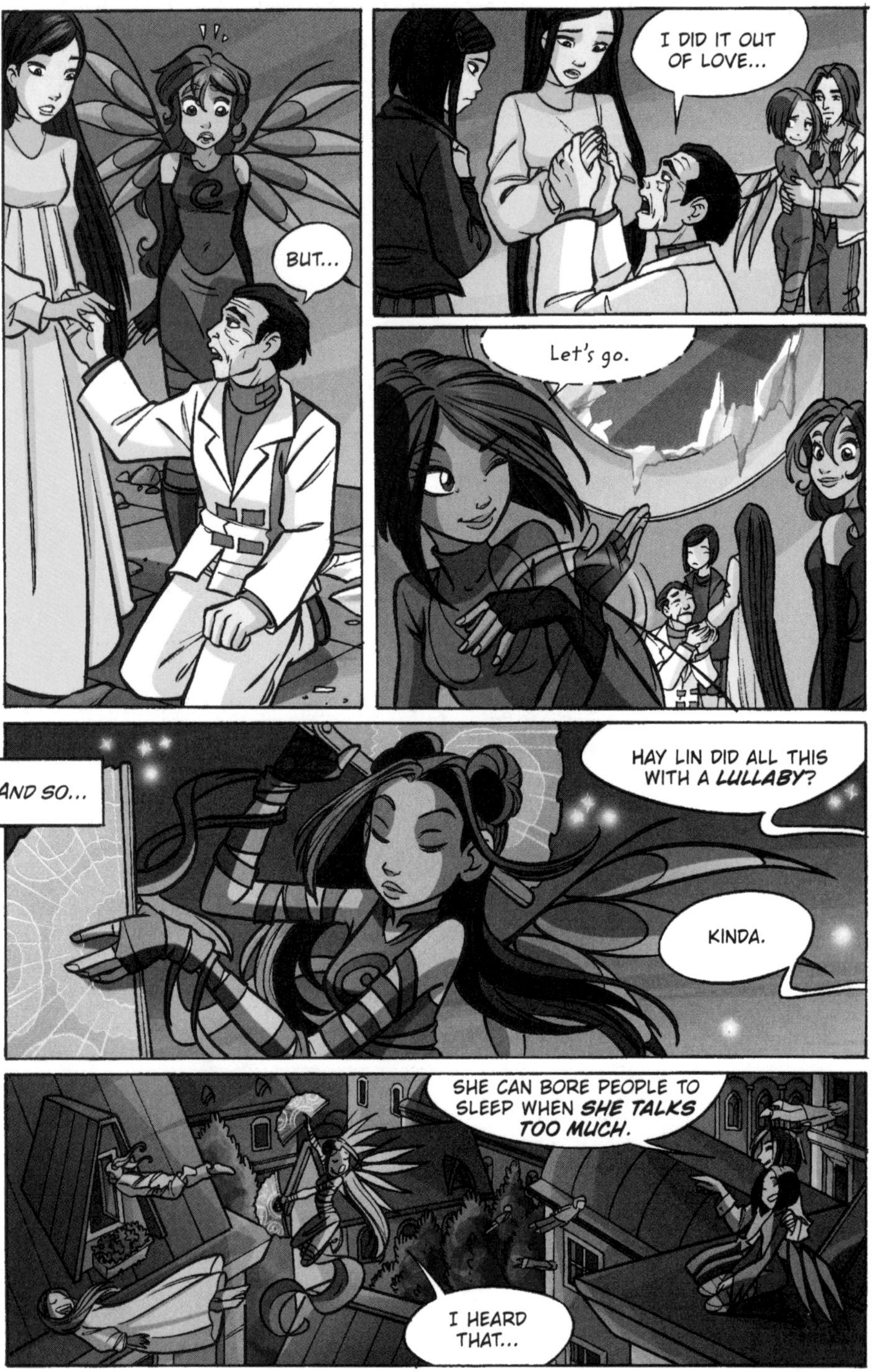
BUT...
I DID IT OUT OF LOVE...
Let's go.
AND SO...
HAY LIN DID ALL THIS WITH A LULLABY?
KINDA.
SHE CAN BORE PEOPLE TO SLEEP WHEN SHE TALKS TOO MUCH.
I HEARD THAT...

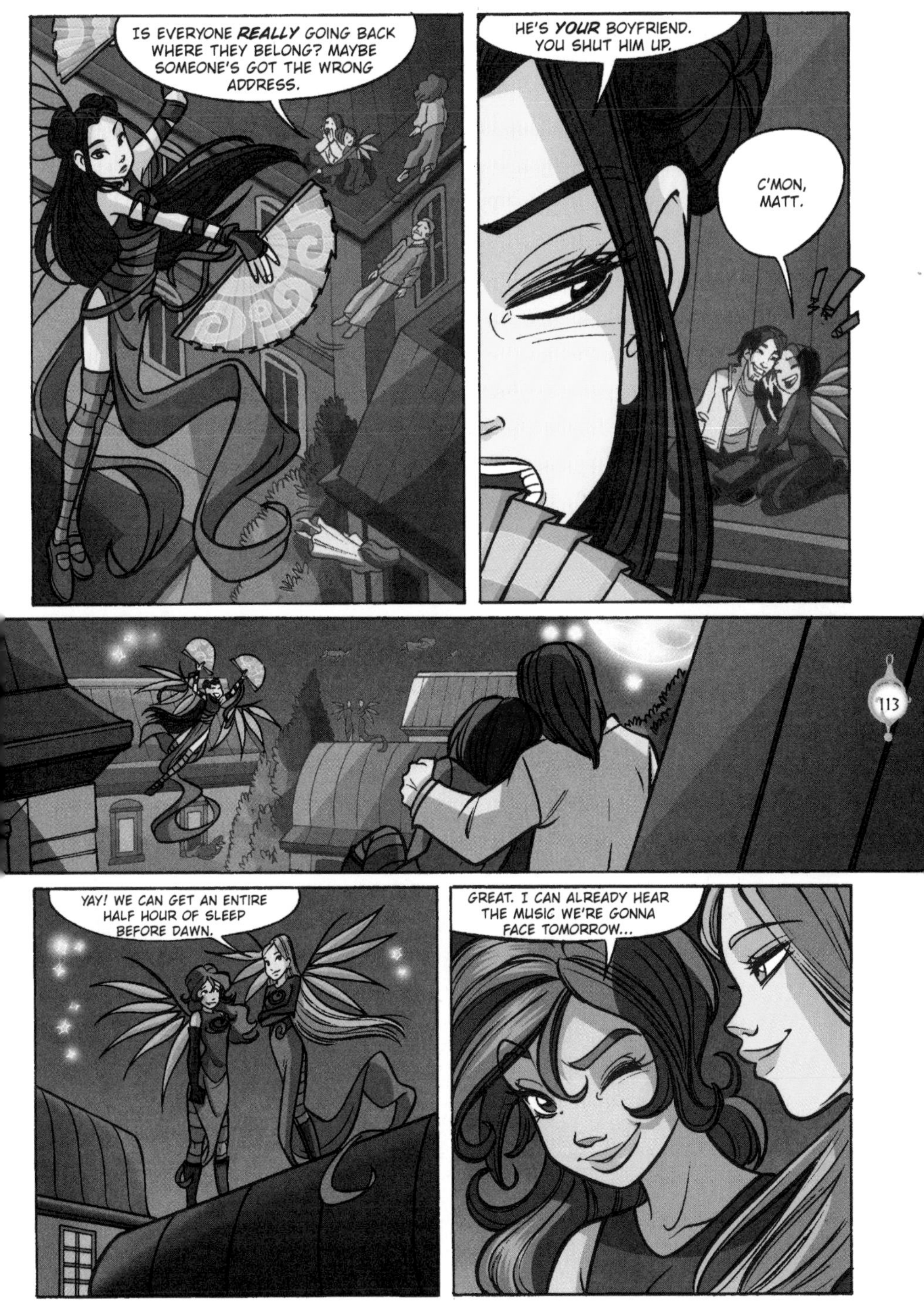
IS EVERYONE REALLY GOING BACK WHERE THEY BELONG? MAYBE SOMEONE'S GOT THE WRONG ADDRESS.
HE'S YOUR BOYFRIEND. YOU SHUT HIM UP.
C'MON, MATT.
YAY! WE CAN GET AN ENTIRE HALF HOUR OF SLEEP BEFORE DAWN.
GREAT. I CAN ALREADY HEAR THE MUSIC WE'RE GONNA FACE TOMORROW...

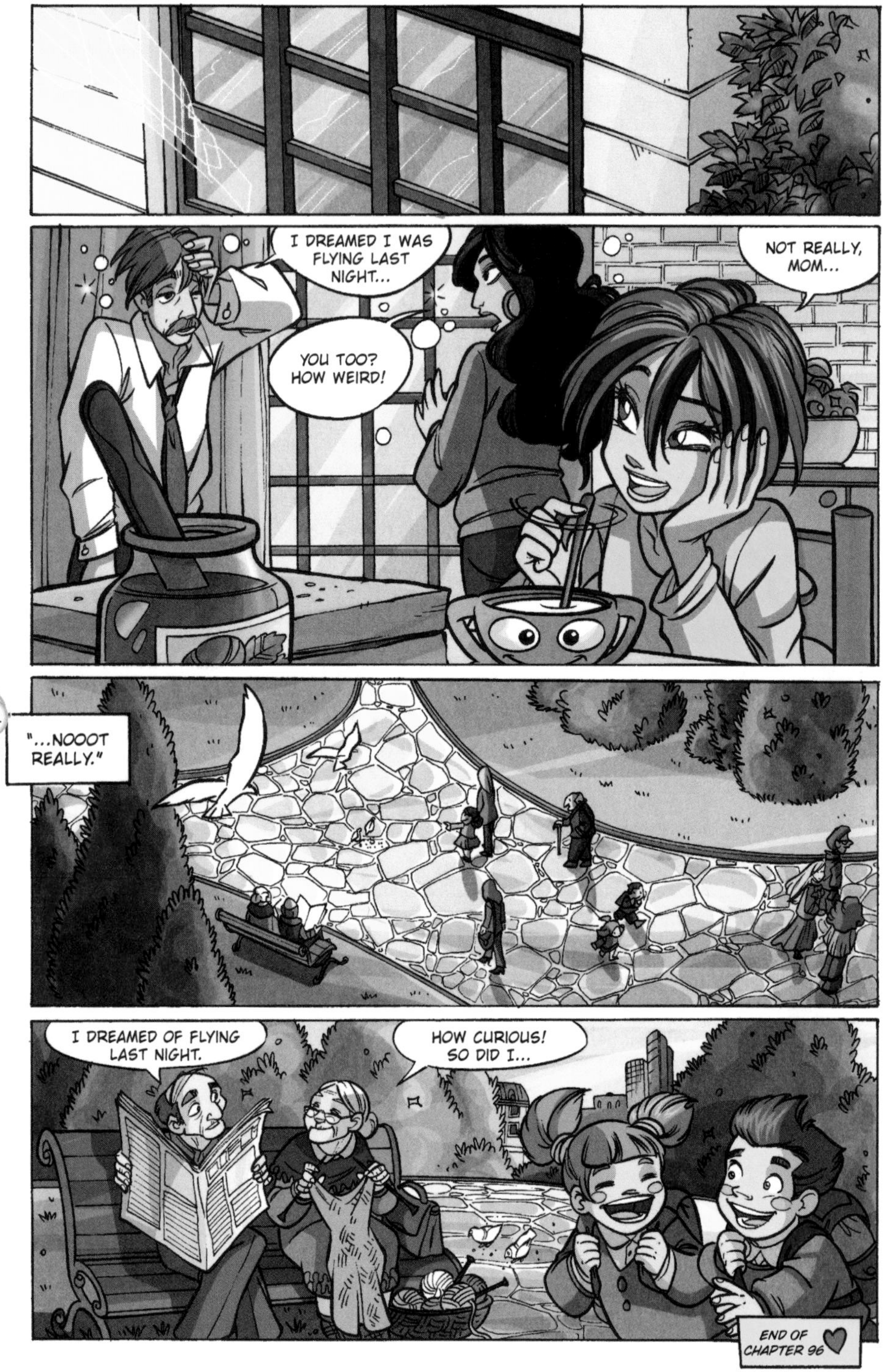
I DREAMED I WAS FLYING LAST NIGHT...
YOU TOO? HOW WEIRD!
NOT REALLY, MOM...
"...NOOOT REALLY."
I DREAMED OF FLYING LAST NIGHT.
HOW CURIOUS! SO DID I...
END OF CHAPTER 96

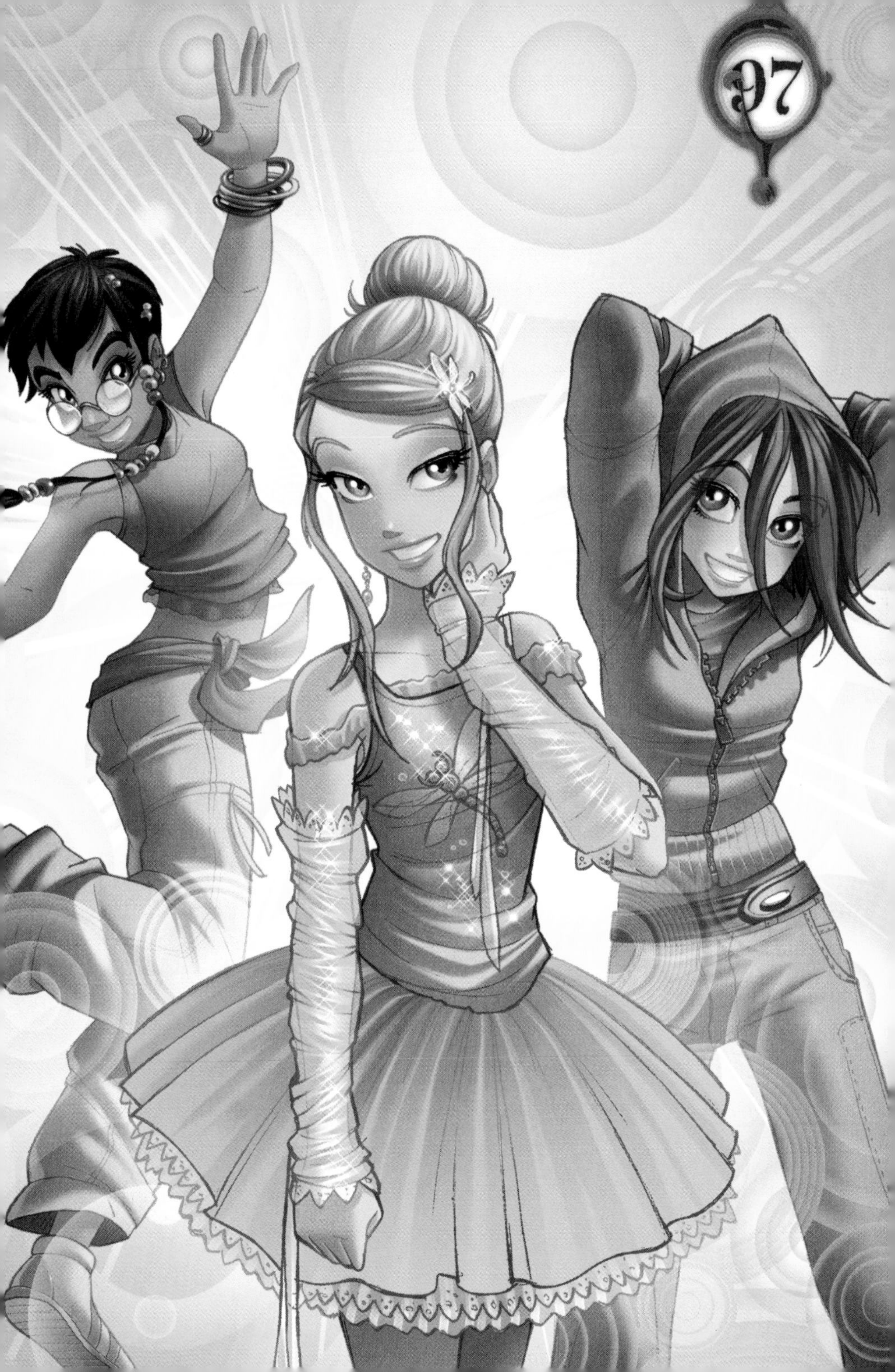

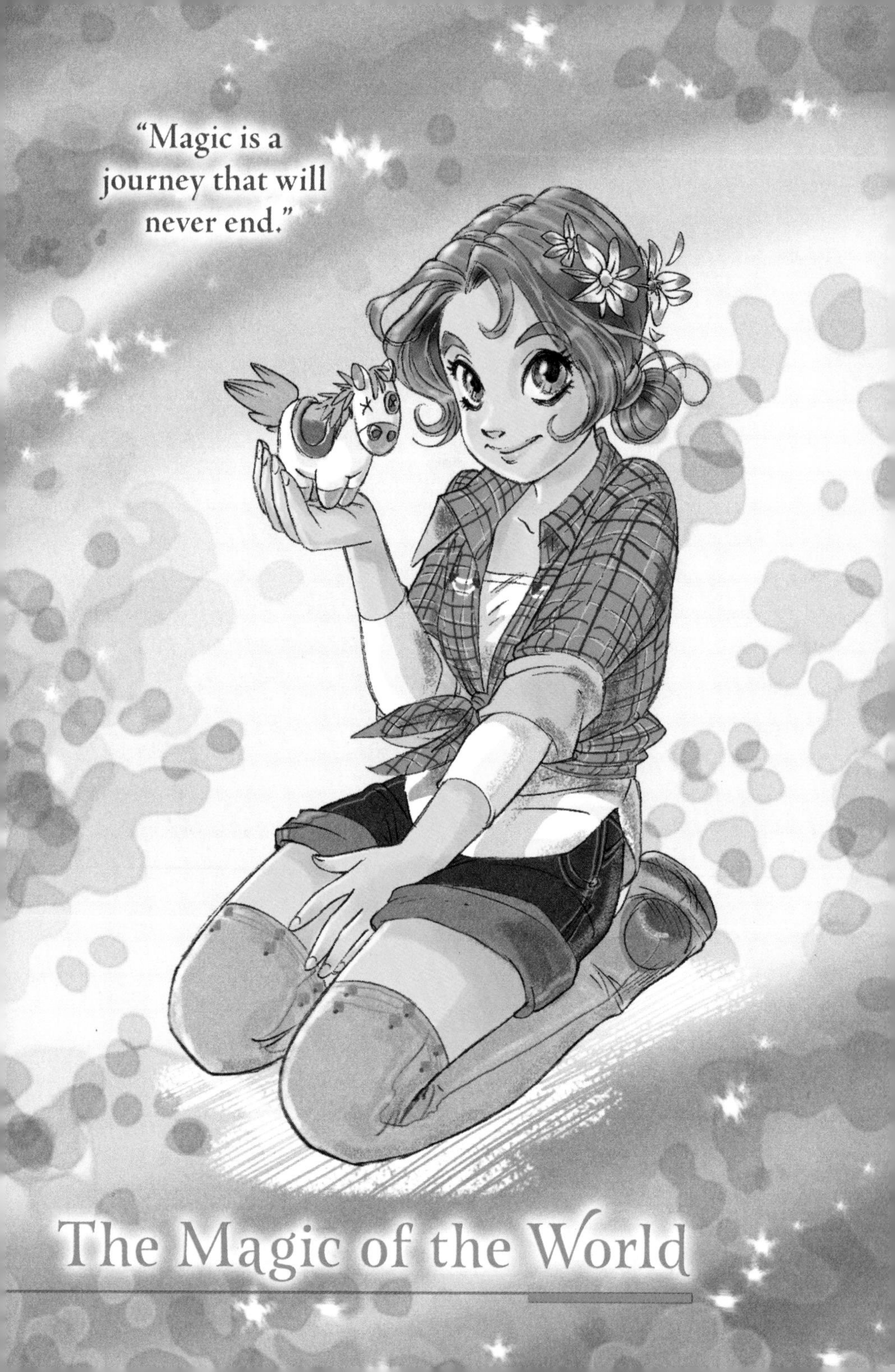
"Magic is a
journey that will
never end."

The Magic of the World

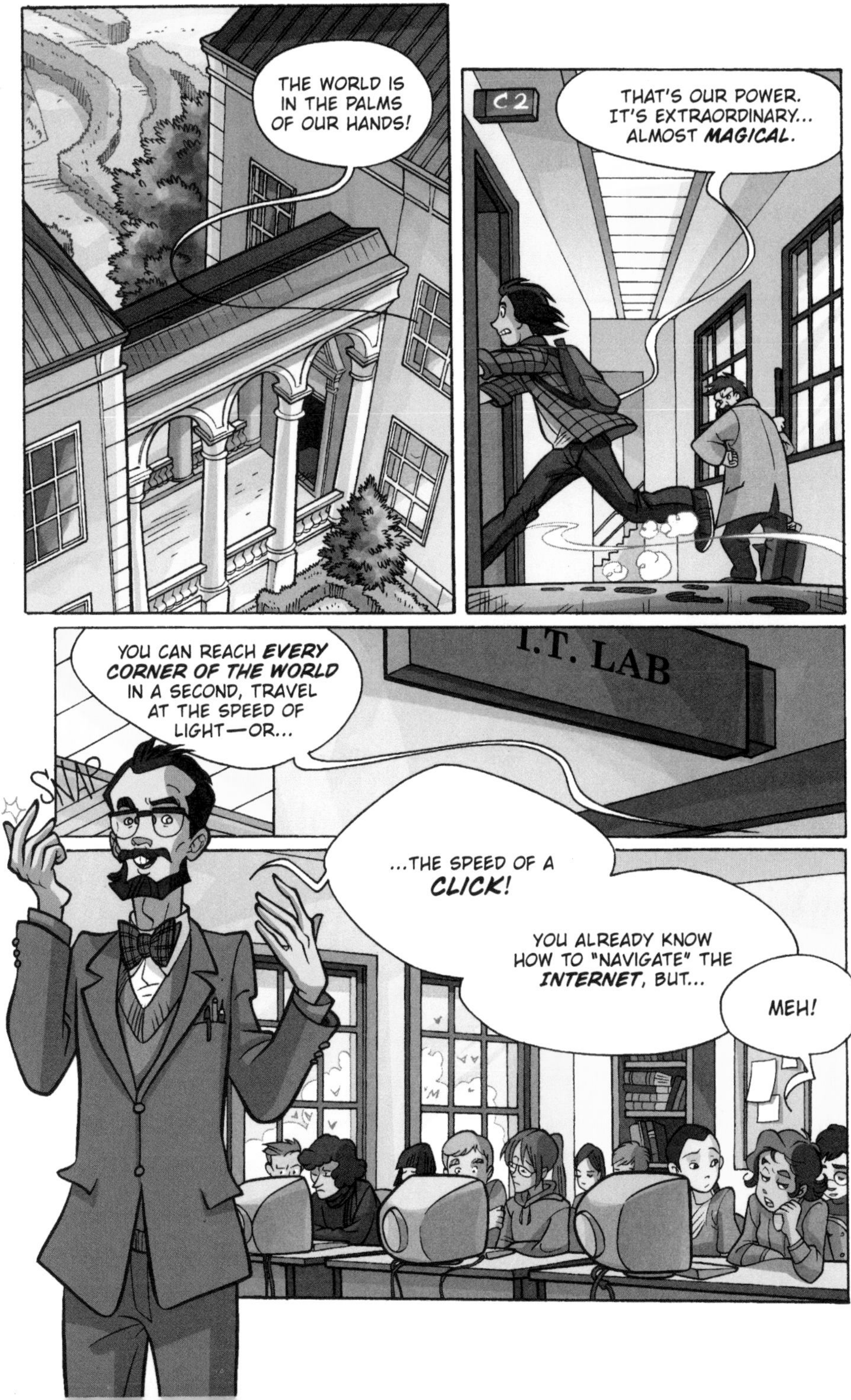
THE WORLD IS IN THE PALMS OF OUR HANDS!
C2
THAT'S OUR POWER. IT'S EXTRAORDINARY... ALMOST MAGICAL.
I.T. LAB
YOU CAN REACH EVERY CORNER OF THE WORLD IN A SECOND, TRAVEL AT THE SPEED OF LIGHT—OR...
SNAP
...THE SPEED OF A CLICK!
YOU ALREADY KNOW HOW TO "NAVIGATE" THE INTERNET, BUT...
MEH!

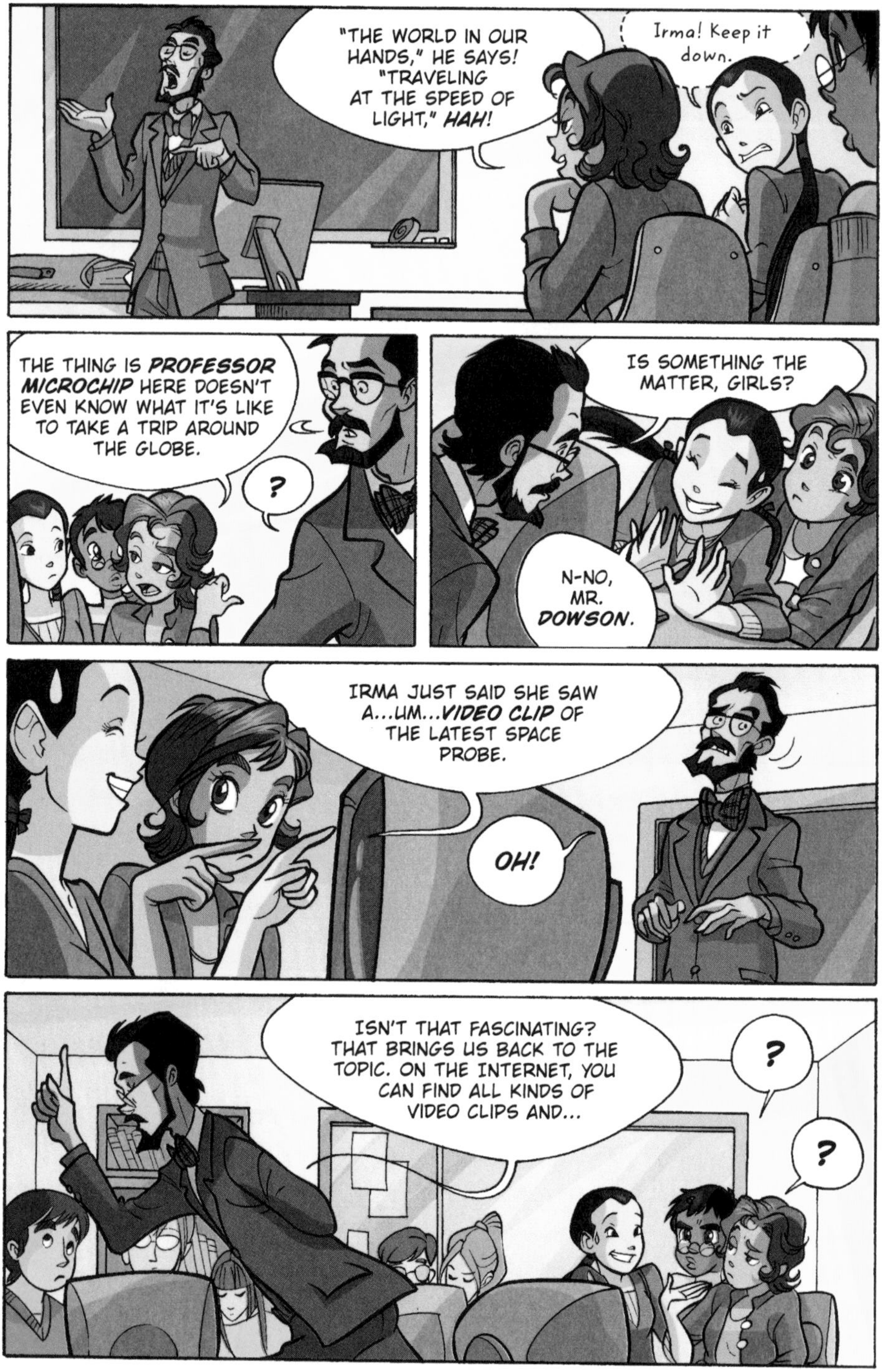
"THE WORLD IN OUR HANDS," HE SAYS! "TRAVELING AT THE SPEED OF LIGHT," HAH!
Irma! Keep it down.
THE THING IS PROFESSOR MICROCHIP HERE DOESN'T EVEN KNOW WHAT IT'S LIKE TO TAKE A TRIP AROUND THE GLOBE.
?
IS SOMETHING THE MATTER, GIRLS?
N-NO, MR. DOWSON.
IRMA JUST SAID SHE SAW A...UM...VIDEO CLIP OF THE LATEST SPACE PROBE.
OH!
ISN'T THAT FASCINATING? THAT BRINGS US BACK TO THE TOPIC. ON THE INTERNET, YOU CAN FIND ALL KINDS OF VIDEO CLIPS AND...
?
?

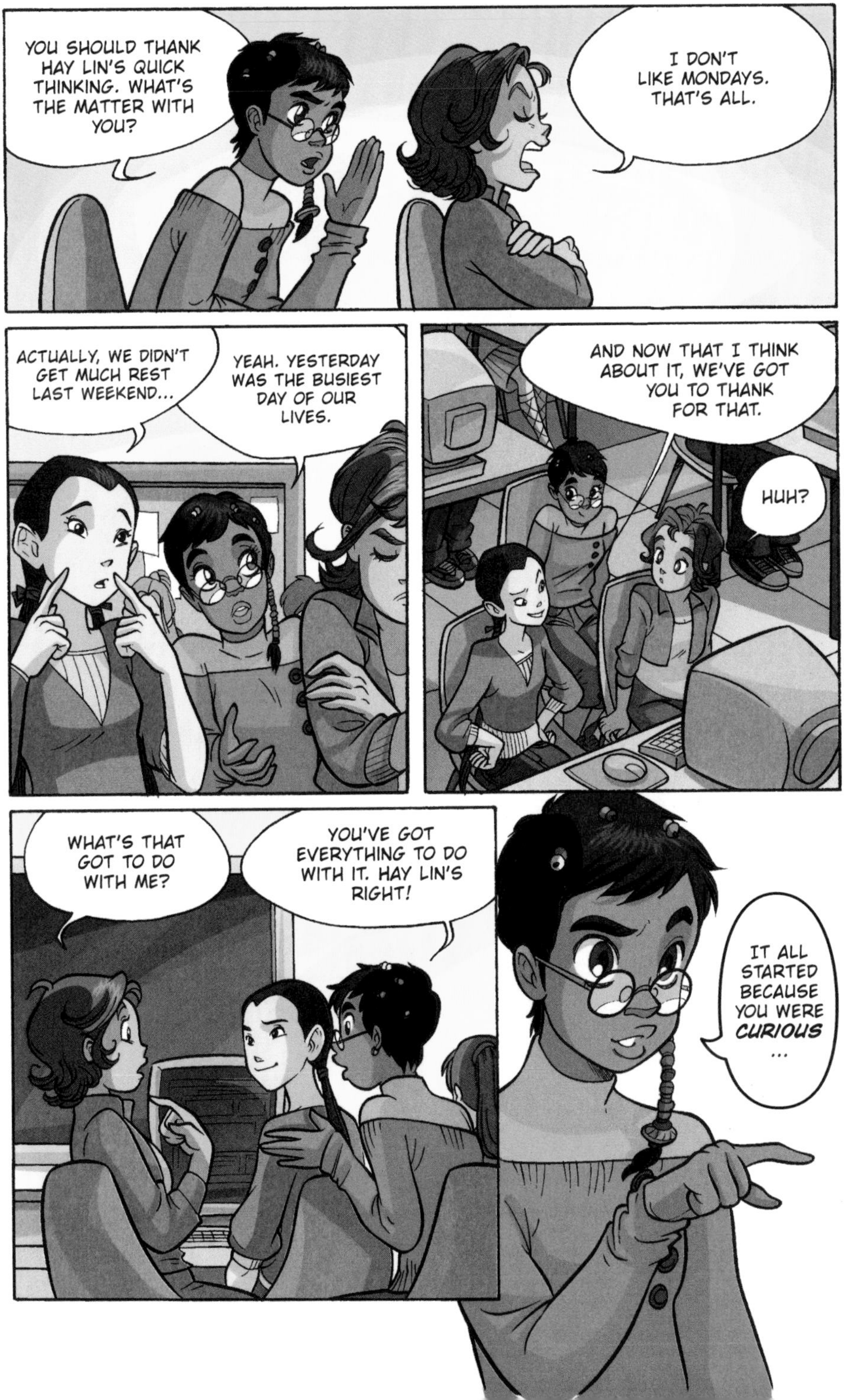
YOU SHOULD THANK HAY LIN'S QUICK THINKING. WHAT'S THE MATTER WITH YOU?
I DON'T LIKE MONDAYS. THAT'S ALL.
ACTUALLY, WE DIDN'T GET MUCH REST LAST WEEKEND...
YEAH. YESTERDAY WAS THE BUSIEST DAY OF OUR LIVES.
AND NOW THAT I THINK ABOUT IT, WE'VE GOT YOU TO THANK FOR THAT.
HUH?
WHAT'S THAT GOT TO DO WITH ME?
YOU'VE GOT EVERYTHING TO DO WITH IT. HAY LIN'S RIGHT!
IT ALL STARTED BECAUSE YOU WERE *CURIOUS* ...

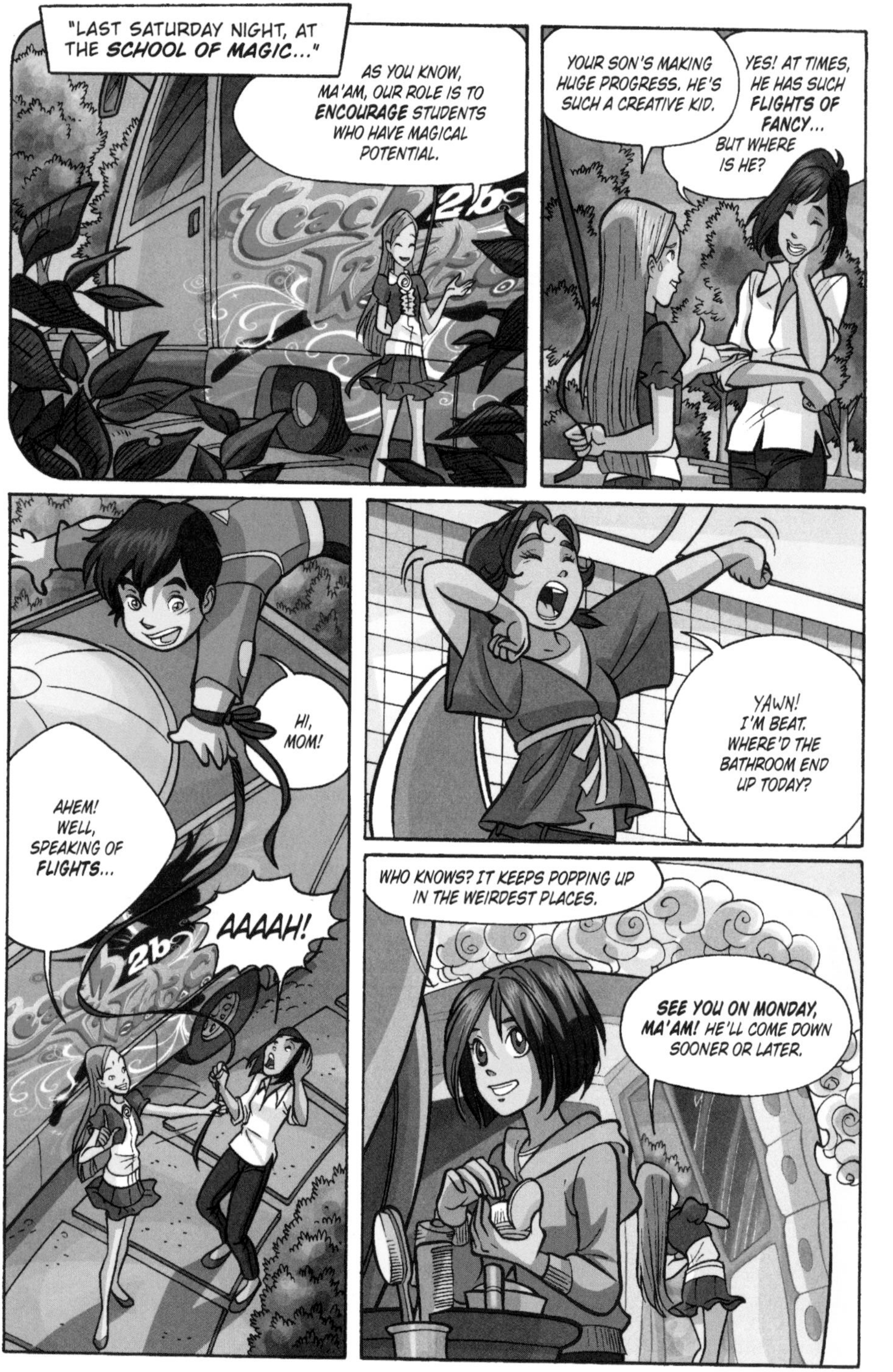
"LAST SATURDAY NIGHT, AT THE SCHOOL OF MAGIC..."
AS YOU KNOW, MA'AM, OUR ROLE IS TO ENCOURAGE STUDENTS WHO HAVE MAGICAL POTENTIAL.
teach 2b witch
YOUR SON'S MAKING HUGE PROGRESS. HE'S SUCH A CREATIVE KID.
YES! AT TIMES, HE HAS SUCH FLIGHTS OF FANCY...
BUT WHERE IS HE?
HI, MOM!
AHEM! WELL, SPEAKING OF FLIGHTS...
AAAAH!
YAWN! I'M BEAT. WHERE'D THE BATHROOM END UP TODAY?
WHO KNOWS? IT KEEPS POPPING UP IN THE WEIRDEST PLACES.
SEE YOU ON MONDAY, MA'AM! HE'LL COME DOWN SOONER OR LATER.

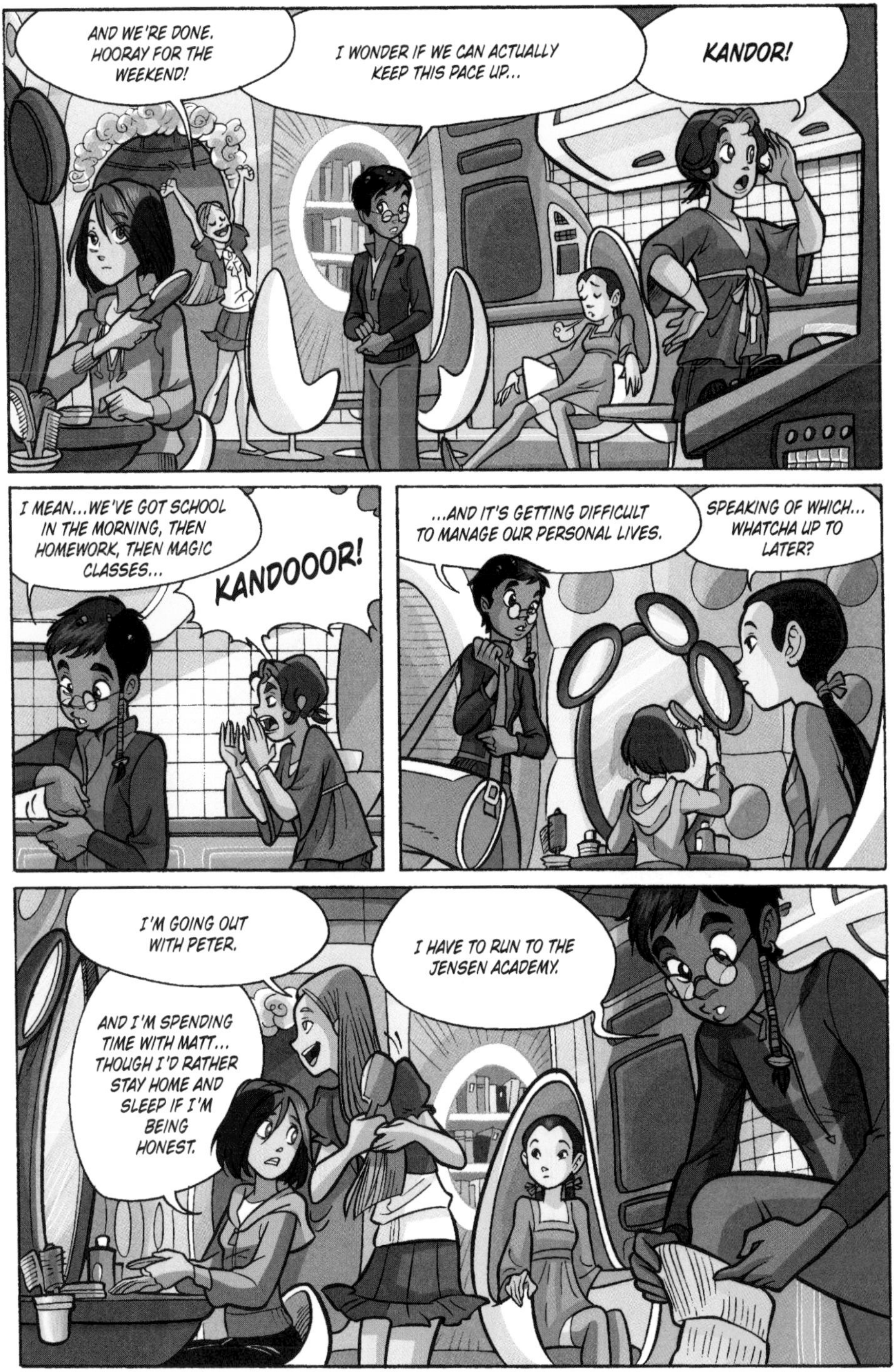
AND WE'RE DONE. HOORAY FOR THE WEEKEND!
I WONDER IF WE CAN ACTUALLY KEEP THIS PACE UP...
KANDOR!
I MEAN...WE'VE GOT SCHOOL IN THE MORNING, THEN HOMEWORK, THEN MAGIC CLASSES...
KANDOOOR!
...AND IT'S GETTING DIFFICULT TO MANAGE OUR PERSONAL LIVES.
SPEAKING OF WHICH... WHATCHA UP TO LATER?
I'M GOING OUT WITH PETER.
I HAVE TO RUN TO THE JENSEN ACADEMY.
AND I'M SPENDING TIME WITH MATT... THOUGH I'D RATHER STAY HOME AND SLEEP IF I'M BEING HONEST.

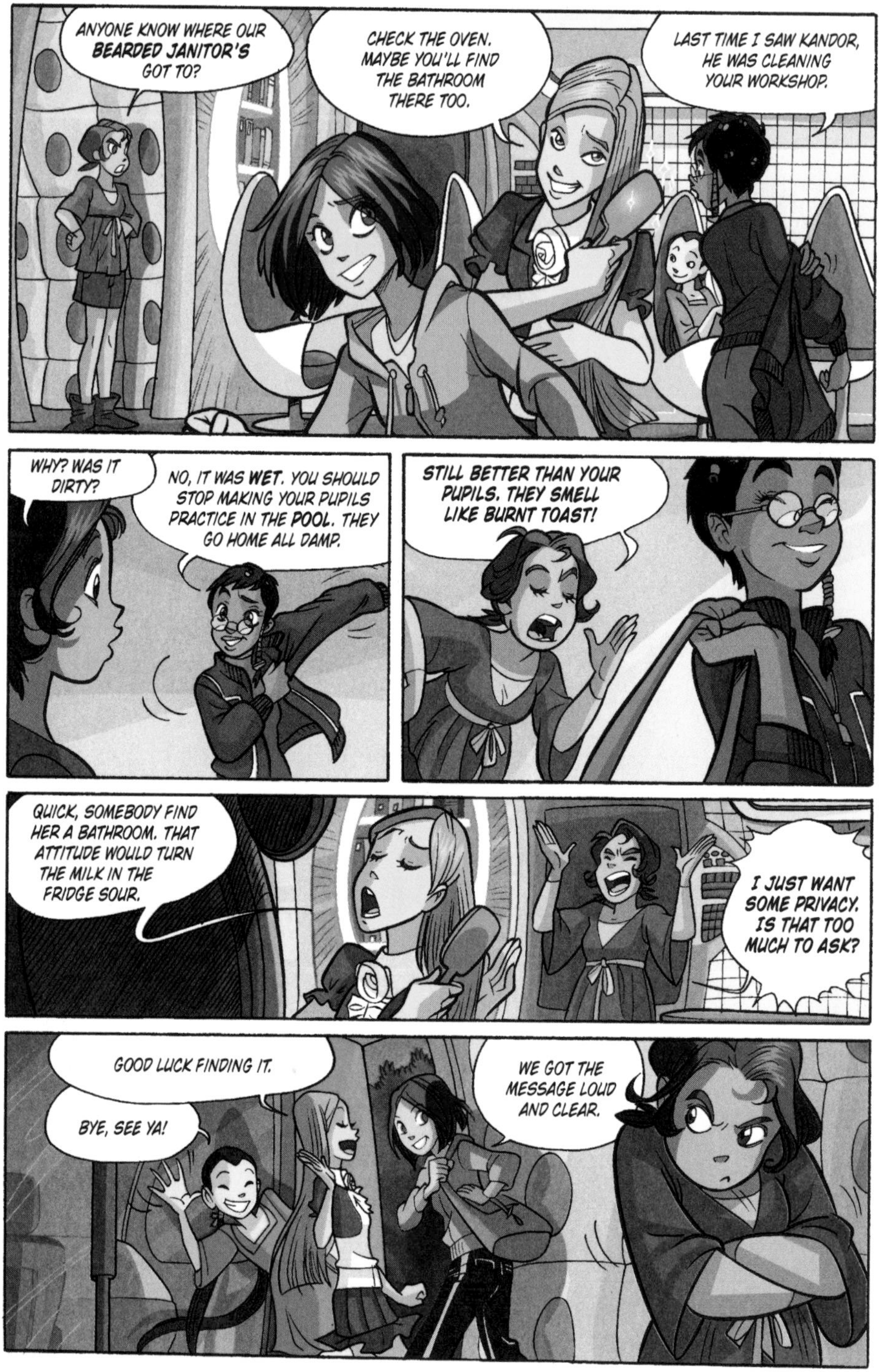
ANYONE KNOW WHERE OUR BEARDED JANITOR'S GOT TO?
CHECK THE OVEN. MAYBE YOU'LL FIND THE BATHROOM THERE TOO.
LAST TIME I SAW KANDOR, HE WAS CLEANING YOUR WORKSHOP.
WHY? WAS IT DIRTY?
NO, IT WAS WET. YOU SHOULD STOP MAKING YOUR PUPILS PRACTICE IN THE POOL. THEY GO HOME ALL DAMP.
STILL BETTER THAN YOUR PUPILS. THEY SMELL LIKE BURNT TOAST!
QUICK, SOMEBODY FIND HER A BATHROOM. THAT ATTITUDE WOULD TURN THE MILK IN THE FRIDGE SOUR.
I JUST WANT SOME PRIVACY. IS THAT TOO MUCH TO ASK?
GOOD LUCK FINDING IT.
BYE, SEE YA!
WE GOT THE MESSAGE LOUD AND CLEAR.

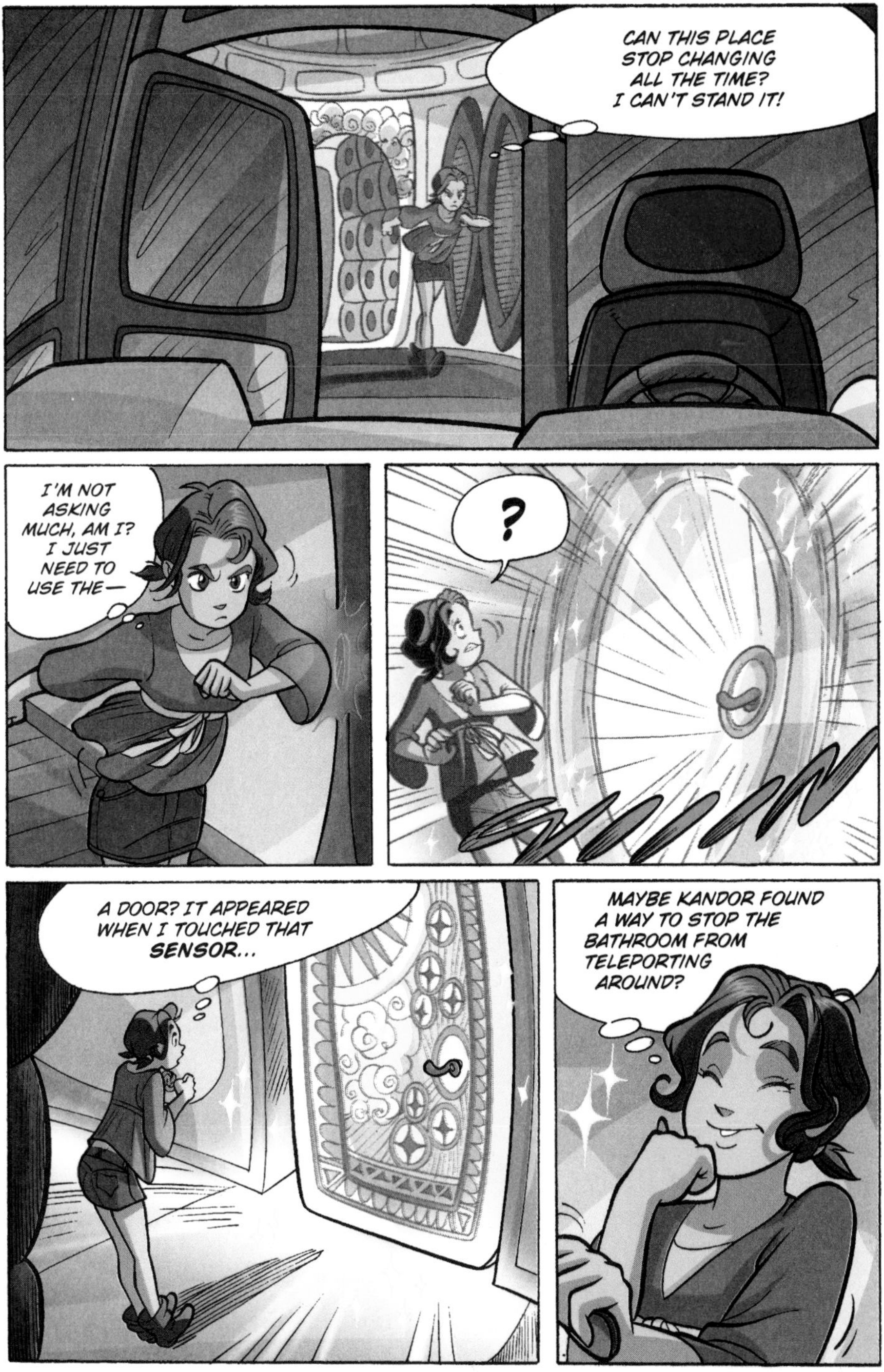
CAN THIS PLACE STOP CHANGING ALL THE TIME? I CAN'T STAND IT!
I'M NOT ASKING MUCH, AM I? I JUST NEED TO USE THE—
?
A DOOR? IT APPEARED WHEN I TOUCHED THAT SENSOR...
MAYBE KANDOR FOUND A WAY TO STOP THE BATHROOM FROM TELEPORTING AROUND?

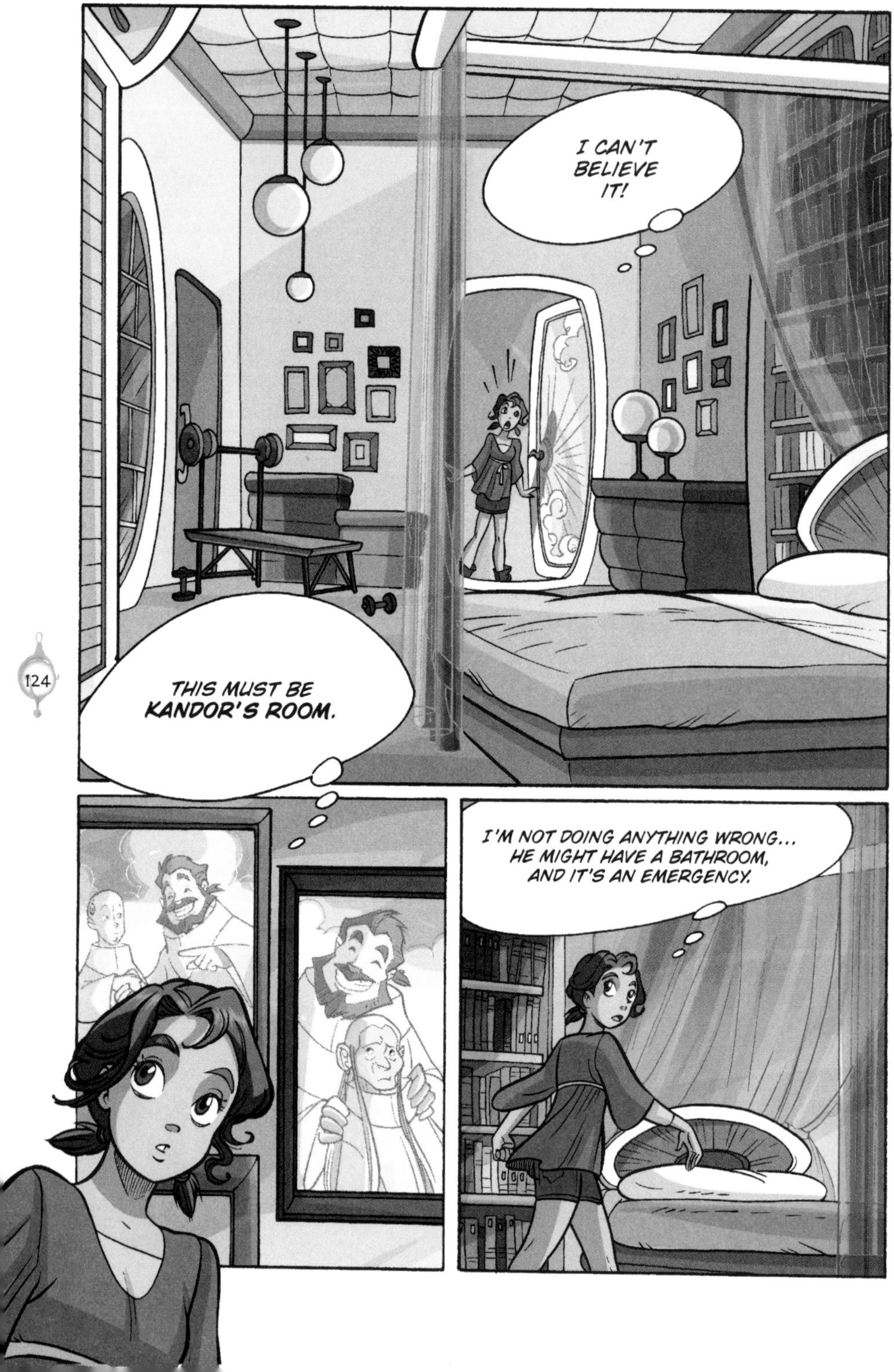
I CAN'T BELIEVE IT!
THIS MUST BE KANDOR'S ROOM.
I'M NOT DOING ANYTHING WRONG... HE MIGHT HAVE A BATHROOM, AND IT'S AN EMERGENCY.

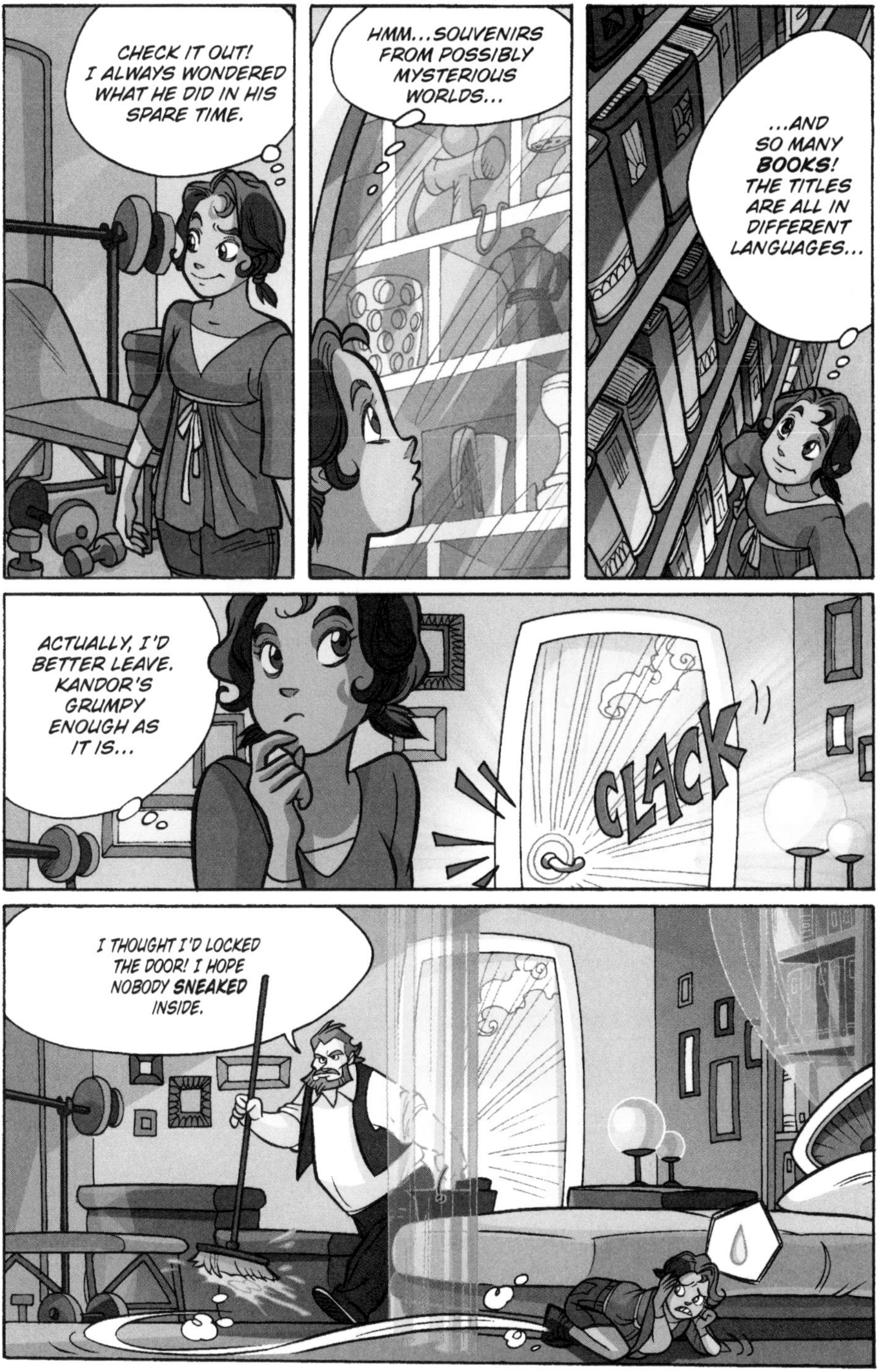
CHECK IT OUT! I ALWAYS WONDERED WHAT HE DID IN HIS SPARE TIME.
HMM...SOUVENIRS FROM POSSIBLY MYSTERIOUS WORLDS...
...AND SO MANY BOOKS! THE TITLES ARE ALL IN DIFFERENT LANGUAGES...
ACTUALLY, I'D BETTER LEAVE. KANDOR'S GRUMPY ENOUGH AS IT IS...
CLACK
I THOUGHT I'D LOCKED THE DOOR! I HOPE NOBODY SNEAKED INSIDE.

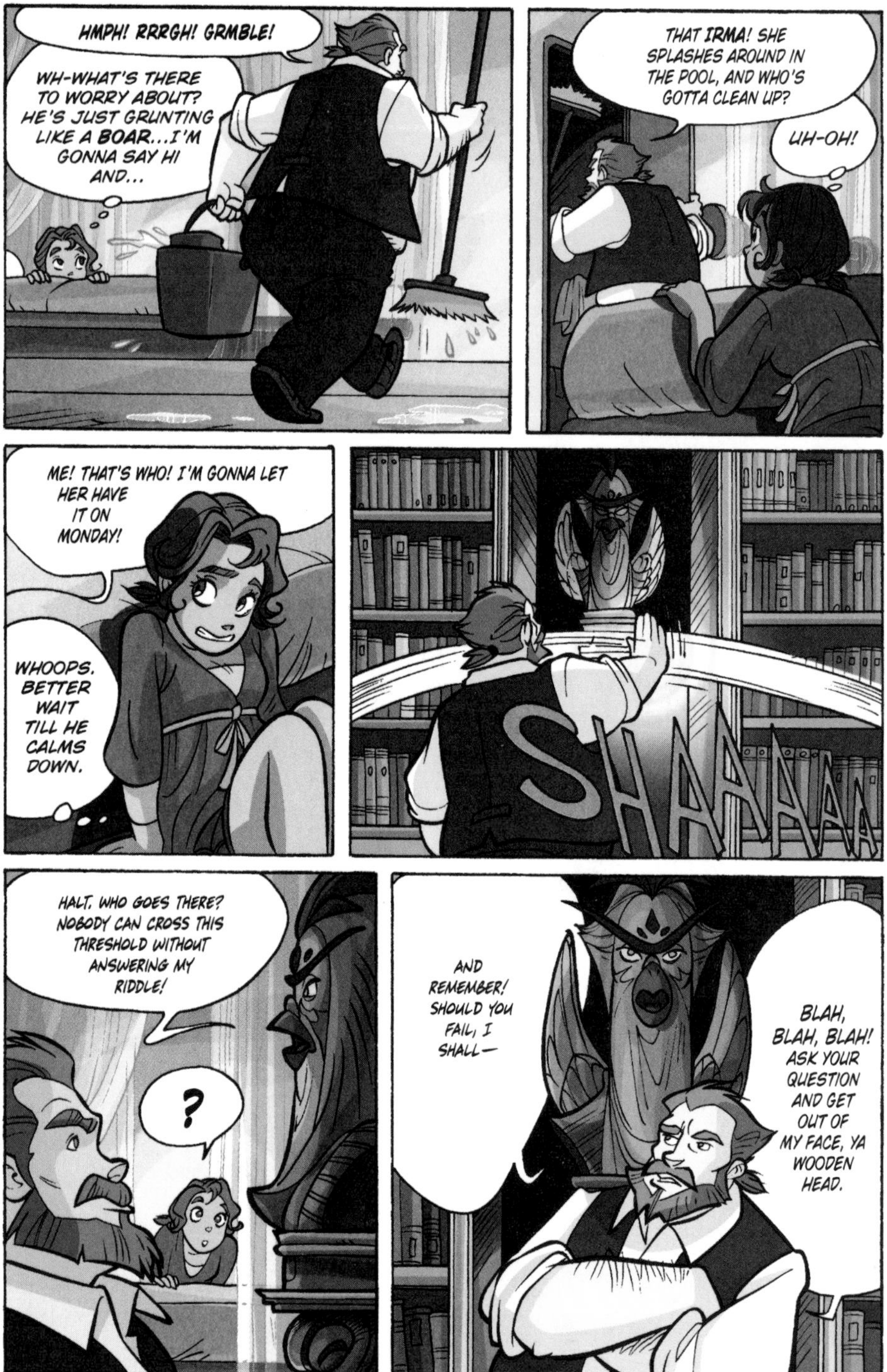

HMPH! RRRGH! GRMBLE!
WH-WHAT'S THERE TO WORRY ABOUT? HE'S JUST GRUNTING LIKE A BOAR...I'M GONNA SAY HI AND...
THAT IRMA! SHE SPLASHES AROUND IN THE POOL, AND WHO'S GOTTA CLEAN UP?
UH-OH!
ME! THAT'S WHO! I'M GONNA LET HER HAVE IT ON MONDAY!
WHOOPS. BETTER WAIT TILL HE CALMS DOWN.
SHAAAAA
HALT. WHO GOES THERE? NOBODY CAN CROSS THIS THRESHOLD WITHOUT ANSWERING MY RIDDLE!
?
AND REMEMBER! SHOULD YOU FAIL, I SHALL—
BLAH, BLAH, BLAH! ASK YOUR QUESTION AND GET OUT OF MY FACE, YA WOODEN HEAD.

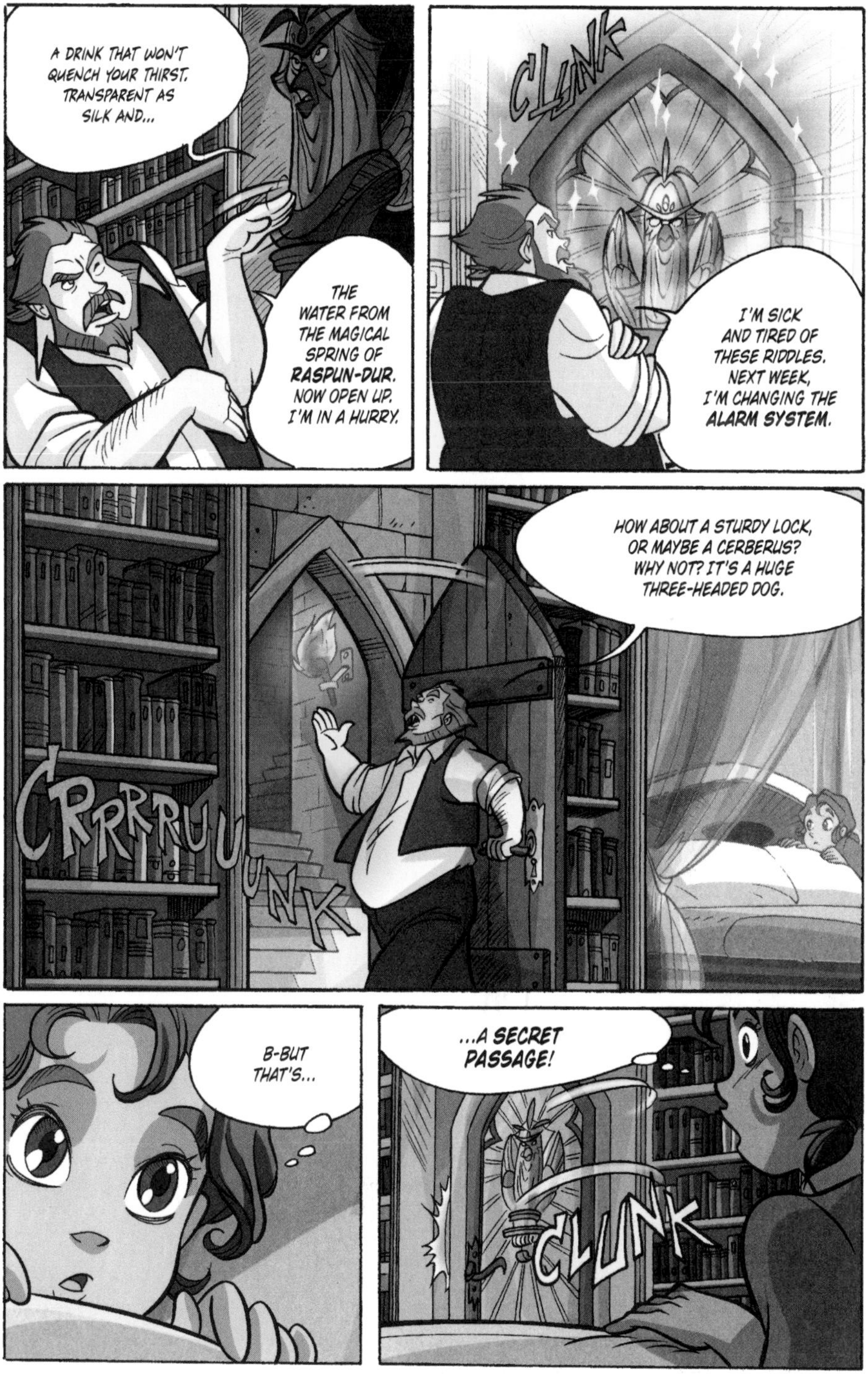
A DRINK THAT WON'T QUENCH YOUR THIRST. TRANSPARENT AS SILK AND...
THE WATER FROM THE MAGICAL SPRING OF RASPUN-DUR. NOW OPEN UP. I'M IN A HURRY.
CLUNK
I'M SICK AND TIRED OF THESE RIDDLES. NEXT WEEK, I'M CHANGING THE ALARM SYSTEM.
HOW ABOUT A STURDY LOCK, OR MAYBE A CERBERUS? WHY NOT? IT'S A HUGE THREE-HEADED DOG.
CRRRRUUUUNK
B-BUT THAT'S...
...A SECRET PASSAGE!
CLUNK

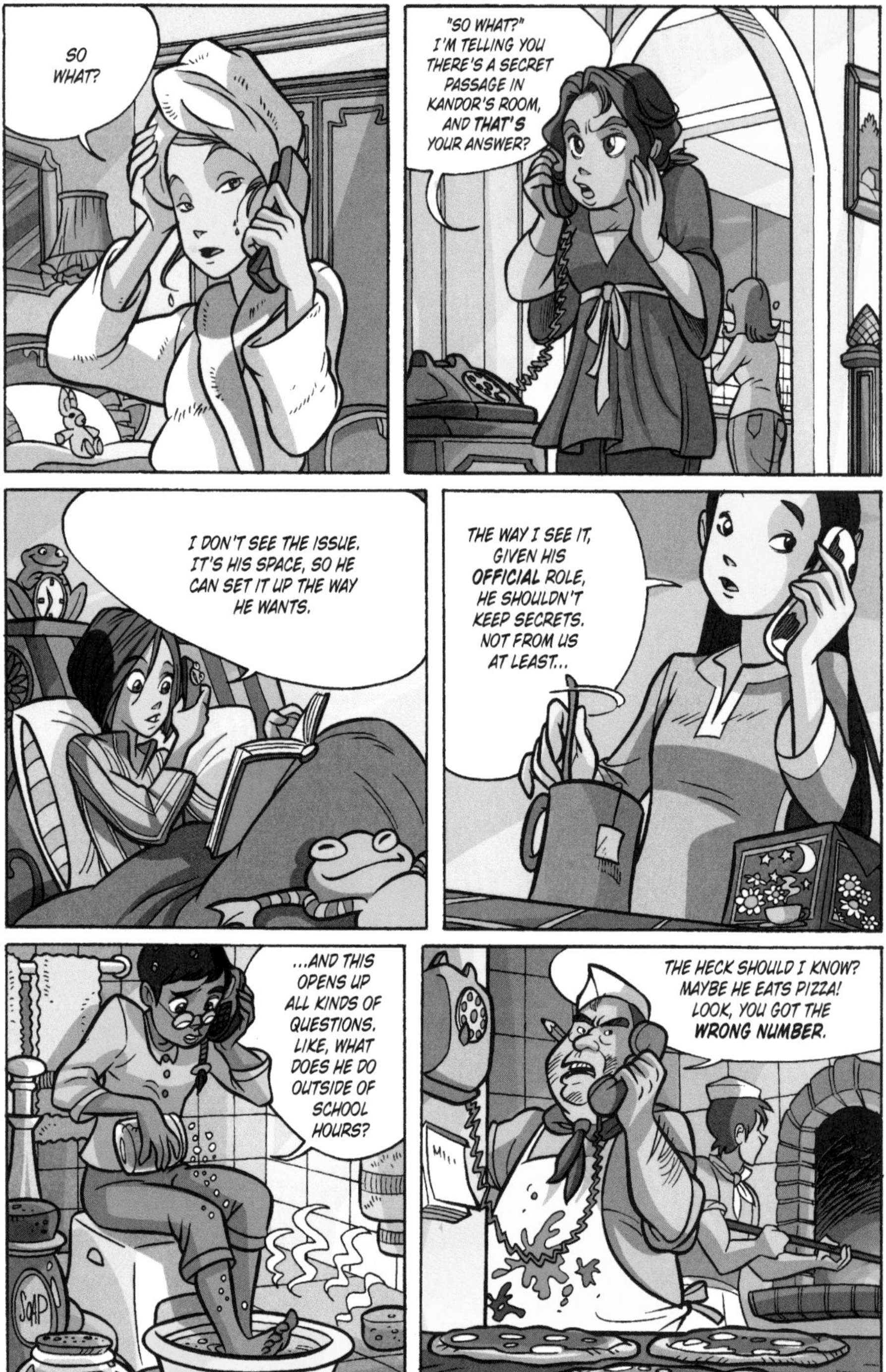
SO WHAT?
"SO WHAT?" I'M TELLING YOU THERE'S A SECRET PASSAGE IN KANDOR'S ROOM, AND THAT'S YOUR ANSWER?
I DON'T SEE THE ISSUE. IT'S HIS SPACE, SO HE CAN SET IT UP THE WAY HE WANTS.
THE WAY I SEE IT, GIVEN HIS OFFICIAL ROLE, HE SHOULDN'T KEEP SECRETS. NOT FROM US AT LEAST...
...AND THIS OPENS UP ALL KINDS OF QUESTIONS. LIKE, WHAT DOES HE DO OUTSIDE OF SCHOOL HOURS?
THE HECK SHOULD I KNOW? MAYBE HE EATS PIZZA! LOOK, YOU GOT THE WRONG NUMBER.
SOAP

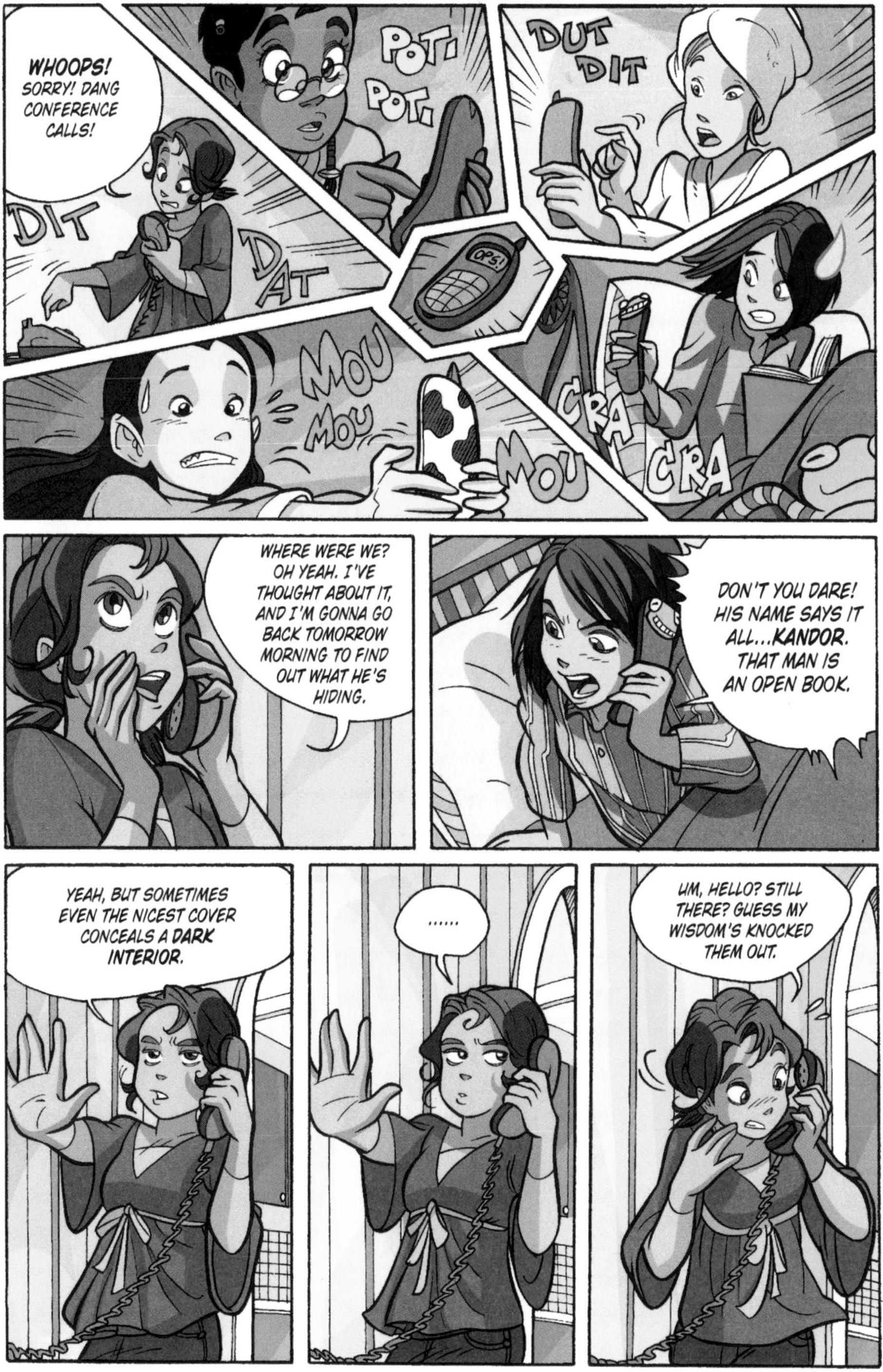

WHOOPS! SORRY! DANG CONFERENCE CALLS!
DIT
DAT
POT! POT!
DUT DIT
OPS!
MOU MOU
MOU
CRA
CRA
WHERE WERE WE? OH YEAH. I'VE THOUGHT ABOUT IT, AND I'M GONNA GO BACK TOMORROW MORNING TO FIND OUT WHAT HE'S HIDING.
DON'T YOU DARE! HIS NAME SAYS IT ALL...KANDOR. THAT MAN IS AN OPEN BOOK.
YEAH, BUT SOMETIMES EVEN THE NICEST COVER CONCEALS A DARK INTERIOR.
......
UM, HELLO? STILL THERE? GUESS MY WISDOM'S KNOCKED THEM OUT.

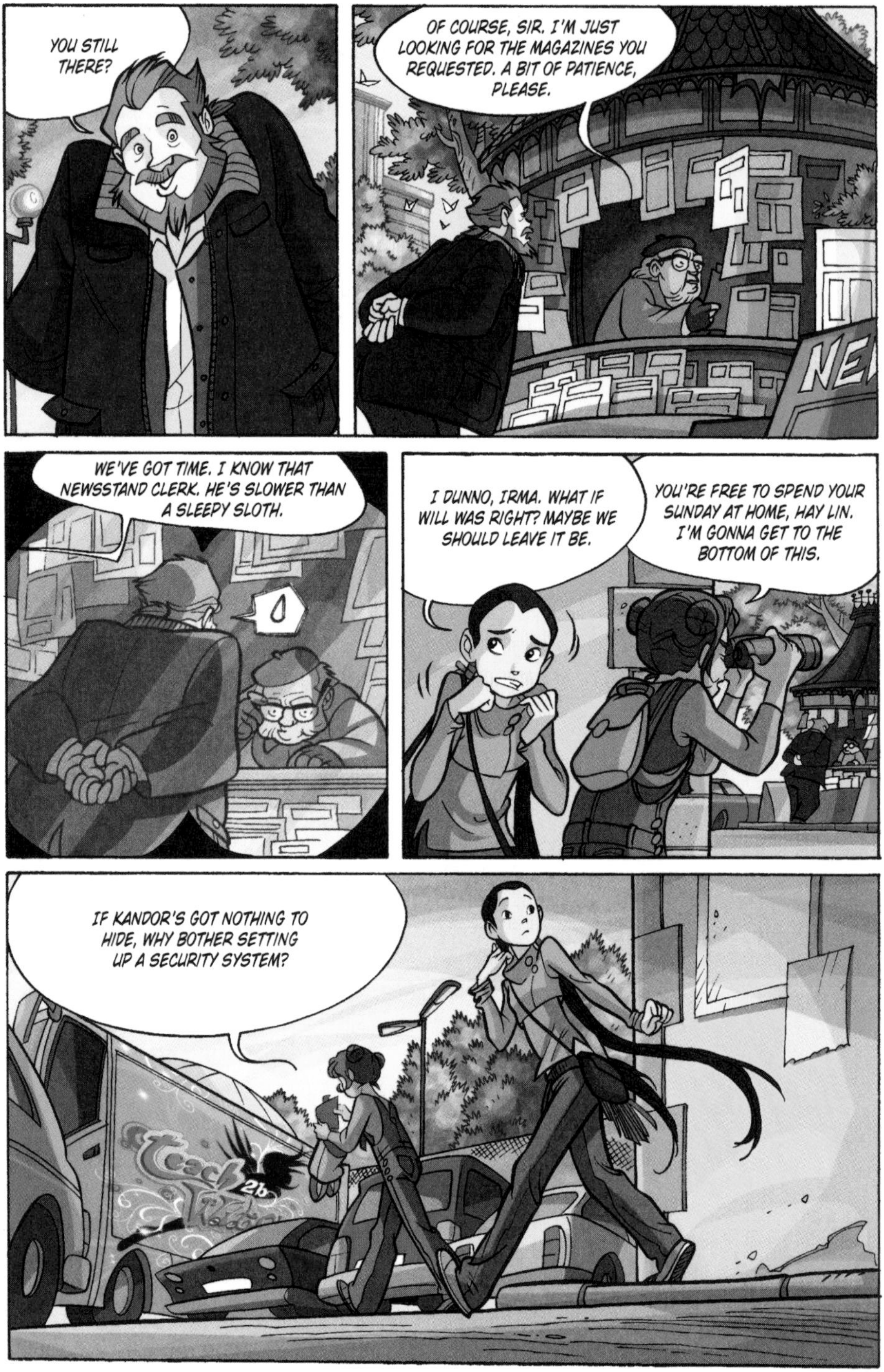
YOU STILL THERE?
OF COURSE, SIR. I'M JUST LOOKING FOR THE MAGAZINES YOU REQUESTED. A BIT OF PATIENCE, PLEASE.
NE
WE'VE GOT TIME. I KNOW THAT NEWSSTAND CLERK. HE'S SLOWER THAN A SLEEPY SLOTH.
I DUNNO, IRMA. WHAT IF WILL WAS RIGHT? MAYBE WE SHOULD LEAVE IT BE.
YOU'RE FREE TO SPEND YOUR SUNDAY AT HOME, HAY LIN. I'M GONNA GET TO THE BOTTOM OF THIS.
IF KANDOR'S GOT NOTHING TO HIDE, WHY BOTHER SETTING UP A SECURITY SYSTEM?

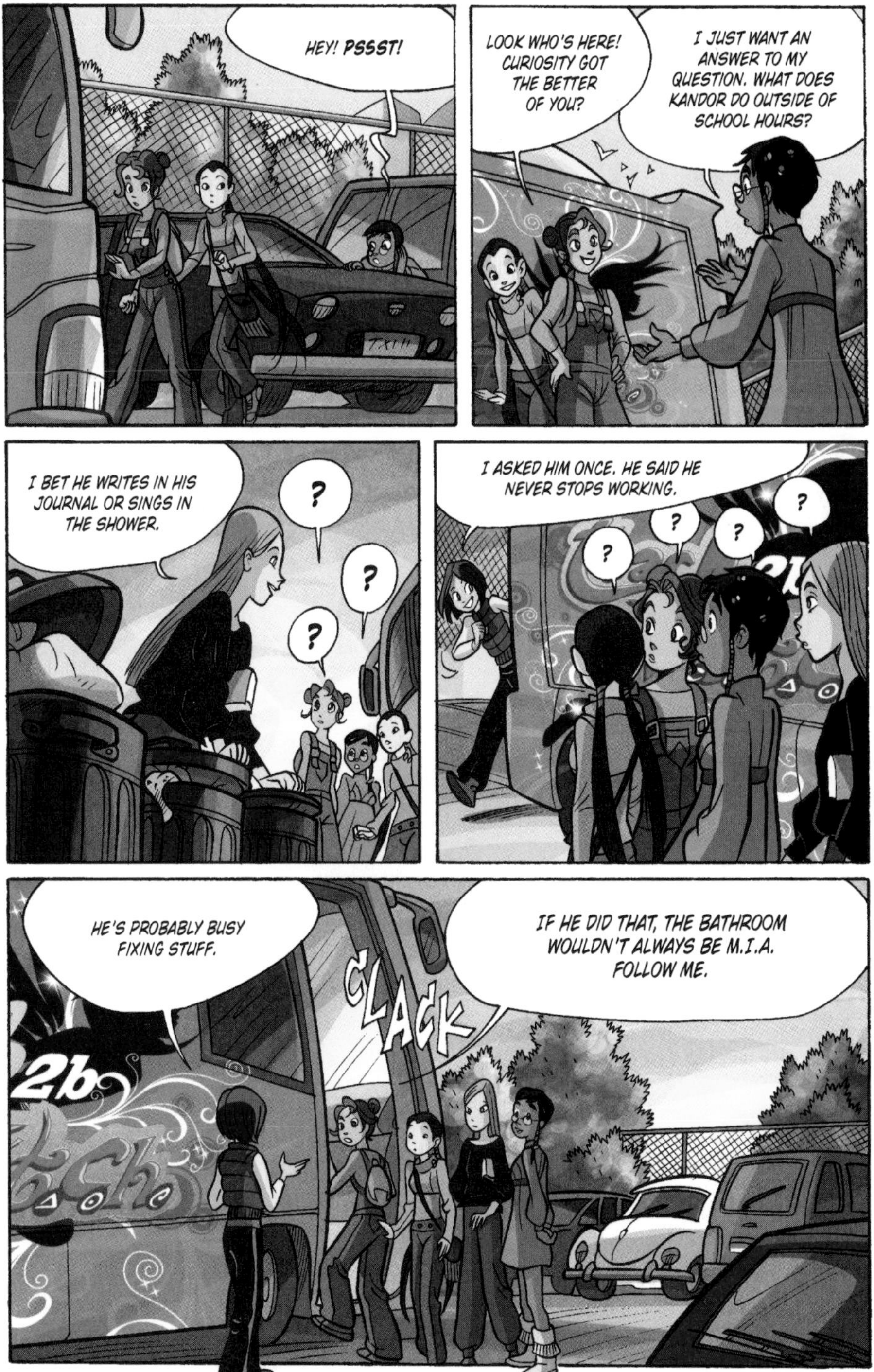
HEY! PSSST!
LOOK WHO'S HERE! CURIOSITY GOT THE BETTER OF YOU?
I JUST WANT AN ANSWER TO MY QUESTION. WHAT DOES KANDOR DO OUTSIDE OF SCHOOL HOURS?
I BET HE WRITES IN HIS JOURNAL OR SINGS IN THE SHOWER.
?
?
?
I ASKED HIM ONCE. HE SAID HE NEVER STOPS WORKING.
?
?
?
?
HE'S PROBABLY BUSY FIXING STUFF.
CLACK
IF HE DID THAT, THE BATHROOM WOULDN'T ALWAYS BE M.I.A. FOLLOW ME.

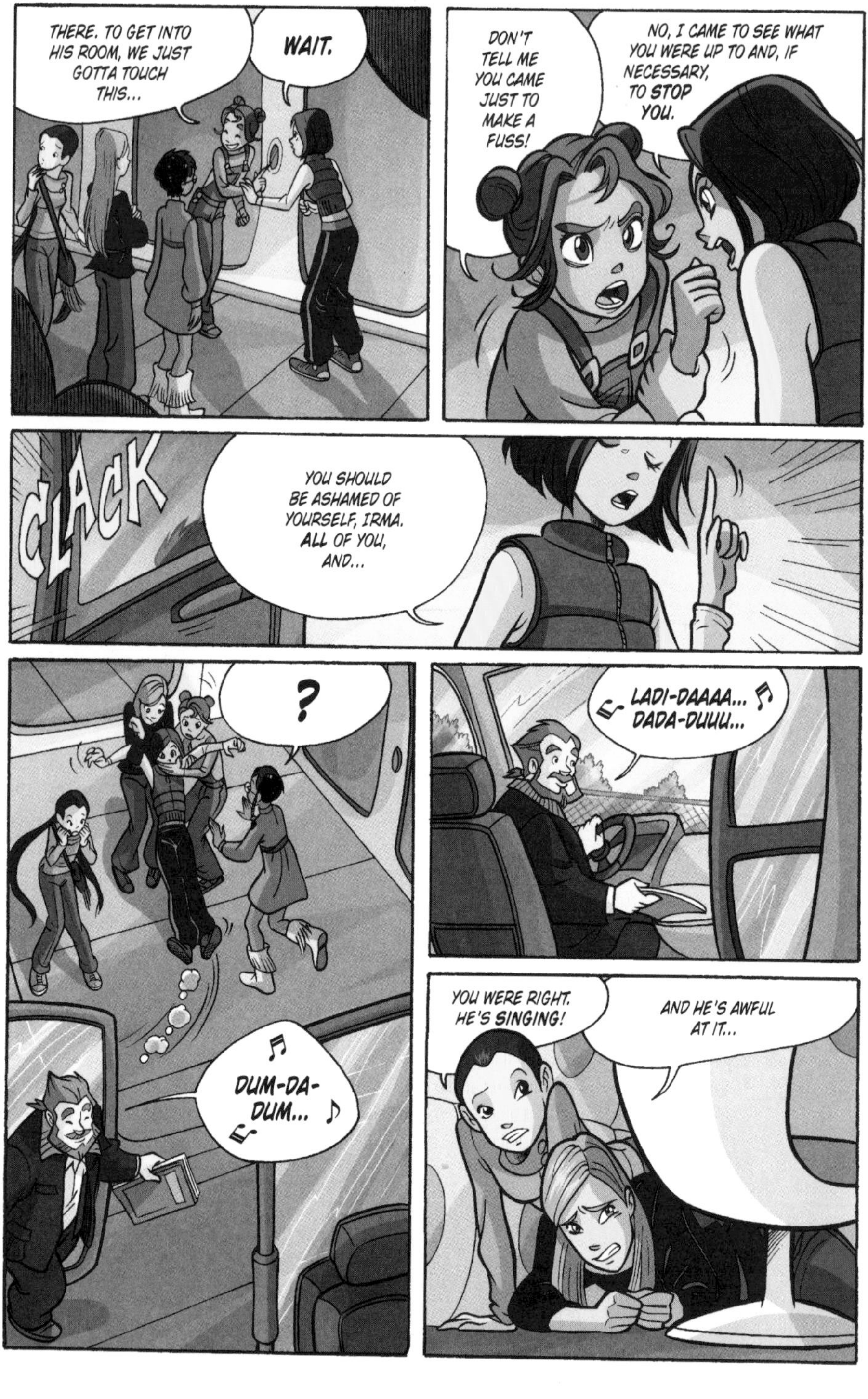
THERE. TO GET INTO HIS ROOM, WE JUST GOTTA TOUCH THIS...
WAIT.
DON'T TELL ME YOU CAME JUST TO MAKE A FUSS!
NO, I CAME TO SEE WHAT YOU WERE UP TO AND, IF NECESSARY, TO STOP YOU.
CLACK
YOU SHOULD BE ASHAMED OF YOURSELF, IRMA. ALL OF YOU, AND...
?
LADI-DAAAA... DADA-DUUU...
DUM-DA-DUM...
YOU WERE RIGHT. HE'S SINGING!
AND HE'S AWFUL AT IT...

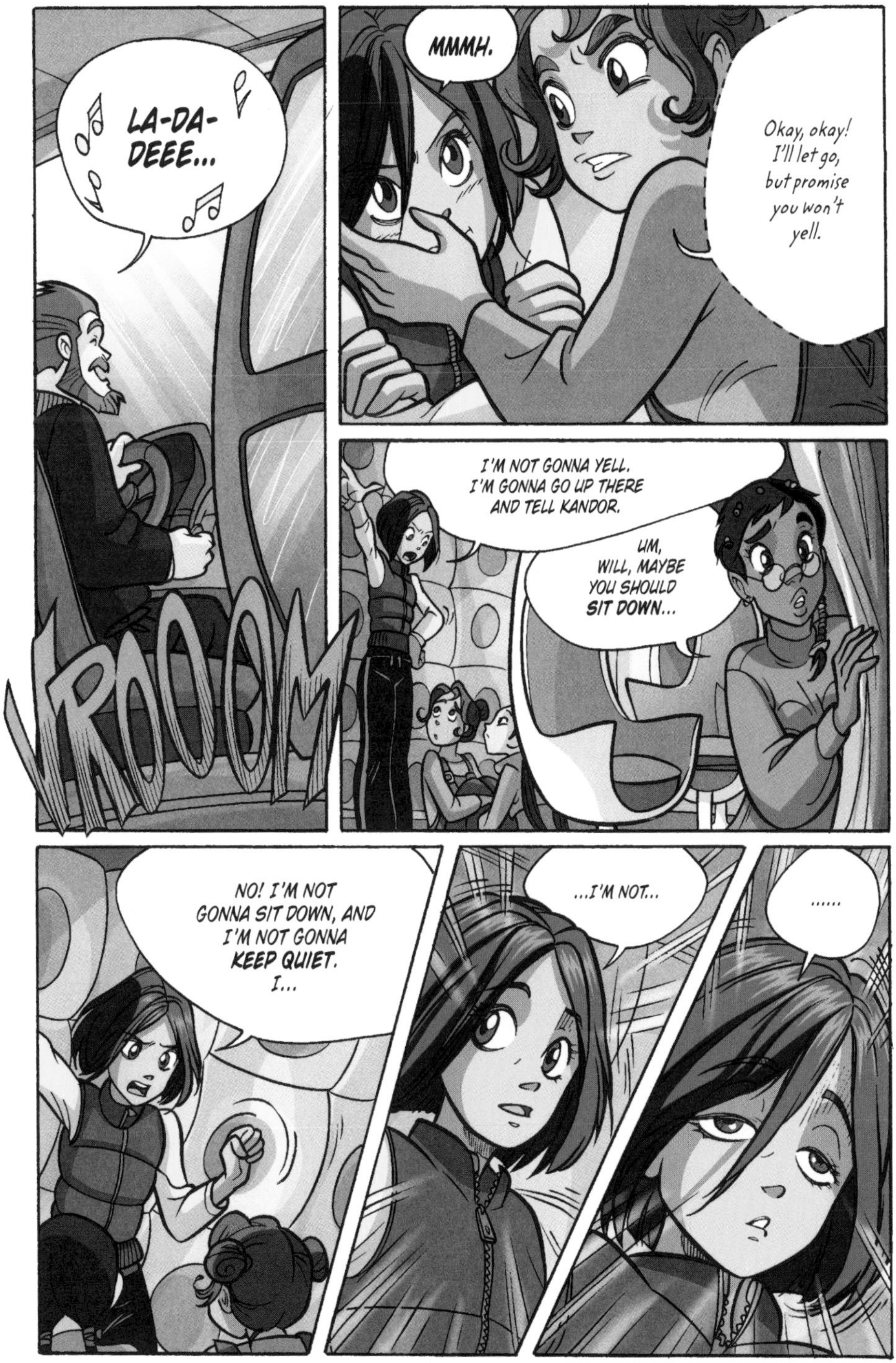
LA-DA-DEEE...
VROOOM
MMMH.
Okay, okay! I'll let go, but promise you won't yell.
I'M NOT GONNA YELL. I'M GONNA GO UP THERE AND TELL KANDOR.
UM, WILL, MAYBE YOU SHOULD SIT DOWN...
NO! I'M NOT GONNA SIT DOWN, AND I'M NOT GONNA KEEP QUIET. I...
...I'M NOT...
......

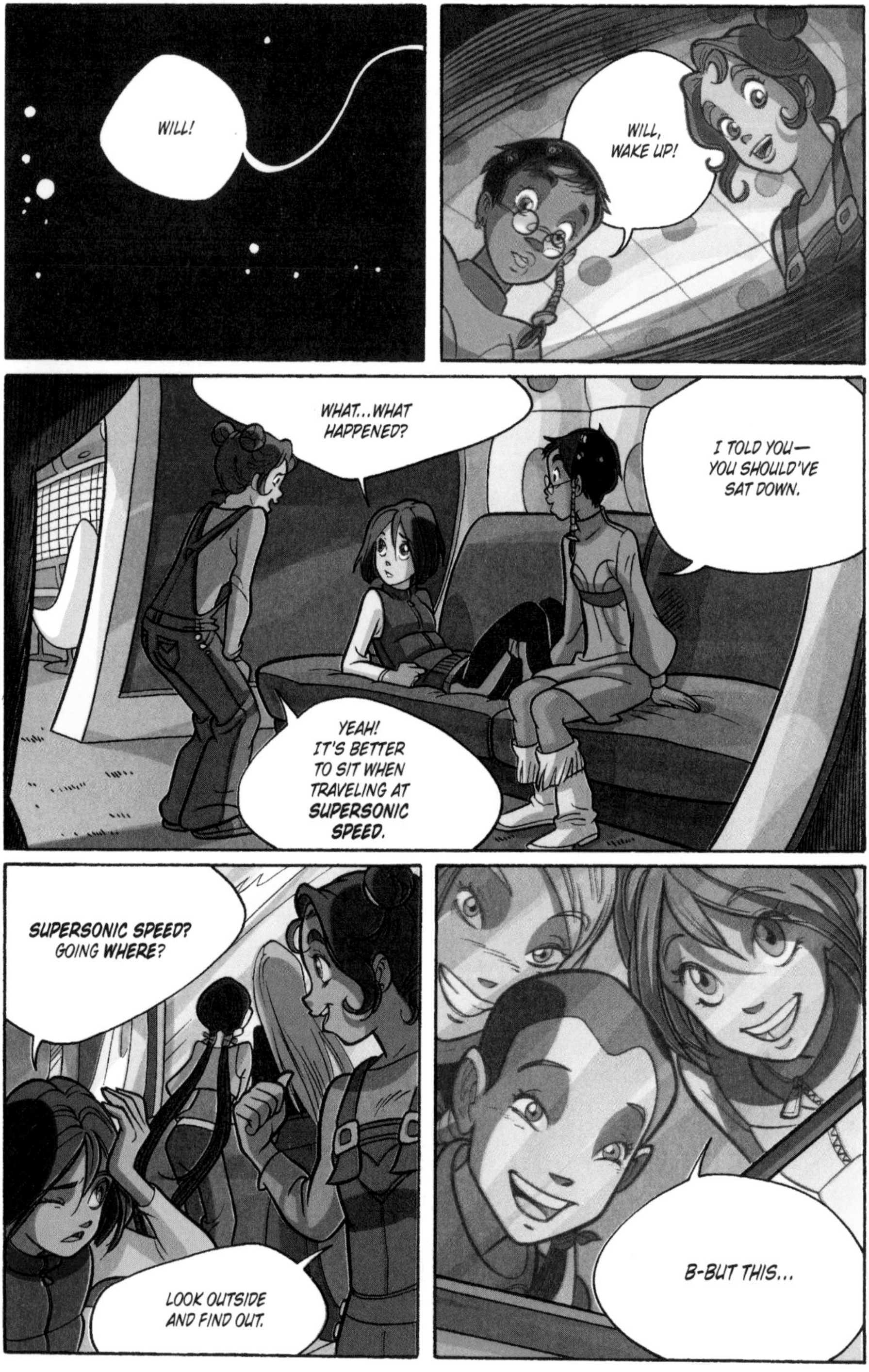
WILL!
WILL, WAKE UP!
WHAT...WHAT HAPPENED?
I TOLD YOU— YOU SHOULD'VE SAT DOWN.
YEAH! IT'S BETTER TO SIT WHEN TRAVELING AT SUPERSONIC SPEED.
SUPERSONIC SPEED? GOING WHERE?
LOOK OUTSIDE AND FIND OUT.
B-BUT THIS...

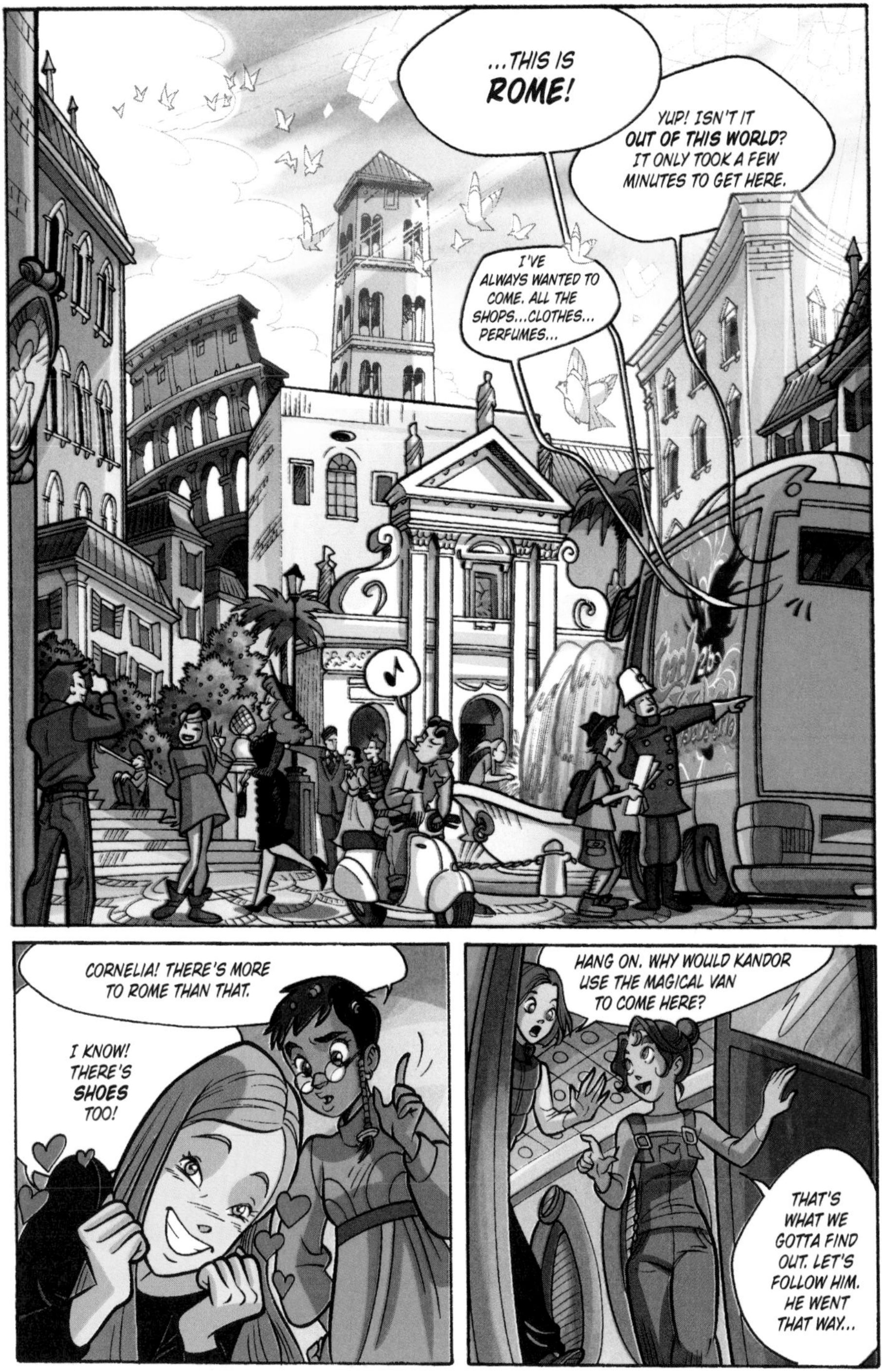
...THIS IS ROME!
YUP! ISN'T IT OUT OF THIS WORLD? IT ONLY TOOK A FEW MINUTES TO GET HERE.
I'VE ALWAYS WANTED TO COME. ALL THE SHOPS...CLOTHES... PERFUMES...
CORNELIA! THERE'S MORE TO ROME THAN THAT.
I KNOW! THERE'S SHOES TOO!
HANG ON. WHY WOULD KANDOR USE THE MAGICAL VAN TO COME HERE?
THAT'S WHAT WE GOTTA FIND OUT. LET'S FOLLOW HIM. HE WENT THAT WAY...

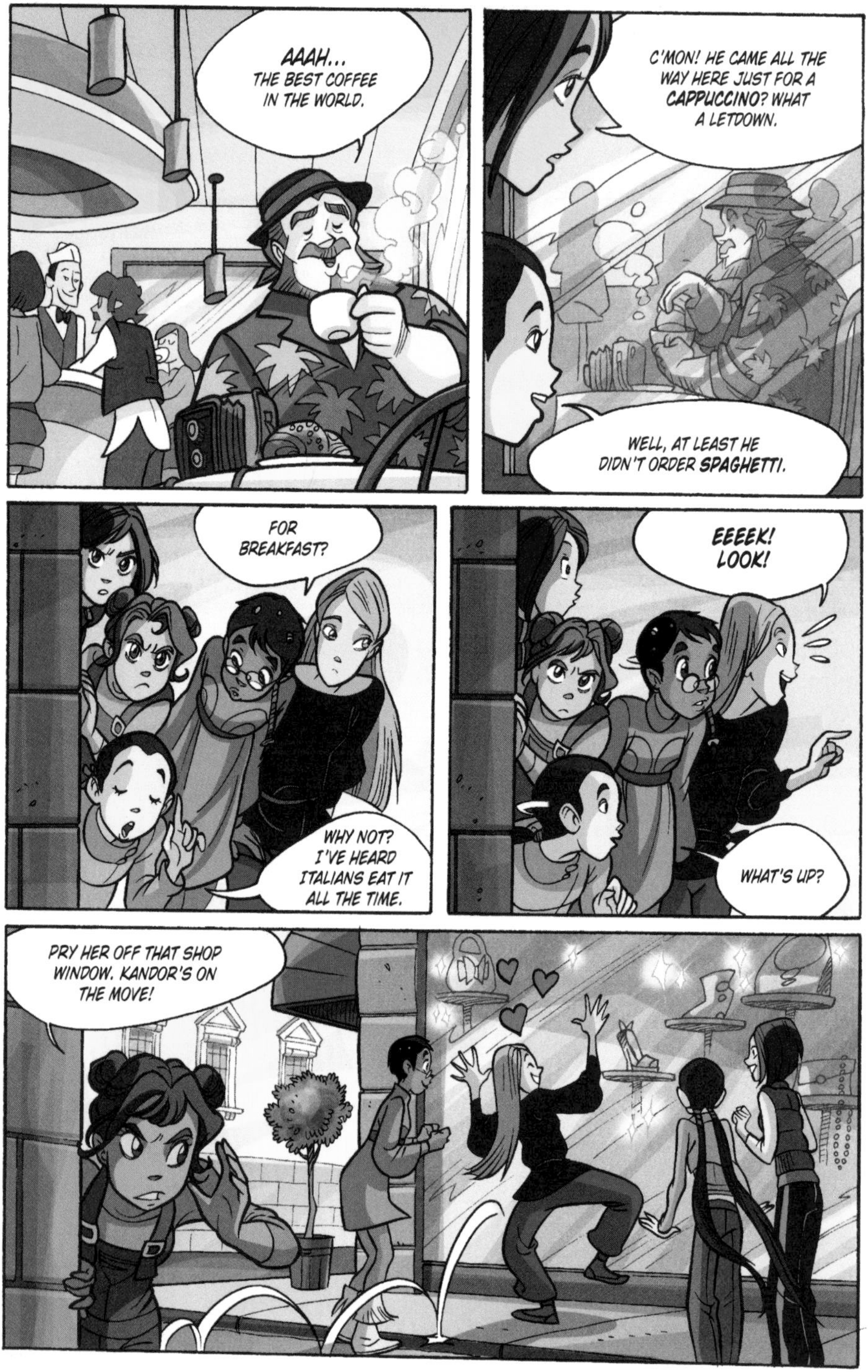
AAAH... THE BEST COFFEE IN THE WORLD.
C'MON! HE CAME ALL THE WAY HERE JUST FOR A CAPPUCCINO? WHAT A LETDOWN.
WELL, AT LEAST HE DIDN'T ORDER SPAGHETTI.
FOR BREAKFAST?
WHY NOT? I'VE HEARD ITALIANS EAT IT ALL THE TIME.
EEEEK! LOOK!
WHAT'S UP?
PRY HER OFF THAT SHOP WINDOW. KANDOR'S ON THE MOVE!

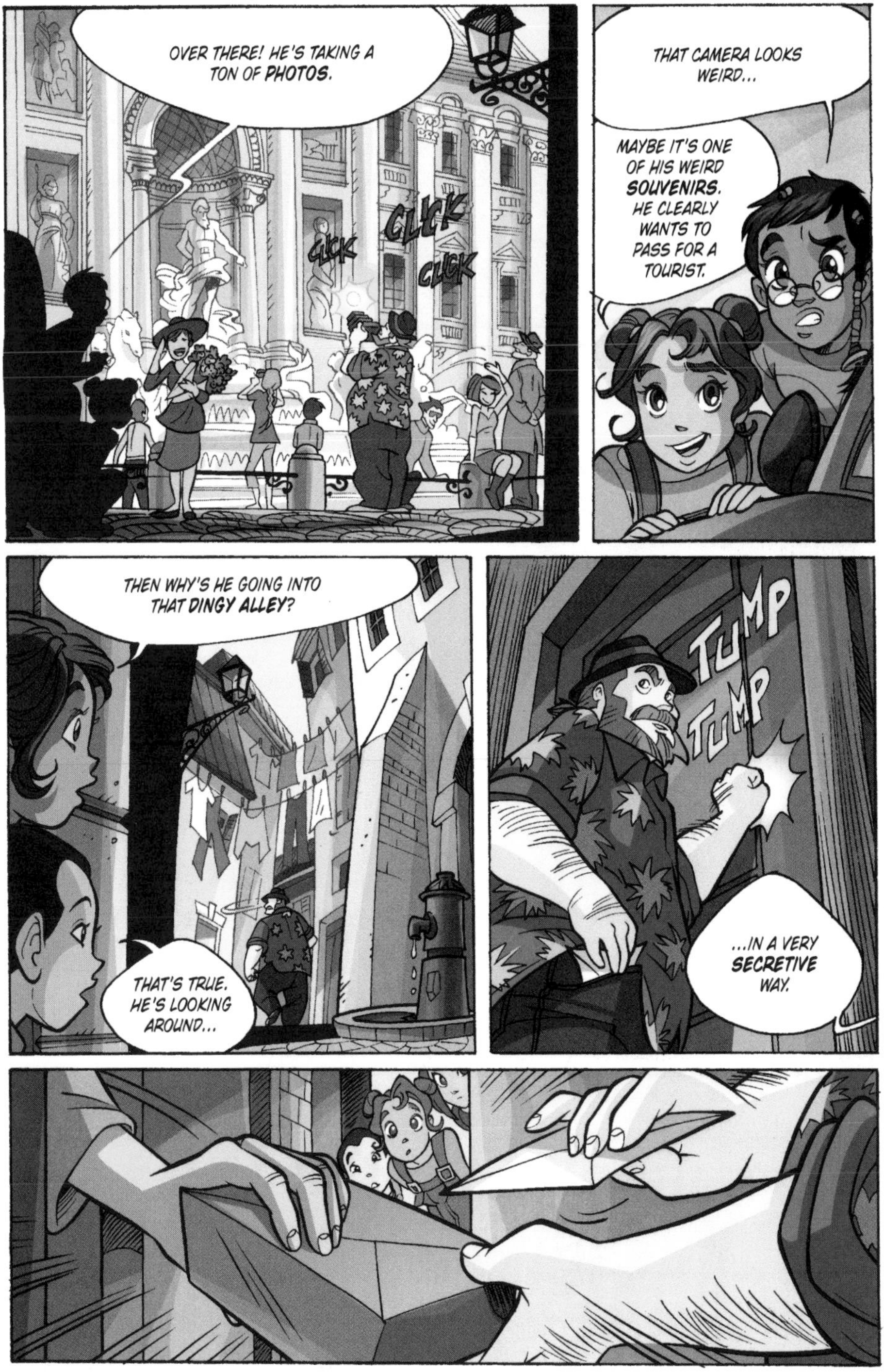
OVER THERE! HE'S TAKING A TON OF **PHOTOS**.
CLICK
CLICK
CLICK
THAT CAMERA LOOKS WEIRD...
MAYBE IT'S ONE OF HIS WEIRD **SOUVENIRS**. HE CLEARLY WANTS TO PASS FOR A TOURIST.
THEN WHY'S HE GOING INTO THAT **DINGY ALLEY**?
THAT'S TRUE. HE'S LOOKING AROUND...
TUMP
TUMP
...IN A VERY **SECRETIVE** WAY.

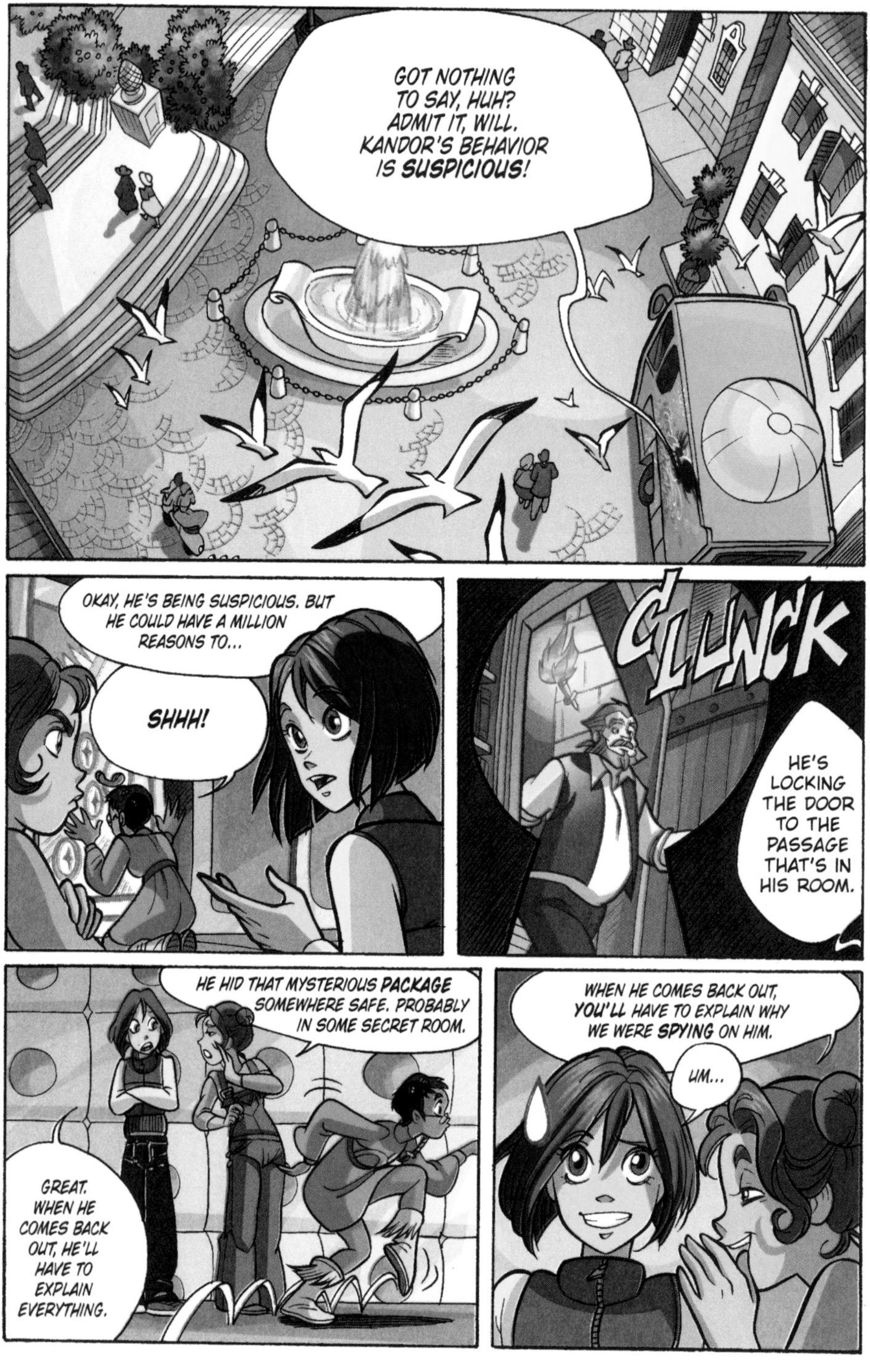
GOT NOTHING TO SAY, HUH? ADMIT IT, WILL. KANDOR'S BEHAVIOR IS SUSPICIOUS!
OKAY, HE'S BEING SUSPICIOUS. BUT HE COULD HAVE A MILLION REASONS TO...
SHHH!
CLUNCK
HE'S LOCKING THE DOOR TO THE PASSAGE THAT'S IN HIS ROOM.
HE HID THAT MYSTERIOUS PACKAGE SOMEWHERE SAFE. PROBABLY IN SOME SECRET ROOM.
GREAT. WHEN HE COMES BACK OUT, HE'LL HAVE TO EXPLAIN EVERYTHING.
WHEN HE COMES BACK OUT, YOU'LL HAVE TO EXPLAIN WHY WE WERE SPYING ON HIM.
UM...

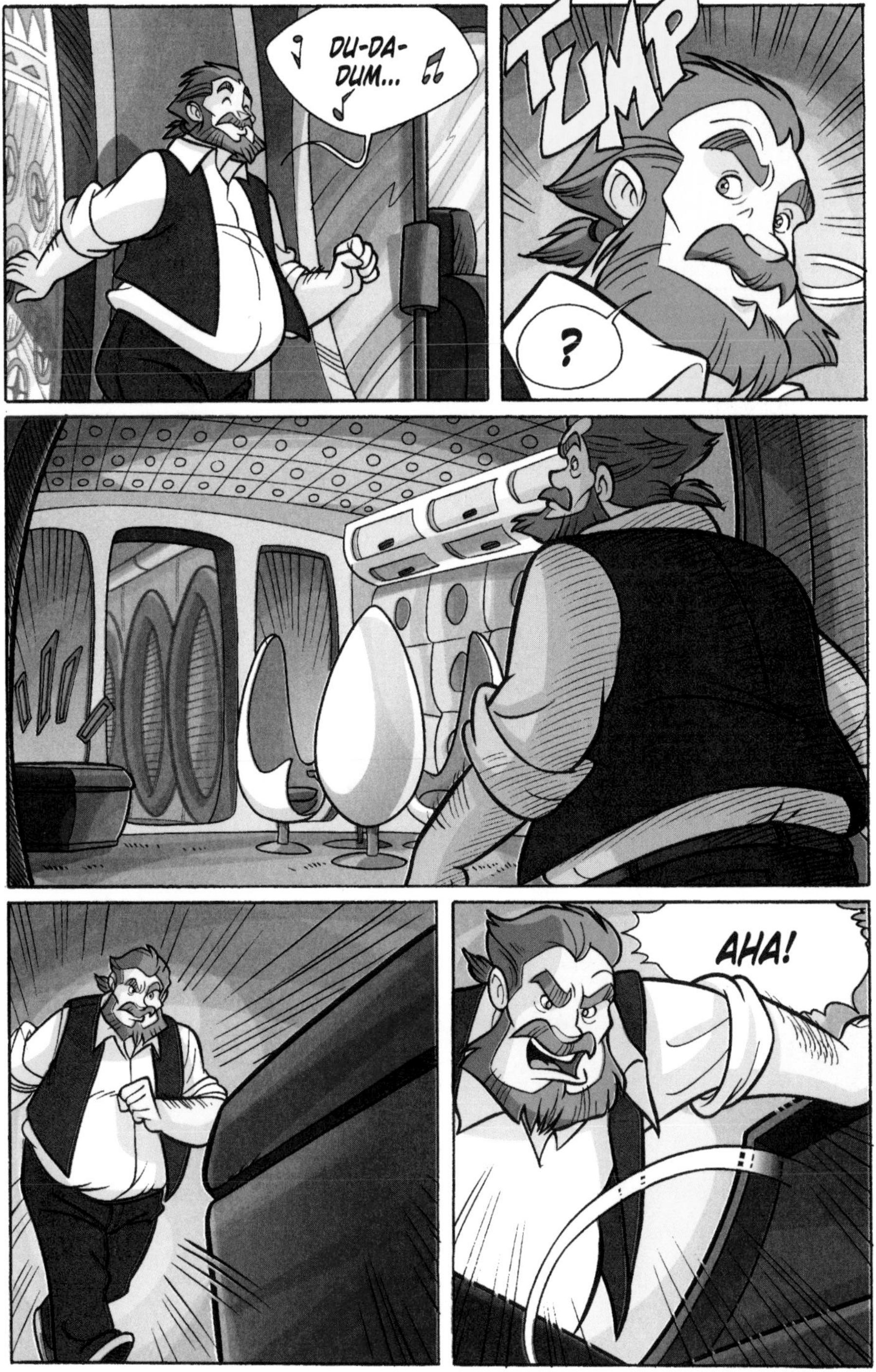
DU-DA-DUM...
TUMP
?
AHA!

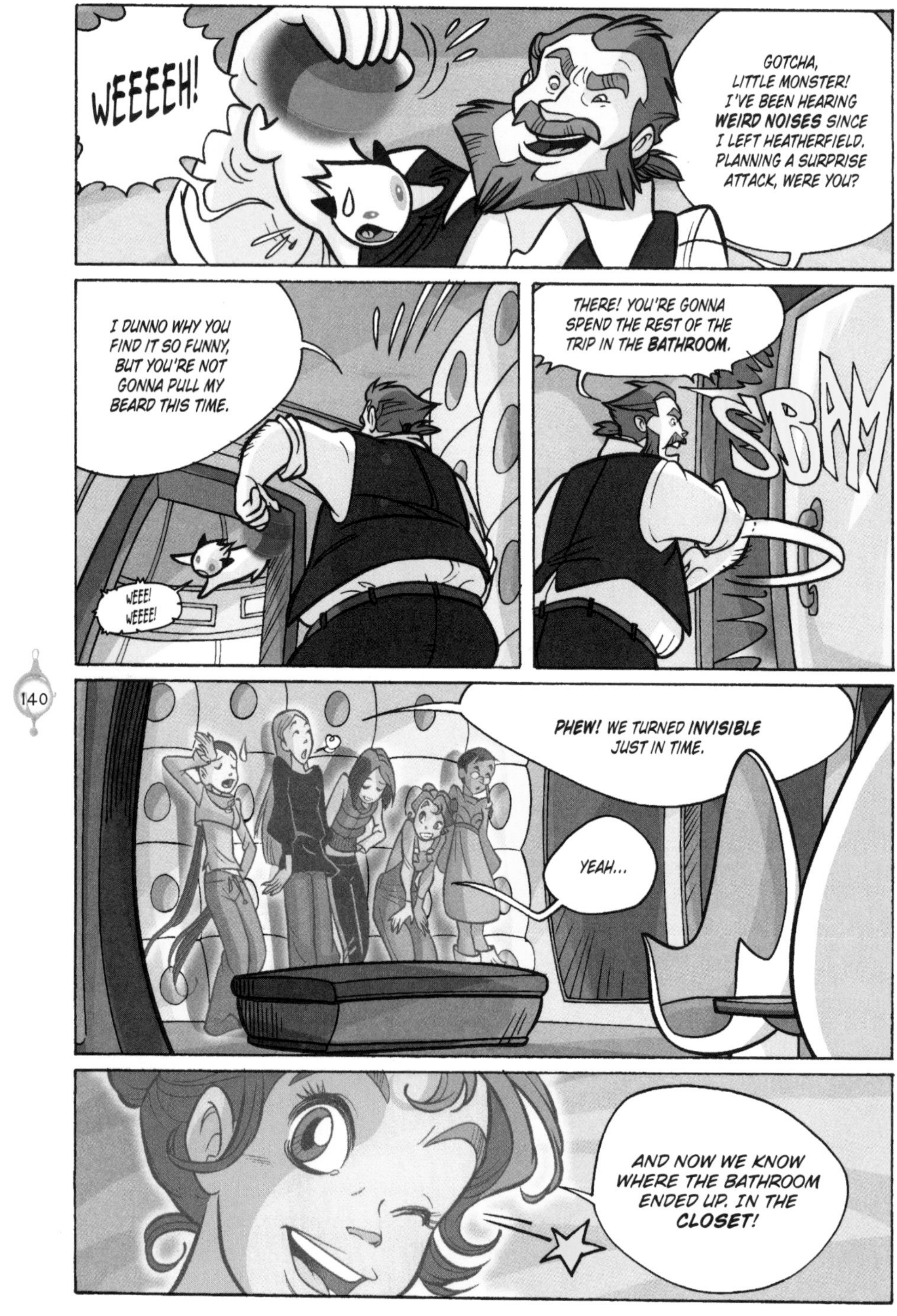
WEEEEH!
GOTCHA, LITTLE MONSTER! I'VE BEEN HEARING WEIRD NOISES SINCE I LEFT HEATHERFIELD. PLANNING A SURPRISE ATTACK, WERE YOU?
I DUNNO WHY YOU FIND IT SO FUNNY, BUT YOU'RE NOT GONNA PULL MY BEARD THIS TIME.
WEEE! WEEEE!
THERE! YOU'RE GONNA SPEND THE REST OF THE TRIP IN THE BATHROOM.
SBAM
PHEW! WE TURNED INVISIBLE JUST IN TIME.
YEAH...
AND NOW WE KNOW WHERE THE BATHROOM ENDED UP. IN THE CLOSET!

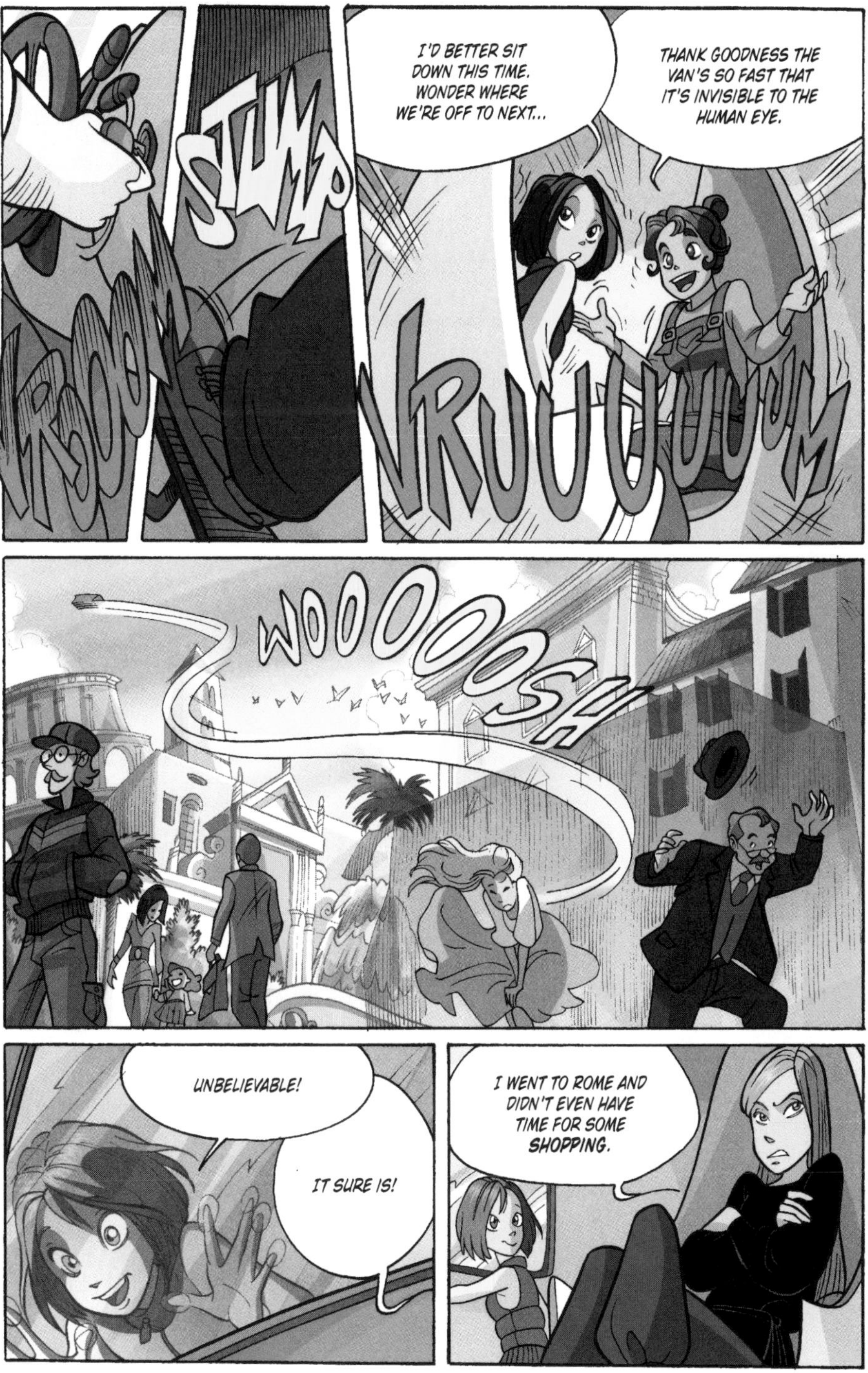
VROOOOM
STUMP
I'D BETTER SIT DOWN THIS TIME. WONDER WHERE WE'RE OFF TO NEXT...
THANK GOODNESS THE VAN'S SO FAST THAT IT'S INVISIBLE TO THE HUMAN EYE.
VRUUUUUUM
WOOOOOSH
UNBELIEVABLE!
IT SURE IS!
I WENT TO ROME AND DIDN'T EVEN HAVE TIME FOR SOME SHOPPING.

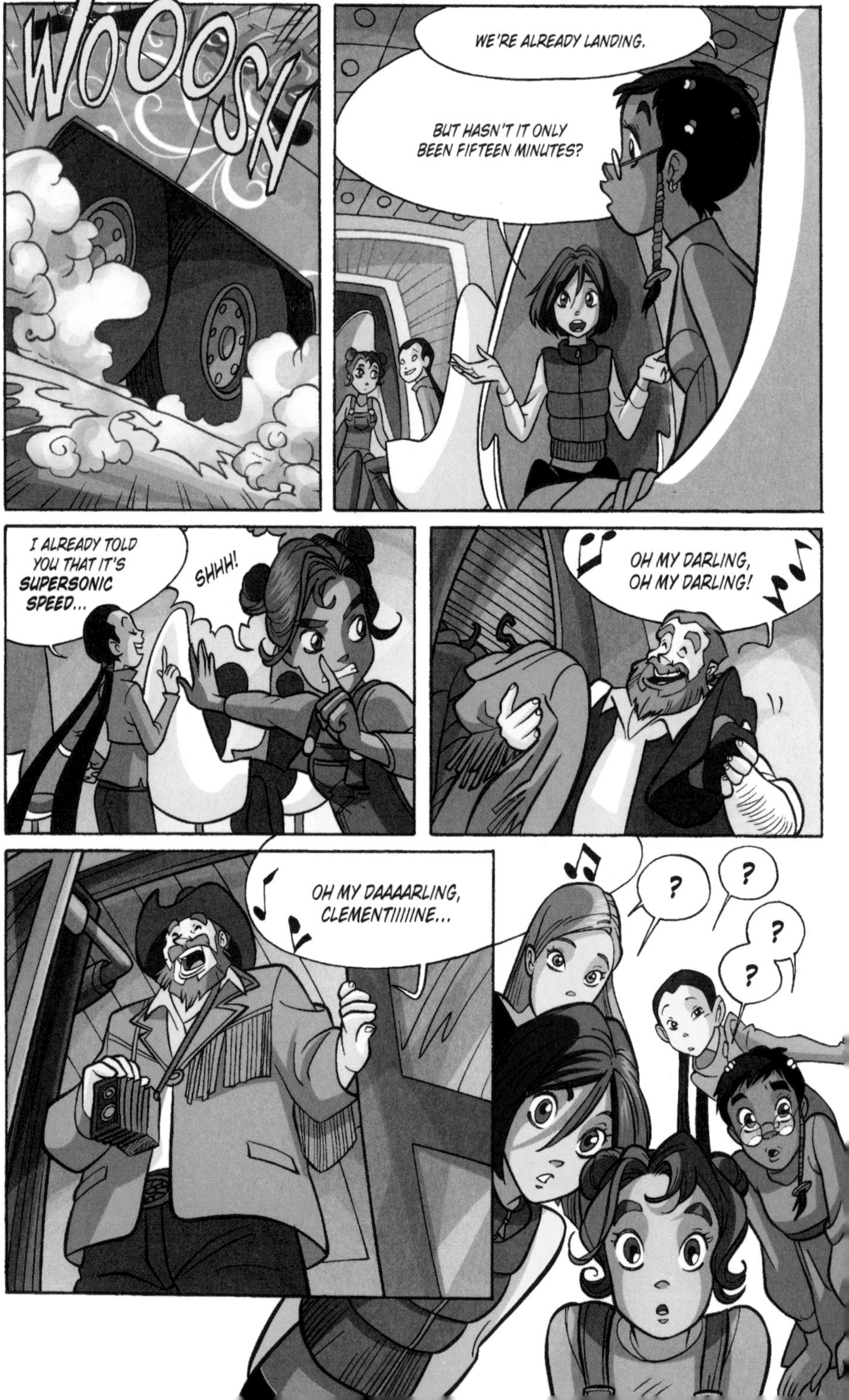
WOOOSH
WE'RE ALREADY LANDING.
BUT HASN'T IT ONLY BEEN FIFTEEN MINUTES?
I ALREADY TOLD YOU THAT IT'S SUPERSONIC SPEED...
SHHH!
OH MY DARLING, OH MY DARLING!
OH MY DAAAARLING, CLEMENTIIIIINE...
?
?
?
?

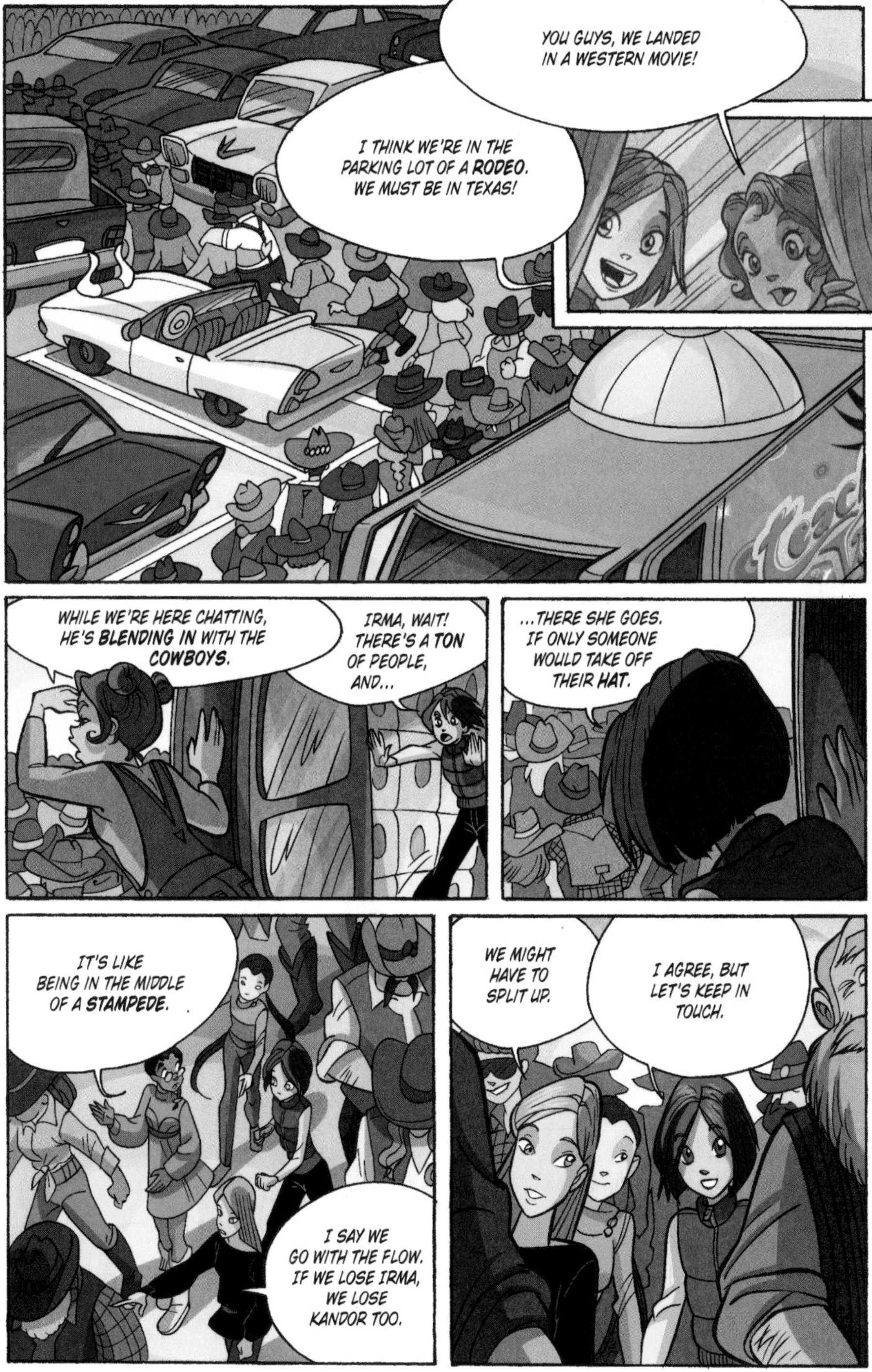

YOU GUYS, WE LANDED IN A WESTERN MOVIE!
I THINK WE'RE IN THE PARKING LOT OF A RODEO. WE MUST BE IN TEXAS!
WHILE WE'RE HERE CHATTING, HE'S BLENDING IN WITH THE COWBOYS.
IRMA, WAIT! THERE'S A TON OF PEOPLE, AND...
...THERE SHE GOES. IF ONLY SOMEONE WOULD TAKE OFF THEIR HAT.
IT'S LIKE BEING IN THE MIDDLE OF A STAMPEDE.
I SAY WE GO WITH THE FLOW. IF WE LOSE IRMA, WE LOSE KANDOR TOO.
WE MIGHT HAVE TO SPLIT UP.
I AGREE, BUT LET'S KEEP IN TOUCH.

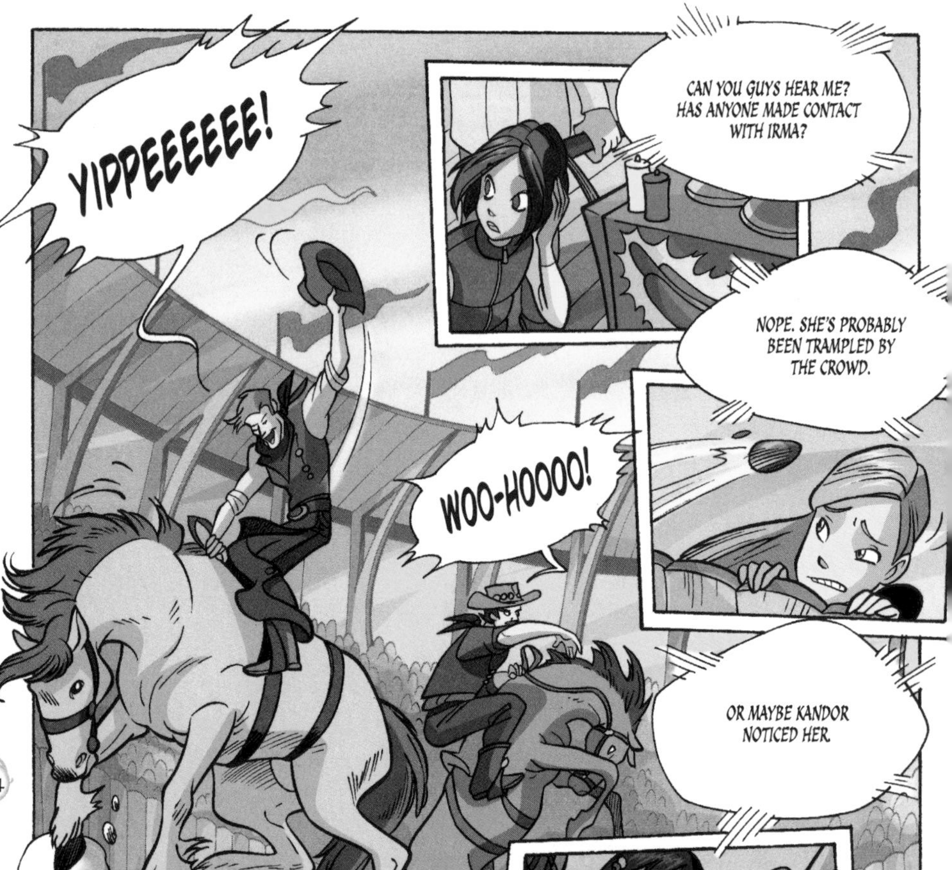
YIPPEEEEEE!
CAN YOU GUYS HEAR ME? HAS ANYONE MADE CONTACT WITH IRMA?
NOPE. SHE'S PROBABLY BEEN TRAMPLED BY THE CROWD.
WOO-HOOOO!
OR MAYBE KANDOR NOTICED HER.

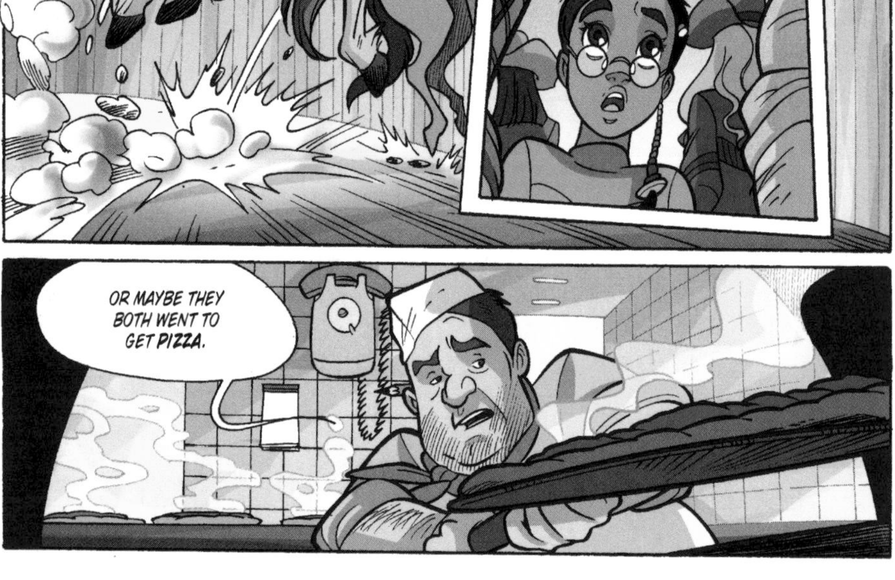
OR MAYBE THEY BOTH WENT TO GET PIZZA.

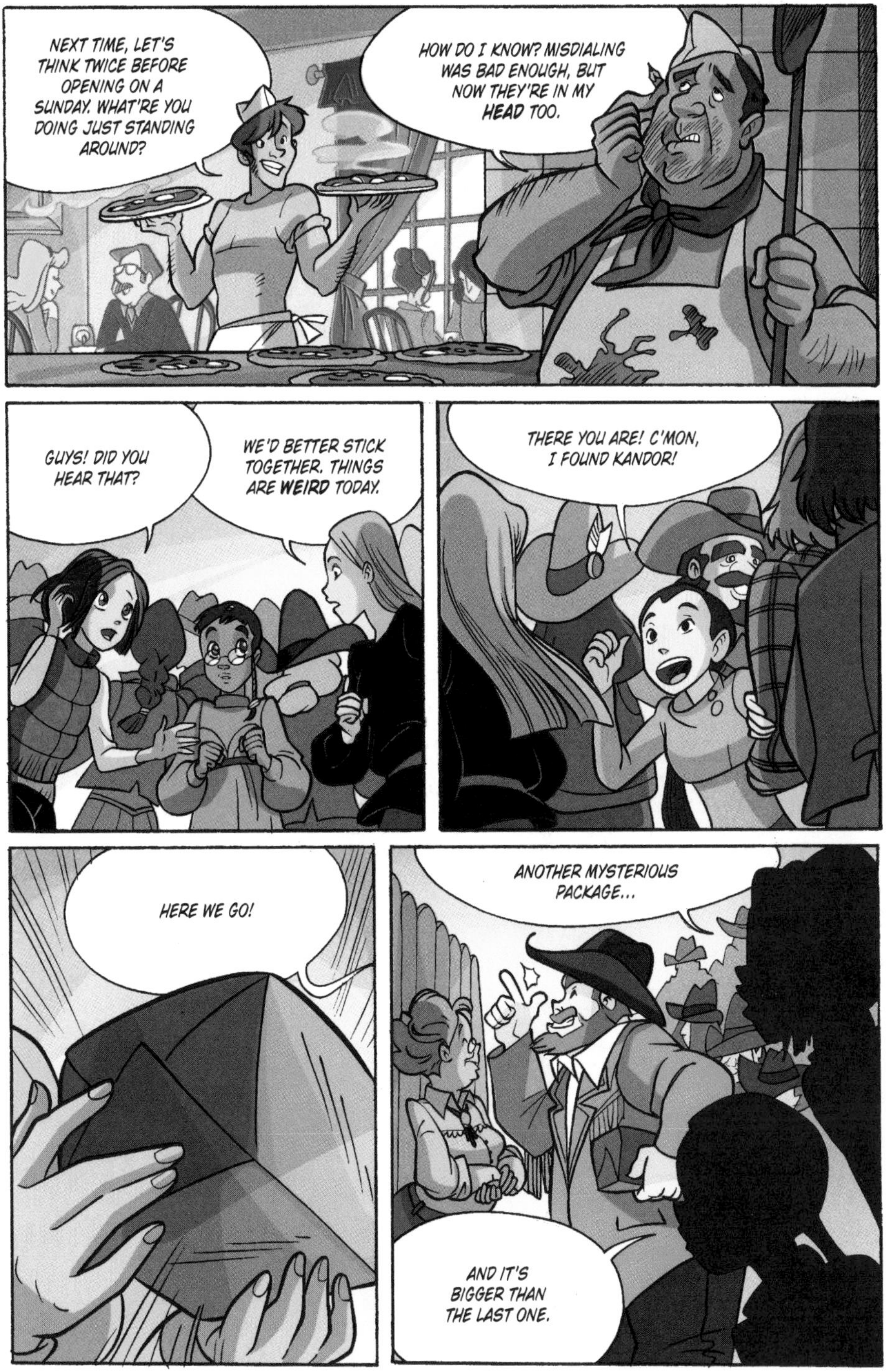
NEXT TIME, LET'S THINK TWICE BEFORE OPENING ON A SUNDAY. WHAT'RE YOU DOING JUST STANDING AROUND?
HOW DO I KNOW? MISDIALING WAS BAD ENOUGH, BUT NOW THEY'RE IN MY HEAD TOO.
GUYS! DID YOU HEAR THAT?
WE'D BETTER STICK TOGETHER. THINGS ARE WEIRD TODAY.
THERE YOU ARE! C'MON, I FOUND KANDOR!
HERE WE GO!
ANOTHER MYSTERIOUS PACKAGE...
AND IT'S BIGGER THAN THE LAST ONE.

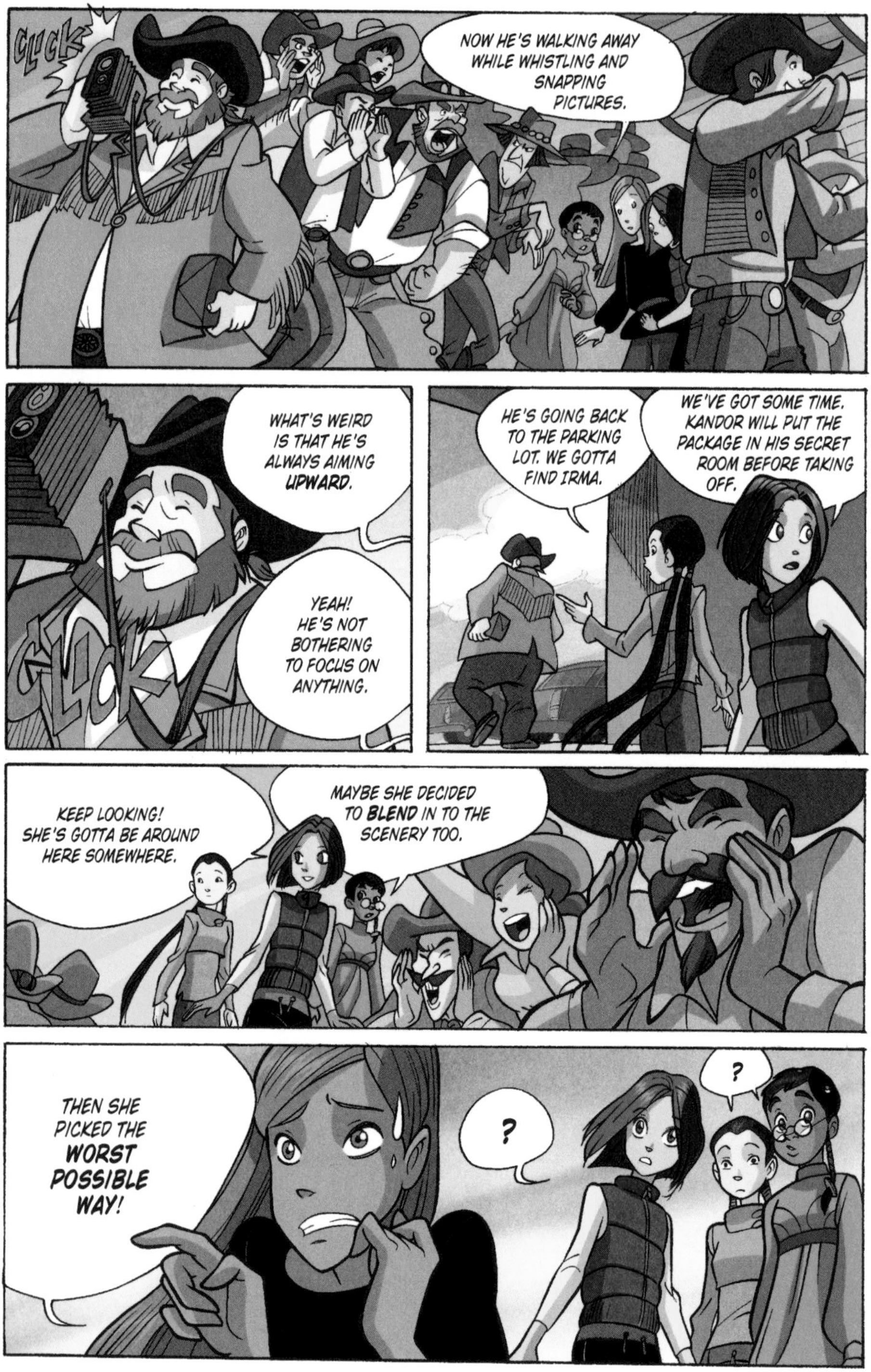
CLICK
NOW HE'S WALKING AWAY WHILE WHISTLING AND SNAPPING PICTURES.
WHAT'S WEIRD IS THAT HE'S ALWAYS AIMING **UPWARD**.
YEAH! HE'S NOT BOTHERING TO FOCUS ON ANYTHING.
CLICK
HE'S GOING BACK TO THE PARKING LOT. WE GOTTA FIND IRMA.
WE'VE GOT SOME TIME. KANDOR WILL PUT THE PACKAGE IN HIS SECRET ROOM BEFORE TAKING OFF.
KEEP LOOKING! SHE'S GOTTA BE AROUND HERE SOMEWHERE.
MAYBE SHE DECIDED TO **BLEND** IN TO THE SCENERY TOO.
THEN SHE PICKED THE **WORST POSSIBLE WAY!**
?
?

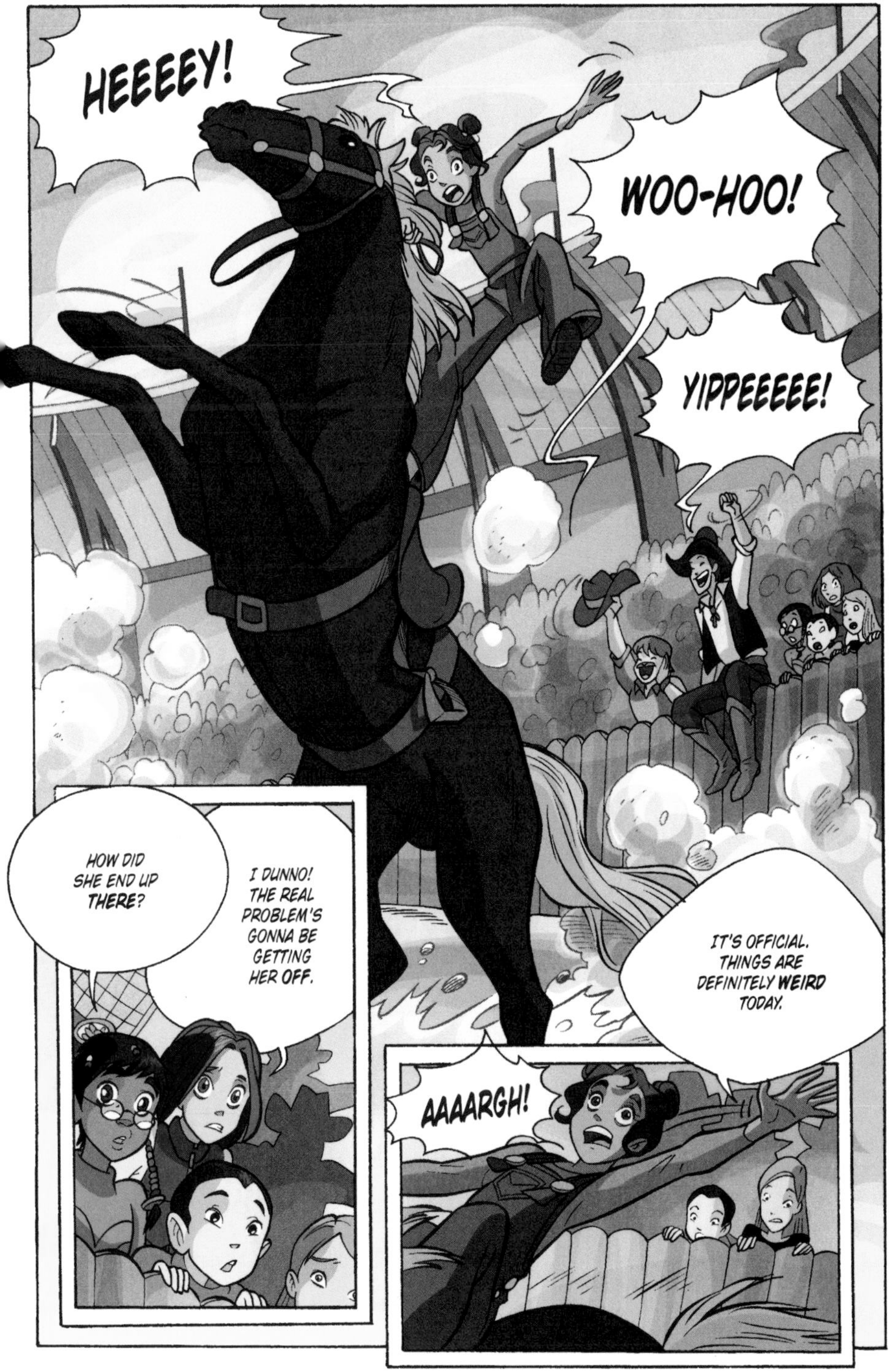
HEEEEY!
WOO-HOO!
YIPPEEEEE!
HOW DID SHE END UP THERE?
I DUNNO! THE REAL PROBLEM'S GONNA BE GETTING HER OFF.
IT'S OFFICIAL. THINGS ARE DEFINITELY WEIRD TODAY.
AAAARGH!

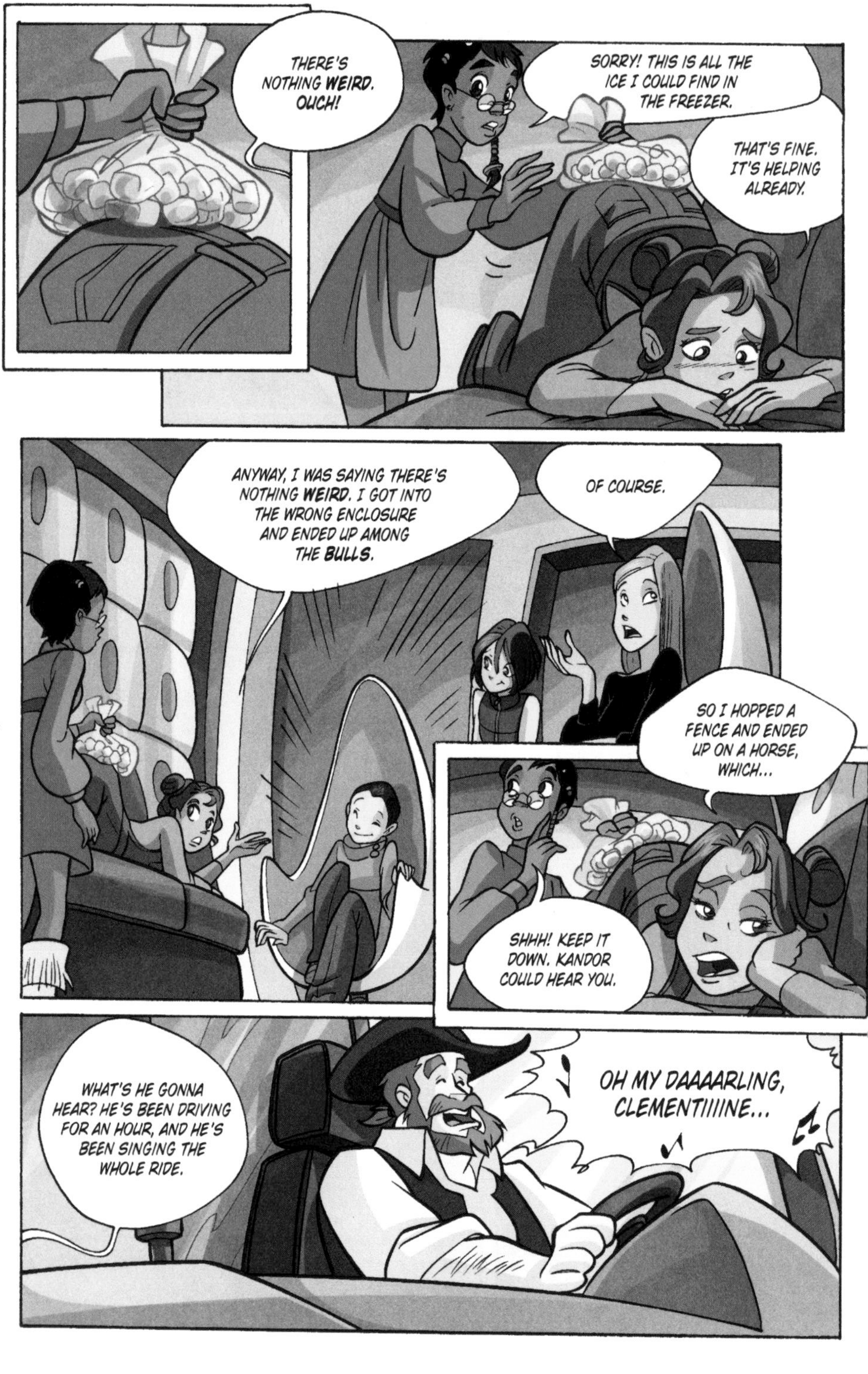
THERE'S NOTHING WEIRD. OUCH!
SORRY! THIS IS ALL THE ICE I COULD FIND IN THE FREEZER.
THAT'S FINE. IT'S HELPING ALREADY.
ANYWAY, I WAS SAYING THERE'S NOTHING WEIRD. I GOT INTO THE WRONG ENCLOSURE AND ENDED UP AMONG THE BULLS.
OF COURSE.
SO I HOPPED A FENCE AND ENDED UP ON A HORSE, WHICH...
SHHH! KEEP IT DOWN. KANDOR COULD HEAR YOU.
WHAT'S HE GONNA HEAR? HE'S BEEN DRIVING FOR AN HOUR, AND HE'S BEEN SINGING THE WHOLE RIDE.
OH MY DAAAARLING, CLEMENTIIIINE...

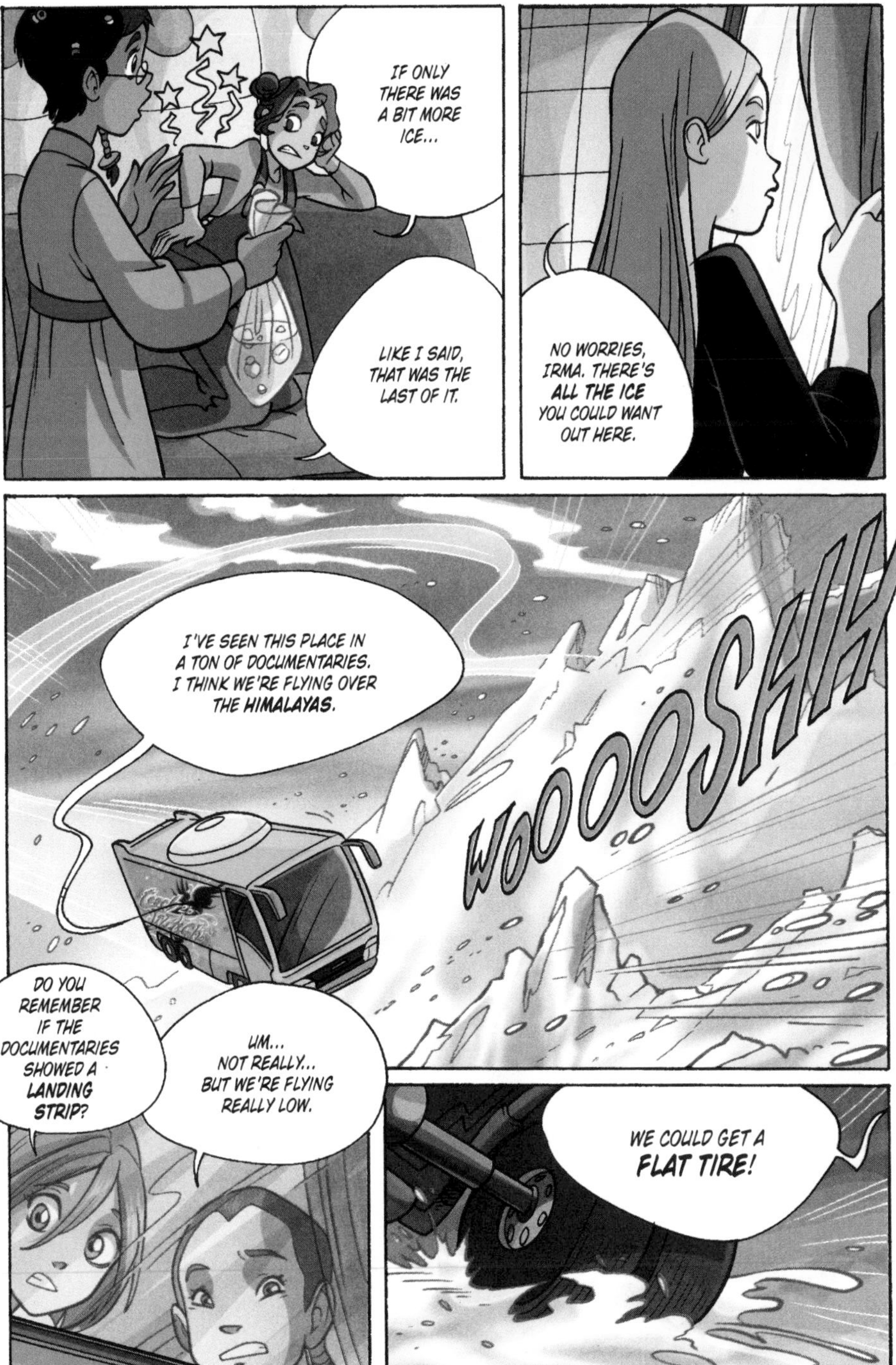

IF ONLY THERE WAS A BIT MORE ICE...
LIKE I SAID, THAT WAS THE LAST OF IT.
NO WORRIES, IRMA. THERE'S ALL THE ICE YOU COULD WANT OUT HERE.
I'VE SEEN THIS PLACE IN A TON OF DOCUMENTARIES. I THINK WE'RE FLYING OVER THE HIMALAYAS.
WOOOOOSHH
DO YOU REMEMBER IF THE DOCUMENTARIES SHOWED A LANDING STRIP?
UM... NOT REALLY... BUT WE'RE FLYING REALLY LOW.
WE COULD GET A FLAT TIRE!

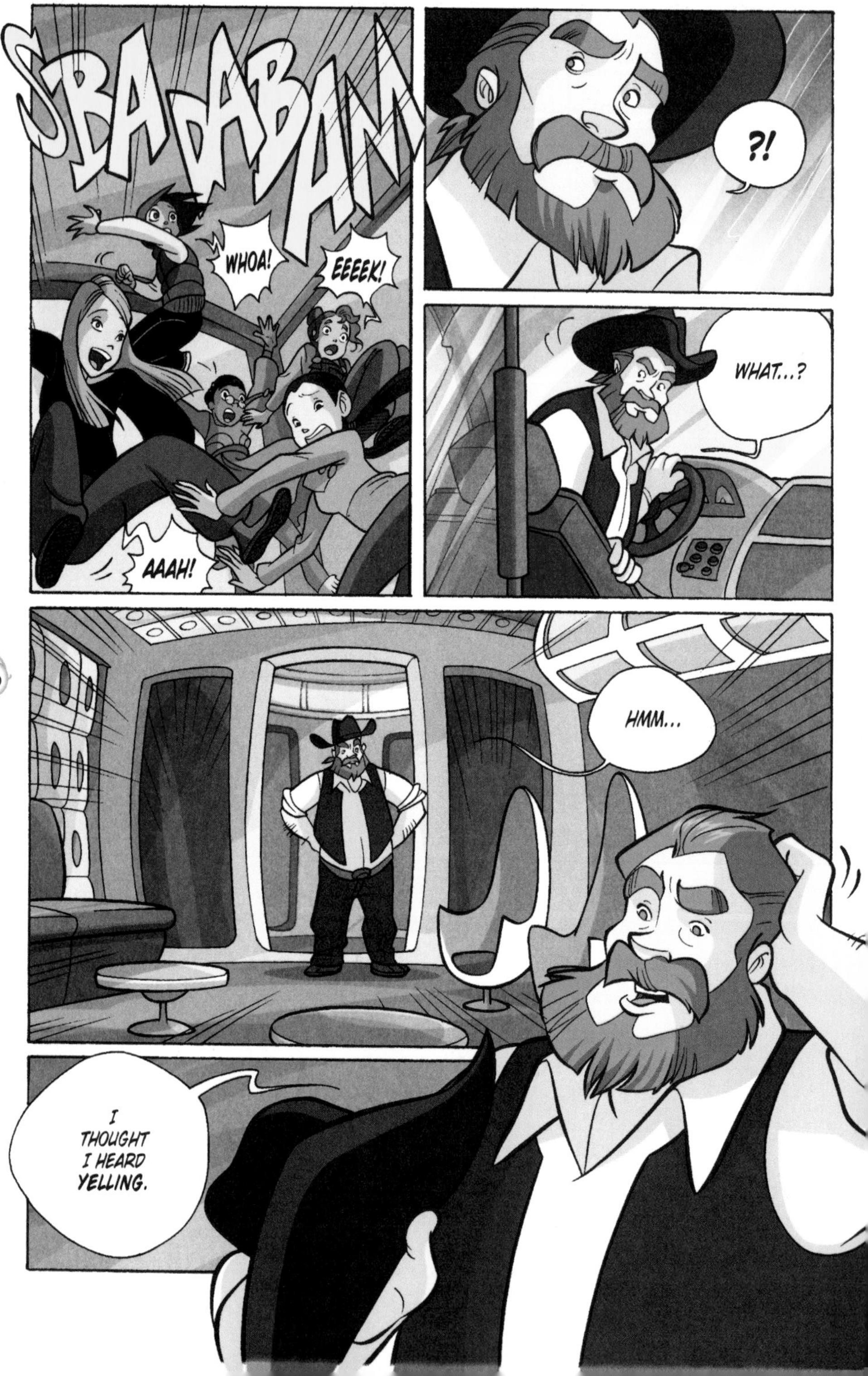
SBADABAM
WHOA!
EEEEK!
AAAH!
?!
WHAT...?
HMM...
I THOUGHT I HEARD YELLING.

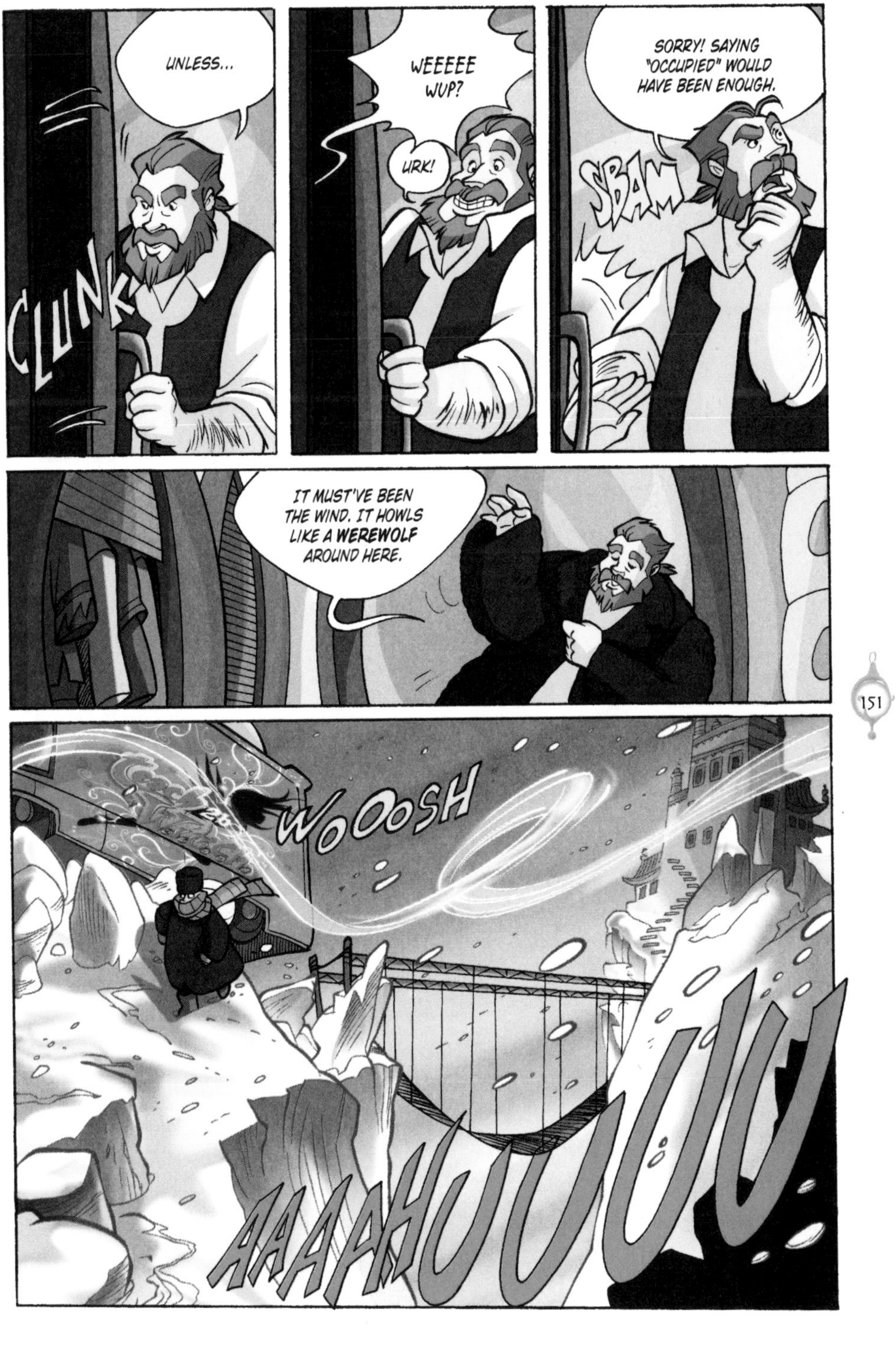
UNLESS...
CLUNK
WEEEEE WUP?
URK!
SORRY! SAYING "OCCUPIED" WOULD HAVE BEEN ENOUGH.
SBAM
IT MUST'VE BEEN THE WIND. IT HOWLS LIKE A **WEREWOLF** AROUND HERE.
WOOOSH
AAAAHUUUUU

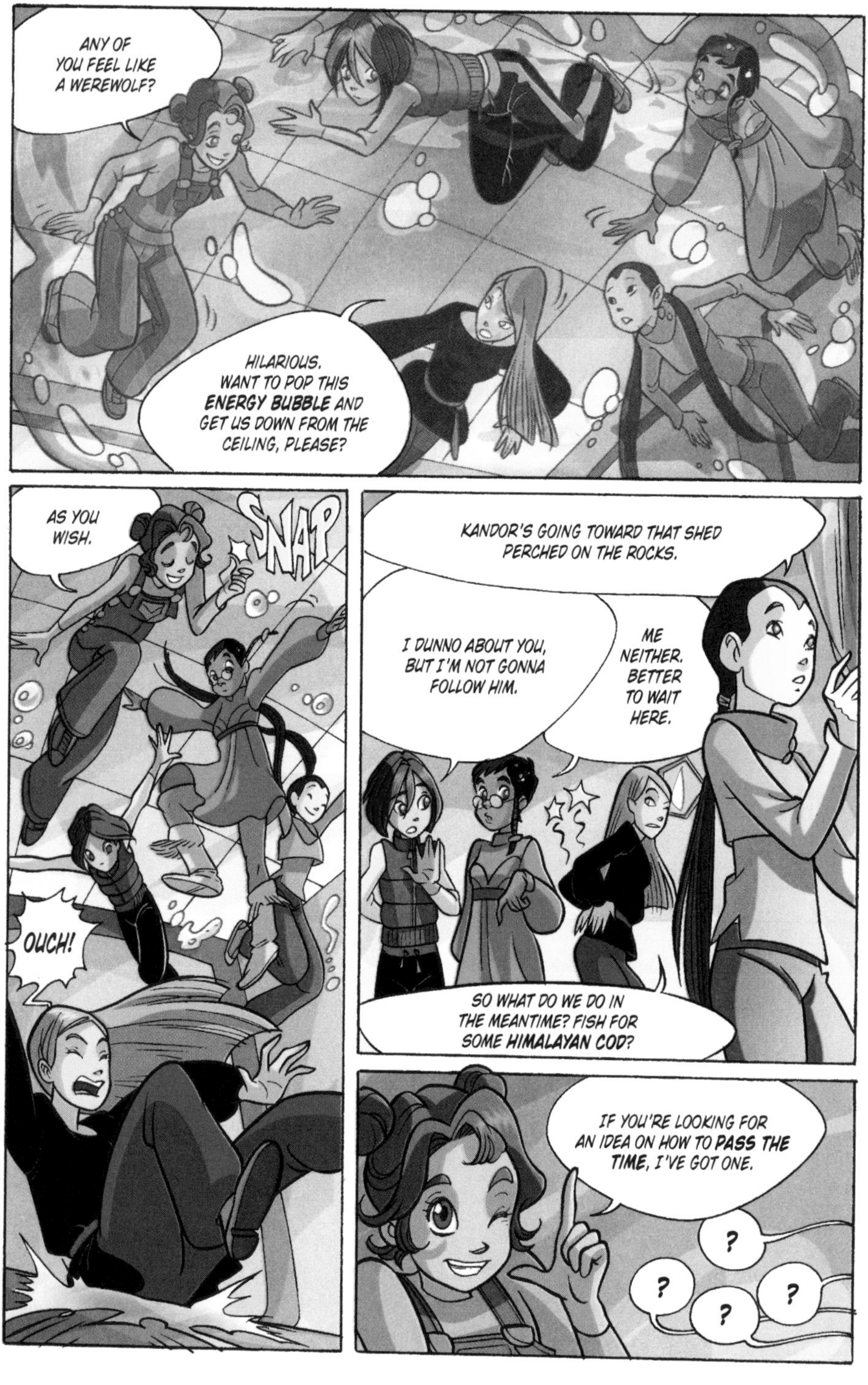

ANY OF YOU FEEL LIKE A WEREWOLF?
HILARIOUS. WANT TO POP THIS **ENERGY BUBBLE** AND GET US DOWN FROM THE CEILING, PLEASE?
AS YOU WISH.
SNAP
OUCH!
KANDOR'S GOING TOWARD THAT SHED PERCHED ON THE ROCKS.
I DUNNO ABOUT YOU, BUT I'M NOT GONNA FOLLOW HIM.
ME NEITHER. BETTER TO WAIT HERE.
SO WHAT DO WE DO IN THE MEANTIME? FISH FOR SOME **HIMALAYAN COD**?
IF YOU'RE LOOKING FOR AN IDEA ON HOW TO **PASS THE TIME**, I'VE GOT ONE.
?
?
?
?

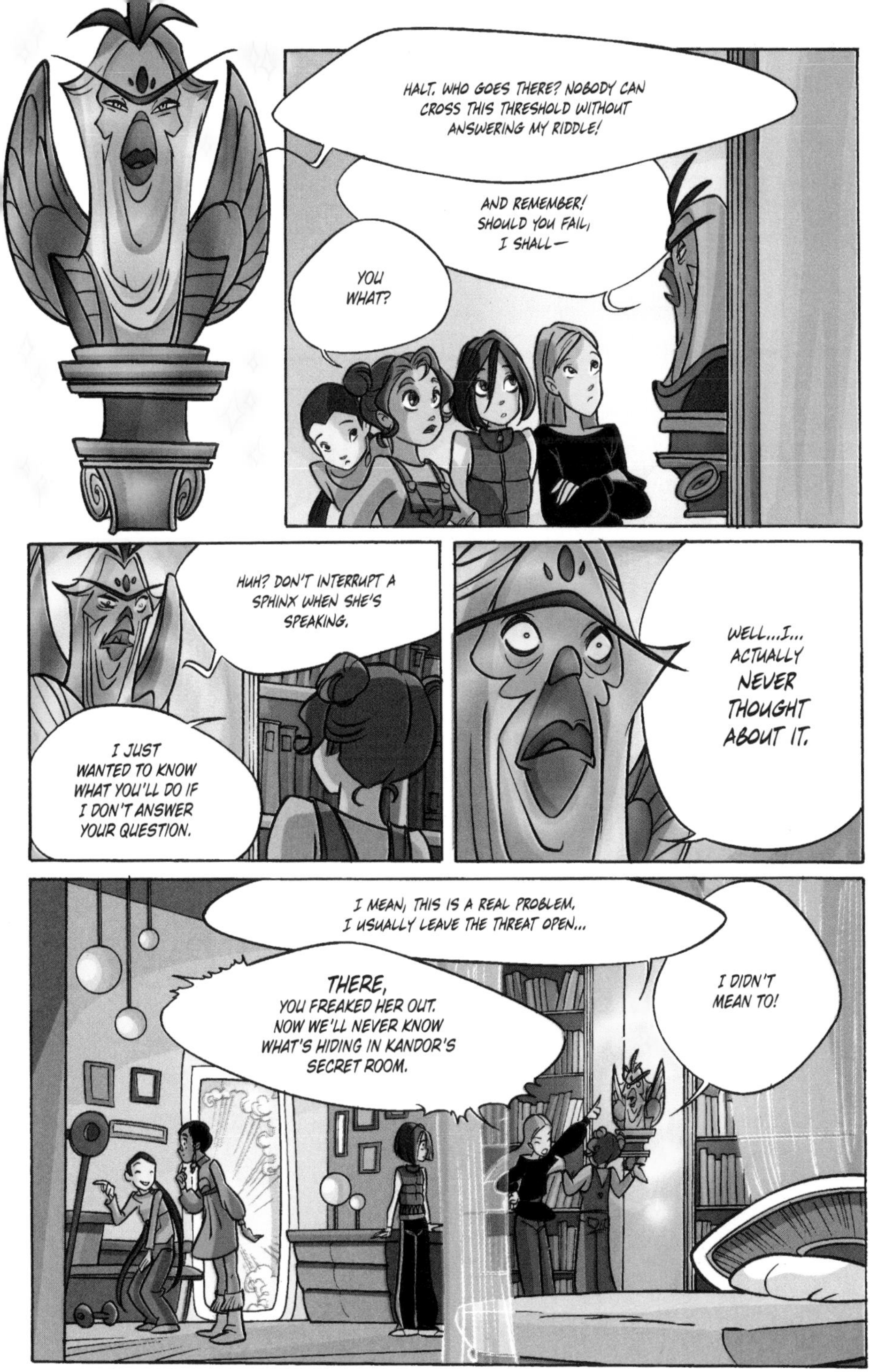
HALT. WHO GOES THERE? NOBODY CAN CROSS THIS THRESHOLD WITHOUT ANSWERING MY RIDDLE!
AND REMEMBER! SHOULD YOU FAIL, I SHALL—
YOU WHAT?
HUH? DON'T INTERRUPT A SPHINX WHEN SHE'S SPEAKING.
I JUST WANTED TO KNOW WHAT YOU'LL DO IF I DON'T ANSWER YOUR QUESTION.
WELL...I... ACTUALLY NEVER THOUGHT ABOUT IT.
I MEAN, THIS IS A REAL PROBLEM. I USUALLY LEAVE THE THREAT OPEN...
THERE, YOU FREAKED HER OUT. NOW WE'LL NEVER KNOW WHAT'S HIDING IN KANDOR'S SECRET ROOM.
I DIDN'T MEAN TO!

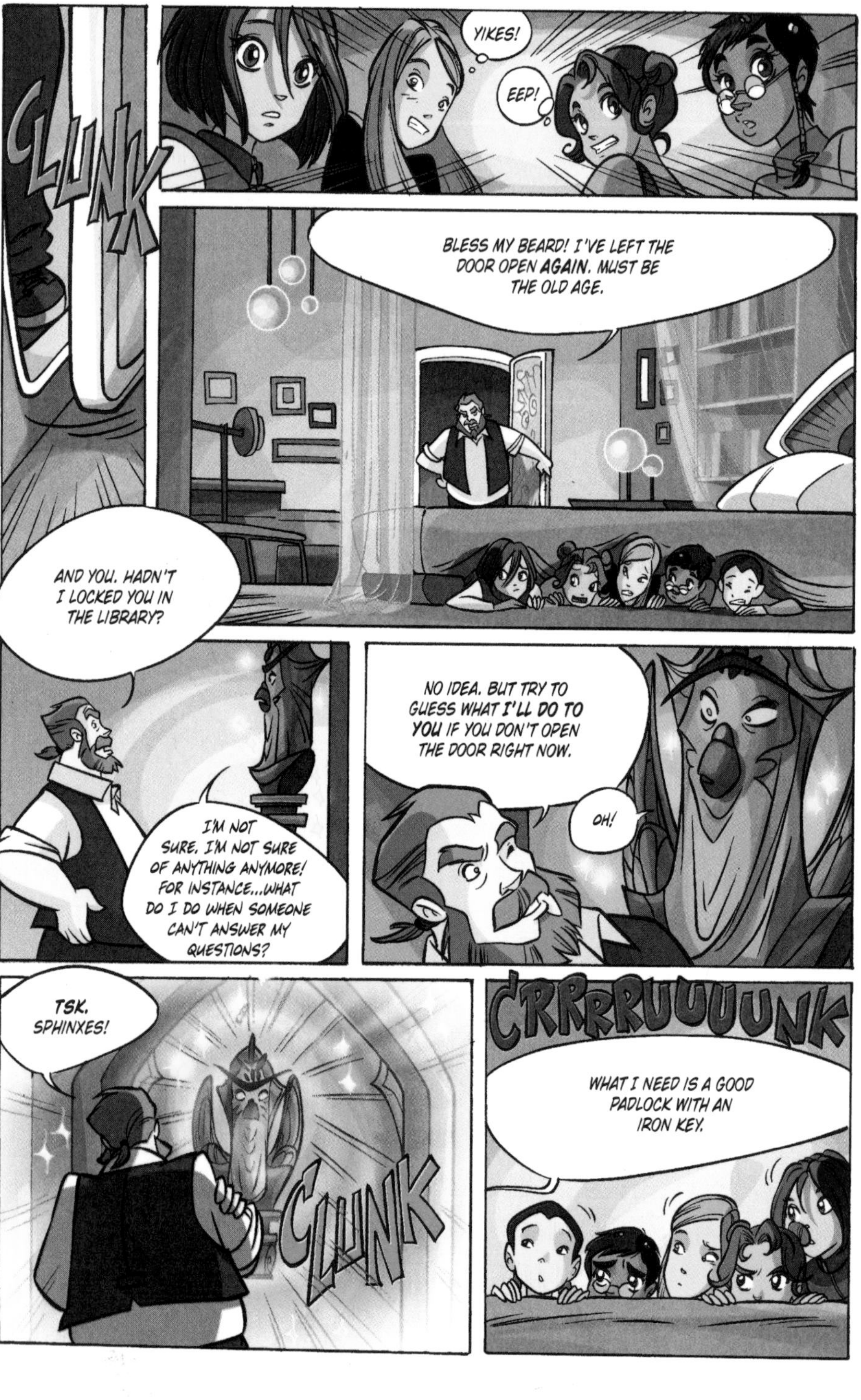
CLUNK
YIKES!
EEP!
BLESS MY BEARD! I'VE LEFT THE DOOR OPEN AGAIN. MUST BE THE OLD AGE.
AND YOU. HADN'T I LOCKED YOU IN THE LIBRARY?
I'M NOT SURE. I'M NOT SURE OF ANYTHING ANYMORE! FOR INSTANCE...WHAT DO I DO WHEN SOMEONE CAN'T ANSWER MY QUESTIONS?
NO IDEA. BUT TRY TO GUESS WHAT I'LL DO TO YOU IF YOU DON'T OPEN THE DOOR RIGHT NOW.
OH!
TSK. SPHINXES!
CLUNK
CRRRRUUUUNK
WHAT I NEED IS A GOOD PADLOCK WITH AN IRON KEY.

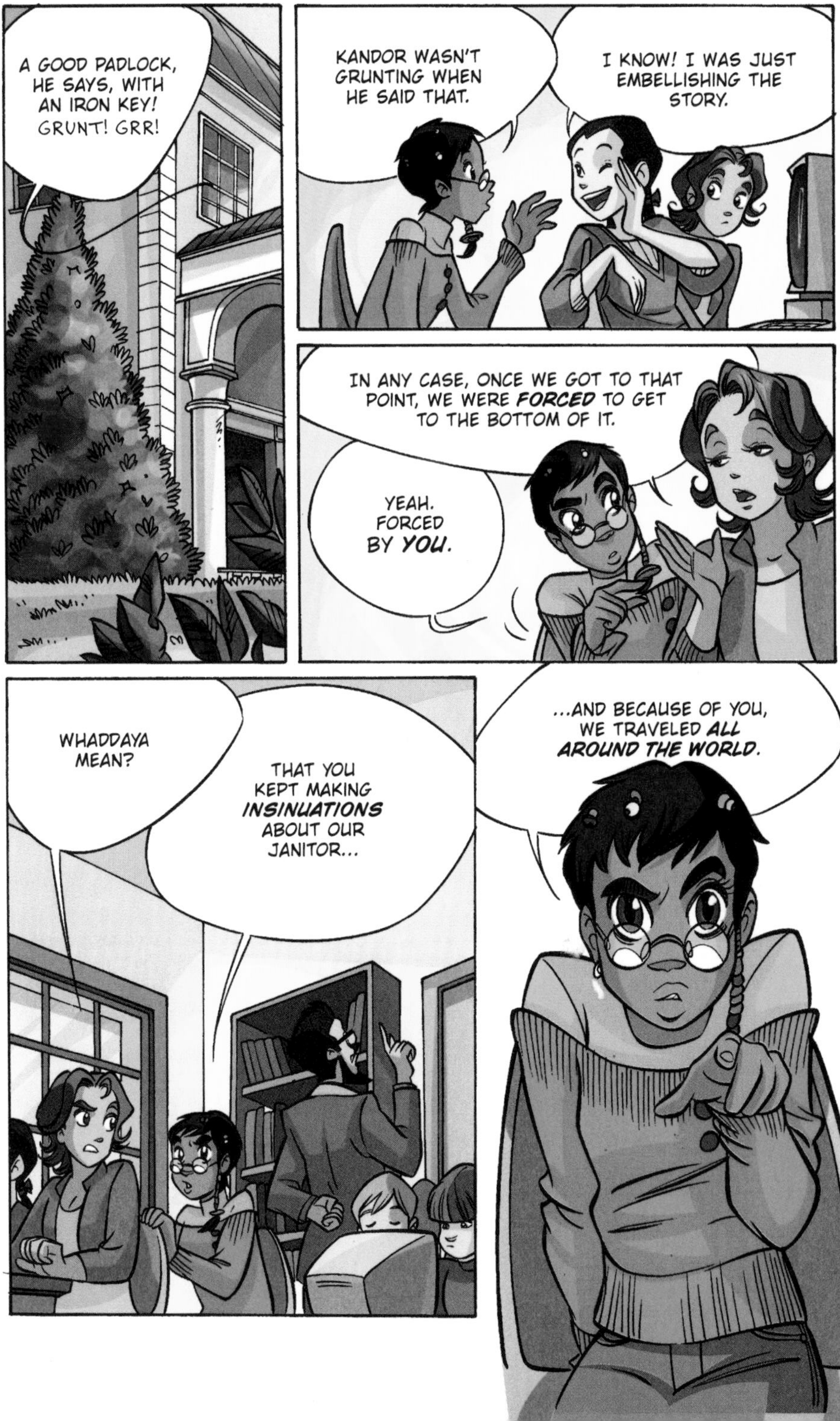
A GOOD PADLOCK, HE SAYS, WITH AN IRON KEY! GRUNT! GRR!
KANDOR WASN'T GRUNTING WHEN HE SAID THAT.
I KNOW! I WAS JUST EMBELLISHING THE STORY.
IN ANY CASE, ONCE WE GOT TO THAT POINT, WE WERE *FORCED* TO GET TO THE BOTTOM OF IT.
YEAH. FORCED BY *YOU*.
WHADDAYA MEAN?
THAT YOU KEPT MAKING *INSINUATIONS* ABOUT OUR JANITOR...
...AND BECAUSE OF YOU, WE TRAVELED *ALL AROUND THE WORLD*.

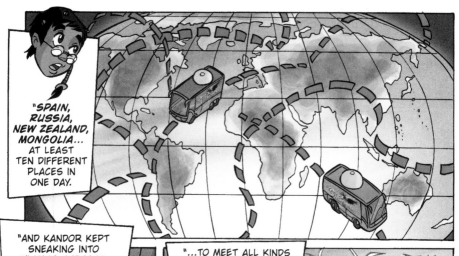

"SPAIN, RUSSIA, NEW ZEALAND, MONGOLIA... AT LEAST TEN DIFFERENT PLACES IN ONE DAY.

"AND KANDOR KEPT SNEAKING INTO WINDING STREETS, HIDDEN MARKETPLACES, AND OBSCURE SHOPS...

"...TO MEET ALL KINDS OF STRANGE PEOPLE AND COLLECT MYSTERIOUS PACKAGES.

"HE ALMOST *BUSTED* US MORE THAN ONCE...

"...AND KEPT TAKING PICTURES OF *NOTHING.*

CLICK

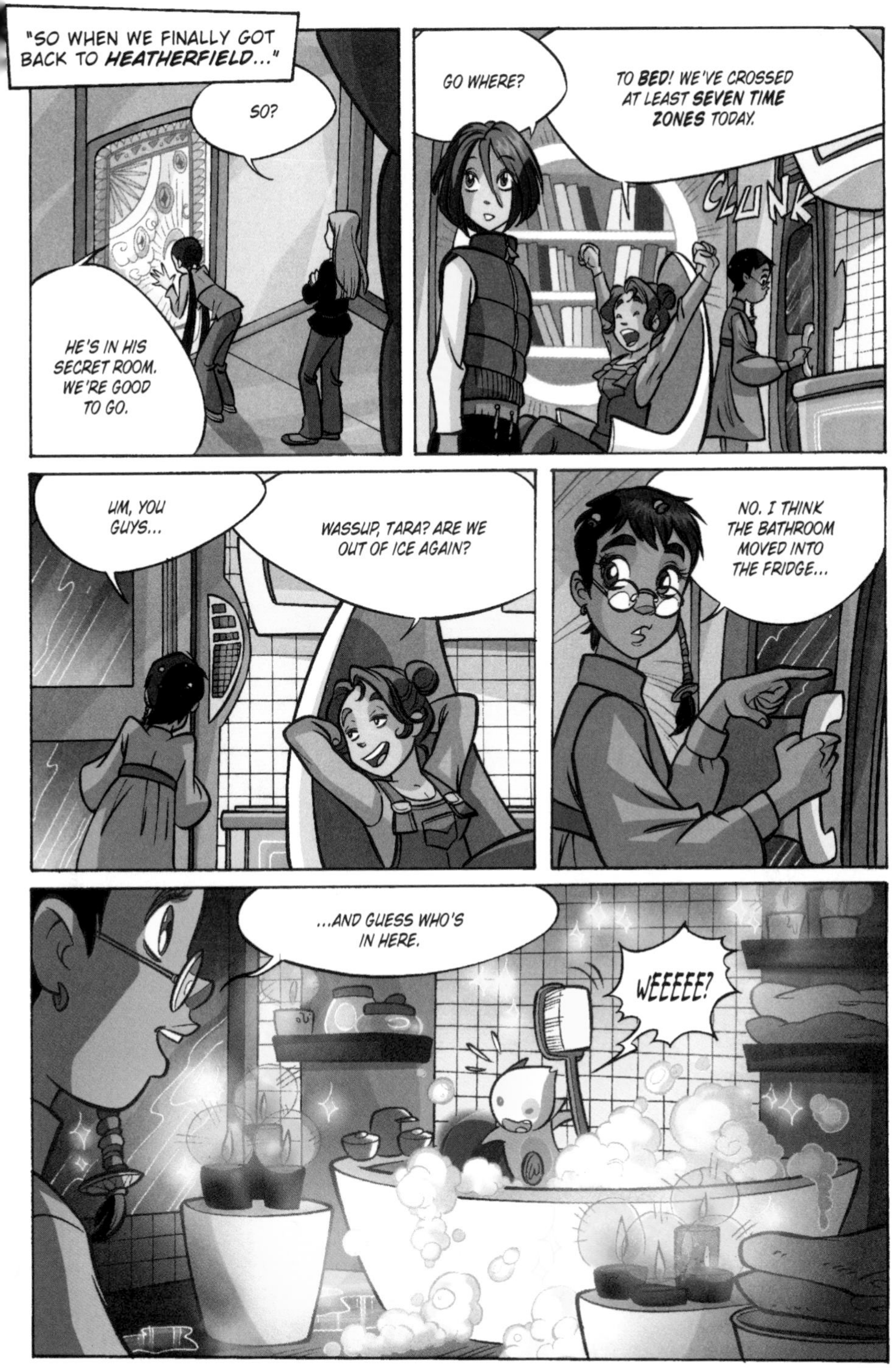
"SO WHEN WE FINALLY GOT BACK TO HEATHERFIELD..."
SO?
HE'S IN HIS SECRET ROOM. WE'RE GOOD TO GO.
GO WHERE?
TO BED! WE'VE CROSSED AT LEAST SEVEN TIME ZONES TODAY.
CLUNK
UM, YOU GUYS...
WASSUP, TARA? ARE WE OUT OF ICE AGAIN?
NO. I THINK THE BATHROOM MOVED INTO THE FRIDGE...
...AND GUESS WHO'S IN HERE.
WEEEEE?

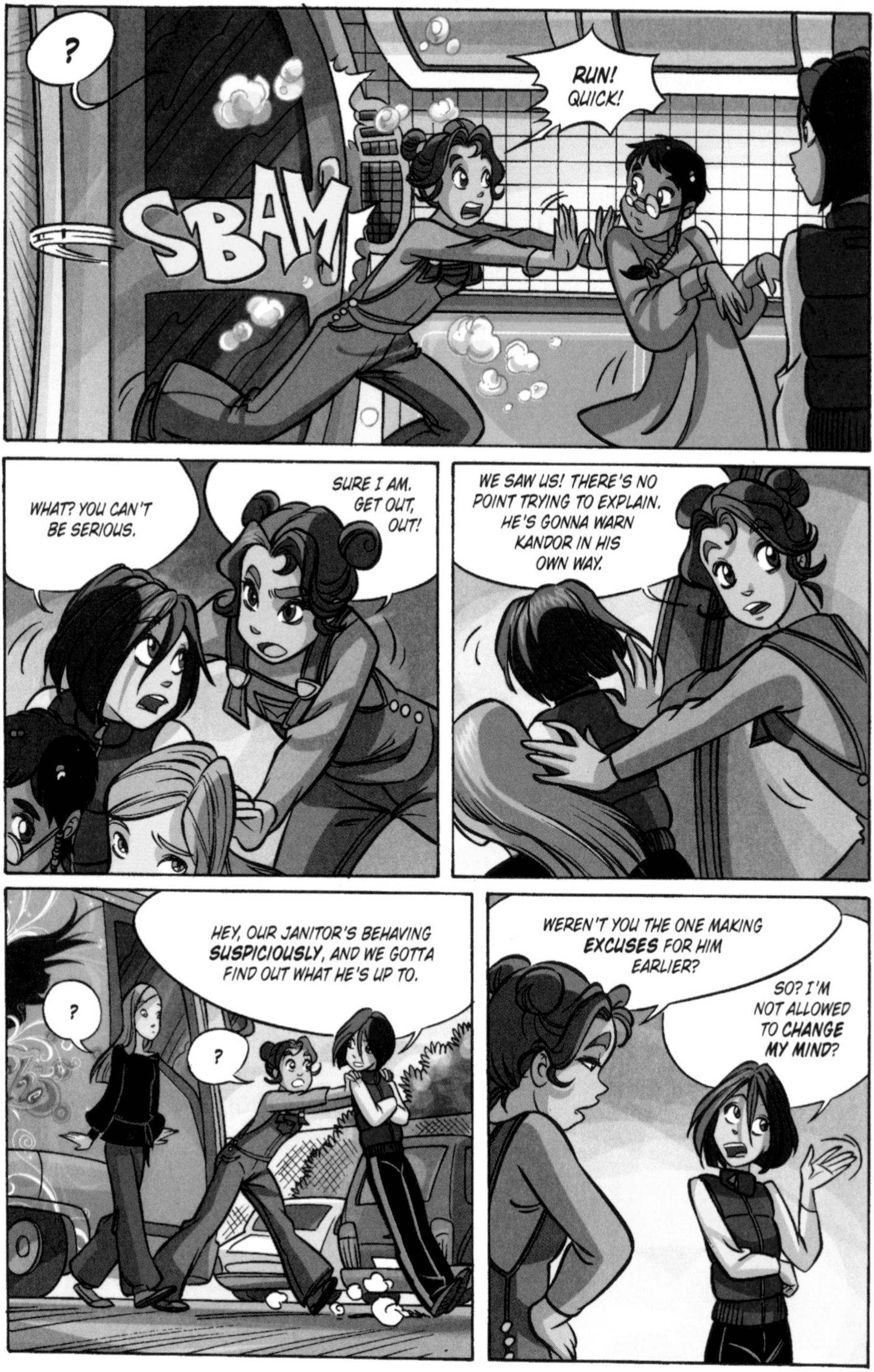
?
RUN! QUICK!
SBAM
WHAT? YOU CAN'T BE SERIOUS.
SURE I AM. GET OUT, OUT!
WE SAW US! THERE'S NO POINT TRYING TO EXPLAIN. HE'S GONNA WARN KANDOR IN HIS OWN WAY.
HEY, OUR JANITOR'S BEHAVING **SUSPICIOUSLY**, AND WE GOTTA FIND OUT WHAT HE'S UP TO.
?
?
WEREN'T YOU THE ONE MAKING **EXCUSES** FOR HIM EARLIER?
SO? I'M NOT ALLOWED TO **CHANGE MY MIND**?

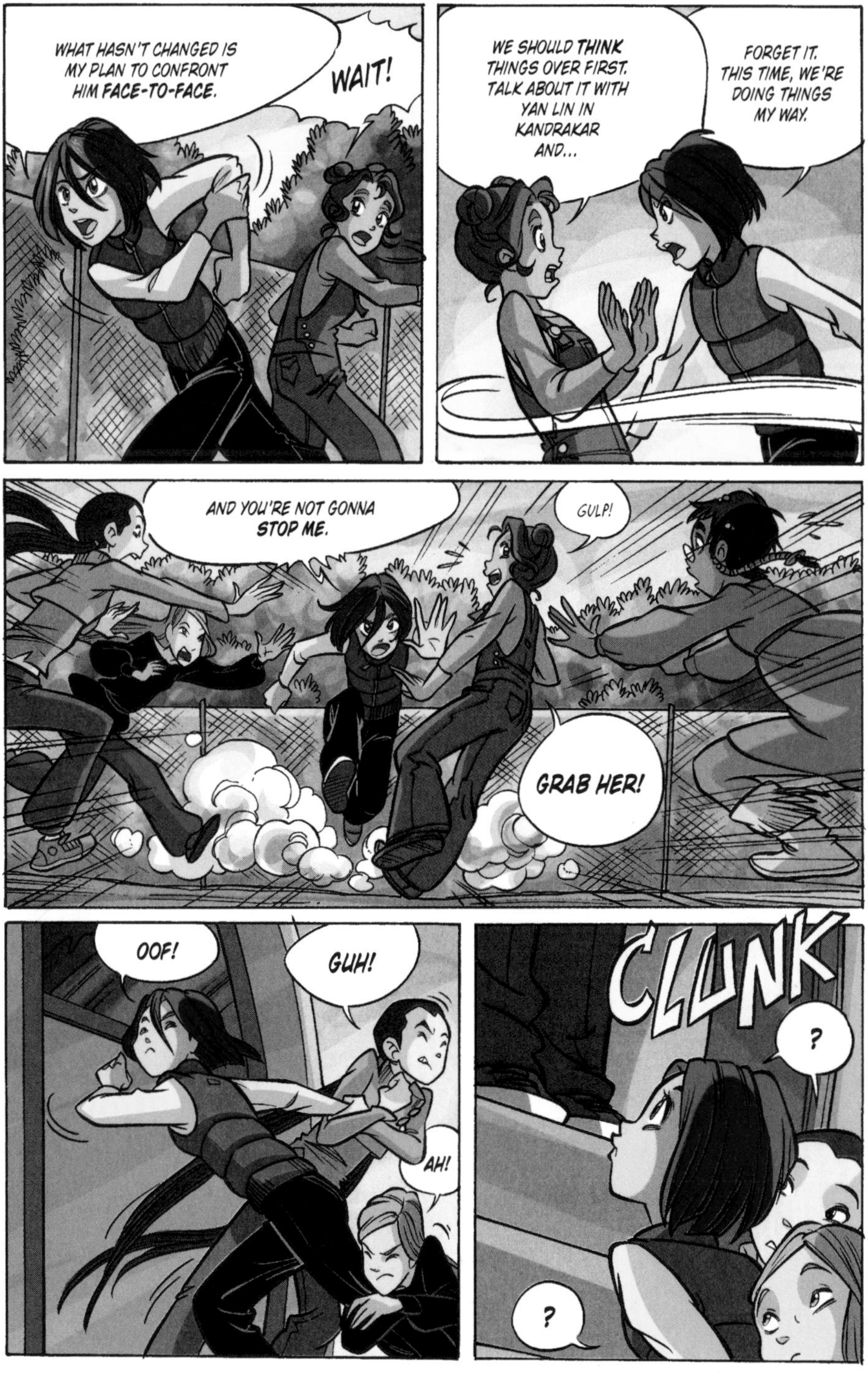
WHAT HASN'T CHANGED IS MY PLAN TO CONFRONT HIM FACE-TO-FACE.
WAIT!
WE SHOULD THINK THINGS OVER FIRST. TALK ABOUT IT WITH YAN LIN IN KANDRAKAR AND...
FORGET IT. THIS TIME, WE'RE DOING THINGS MY WAY.
AND YOU'RE NOT GONNA STOP ME.
GULP!
GRAB HER!
OOF!
GUH!
AH!
CLUNK
?
?

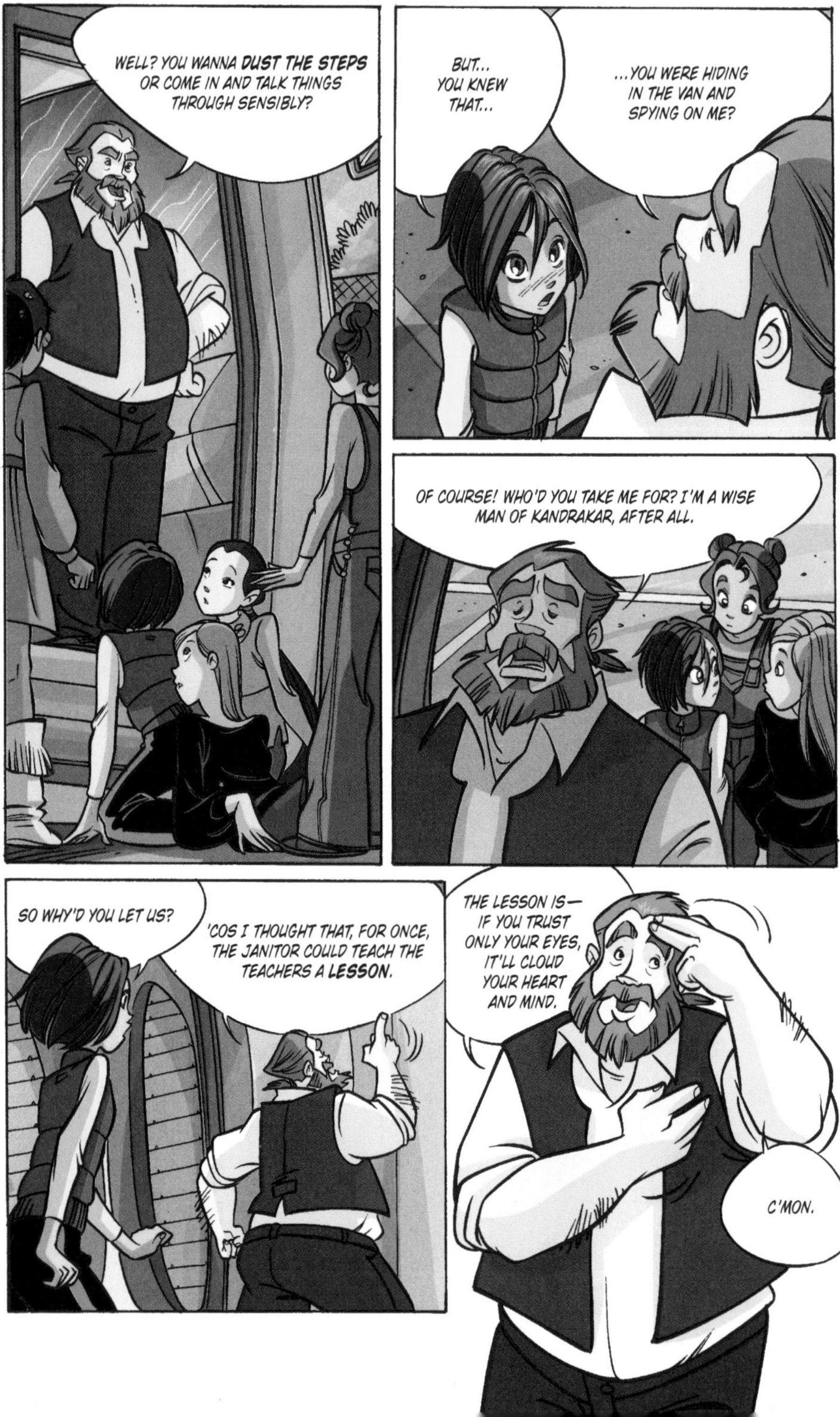
WELL? YOU WANNA **DUST THE STEPS** OR COME IN AND TALK THINGS THROUGH SENSIBLY?
BUT... YOU KNEW THAT...
...YOU WERE HIDING IN THE VAN AND SPYING ON ME?
OF COURSE! WHO'D YOU TAKE ME FOR? I'M A WISE MAN OF KANDRAKAR, AFTER ALL.
SO WHY'D YOU LET US?
'COS I THOUGHT THAT, FOR ONCE, THE JANITOR COULD TEACH THE TEACHERS A **LESSON**.
THE LESSON IS— IF YOU TRUST ONLY YOUR EYES, IT'LL CLOUD YOUR HEART AND MIND.
C'MON.

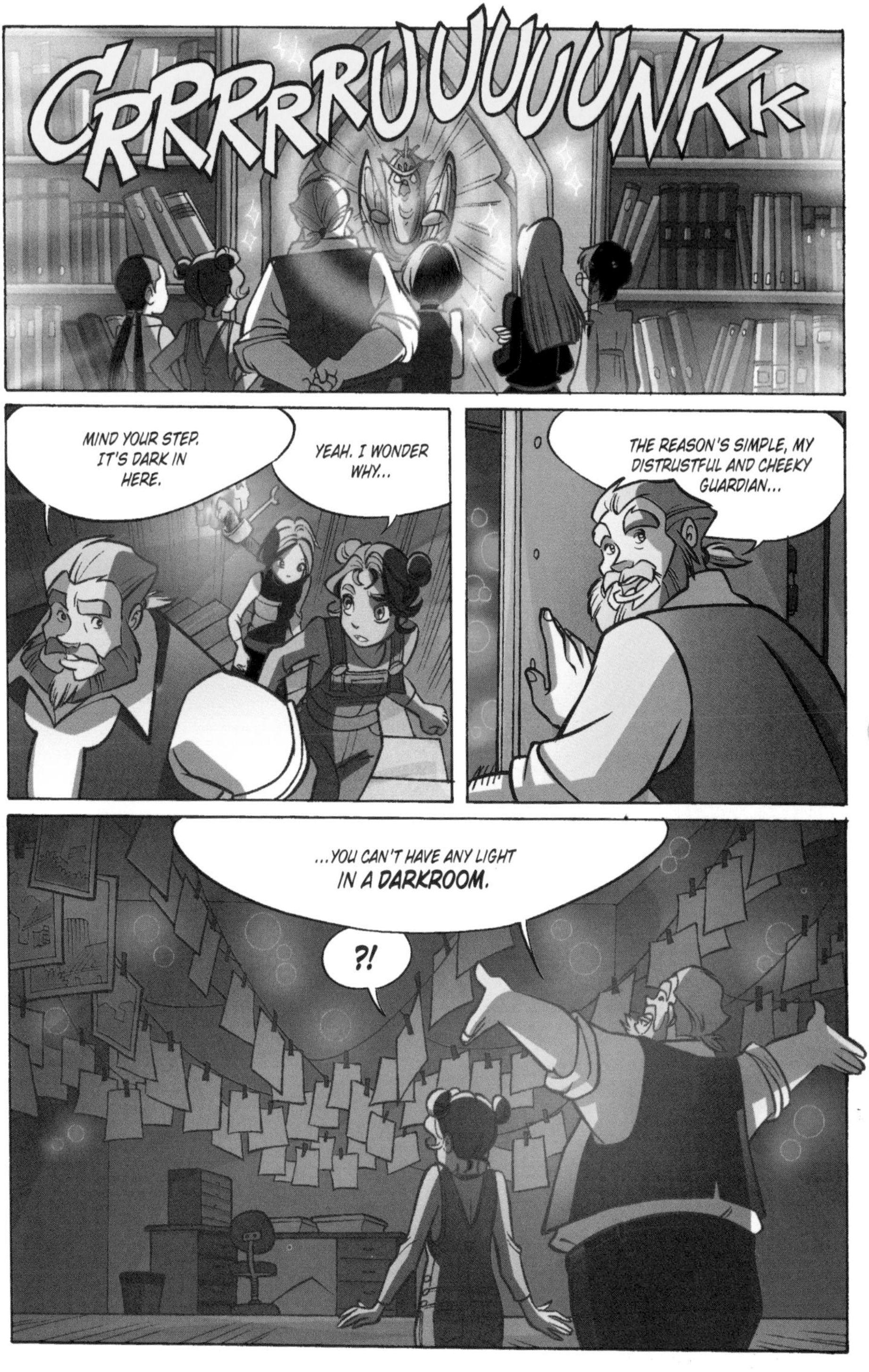
CRRRRRUUUUUNKK
MIND YOUR STEP. IT'S DARK IN HERE.
YEAH. I WONDER WHY...
THE REASON'S SIMPLE, MY DISTRUSTFUL AND CHEEKY GUARDIAN...
...YOU CAN'T HAVE ANY LIGHT IN A DARKROOM.
?!

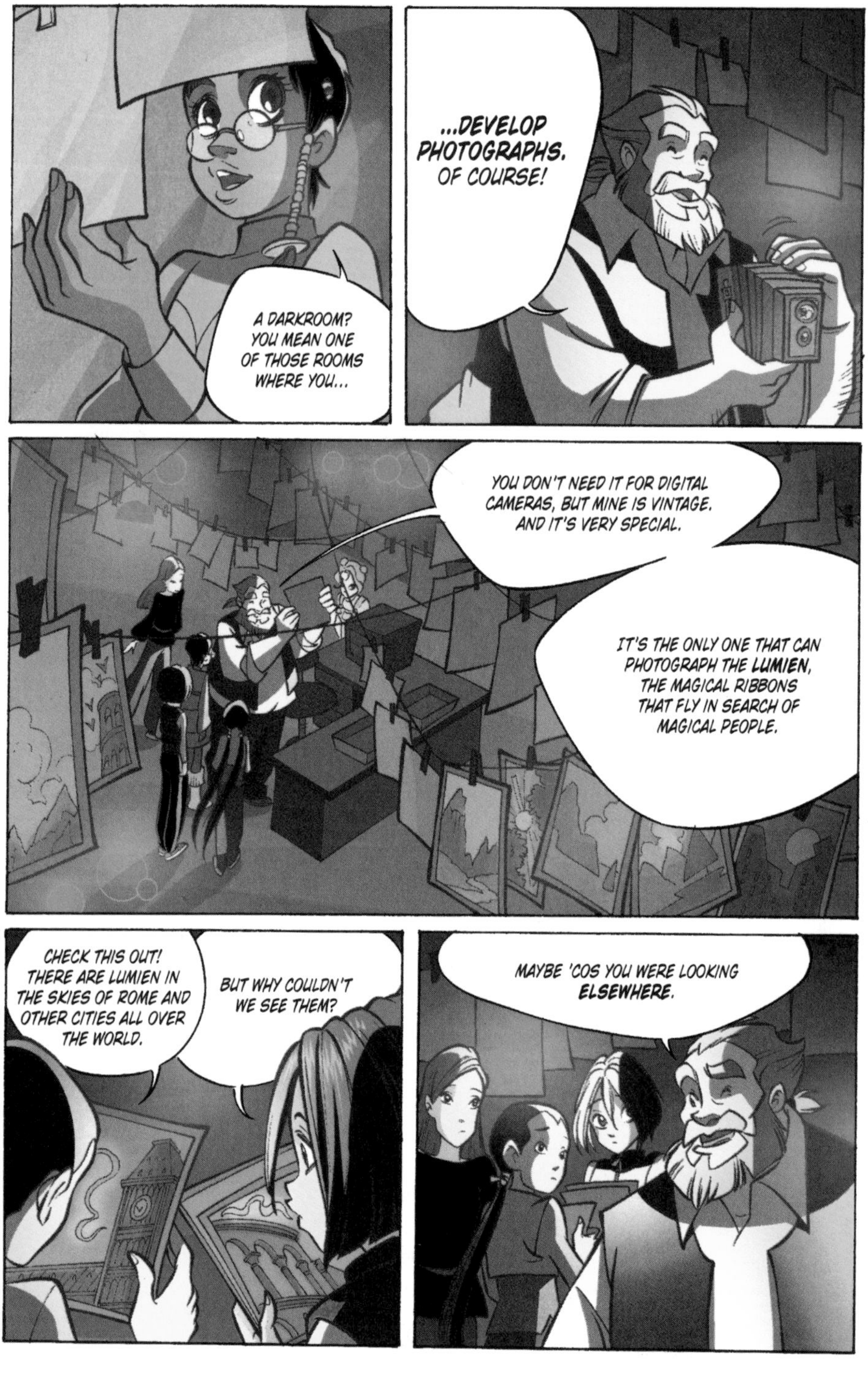
A DARKROOM? YOU MEAN ONE OF THOSE ROOMS WHERE YOU...
...DEVELOP PHOTOGRAPHS. OF COURSE!
YOU DON'T NEED IT FOR DIGITAL CAMERAS, BUT MINE IS VINTAGE. AND IT'S VERY SPECIAL.
IT'S THE ONLY ONE THAT CAN PHOTOGRAPH THE LUMIEN, THE MAGICAL RIBBONS THAT FLY IN SEARCH OF MAGICAL PEOPLE.
CHECK THIS OUT! THERE ARE LUMIEN IN THE SKIES OF ROME AND OTHER CITIES ALL OVER THE WORLD.
BUT WHY COULDN'T WE SEE THEM?
MAYBE 'COS YOU WERE LOOKING ELSEWHERE.

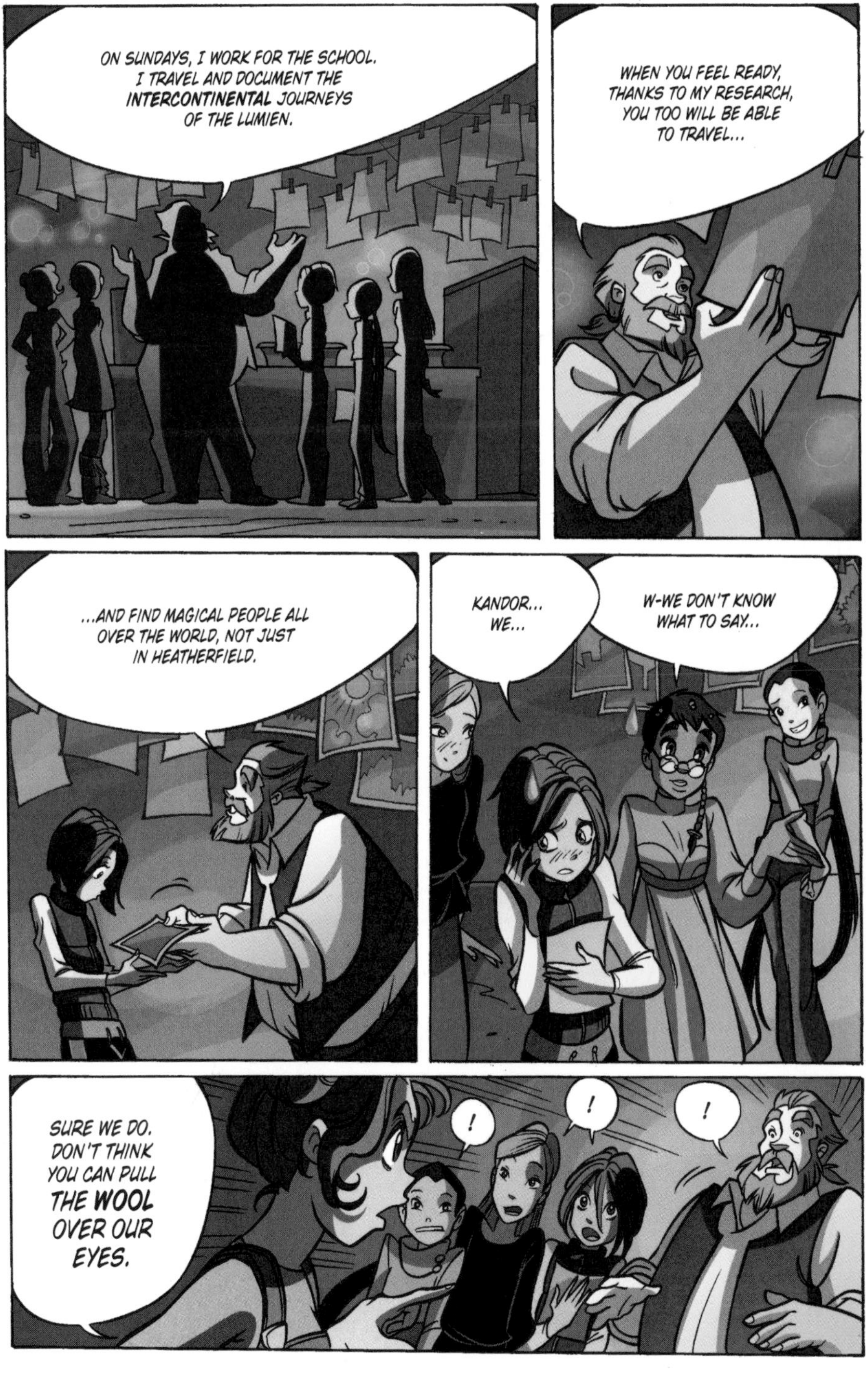
ON SUNDAYS, I WORK FOR THE SCHOOL. I TRAVEL AND DOCUMENT THE **INTERCONTINENTAL** JOURNEYS OF THE LUMIEN.
WHEN YOU FEEL READY, THANKS TO MY RESEARCH, YOU TOO WILL BE ABLE TO TRAVEL...
...AND FIND MAGICAL PEOPLE ALL OVER THE WORLD, NOT JUST IN HEATHERFIELD.
KANDOR... WE...
W-WE DON'T KNOW WHAT TO SAY...
SURE WE DO. DON'T THINK YOU CAN PULL **THE WOOL** OVER OUR EYES.
!
!
!

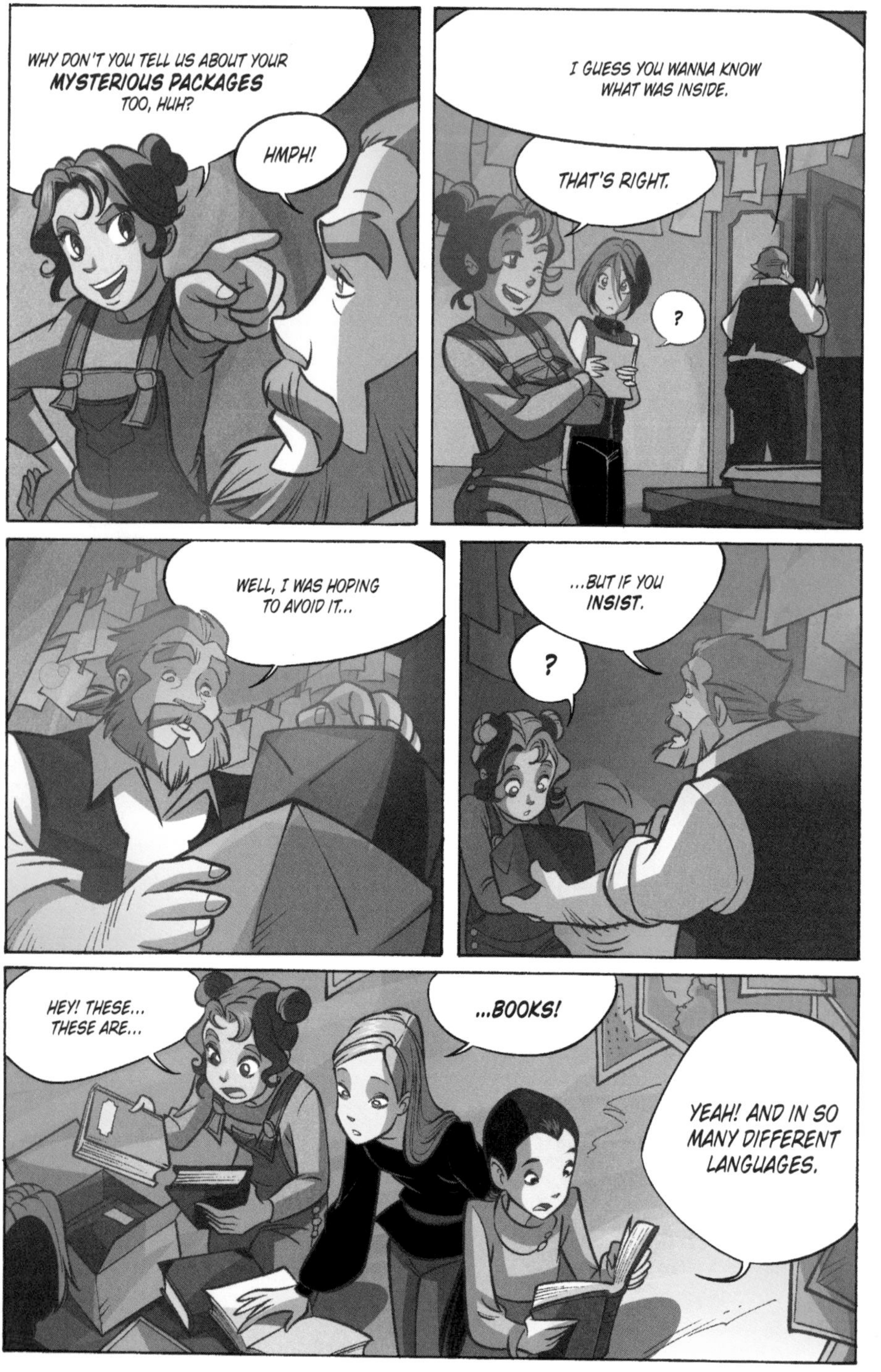
WHY DON'T YOU TELL US ABOUT YOUR **MYSTERIOUS PACKAGES** TOO, HUH?
HMPH!
I GUESS YOU WANNA KNOW WHAT WAS INSIDE.
THAT'S RIGHT.
?
WELL, I WAS HOPING TO AVOID IT...
...BUT IF YOU **INSIST**.
?
HEY! THESE... THESE ARE...
...BOOKS!
YEAH! AND IN SO MANY DIFFERENT LANGUAGES.

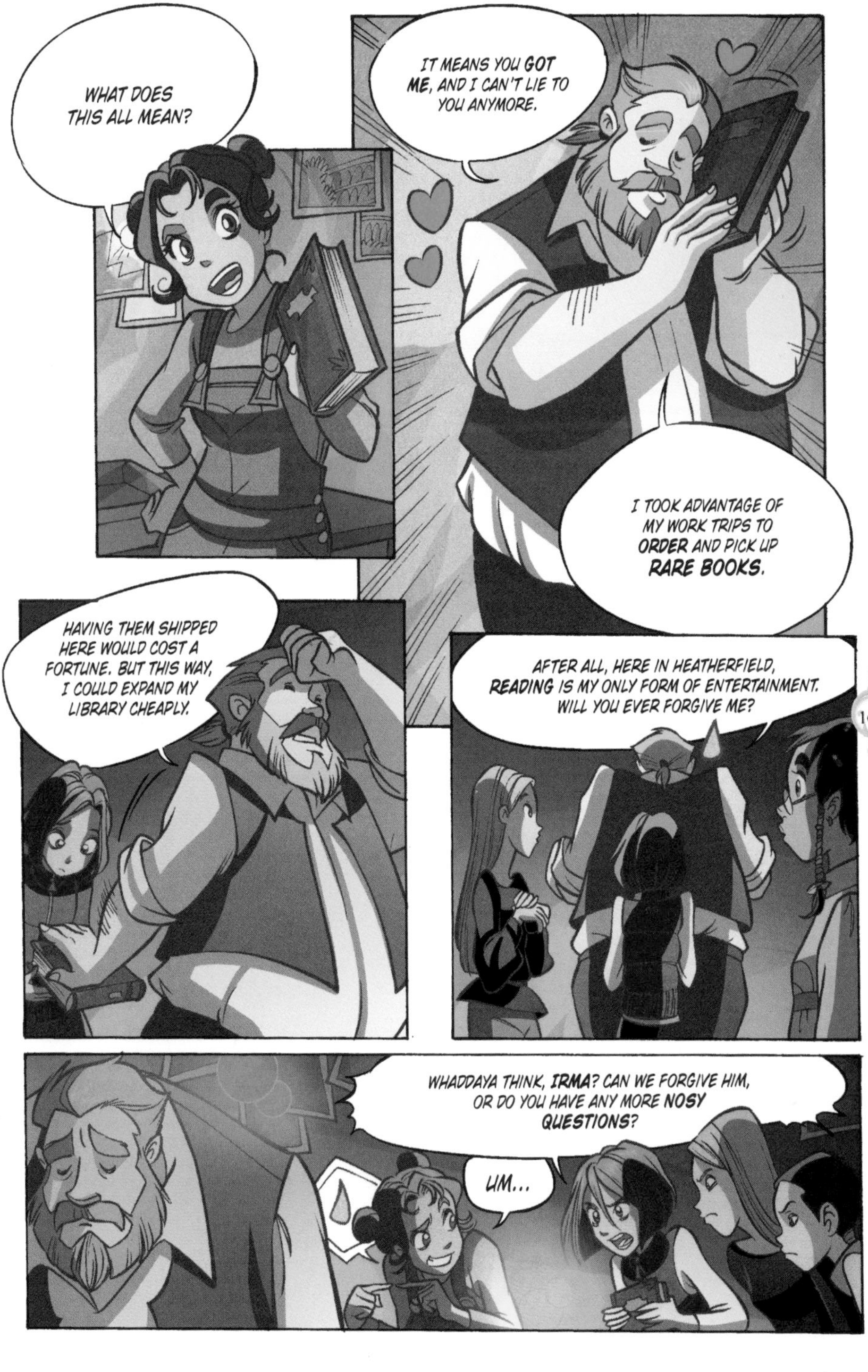
WHAT DOES THIS ALL MEAN?
IT MEANS YOU GOT ME, AND I CAN'T LIE TO YOU ANYMORE.
I TOOK ADVANTAGE OF MY WORK TRIPS TO ORDER AND PICK UP RARE BOOKS.
HAVING THEM SHIPPED HERE WOULD COST A FORTUNE. BUT THIS WAY, I COULD EXPAND MY LIBRARY CHEAPLY.
AFTER ALL, HERE IN HEATHERFIELD, READING IS MY ONLY FORM OF ENTERTAINMENT. WILL YOU EVER FORGIVE ME?
WHADDAYA THINK, IRMA? CAN WE FORGIVE HIM, OR DO YOU HAVE ANY MORE NOSY QUESTIONS?
UM...

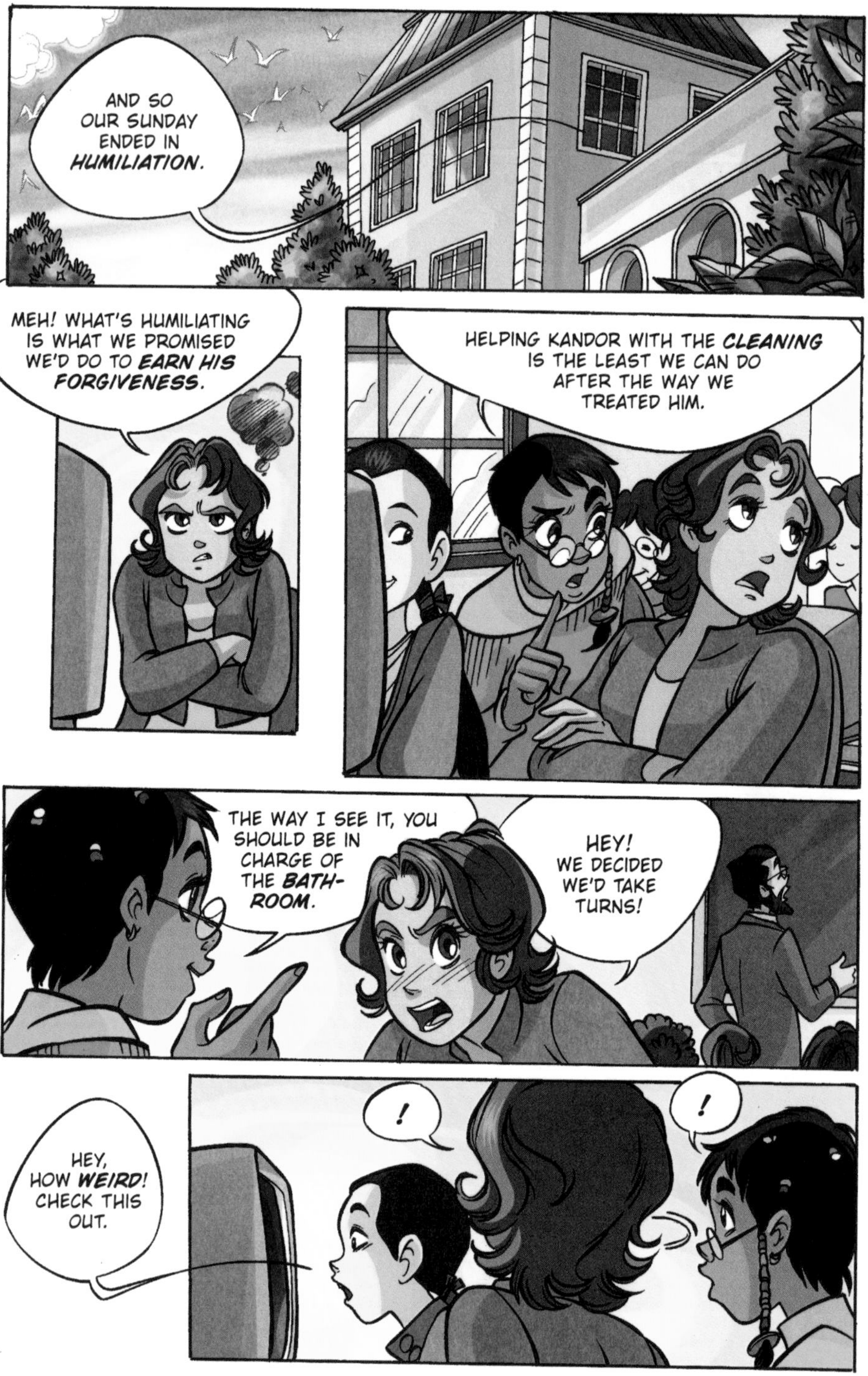
AND SO OUR SUNDAY ENDED IN HUMILIATION.
MEH! WHAT'S HUMILIATING IS WHAT WE PROMISED WE'D DO TO EARN HIS FORGIVENESS.
HELPING KANDOR WITH THE CLEANING IS THE LEAST WE CAN DO AFTER THE WAY WE TREATED HIM.
THE WAY I SEE IT, YOU SHOULD BE IN CHARGE OF THE BATH-ROOM.
HEY! WE DECIDED WE'D TAKE TURNS!
HEY, HOW WEIRD! CHECK THIS OUT.
!
!

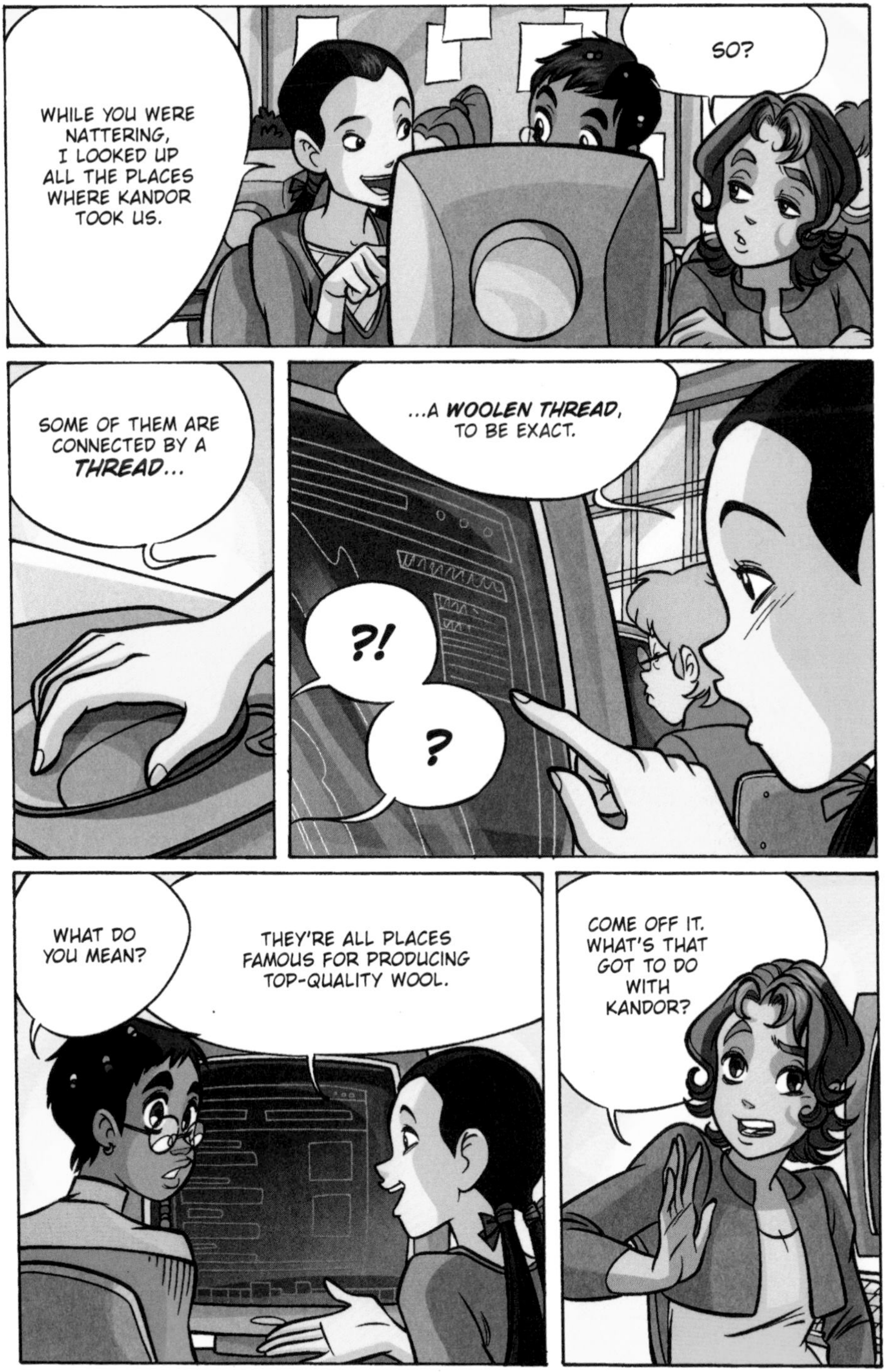
WHILE YOU WERE NATTERING, I LOOKED UP ALL THE PLACES WHERE KANDOR TOOK US.
SO?
SOME OF THEM ARE CONNECTED BY A THREAD...
...A WOOLEN THREAD, TO BE EXACT.
?!
?
WHAT DO YOU MEAN?
THEY'RE ALL PLACES FAMOUS FOR PRODUCING TOP-QUALITY WOOL.
COME OFF IT. WHAT'S THAT GOT TO DO WITH KANDOR?

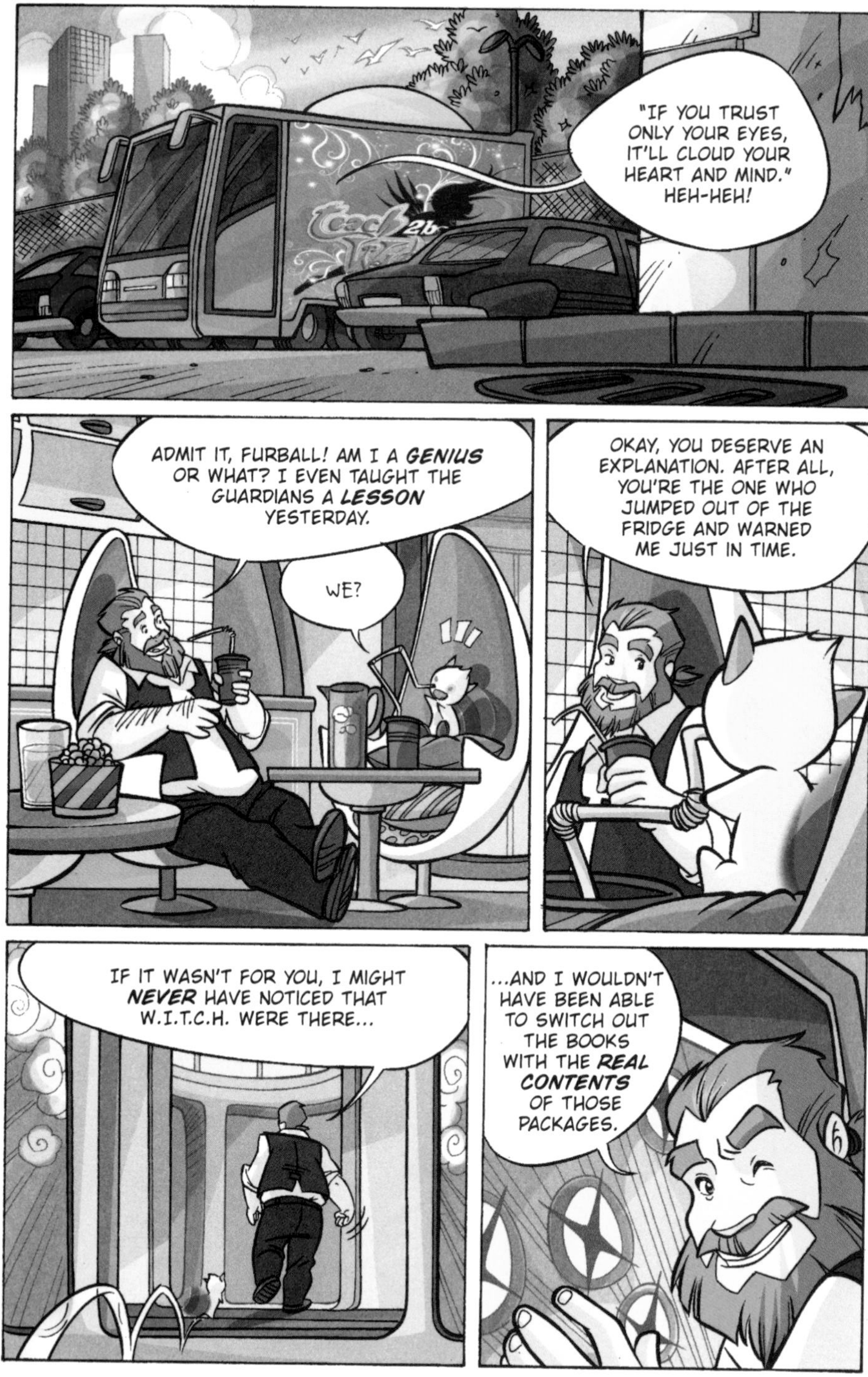
"IF YOU TRUST ONLY YOUR EYES, IT'LL CLOUD YOUR HEART AND MIND." HEH-HEH!
ADMIT IT, FURBALL! AM I A GENIUS OR WHAT? I EVEN TAUGHT THE GUARDIANS A LESSON YESTERDAY.
WE?
OKAY, YOU DESERVE AN EXPLANATION. AFTER ALL, YOU'RE THE ONE WHO JUMPED OUT OF THE FRIDGE AND WARNED ME JUST IN TIME.
IF IT WASN'T FOR YOU, I MIGHT NEVER HAVE NOTICED THAT W.I.T.C.H. WERE THERE...
...AND I WOULDN'T HAVE BEEN ABLE TO SWITCH OUT THE BOOKS WITH THE REAL CONTENTS OF THOSE PACKAGES.

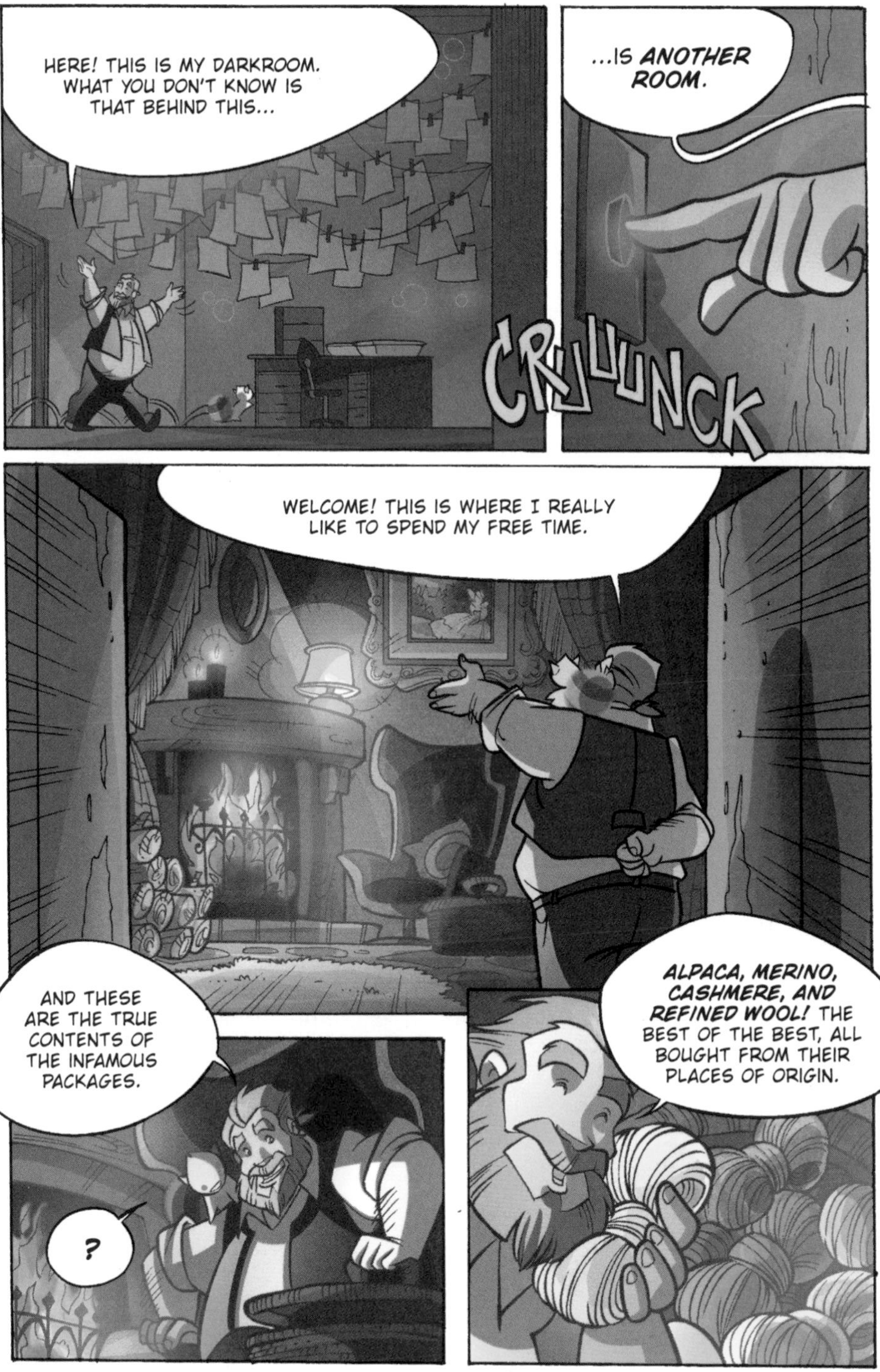
HERE! THIS IS MY DARKROOM. WHAT YOU DON'T KNOW IS THAT BEHIND THIS...
...IS ANOTHER ROOM.
CRUUUNCK
WELCOME! THIS IS WHERE I REALLY LIKE TO SPEND MY FREE TIME.
AND THESE ARE THE TRUE CONTENTS OF THE INFAMOUS PACKAGES.
?
ALPACA, MERINO, CASHMERE, AND REFINED WOOL! THE BEST OF THE BEST, ALL BOUGHT FROM THEIR PLACES OF ORIGIN.

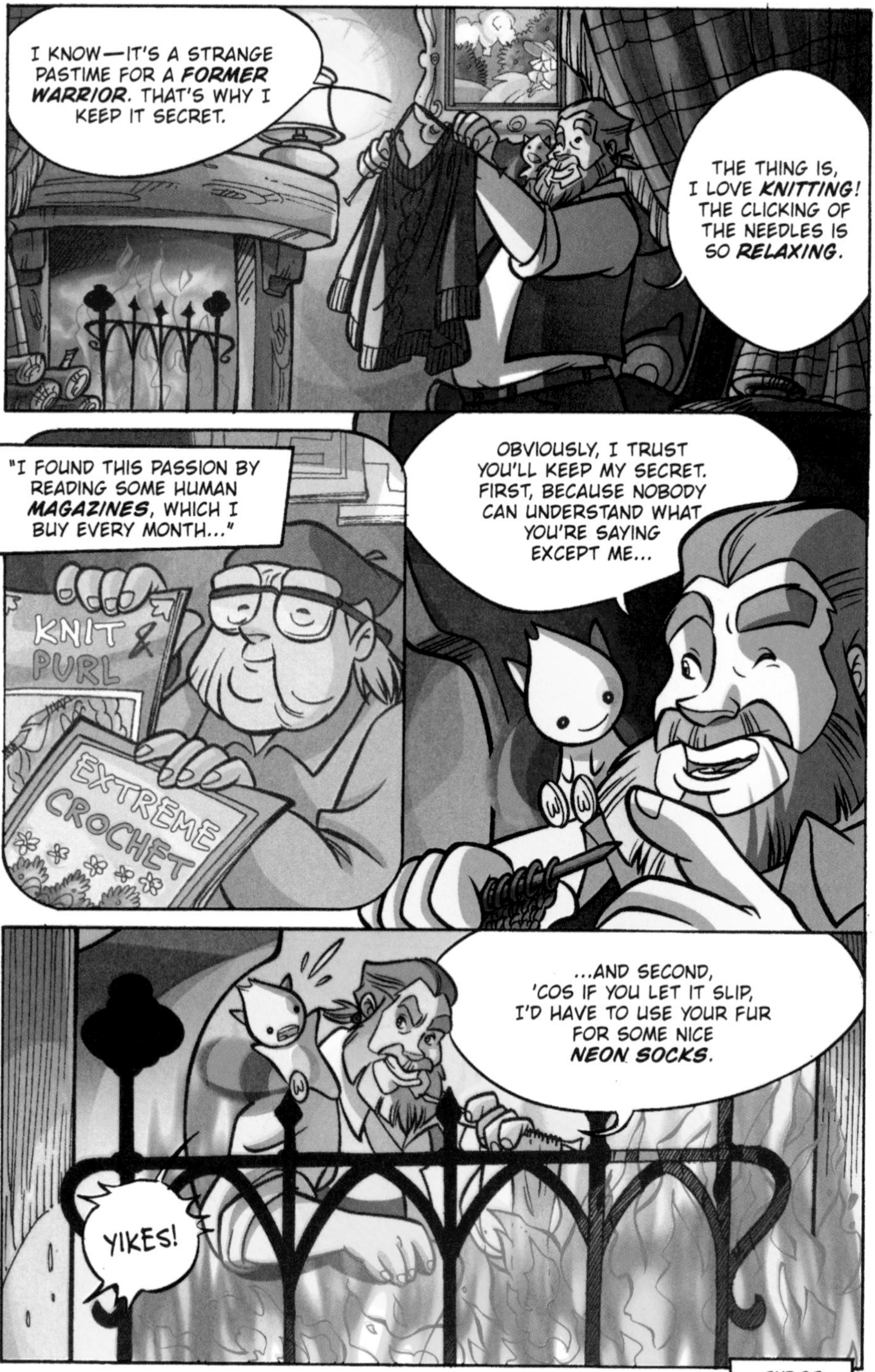

I KNOW—IT'S A STRANGE PASTIME FOR A FORMER WARRIOR. THAT'S WHY I KEEP IT SECRET.
THE THING IS, I LOVE KNITTING! THE CLICKING OF THE NEEDLES IS SO RELAXING.
"I FOUND THIS PASSION BY READING SOME HUMAN MAGAZINES, WHICH I BUY EVERY MONTH..."
KNIT & PURL
EXTREME CROCHET
OBVIOUSLY, I TRUST YOU'LL KEEP MY SECRET. FIRST, BECAUSE NOBODY CAN UNDERSTAND WHAT YOU'RE SAYING EXCEPT ME...
...AND SECOND, 'COS IF YOU LET IT SLIP, I'D HAVE TO USE YOUR FUR FOR SOME NICE NEON SOCKS.
YIKES!

END OF CHAPTER 97

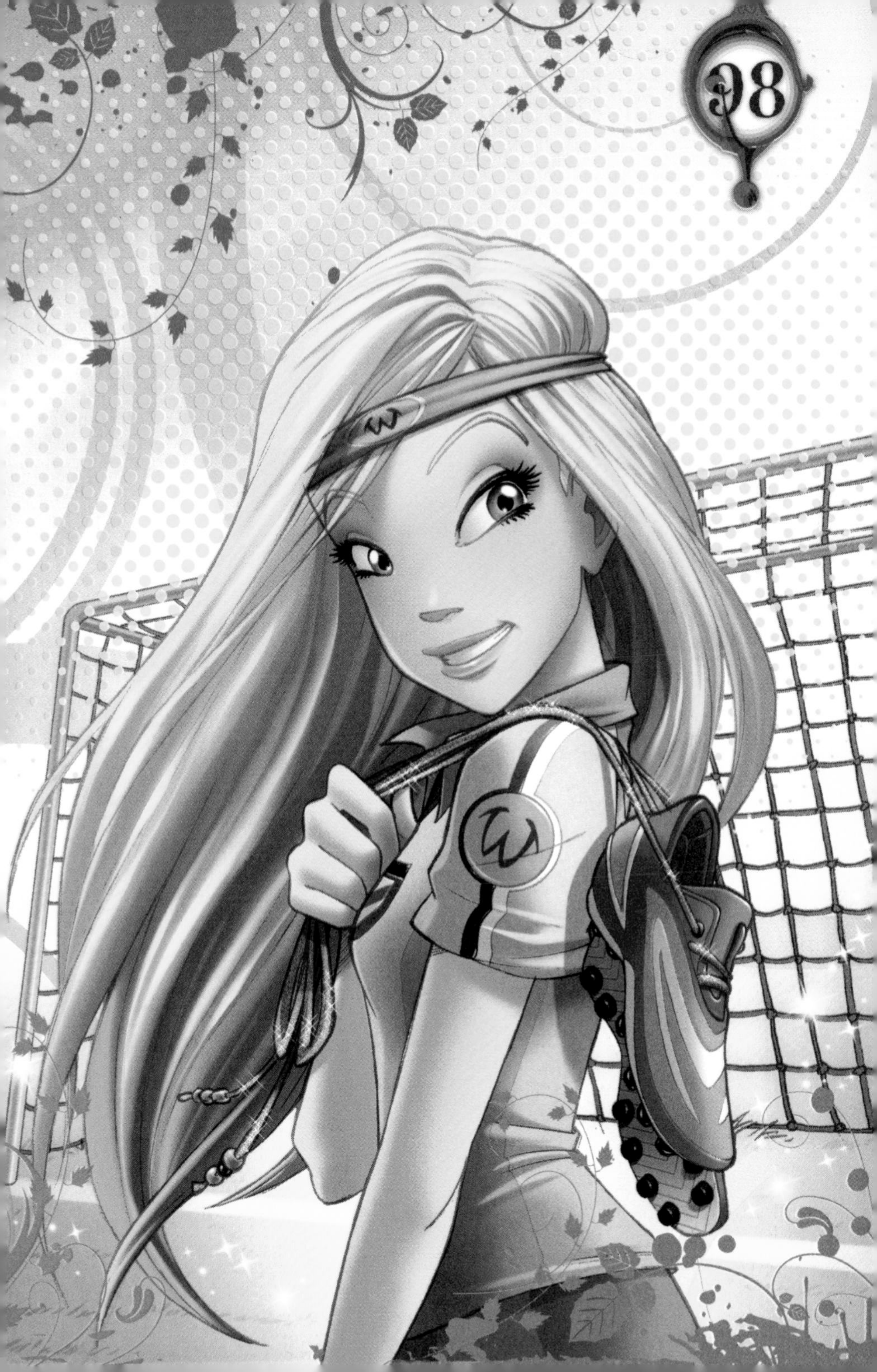
08

98

Sweet, in the End

"We'll leaf through the pages of time. We'll read them all!"

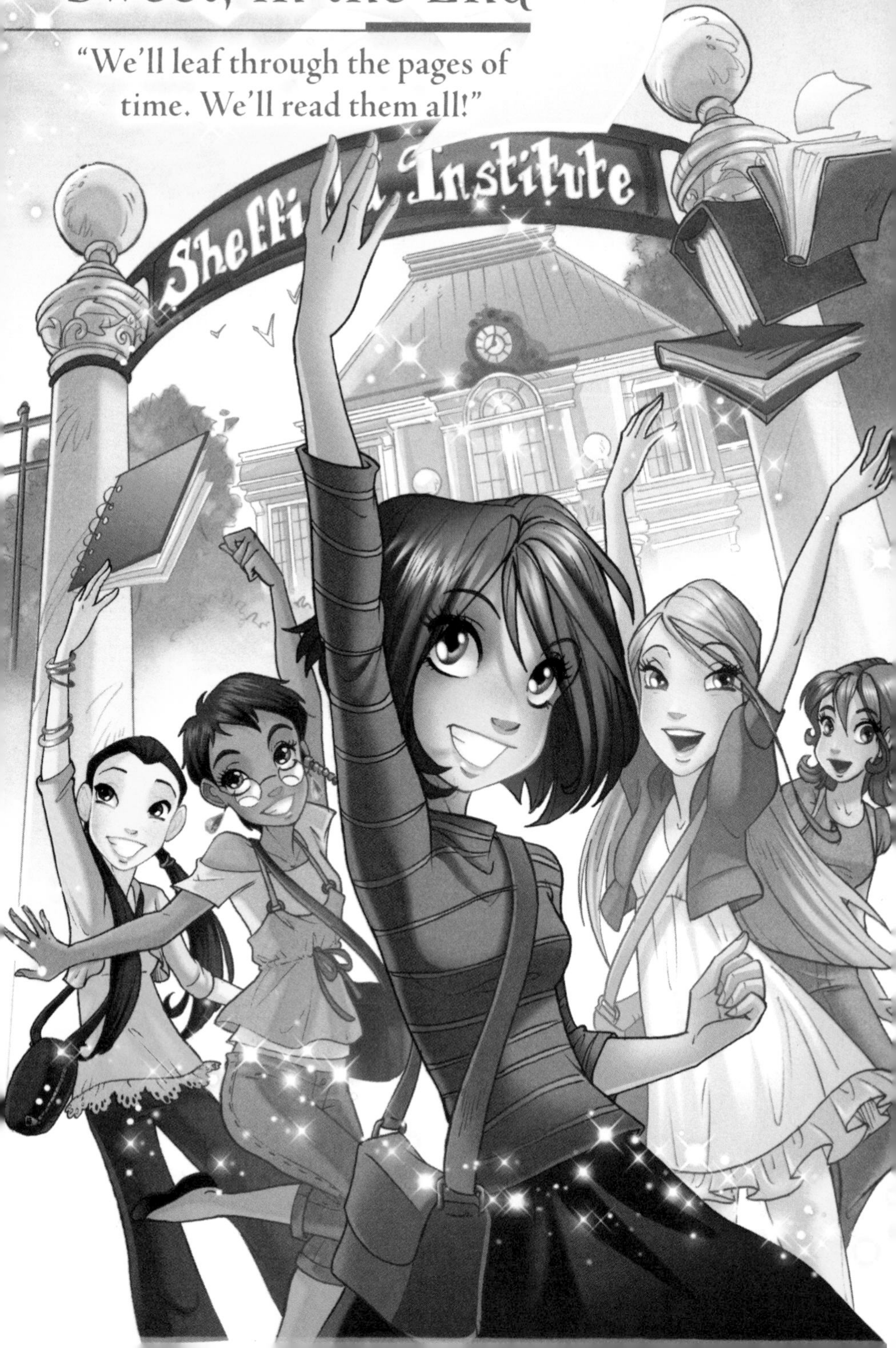
Institute

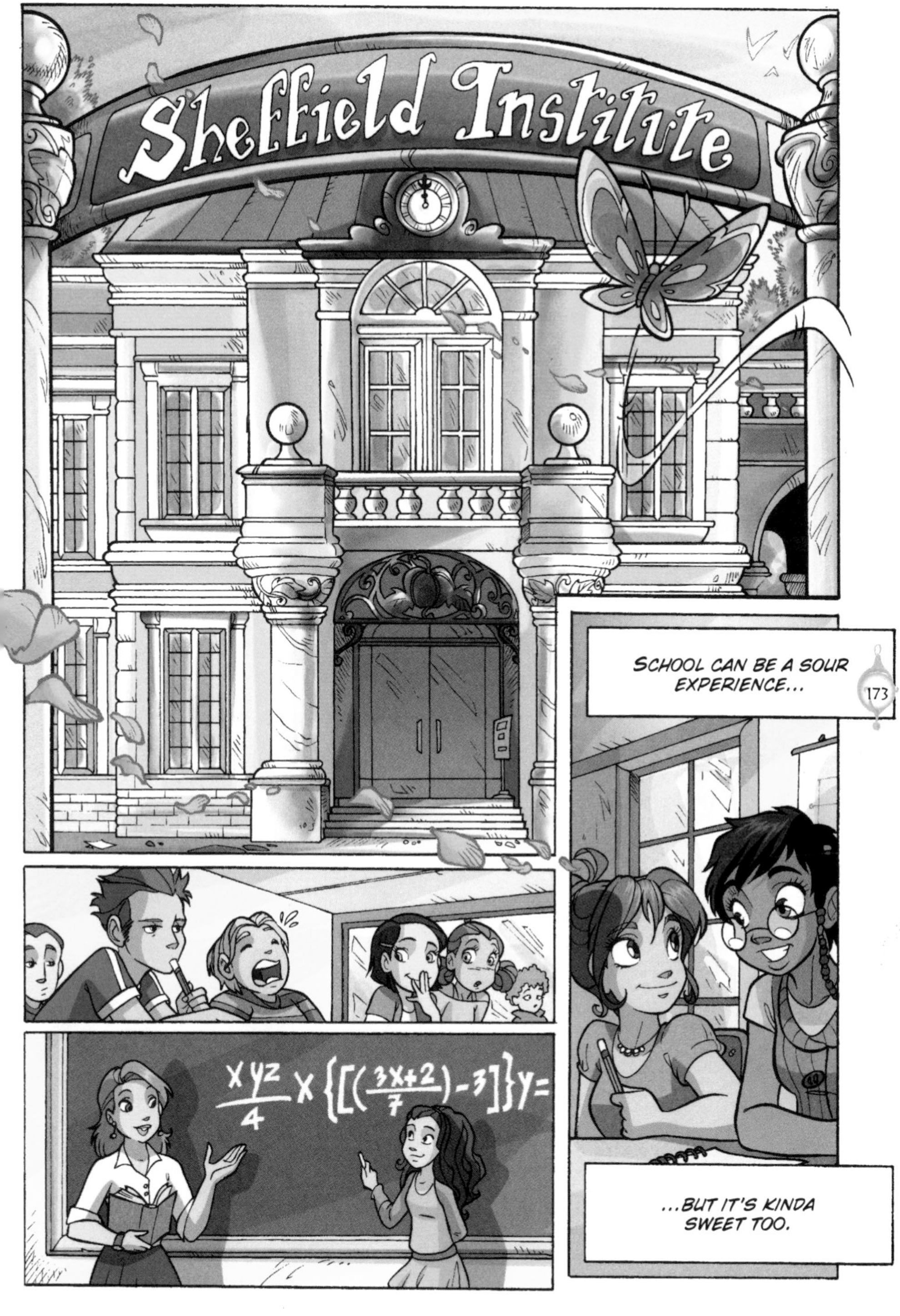
Sheffield Institute
SCHOOL CAN BE A SOUR EXPERIENCE...
...BUT IT'S KINDA SWEET TOO.

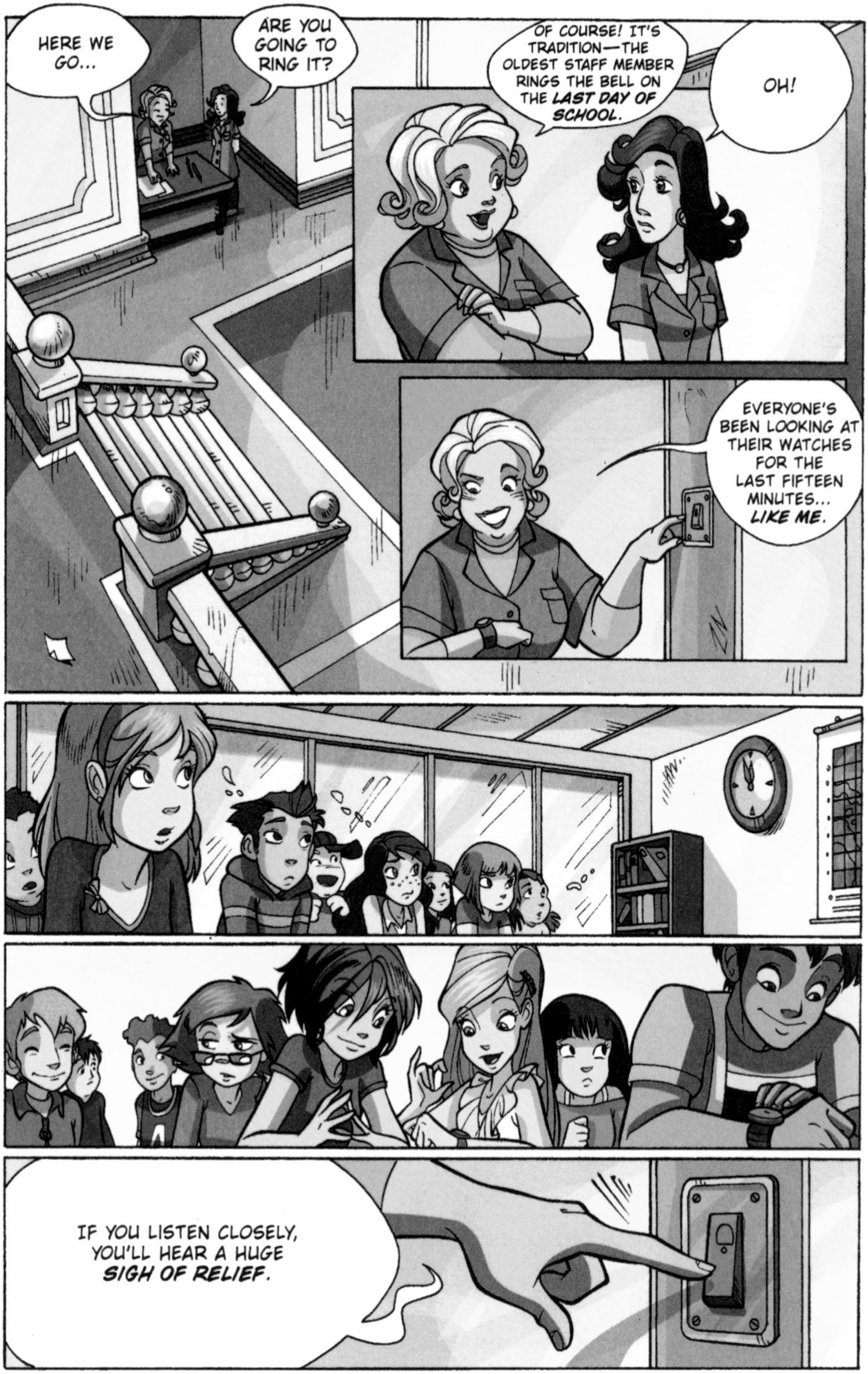
HERE WE GO...
ARE YOU GOING TO RING IT?
OF COURSE! IT'S TRADITION—THE OLDEST STAFF MEMBER RINGS THE BELL ON THE LAST DAY OF SCHOOL.
OH!
EVERYONE'S BEEN LOOKING AT THEIR WATCHES FOR THE LAST FIFTEEN MINUTES... LIKE ME.
IF YOU LISTEN CLOSELY, YOU'LL HEAR A HUGE SIGH OF RELIEF.

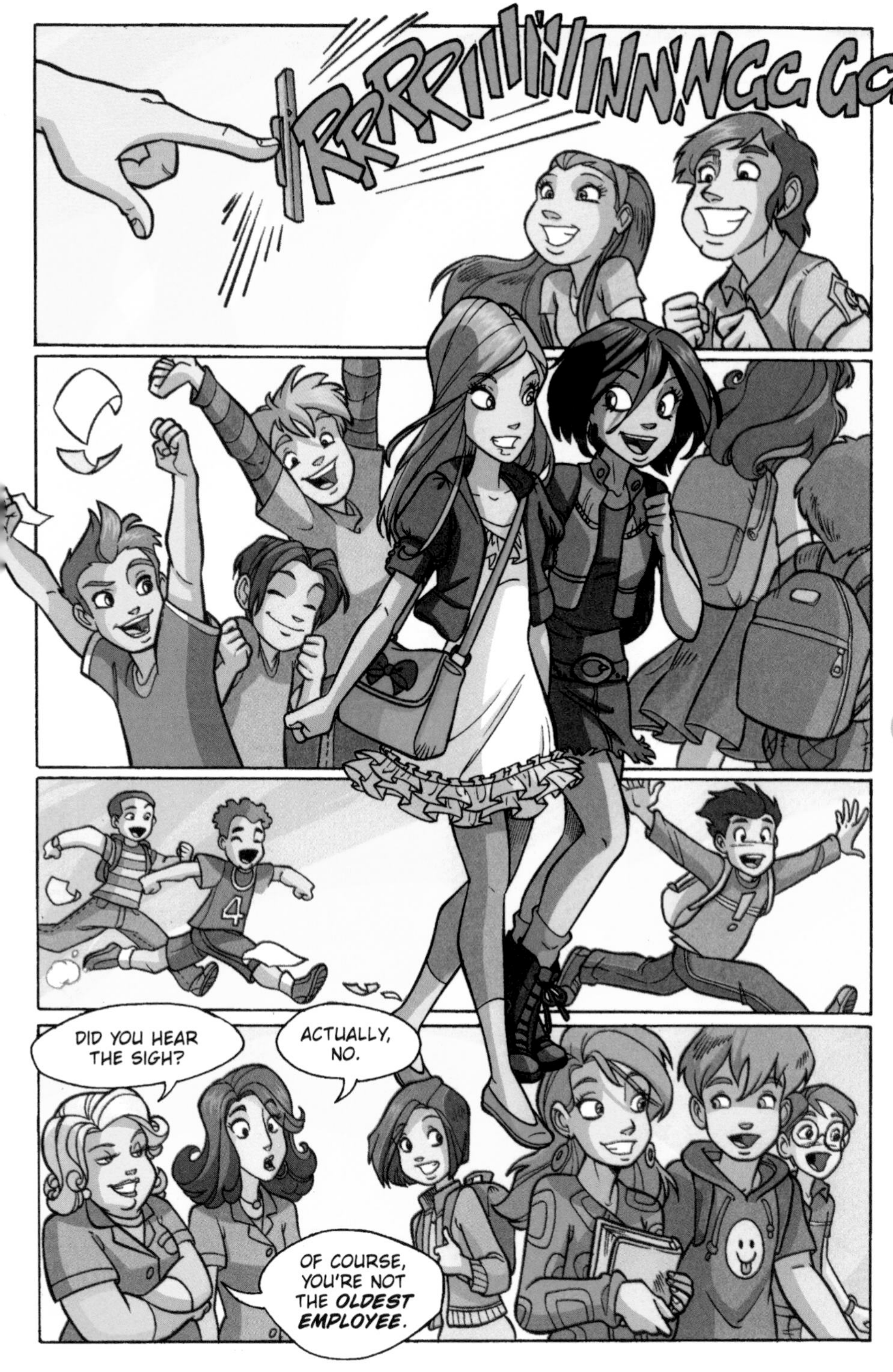
RRRRIIIIIIINNNNGG GG
DID YOU HEAR THE SIGH?
ACTUALLY, NO.
OF COURSE, YOU'RE NOT THE OLDEST EMPLOYEE.

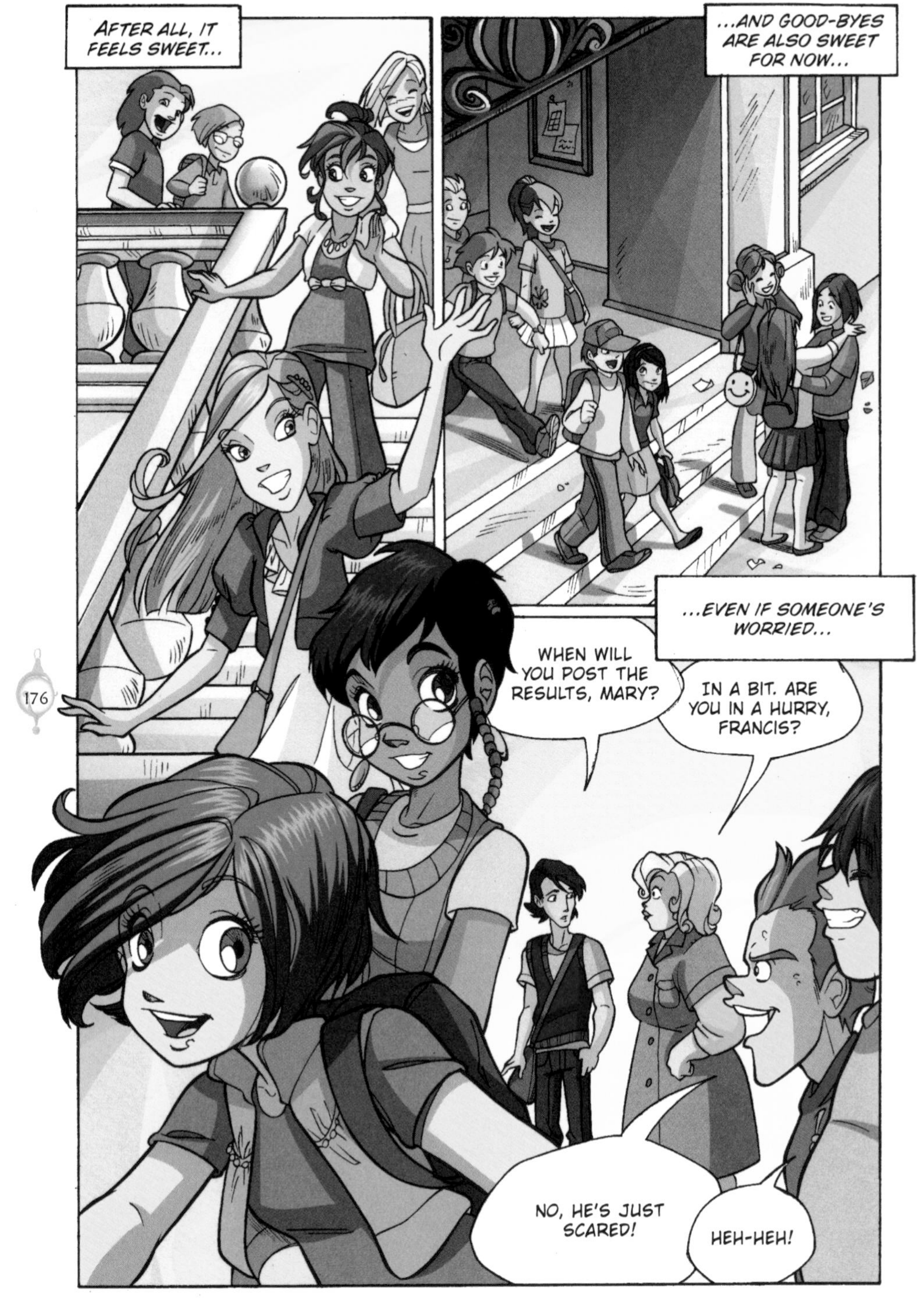
AFTER ALL, IT FEELS SWEET...
...AND GOOD-BYES ARE ALSO SWEET FOR NOW...
...EVEN IF SOMEONE'S WORRIED...
WHEN WILL YOU POST THE RESULTS, MARY?
IN A BIT. ARE YOU IN A HURRY, FRANCIS?
NO, HE'S JUST SCARED!
HEH-HEH!

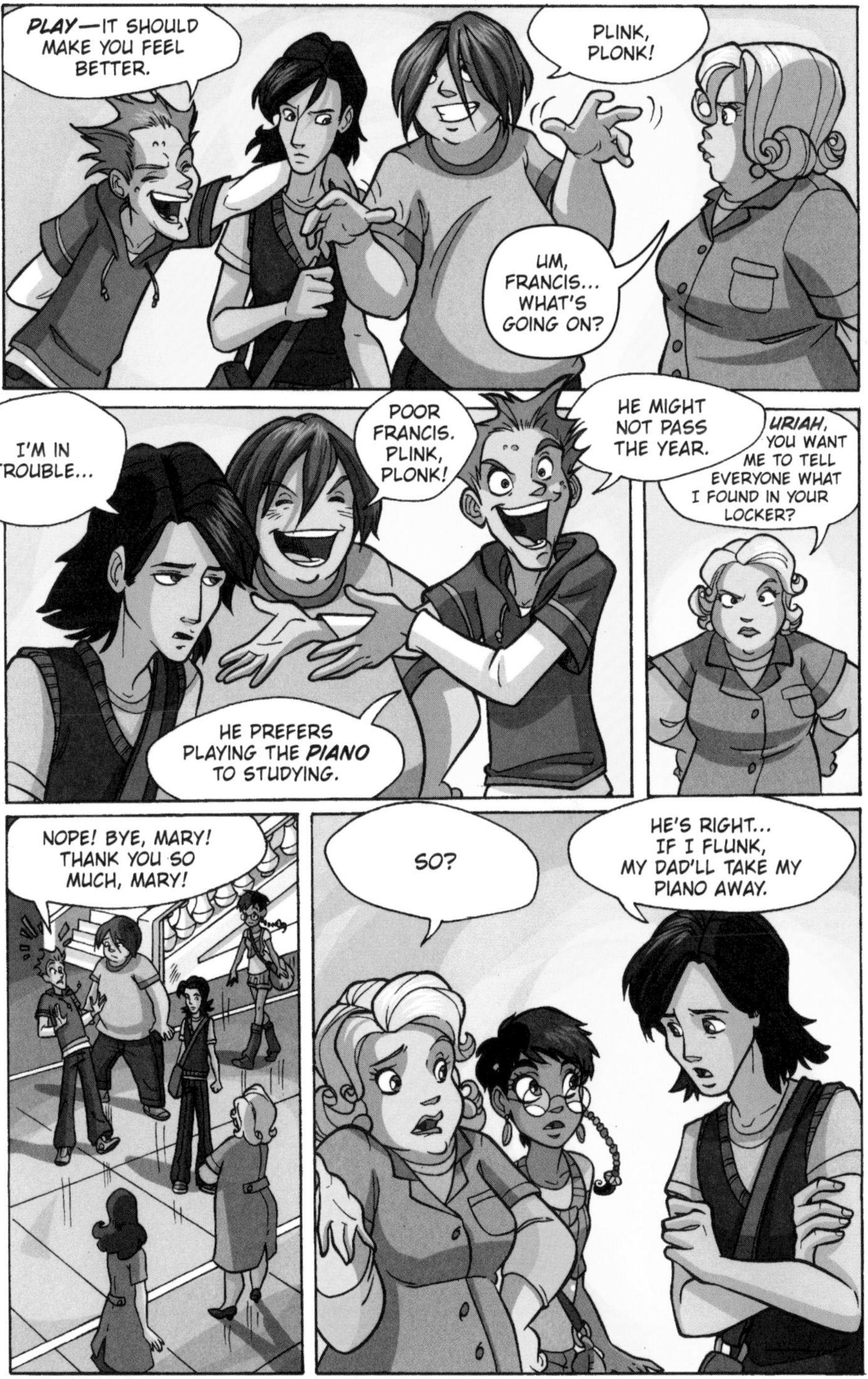
PLAY—IT SHOULD MAKE YOU FEEL BETTER.
PLINK, PLONK!
UM, FRANCIS... WHAT'S GOING ON?
I'M IN TROUBLE...
POOR FRANCIS. PLINK, PLONK!
HE MIGHT NOT PASS THE YEAR.
HE PREFERS PLAYING THE PIANO TO STUDYING.
URIAH, YOU WANT ME TO TELL EVERYONE WHAT I FOUND IN YOUR LOCKER?
NOPE! BYE, MARY! THANK YOU SO MUCH, MARY!
SO?
HE'S RIGHT... IF I FLUNK, MY DAD'LL TAKE MY PIANO AWAY.

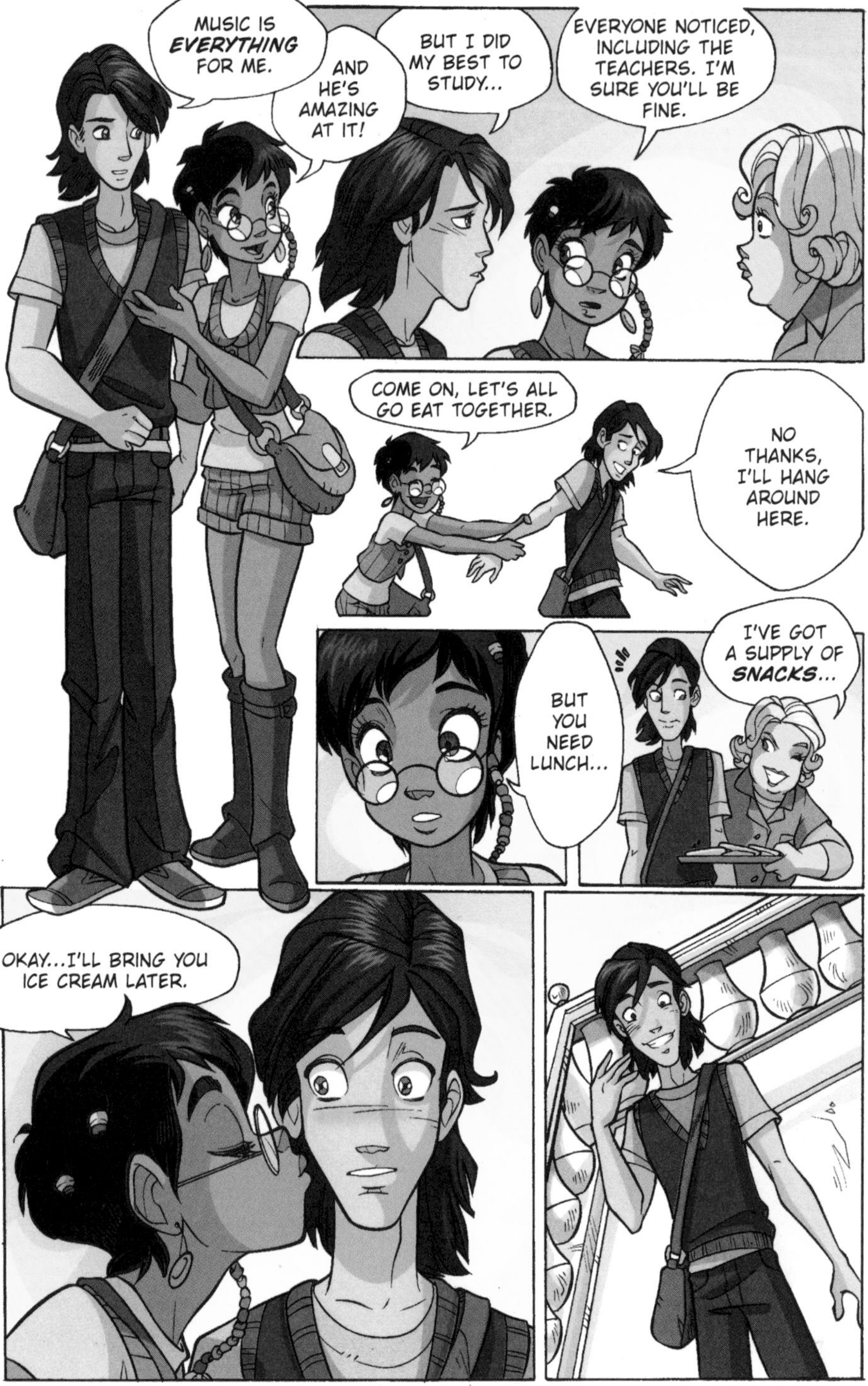
MUSIC IS ***EVERYTHING*** FOR ME.
AND HE'S AMAZING AT IT!
BUT I DID MY BEST TO STUDY...
EVERYONE NOTICED, INCLUDING THE TEACHERS. I'M SURE YOU'LL BE FINE.
COME ON, LET'S ALL GO EAT TOGETHER.
NO THANKS, I'LL HANG AROUND HERE.
BUT YOU NEED LUNCH...
I'VE GOT A SUPPLY OF ***SNACKS***...
OKAY...I'LL BRING YOU ICE CREAM LATER.

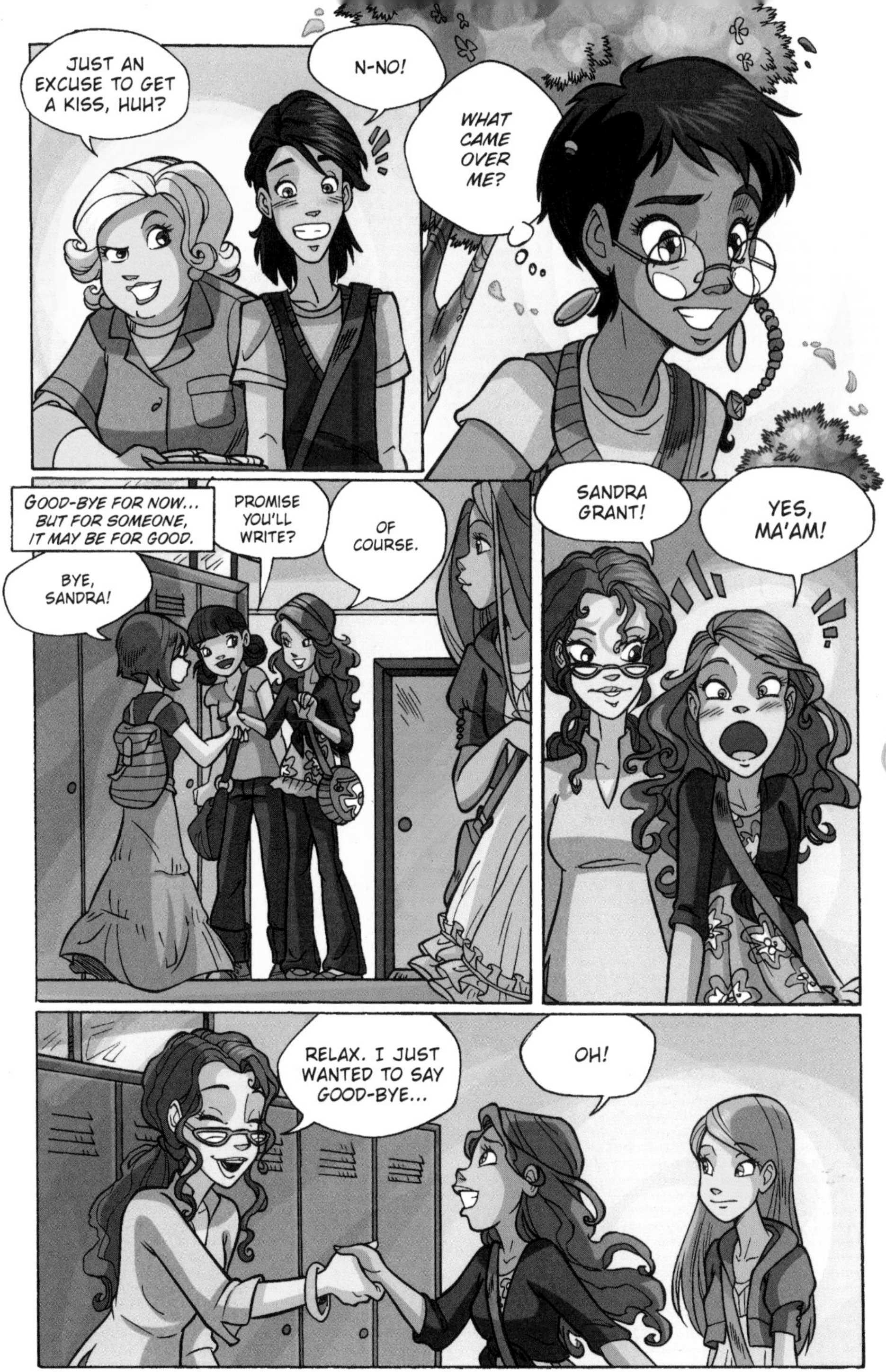
JUST AN EXCUSE TO GET A KISS, HUH?
N-NO!
WHAT CAME OVER ME?
GOOD-BYE FOR NOW... BUT FOR SOMEONE, IT MAY BE FOR GOOD.
PROMISE YOU'LL WRITE?
OF COURSE.
BYE, SANDRA!
SANDRA GRANT!
YES, MA'AM!
RELAX. I JUST WANTED TO SAY GOOD-BYE...
OH!

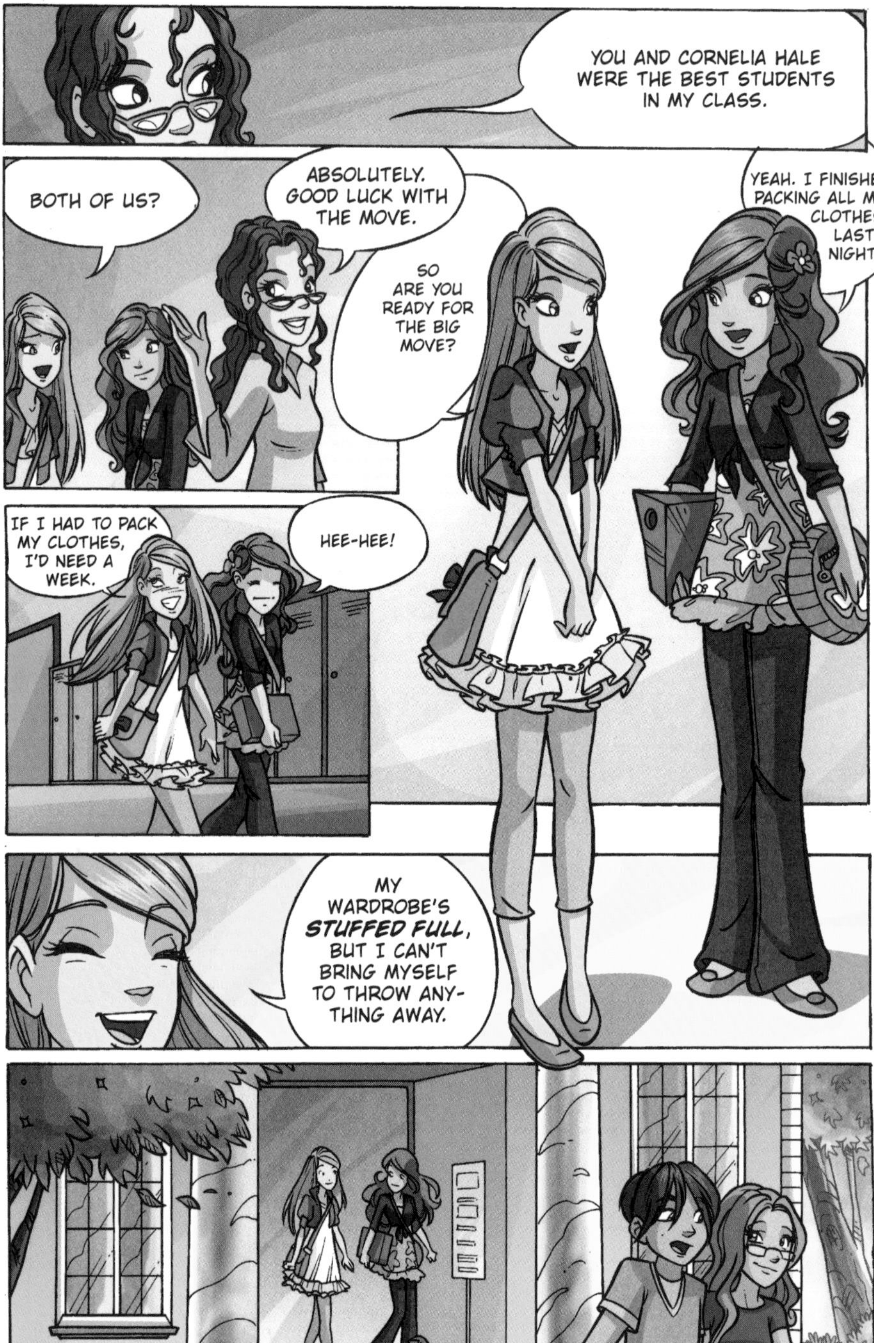
YOU AND CORNELIA HALE WERE THE BEST STUDENTS IN MY CLASS.
BOTH OF US?
ABSOLUTELY. GOOD LUCK WITH THE MOVE.
SO ARE YOU READY FOR THE BIG MOVE?
YEAH. I FINISHED PACKING ALL MY CLOTHES LAST NIGHT.
IF I HAD TO PACK MY CLOTHES, I'D NEED A WEEK.
HEE-HEE!
MY WARDROBE'S STUFFED FULL, BUT I CAN'T BRING MYSELF TO THROW ANYTHING AWAY.

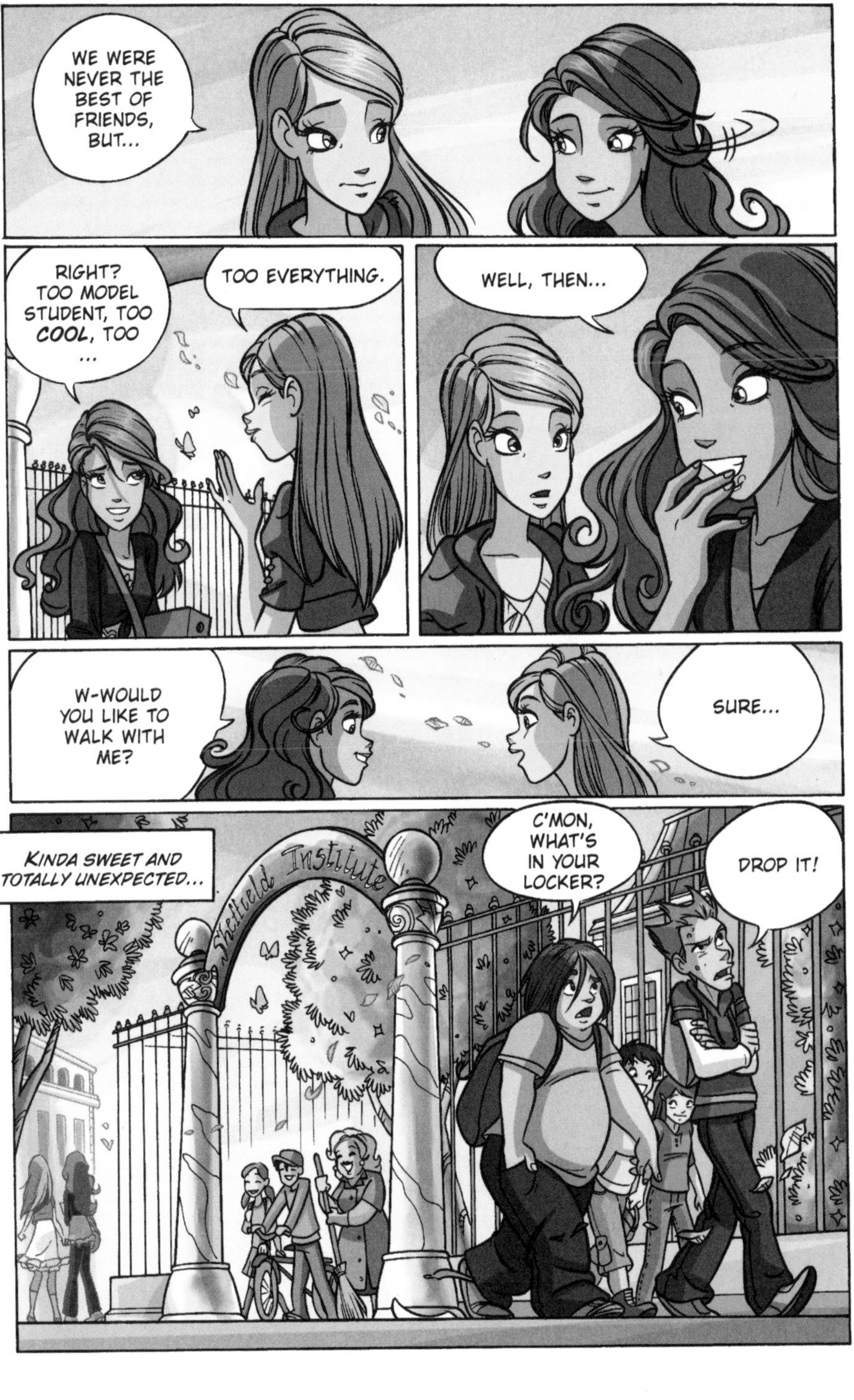
WE WERE NEVER THE BEST OF FRIENDS, BUT...
RIGHT? TOO MODEL STUDENT, TOO COOL, TOO ...
TOO EVERYTHING.
WELL, THEN...
W-WOULD YOU LIKE TO WALK WITH ME?
SURE...
KINDA SWEET AND TOTALLY UNEXPECTED...
Sheffield Institute
C'MON, WHAT'S IN YOUR LOCKER?
DROP IT!

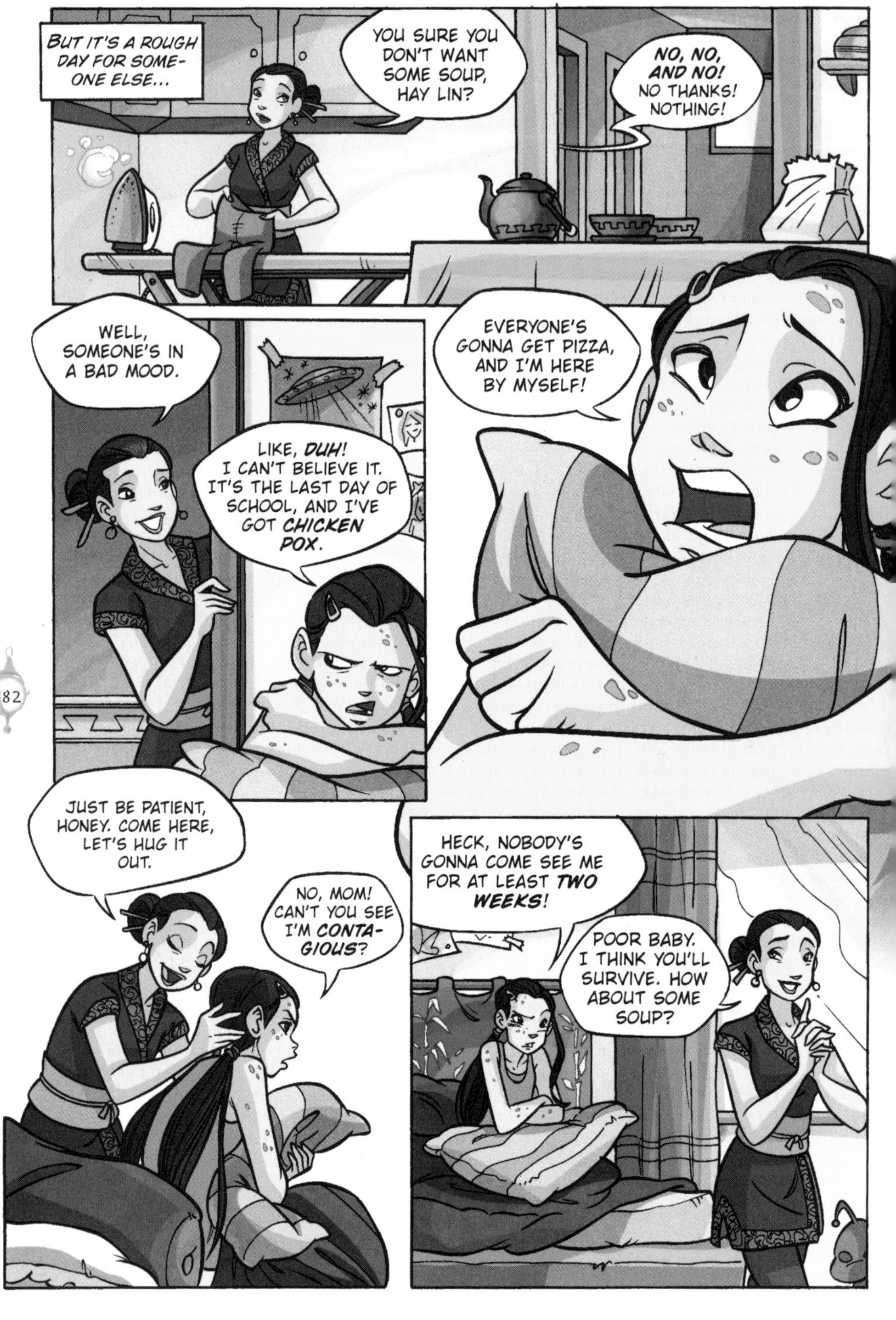
BUT IT'S A ROUGH DAY FOR SOME-ONE ELSE...
YOU SURE YOU DON'T WANT SOME SOUP, HAY LIN?
NO, NO, AND NO! NO THANKS! NOTHING!
WELL, SOMEONE'S IN A BAD MOOD.
LIKE, DUH! I CAN'T BELIEVE IT. IT'S THE LAST DAY OF SCHOOL, AND I'VE GOT CHICKEN POX.
EVERYONE'S GONNA GET PIZZA, AND I'M HERE BY MYSELF!
JUST BE PATIENT, HONEY. COME HERE, LET'S HUG IT OUT.
NO, MOM! CAN'T YOU SEE I'M CONTA-GIOUS?
HECK, NOBODY'S GONNA COME SEE ME FOR AT LEAST TWO WEEKS!
POOR BABY. I THINK YOU'LL SURVIVE. HOW ABOUT SOME SOUP?

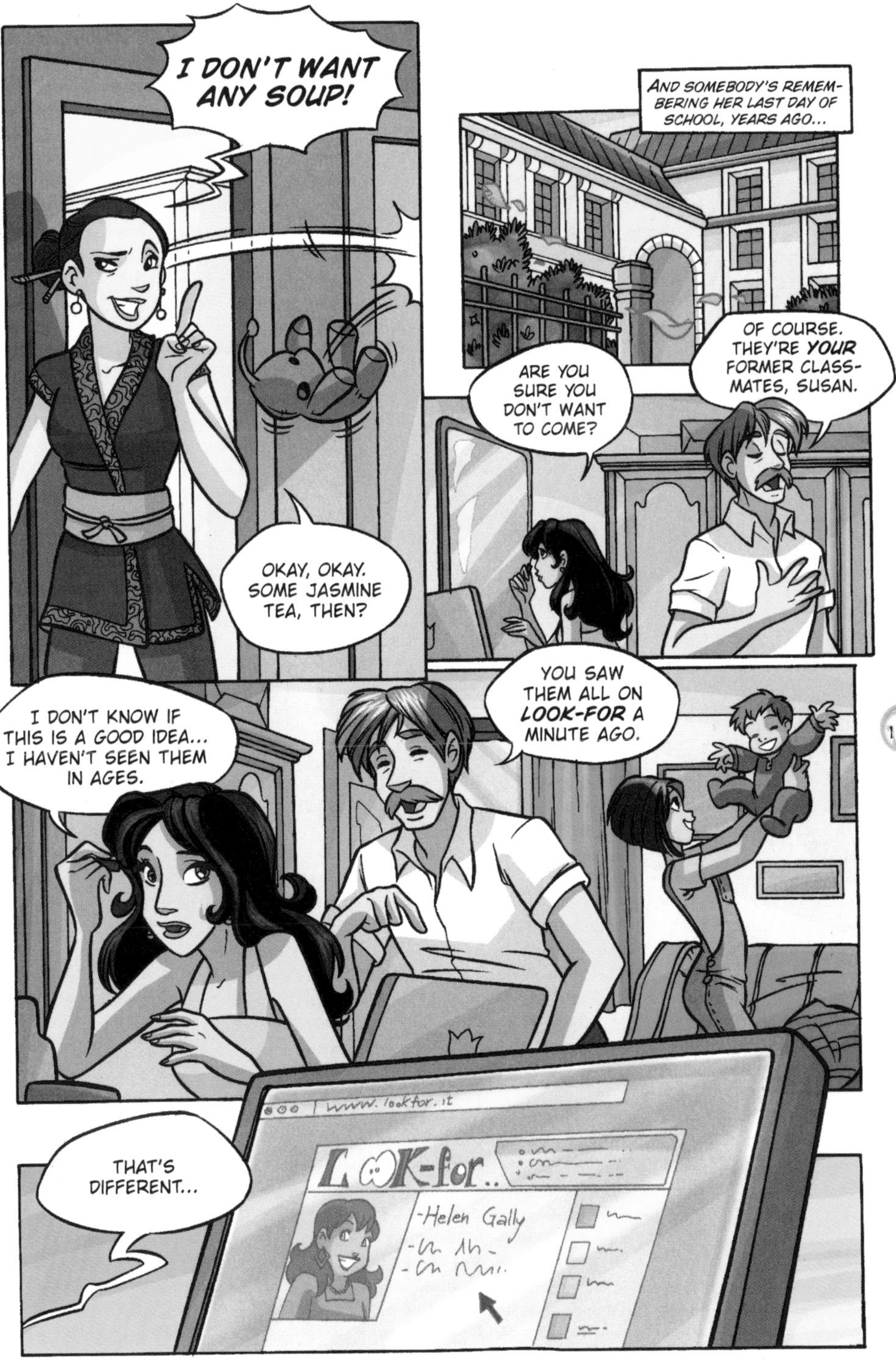
I DON'T WANT ANY SOUP!
OKAY, OKAY. SOME JASMINE TEA, THEN?
AND SOMEBODY'S REMEMBERING HER LAST DAY OF SCHOOL, YEARS AGO...
ARE YOU SURE YOU DON'T WANT TO COME?
OF COURSE. THEY'RE YOUR FORMER CLASSMATES, SUSAN.
I DON'T KNOW IF THIS IS A GOOD IDEA... I HAVEN'T SEEN THEM IN AGES.
YOU SAW THEM ALL ON LOOK-FOR A MINUTE AGO.
THAT'S DIFFERENT...
www.lookfor.it
LOOK-for..
-Helen Gally

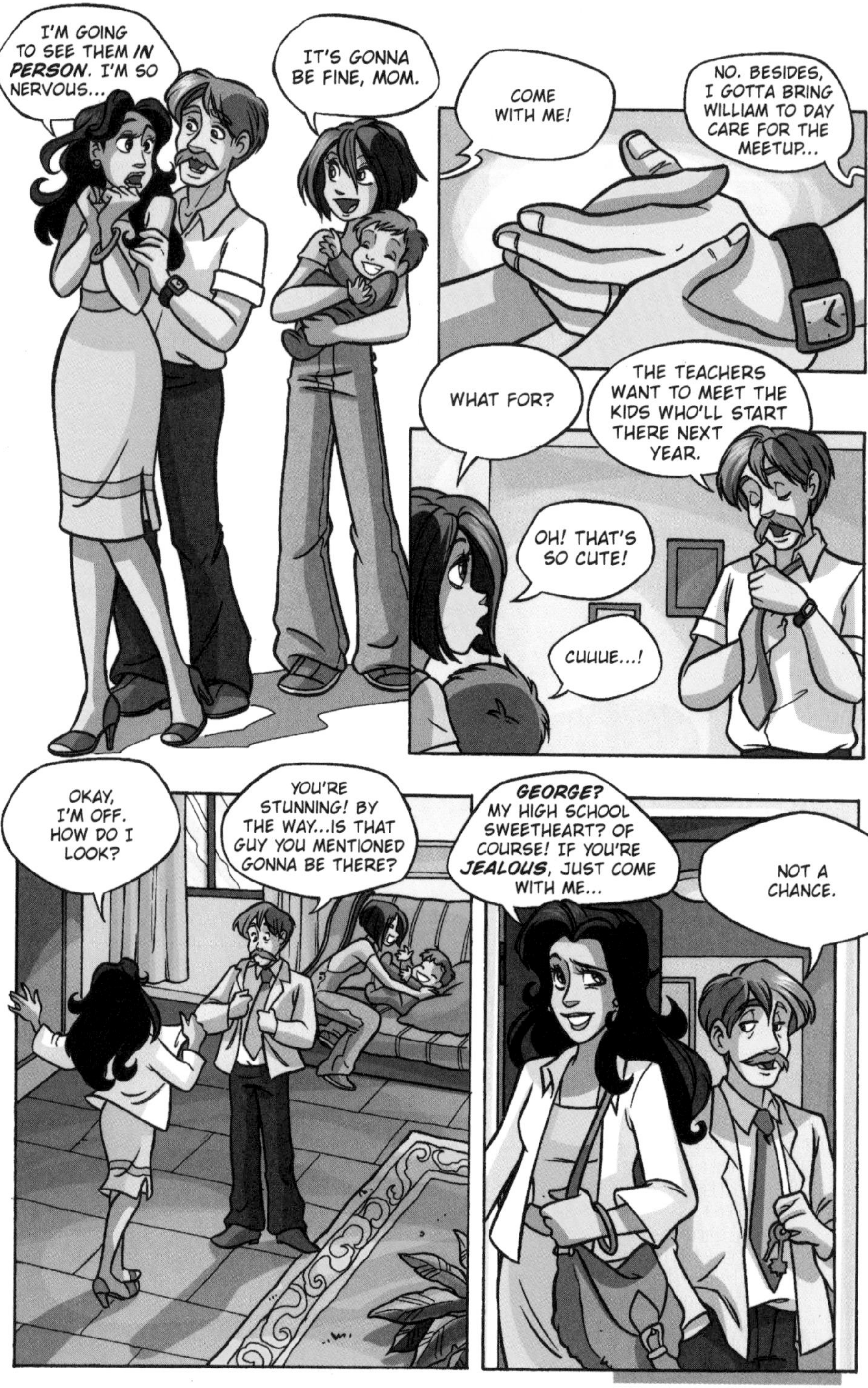
I'M GOING TO SEE THEM *IN PERSON*. I'M SO NERVOUS...
IT'S GONNA BE FINE, MOM.
COME WITH ME!
NO. BESIDES, I GOTTA BRING WILLIAM TO DAY CARE FOR THE MEETUP...
WHAT FOR?
THE TEACHERS WANT TO MEET THE KIDS WHO'LL START THERE NEXT YEAR.
OH! THAT'S SO CUTE!
CUUUE...!
OKAY, I'M OFF. HOW DO I LOOK?
YOU'RE STUNNING! BY THE WAY...IS THAT GUY YOU MENTIONED GONNA BE THERE?
GEORGE? MY HIGH SCHOOL SWEETHEART? OF COURSE! IF YOU'RE *JEALOUS*, JUST COME WITH ME...
NOT A CHANCE.

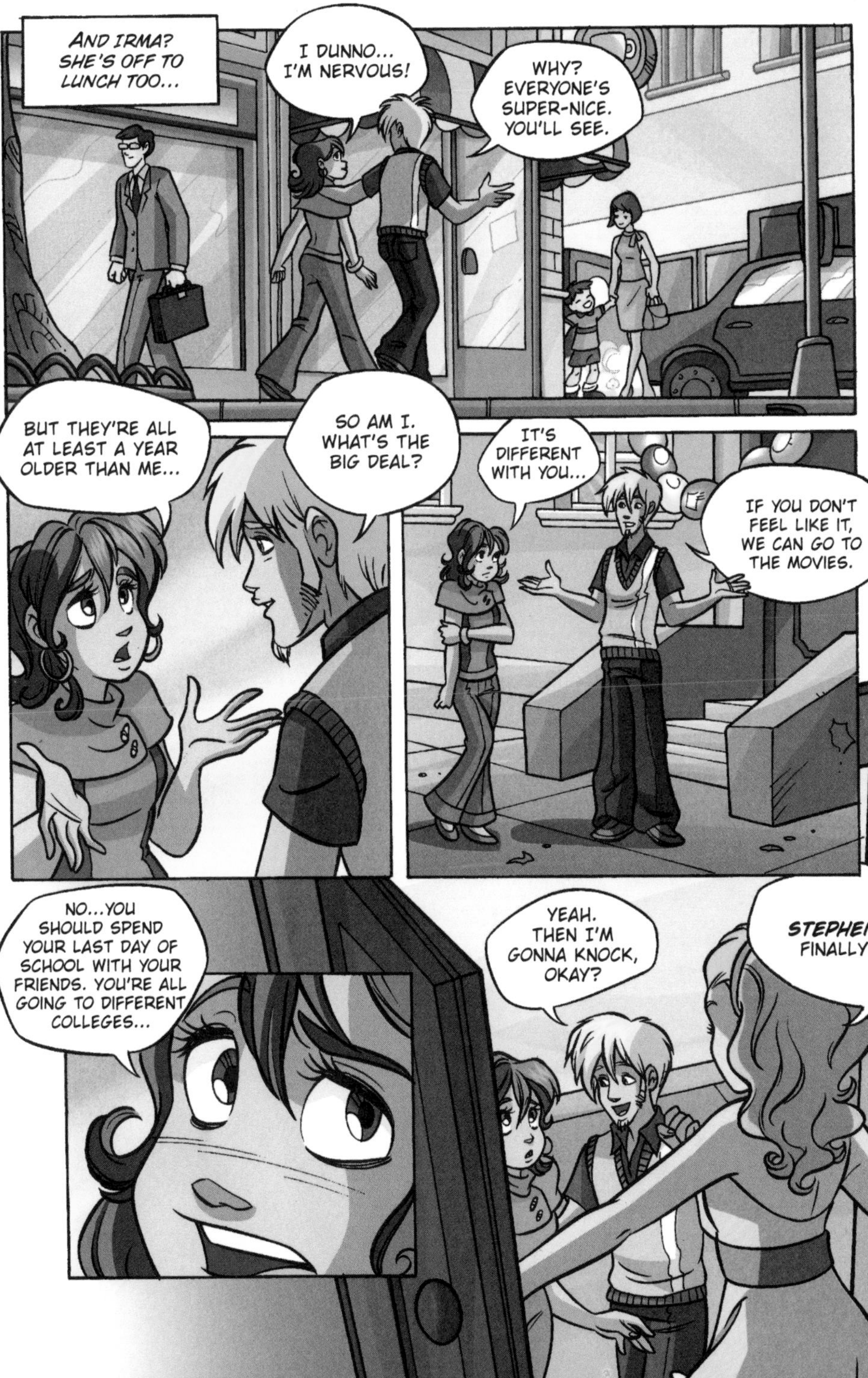
AND IRMA? SHE'S OFF TO LUNCH TOO...
I DUNNO... I'M NERVOUS!
WHY? EVERYONE'S SUPER-NICE. YOU'LL SEE.
BUT THEY'RE ALL AT LEAST A YEAR OLDER THAN ME...
SO AM I. WHAT'S THE BIG DEAL?
IT'S DIFFERENT WITH YOU...
IF YOU DON'T FEEL LIKE IT, WE CAN GO TO THE MOVIES.
NO...YOU SHOULD SPEND YOUR LAST DAY OF SCHOOL WITH YOUR FRIENDS. YOU'RE ALL GOING TO DIFFERENT COLLEGES...
YEAH. THEN I'M GONNA KNOCK, OKAY?
STEPHEN! FINALLY!

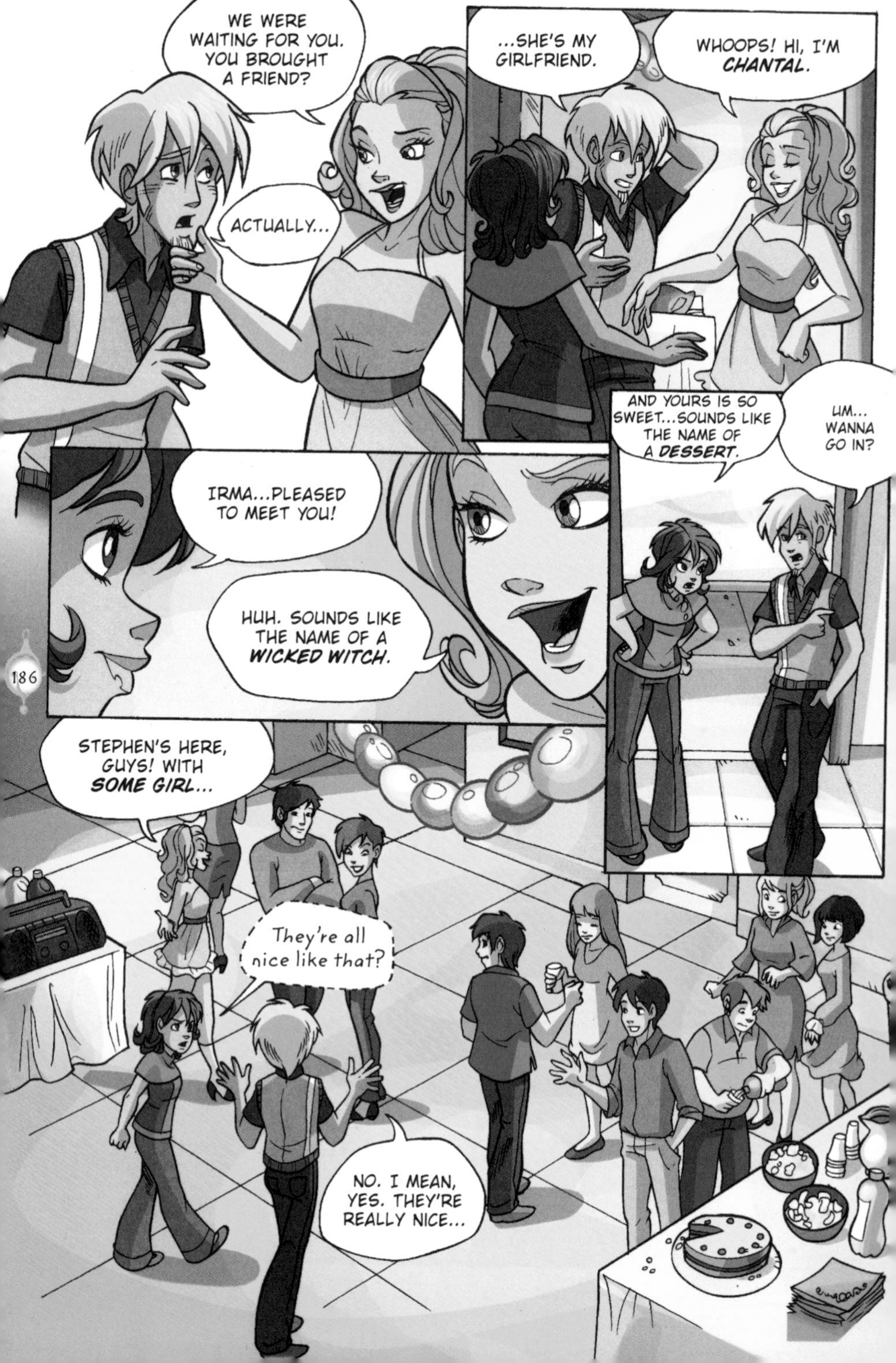
WE WERE WAITING FOR YOU. YOU BROUGHT A FRIEND?
ACTUALLY...
...SHE'S MY GIRLFRIEND.
WHOOPS! HI, I'M *CHANTAL.*
IRMA...PLEASED TO MEET YOU!
HUH. SOUNDS LIKE THE NAME OF A *WICKED WITCH.*
AND YOURS IS SO SWEET...SOUNDS LIKE THE NAME OF A *DESSERT.*
UM... WANNA GO IN?
STEPHEN'S HERE, GUYS! WITH *SOME GIRL...*
They're all nice like that?
NO. I MEAN, YES. THEY'RE REALLY NICE...

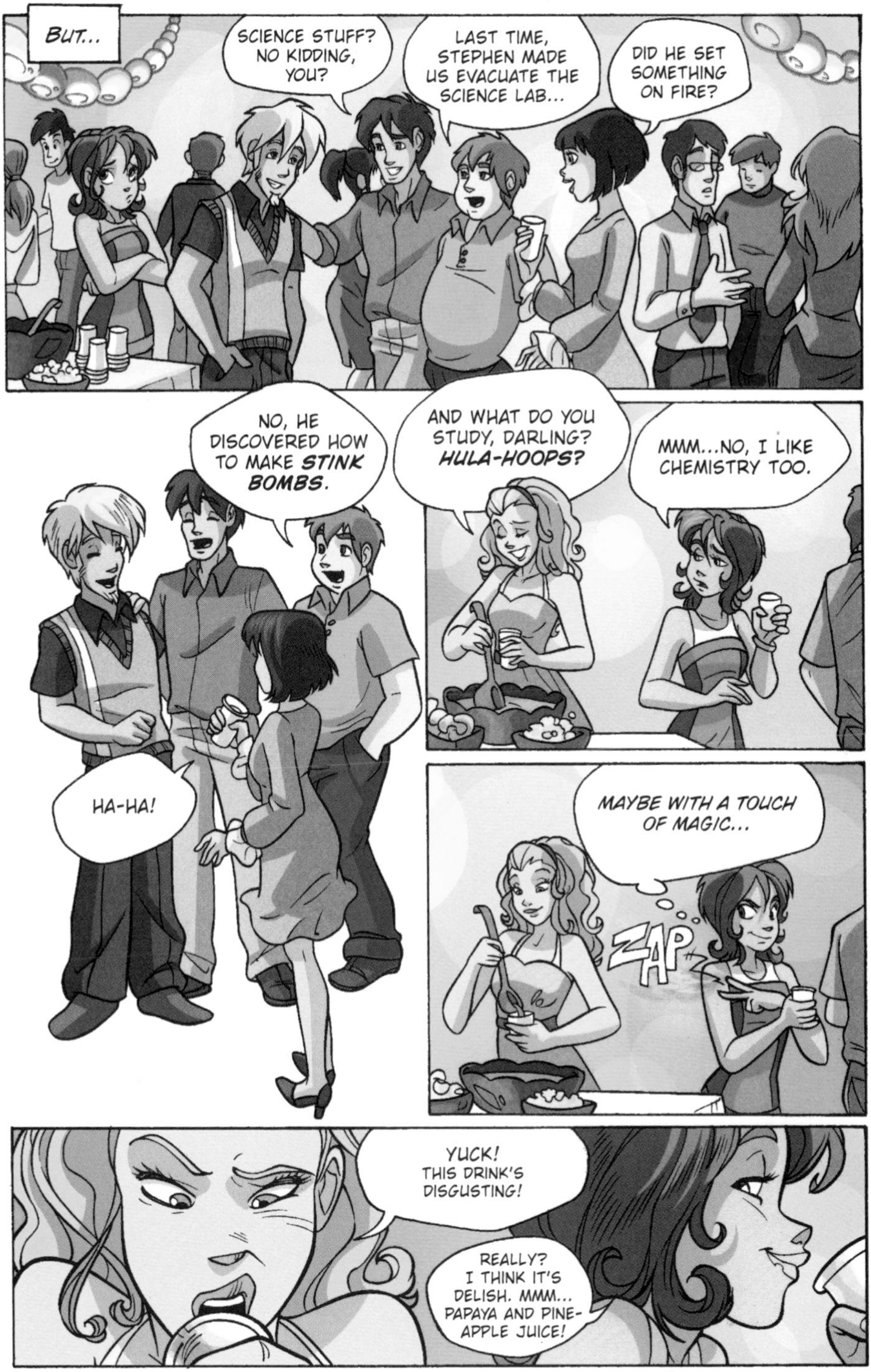
BUT...
SCIENCE STUFF? NO KIDDING, YOU?
LAST TIME, STEPHEN MADE US EVACUATE THE SCIENCE LAB...
DID HE SET SOMETHING ON FIRE?
NO, HE DISCOVERED HOW TO MAKE STINK BOMBS.
HA-HA!
AND WHAT DO YOU STUDY, DARLING? HULA-HOOPS?
MMM...NO, I LIKE CHEMISTRY TOO.
MAYBE WITH A TOUCH OF MAGIC...
ZAP
YUCK! THIS DRINK'S DISGUSTING!
REALLY? I THINK IT'S DELISH. MMM... PAPAYA AND PINE-APPLE JUICE!

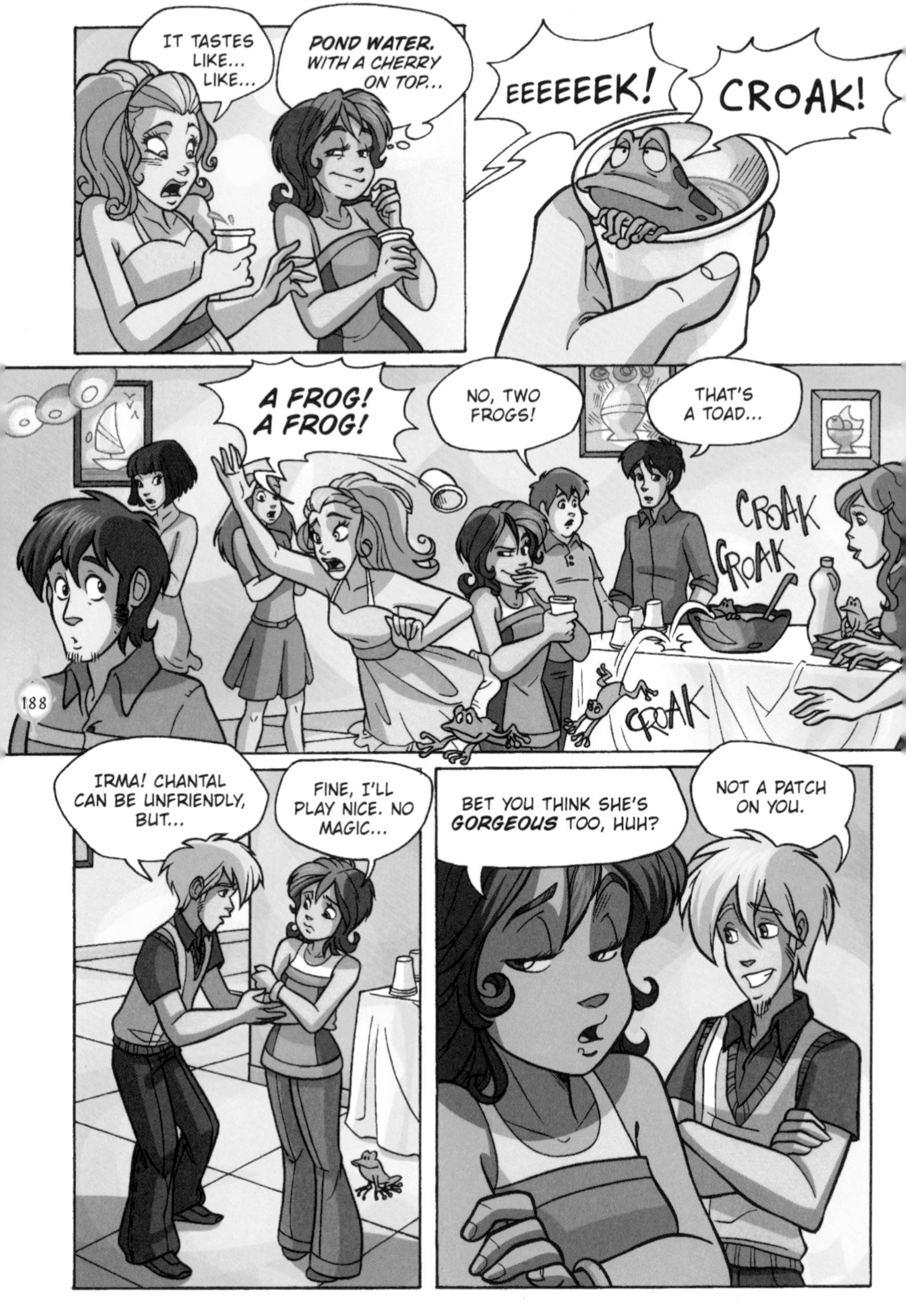
IT TASTES LIKE... LIKE...
POND WATER. WITH A CHERRY ON TOP...
EEEEEEK!
CROAK!
A FROG! A FROG!
NO, TWO FROGS!
THAT'S A TOAD...
CROAK
CROAK
CROAK
IRMA! CHANTAL CAN BE UNFRIENDLY, BUT...
FINE, I'LL PLAY NICE. NO MAGIC...
BET YOU THINK SHE'S GORGEOUS TOO, HUH?
NOT A PATCH ON YOU.

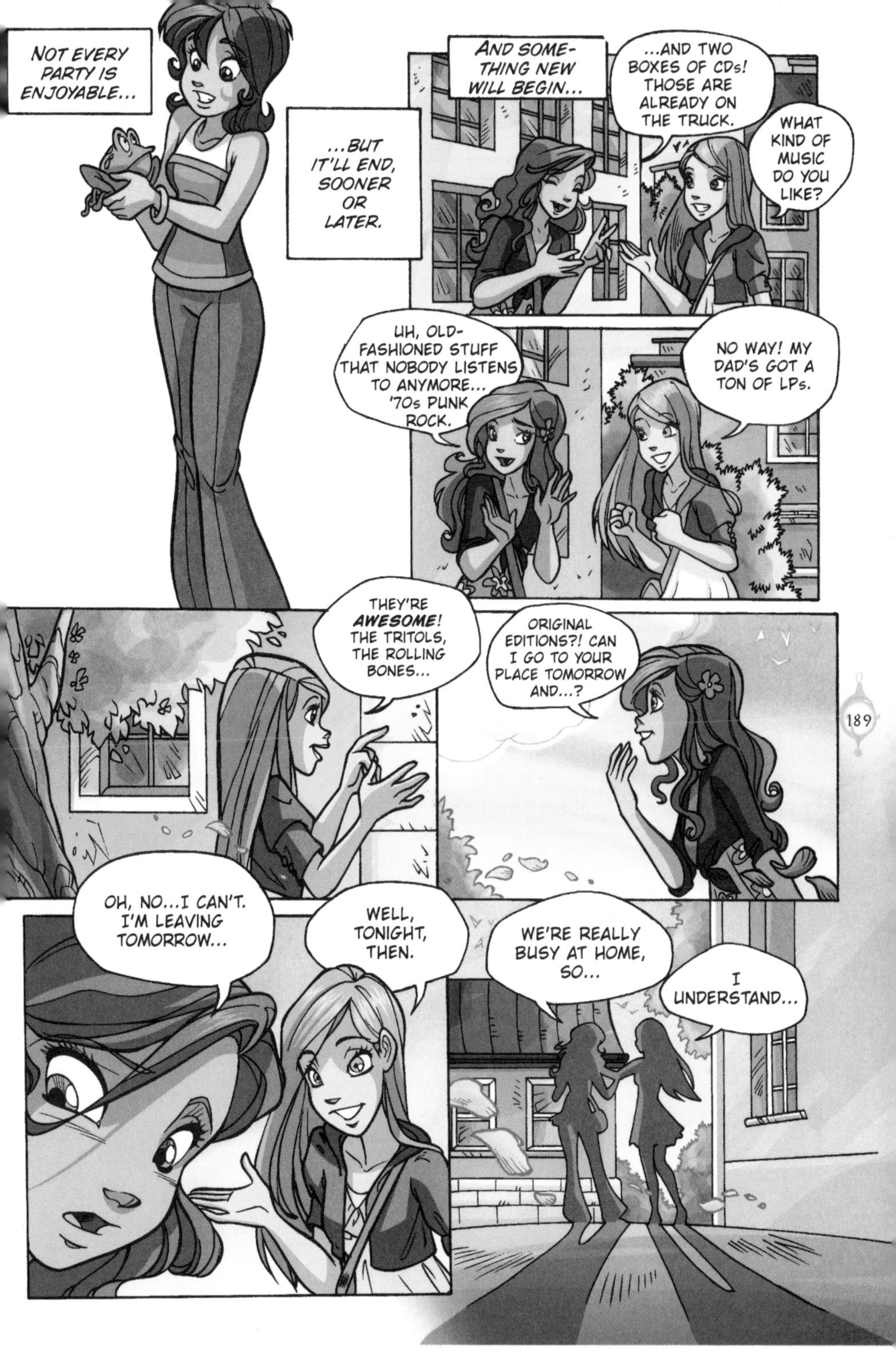
NOT EVERY PARTY IS ENJOYABLE...
...BUT IT'LL END, SOONER OR LATER.
AND SOMETHING NEW WILL BEGIN...
...AND TWO BOXES OF CDs! THOSE ARE ALREADY ON THE TRUCK.
WHAT KIND OF MUSIC DO YOU LIKE?
UH, OLD-FASHIONED STUFF THAT NOBODY LISTENS TO ANYMORE... '70s PUNK ROCK.
NO WAY! MY DAD'S GOT A TON OF LPs.
THEY'RE AWESOME! THE TRITOLS, THE ROLLING BONES...
ORIGINAL EDITIONS?! CAN I GO TO YOUR PLACE TOMORROW AND...?
OH, NO...I CAN'T. I'M LEAVING TOMORROW...
WELL, TONIGHT, THEN.
WE'RE REALLY BUSY AT HOME, SO...
I UNDERSTAND...

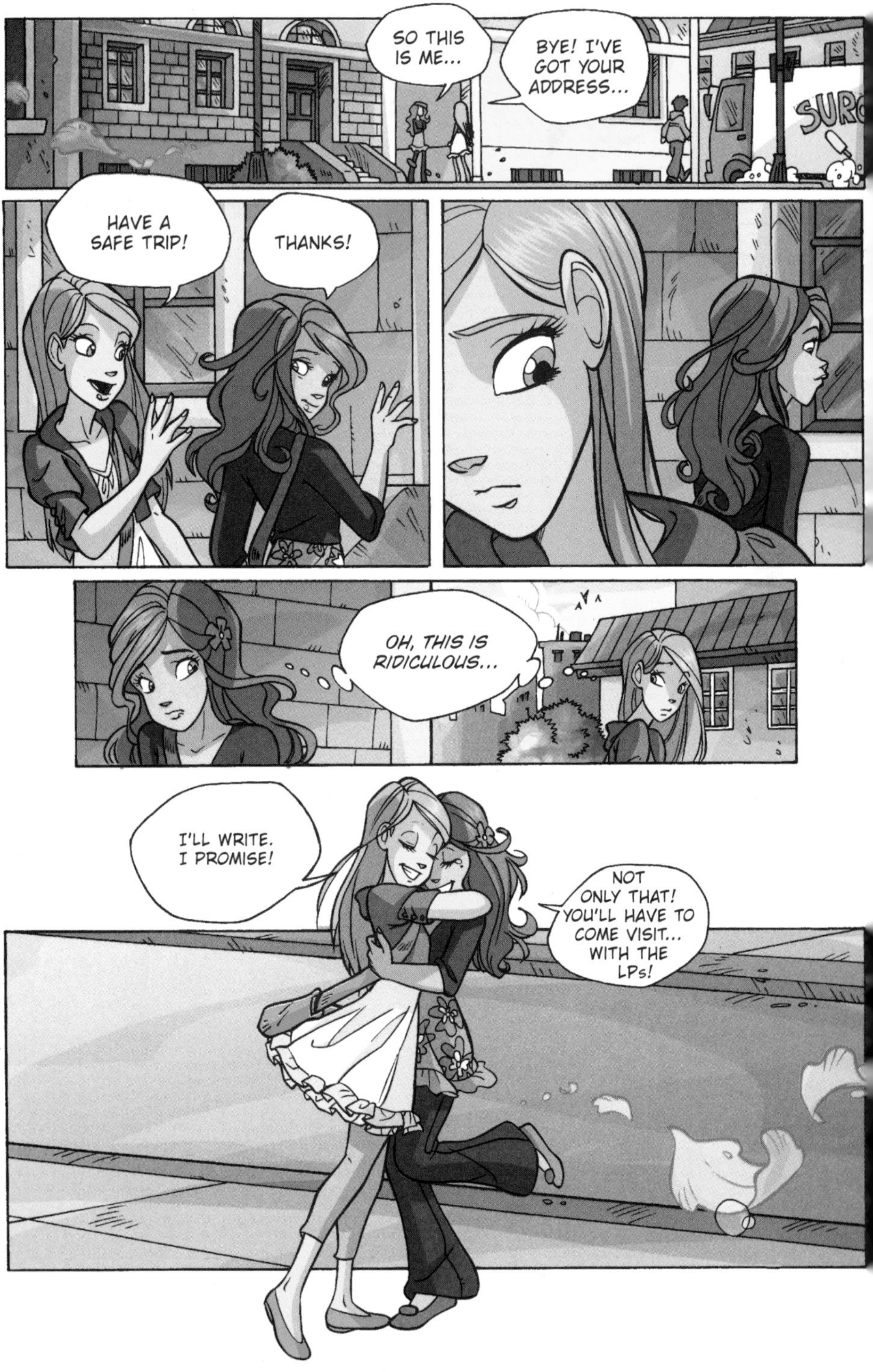
SO THIS IS ME...
BYE! I'VE GOT YOUR ADDRESS...
SURO
HAVE A SAFE TRIP!
THANKS!
OH, THIS IS RIDICULOUS...
I'LL WRITE. I PROMISE!
NOT ONLY THAT! YOU'LL HAVE TO COME VISIT... WITH THE LPs!

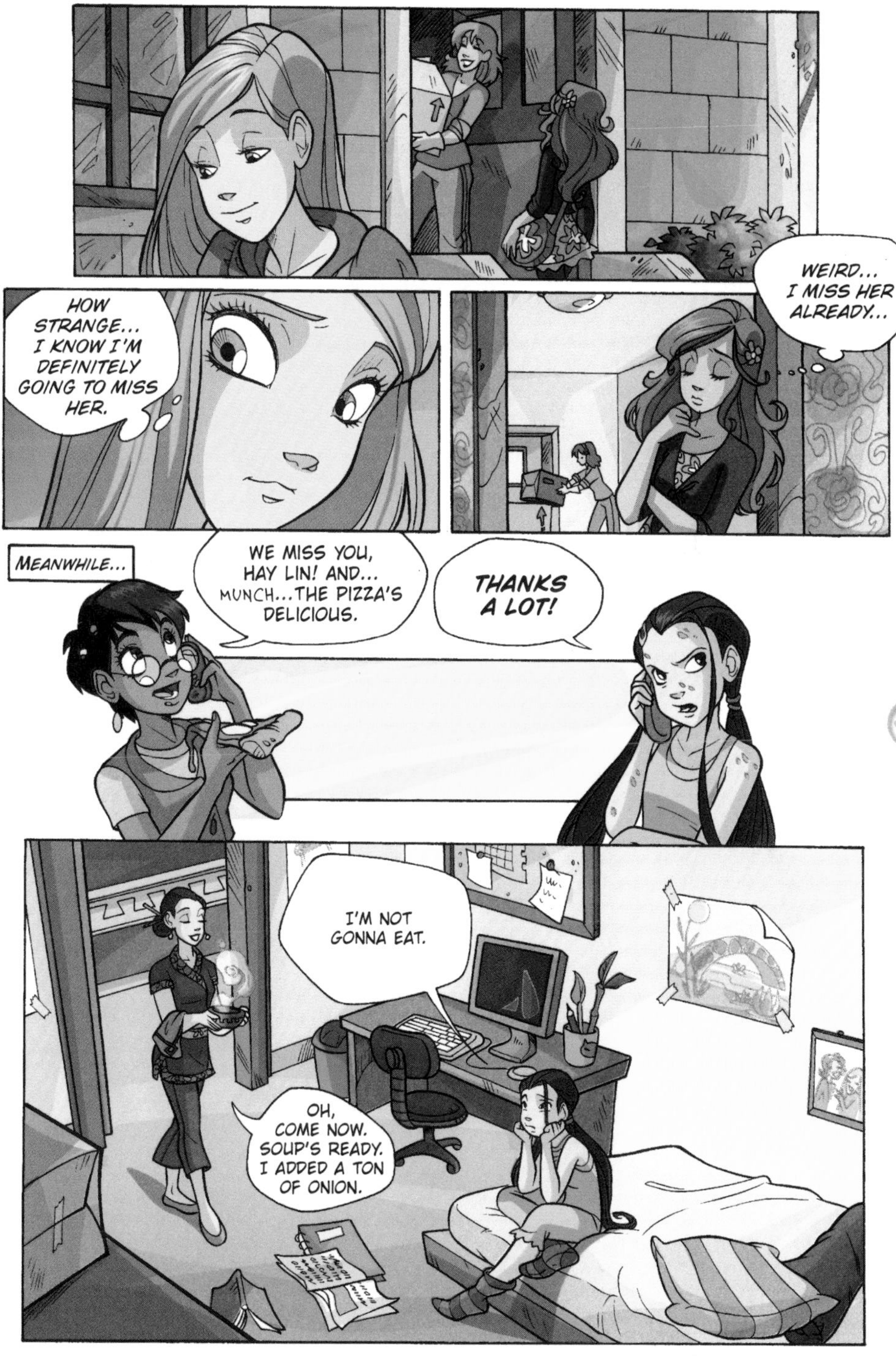
HOW STRANGE... I KNOW I'M DEFINITELY GOING TO MISS HER.
WEIRD... I MISS HER ALREADY...
MEANWHILE...
WE MISS YOU, HAY LIN! AND... MUNCH...THE PIZZA'S DELICIOUS.
THANKS A LOT!
I'M NOT GONNA EAT.
OH, COME NOW. SOUP'S READY. I ADDED A TON OF ONION.

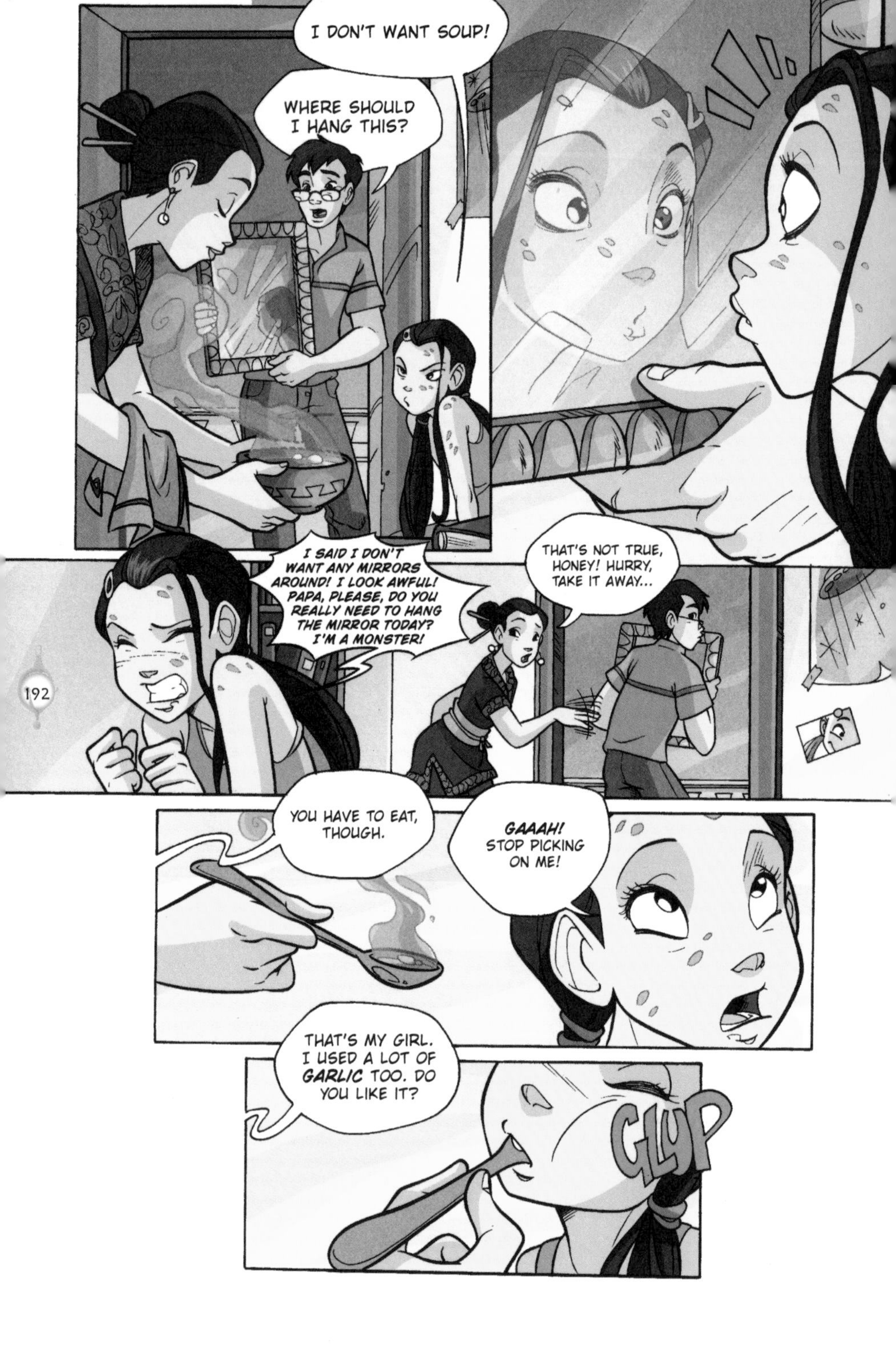
I DON'T WANT SOUP!
WHERE SHOULD I HANG THIS?
I SAID I DON'T WANT ANY MIRRORS AROUND! I LOOK AWFUL! PAPA, PLEASE, DO YOU REALLY NEED TO HANG THE MIRROR TODAY? I'M A MONSTER!
THAT'S NOT TRUE, HONEY! HURRY, TAKE IT AWAY...
YOU HAVE TO EAT, THOUGH.
GAAAH! STOP PICKING ON ME!
THAT'S MY GIRL. I USED A LOT OF GARLIC TOO. DO YOU LIKE IT?
GLUP

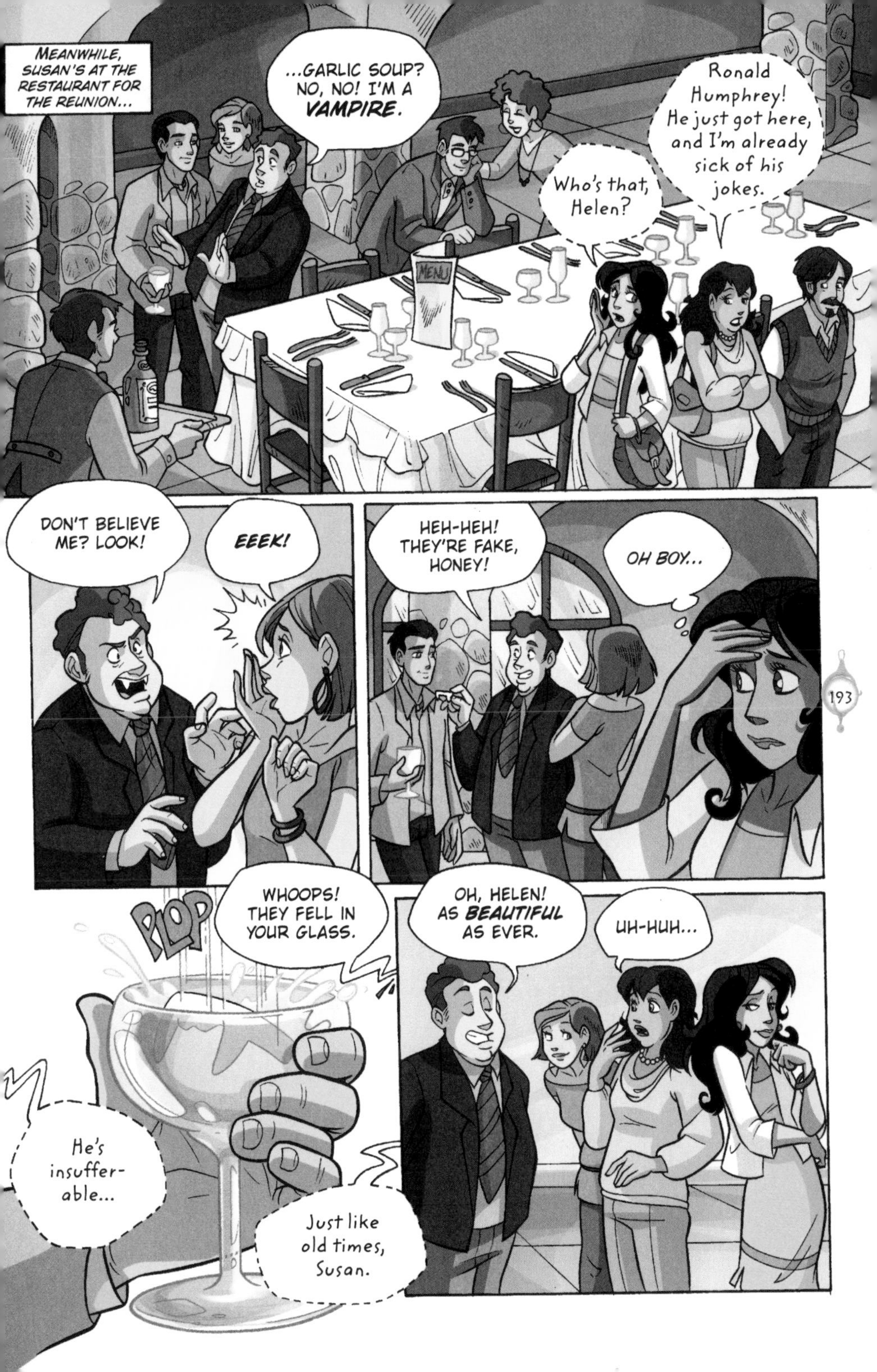
MEANWHILE, SUSAN'S AT THE RESTAURANT FOR THE REUNION...
...GARLIC SOUP? NO, NO! I'M A *VAMPIRE*.
Who's that, Helen?
Ronald Humphrey! He just got here, and I'm already sick of his jokes.
MENU
DON'T BELIEVE ME? LOOK!
EEEK!
HEH-HEH! THEY'RE FAKE, HONEY!
OH BOY...
PLOP
WHOOPS! THEY FELL IN YOUR GLASS.
He's insuffer-able...
Just like old times, Susan.
OH, HELEN! AS *BEAUTIFUL* AS EVER.
UH-HUH...

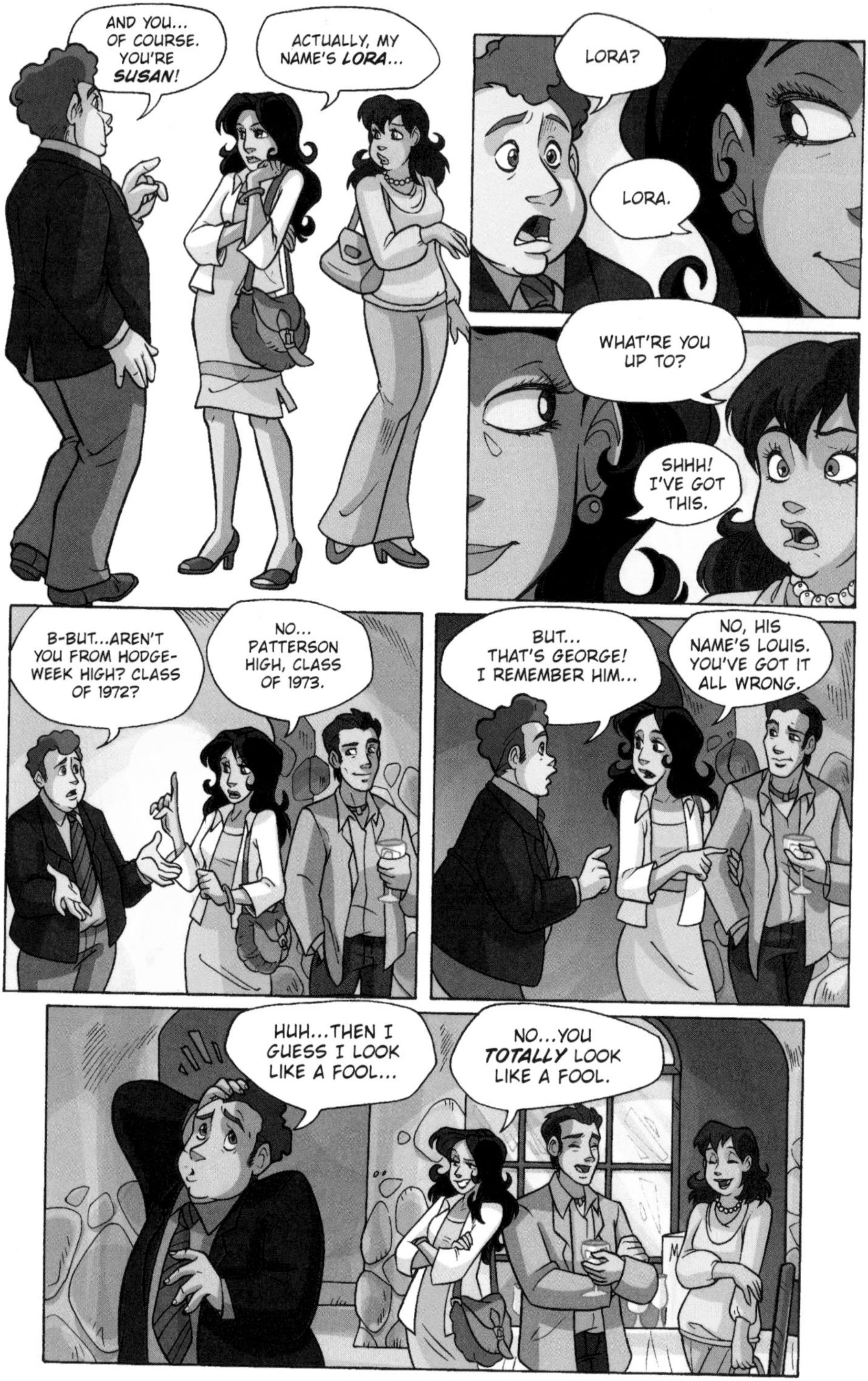
AND YOU... OF COURSE. YOU'RE **SUSAN**!
ACTUALLY, MY NAME'S **LORA**...
LORA?
LORA.
WHAT'RE YOU UP TO?
SHHH! I'VE GOT THIS.
B-BUT...AREN'T YOU FROM HODGE-WEEK HIGH? CLASS OF 1972?
NO... PATTERSON HIGH, CLASS OF 1973.
BUT... THAT'S GEORGE! I REMEMBER HIM...
NO, HIS NAME'S LOUIS. YOU'VE GOT IT ALL WRONG.
HUH...THEN I GUESS I LOOK LIKE A FOOL...
NO...YOU **TOTALLY** LOOK LIKE A FOOL.

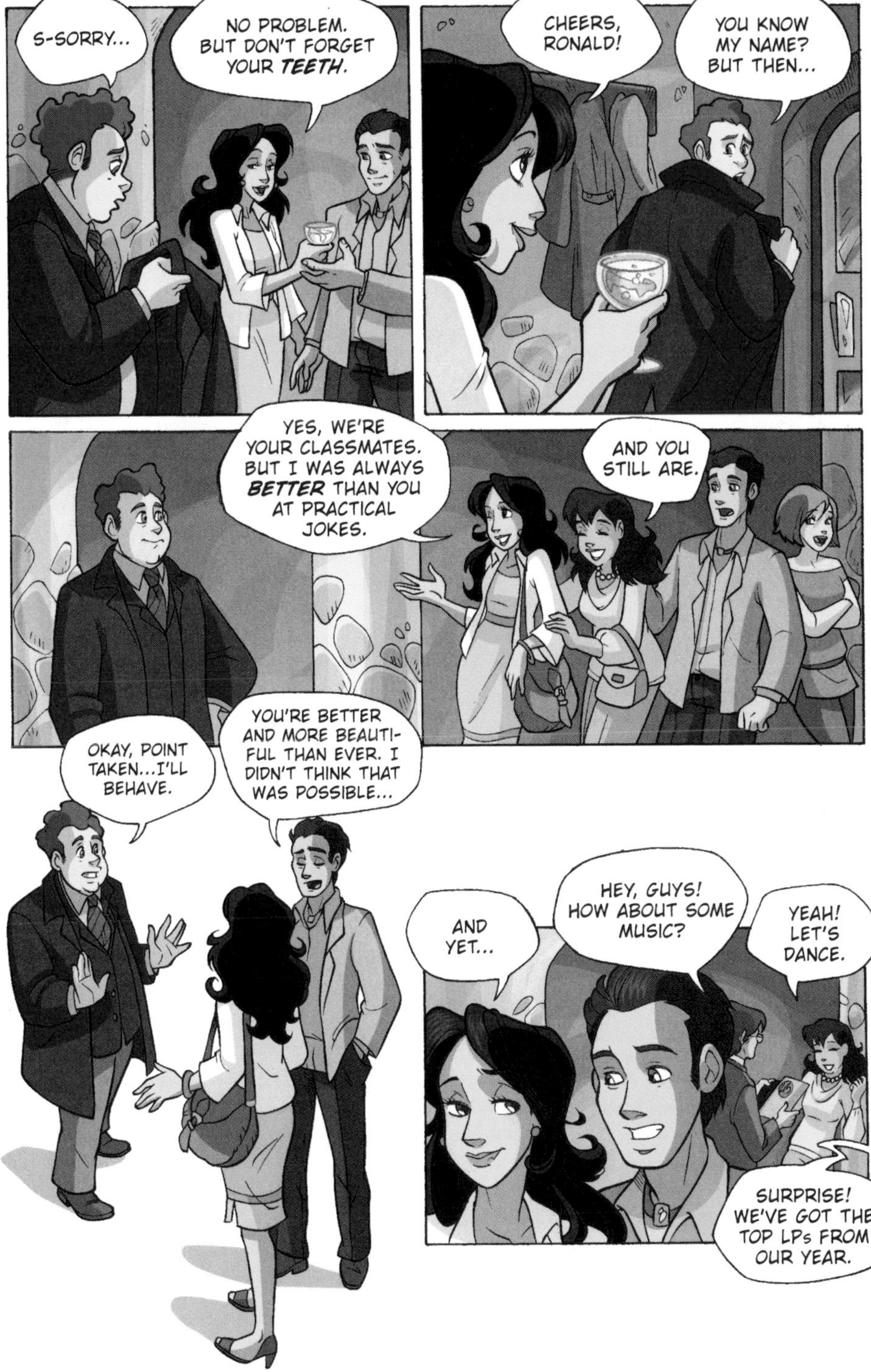
S-SORRY...
NO PROBLEM. BUT DON'T FORGET YOUR TEETH.
CHEERS, RONALD!
YOU KNOW MY NAME? BUT THEN...
YES, WE'RE YOUR CLASSMATES. BUT I WAS ALWAYS BETTER THAN YOU AT PRACTICAL JOKES.
AND YOU STILL ARE.
OKAY, POINT TAKEN...I'LL BEHAVE.
YOU'RE BETTER AND MORE BEAUTIFUL THAN EVER. I DIDN'T THINK THAT WAS POSSIBLE...
AND YET...
HEY, GUYS! HOW ABOUT SOME MUSIC?
YEAH! LET'S DANCE.
SURPRISE! WE'VE GOT THE TOP LPs FROM OUR YEAR.

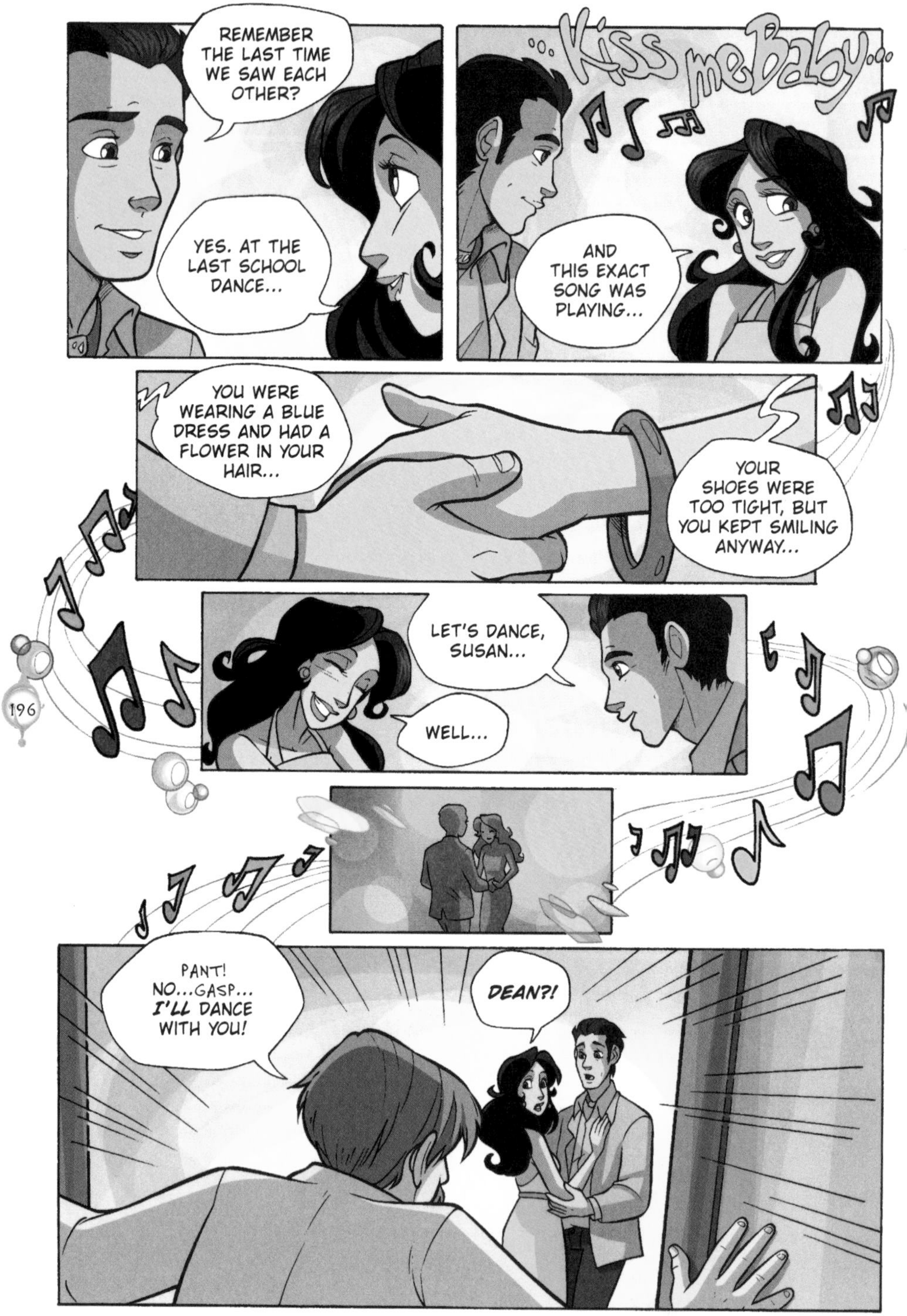
REMEMBER THE LAST TIME WE SAW EACH OTHER?
YES. AT THE LAST SCHOOL DANCE...
...Kiss me Baby...
AND THIS EXACT SONG WAS PLAYING...
YOU WERE WEARING A BLUE DRESS AND HAD A FLOWER IN YOUR HAIR...
YOUR SHOES WERE TOO TIGHT, BUT YOU KEPT SMILING ANYWAY...
LET'S DANCE, SUSAN...
WELL...
PANT! NO...GASP... I'LL DANCE WITH YOU!
DEAN?!

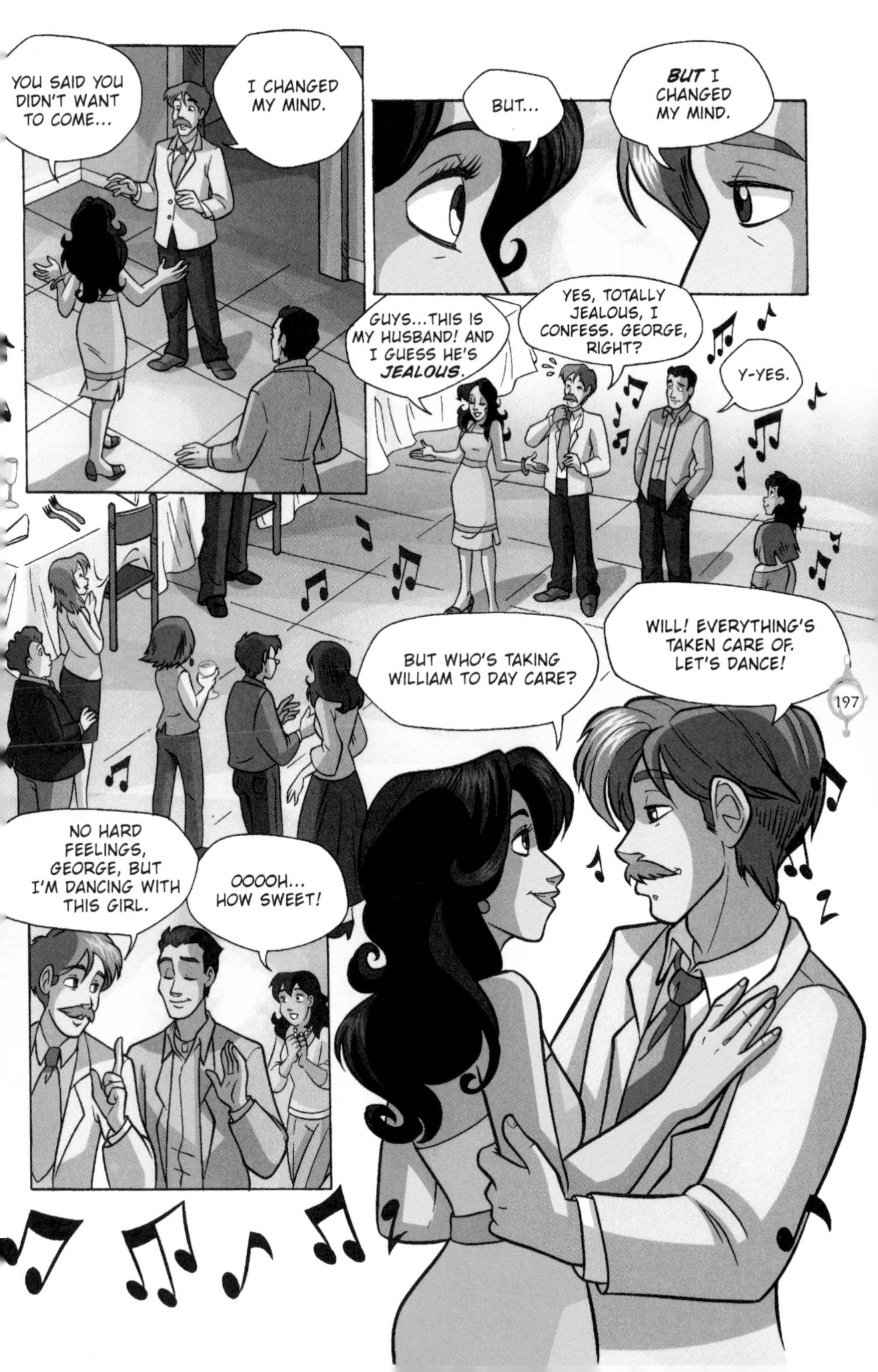

YOU SAID YOU DIDN'T WANT TO COME...
I CHANGED MY MIND.
BUT...
BUT I CHANGED MY MIND.
GUYS...THIS IS MY HUSBAND! AND I GUESS HE'S JEALOUS.
YES, TOTALLY JEALOUS, I CONFESS. GEORGE, RIGHT?
Y-YES.
BUT WHO'S TAKING WILLIAM TO DAY CARE?
WILL! EVERYTHING'S TAKEN CARE OF. LET'S DANCE!
NO HARD FEELINGS, GEORGE, BUT I'M DANCING WITH THIS GIRL.
OOOOH... HOW SWEET!

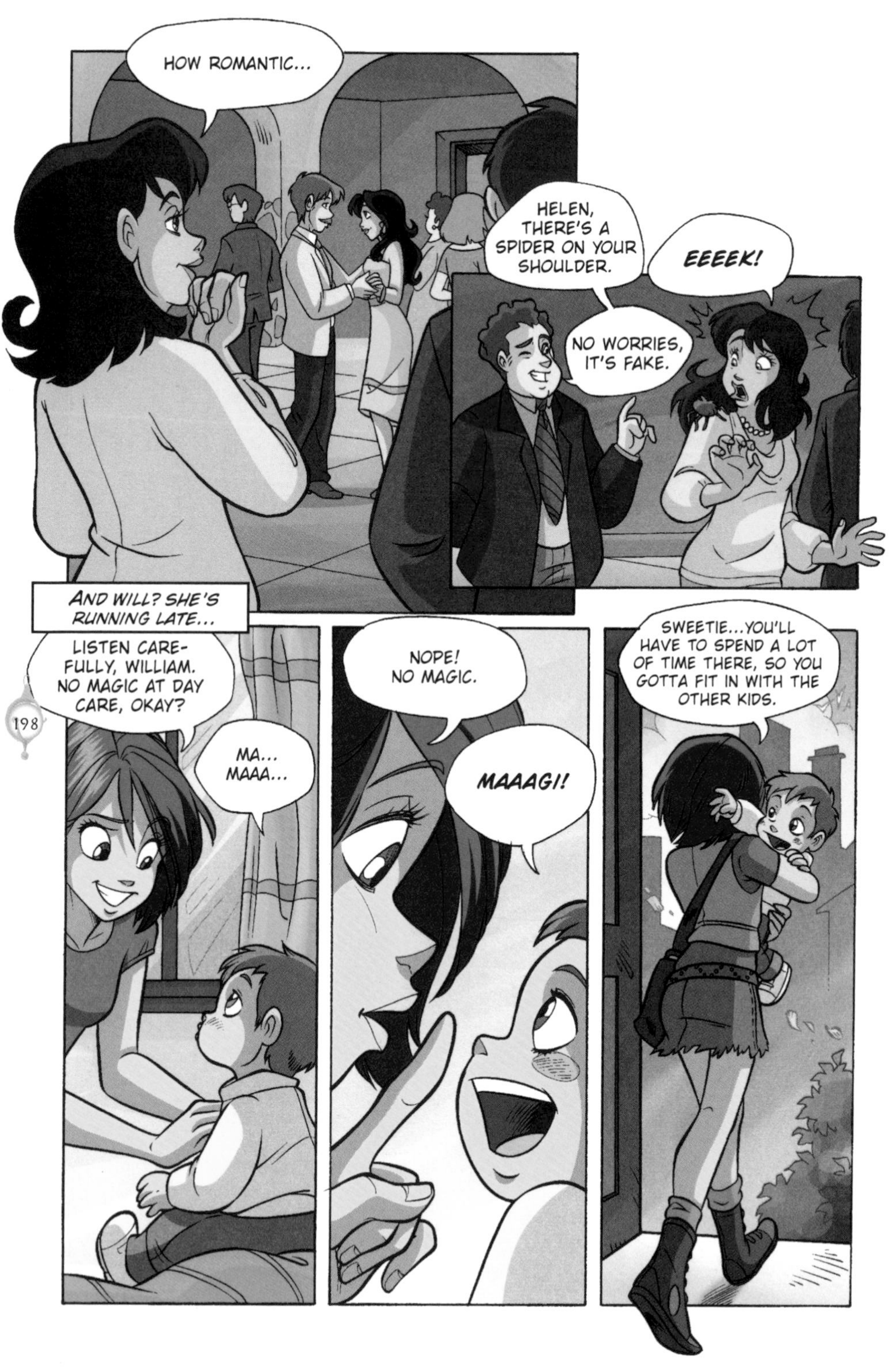
HOW ROMANTIC...
HELEN, THERE'S A SPIDER ON YOUR SHOULDER.
EEEEK!
NO WORRIES, IT'S FAKE.
AND WILL? SHE'S RUNNING LATE...
LISTEN CARE-FULLY, WILLIAM. NO MAGIC AT DAY CARE, OKAY?
MA... MAAA...
NOPE! NO MAGIC.
MAAAGI!
SWEETIE...YOU'LL HAVE TO SPEND A LOT OF TIME THERE, SO YOU GOTTA FIT IN WITH THE OTHER KIDS.

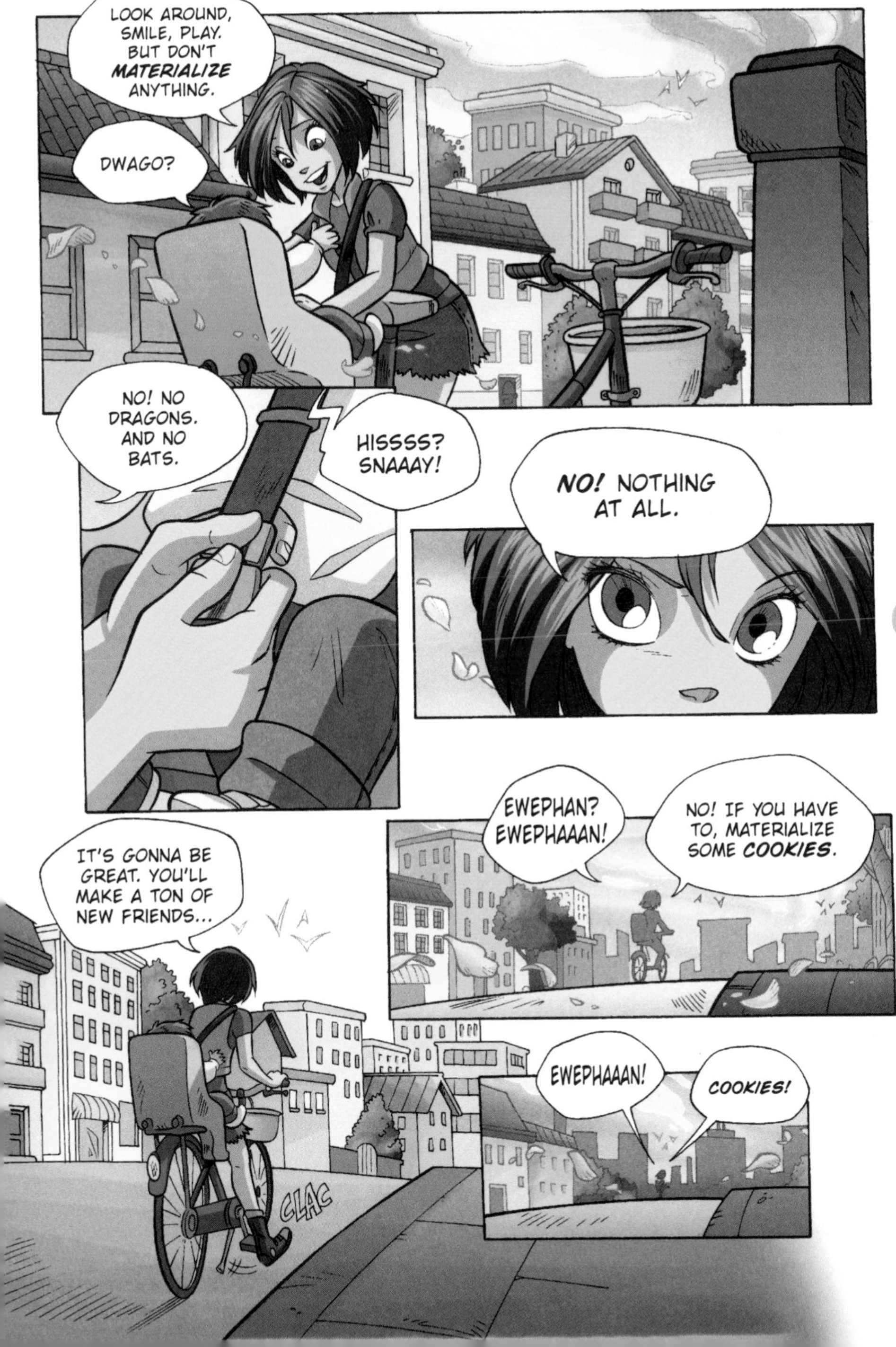

LOOK AROUND, SMILE, PLAY. BUT DON'T MATERIALIZE ANYTHING.
DWAGO?
NO! NO DRAGONS. AND NO BATS.
HISSSS? SNAAAY!
NO! NOTHING AT ALL.
IT'S GONNA BE GREAT. YOU'LL MAKE A TON OF NEW FRIENDS...
CLAC
EWEPHAN? EWEPHAAAN!
NO! IF YOU HAVE TO, MATERIALIZE SOME COOKIES.
EWEPHAAAN!
COOKIES!

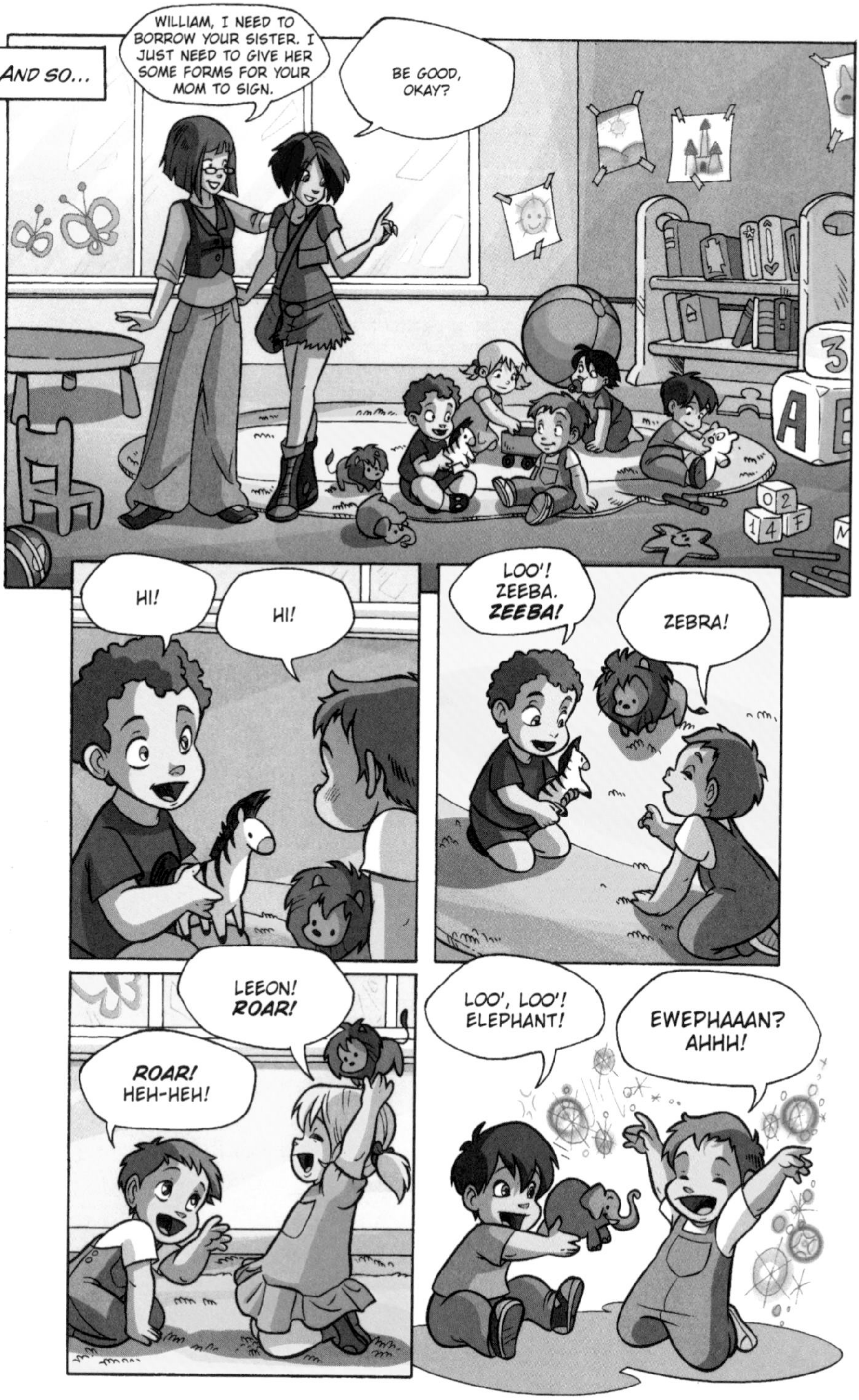
AND SO...
WILLIAM, I NEED TO BORROW YOUR SISTER. I JUST NEED TO GIVE HER SOME FORMS FOR YOUR MOM TO SIGN.
BE GOOD, OKAY?
HI!
HI!
LOO'! ZEEBA. ZEEBA!
ZEBRA!
LEEON! ROAR!
ROAR! HEH-HEH!
LOO', LOO'! ELEPHANT!
EWEPHAAAN? AHHH!

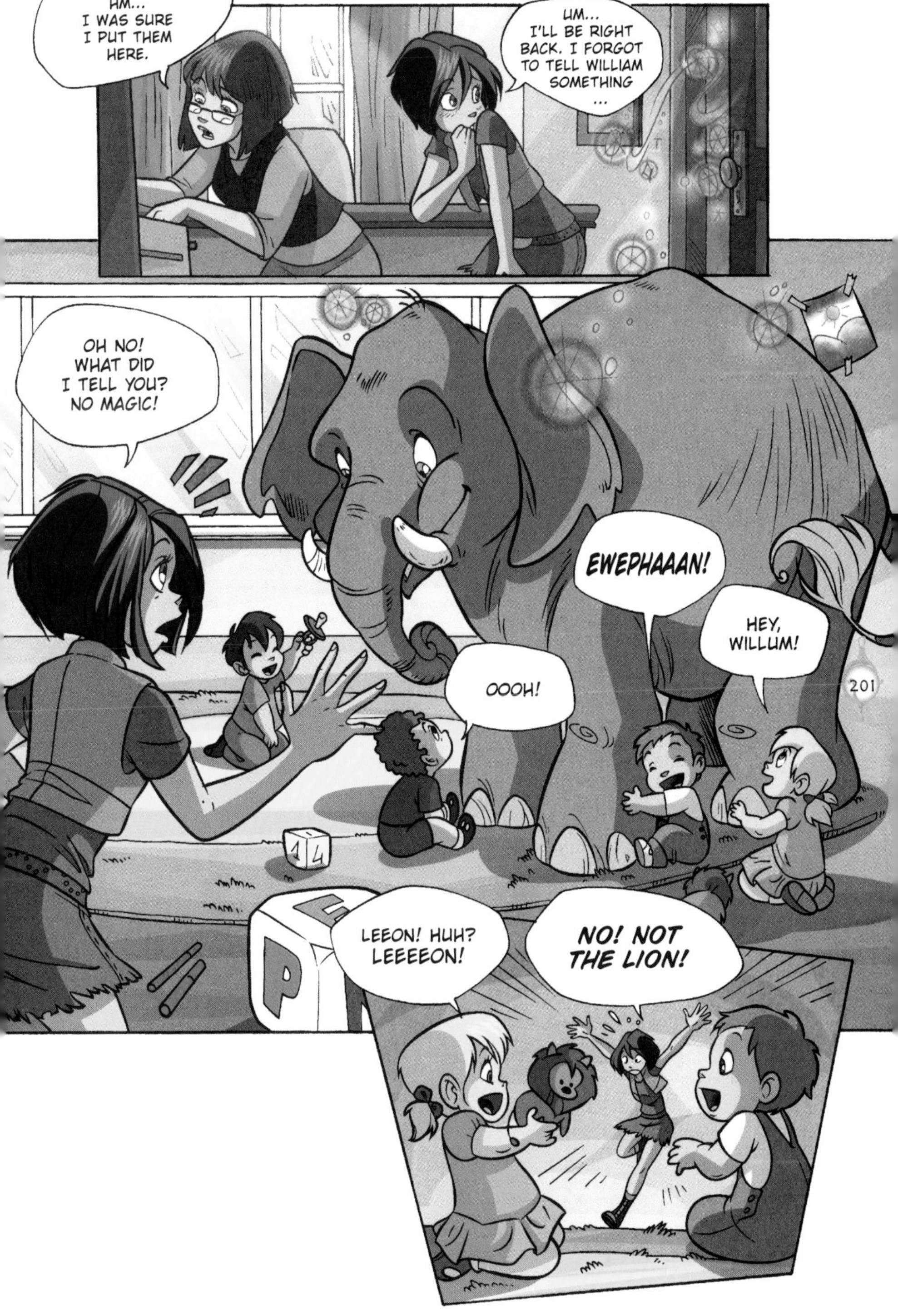
HM... I WAS SURE I PUT THEM HERE.
UM... I'LL BE RIGHT BACK. I FORGOT TO TELL WILLIAM SOMETHING ...
OH NO! WHAT DID I TELL YOU? NO MAGIC!
EWEPHAAAN!
HEY, WILLUM!
OOOH!
LEEON! HUH? LEEEEON!
NO! NOT THE LION!

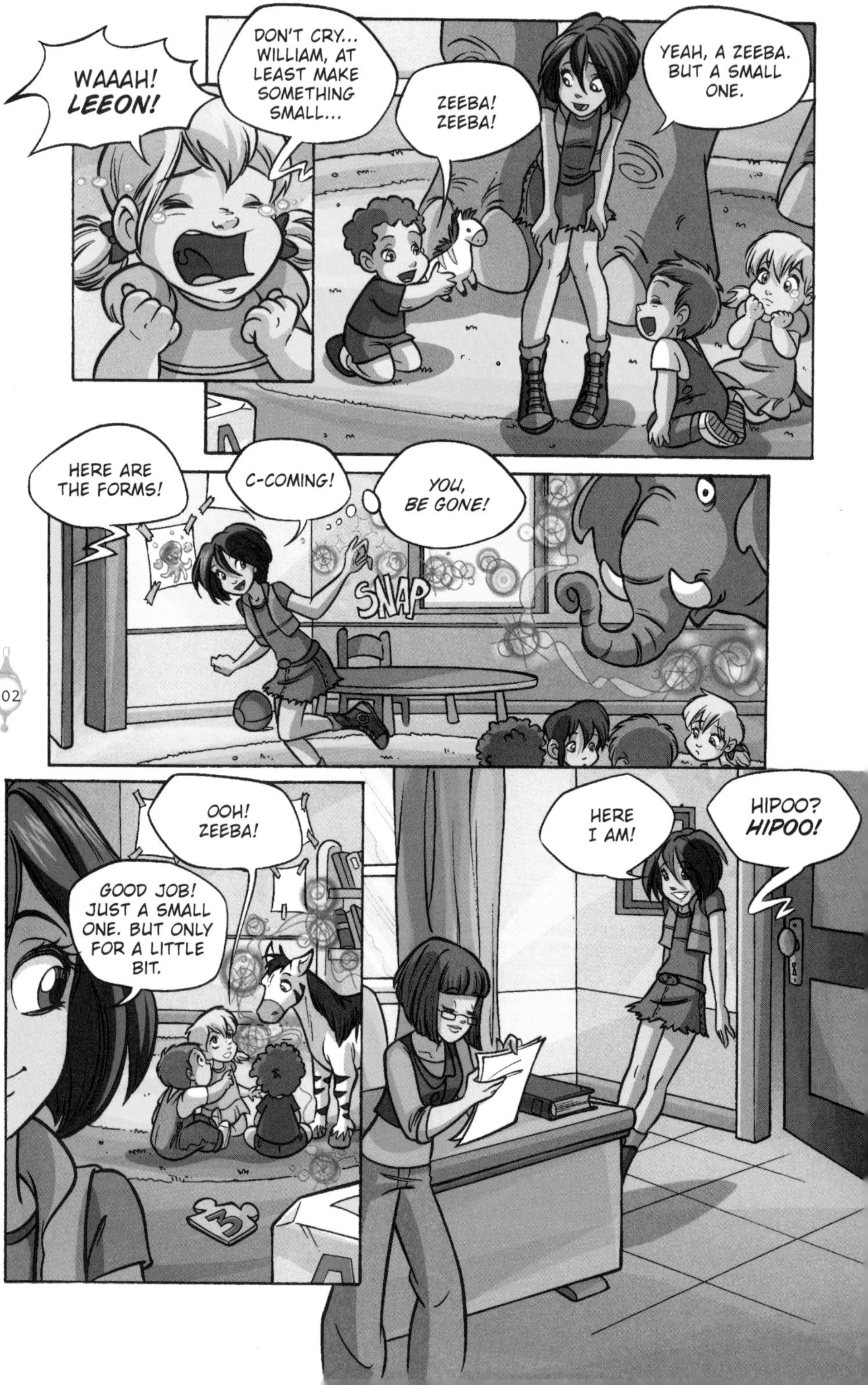
WAAAH! LEEON!
DON'T CRY... WILLIAM, AT LEAST MAKE SOMETHING SMALL...
ZEEBA! ZEEBA!
YEAH, A ZEEBA. BUT A SMALL ONE.
HERE ARE THE FORMS!
C-COMING!
YOU, BE GONE!
SNAP
OOH! ZEEBA!
GOOD JOB! JUST A SMALL ONE. BUT ONLY FOR A LITTLE BIT.
HERE I AM!
HIPOO? HIPOO!

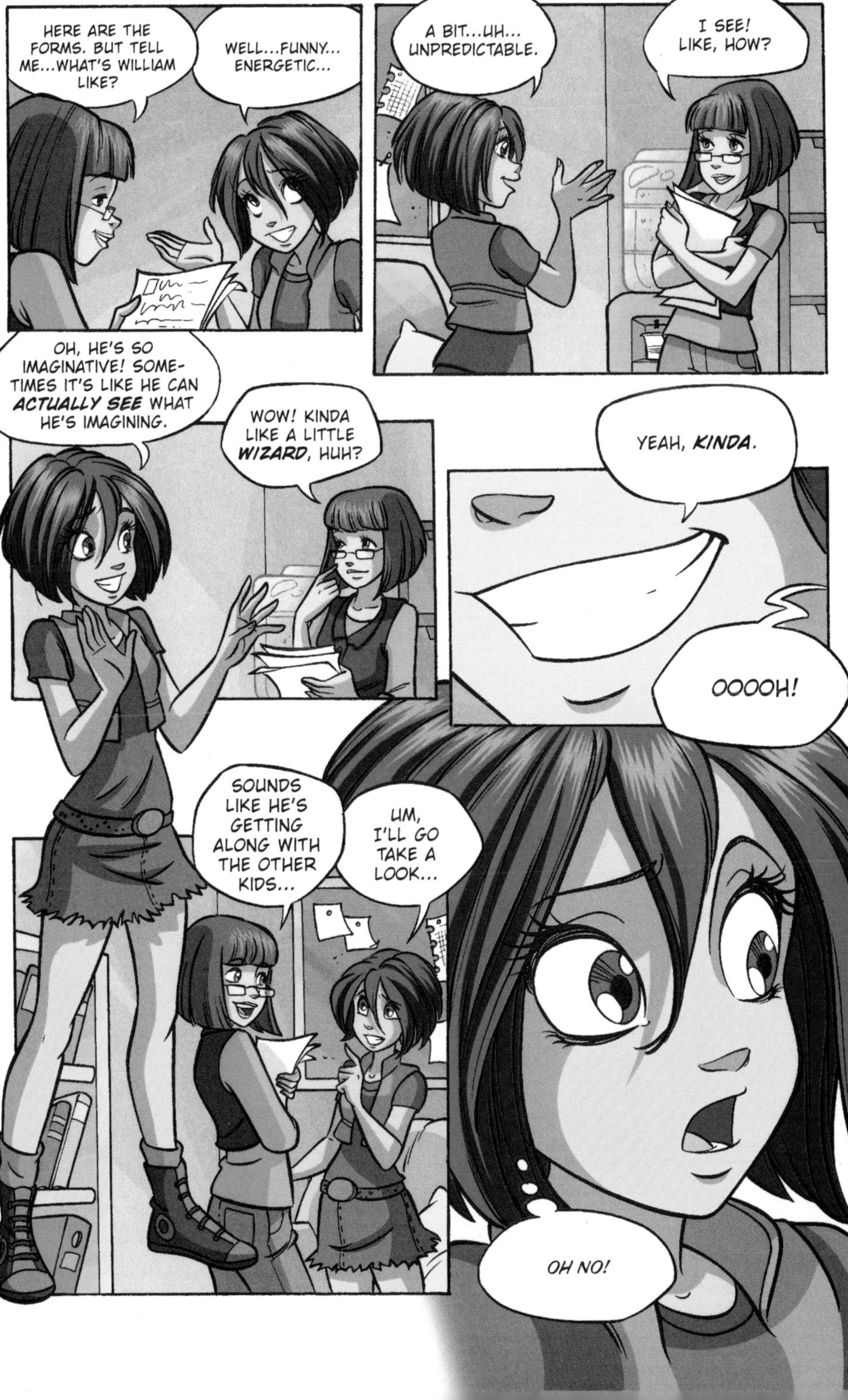
HERE ARE THE FORMS. BUT TELL ME...WHAT'S WILLIAM LIKE?
WELL...FUNNY... ENERGETIC...
A BIT...UH... UNPREDICTABLE.
I SEE! LIKE, HOW?
OH, HE'S SO IMAGINATIVE! SOMETIMES IT'S LIKE HE CAN ACTUALLY SEE WHAT HE'S IMAGINING.
WOW! KINDA LIKE A LITTLE WIZARD, HUH?
YEAH, KINDA.
OOOOH!
SOUNDS LIKE HE'S GETTING ALONG WITH THE OTHER KIDS...
UM, I'LL GO TAKE A LOOK...
OH NO!

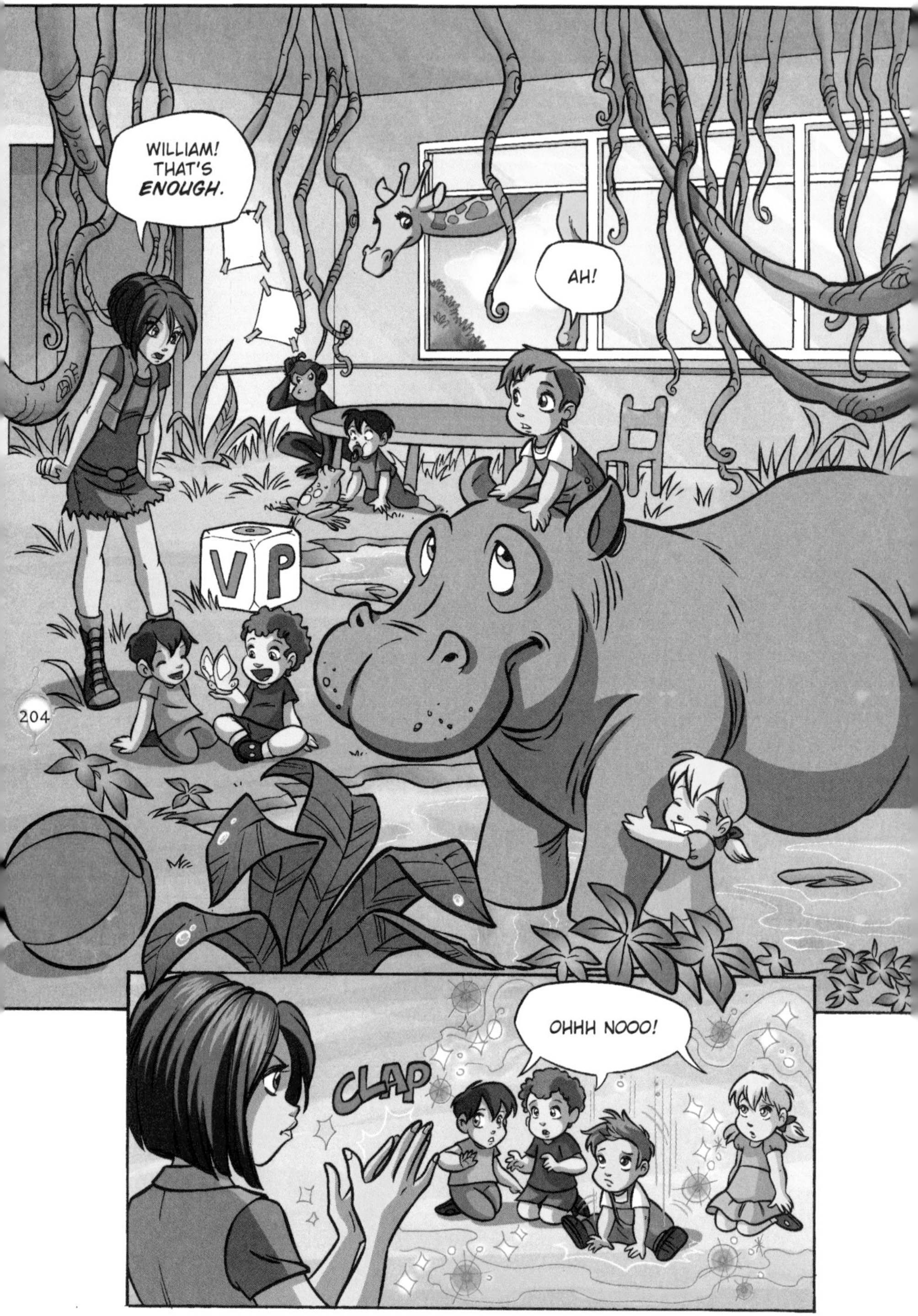
WILLIAM! THAT'S ENOUGH.
AH!
V P
CLAP
OHHH NOOO!

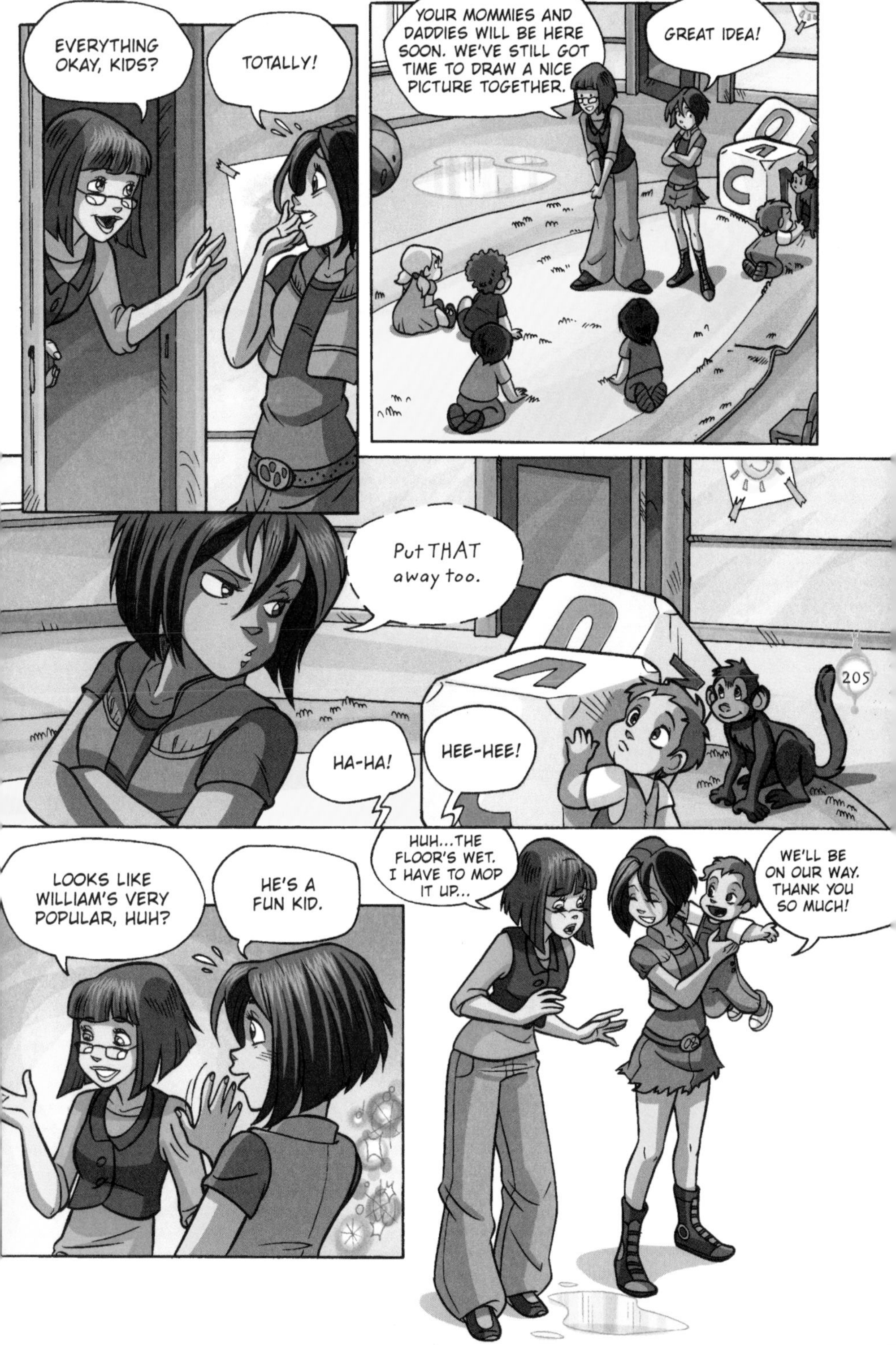
EVERYTHING OKAY, KIDS?
TOTALLY!
YOUR MOMMIES AND DADDIES WILL BE HERE SOON. WE'VE STILL GOT TIME TO DRAW A NICE PICTURE TOGETHER.
GREAT IDEA!
Put THAT away too.
HA-HA!
HEE-HEE!
LOOKS LIKE WILLIAM'S VERY POPULAR, HUH?
HE'S A FUN KID.
HUH...THE FLOOR'S WET. I HAVE TO MOP IT UP...
WE'LL BE ON OUR WAY. THANK YOU SO MUCH!

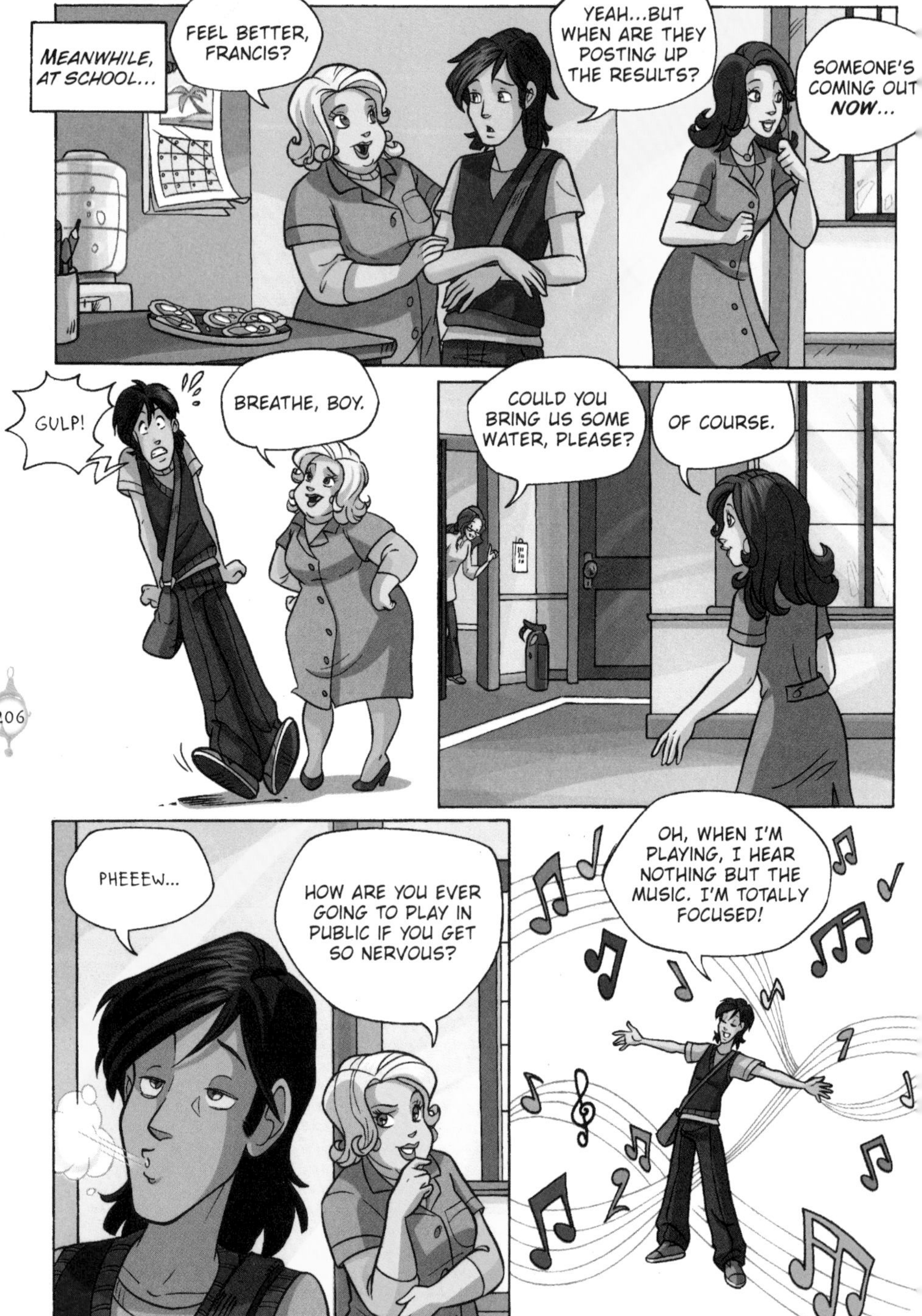
MEANWHILE, AT SCHOOL...
FEEL BETTER, FRANCIS?
YEAH...BUT WHEN ARE THEY POSTING UP THE RESULTS?
SOMEONE'S COMING OUT NOW...
GULP!
BREATHE, BOY.
COULD YOU BRING US SOME WATER, PLEASE?
OF COURSE.
PHEEEW...
HOW ARE YOU EVER GOING TO PLAY IN PUBLIC IF YOU GET SO NERVOUS?
OH, WHEN I'M PLAYING, I HEAR NOTHING BUT THE MUSIC. I'M TOTALLY FOCUSED!

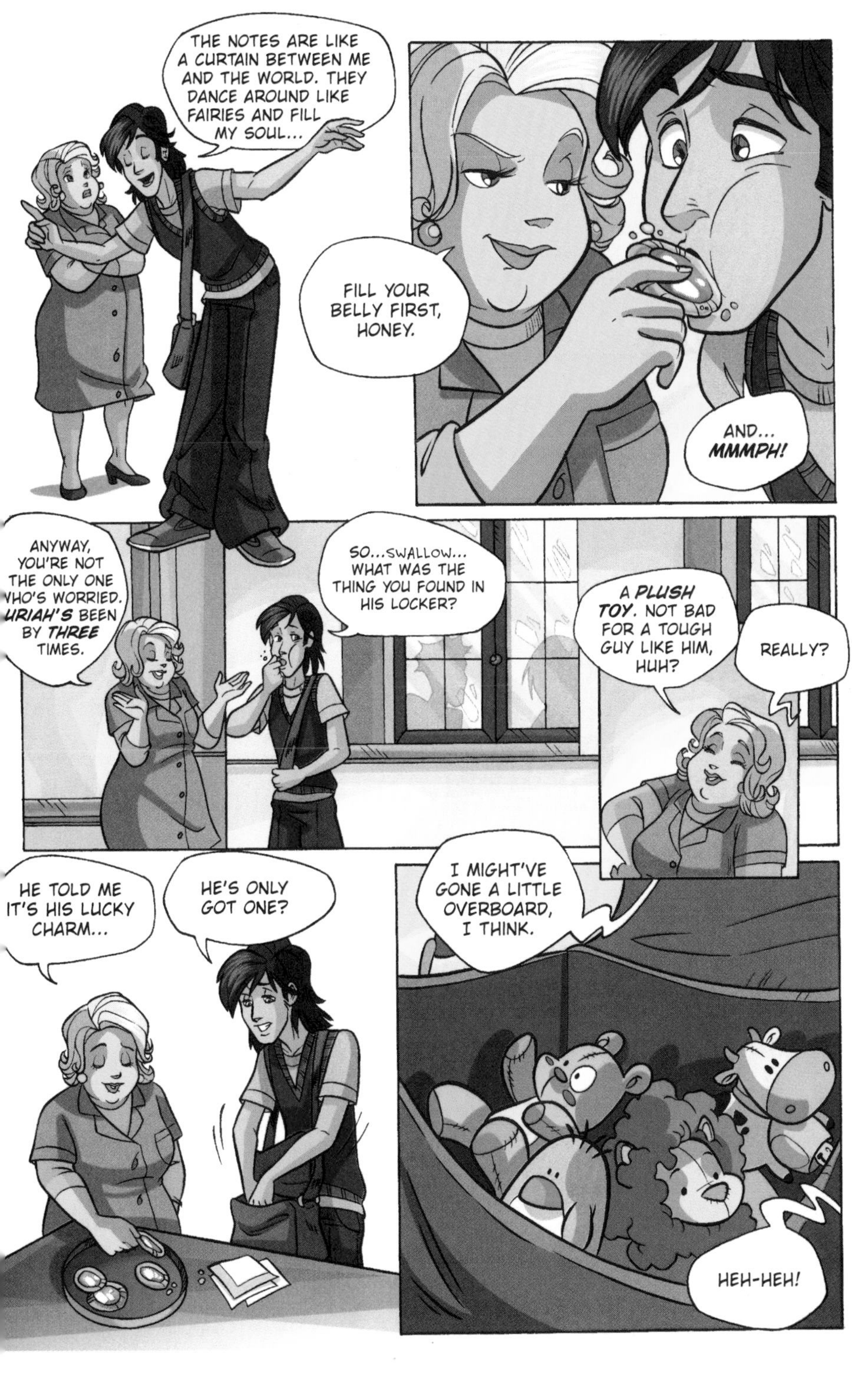

THE NOTES ARE LIKE A CURTAIN BETWEEN ME AND THE WORLD. THEY DANCE AROUND LIKE FAIRIES AND FILL MY SOUL...
FILL YOUR BELLY FIRST, HONEY.
AND... MMMPH!
ANYWAY, YOU'RE NOT THE ONLY ONE WHO'S WORRIED. URIAH'S BEEN BY THREE TIMES.
SO...SWALLOW... WHAT WAS THE THING YOU FOUND IN HIS LOCKER?
A PLUSH TOY. NOT BAD FOR A TOUGH GUY LIKE HIM, HUH?
REALLY?
HE TOLD ME IT'S HIS LUCKY CHARM...
HE'S ONLY GOT ONE?
I MIGHT'VE GONE A LITTLE OVERBOARD, I THINK.
HEH-HEH!

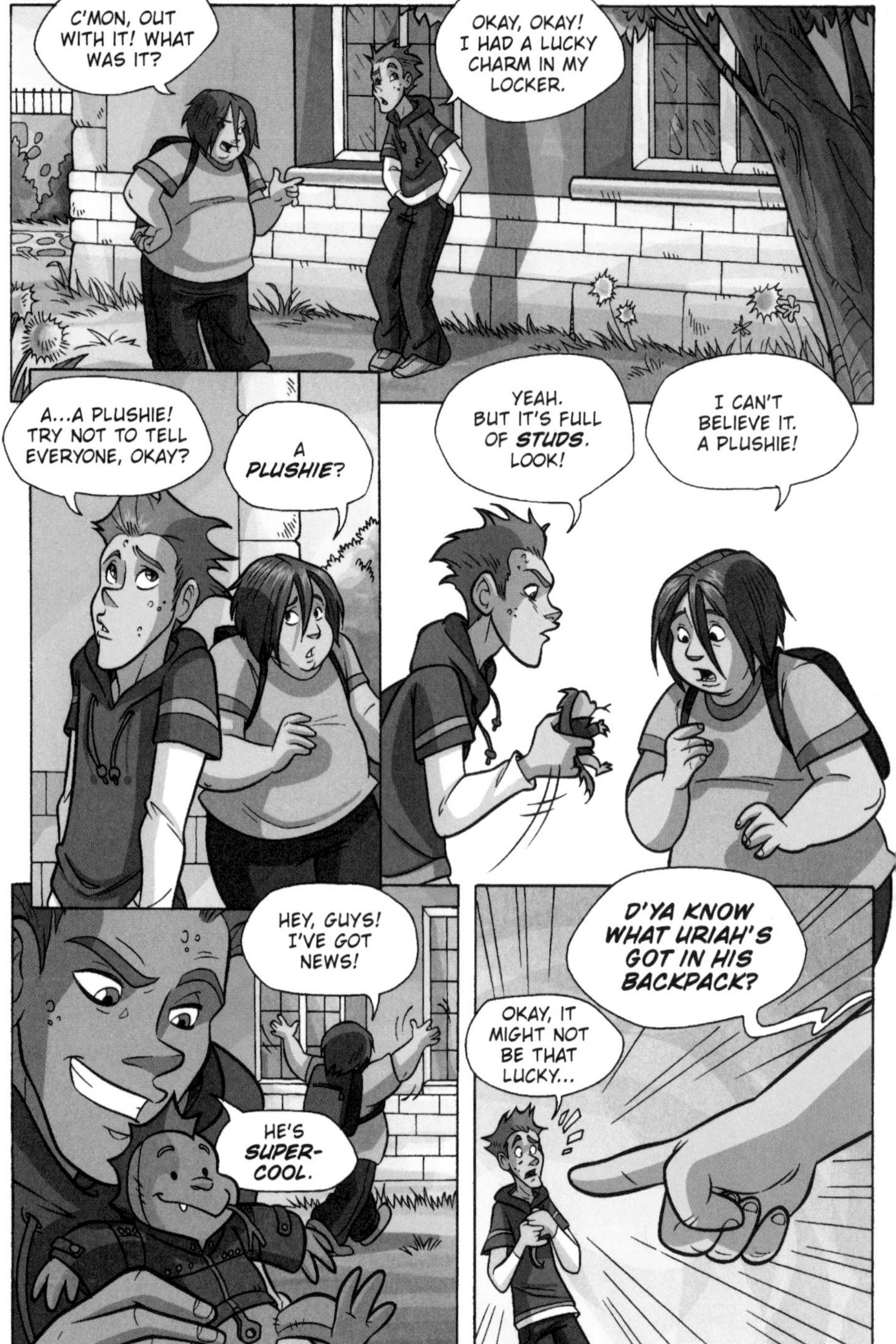
C'MON, OUT WITH IT! WHAT WAS IT?
OKAY, OKAY! I HAD A LUCKY CHARM IN MY LOCKER.
A...A PLUSHIE! TRY NOT TO TELL EVERYONE, OKAY?
A PLUSHIE?
YEAH. BUT IT'S FULL OF STUDS. LOOK!
I CAN'T BELIEVE IT. A PLUSHIE!
HEY, GUYS! I'VE GOT NEWS!
HE'S SUPER-COOL.
D'YA KNOW WHAT URIAH'S GOT IN HIS BACKPACK?
OKAY, IT MIGHT NOT BE THAT LUCKY...

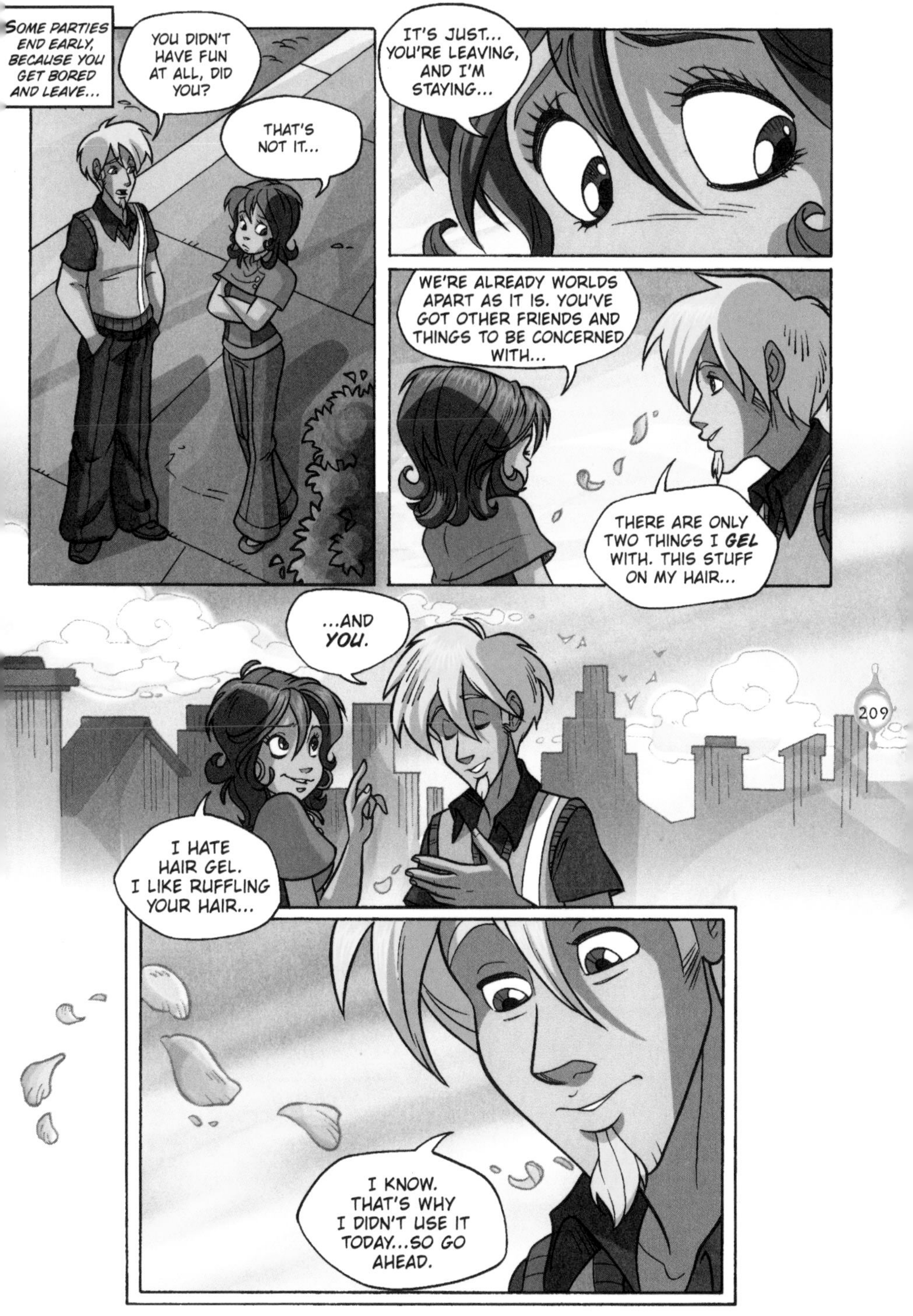
SOME PARTIES END EARLY, BECAUSE YOU GET BORED AND LEAVE...
YOU DIDN'T HAVE FUN AT ALL, DID YOU?
THAT'S NOT IT...
IT'S JUST... YOU'RE LEAVING, AND I'M STAYING...
WE'RE ALREADY WORLDS APART AS IT IS. YOU'VE GOT OTHER FRIENDS AND THINGS TO BE CONCERNED WITH...
THERE ARE ONLY TWO THINGS I GEL WITH. THIS STUFF ON MY HAIR...
...AND YOU.
I HATE HAIR GEL. I LIKE RUFFLING YOUR HAIR...
I KNOW. THAT'S WHY I DIDN'T USE IT TODAY...SO GO AHEAD.

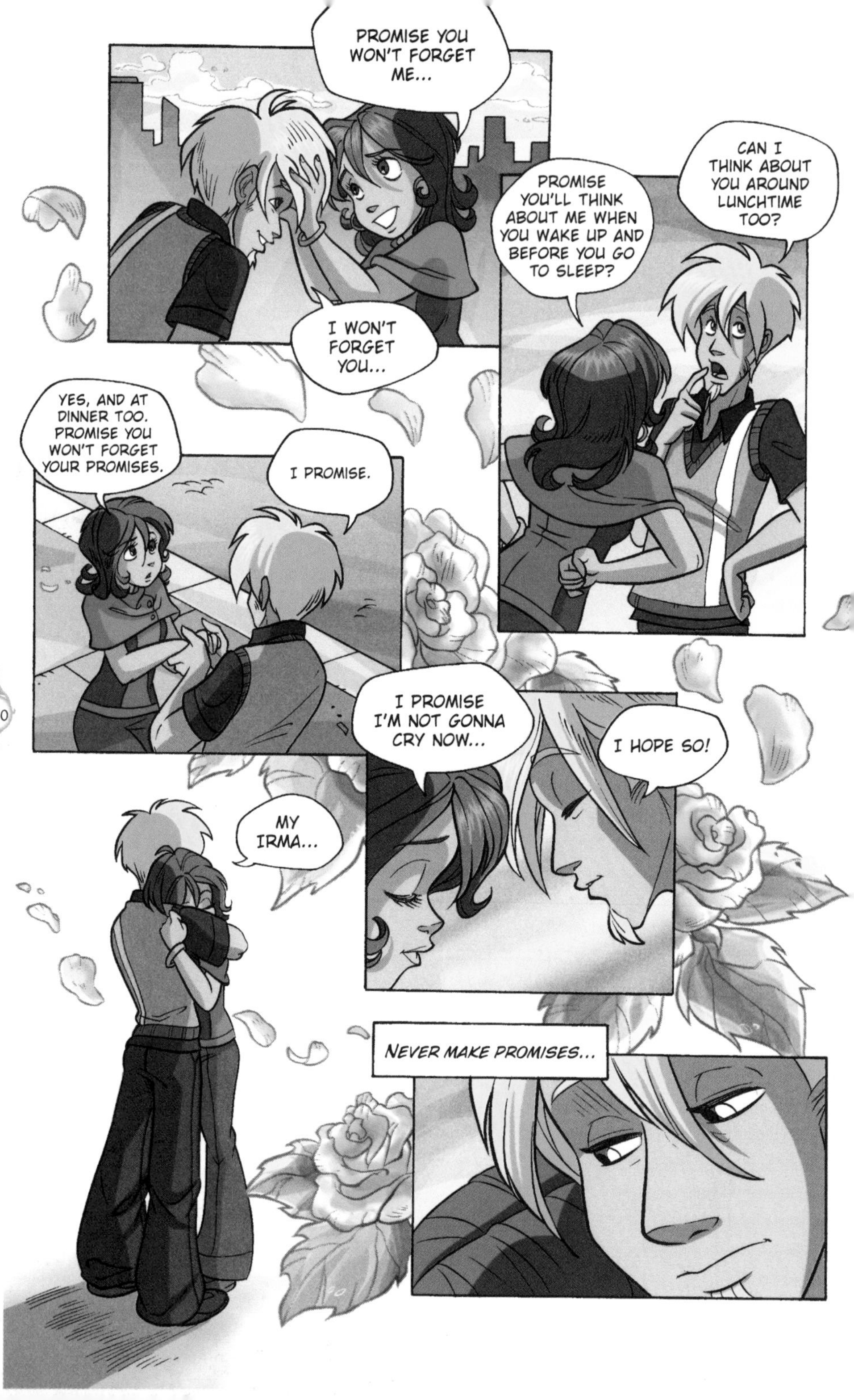
PROMISE YOU WON'T FORGET ME...
I WON'T FORGET YOU...
PROMISE YOU'LL THINK ABOUT ME WHEN YOU WAKE UP AND BEFORE YOU GO TO SLEEP?
CAN I THINK ABOUT YOU AROUND LUNCHTIME TOO?
YES, AND AT DINNER TOO. PROMISE YOU WON'T FORGET YOUR PROMISES.
I PROMISE.
I PROMISE I'M NOT GONNA CRY NOW...
I HOPE SO!
MY IRMA...
NEVER MAKE PROMISES...

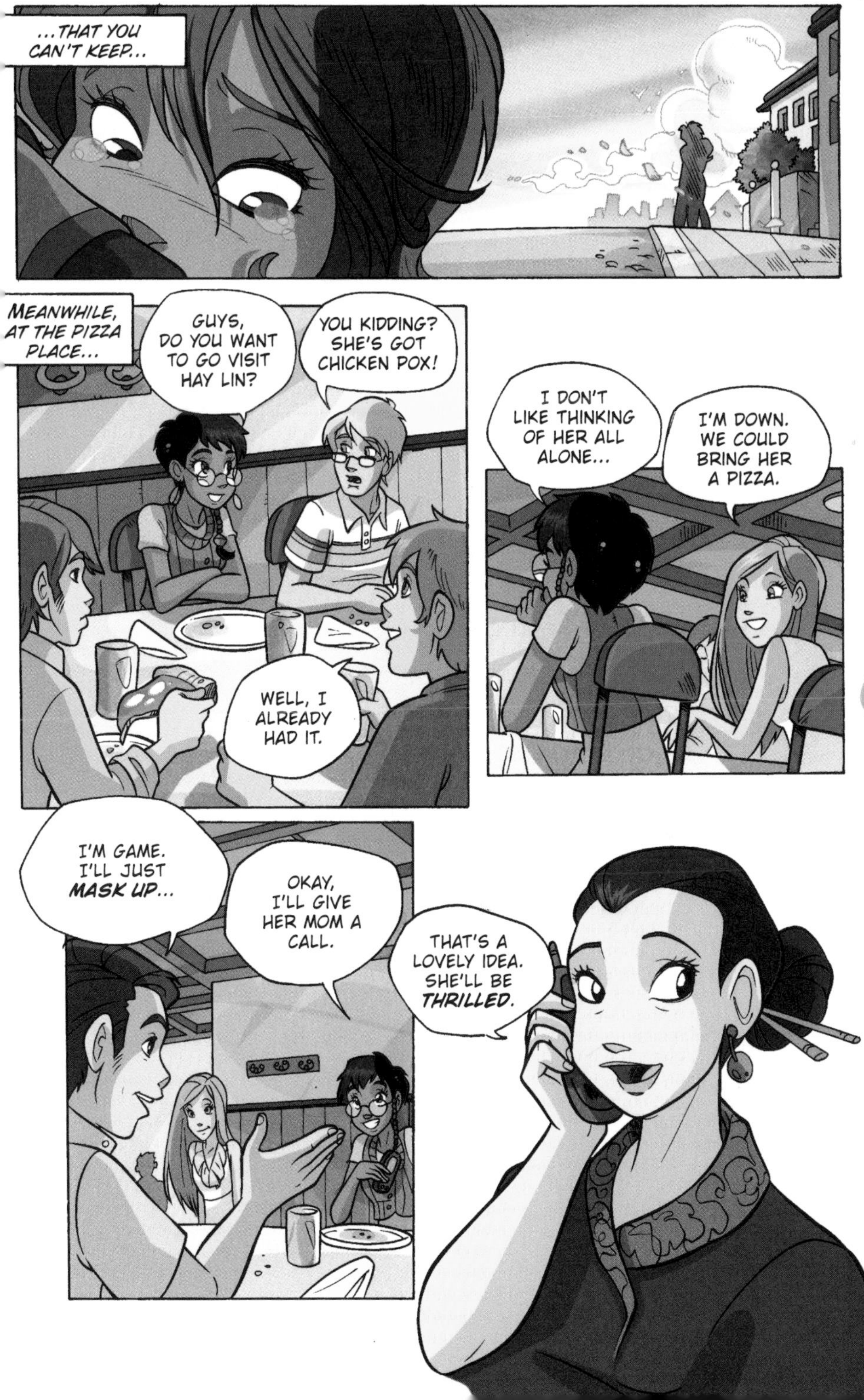
...THAT YOU CAN'T KEEP...
MEANWHILE, AT THE PIZZA PLACE...
GUYS, DO YOU WANT TO GO VISIT HAY LIN?
YOU KIDDING? SHE'S GOT CHICKEN POX!
WELL, I ALREADY HAD IT.
I DON'T LIKE THINKING OF HER ALL ALONE...
I'M DOWN. WE COULD BRING HER A PIZZA.
I'M GAME. I'LL JUST **MASK UP**...
OKAY, I'LL GIVE HER MOM A CALL.
THAT'S A LOVELY IDEA. SHE'LL BE ***THRILLED***.

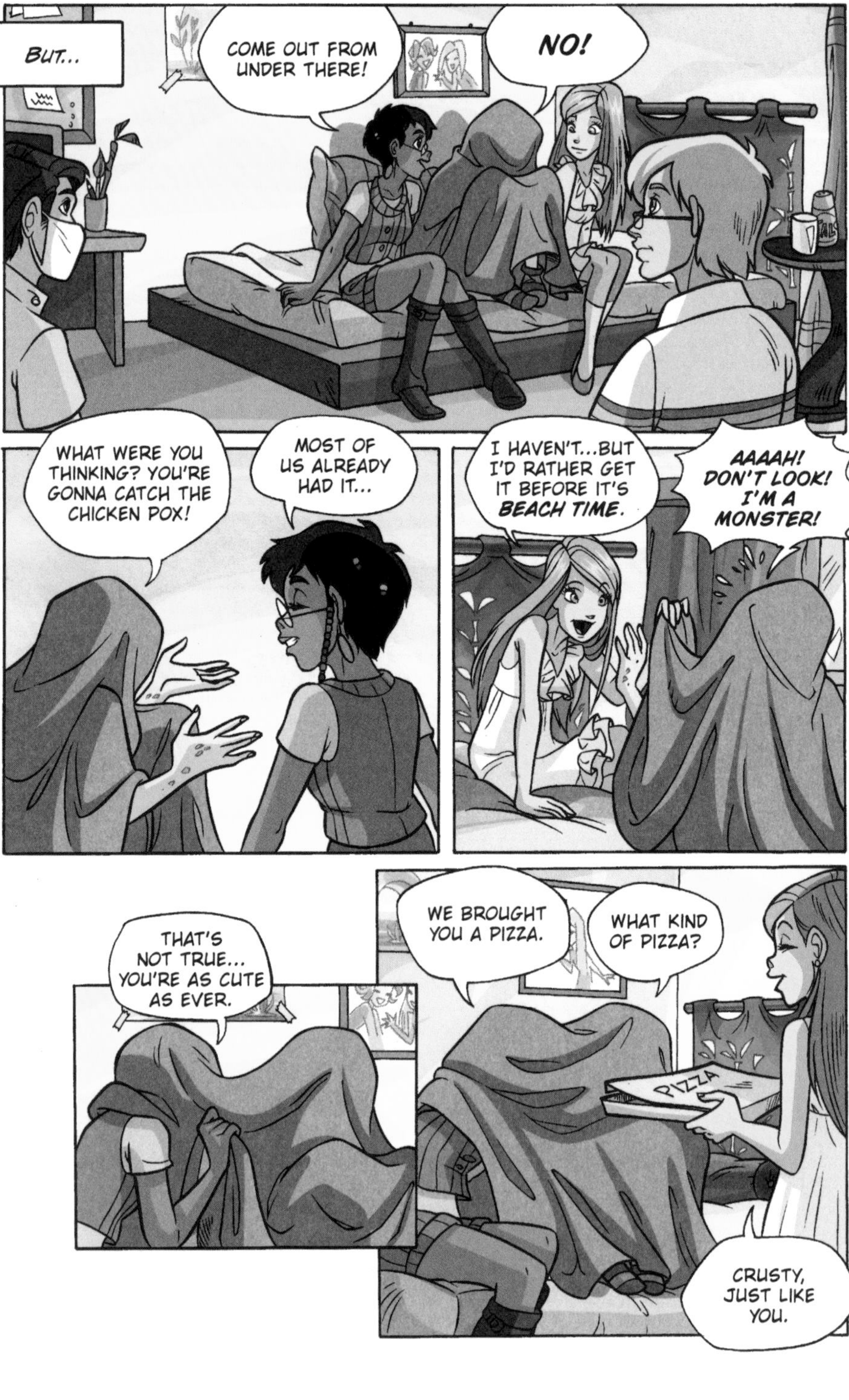
BUT...
COME OUT FROM UNDER THERE!
NO!
WHAT WERE YOU THINKING? YOU'RE GONNA CATCH THE CHICKEN POX!
MOST OF US ALREADY HAD IT...
I HAVEN'T...BUT I'D RATHER GET IT BEFORE IT'S BEACH TIME.
AAAAH! DON'T LOOK! I'M A MONSTER!
THAT'S NOT TRUE... YOU'RE AS CUTE AS EVER.
WE BROUGHT YOU A PIZZA.
WHAT KIND OF PIZZA?
PIZZA
CRUSTY, JUST LIKE YOU.

212

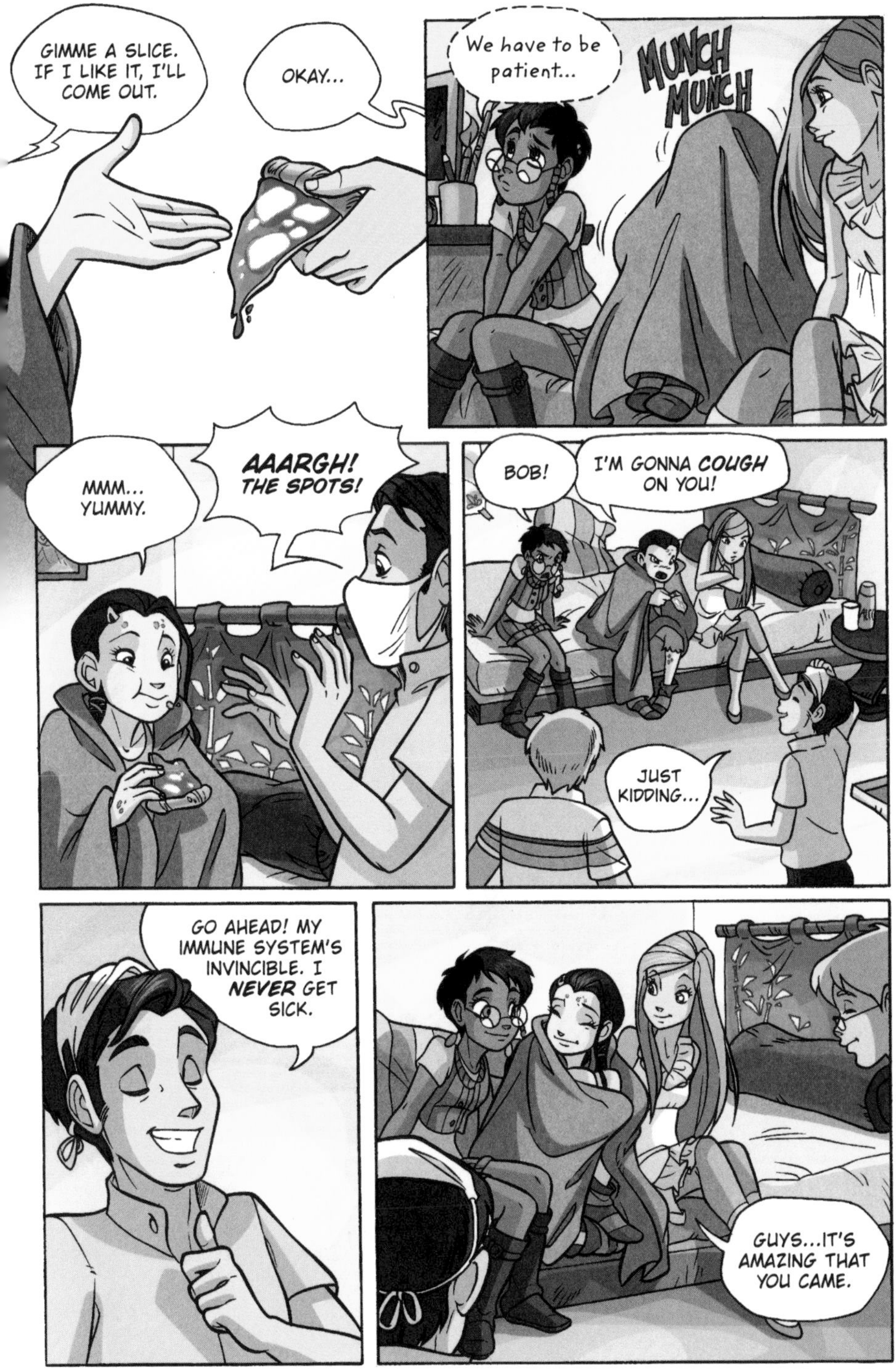
GIMME A SLICE. IF I LIKE IT, I'LL COME OUT.
OKAY...
We have to be patient...
MUNCH MUNCH
MMM... YUMMY.
AAARGH! THE SPOTS!
BOB!
I'M GONNA COUGH ON YOU!
JUST KIDDING...
GO AHEAD! MY IMMUNE SYSTEM'S INVINCIBLE. I NEVER GET SICK.
GUYS...IT'S AMAZING THAT YOU CAME.

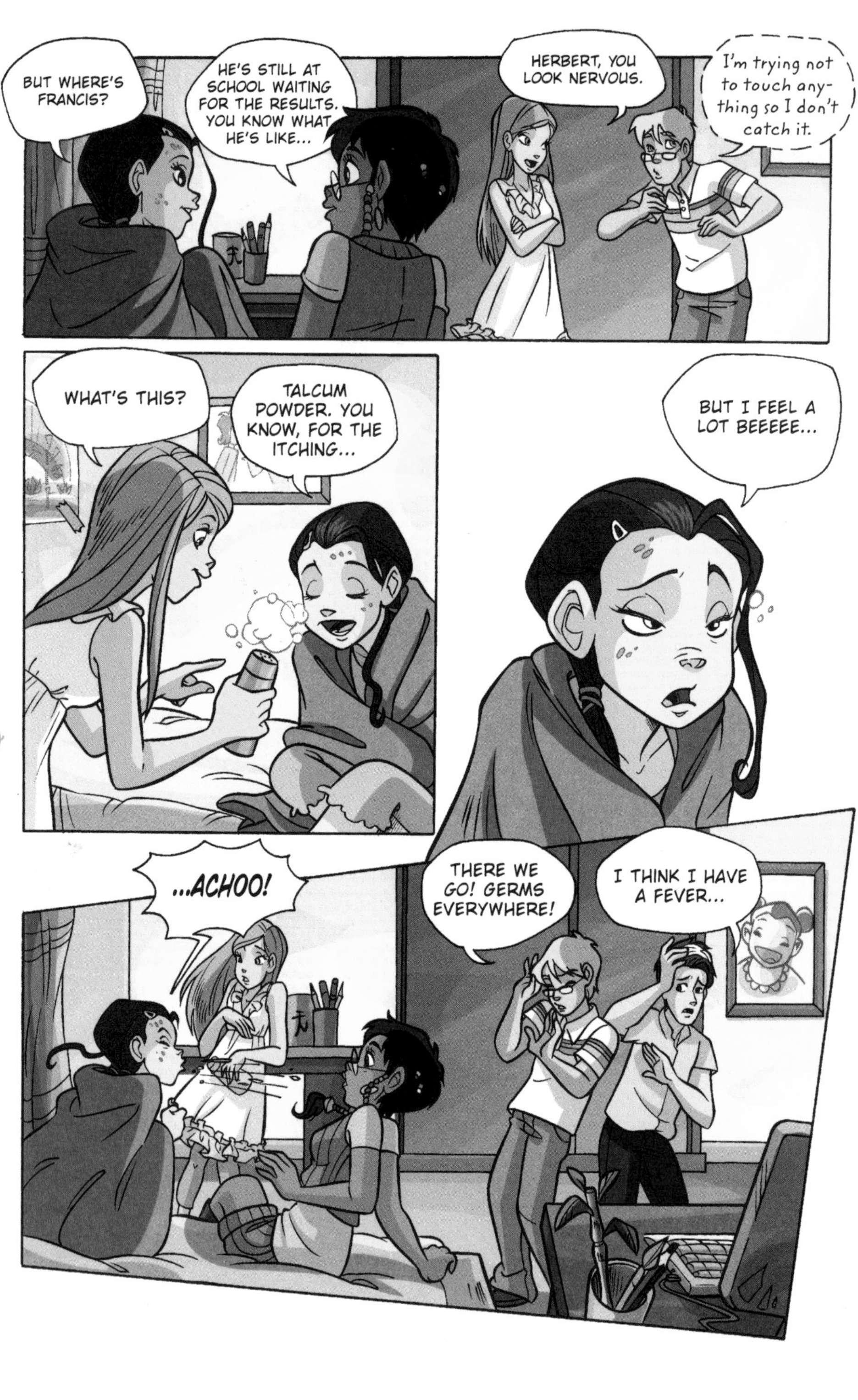
BUT WHERE'S FRANCIS?
HE'S STILL AT SCHOOL WAITING FOR THE RESULTS. YOU KNOW WHAT HE'S LIKE...
HERBERT, YOU LOOK NERVOUS.
I'm trying not to touch anything so I don't catch it.
WHAT'S THIS?
TALCUM POWDER. YOU KNOW, FOR THE ITCHING...
BUT I FEEL A LOT BEEEEE...
...ACHOO!
THERE WE GO! GERMS EVERYWHERE!
I THINK I HAVE A FEVER...

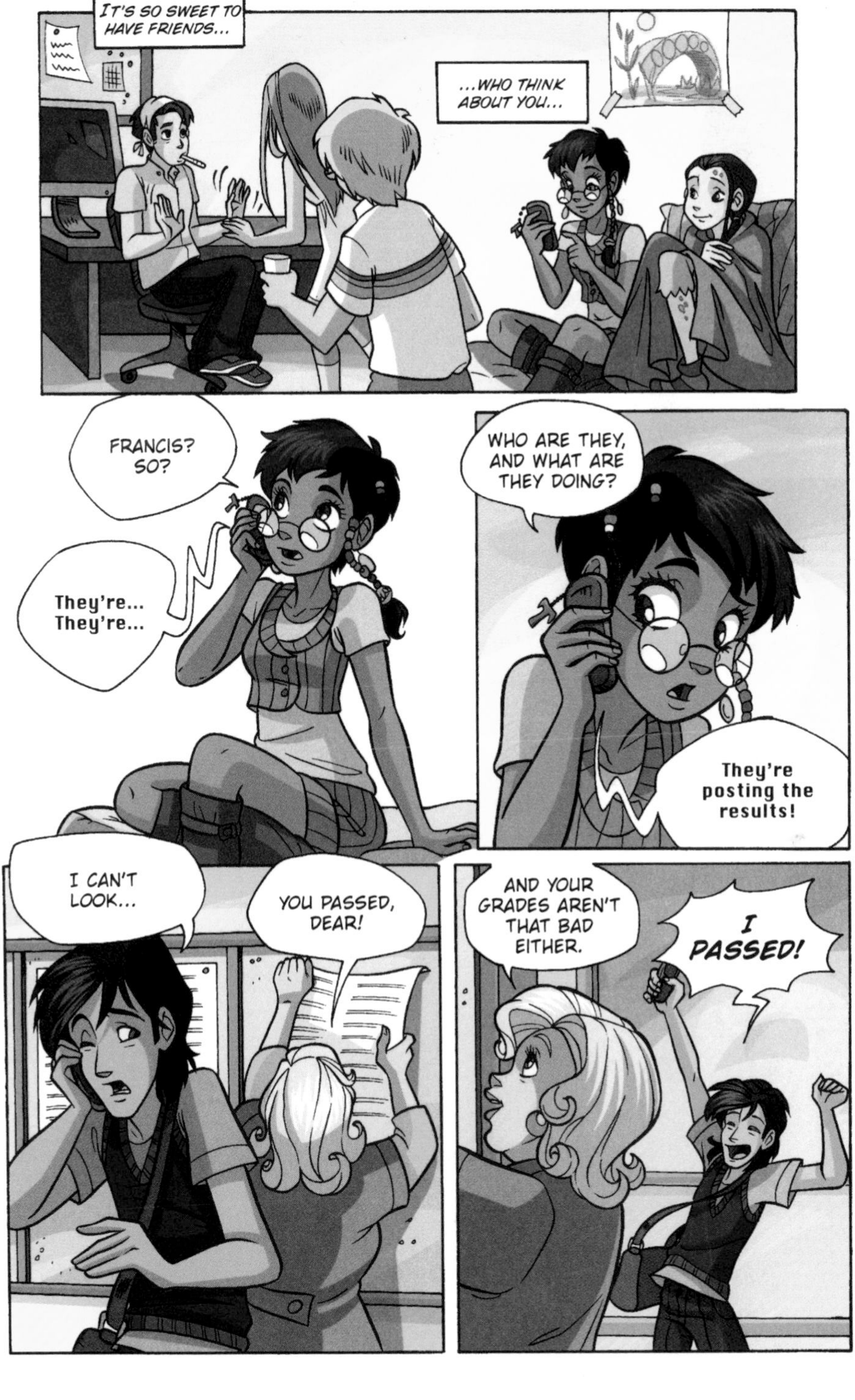
IT'S SO SWEET TO HAVE FRIENDS...
...WHO THINK ABOUT YOU...
FRANCIS? SO?
They're... They're...
WHO ARE THEY, AND WHAT ARE THEY DOING?
They're posting the results!
I CAN'T LOOK...
YOU PASSED, DEAR!
AND YOUR GRADES AREN'T THAT BAD EITHER.
I PASSED!

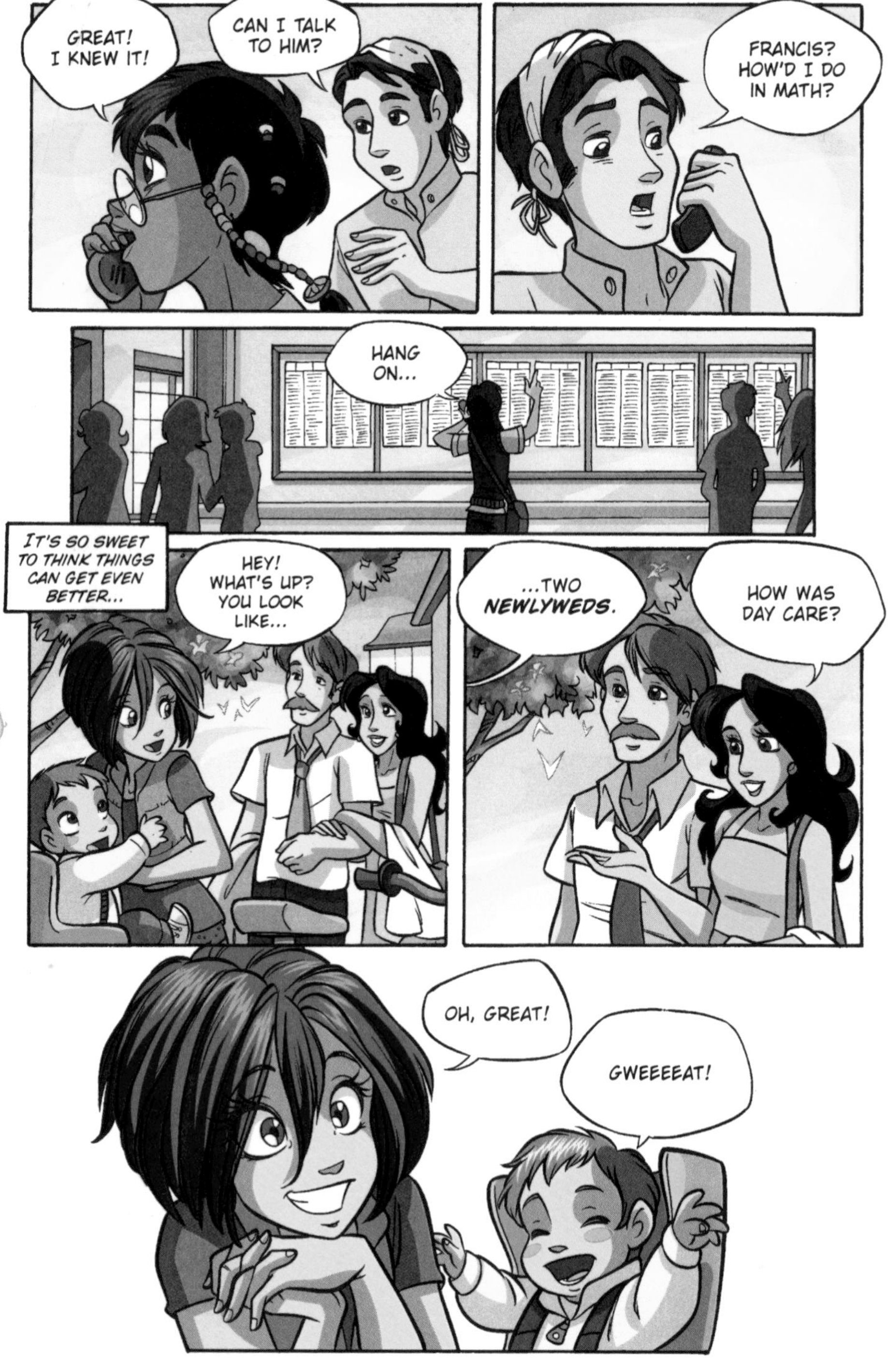
GREAT! I KNEW IT!
CAN I TALK TO HIM?
FRANCIS? HOW'D I DO IN MATH?
HANG ON...
IT'S SO SWEET TO THINK THINGS CAN GET EVEN BETTER...
HEY! WHAT'S UP? YOU LOOK LIKE...
...TWO NEWLYWEDS.
HOW WAS DAY CARE?
OH, GREAT!
GWEEEEAT!

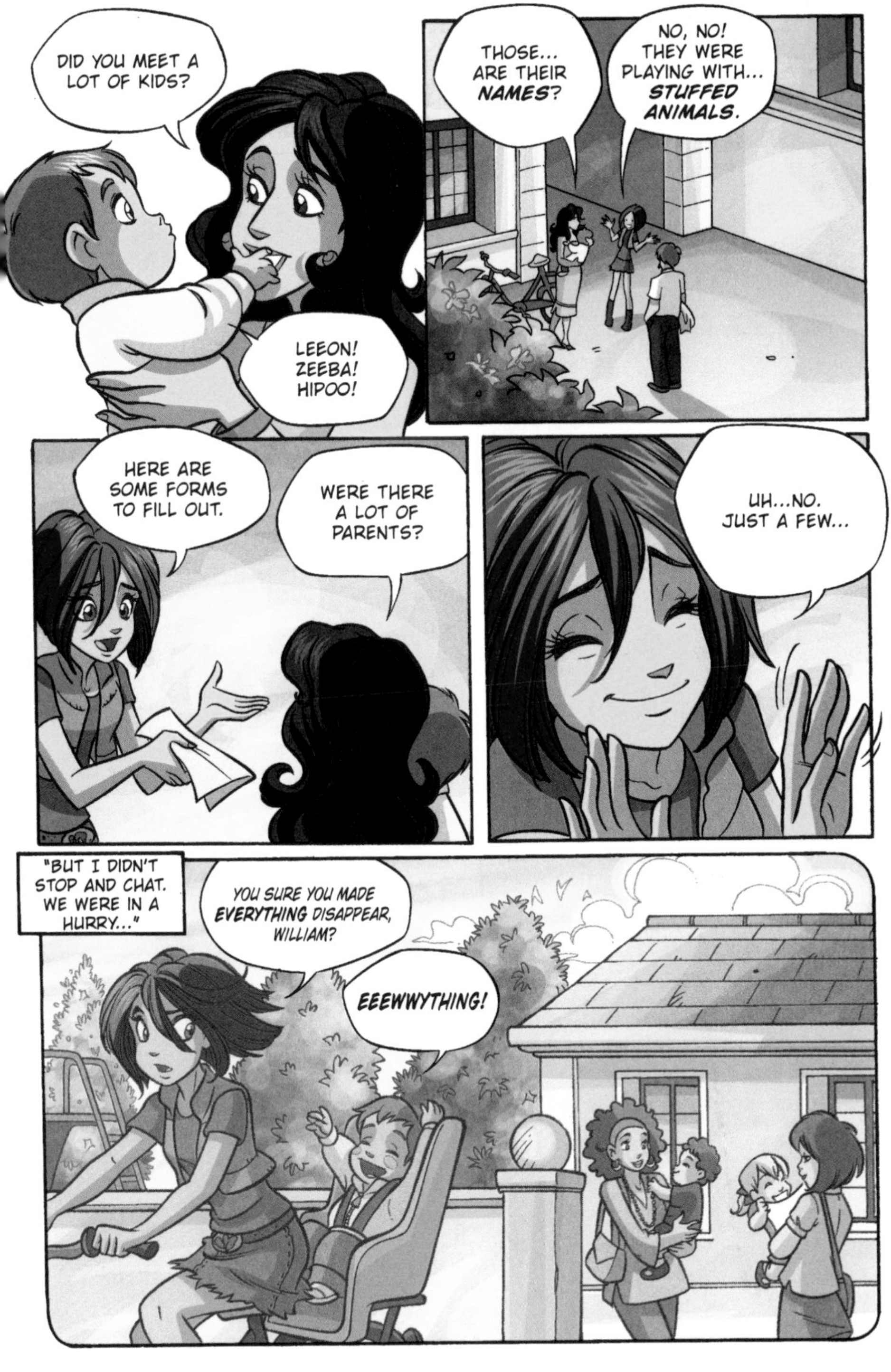
DID YOU MEET A LOT OF KIDS?
LEEON! ZEEBA! HIPOO!
THOSE... ARE THEIR NAMES?
NO, NO! THEY WERE PLAYING WITH... STUFFED ANIMALS.
HERE ARE SOME FORMS TO FILL OUT.
WERE THERE A LOT OF PARENTS?
UH...NO. JUST A FEW...
"BUT I DIDN'T STOP AND CHAT. WE WERE IN A HURRY..."
YOU SURE YOU MADE EVERYTHING DISAPPEAR, WILLIAM?
EEEWWYTHING!

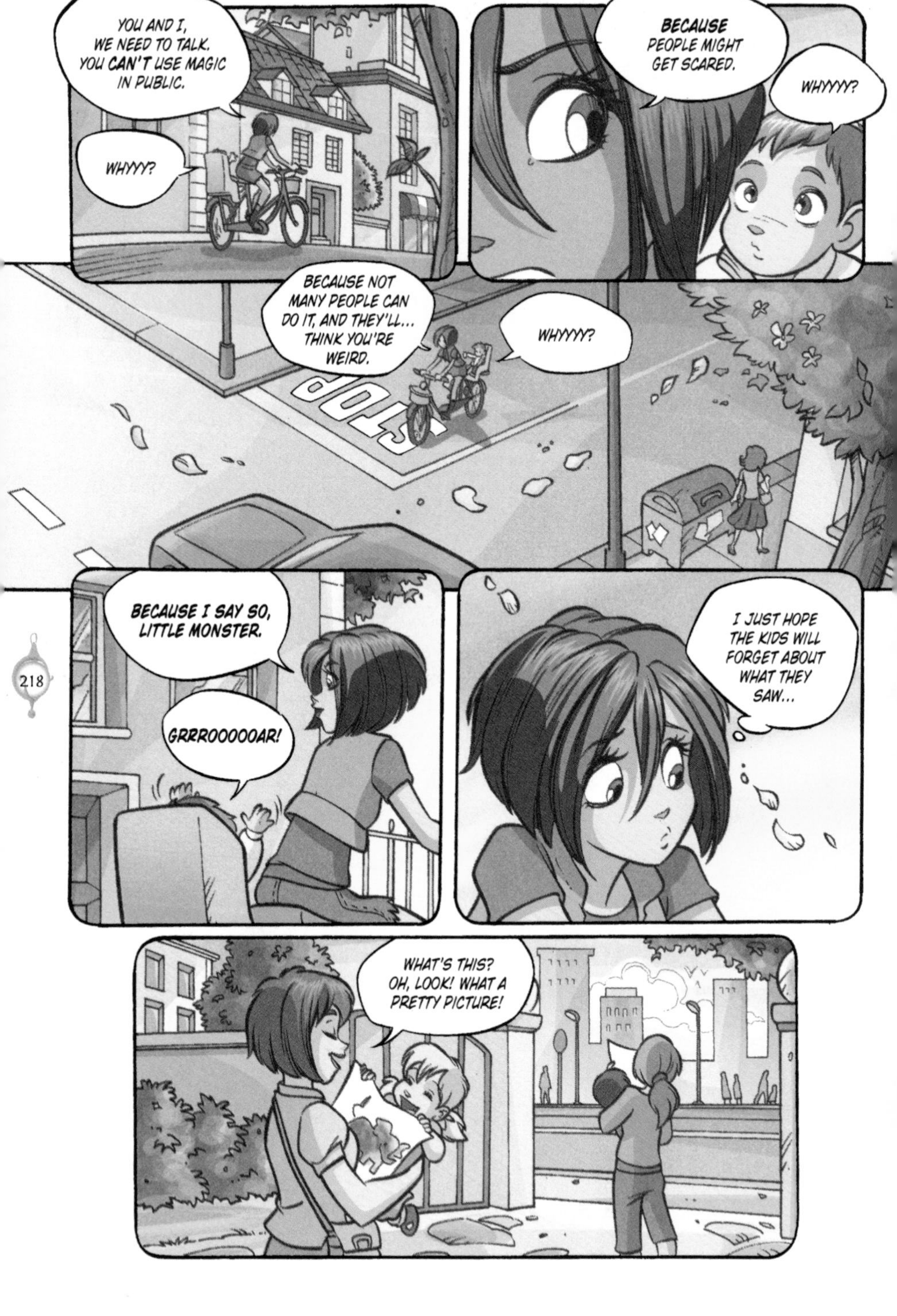
YOU AND I, WE NEED TO TALK. YOU CAN'T USE MAGIC IN PUBLIC.
WHYYY?
BECAUSE PEOPLE MIGHT GET SCARED.
WHYYYY?
BECAUSE NOT MANY PEOPLE CAN DO IT, AND THEY'LL... THINK YOU'RE WEIRD.
WHYYYY?
STOP
BECAUSE I SAY SO, LITTLE MONSTER.
GRRROOOOOAR!
I JUST HOPE THE KIDS WILL FORGET ABOUT WHAT THEY SAW...
WHAT'S THIS? OH, LOOK! WHAT A PRETTY PICTURE!

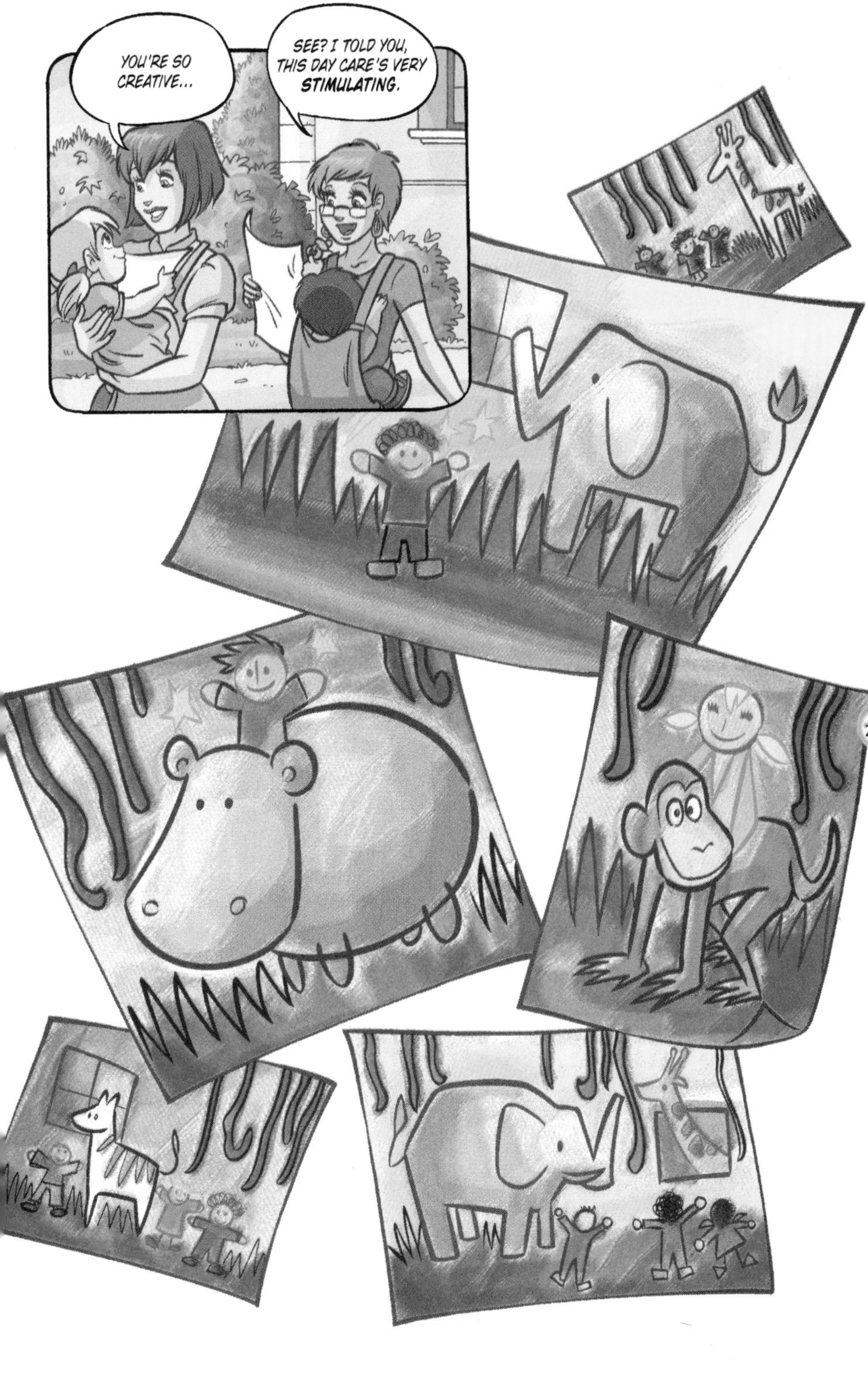
YOU'RE SO CREATIVE...
SEE? I TOLD YOU, THIS DAY CARE'S VERY **STIMULATING**.

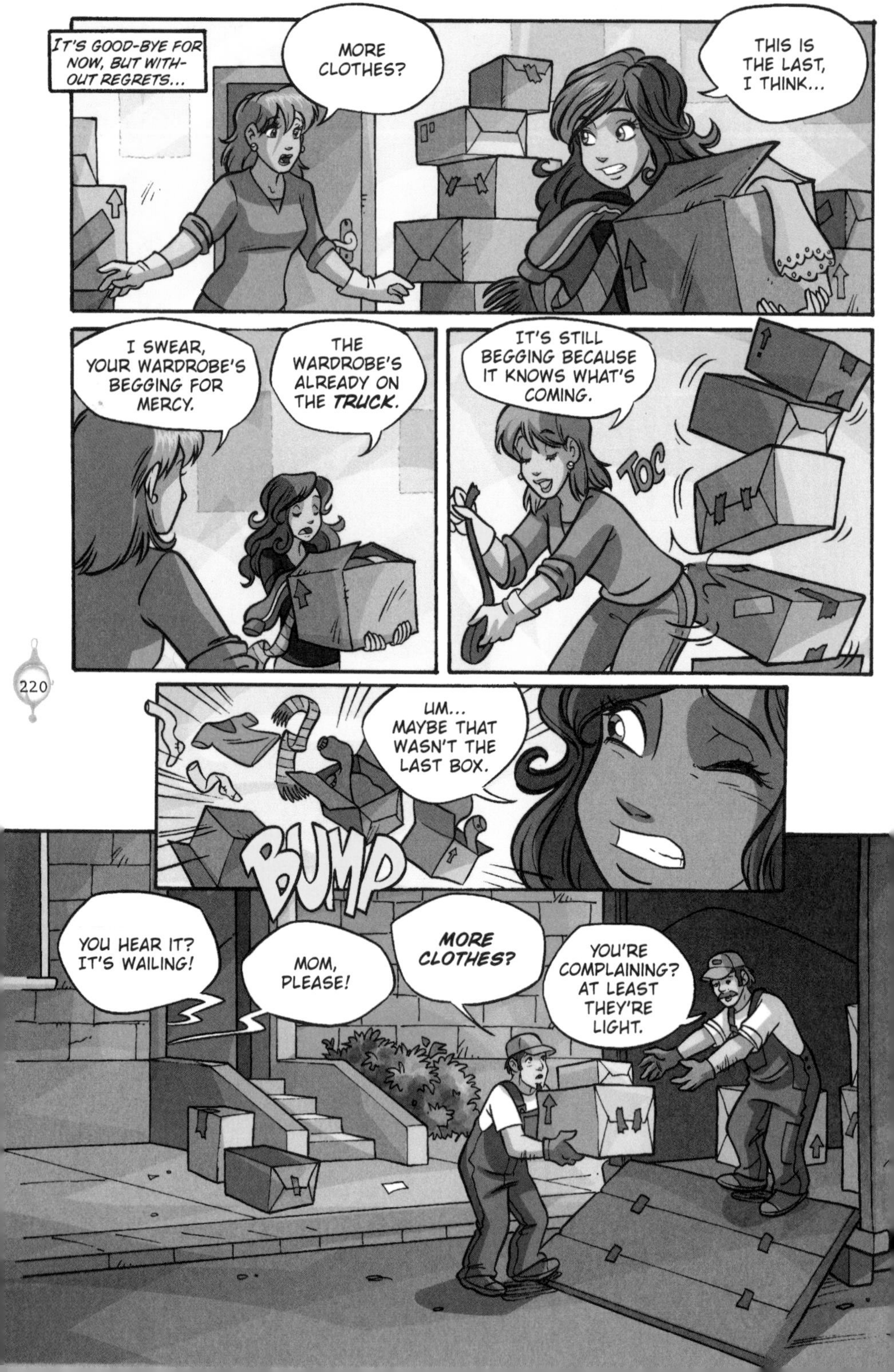

IT'S GOOD-BYE FOR NOW, BUT WITH-OUT REGRETS...
MORE CLOTHES?
THIS IS THE LAST, I THINK...
I SWEAR, YOUR WARDROBE'S BEGGING FOR MERCY.
THE WARDROBE'S ALREADY ON THE TRUCK.
IT'S STILL BEGGING BECAUSE IT KNOWS WHAT'S COMING.
TOC
UM... MAYBE THAT WASN'T THE LAST BOX.
BUMP
YOU HEAR IT? IT'S WAILING!
MOM, PLEASE!
MORE CLOTHES?
YOU'RE COMPLAINING? AT LEAST THEY'RE LIGHT.

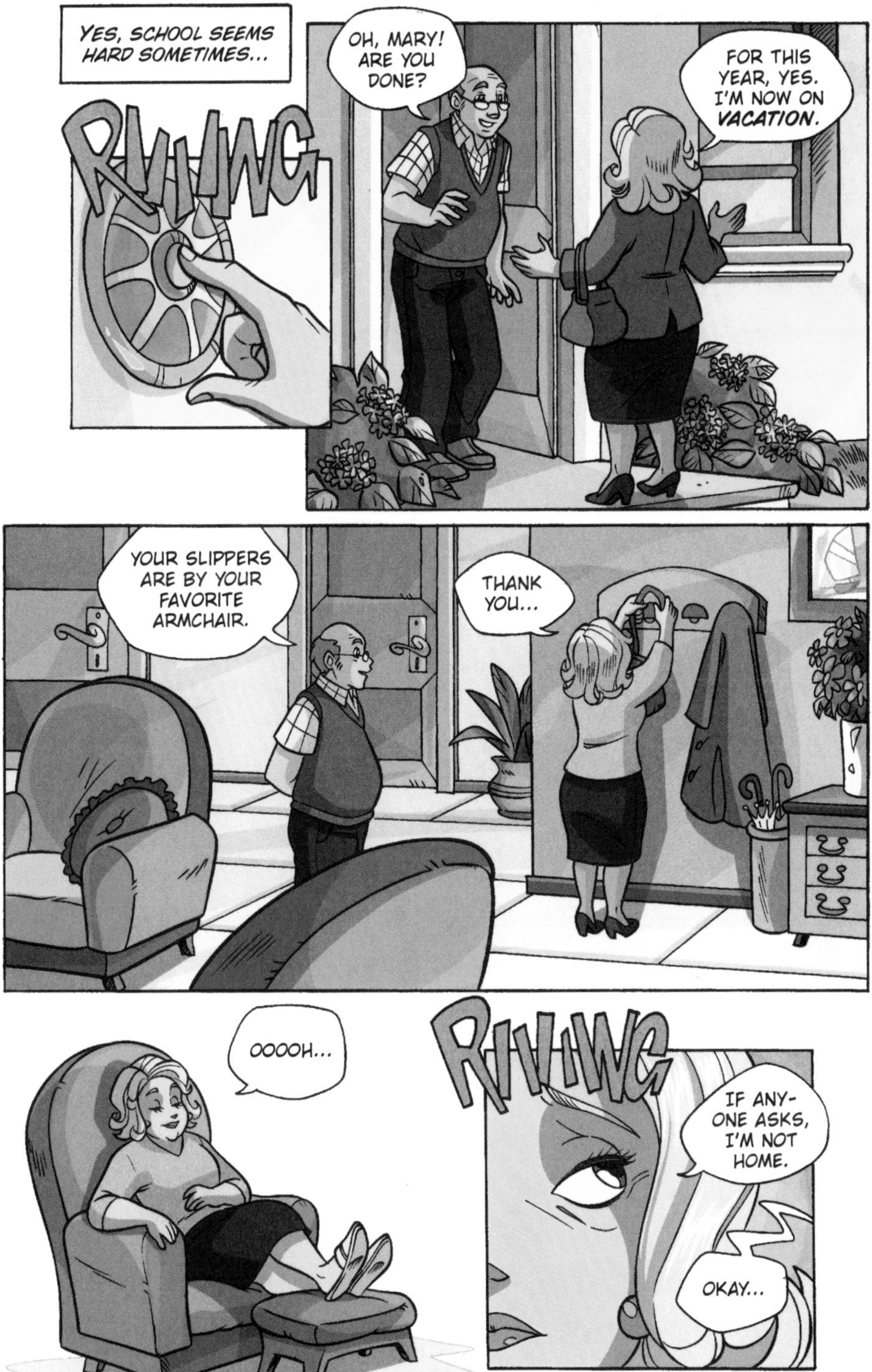
YES, SCHOOL SEEMS HARD SOMETIMES...
RIIIING
OH, MARY! ARE YOU DONE?
FOR THIS YEAR, YES. I'M NOW ON VACATION.
YOUR SLIPPERS ARE BY YOUR FAVORITE ARMCHAIR.
THANK YOU...
OOOOH...
RIIIING
IF ANY-ONE ASKS, I'M NOT HOME.
OKAY...

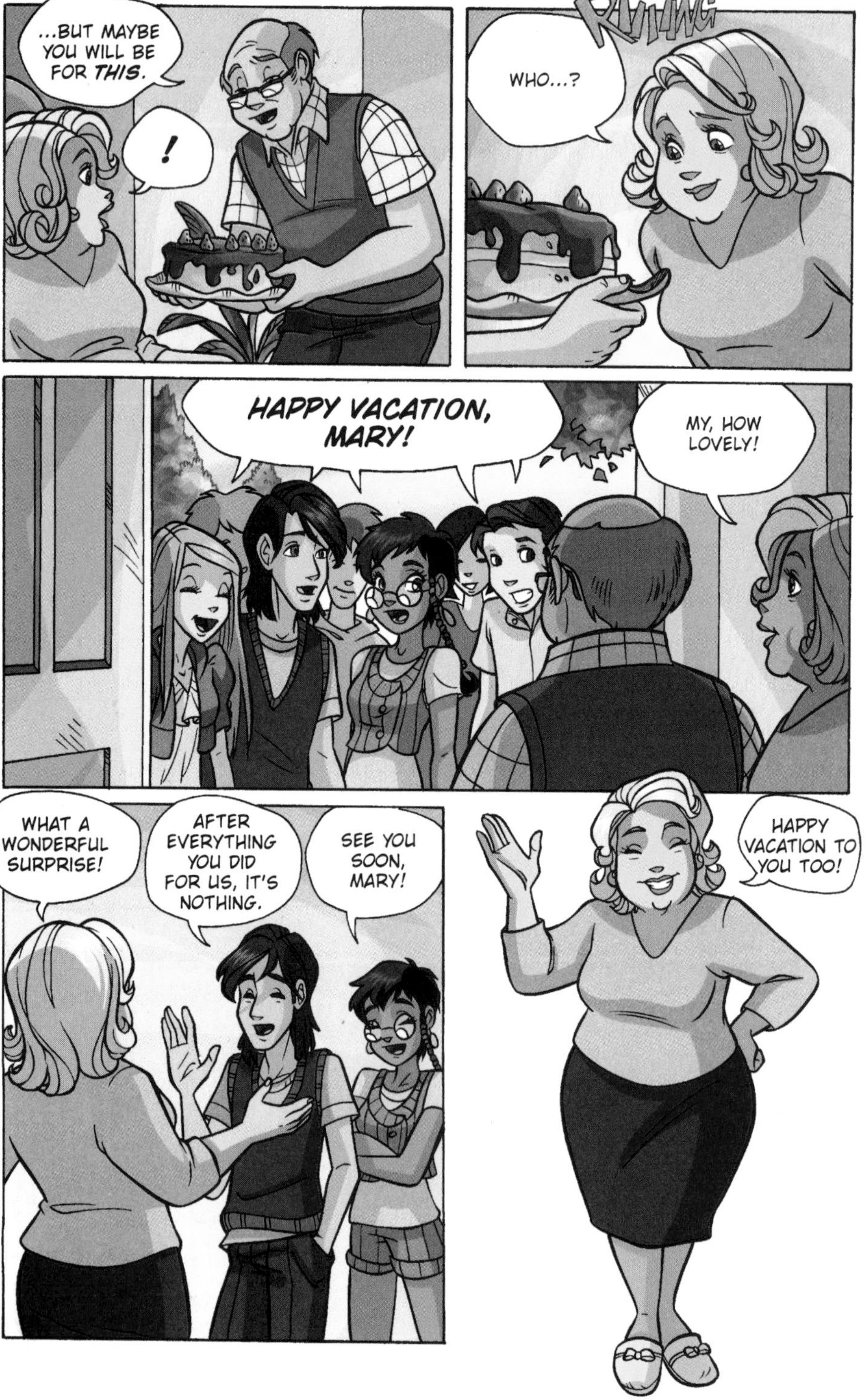
...BUT MAYBE YOU WILL BE FOR THIS.
!
RIIING
WHO...?
HAPPY VACATION, MARY!
MY, HOW LOVELY!
WHAT A WONDERFUL SURPRISE!
AFTER EVERYTHING YOU DID FOR US, IT'S NOTHING.
SEE YOU SOON, MARY!
HAPPY VACATION TO YOU TOO!

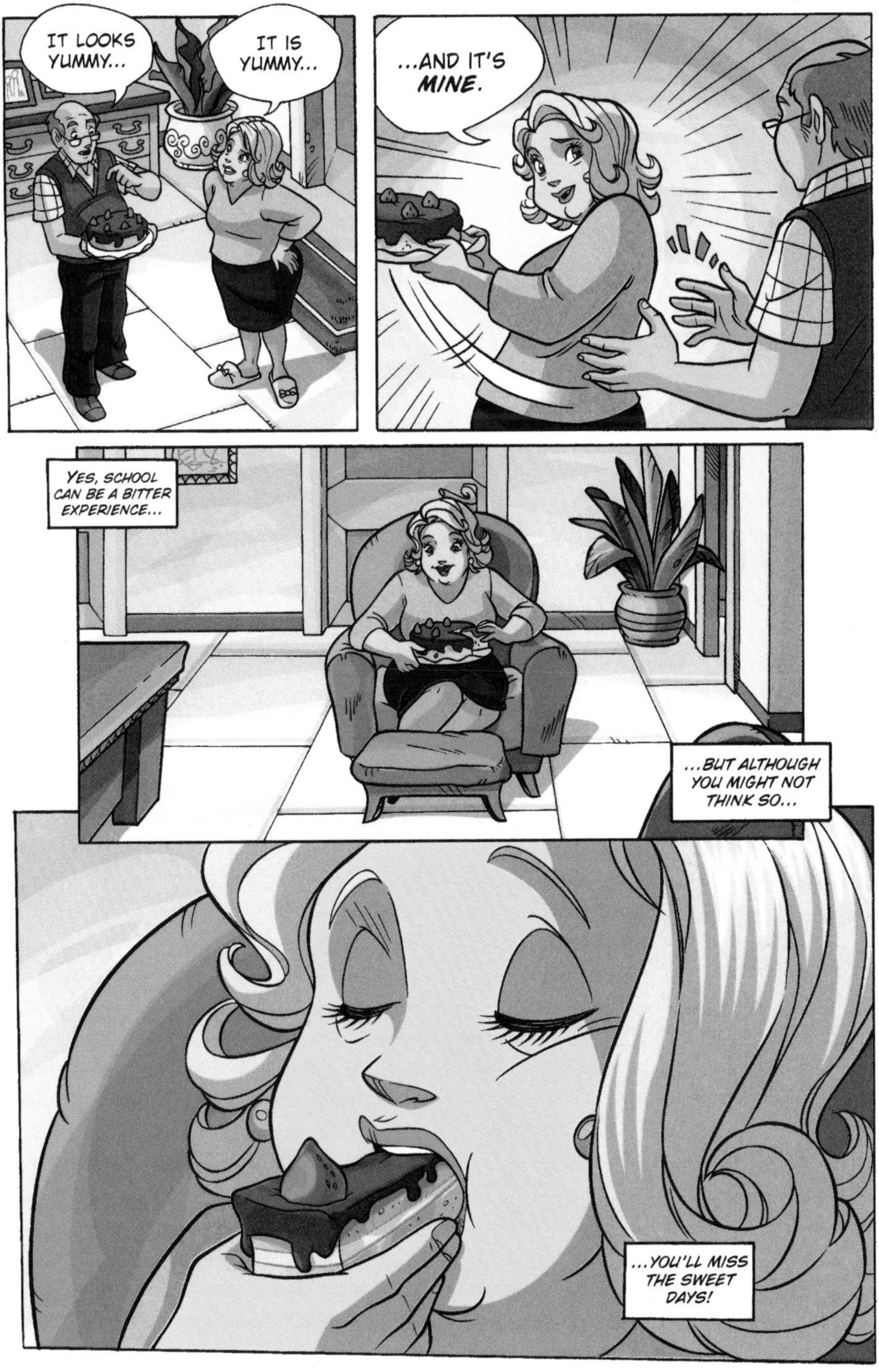
IT LOOKS YUMMY...
IT IS YUMMY...
...AND IT'S MINE.
YES, SCHOOL CAN BE A BITTER EXPERIENCE...
...BUT ALTHOUGH YOU MIGHT NOT THINK SO...
...YOU'LL MISS THE SWEET DAYS!

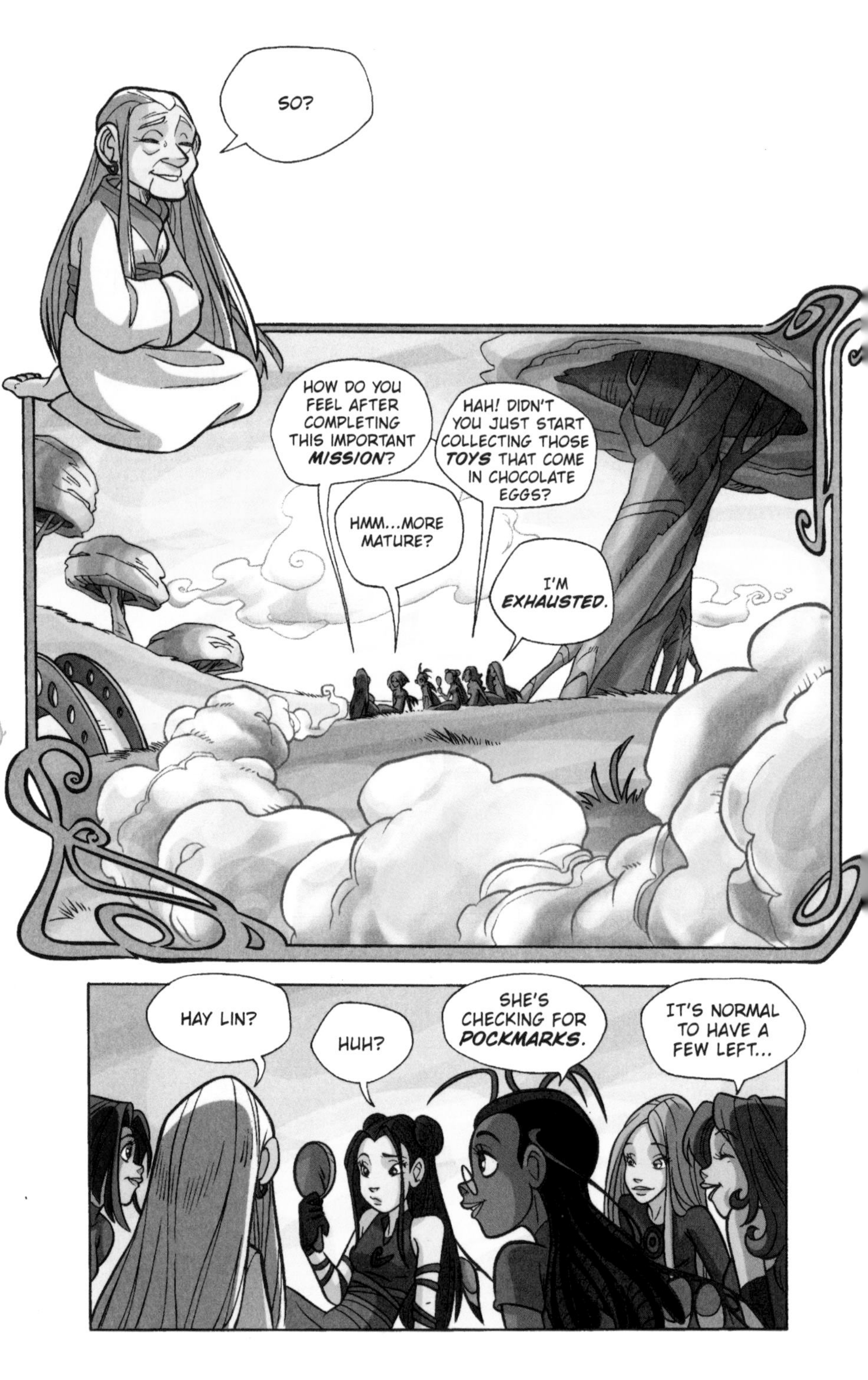
SO?
HOW DO YOU FEEL AFTER COMPLETING THIS IMPORTANT *MISSION*?
HMM...MORE MATURE?
HAH! DIDN'T YOU JUST START COLLECTING THOSE *TOYS* THAT COME IN CHOCOLATE EGGS?
I'M *EXHAUSTED*.
HAY LIN?
HUH?
SHE'S CHECKING FOR *POCKMARKS*.
IT'S NORMAL TO HAVE A FEW LEFT...

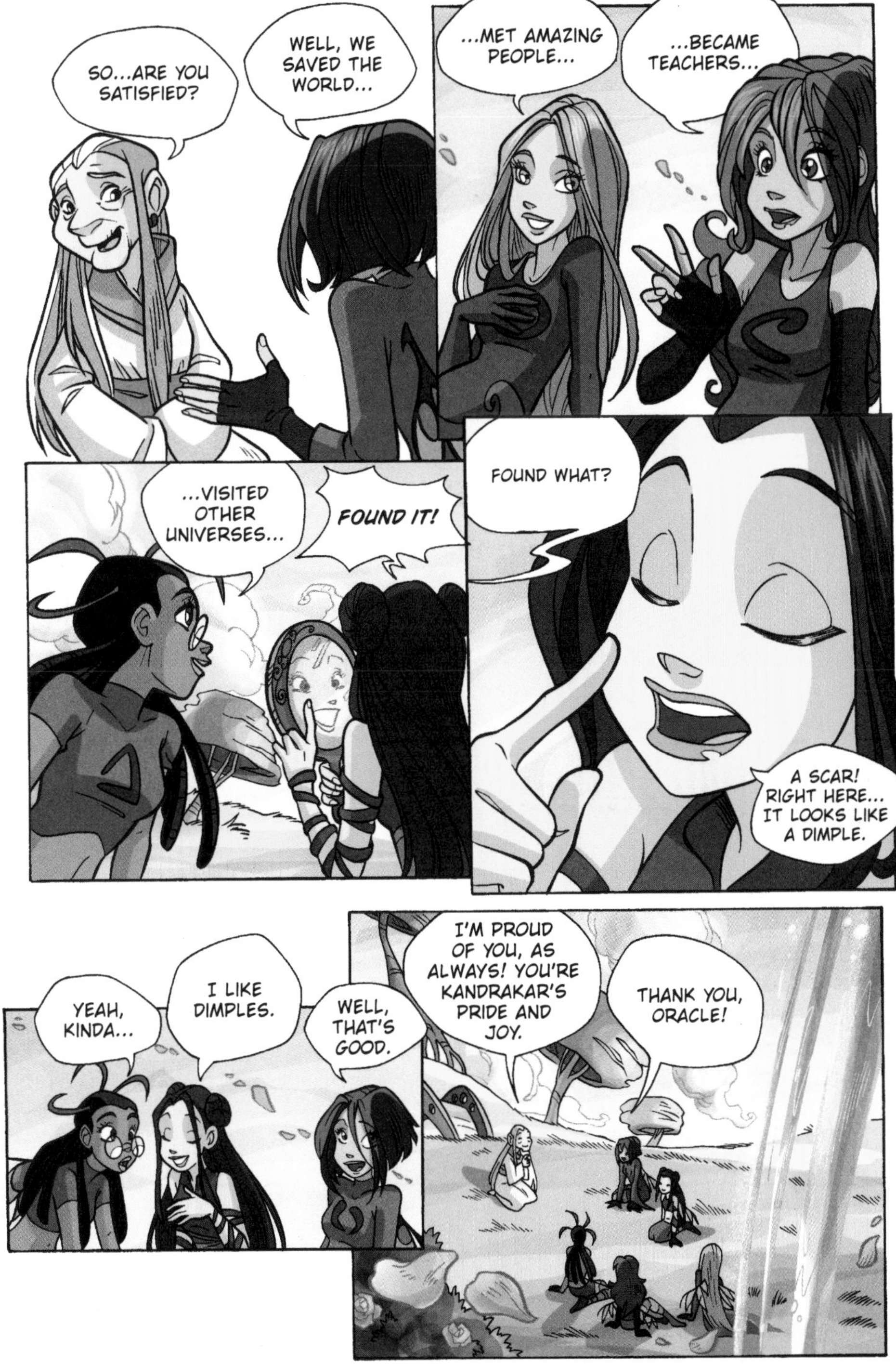
SO...ARE YOU SATISFIED?
WELL, WE SAVED THE WORLD...
...MET AMAZING PEOPLE...
...BECAME TEACHERS...
...VISITED OTHER UNIVERSES...
FOUND IT!
FOUND WHAT?
A SCAR! RIGHT HERE... IT LOOKS LIKE A DIMPLE.
YEAH, KINDA...
I LIKE DIMPLES.
WELL, THAT'S GOOD.
I'M PROUD OF YOU, AS ALWAYS! YOU'RE KANDRAKAR'S PRIDE AND JOY.
THANK YOU, ORACLE!

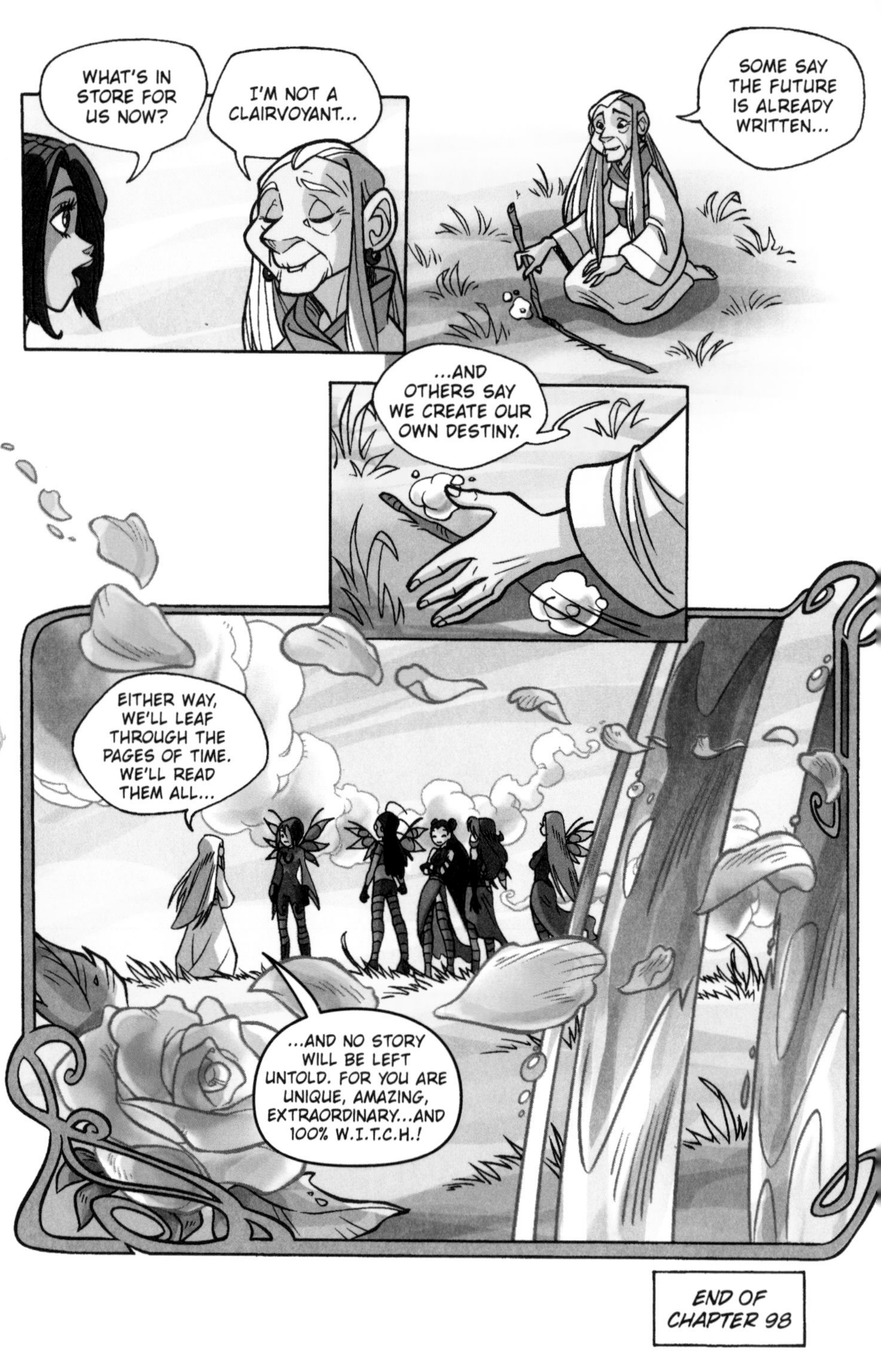
WHAT'S IN STORE FOR US NOW?
I'M NOT A CLAIRVOYANT...
SOME SAY THE FUTURE IS ALREADY WRITTEN...
...AND OTHERS SAY WE CREATE OUR OWN DESTINY.
EITHER WAY, WE'LL LEAF THROUGH THE PAGES OF TIME. WE'LL READ THEM ALL...
...AND NO STORY WILL BE LEFT UNTOLD. FOR YOU ARE UNIQUE, AMAZING, EXTRAORDINARY...AND 100% W.I.T.C.H.!

END OF CHAPTER 98

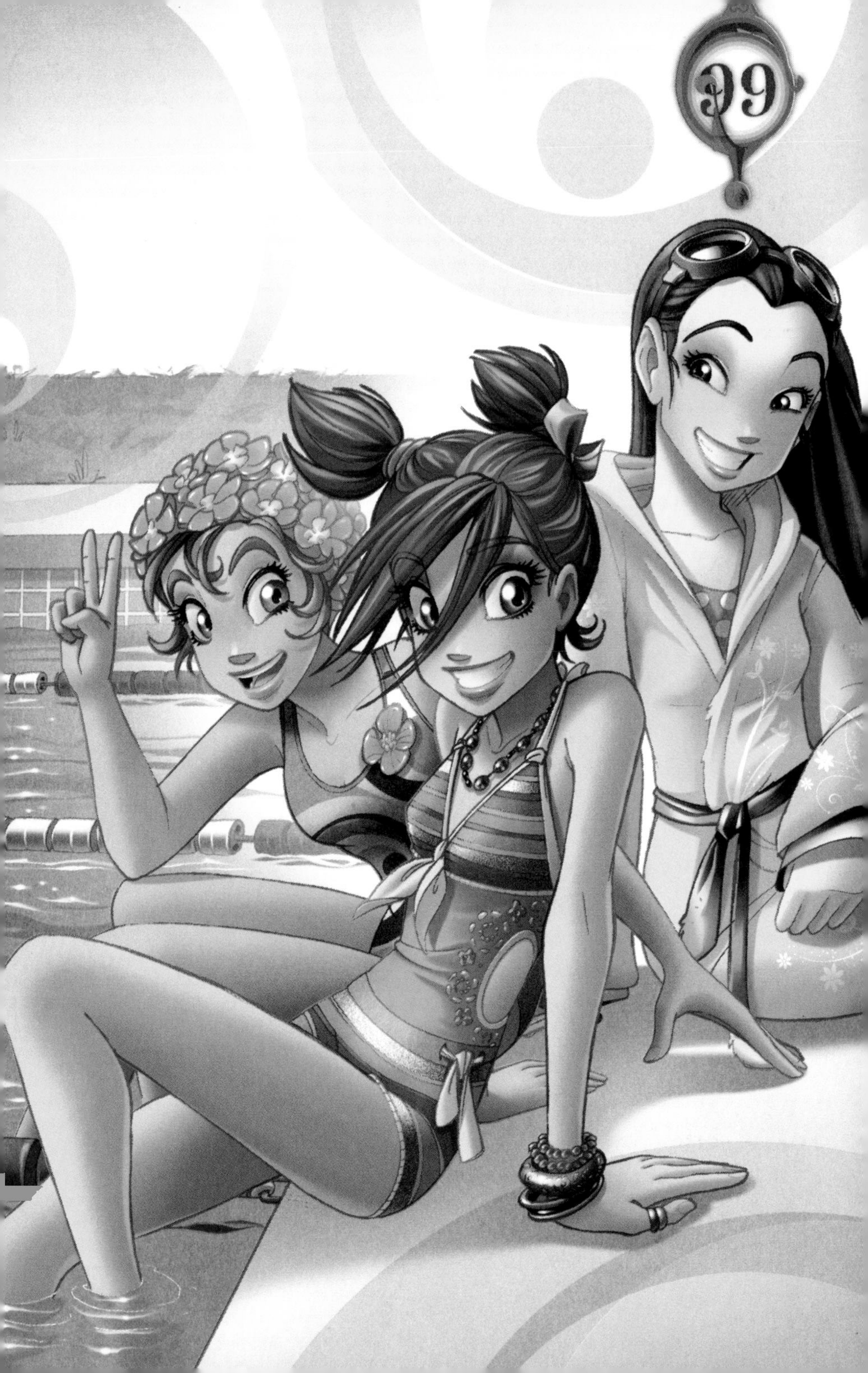
39

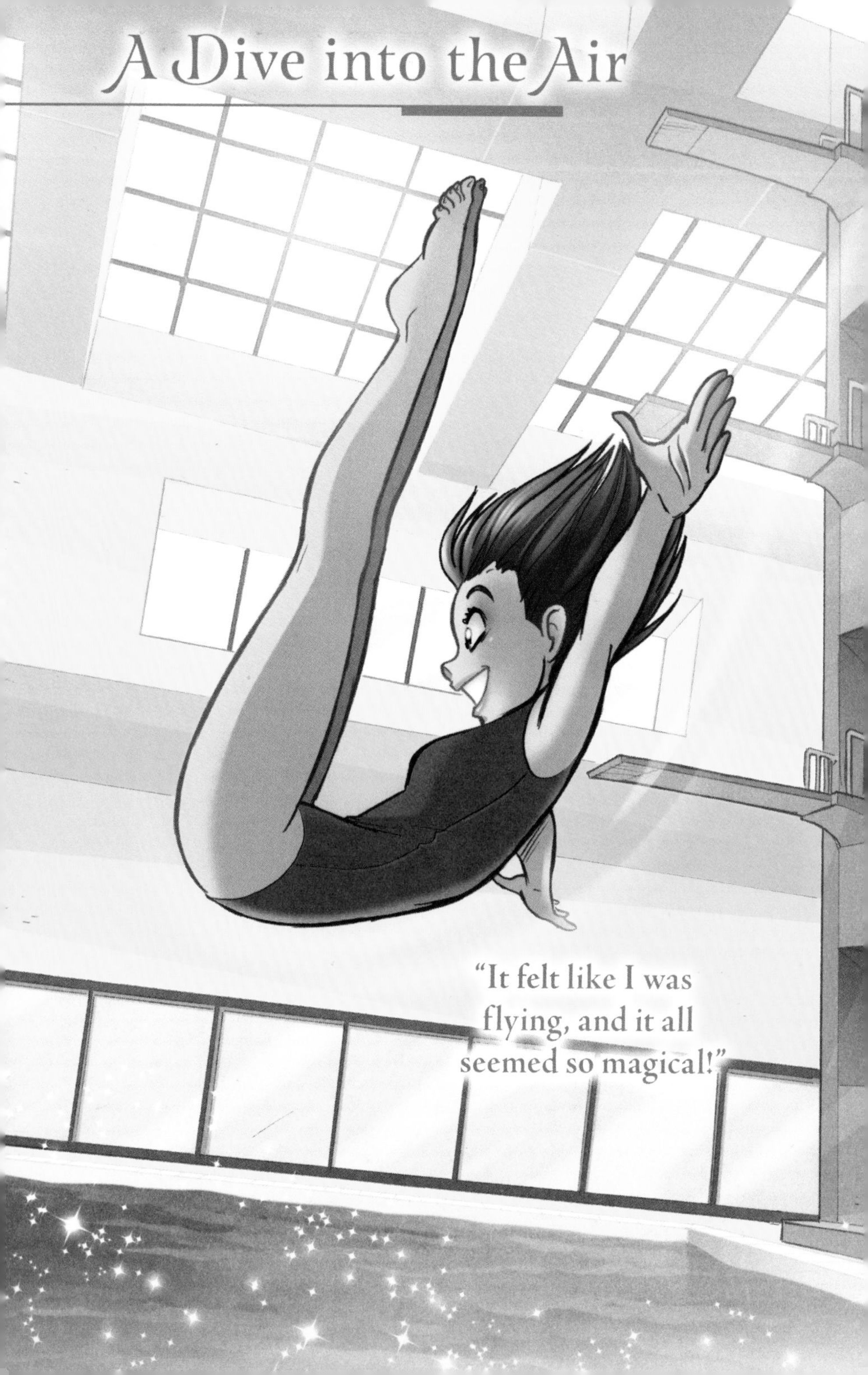
A Dive into the Air
"It felt like I was flying, and it all seemed so magical!"

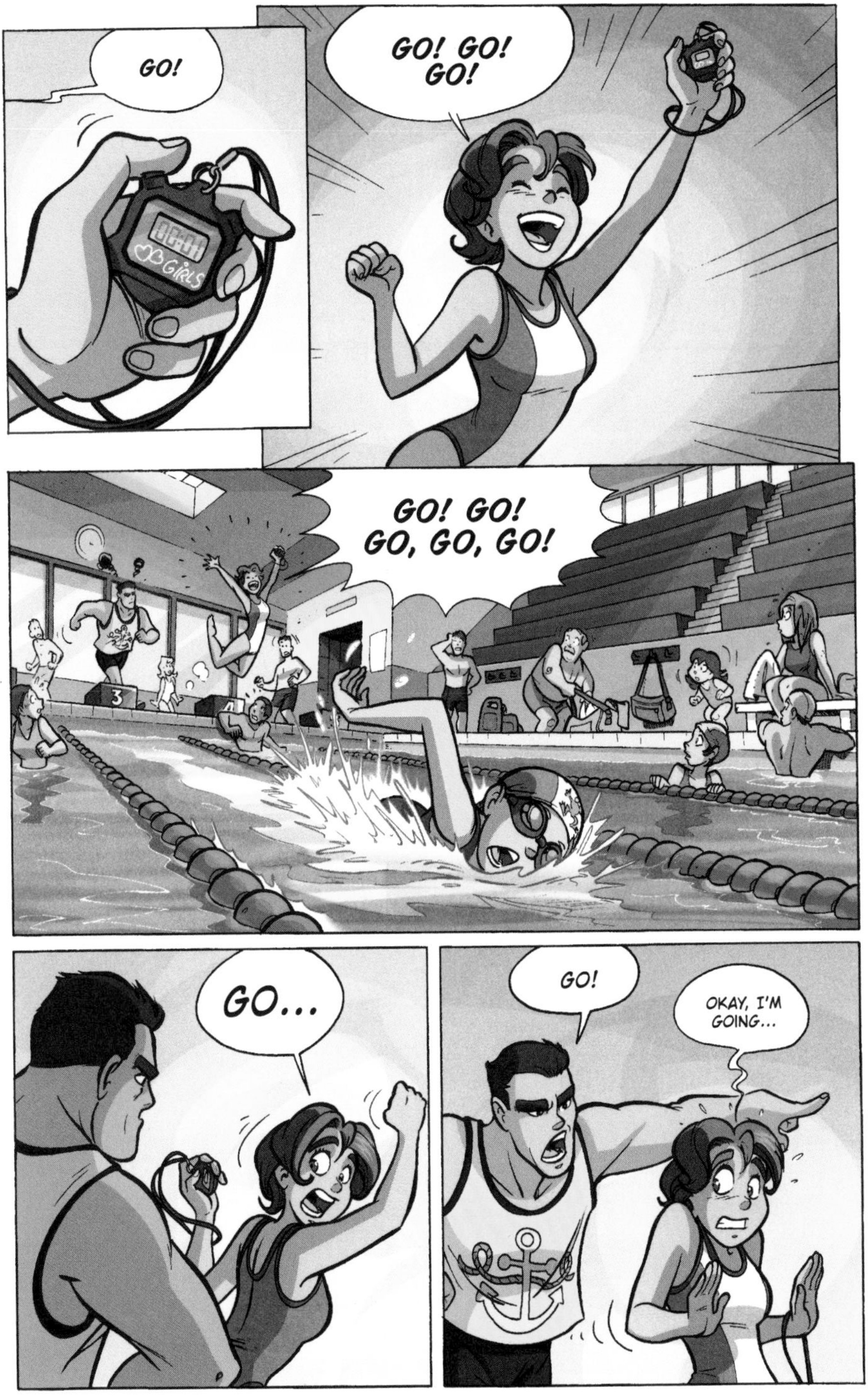
GO!
GIRLS
GO! GO! GO!
GO! GO! GO, GO, GO!
GO...
GO!
OKAY, I'M GOING...

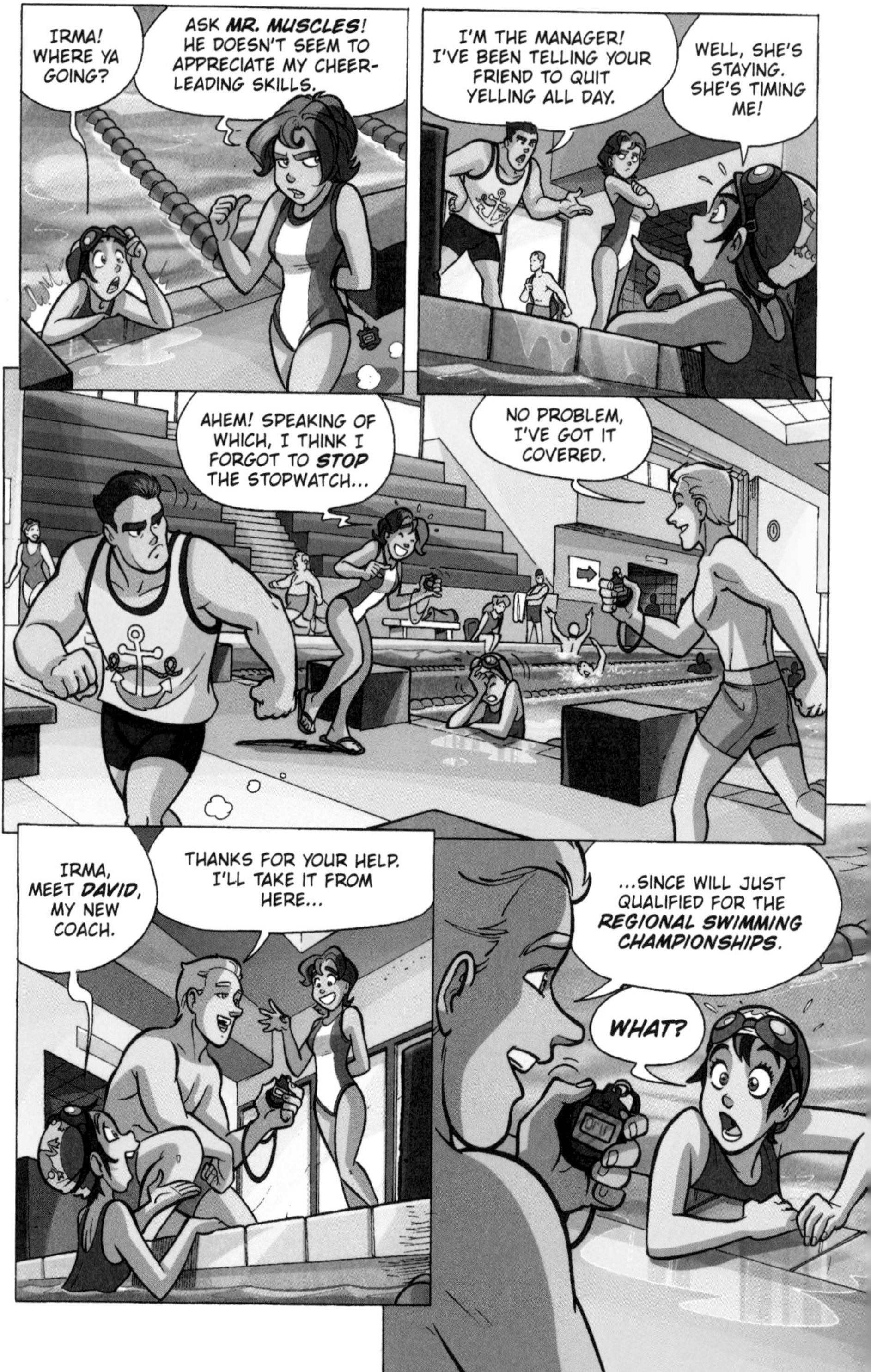
IRMA! WHERE YA GOING?
ASK **MR. MUSCLES**! HE DOESN'T SEEM TO APPRECIATE MY CHEER-LEADING SKILLS.
I'M THE MANAGER! I'VE BEEN TELLING YOUR FRIEND TO QUIT YELLING ALL DAY.
WELL, SHE'S STAYING. SHE'S TIMING ME!
AHEM! SPEAKING OF WHICH, I THINK I FORGOT TO **STOP** THE STOPWATCH...
NO PROBLEM, I'VE GOT IT COVERED.
IRMA, MEET **DAVID**, MY NEW COACH.
THANKS FOR YOUR HELP. I'LL TAKE IT FROM HERE...
...SINCE WILL JUST QUALIFIED FOR THE **REGIONAL SWIMMING CHAMPIONSHIPS**.
WHAT?

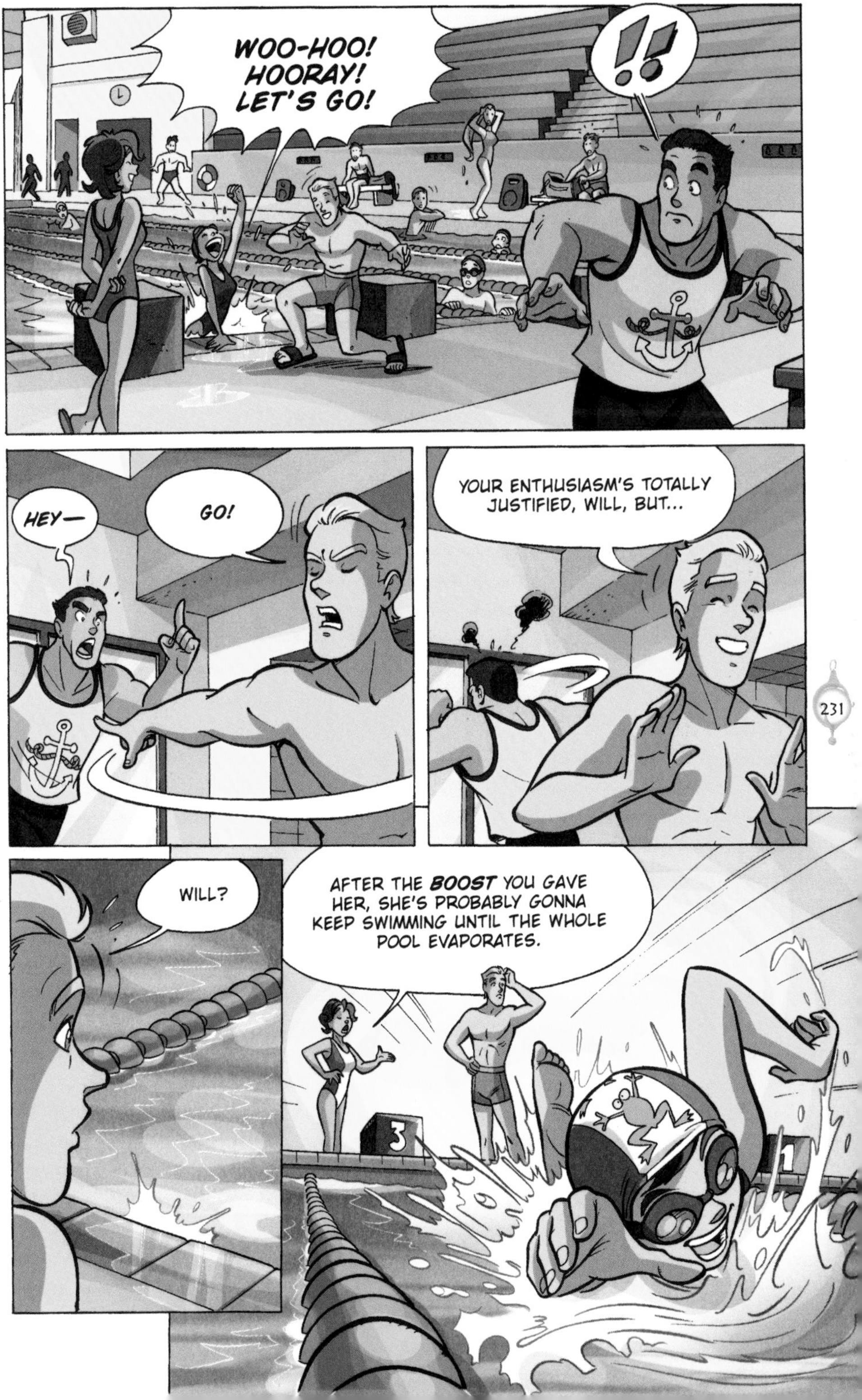
WOO-HOO! HOORAY! LET'S GO!
!!
HEY—
GO!
YOUR ENTHUSIASM'S TOTALLY JUSTIFIED, WILL, BUT...
WILL?
AFTER THE BOOST YOU GAVE HER, SHE'S PROBABLY GONNA KEEP SWIMMING UNTIL THE WHOLE POOL EVAPORATES.

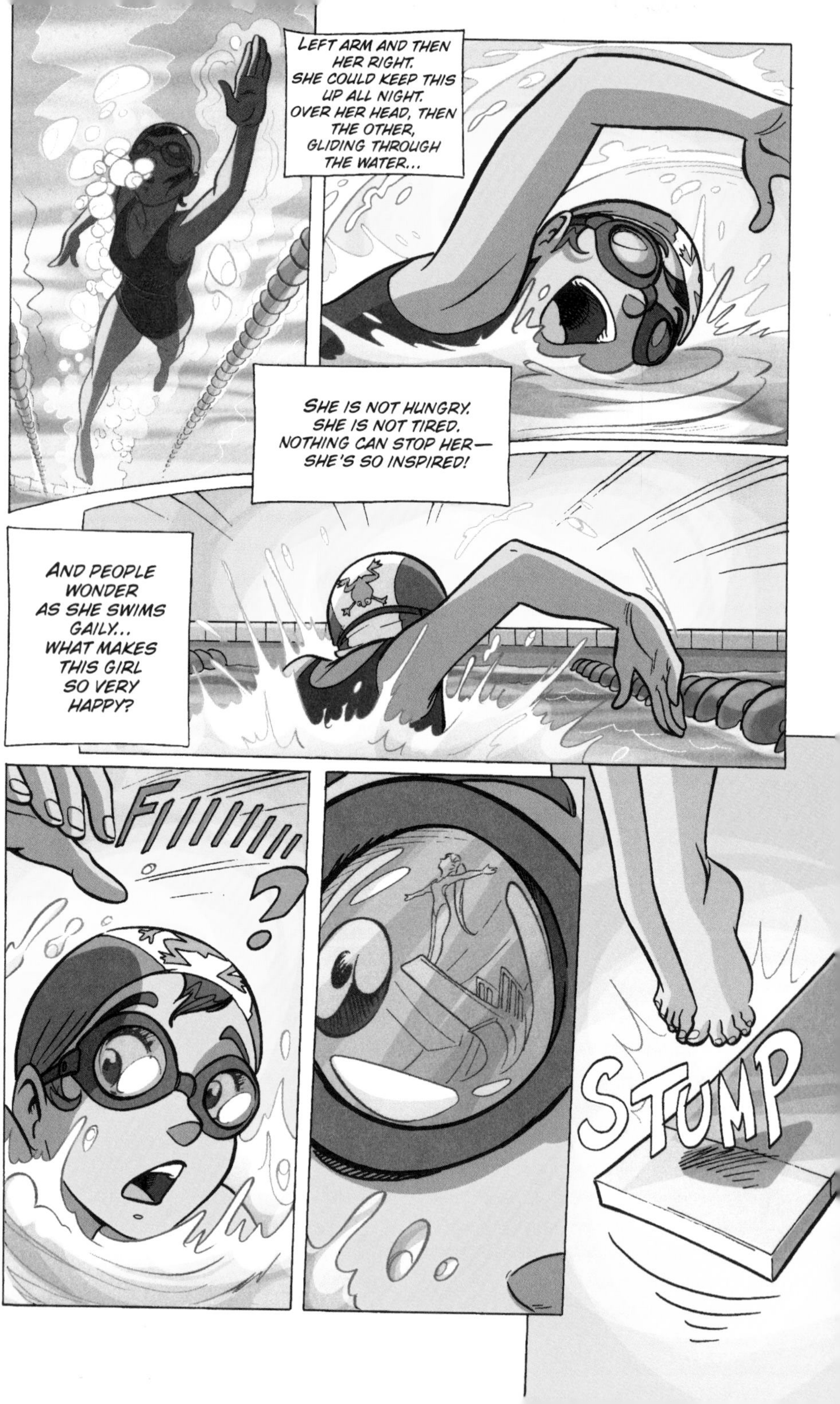
LEFT ARM AND THEN HER RIGHT. SHE COULD KEEP THIS UP ALL NIGHT. OVER HER HEAD, THEN THE OTHER, GLIDING THROUGH THE WATER...
SHE IS NOT HUNGRY. SHE IS NOT TIRED. NOTHING CAN STOP HER— SHE'S SO INSPIRED!
AND PEOPLE WONDER AS SHE SWIMS GAILY... WHAT MAKES THIS GIRL SO VERY HAPPY?
FIIIIIIII
?
STUMP

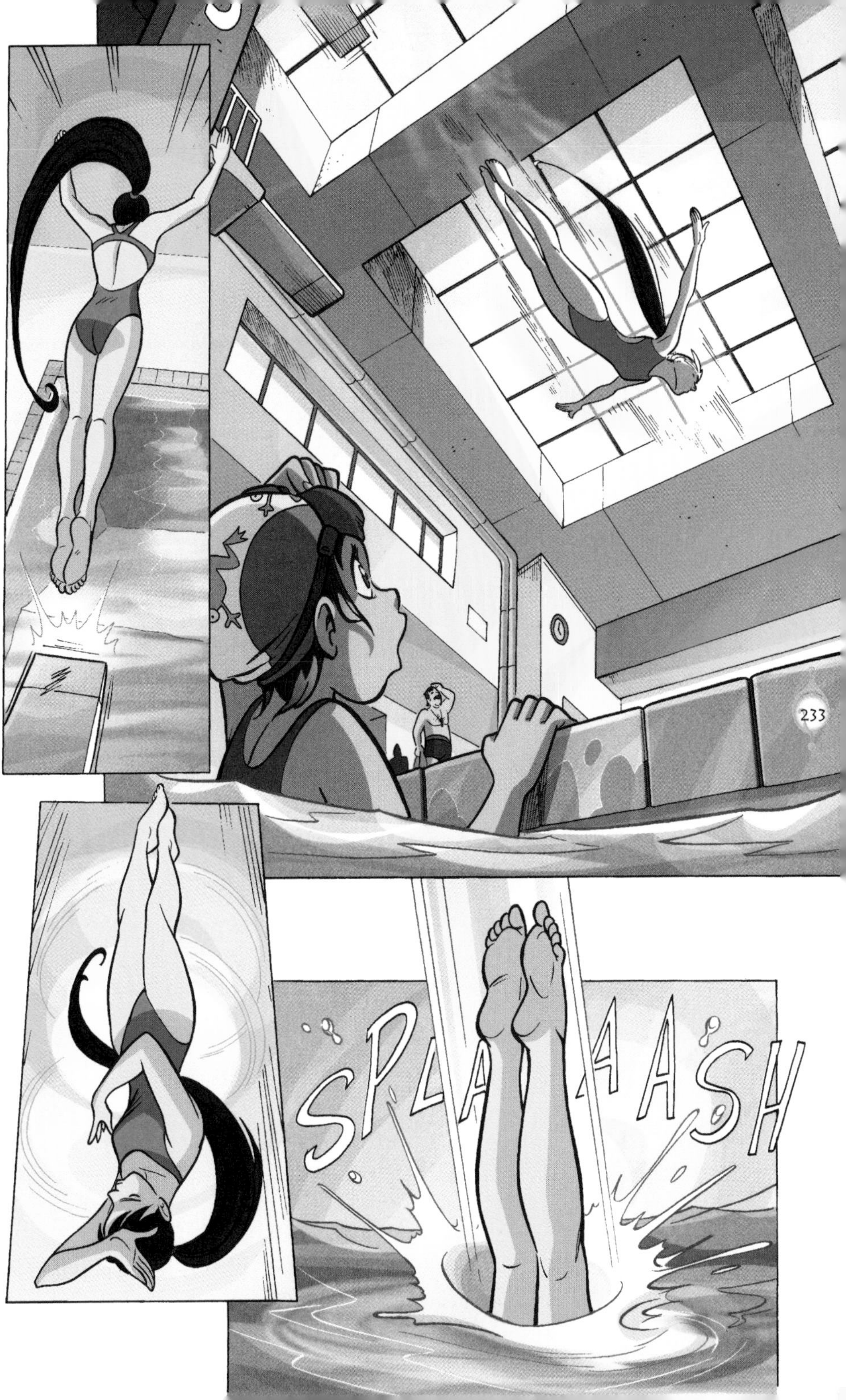
SPLAAAASH

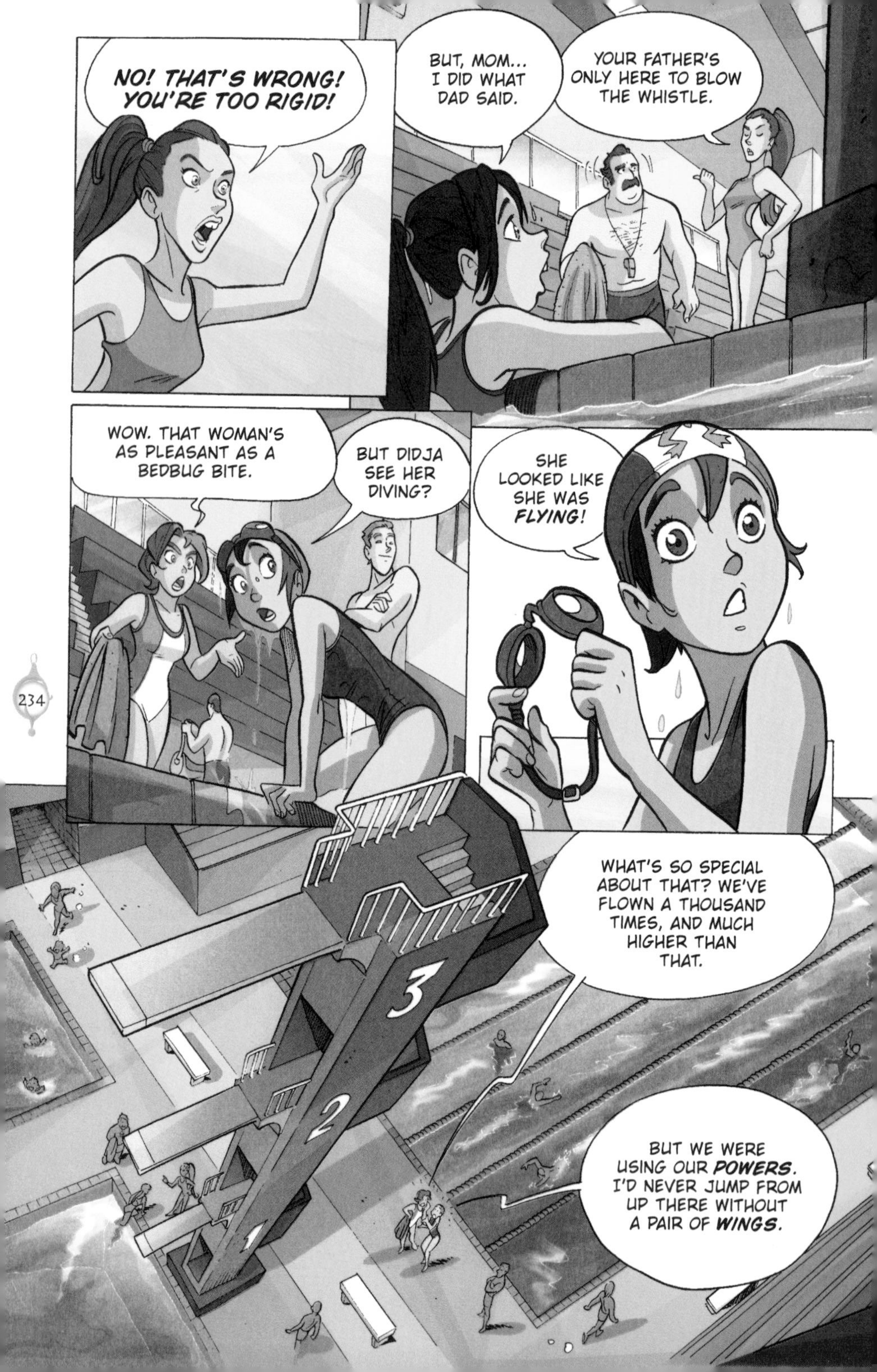
NO! THAT'S WRONG! YOU'RE TOO RIGID!
BUT, MOM... I DID WHAT DAD SAID.
YOUR FATHER'S ONLY HERE TO BLOW THE WHISTLE.
WOW. THAT WOMAN'S AS PLEASANT AS A BEDBUG BITE.
BUT DIDJA SEE HER DIVING?
SHE LOOKED LIKE SHE WAS FLYING!
WHAT'S SO SPECIAL ABOUT THAT? WE'VE FLOWN A THOUSAND TIMES, AND MUCH HIGHER THAN THAT.
BUT WE WERE USING OUR POWERS. I'D NEVER JUMP FROM UP THERE WITHOUT A PAIR OF WINGS.
3
2
1

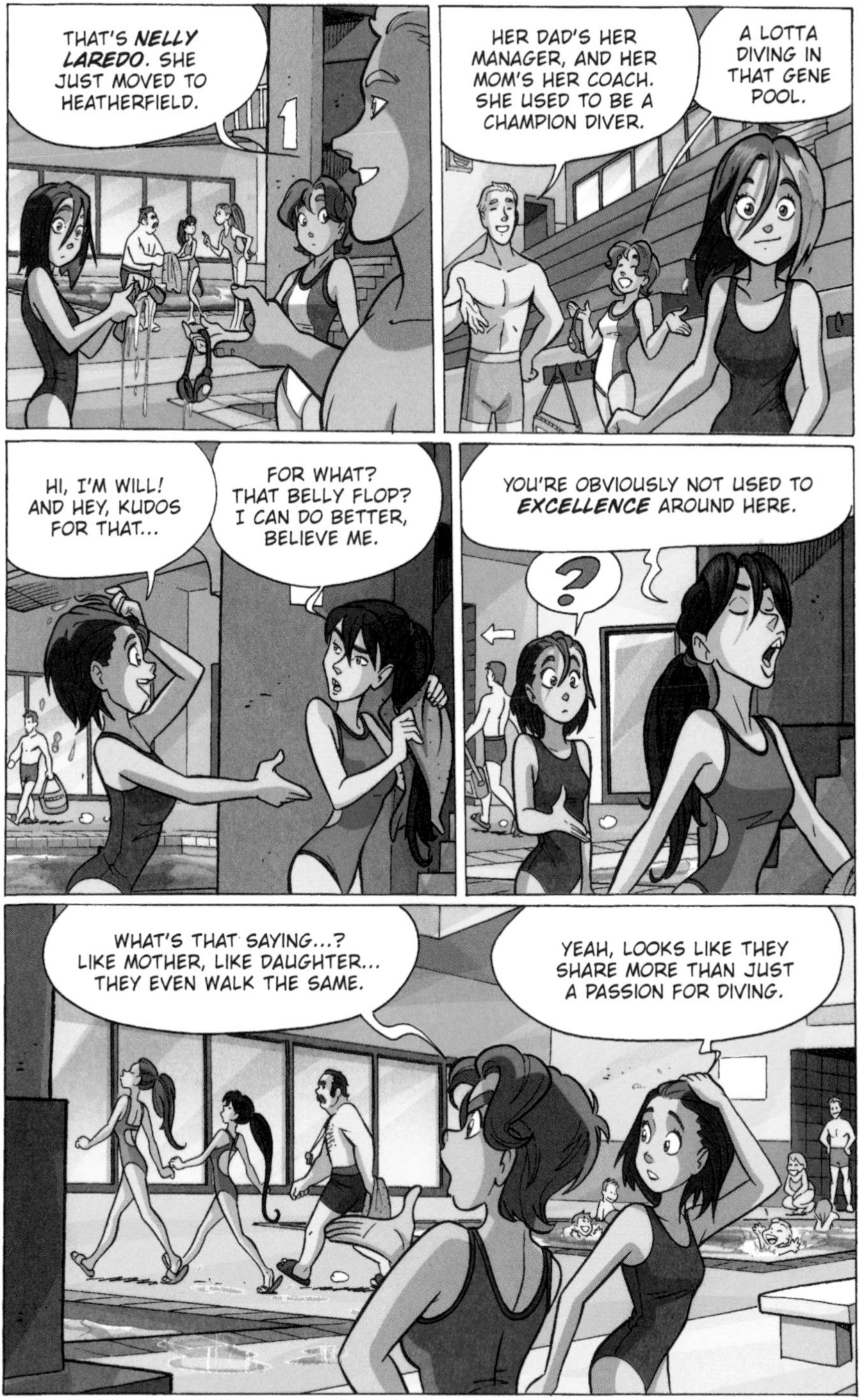
THAT'S NELLY LAREDO. SHE JUST MOVED TO HEATHERFIELD.
HER DAD'S HER MANAGER, AND HER MOM'S HER COACH. SHE USED TO BE A CHAMPION DIVER.
A LOTTA DIVING IN THAT GENE POOL.
HI, I'M WILL! AND HEY, KUDOS FOR THAT...
FOR WHAT? THAT BELLY FLOP? I CAN DO BETTER, BELIEVE ME.
YOU'RE OBVIOUSLY NOT USED TO EXCELLENCE AROUND HERE.
?
WHAT'S THAT SAYING...? LIKE MOTHER, LIKE DAUGHTER... THEY EVEN WALK THE SAME.
YEAH, LOOKS LIKE THEY SHARE MORE THAN JUST A PASSION FOR DIVING.

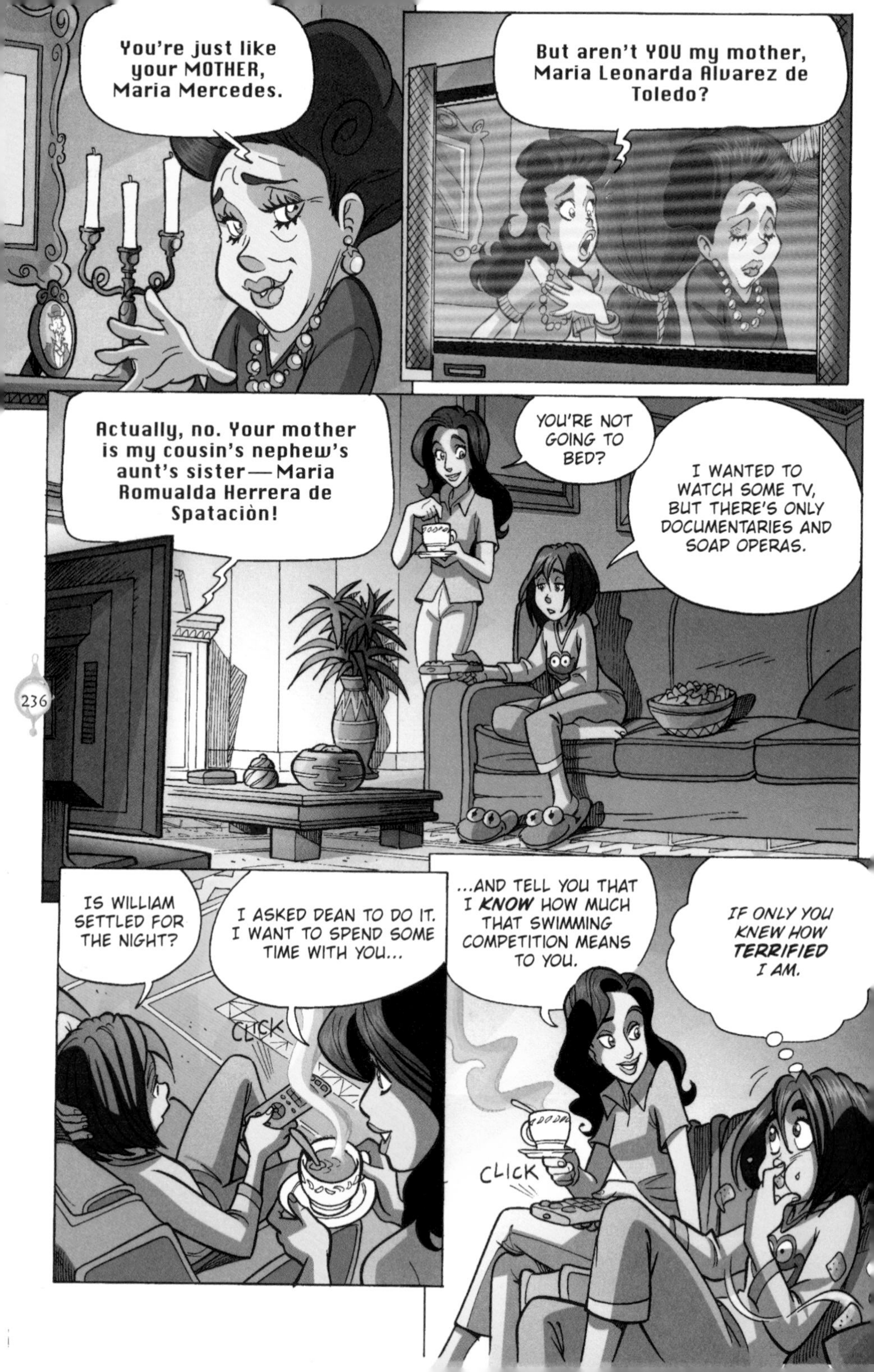

You're just like your MOTHER, Maria Mercedes.
But aren't YOU my mother, Maria Leonarda Alvarez de Toledo?
Actually, no. Your mother is my cousin's nephew's aunt's sister—Maria Romualda Herrera de Spataciòn!
YOU'RE NOT GOING TO BED?
I WANTED TO WATCH SOME TV, BUT THERE'S ONLY DOCUMENTARIES AND SOAP OPERAS.
IS WILLIAM SETTLED FOR THE NIGHT?
I ASKED DEAN TO DO IT. I WANT TO SPEND SOME TIME WITH YOU...
CLICK
...AND TELL YOU THAT I *KNOW* HOW MUCH THAT SWIMMING COMPETITION MEANS TO YOU.
*IF ONLY YOU KNEW HOW **TERRIFIED** I AM.*
CLICK

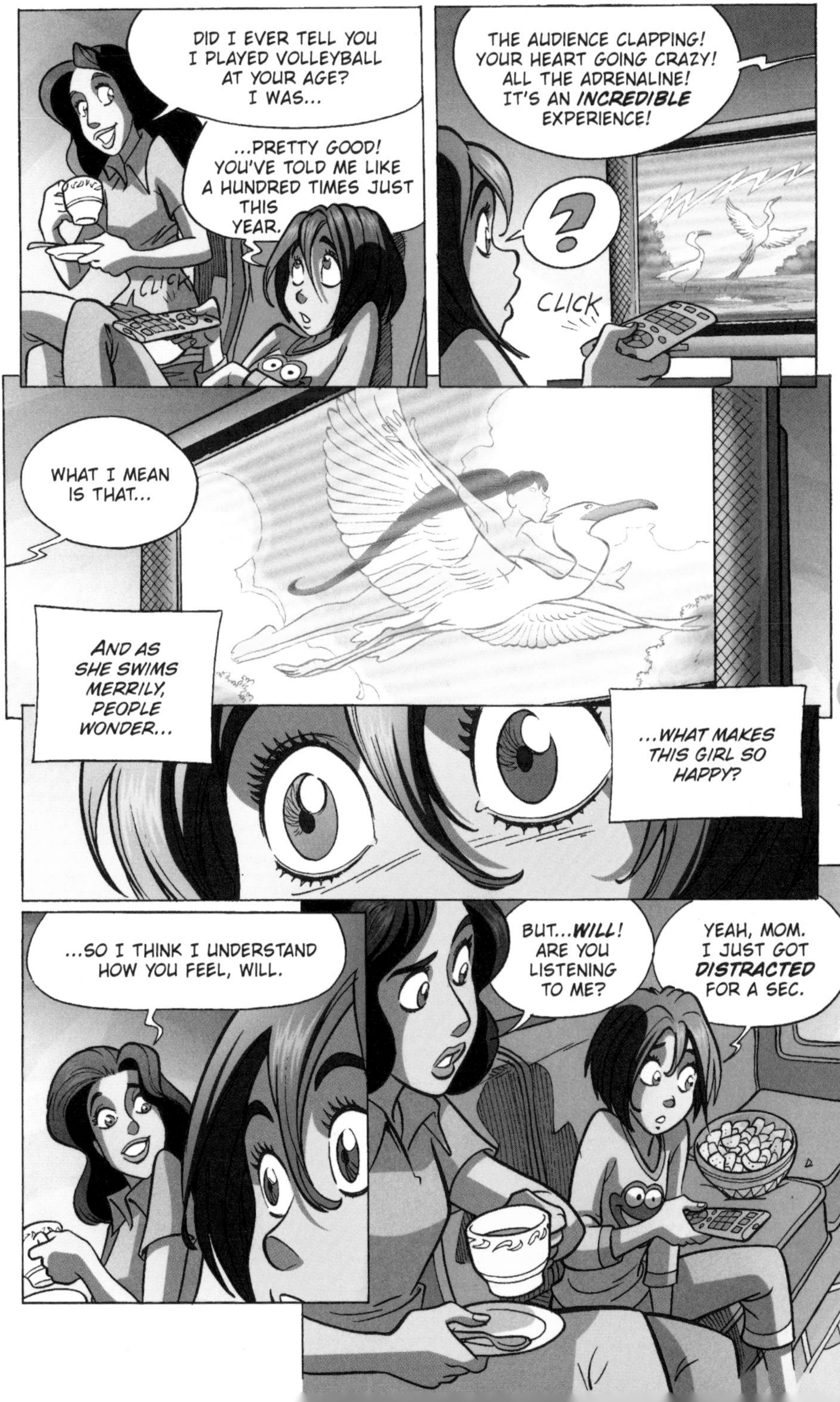
DID I EVER TELL YOU I PLAYED VOLLEYBALL AT YOUR AGE? I WAS...
...PRETTY GOOD! YOU'VE TOLD ME LIKE A HUNDRED TIMES JUST THIS YEAR.
CLICK
THE AUDIENCE CLAPPING! YOUR HEART GOING CRAZY! ALL THE ADRENALINE! IT'S AN *INCREDIBLE* EXPERIENCE!
?
CLICK
WHAT I MEAN IS THAT...
AND AS SHE SWIMS MERRILY, PEOPLE WONDER...
...WHAT MAKES THIS GIRL SO HAPPY?
...SO I THINK I UNDERSTAND HOW YOU FEEL, WILL.
BUT...*WILL*! ARE YOU LISTENING TO ME?
YEAH, MOM. I JUST GOT *DISTRACTED* FOR A SEC.

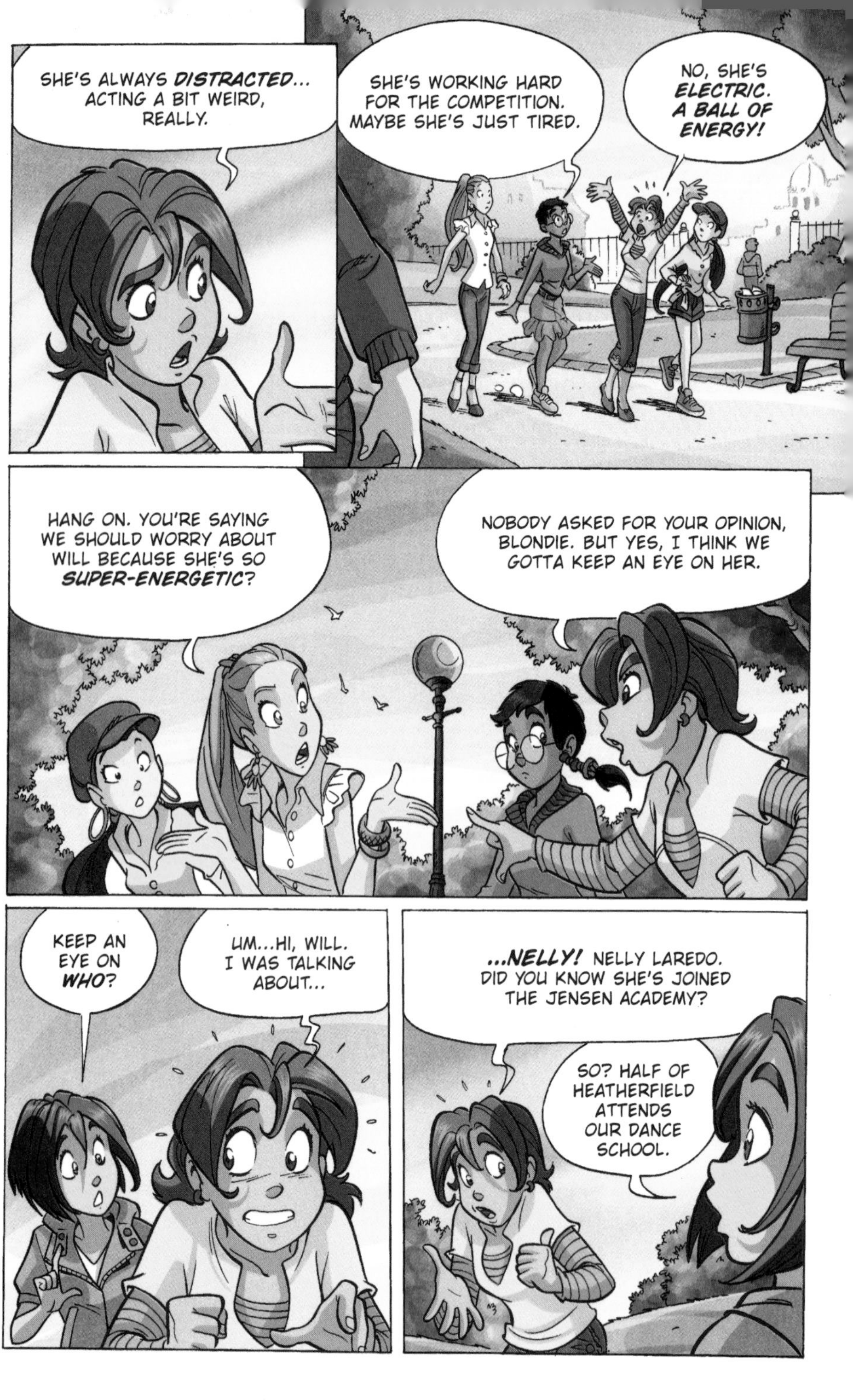
SHE'S ALWAYS DISTRACTED... ACTING A BIT WEIRD, REALLY.
SHE'S WORKING HARD FOR THE COMPETITION. MAYBE SHE'S JUST TIRED.
NO, SHE'S ELECTRIC. A BALL OF ENERGY!
HANG ON. YOU'RE SAYING WE SHOULD WORRY ABOUT WILL BECAUSE SHE'S SO SUPER-ENERGETIC?
NOBODY ASKED FOR YOUR OPINION, BLONDIE. BUT YES, I THINK WE GOTTA KEEP AN EYE ON HER.
KEEP AN EYE ON WHO?
UM...HI, WILL. I WAS TALKING ABOUT...
...NELLY! NELLY LAREDO. DID YOU KNOW SHE'S JOINED THE JENSEN ACADEMY?
SO? HALF OF HEATHERFIELD ATTENDS OUR DANCE SCHOOL.

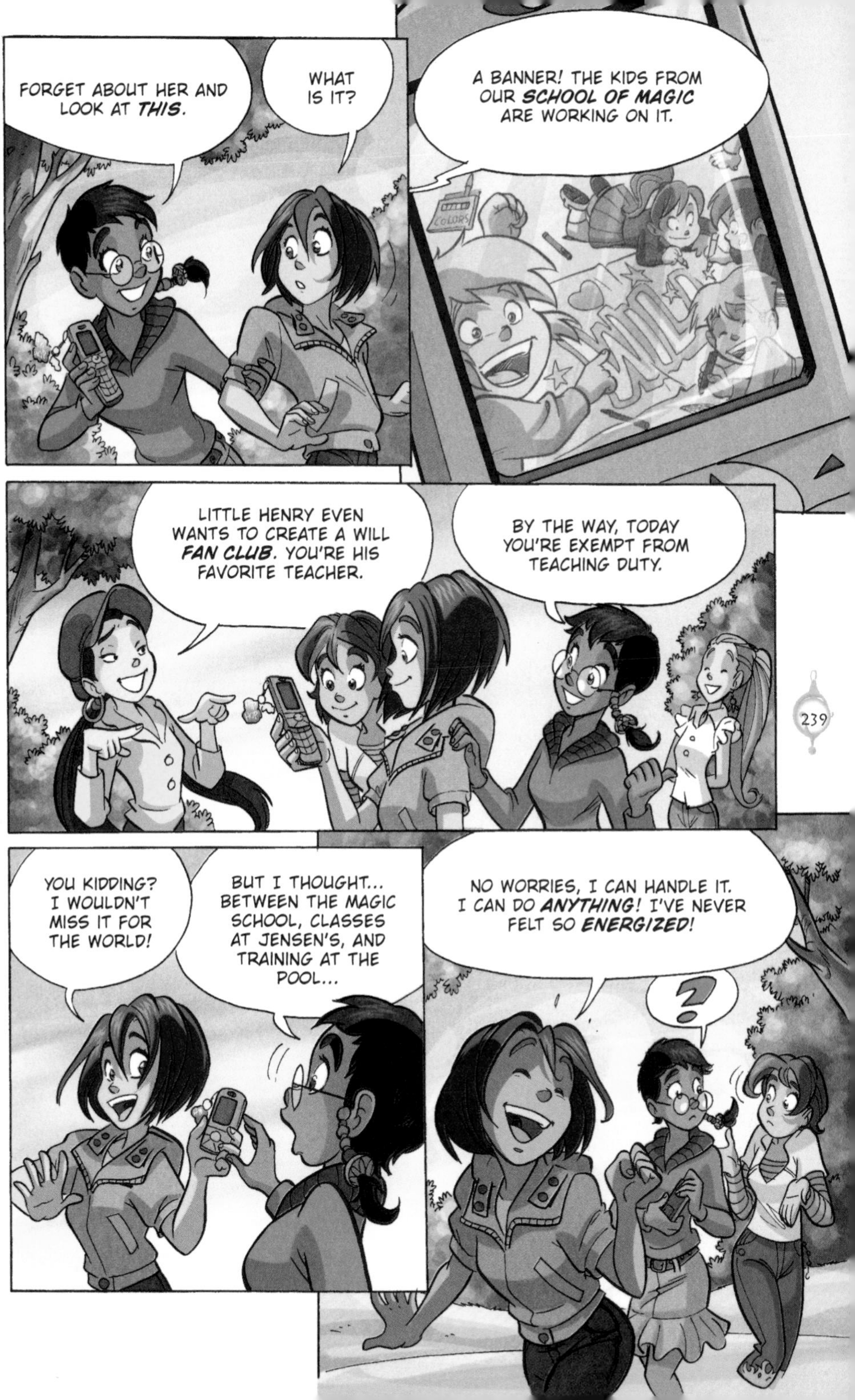
FORGET ABOUT HER AND LOOK AT *THIS*.
WHAT IS IT?
A BANNER! THE KIDS FROM OUR *SCHOOL OF MAGIC* ARE WORKING ON IT.
COLORS
LITTLE HENRY EVEN WANTS TO CREATE A WILL *FAN CLUB*. YOU'RE HIS FAVORITE TEACHER.
BY THE WAY, TODAY YOU'RE EXEMPT FROM TEACHING DUTY.
YOU KIDDING? I WOULDN'T MISS IT FOR THE WORLD!
BUT I THOUGHT... BETWEEN THE MAGIC SCHOOL, CLASSES AT JENSEN'S, AND TRAINING AT THE POOL...
NO WORRIES, I CAN HANDLE IT. I CAN DO *ANYTHING*! I'VE NEVER FELT SO *ENERGIZED*!
?

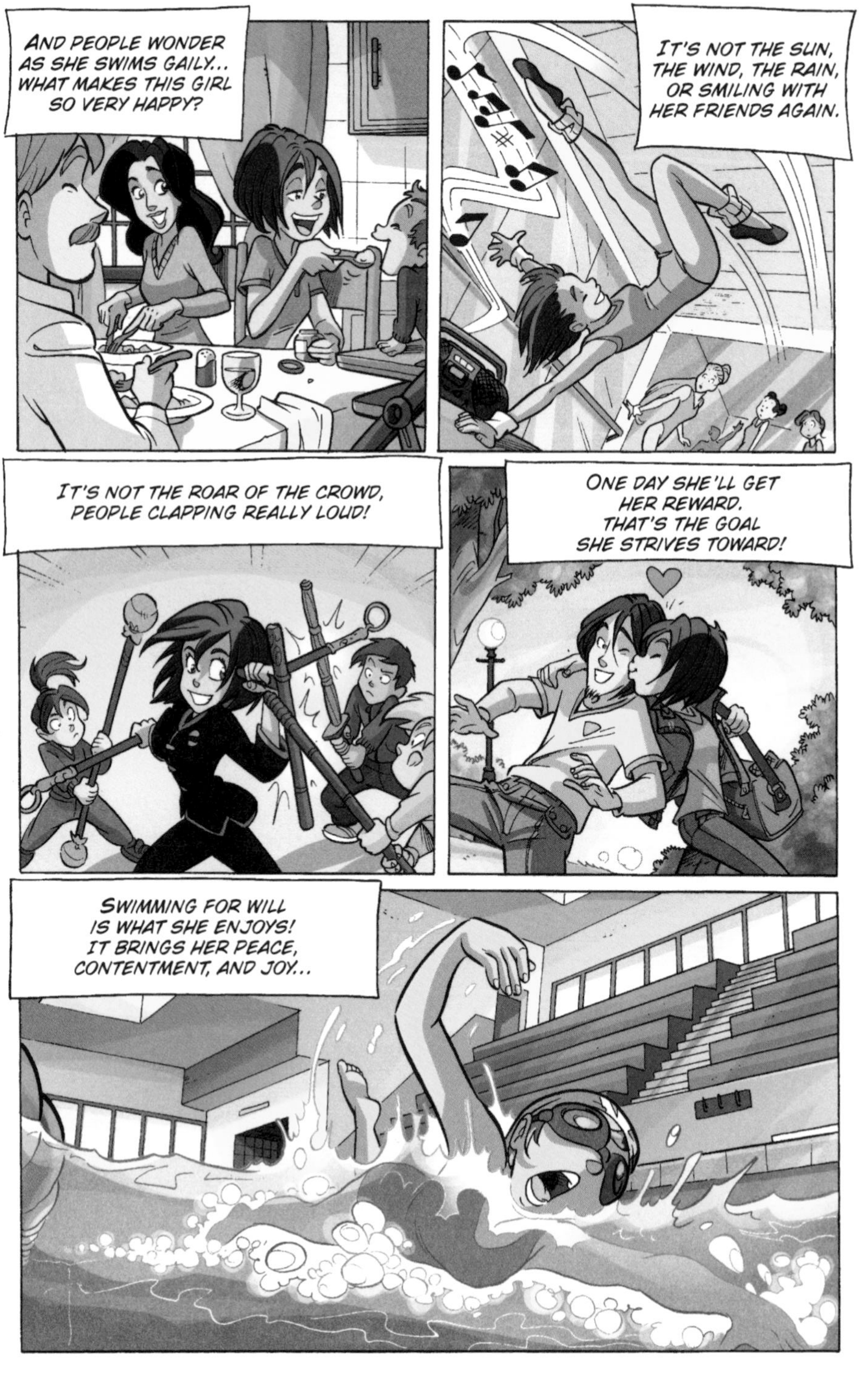
AND PEOPLE WONDER
AS SHE SWIMS GAILY...
WHAT MAKES THIS GIRL
SO VERY HAPPY?
IT'S NOT THE SUN,
THE WIND, THE RAIN,
OR SMILING WITH
HER FRIENDS AGAIN.
IT'S NOT THE ROAR OF THE CROWD,
PEOPLE CLAPPING REALLY LOUD!
ONE DAY SHE'LL GET
HER REWARD.
THAT'S THE GOAL
SHE STRIVES TOWARD!
SWIMMING FOR WILL
IS WHAT SHE ENJOYS!
IT BRINGS HER PEACE,
CONTENTMENT, AND JOY...

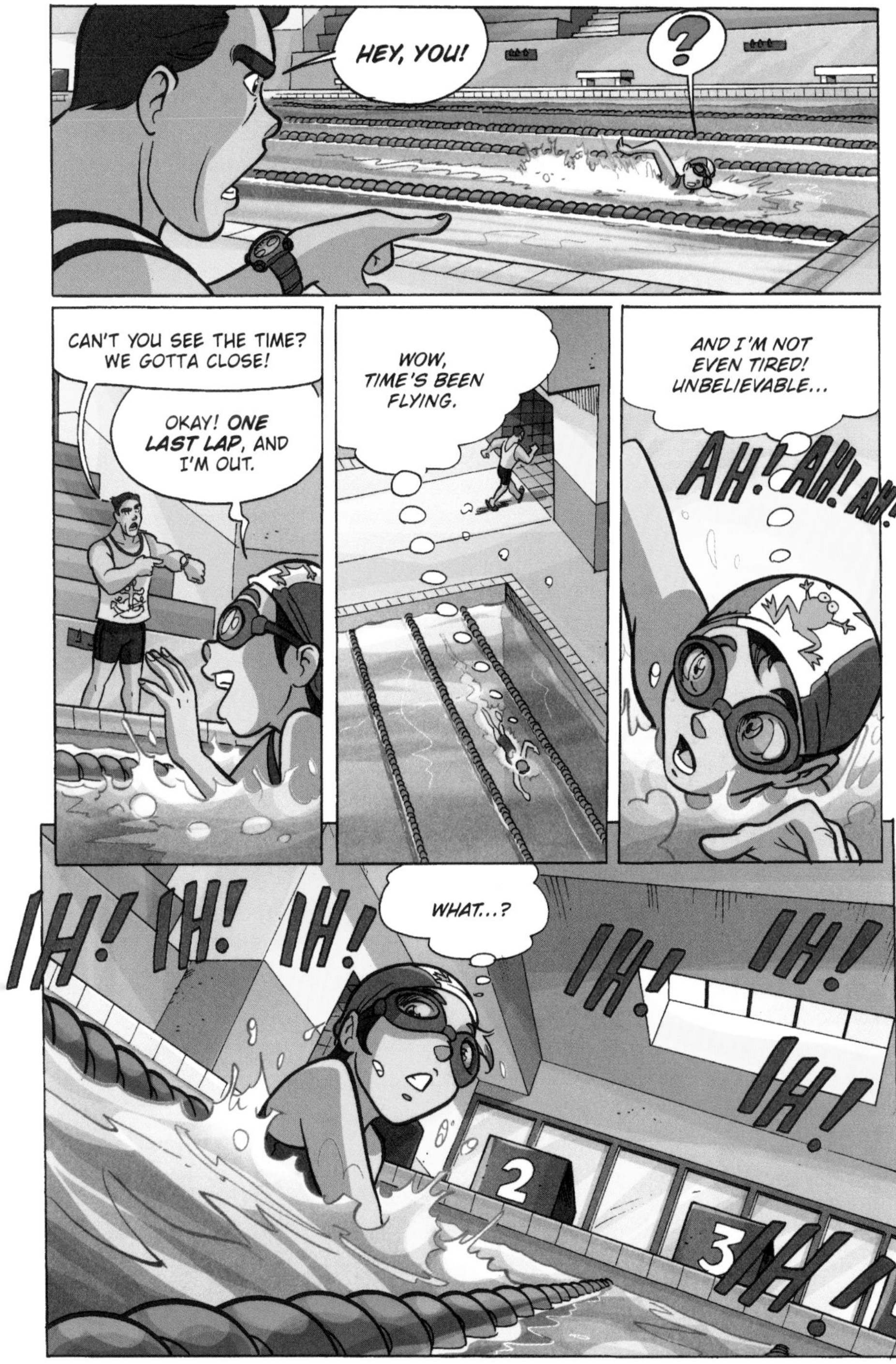
HEY, YOU!
?
CAN'T YOU SEE THE TIME? WE GOTTA CLOSE!
OKAY! ONE LAST LAP, AND I'M OUT.
WOW, TIME'S BEEN FLYING.
AND I'M NOT EVEN TIRED! UNBELIEVABLE...
AH! AH! AH!
IH! IH! IH!
WHAT...?
IH! IH! IH!
2
3
AH!

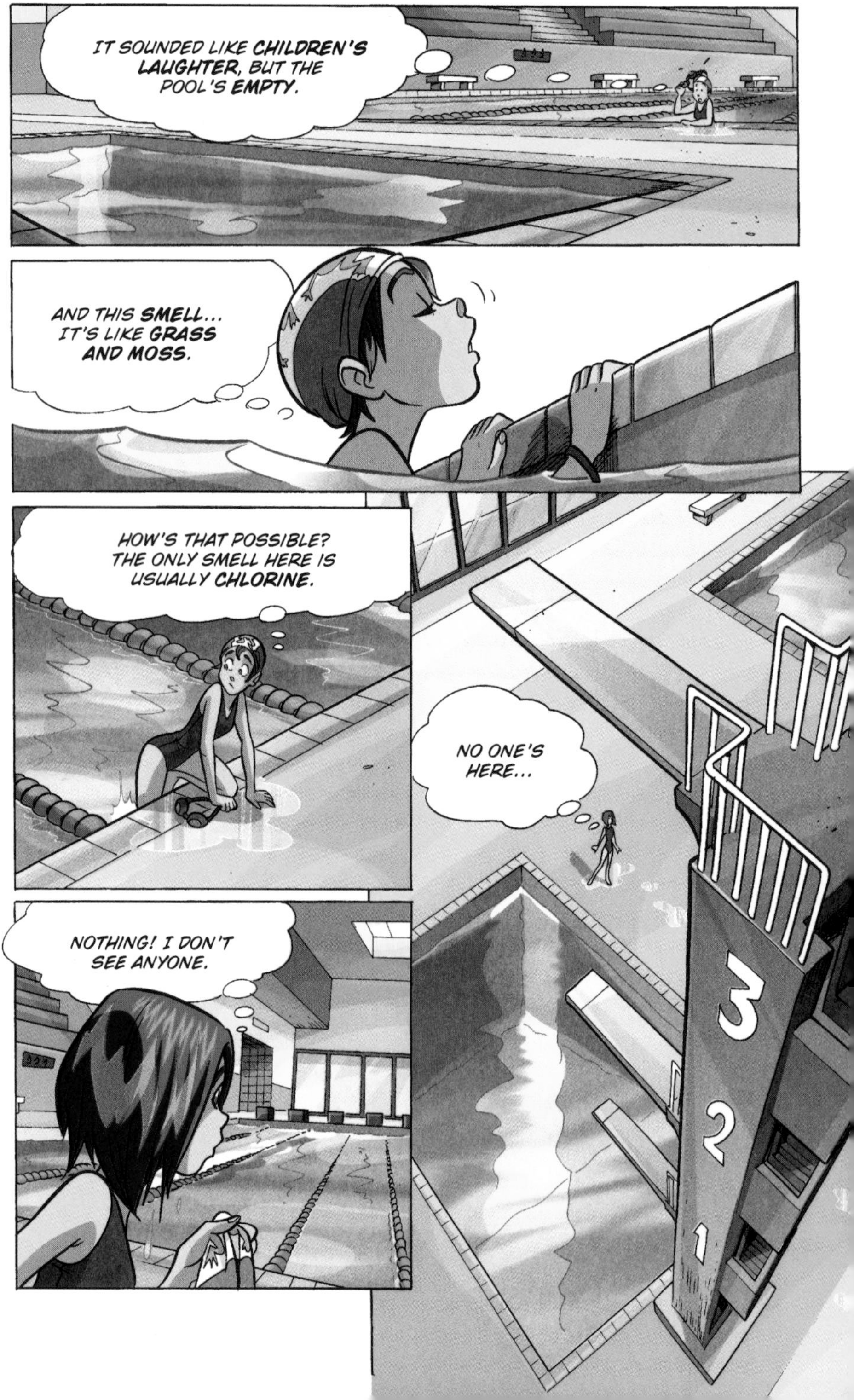
IT SOUNDED LIKE CHILDREN'S LAUGHTER, BUT THE POOL'S EMPTY.
AND THIS SMELL... IT'S LIKE GRASS AND MOSS.
HOW'S THAT POSSIBLE? THE ONLY SMELL HERE IS USUALLY CHLORINE.
NO ONE'S HERE...
NOTHING! I DON'T SEE ANYONE.
3
2
1

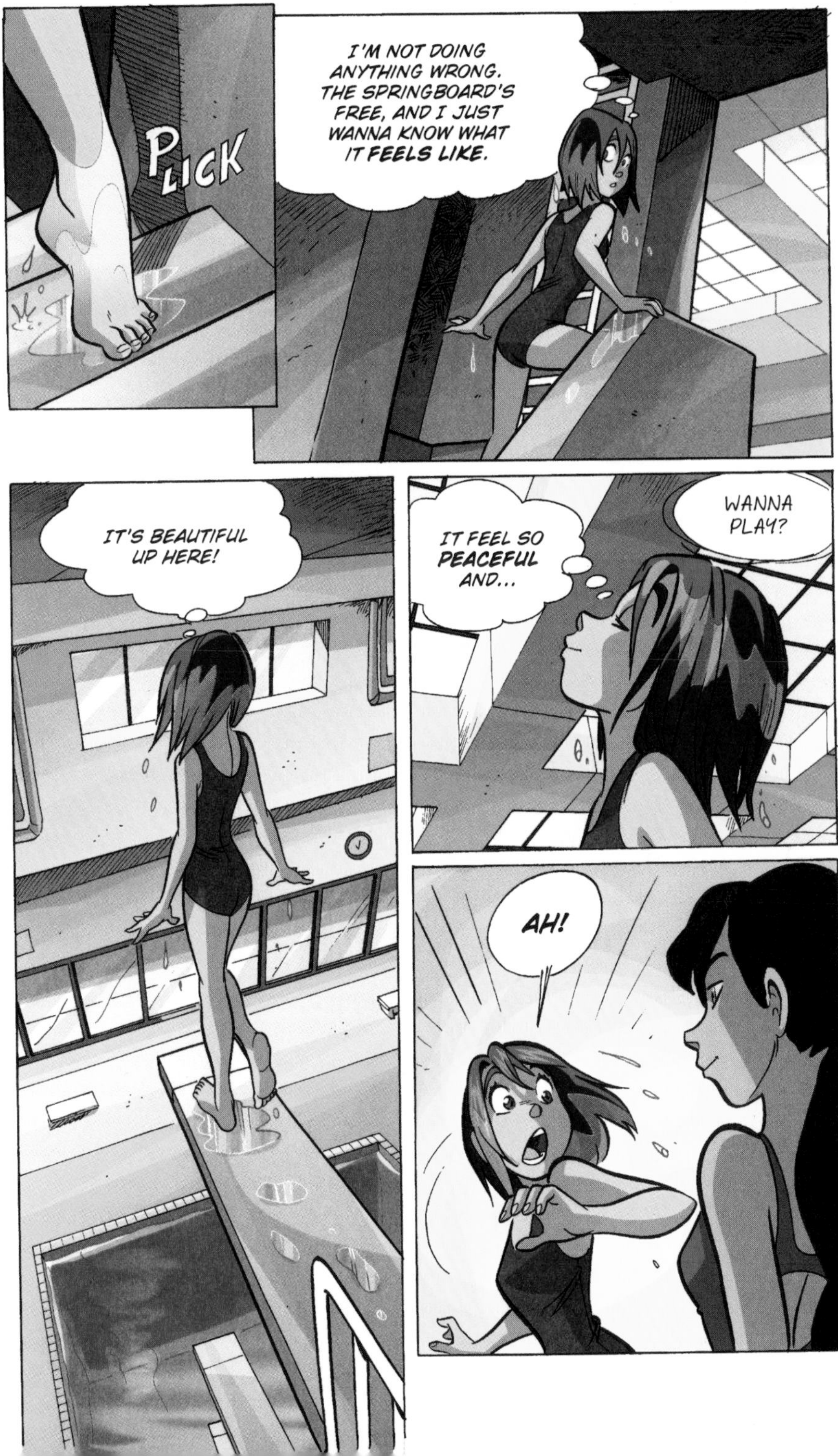
PLICK
I'M NOT DOING ANYTHING WRONG. THE SPRINGBOARD'S FREE, AND I JUST WANNA KNOW WHAT IT **FEELS LIKE.**
IT'S BEAUTIFUL UP HERE!
IT FEEL SO **PEACEFUL** AND...
WANNA PLAY?
AH!

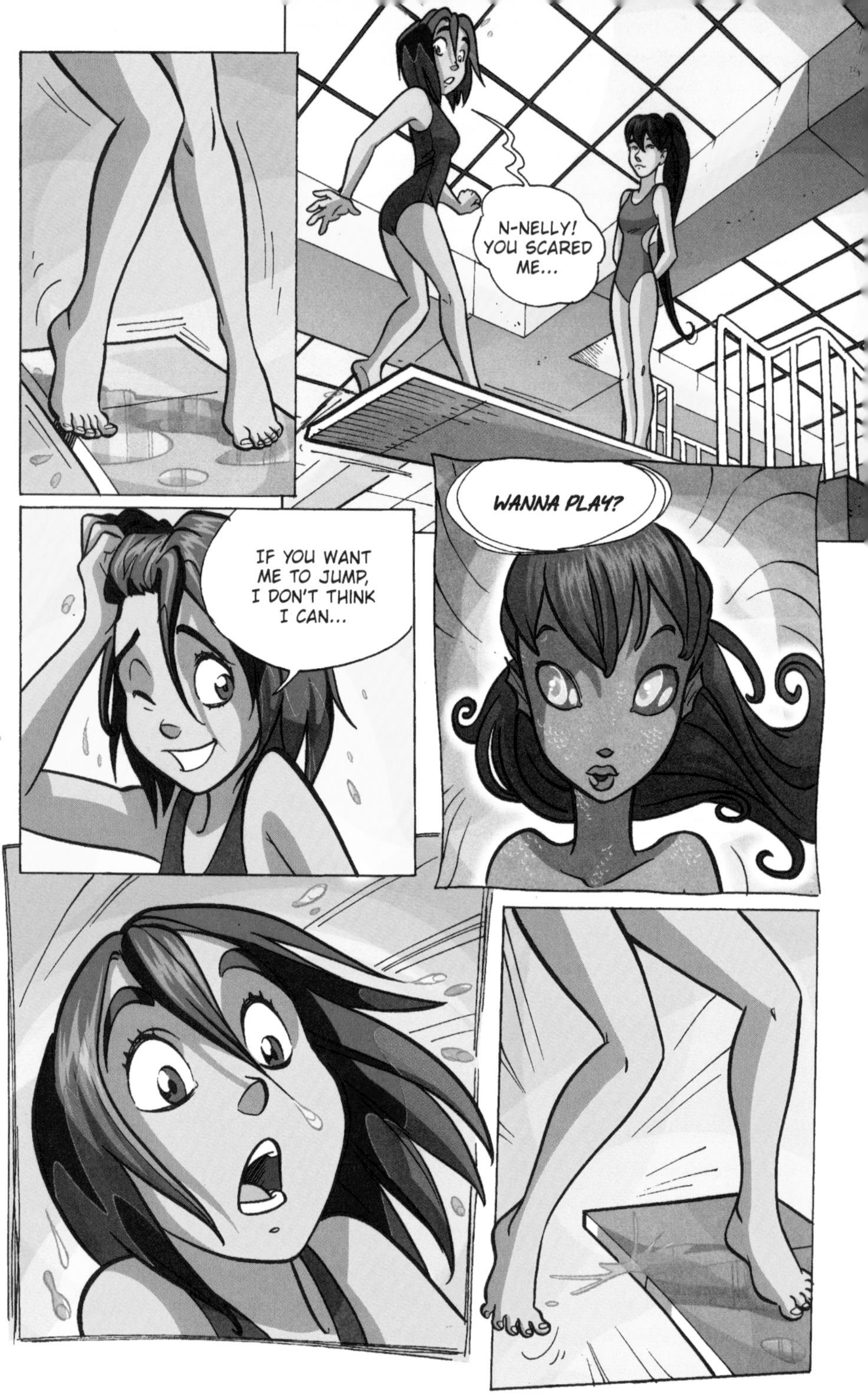

N-NELLY! YOU SCARED ME...
WANNA PLAY?
IF YOU WANT ME TO JUMP, I DON'T THINK I CAN...

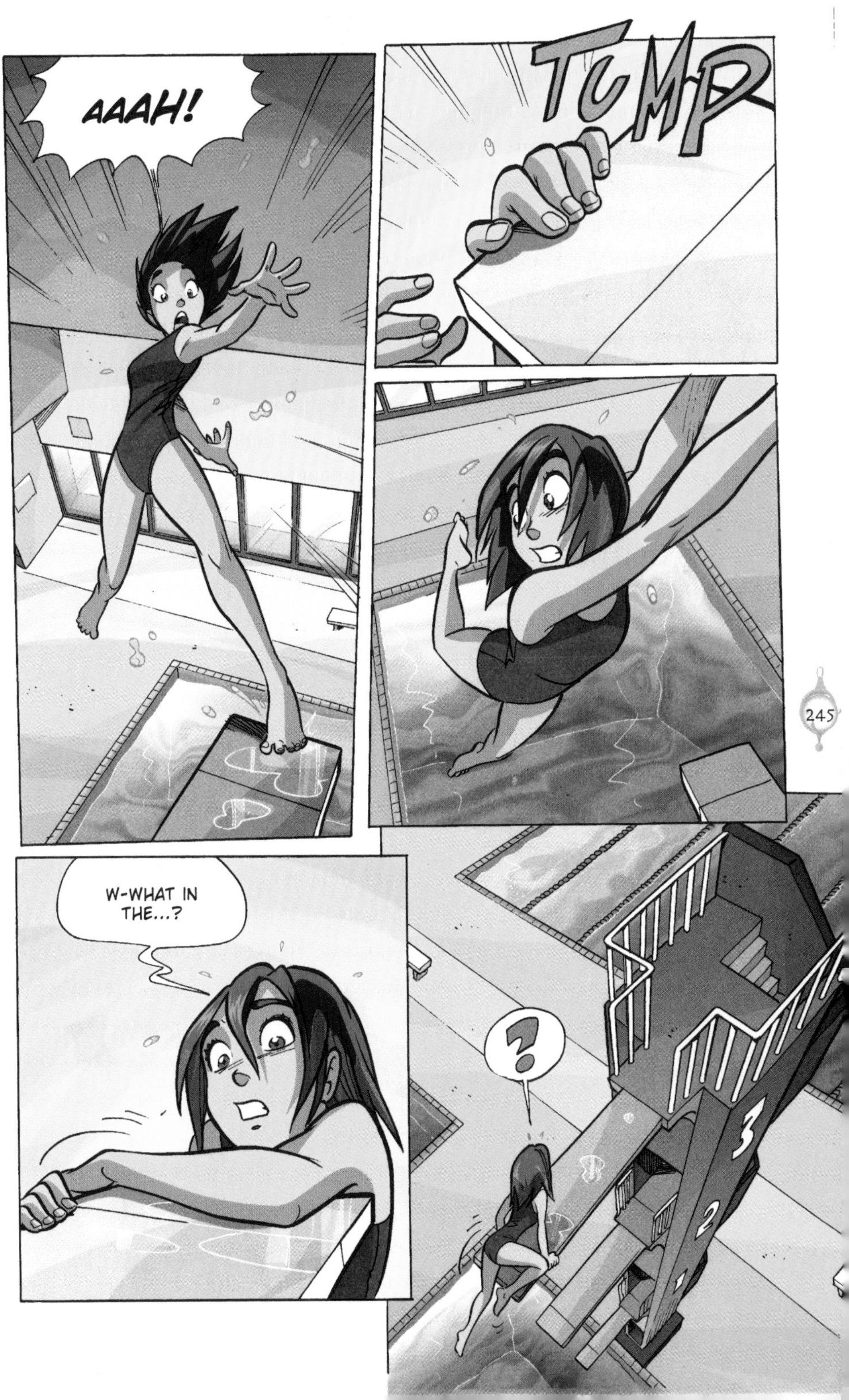

AAAH!
TUMP
W-WHAT IN THE...?
?
3
2

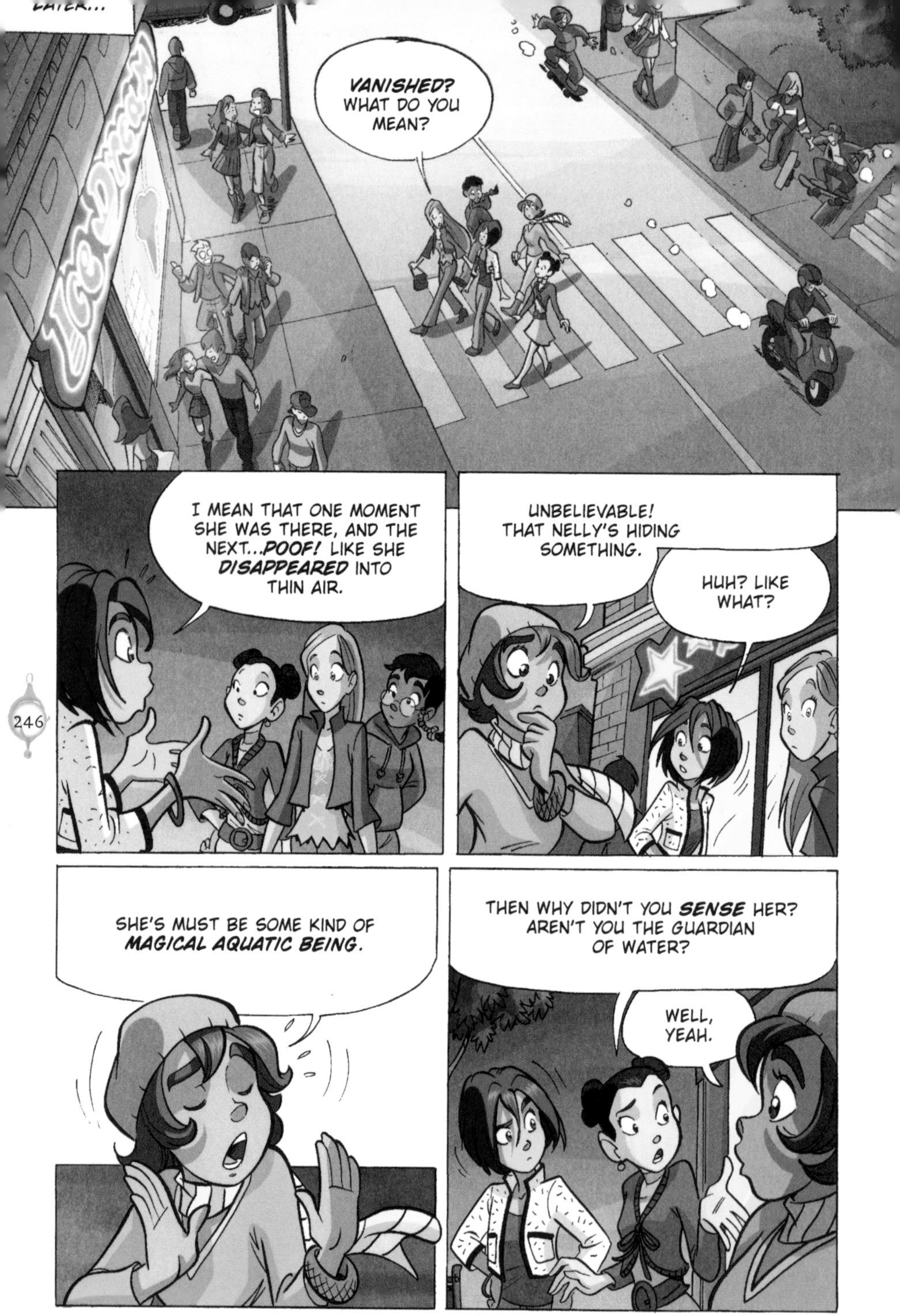

VANISHED? WHAT DO YOU MEAN?
I MEAN THAT ONE MOMENT SHE WAS THERE, AND THE NEXT...POOF! LIKE SHE DISAPPEARED INTO THIN AIR.
UNBELIEVABLE! THAT NELLY'S HIDING SOMETHING.
HUH? LIKE WHAT?
SHE'S MUST BE SOME KIND OF MAGICAL AQUATIC BEING.
THEN WHY DIDN'T YOU SENSE HER? AREN'T YOU THE GUARDIAN OF WATER?
WELL, YEAH.

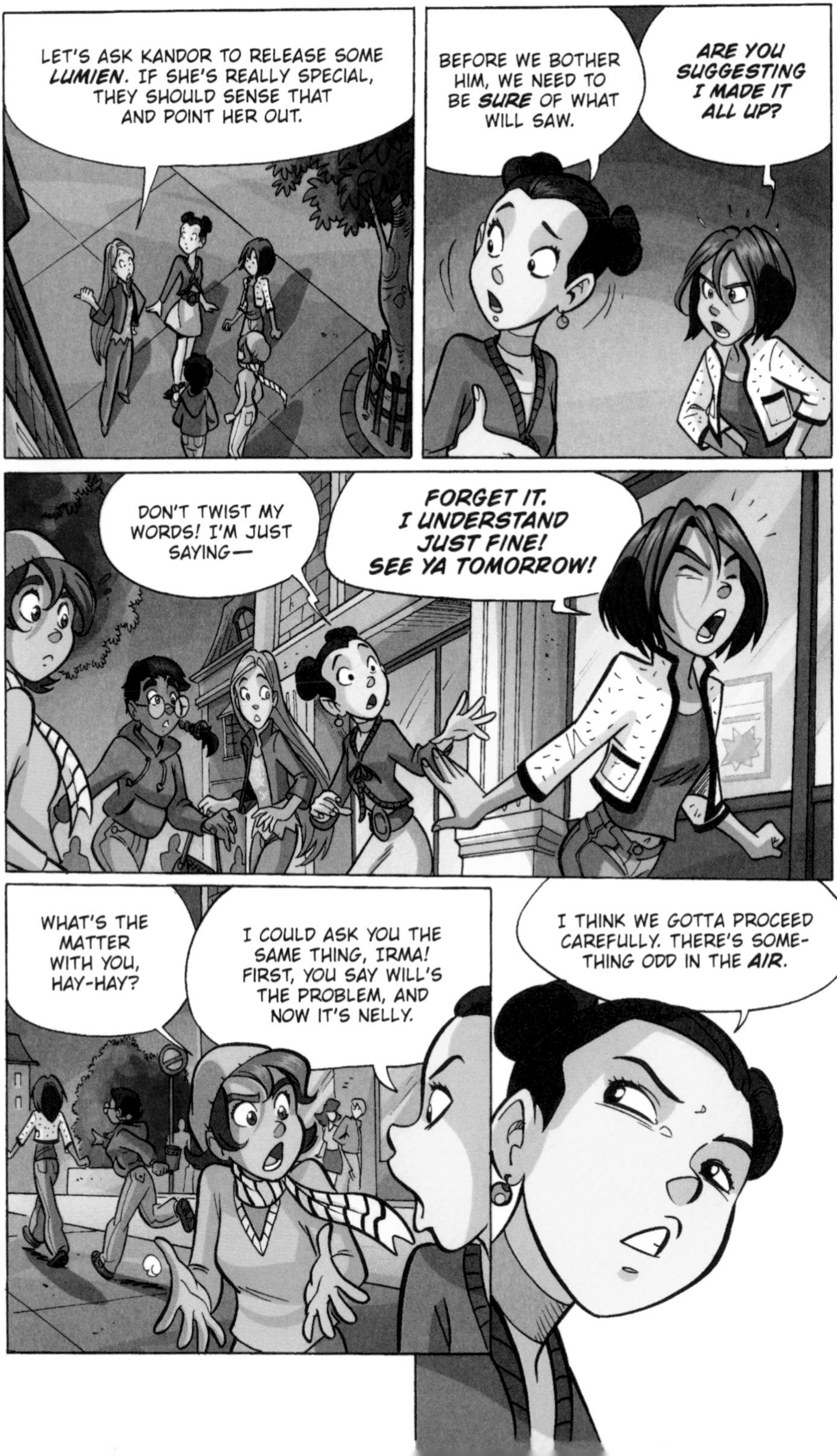
LET'S ASK KANDOR TO RELEASE SOME *LUMIEN*. IF SHE'S REALLY SPECIAL, THEY SHOULD SENSE THAT AND POINT HER OUT.
BEFORE WE BOTHER HIM, WE NEED TO BE *SURE* OF WHAT WILL SAW.
ARE YOU SUGGESTING I MADE IT ALL UP?
DON'T TWIST MY WORDS! I'M JUST SAYING—
FORGET IT. I UNDERSTAND JUST FINE! SEE YA TOMORROW!
WHAT'S THE MATTER WITH YOU, HAY-HAY?
I COULD ASK YOU THE SAME THING, IRMA! FIRST, YOU SAY WILL'S THE PROBLEM, AND NOW IT'S NELLY.
I THINK WE GOTTA PROCEED CAREFULLY. THERE'S SOMETHING ODD IN THE *AIR*.

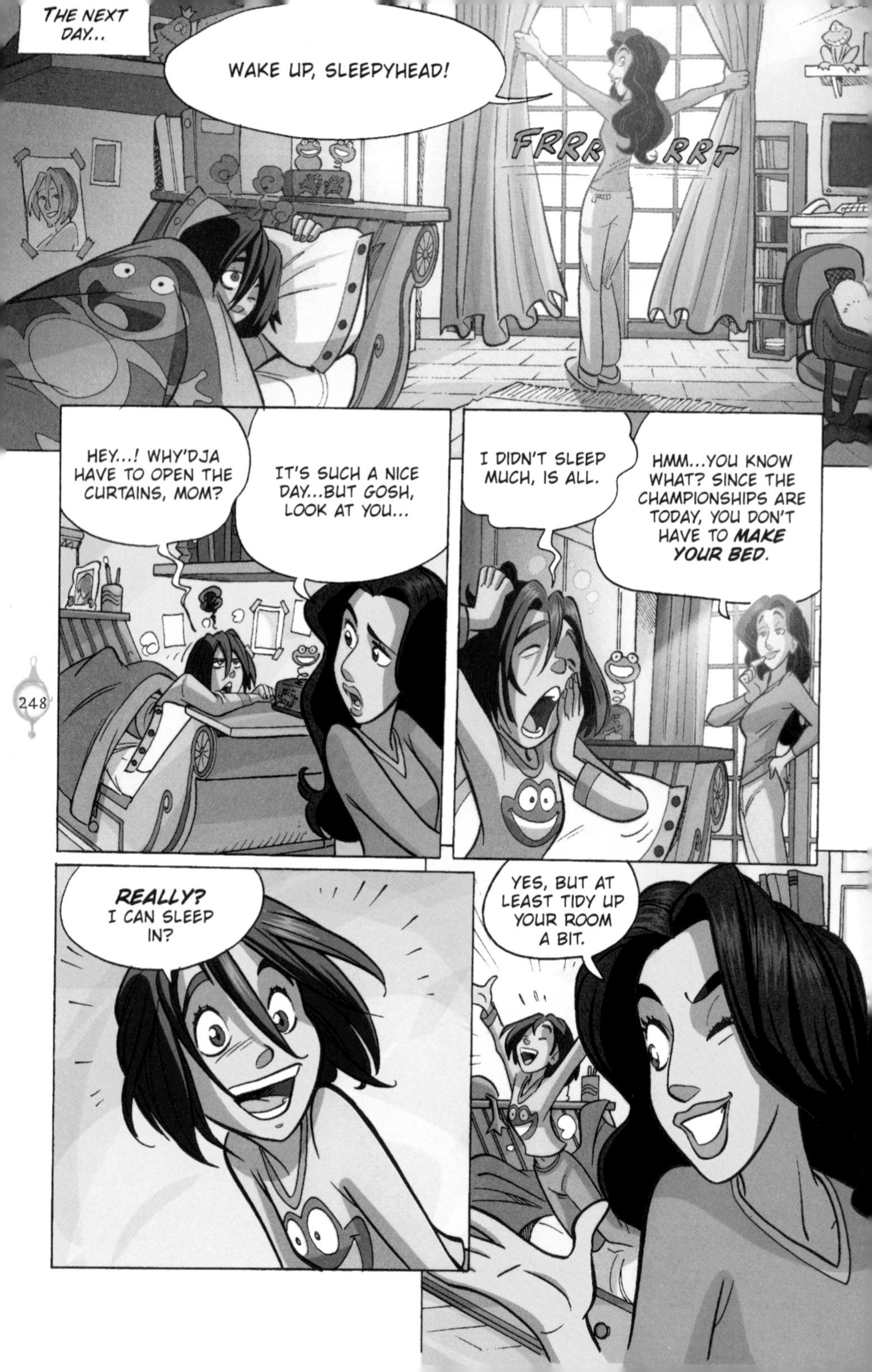

THE NEXT DAY...
WAKE UP, SLEEPYHEAD!
FRRRRRRT
HEY...! WHY'DJA HAVE TO OPEN THE CURTAINS, MOM?
IT'S SUCH A NICE DAY...BUT GOSH, LOOK AT YOU...
I DIDN'T SLEEP MUCH, IS ALL.
HMM...YOU KNOW WHAT? SINCE THE CHAMPIONSHIPS ARE TODAY, YOU DON'T HAVE TO ***MAKE YOUR BED.***
REALLY? I CAN SLEEP IN?
YES, BUT AT LEAST TIDY UP YOUR ROOM A BIT.

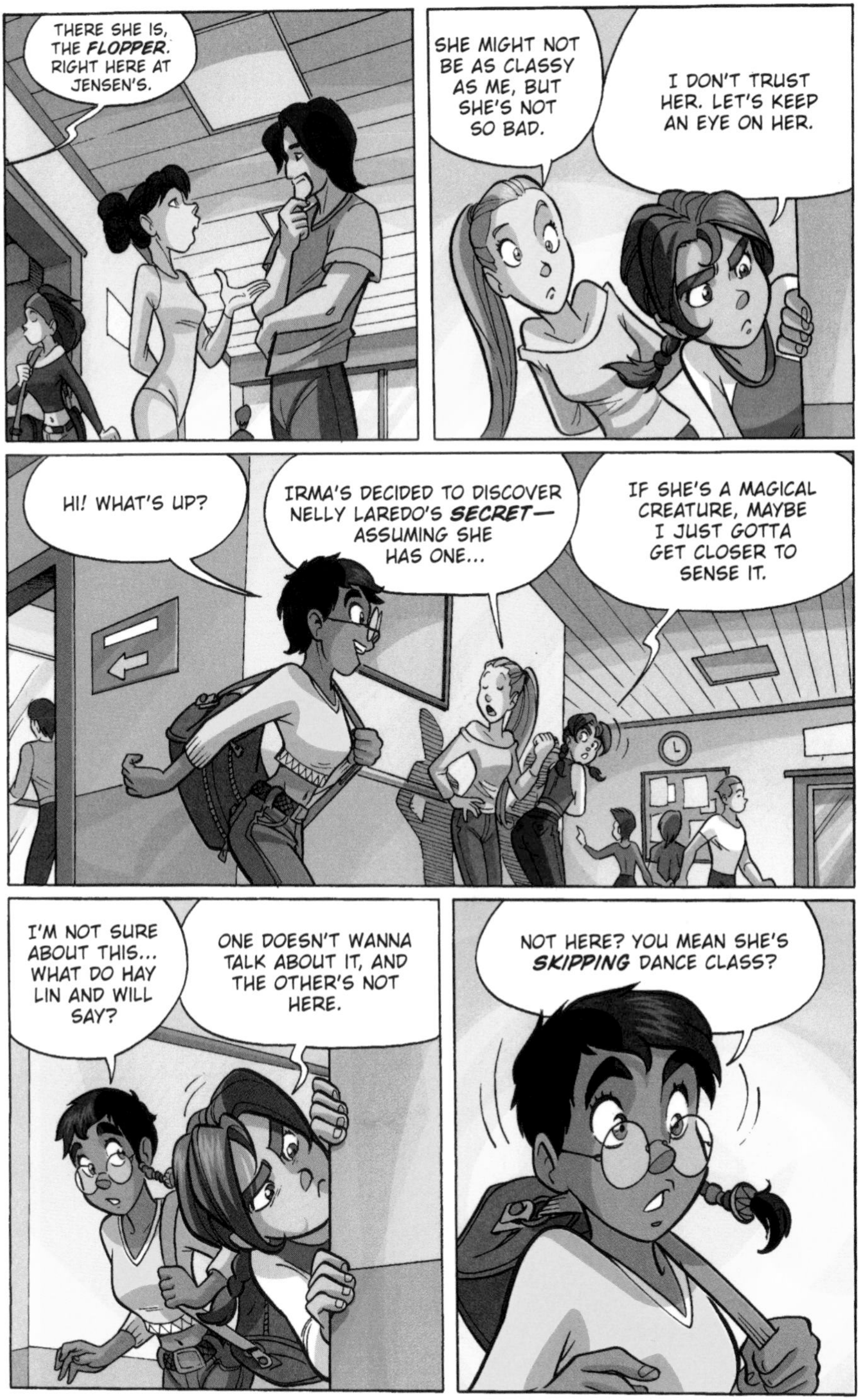
THERE SHE IS, THE FLOPPER. RIGHT HERE AT JENSEN'S.
SHE MIGHT NOT BE AS CLASSY AS ME, BUT SHE'S NOT SO BAD.
I DON'T TRUST HER. LET'S KEEP AN EYE ON HER.
HI! WHAT'S UP?
IRMA'S DECIDED TO DISCOVER NELLY LAREDO'S SECRET— ASSUMING SHE HAS ONE...
IF SHE'S A MAGICAL CREATURE, MAYBE I JUST GOTTA GET CLOSER TO SENSE IT.
I'M NOT SURE ABOUT THIS... WHAT DO HAY LIN AND WILL SAY?
ONE DOESN'T WANNA TALK ABOUT IT, AND THE OTHER'S NOT HERE.
NOT HERE? YOU MEAN SHE'S SKIPPING DANCE CLASS?

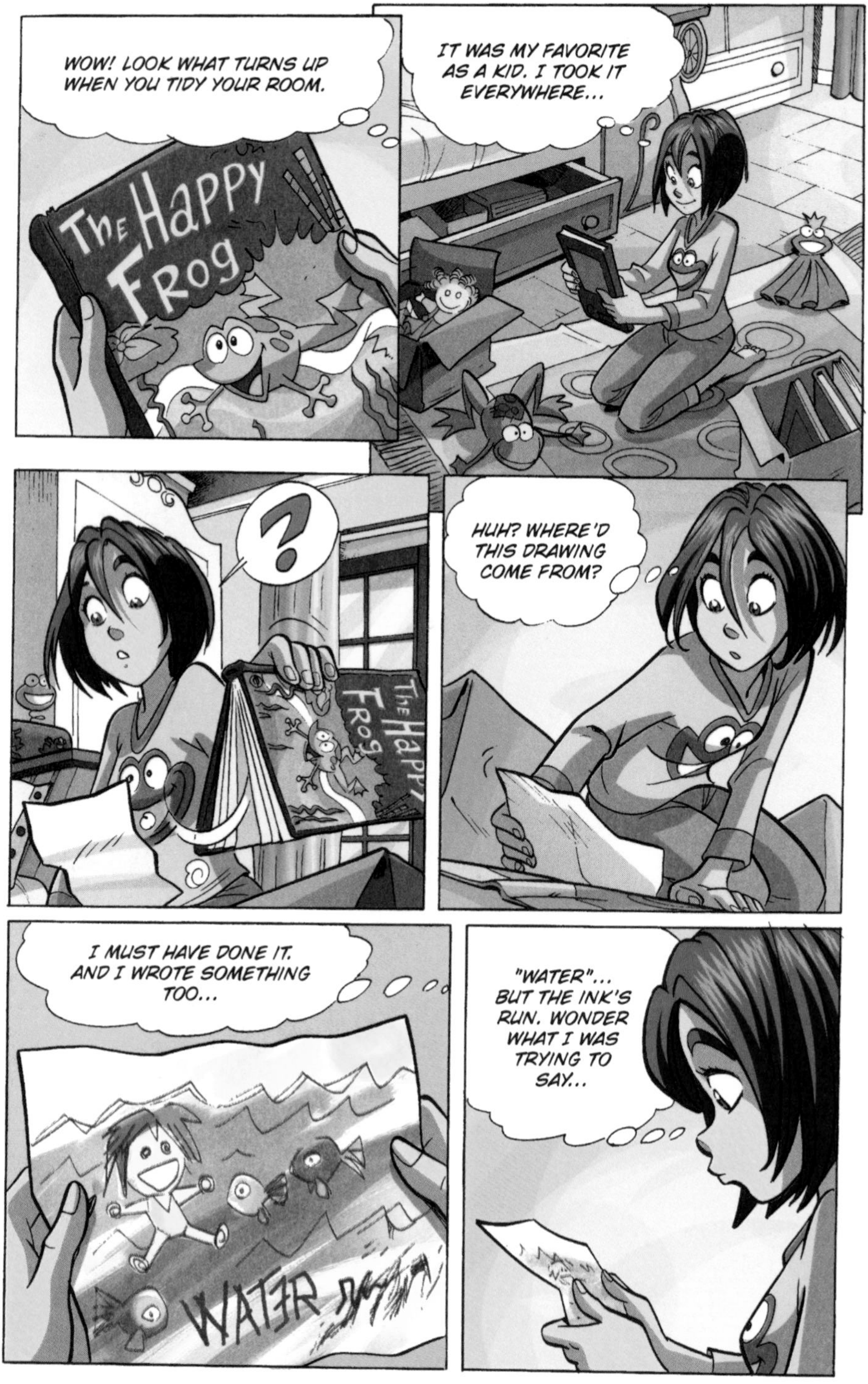

WOW! LOOK WHAT TURNS UP WHEN YOU TIDY YOUR ROOM.
THE HAPPY FROG
IT WAS MY FAVORITE AS A KID. I TOOK IT EVERYWHERE...
?
HUH? WHERE'D THIS DRAWING COME FROM?
I MUST HAVE DONE IT. AND I WROTE SOMETHING TOO...
WATER
"WATER"... BUT THE INK'S RUN. WONDER WHAT I WAS TRYING TO SAY...

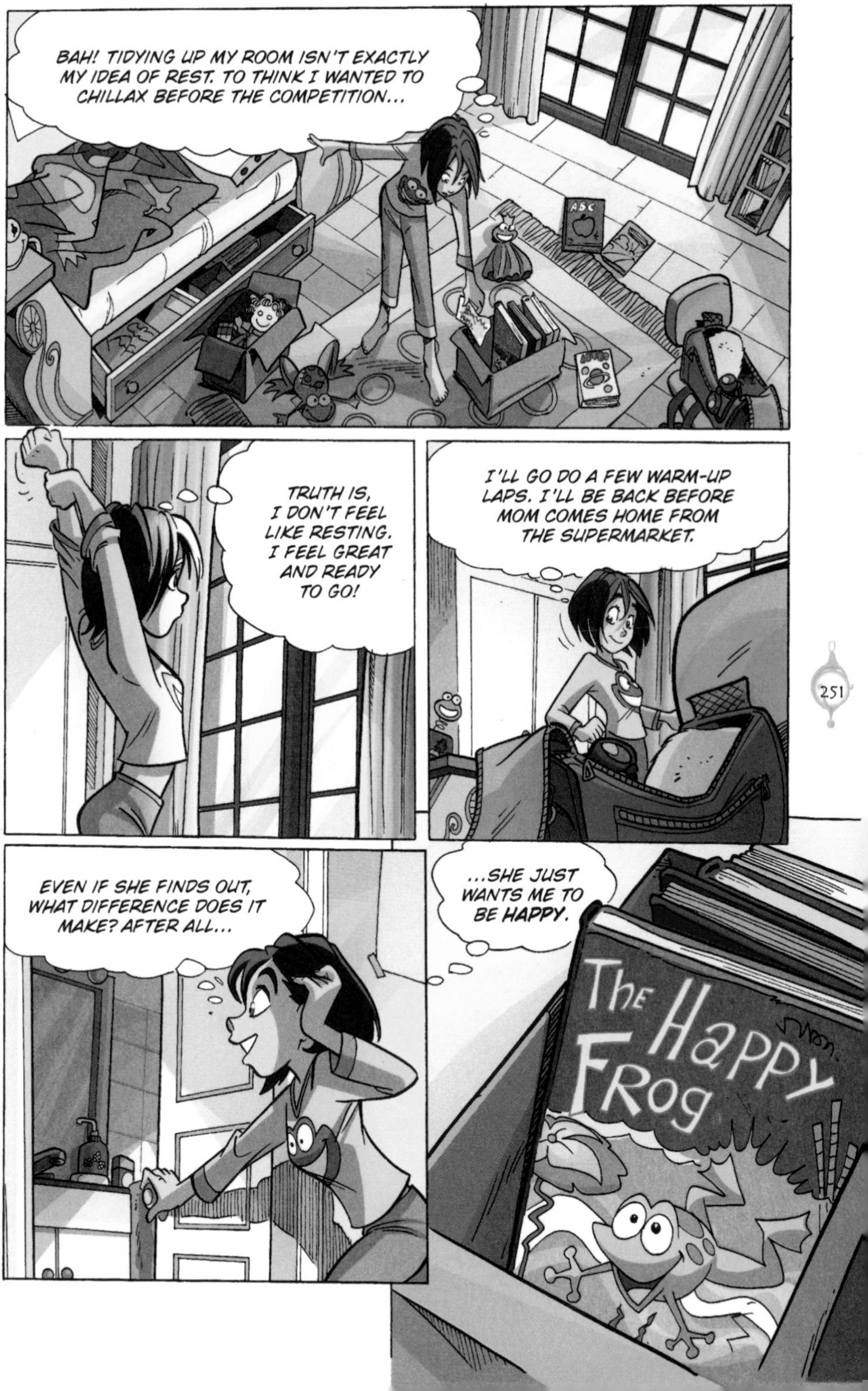
BAH! TIDYING UP MY ROOM ISN'T EXACTLY MY IDEA OF REST. TO THINK I WANTED TO CHILLAX BEFORE THE COMPETITION...
TRUTH IS, I DON'T FEEL LIKE RESTING. I FEEL GREAT AND READY TO GO!
I'LL GO DO A FEW WARM-UP LAPS. I'LL BE BACK BEFORE MOM COMES HOME FROM THE SUPERMARKET.
EVEN IF SHE FINDS OUT, WHAT DIFFERENCE DOES IT MAKE? AFTER ALL...
...SHE JUST WANTS ME TO BE HAPPY.
The Happy Frog

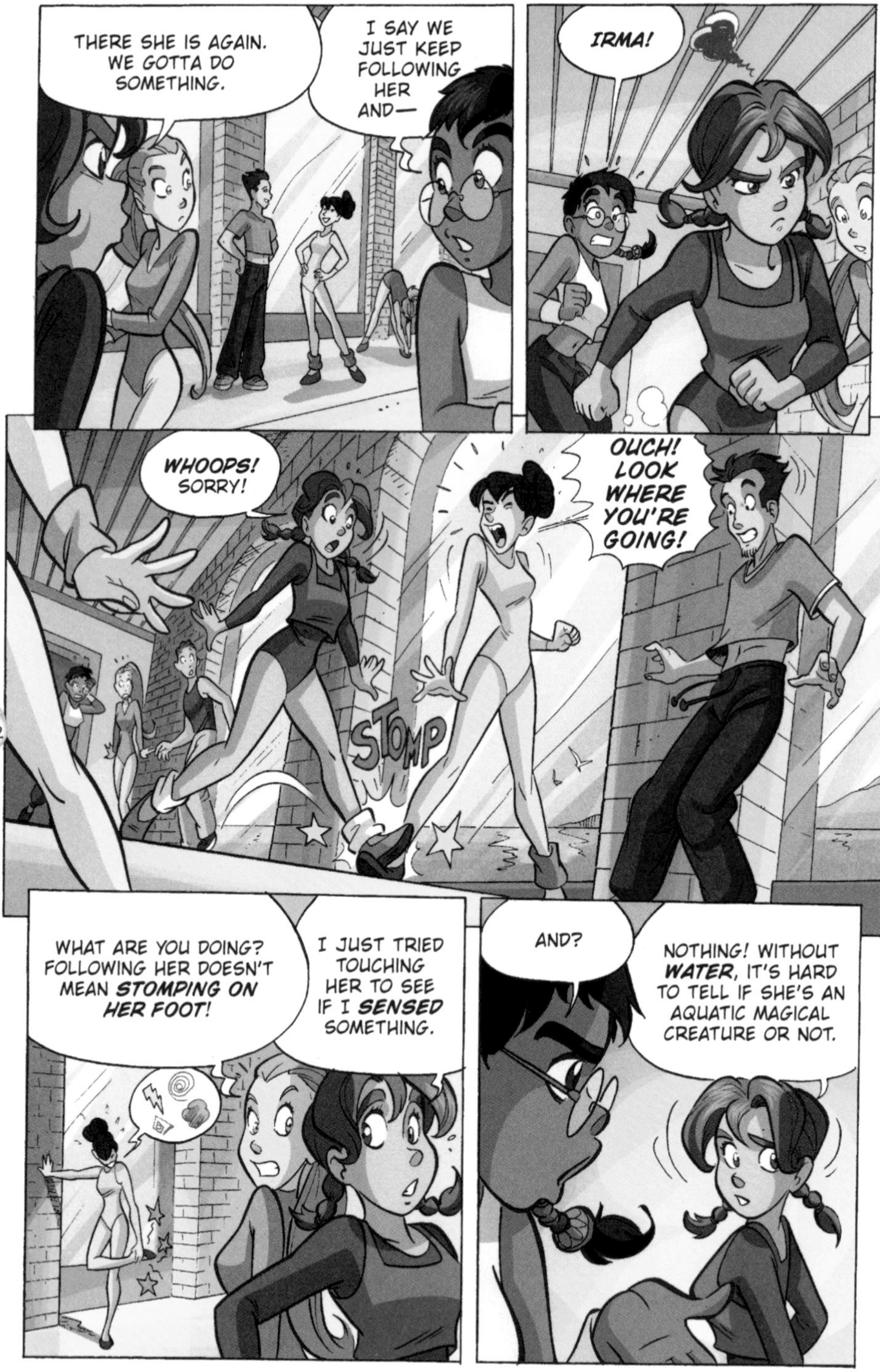

THERE SHE IS AGAIN. WE GOTTA DO SOMETHING.
I SAY WE JUST KEEP FOLLOWING HER AND—
IRMA!
WHOOPS! SORRY!
OUCH! LOOK WHERE YOU'RE GOING!
STOMP
WHAT ARE YOU DOING? FOLLOWING HER DOESN'T MEAN STOMPING ON HER FOOT!
I JUST TRIED TOUCHING HER TO SEE IF I SENSED SOMETHING.
AND?
NOTHING! WITHOUT WATER, IT'S HARD TO TELL IF SHE'S AN AQUATIC MAGICAL CREATURE OR NOT.

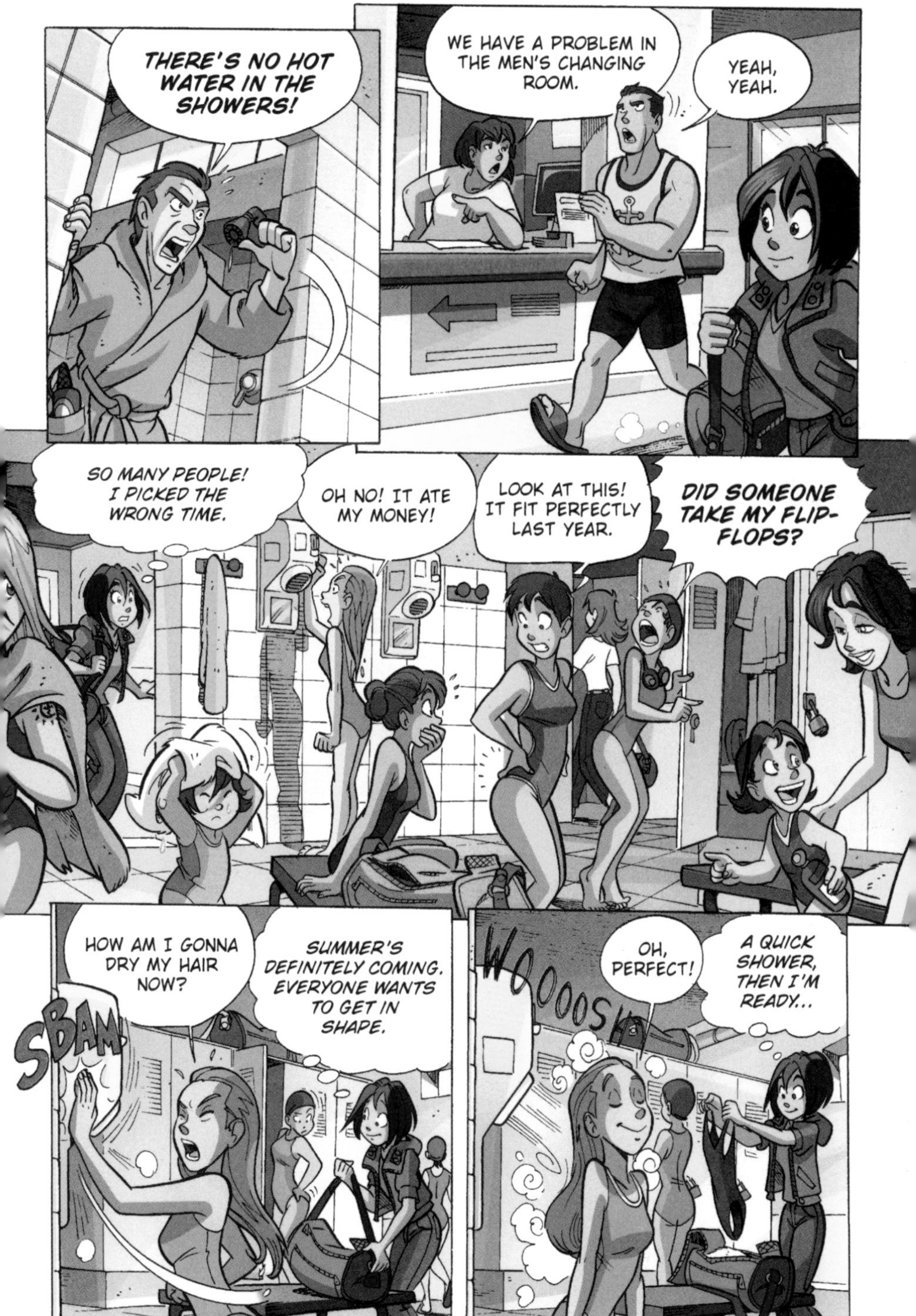
THERE'S NO HOT WATER IN THE SHOWERS!
WE HAVE A PROBLEM IN THE MEN'S CHANGING ROOM.
YEAH, YEAH.
SO MANY PEOPLE! I PICKED THE WRONG TIME.
OH NO! IT ATE MY MONEY!
LOOK AT THIS! IT FIT PERFECTLY LAST YEAR.
DID SOMEONE TAKE MY FLIP-FLOPS?
SBAM
HOW AM I GONNA DRY MY HAIR NOW?
SUMMER'S DEFINITELY COMING. EVERYONE WANTS TO GET IN SHAPE.
WOOOOSH
OH, PERFECT!
A QUICK SHOWER, THEN I'M READY...

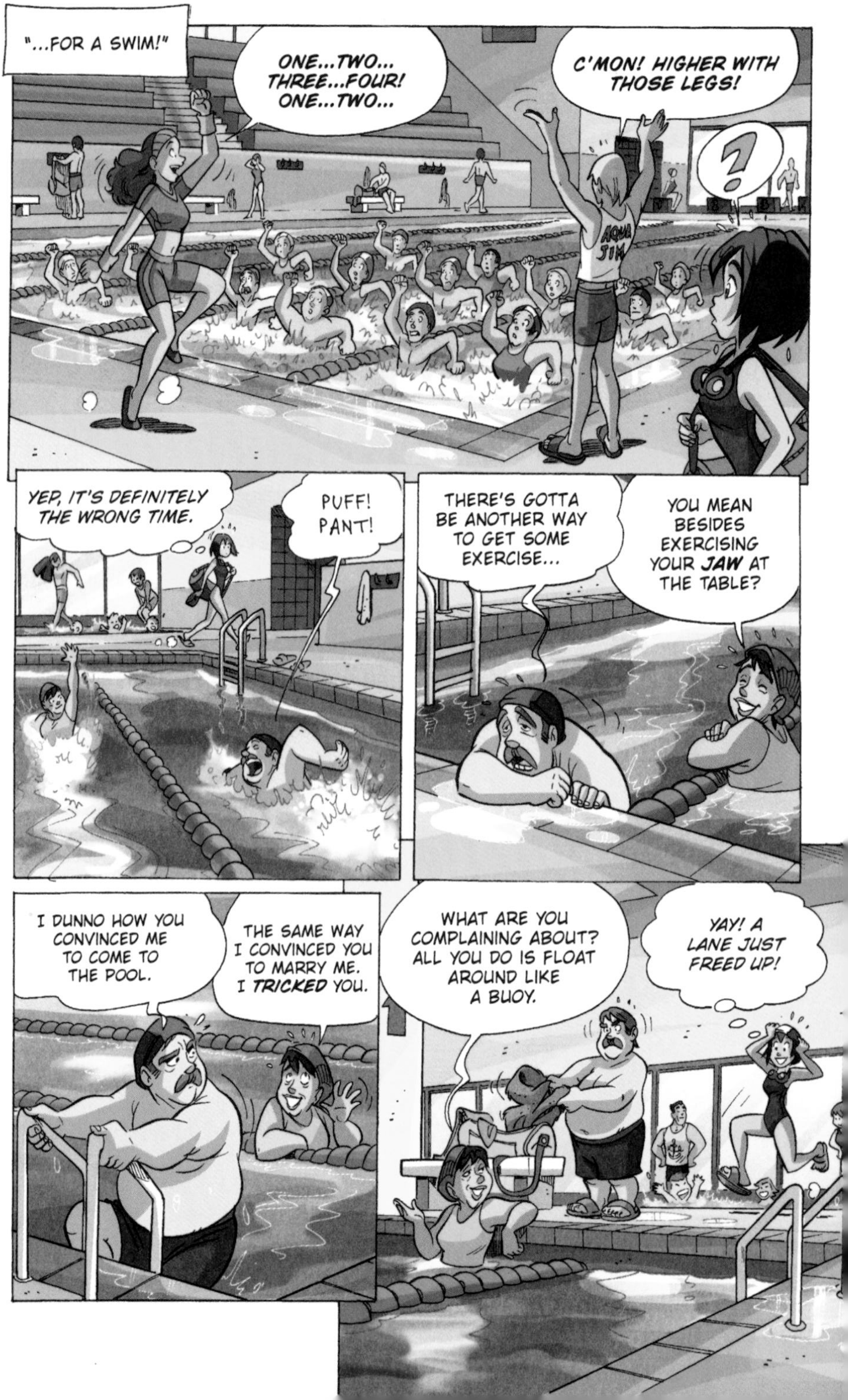
"...FOR A SWIM!"
ONE...TWO... THREE...FOUR! ONE...TWO...
C'MON! HIGHER WITH THOSE LEGS!
?
AQUA JIM
YEP, IT'S DEFINITELY THE WRONG TIME.
PUFF! PANT!
THERE'S GOTTA BE ANOTHER WAY TO GET SOME EXERCISE...
YOU MEAN BESIDES EXERCISING YOUR JAW AT THE TABLE?
I DUNNO HOW YOU CONVINCED ME TO COME TO THE POOL.
THE SAME WAY I CONVINCED YOU TO MARRY ME. I TRICKED YOU.
WHAT ARE YOU COMPLAINING ABOUT? ALL YOU DO IS FLOAT AROUND LIKE A BUOY.
YAY! A LANE JUST FREED UP!

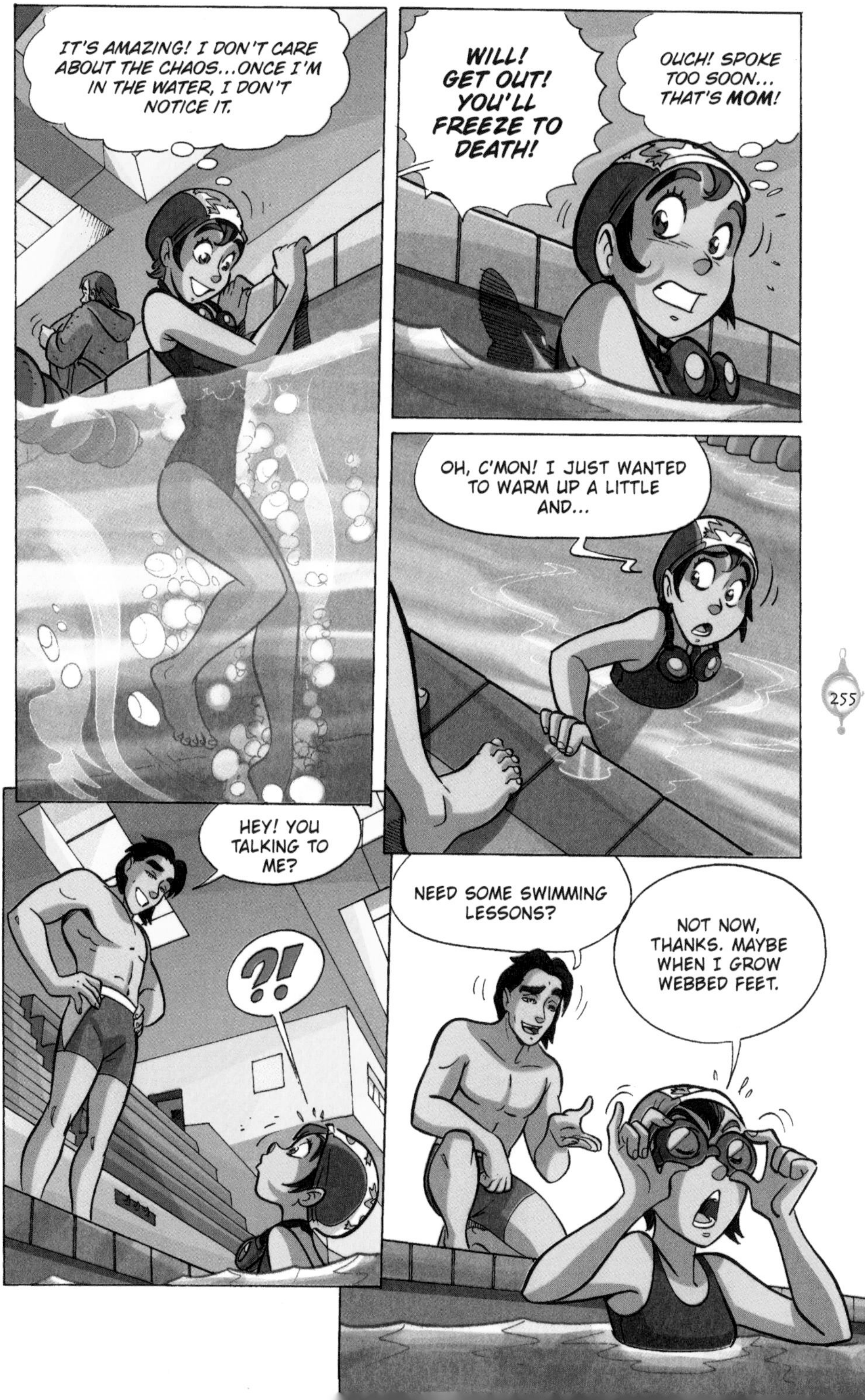
IT'S AMAZING! I DON'T CARE ABOUT THE CHAOS...ONCE I'M IN THE WATER, I DON'T NOTICE IT.
WILL! GET OUT! YOU'LL FREEZE TO DEATH!
OUCH! SPOKE TOO SOON... THAT'S MOM!
OH, C'MON! I JUST WANTED TO WARM UP A LITTLE AND...
HEY! YOU TALKING TO ME?
?!
NEED SOME SWIMMING LESSONS?
NOT NOW, THANKS. MAYBE WHEN I GROW WEBBED FEET.

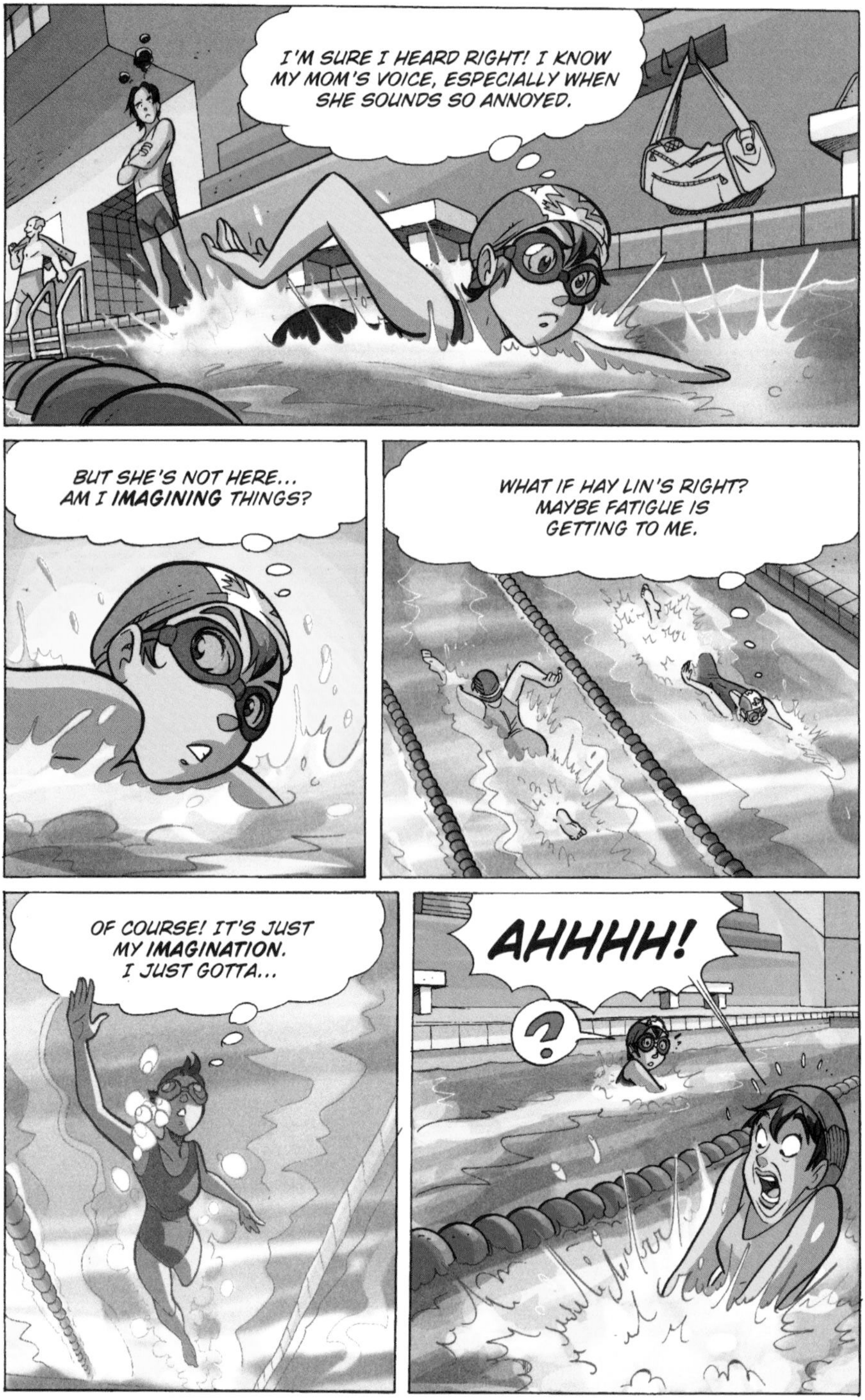
I'M SURE I HEARD RIGHT! I KNOW MY MOM'S VOICE, ESPECIALLY WHEN SHE SOUNDS SO ANNOYED.
BUT SHE'S NOT HERE... AM I IMAGINING THINGS?
WHAT IF HAY LIN'S RIGHT? MAYBE FATIGUE IS GETTING TO ME.
OF COURSE! IT'S JUST MY IMAGINATION. I JUST GOTTA...
AHHHH!
?

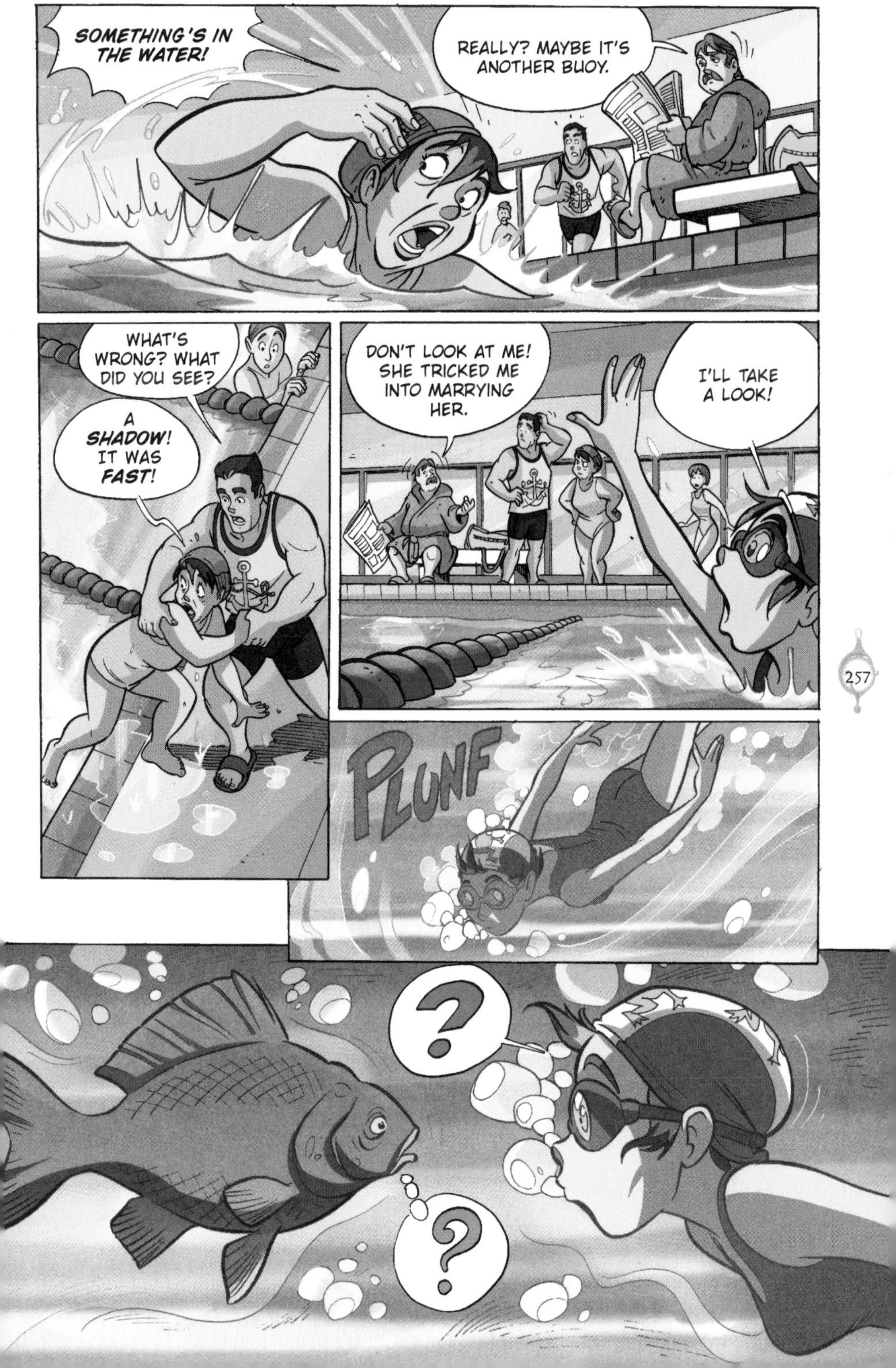
SOMETHING'S IN THE WATER!
REALLY? MAYBE IT'S ANOTHER BUOY.
WHAT'S WRONG? WHAT DID YOU SEE?
A SHADOW! IT WAS FAST!
DON'T LOOK AT ME! SHE TRICKED ME INTO MARRYING HER.
I'LL TAKE A LOOK!
PLUNF
?
?

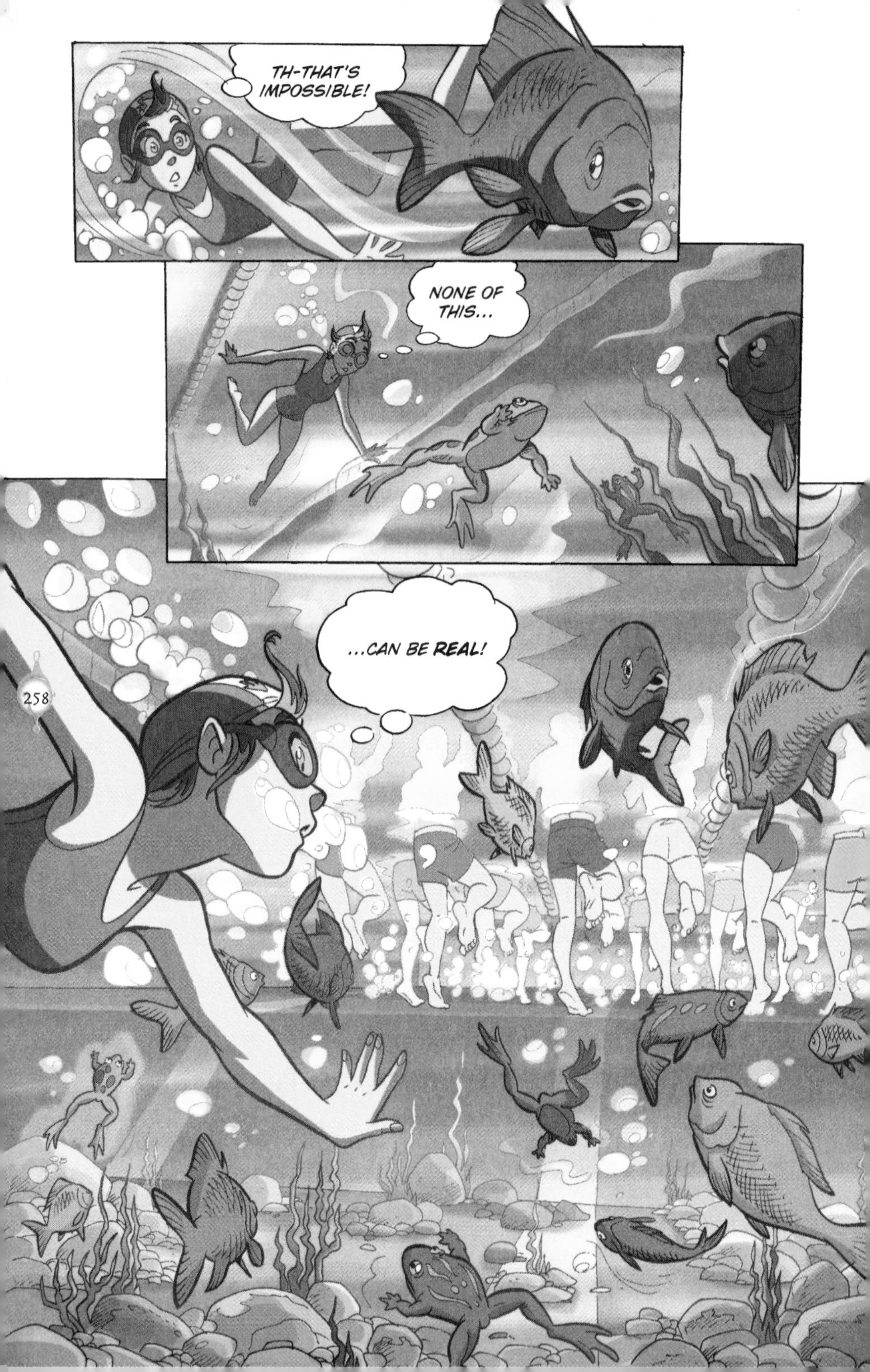
TH-THAT'S IMPOSSIBLE!
NONE OF THIS...
...CAN BE **REAL**!
258

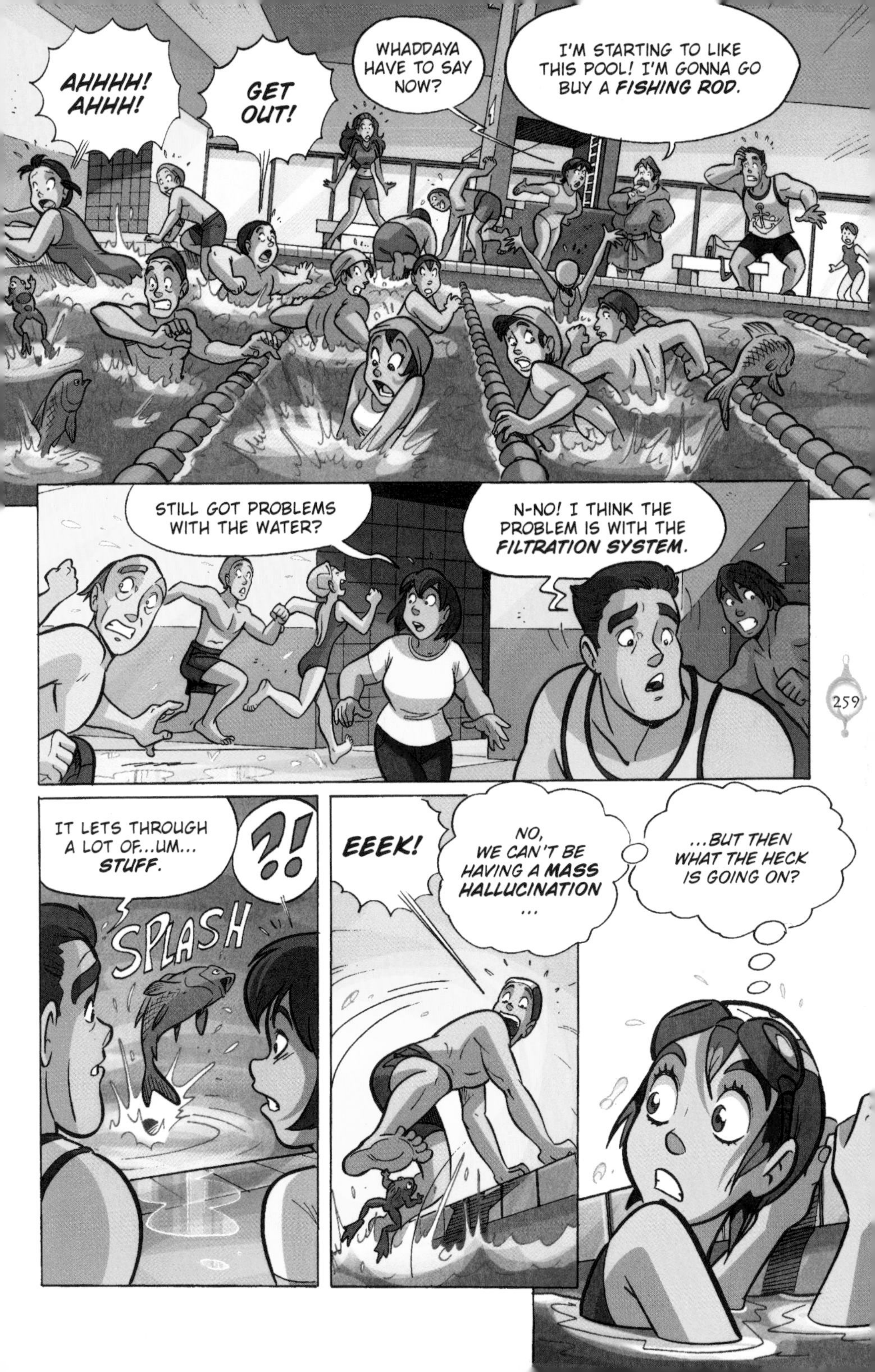
AHHHH! AHHH!
GET OUT!
WHADDAYA HAVE TO SAY NOW?
I'M STARTING TO LIKE THIS POOL! I'M GONNA GO BUY A FISHING ROD.
STILL GOT PROBLEMS WITH THE WATER?
N-NO! I THINK THE PROBLEM IS WITH THE FILTRATION SYSTEM.
IT LETS THROUGH A LOT OF...UM... STUFF.
?!
SPLASH
EEEK!
NO, WE CAN'T BE HAVING A MASS HALLUCINATION ...
...BUT THEN WHAT THE HECK IS GOING ON?

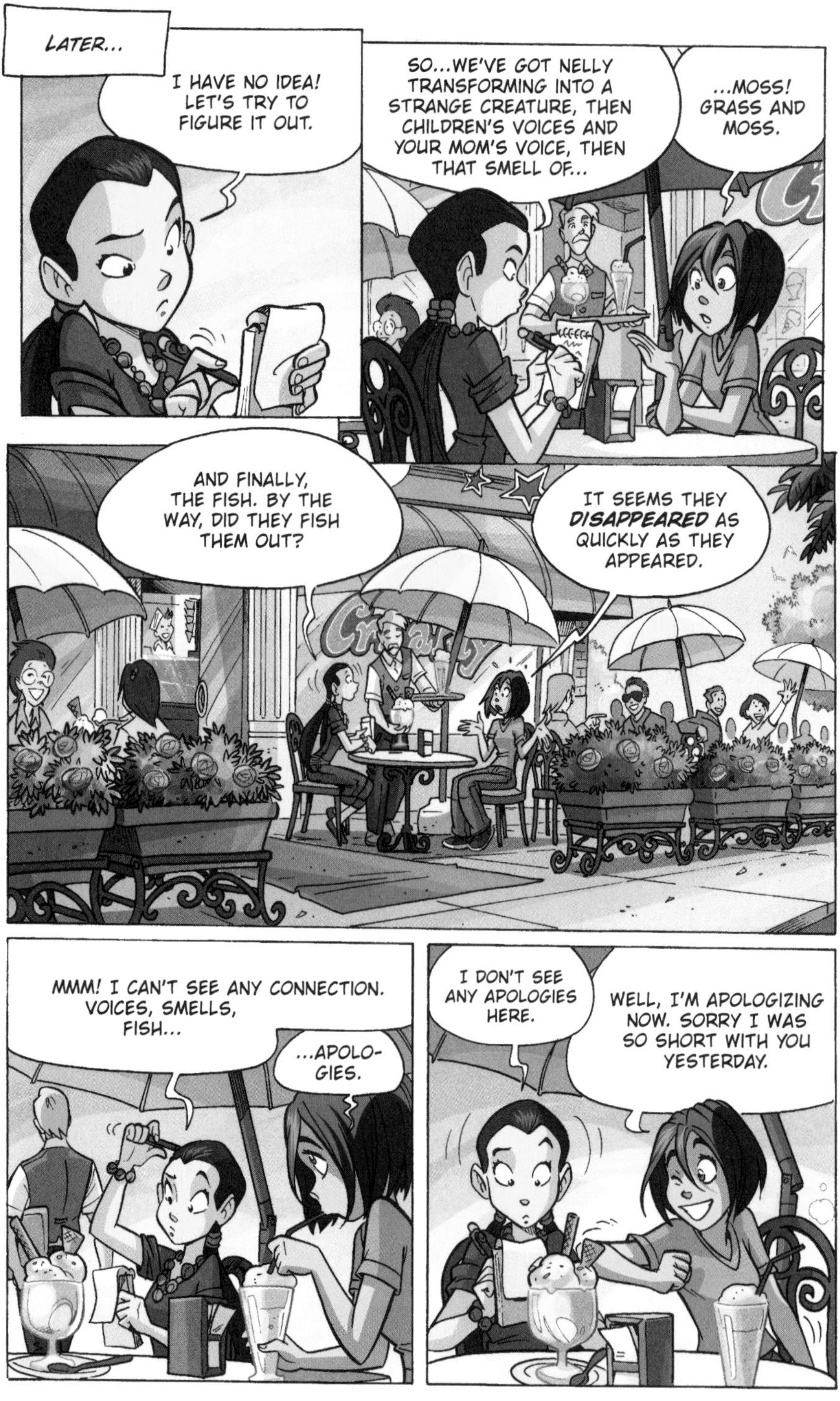
LATER...
I HAVE NO IDEA! LET'S TRY TO FIGURE IT OUT.
SO...WE'VE GOT NELLY TRANSFORMING INTO A STRANGE CREATURE, THEN CHILDREN'S VOICES AND YOUR MOM'S VOICE, THEN THAT SMELL OF...
...MOSS! GRASS AND MOSS.
AND FINALLY, THE FISH. BY THE WAY, DID THEY FISH THEM OUT?
IT SEEMS THEY *DISAPPEARED* AS QUICKLY AS THEY APPEARED.
MMM! I CAN'T SEE ANY CONNECTION. VOICES, SMELLS, FISH...
...APOLOGIES.
I DON'T SEE ANY APOLOGIES HERE.
WELL, I'M APOLOGIZING NOW. SORRY I WAS SO SHORT WITH YOU YESTERDAY.

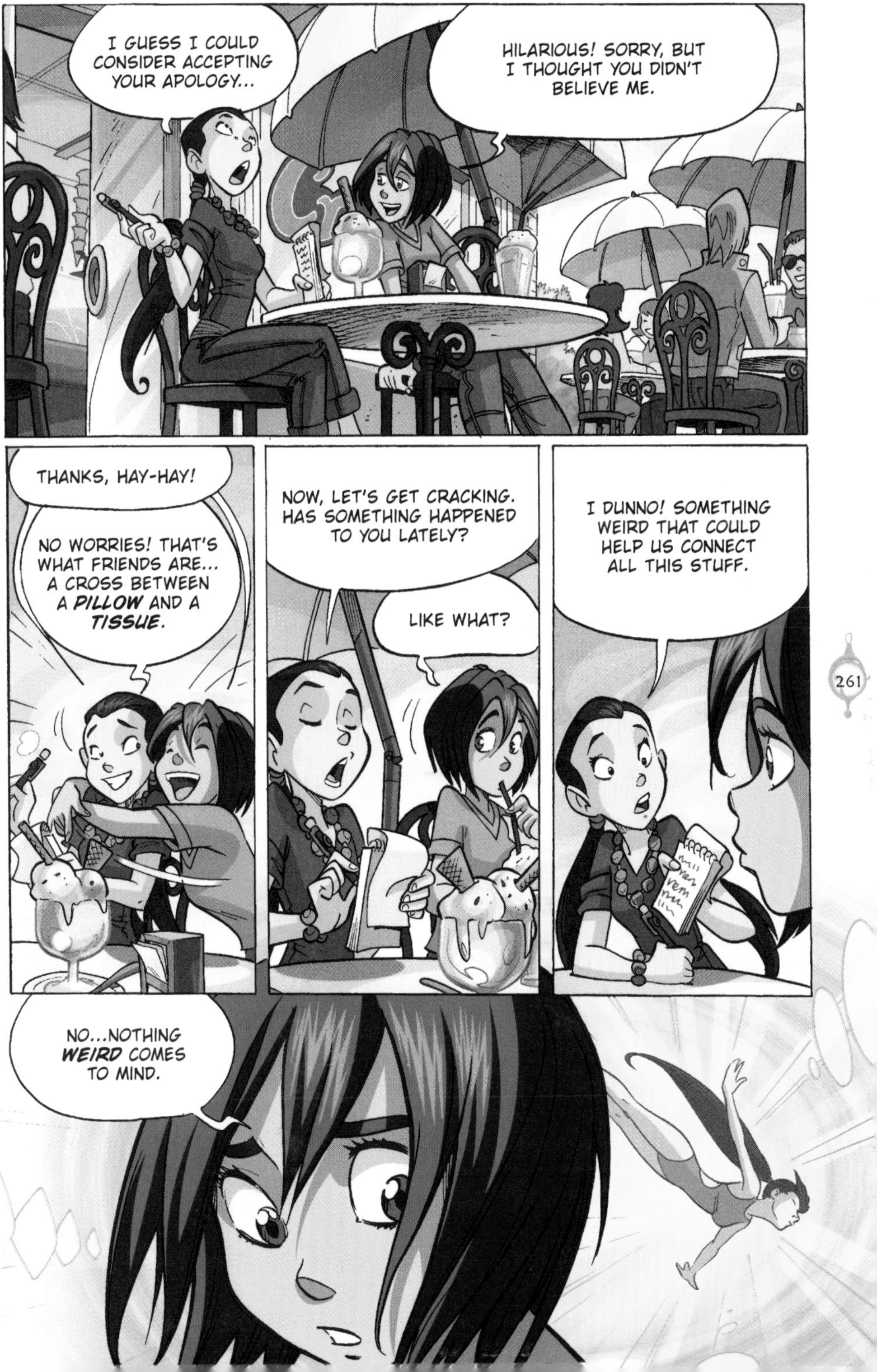
I GUESS I COULD CONSIDER ACCEPTING YOUR APOLOGY...
HILARIOUS! SORRY, BUT I THOUGHT YOU DIDN'T BELIEVE ME.
THANKS, HAY-HAY!
NO WORRIES! THAT'S WHAT FRIENDS ARE... A CROSS BETWEEN A PILLOW AND A TISSUE.
NOW, LET'S GET CRACKING. HAS SOMETHING HAPPENED TO YOU LATELY?
LIKE WHAT?
I DUNNO! SOMETHING WEIRD THAT COULD HELP US CONNECT ALL THIS STUFF.
NO...NOTHING WEIRD COMES TO MIND.

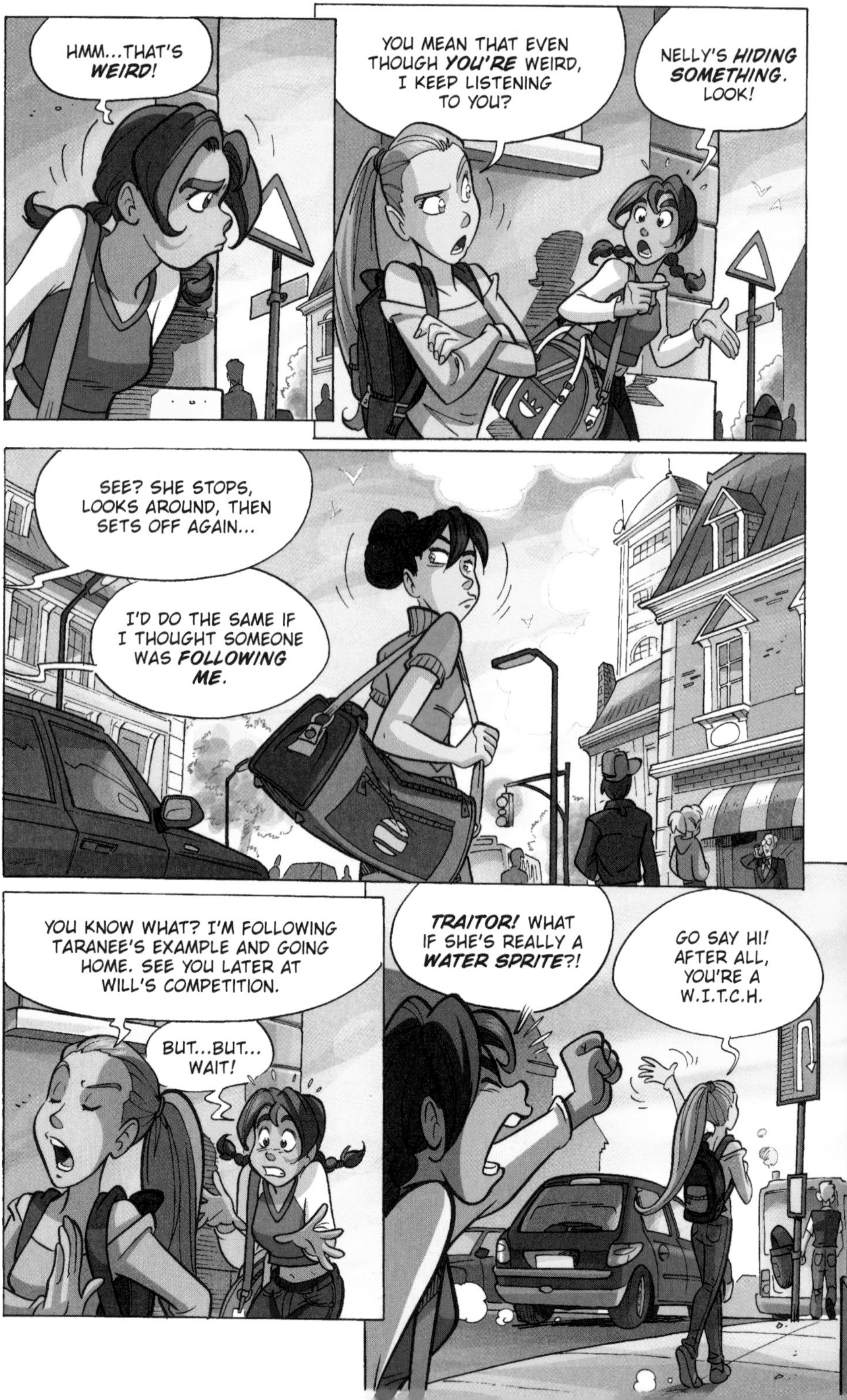
HMM...THAT'S WEIRD!
YOU MEAN THAT EVEN THOUGH YOU'RE WEIRD, I KEEP LISTENING TO YOU?
NELLY'S HIDING SOMETHING. LOOK!
SEE? SHE STOPS, LOOKS AROUND, THEN SETS OFF AGAIN...
I'D DO THE SAME IF I THOUGHT SOMEONE WAS FOLLOWING ME.
YOU KNOW WHAT? I'M FOLLOWING TARANEE'S EXAMPLE AND GOING HOME. SEE YOU LATER AT WILL'S COMPETITION.
BUT...BUT... WAIT!
TRAITOR! WHAT IF SHE'S REALLY A WATER SPRITE?!
GO SAY HI! AFTER ALL, YOU'RE A W.I.T.C.H.

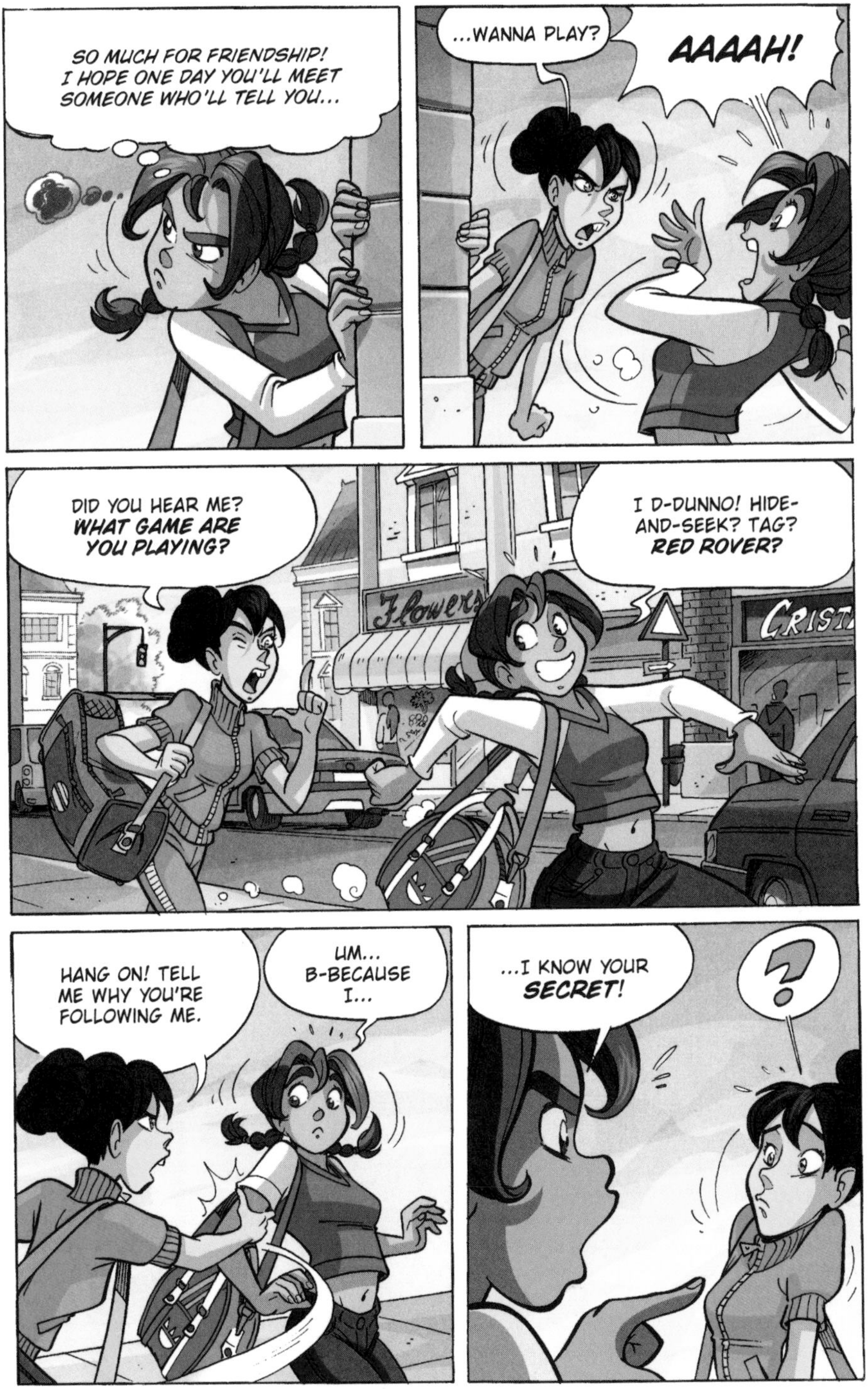
SO MUCH FOR FRIENDSHIP! I HOPE ONE DAY YOU'LL MEET SOMEONE WHO'LL TELL YOU...
...WANNA PLAY?
AAAAH!
DID YOU HEAR ME? WHAT GAME ARE YOU PLAYING?
I D-DUNNO! HIDE-AND-SEEK? TAG? RED ROVER?
Flowers
CRIST
HANG ON! TELL ME WHY YOU'RE FOLLOWING ME.
UM... B-BECAUSE I...
...I KNOW YOUR SECRET!
?

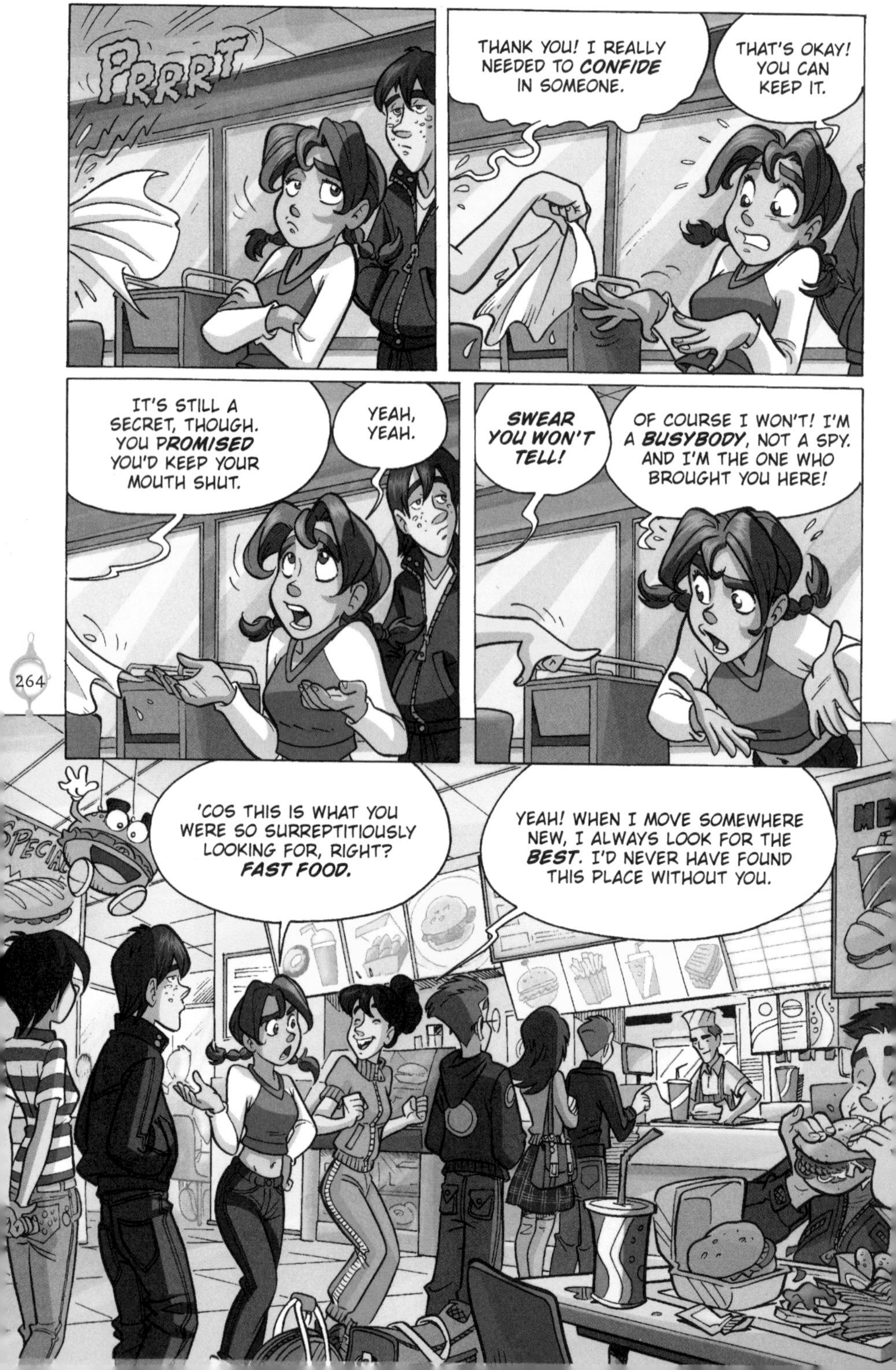
PRRRT
THANK YOU! I REALLY NEEDED TO CONFIDE IN SOMEONE.
THAT'S OKAY! YOU CAN KEEP IT.
IT'S STILL A SECRET, THOUGH. YOU PROMISED YOU'D KEEP YOUR MOUTH SHUT.
YEAH, YEAH.
SWEAR YOU WON'T TELL!
OF COURSE I WON'T! I'M A BUSYBODY, NOT A SPY. AND I'M THE ONE WHO BROUGHT YOU HERE!
SPECIAL
'COS THIS IS WHAT YOU WERE SO SURREPTITIOUSLY LOOKING FOR, RIGHT? FAST FOOD.
YEAH! WHEN I MOVE SOMEWHERE NEW, I ALWAYS LOOK FOR THE BEST. I'D NEVER HAVE FOUND THIS PLACE WITHOUT YOU.

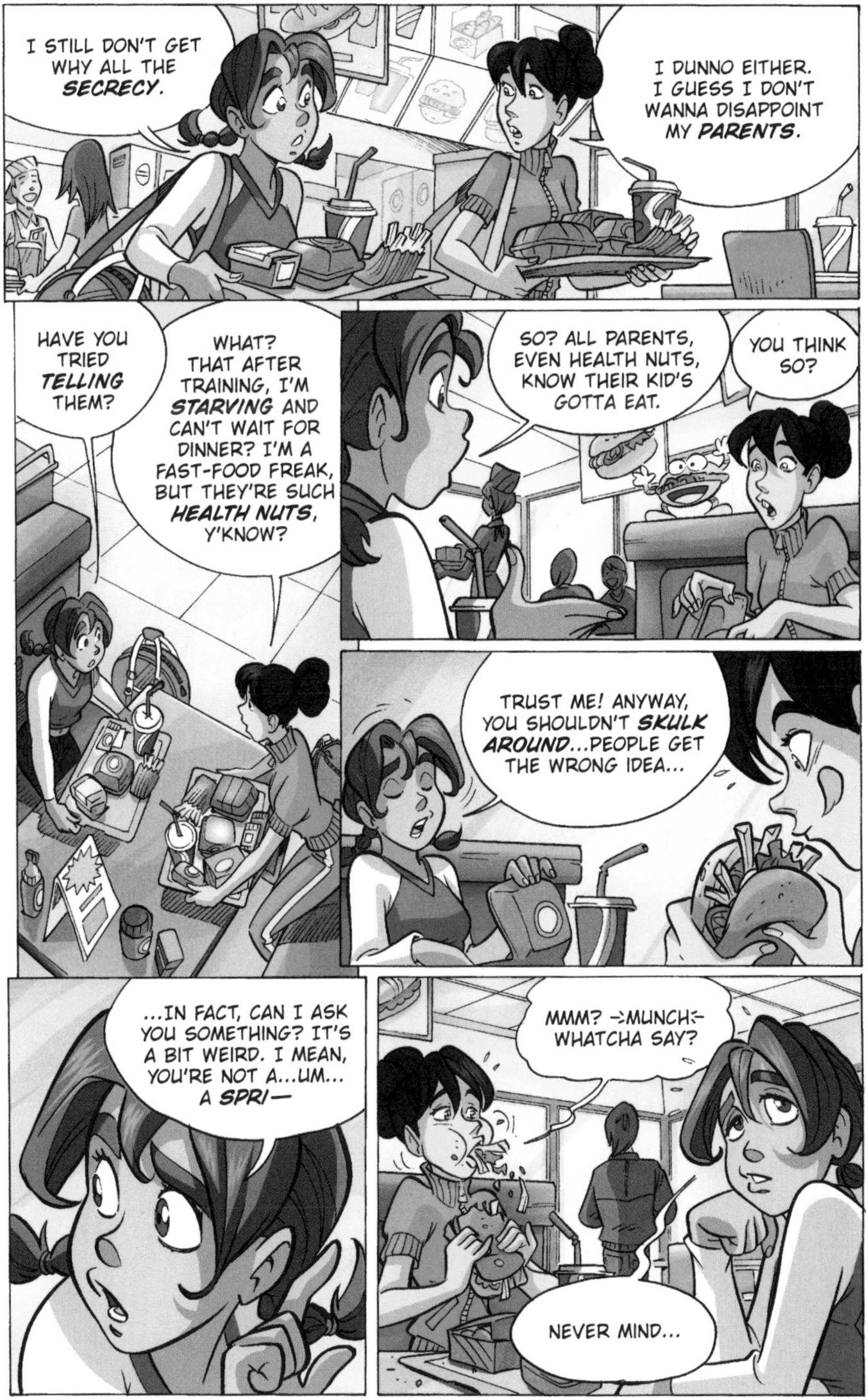
I STILL DON'T GET WHY ALL THE SECRECY.
I DUNNO EITHER. I GUESS I DON'T WANNA DISAPPOINT MY PARENTS.
HAVE YOU TRIED TELLING THEM?
WHAT? THAT AFTER TRAINING, I'M STARVING AND CAN'T WAIT FOR DINNER? I'M A FAST-FOOD FREAK, BUT THEY'RE SUCH HEALTH NUTS, Y'KNOW?
SO? ALL PARENTS, EVEN HEALTH NUTS, KNOW THEIR KID'S GOTTA EAT.
YOU THINK SO?
TRUST ME! ANYWAY, YOU SHOULDN'T SKULK AROUND...PEOPLE GET THE WRONG IDEA...
...IN FACT, CAN I ASK YOU SOMETHING? IT'S A BIT WEIRD. I MEAN, YOU'RE NOT A...UM... A SPRI—
MMM? ⇒MUNCH⇐ WHATCHA SAY?
NEVER MIND...

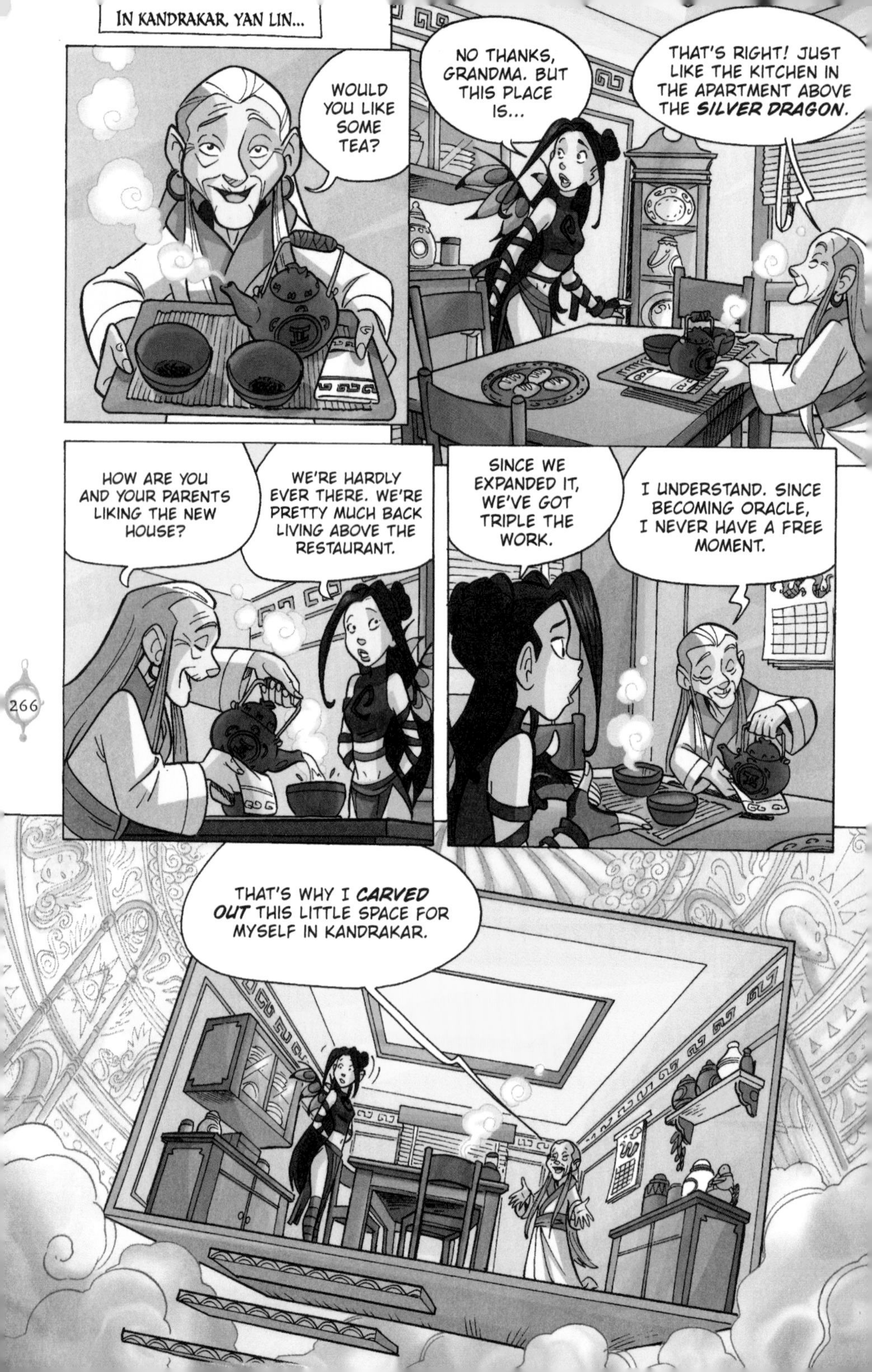
IN KANDRAKAR, YAN LIN...
WOULD YOU LIKE SOME TEA?
NO THANKS, GRANDMA. BUT THIS PLACE IS...
THAT'S RIGHT! JUST LIKE THE KITCHEN IN THE APARTMENT ABOVE THE SILVER DRAGON.
HOW ARE YOU AND YOUR PARENTS LIKING THE NEW HOUSE?
WE'RE HARDLY EVER THERE. WE'RE PRETTY MUCH BACK LIVING ABOVE THE RESTAURANT.
SINCE WE EXPANDED IT, WE'VE GOT TRIPLE THE WORK.
I UNDERSTAND. SINCE BECOMING ORACLE, I NEVER HAVE A FREE MOMENT.
THAT'S WHY I CARVED OUT THIS LITTLE SPACE FOR MYSELF IN KANDRAKAR.

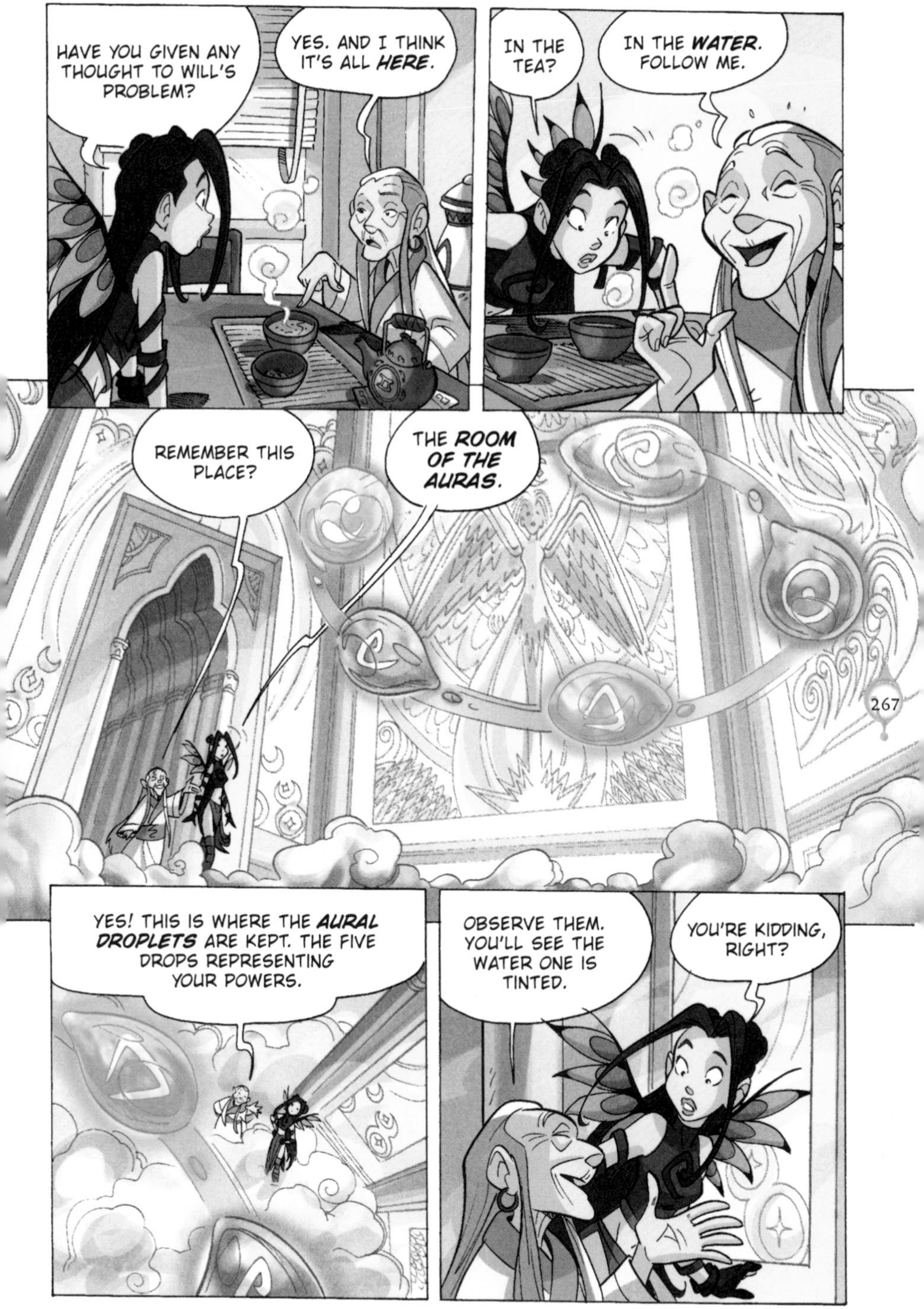
HAVE YOU GIVEN ANY THOUGHT TO WILL'S PROBLEM?
YES. AND I THINK IT'S ALL *HERE*.
IN THE TEA?
IN THE *WATER*. FOLLOW ME.
REMEMBER THIS PLACE?
THE *ROOM OF THE AURAS*.
YES! THIS IS WHERE THE *AURAL DROPLETS* ARE KEPT. THE FIVE DROPS REPRESENTING YOUR POWERS.
OBSERVE THEM. YOU'LL SEE THE WATER ONE IS TINTED.
YOU'RE KIDDING, RIGHT?

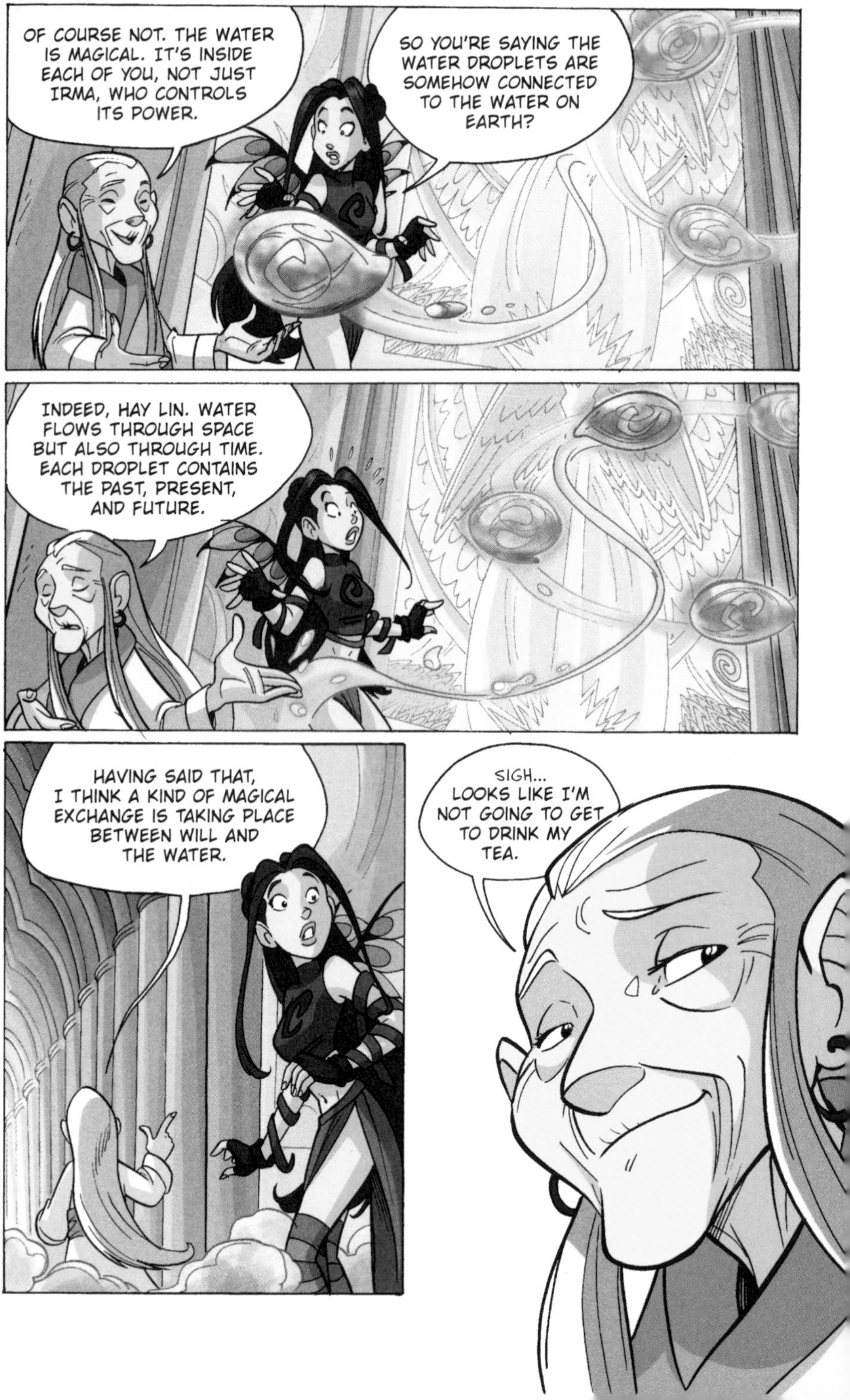
OF COURSE NOT. THE WATER IS MAGICAL. IT'S INSIDE EACH OF YOU, NOT JUST IRMA, WHO CONTROLS ITS POWER.
SO YOU'RE SAYING THE WATER DROPLETS ARE SOMEHOW CONNECTED TO THE WATER ON EARTH?
INDEED, HAY LIN. WATER FLOWS THROUGH SPACE BUT ALSO THROUGH TIME. EACH DROPLET CONTAINS THE PAST, PRESENT, AND FUTURE.
HAVING SAID THAT, I THINK A KIND OF MAGICAL EXCHANGE IS TAKING PLACE BETWEEN WILL AND THE WATER.
SIGH... LOOKS LIKE I'M NOT GOING TO GET TO DRINK MY TEA.

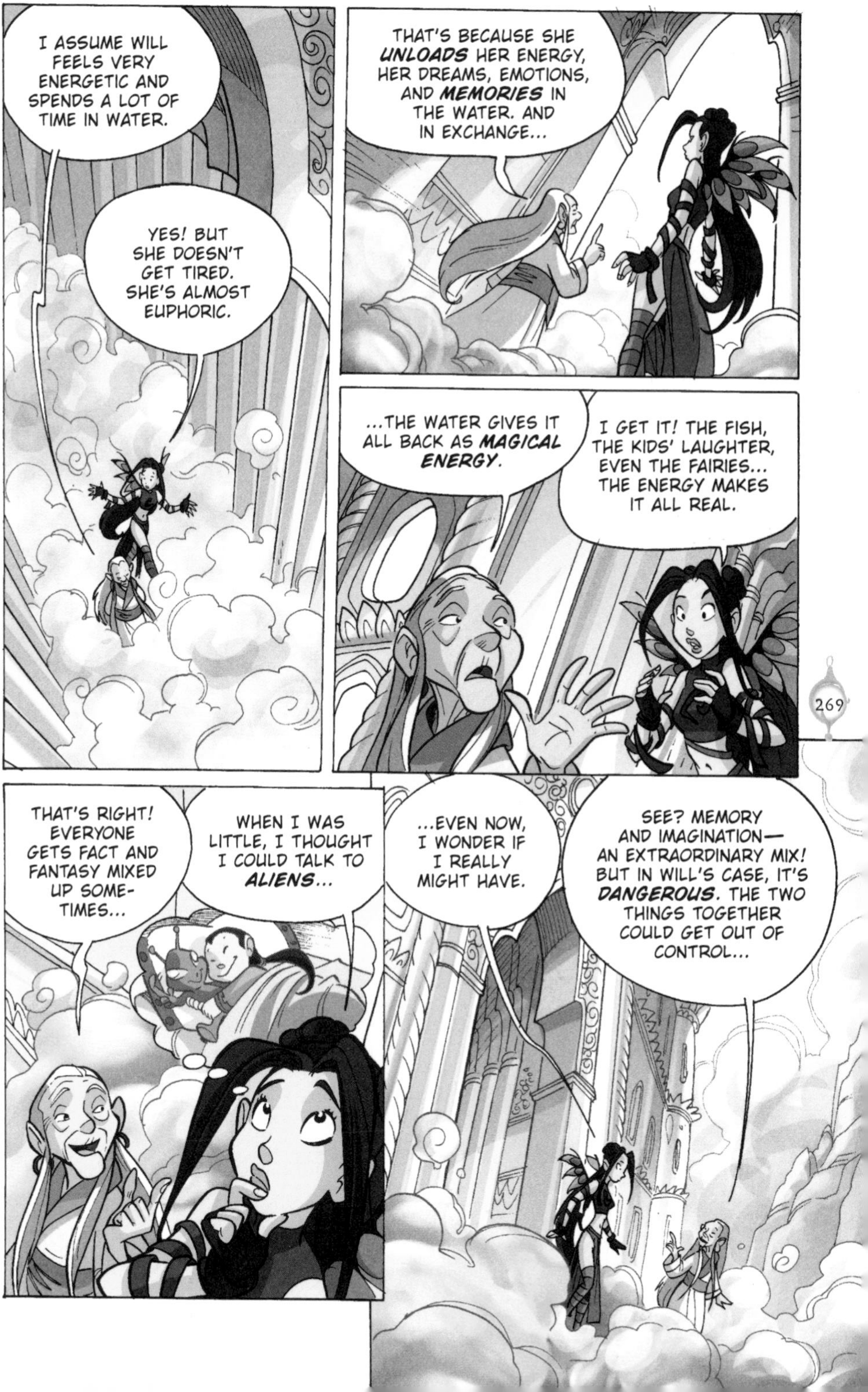
I ASSUME WILL FEELS VERY ENERGETIC AND SPENDS A LOT OF TIME IN WATER.
YES! BUT SHE DOESN'T GET TIRED. SHE'S ALMOST EUPHORIC.
THAT'S BECAUSE SHE *UNLOADS* HER ENERGY, HER DREAMS, EMOTIONS, AND *MEMORIES* IN THE WATER. AND IN EXCHANGE...
...THE WATER GIVES IT ALL BACK AS *MAGICAL ENERGY*.
I GET IT! THE FISH, THE KIDS' LAUGHTER, EVEN THE FAIRIES... THE ENERGY MAKES IT ALL REAL.
THAT'S RIGHT! EVERYONE GETS FACT AND FANTASY MIXED UP SOMETIMES...
WHEN I WAS LITTLE, I THOUGHT I COULD TALK TO *ALIENS*...
...EVEN NOW, I WONDER IF I REALLY MIGHT HAVE.
SEE? MEMORY AND IMAGINATION—AN EXTRAORDINARY MIX! BUT IN WILL'S CASE, IT'S *DANGEROUS*. THE TWO THINGS TOGETHER COULD GET OUT OF CONTROL...

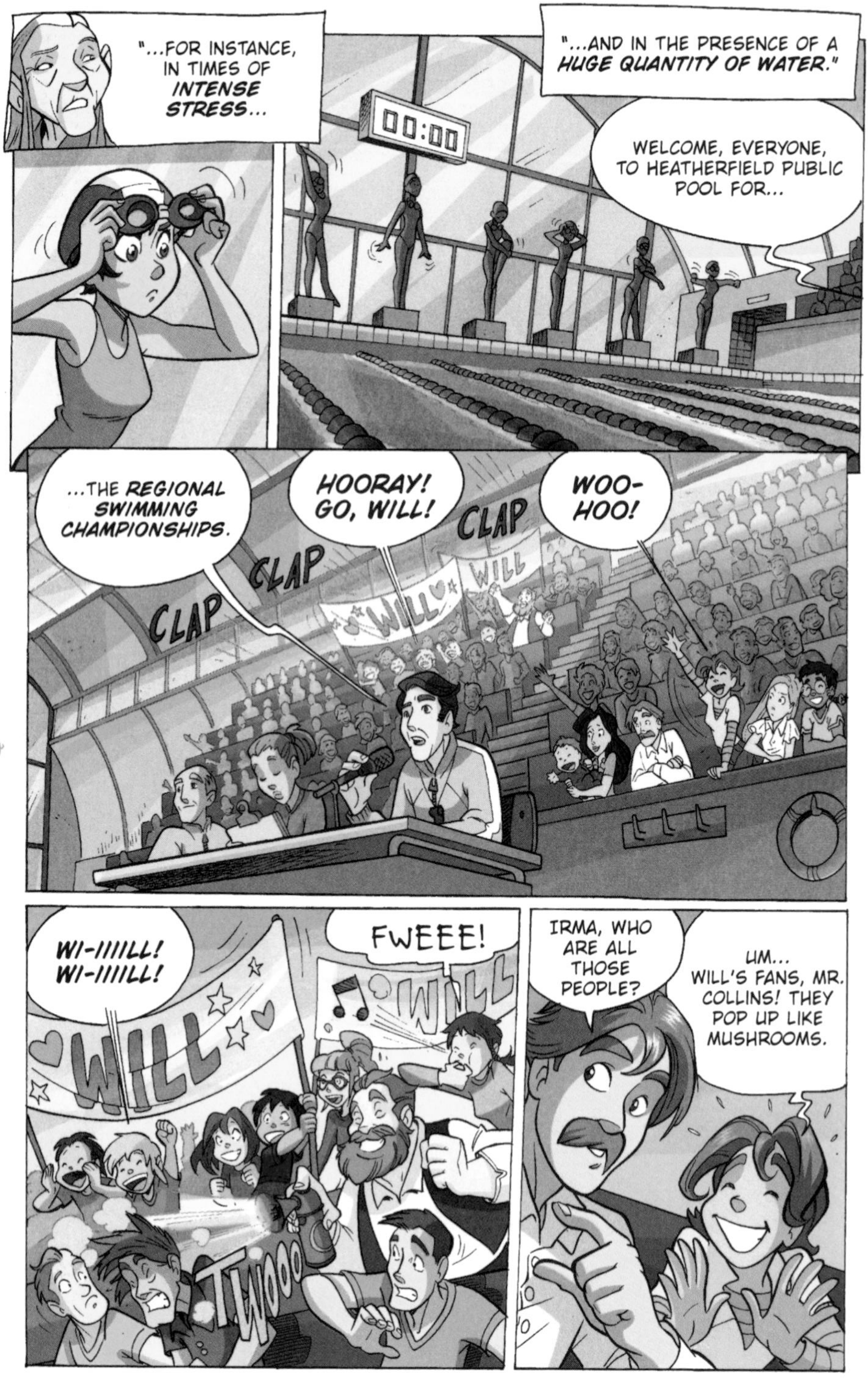
"...FOR INSTANCE, IN TIMES OF INTENSE STRESS...
"...AND IN THE PRESENCE OF A HUGE QUANTITY OF WATER."
00:00
WELCOME, EVERYONE, TO HEATHERFIELD PUBLIC POOL FOR...
...THE REGIONAL SWIMMING CHAMPIONSHIPS.
HOORAY! GO, WILL!
WOO-HOO!
CLAP
CLAP
CLAP
WILL
WILL
WI-IIIILL! WI-IIIILL!
FWEEE!
WILL
WILL
TWOOO
IRMA, WHO ARE ALL THOSE PEOPLE?
UM... WILL'S FANS, MR. COLLINS! THEY POP UP LIKE MUSHROOMS.

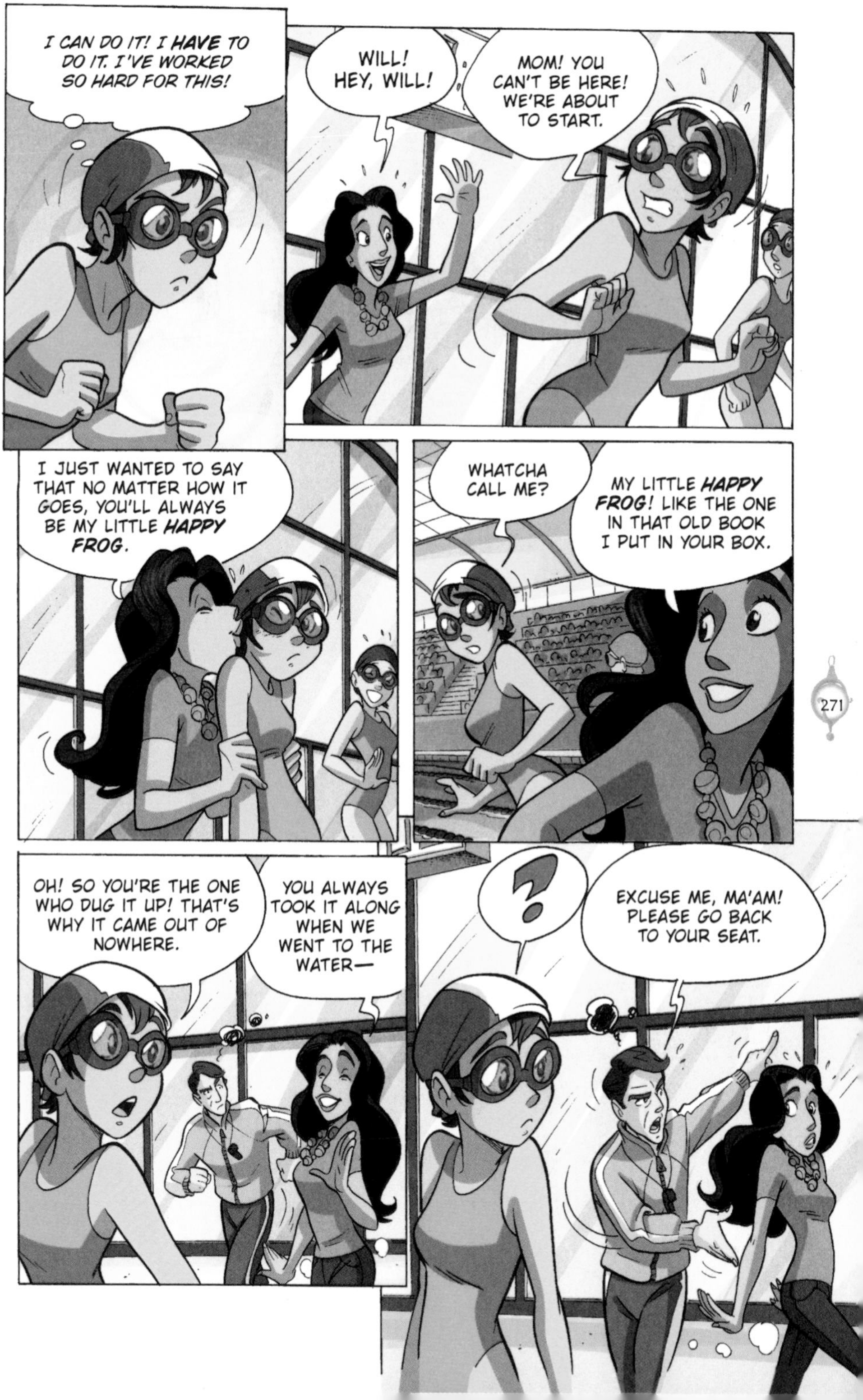
I CAN DO IT! I **HAVE** TO DO IT. I'VE WORKED SO HARD FOR THIS!
WILL! HEY, WILL!
MOM! YOU CAN'T BE HERE! WE'RE ABOUT TO START.
I JUST WANTED TO SAY THAT NO MATTER HOW IT GOES, YOU'LL ALWAYS BE MY LITTLE **HAPPY FROG**.
WHATCHA CALL ME?
MY LITTLE **HAPPY FROG**! LIKE THE ONE IN THAT OLD BOOK I PUT IN YOUR BOX.
OH! SO YOU'RE THE ONE WHO DUG IT UP! THAT'S WHY IT CAME OUT OF NOWHERE.
YOU ALWAYS TOOK IT ALONG WHEN WE WENT TO THE WATER—
?
EXCUSE ME, MA'AM! PLEASE GO BACK TO YOUR SEAT.

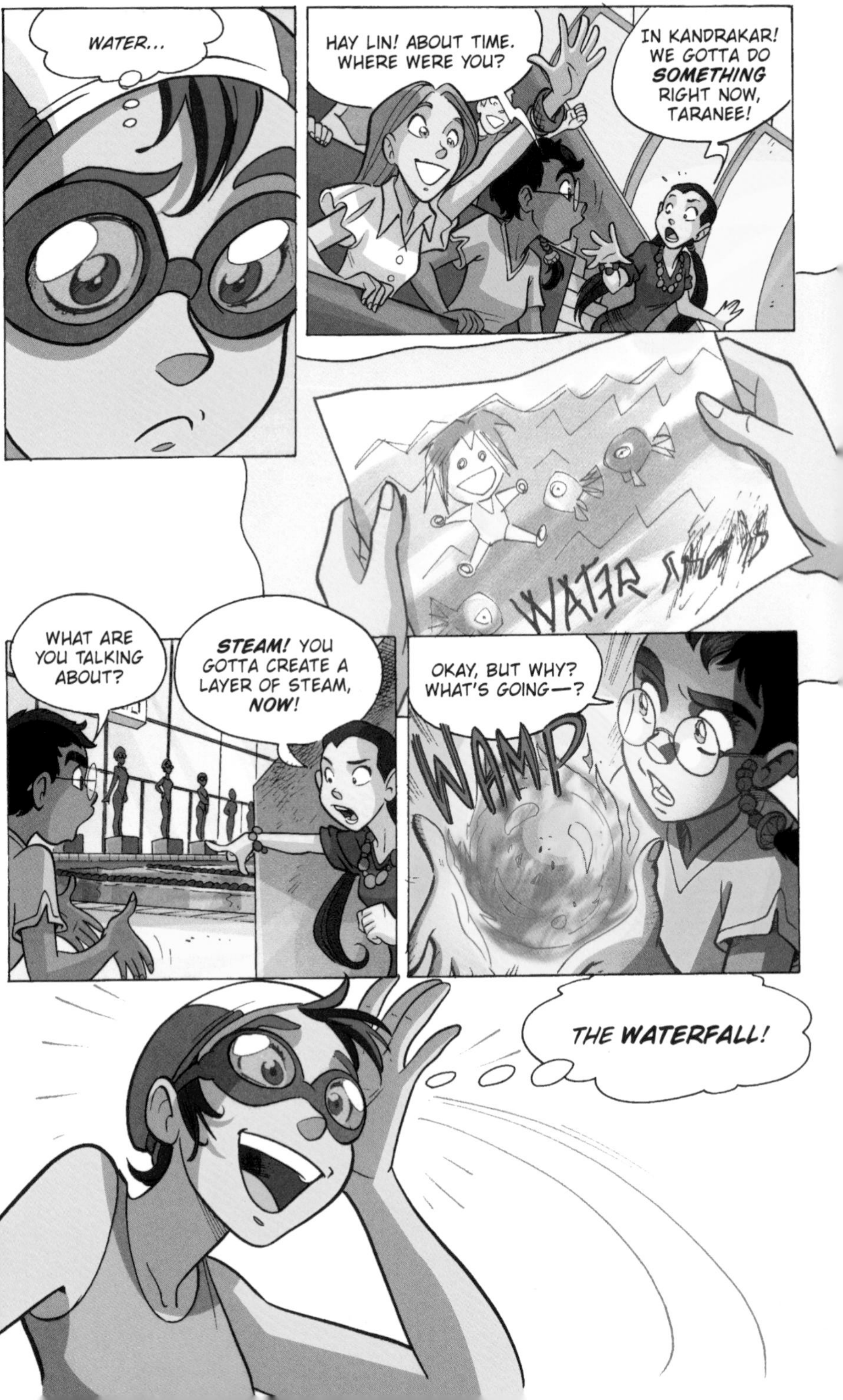
WATER...
HAY LIN! ABOUT TIME. WHERE WERE YOU?
IN KANDRAKAR! WE GOTTA DO **SOMETHING** RIGHT NOW, TARANEE!
WHAT ARE YOU TALKING ABOUT?
STEAM! YOU GOTTA CREATE A LAYER OF STEAM, **NOW**!
OKAY, BUT WHY? WHAT'S GOING—?
WAMP
THE **WATERFALL**!

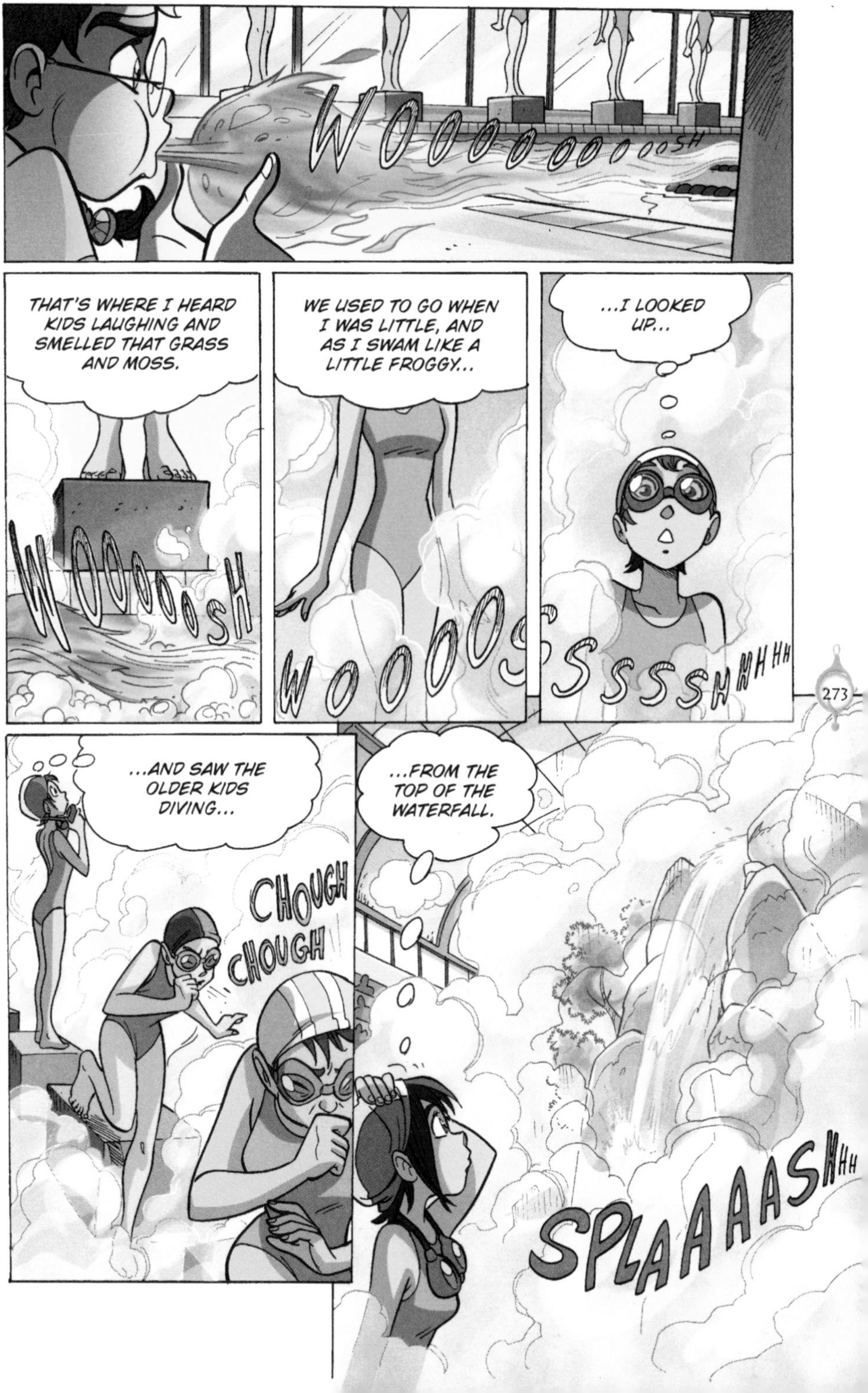
WOOOOOOOOOOOOSH
THAT'S WHERE I HEARD KIDS LAUGHING AND SMELLED THAT GRASS AND MOSS.
WOOOOOSH
WE USED TO GO WHEN I WAS LITTLE, AND AS I SWAM LIKE A LITTLE FROGGY...
...I LOOKED UP...
WOOOOSSSSSHHHH
...AND SAW THE OLDER KIDS DIVING...
CHOUGH
CHOUGH
...FROM THE TOP OF THE WATERFALL.
SPLAAAASHHH

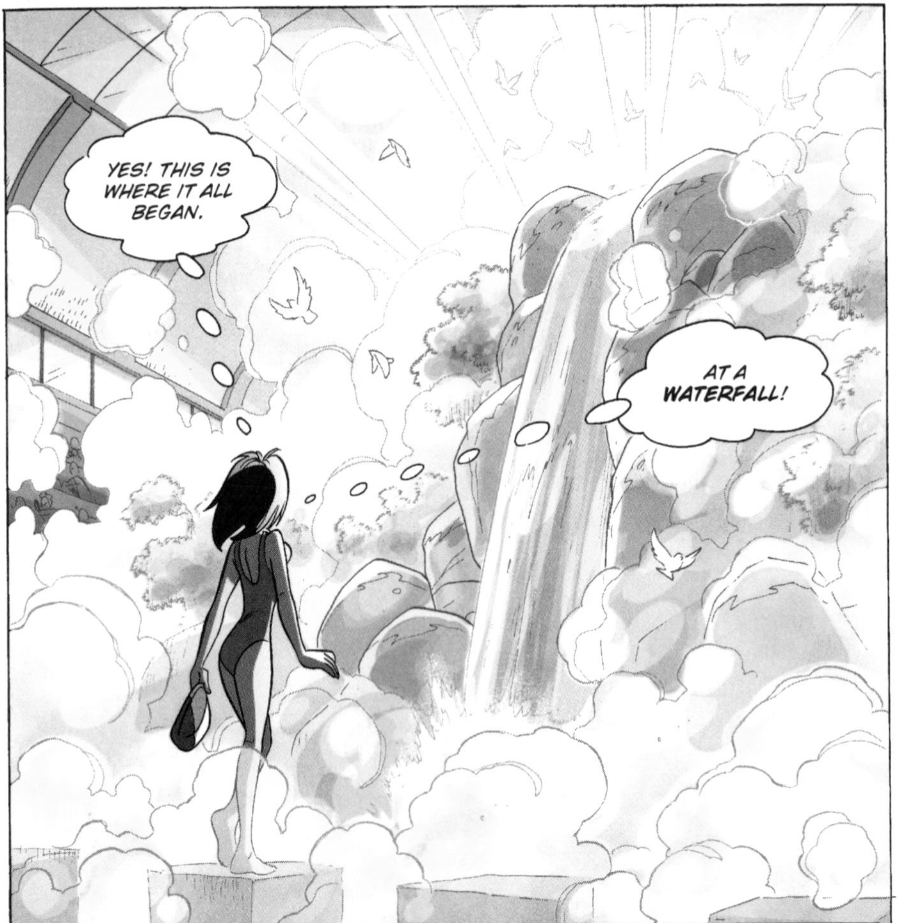
YES! THIS IS WHERE IT ALL BEGAN.
AT A WATERFALL!

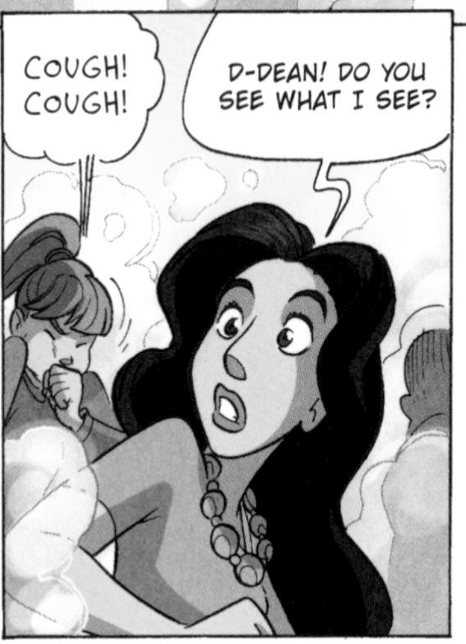
COUGH! COUGH!
D-DEAN! DO YOU SEE WHAT I SEE?

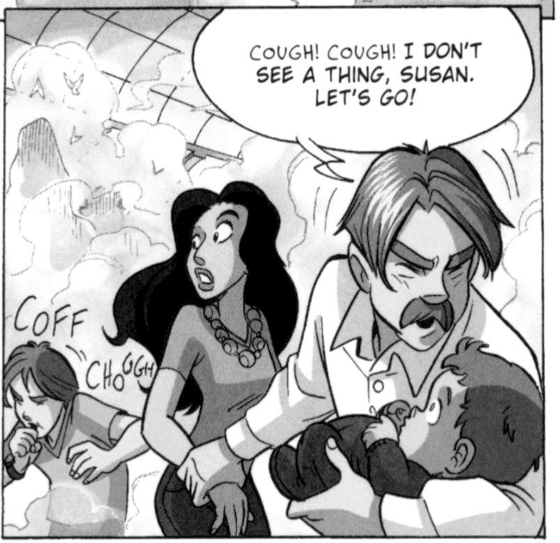
COUGH! COUGH! I DON'T SEE A THING, SUSAN. LET'S GO!
COFF
CHOGGH

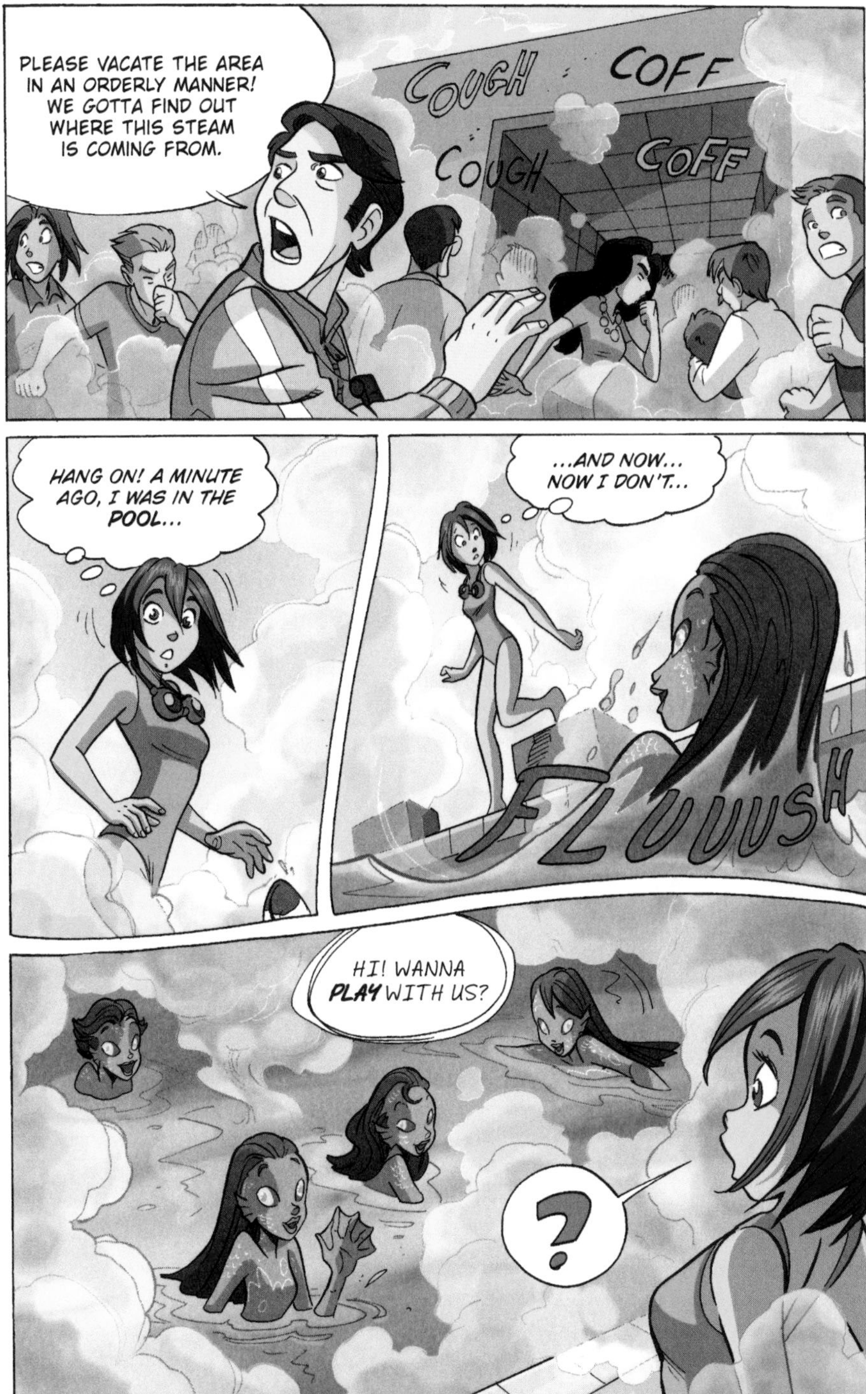
PLEASE VACATE THE AREA IN AN ORDERLY MANNER! WE GOTTA FIND OUT WHERE THIS STEAM IS COMING FROM.
COUGH COFF
COUGH COFF
HANG ON! A MINUTE AGO, I WAS IN THE POOL...
...AND NOW... NOW I DON'T...
FLUUUSH
HI! WANNA PLAY WITH US?
?

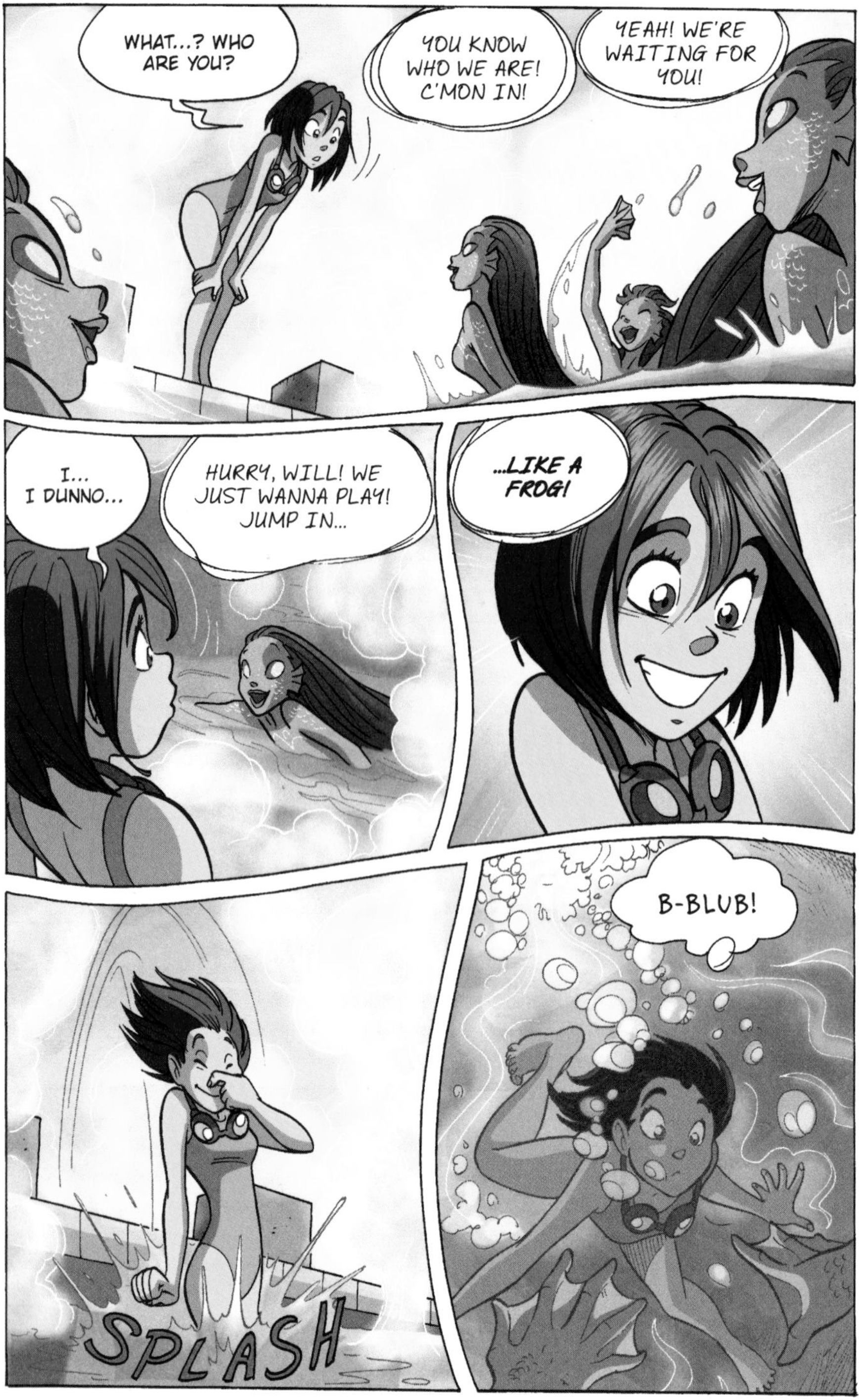
WHAT...? WHO ARE YOU?
YOU KNOW WHO WE ARE! C'MON IN!
YEAH! WE'RE WAITING FOR YOU!
I... I DUNNO...
HURRY, WILL! WE JUST WANNA PLAY! JUMP IN...
...LIKE A FROG!
SPLASH
B-BLUB!

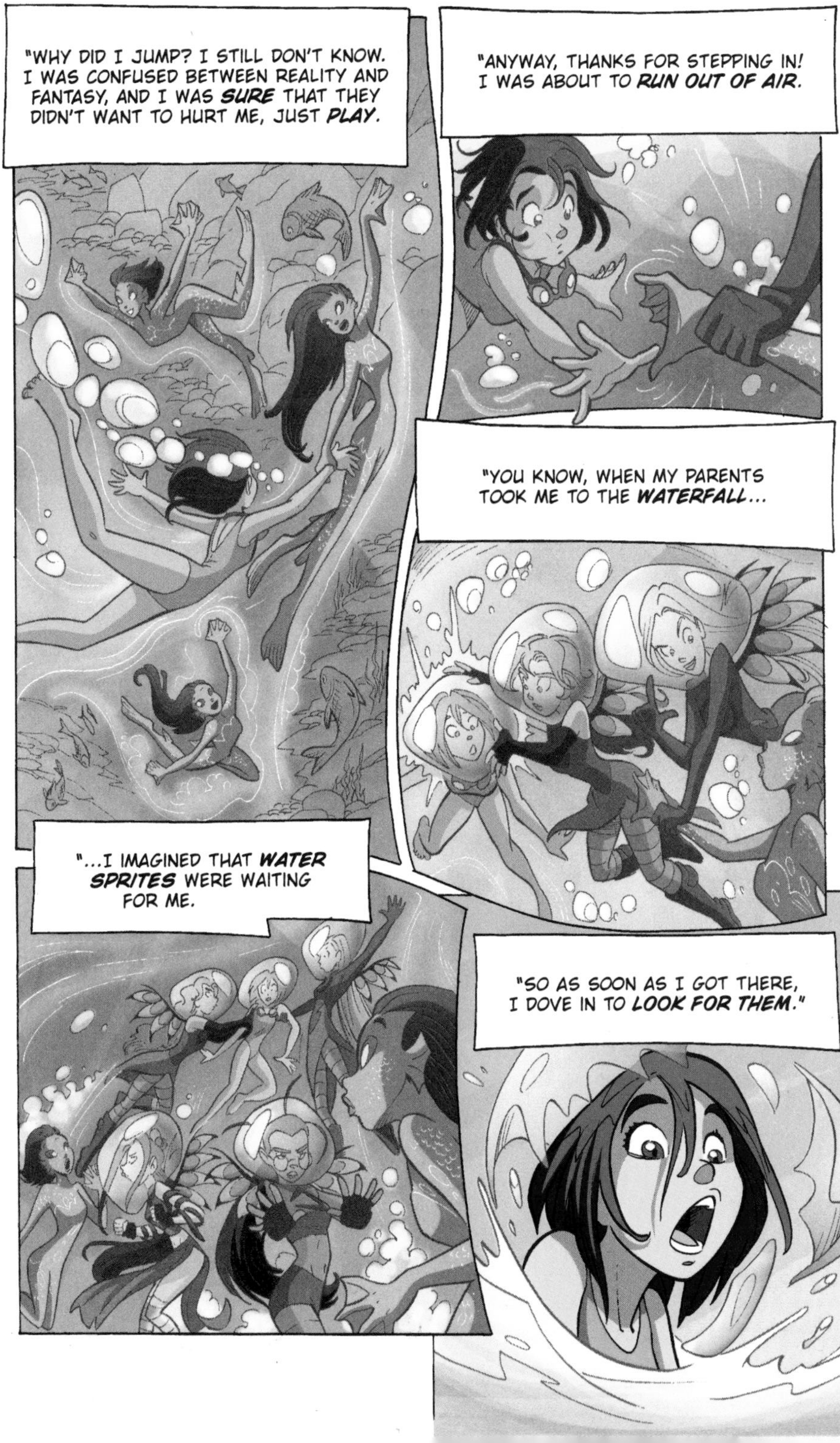

"WHY DID I JUMP? I STILL DON'T KNOW. I WAS CONFUSED BETWEEN REALITY AND FANTASY, AND I WAS *SURE* THAT THEY DIDN'T WANT TO HURT ME, JUST *PLAY*.

"ANYWAY, THANKS FOR STEPPING IN! I WAS ABOUT TO *RUN OUT OF AIR*.

"YOU KNOW, WHEN MY PARENTS TOOK ME TO THE *WATERFALL*...

"...I IMAGINED THAT *WATER SPRITES* WERE WAITING FOR ME.

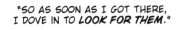

"SO AS SOON AS I GOT THERE, I DOVE IN TO *LOOK FOR THEM*."

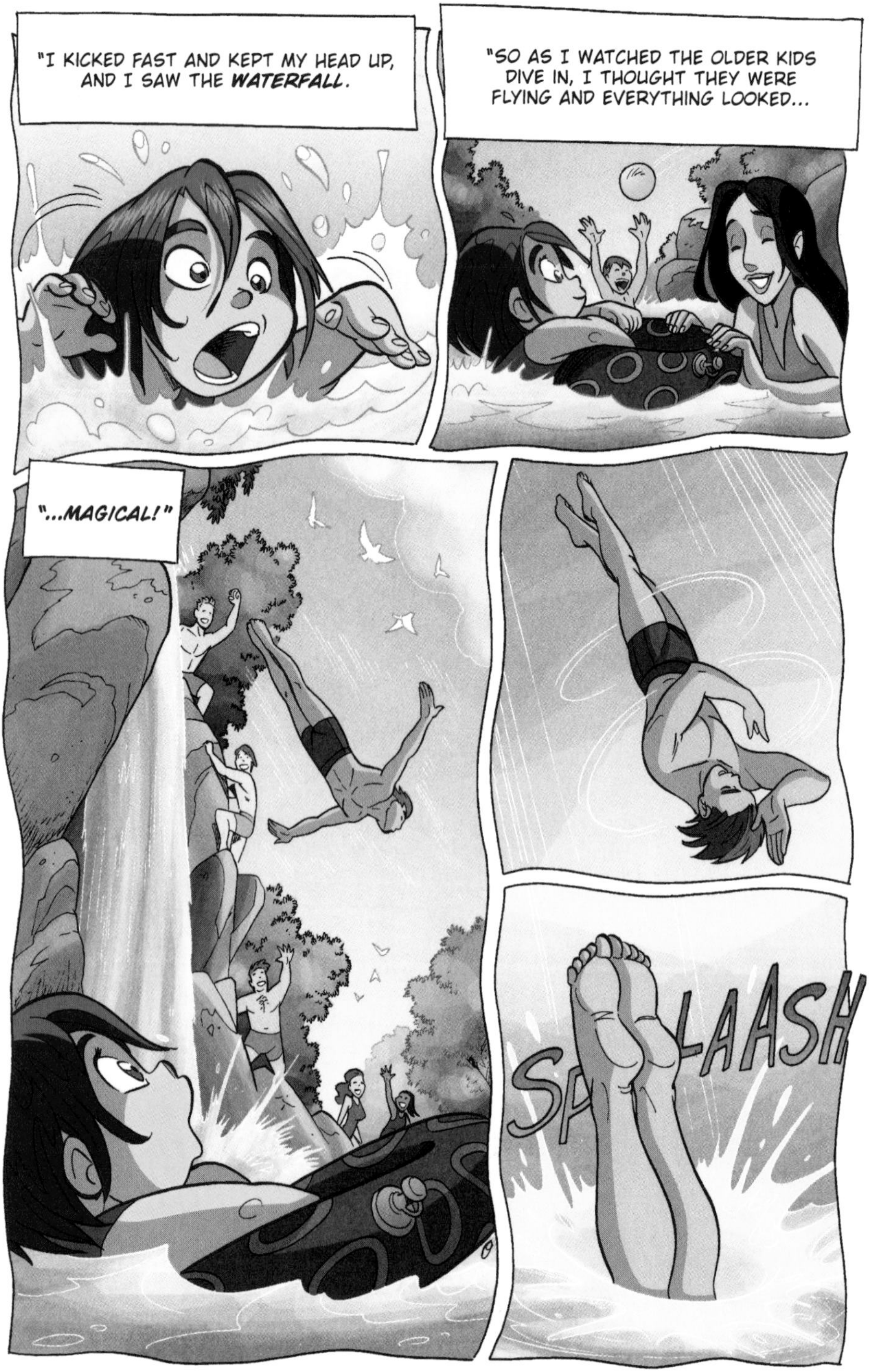
"I KICKED FAST AND KEPT MY HEAD UP, AND I SAW THE WATERFALL.
"SO AS I WATCHED THE OLDER KIDS DIVE IN, I THOUGHT THEY WERE FLYING AND EVERYTHING LOOKED...
"...MAGICAL!"
SPLAASH

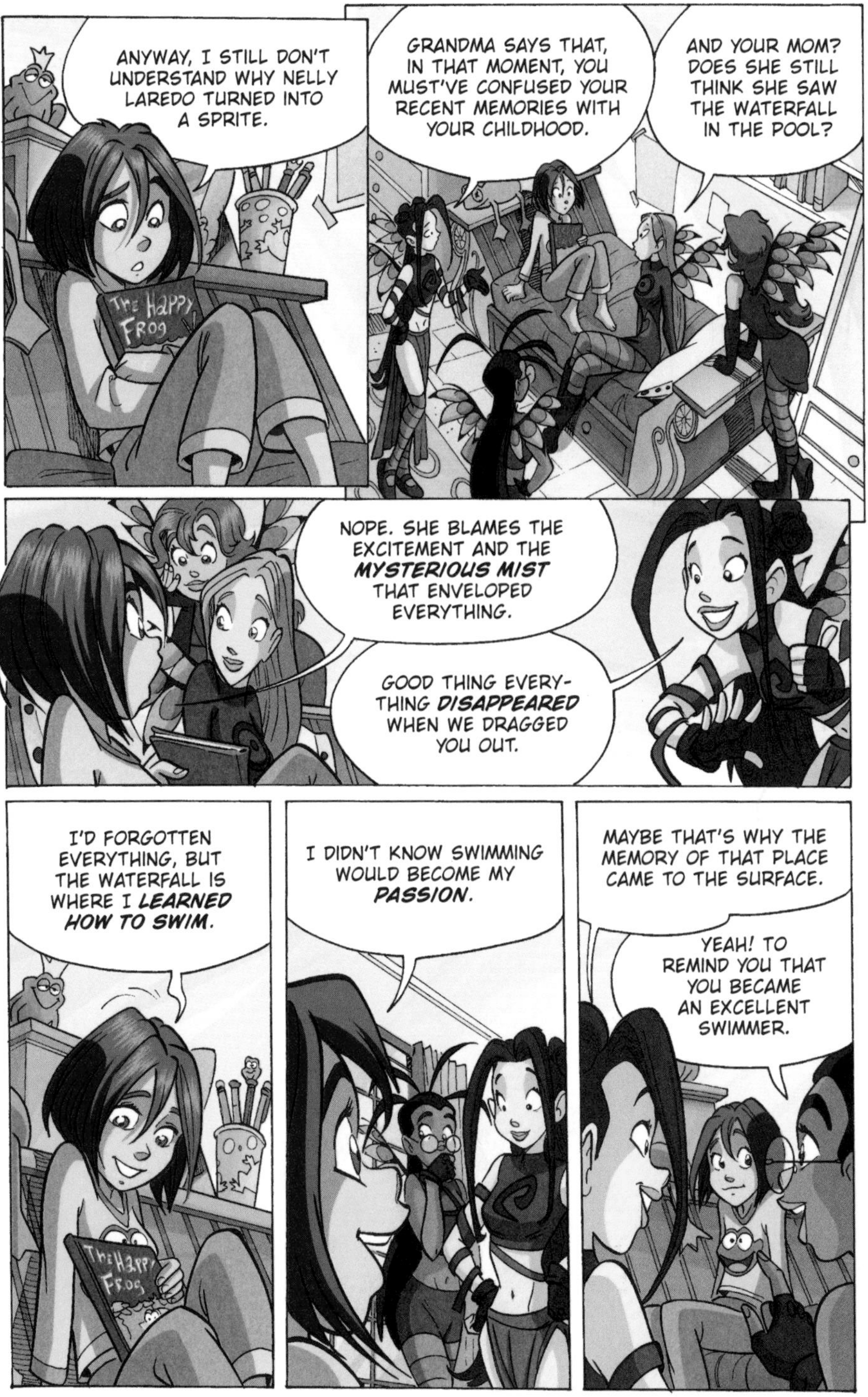
ANYWAY, I STILL DON'T UNDERSTAND WHY NELLY LAREDO TURNED INTO A SPRITE.
THE HAPPY FROG
GRANDMA SAYS THAT, IN THAT MOMENT, YOU MUST'VE CONFUSED YOUR RECENT MEMORIES WITH YOUR CHILDHOOD.
AND YOUR MOM? DOES SHE STILL THINK SHE SAW THE WATERFALL IN THE POOL?
NOPE. SHE BLAMES THE EXCITEMENT AND THE *MYSTERIOUS MIST* THAT ENVELOPED EVERYTHING.
GOOD THING EVERYTHING *DISAPPEARED* WHEN WE DRAGGED YOU OUT.
I'D FORGOTTEN EVERYTHING, BUT THE WATERFALL IS WHERE I *LEARNED HOW TO SWIM*.
THE HAPPY FROG
I DIDN'T KNOW SWIMMING WOULD BECOME MY *PASSION*.
MAYBE THAT'S WHY THE MEMORY OF THAT PLACE CAME TO THE SURFACE.
YEAH! TO REMIND YOU THAT YOU BECAME AN EXCELLENT SWIMMER.

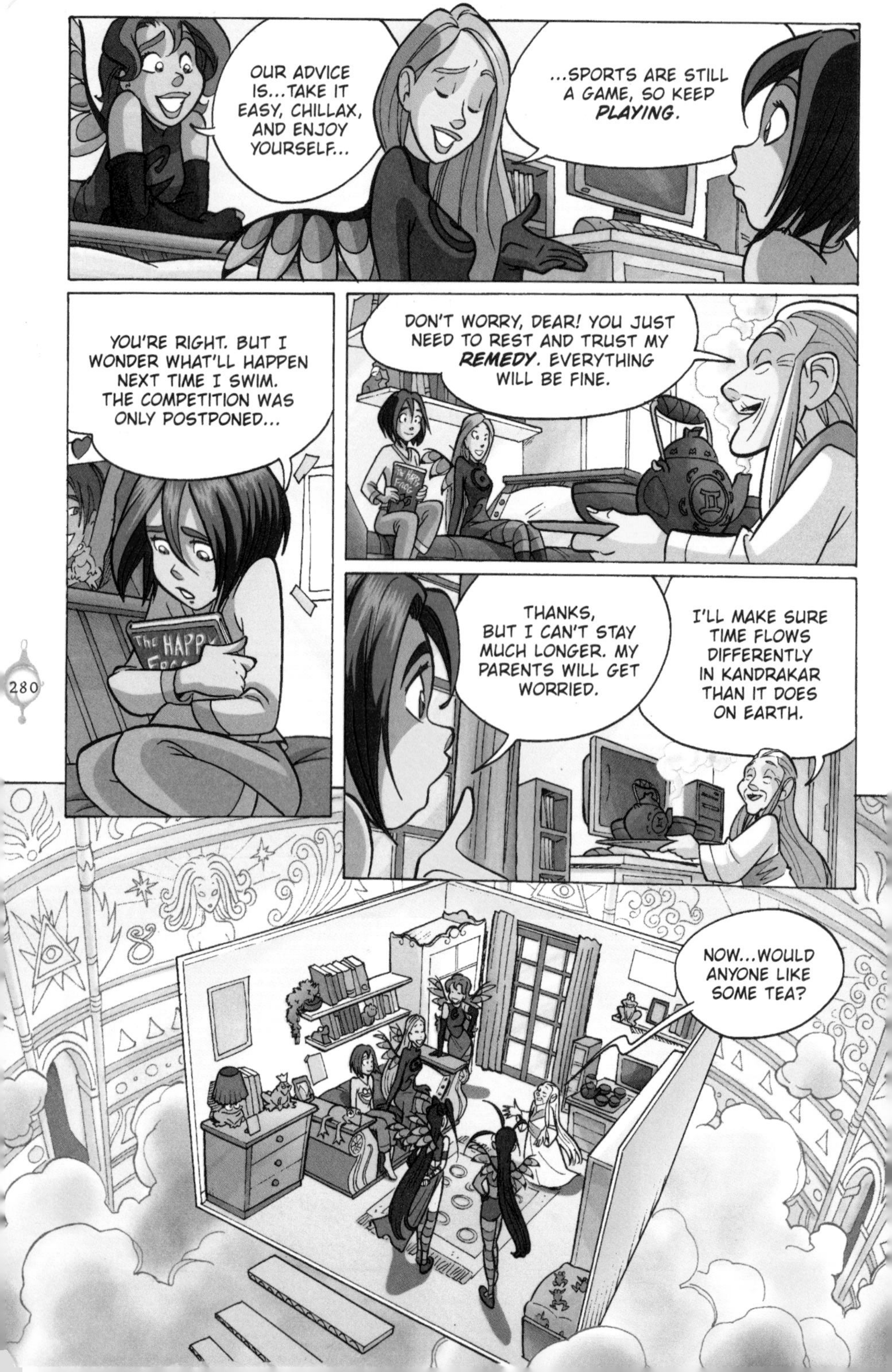

OUR ADVICE IS...TAKE IT EASY, CHILLAX, AND ENJOY YOURSELF...
...SPORTS ARE STILL A GAME, SO KEEP **PLAYING**.
YOU'RE RIGHT. BUT I WONDER WHAT'LL HAPPEN NEXT TIME I SWIM. THE COMPETITION WAS ONLY POSTPONED...
DON'T WORRY, DEAR! YOU JUST NEED TO REST AND TRUST MY **REMEDY**. EVERYTHING WILL BE FINE.
THANKS, BUT I CAN'T STAY MUCH LONGER. MY PARENTS WILL GET WORRIED.
I'LL MAKE SURE TIME FLOWS DIFFERENTLY IN KANDRAKAR THAN IT DOES ON EARTH.
NOW...WOULD ANYONE LIKE SOME TEA?

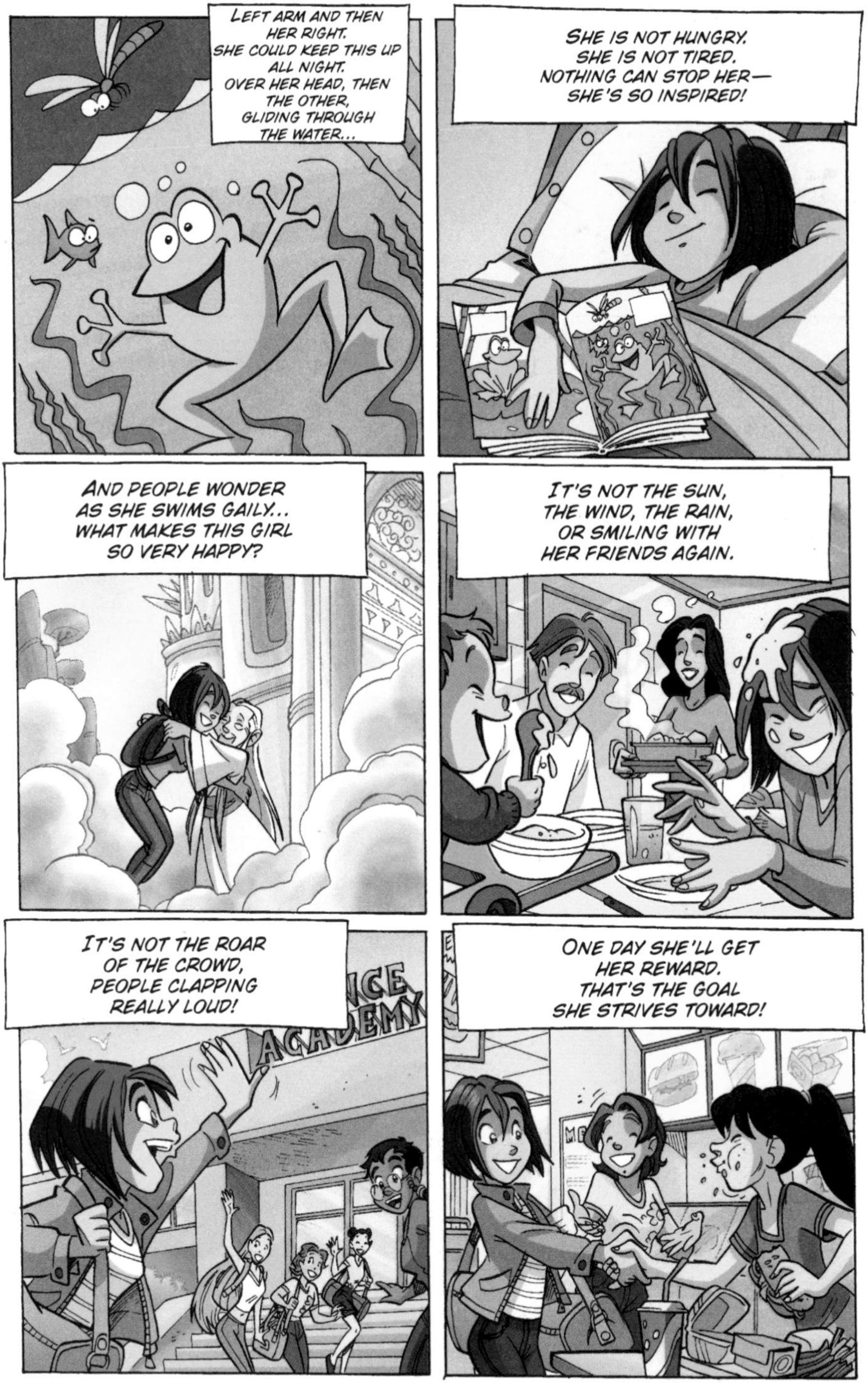
LEFT ARM AND THEN HER RIGHT. SHE COULD KEEP THIS UP ALL NIGHT. OVER HER HEAD, THEN THE OTHER, GLIDING THROUGH THE WATER...
SHE IS NOT HUNGRY. SHE IS NOT TIRED. NOTHING CAN STOP HER— SHE'S SO INSPIRED!
AND PEOPLE WONDER AS SHE SWIMS GAILY... WHAT MAKES THIS GIRL SO VERY HAPPY?
IT'S NOT THE SUN, THE WIND, THE RAIN, OR SMILING WITH HER FRIENDS AGAIN.
IT'S NOT THE ROAR OF THE CROWD, PEOPLE CLAPPING REALLY LOUD!
ACADEMY
ONE DAY SHE'LL GET HER REWARD. THAT'S THE GOAL SHE STRIVES TOWARD!

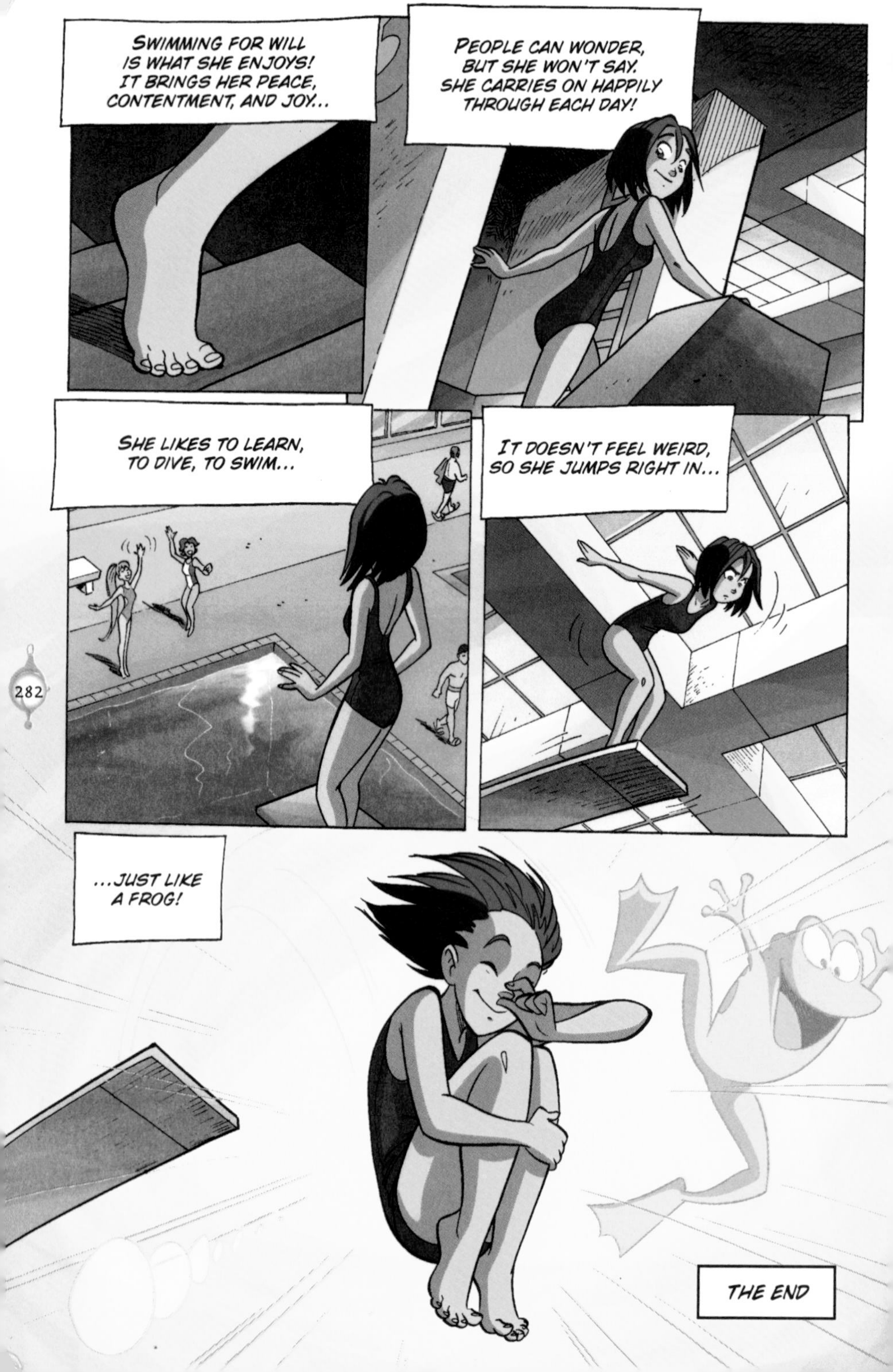
SWIMMING FOR WILL
IS WHAT SHE ENJOYS!
IT BRINGS HER PEACE,
CONTENTMENT, AND JOY...
PEOPLE CAN WONDER,
BUT SHE WON'T SAY.
SHE CARRIES ON HAPPILY
THROUGH EACH DAY!
SHE LIKES TO LEARN,
TO DIVE, TO SWIM...
IT DOESN'T FEEL WEIRD,
SO SHE JUMPS RIGHT IN...
...JUST LIKE
A FROG!
THE END

Read on in Volume 26!

W.i.t.c.h.

Will Irma Taranee Cornelia Hay Lin

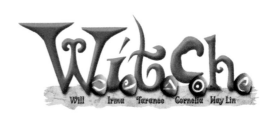

W.i.t.c.h.

Will Irma Taranee Cornelia Hay Lin

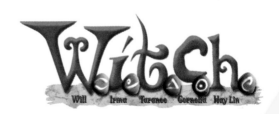

W.i.t.c.h.

Will Irma Taranee Cornelia Hay Lin

Part VIII. Teach 2b W.I.T.C.H. • Volume 3

25

Series Created by Elisabetta Gnone
Comic Art Direction: Alessandro Barbucci, Barbara Canepa

W.I.T.C.H.: The Graphic Novel,
Part VIII: Teach 2b W.I.T.C.H.
© Disney Enterprises, Inc.

English translation © 2021 by Disney Enterprises, Inc.

JY
150 West 30th Street, 19th Floor
New York, NY 10001

Visit us at jyforkids.com
facebook.com/jyforkids
twitter.com/jyforkids
jyforkids.tumblr.com
instagram.com/jyforkids

First JY Edition: August 2021

JY is an imprint of Yen Press, LLC.
The JY name and logo are trademarks of Yen Press, LLC.

The publisher is not responsible for websites (or their content) that are not owned by the publisher.

Library of Congress Control Number: 2017950917

ISBNs:
978-1-9753-1771-3 (paperback)
978-1-9753-1772-0 (ebook)

10 9 8 7 6 5 4 3 2 1

.e United States of America

Cover Art by Giada Perissinotto
Colors by Andrea Cagol

Translation by Linda Ghio and
Stephanie Dagg at Editing Zone
Lettering by Katie Blakeslee

COUNTLESS TEARS

Concept by Augusto Macchetto
Script by Alessandro Ferrari
Art by Alberto Zanon
Inks by Marina Baggio, Cristina Giorgilli, and Roberta Zanotta
Color and Light Direction by Francesco Legramandi
Title Page Art by Alberto Zanon
with colors by Francesco Legramandi

HERE IN YOUR HEART

Concept and Script by Augusto Manchetto
Layout by Giada Perissinotto
Pencils by Davide Baldoni
Inks by Marina Baggio and Roberta Zanotta
Color and Light Direction by Francesco Legramandi
Title Page Art by Giada Perissinotto
with colors by Francesco Legramandi

THE MAGIC OF THE WORLD

Concept by Bruno Enna
Layout and pencils by Daniela Vetro
Inks by Marina Baggio and Roberta Zanotta
Color and Light Direction by Francesco Legramandi
Title Page Art by Daniela Vetro

SWEET, IN THE END

Concept by Augusto Manchetto
Layout by Paolo Campinoti and Danilo Loizedda
Pencils by Federica Salfo
Inks by Marina Baggio and Roberta Zanotta
Color and Light Direction by Francesco Legramandi
Title Page Art by Federica Salfo
with colors by Francesco Legramandi

A DIVE INTO THE AIR

Concept by Bruno Enna
Art by Lucio Leoni
Inks by Marina Baggio and Roberta Zanotta
Color and Light Direction by Francesco Legramandi
Title Page Art by Lucio Leoni
with colors by Francesco Legramandi